Witness of Gor

Witnesses of Gor
John Norman

AN [*e-reads*] BOOK
New York, NY

No part of this publication may be reproduced or transmitted in any form or by any means, electronic, or mechanical, including photocopy, recording, scanning or any information storage retrieval system, without explicit permission in writing from the Author.

This book is a work of fiction. Names, characters, places and incidents are products of the author's imagination or are used fictitiously. Any resemblance to actual events or locals or persons, living or dead, is entirely coincidental.

Copyright © 2002 by John Norman
An E-Reads Edition
www.e-reads.com
ISBN 0-7592-8382-6

The Gor books available from E-Reads:

- 01 - TARNSMAN OF GOR
- 02 - OUTLAW OF GOR
- 03 - PRIEST-KINGS OF GOR
- 04 - NOMADS OF GOR
- 05 - ASSASSIN OF GOR
- 06 - RAIDERS OF GOR
- 07 - CAPTIVE OF GOR
- 08 - HUNTERS OF GOR
- 09 - MARAUDERS OF GOR
- 10 - TRIBESMEN OF GOR
- 11 - SLAVE GIRL OF GOR
- 12 - BEASTS OF GOR
- 13 - EXPLORERS OF GOR
- 14 - FIGHTING SLAVE OF GOR
- 15 - ROGUE OF GOR
- 16 - GUARDSMAN OF GOR
- 17 - SAVAGES OF GOR
- 18 - BLOOD BROTHERS OF GOR
- 19 - KAJIRA OF GOR
- 20 - PLAYERS OF GOR
- 21 - MERCENARIES OF GOR
- 22 - DANCER OF GOR
- 23 - RENEGADES OF GOR
- 24 - VAGABONDS OF GOR
- 25 - MAGICIANS OF GOR
- 26 - WITNESS OF GOR

Table of Contents

Chapter	Page
One	1
Two	3
Three	11
Four	13
Five	38
Six	43
Seven	55
Eight	96
Nine	136
Ten	149
Eleven	185
Twelve	249
Thirteen	282
Fourteen	334
Fifteen	394
Sixteen	400
Seventeen	424
Eighteen	428
Nineteen	443
Twenty	486
Twenty One	487
Twenty Two	489
Twenty Three	493

Chapter	Page
Twenty Four	502
Twenty Five	534
Twenty Six	536
Twenty Seven	539
Twenty Eight	540
Twenty Nine	546
Thirty	582
Thirty One	586
Thirty Two	611
Thirty Three	614
Thirty Four	618
Thirty Five	627
Thirty Six	633
Thirty Seven	637
Thirty Eight	679
Thirty Nine	689
Forty	694
Forty One	706
Forty Two	712
Forty Three	720
Forty Four	726
Forty Five	737
Forty Six	746

One

I looked about. No one was looking.

I crossed the perimeter of small, sharpened stones, a foot or so deep, about ten feet wide, which lined the interior wall of the garden. This hurt my feet, which were small, and soft, and bare. Even the soles of our feet must be soft, and this is seen to, by creams and lotions, and the nature of the surfaces upon which we are permitted to walk, such things.

It was during the heat of the day.

The bangles on my left ankle made a tiny sound, and I stopped, looking about. I was frightened. But no one saw. How pleased I was that I had not been belled! Normally it is a new girl, or even a free woman, who is belled. To be sure, we may be belled at any time, and, naturally, if it is wished, kept that way. But usually one is belled, if at all, in serving, or in the dance. To be sure, it is sometimes required of us in the furs. Bells have many purposes, as might be supposed. Only one of these is security, making it easy, for example, to detect the presence, the movements, of a girl. This is particularly useful at night. One of the reasons, too, why new girls, and sometimes free women, may be belled is that they may begin to understand what they are, or are likely to become. This is not hard to understand when one has bells locked on one's limbs. What sort of girl or woman would be belled? Later, of course, bells are unnecessary for such a purpose. Later, obviously, there will be no doubt as to what one is, either in the minds of others or in one's own mind.

I crept to the wall and put my fingers to the smooth, marbled surface. I looked upward. The wall was some forty feet high. There are trees in the garden, of course, but they are not placed in proximity to the wall. One could not use them, thus, even if they were tall enough, to obtain access to its height. The wall, I had been told, was some ten feet in thickness. I did not know, considering the fashion in which I had been brought here, but presumably only the interior side was marbled. I had been told that the foundation of the wall extended several feet below the surface of the ground. The height of the wall, now that I backed from it, I could see was surmounted by incurved blades. I shuddered. Presumably some similar arrangement, perhaps outcurved blades, characterized its exterior side.

I moved the armlet on my left arm a bit higher on my arm. It was warm to the touch. Many of the others were resting. I looked about. I did not want anyone to see me near the wall. We were not to approach the wall. The sun was reflecting against the wall. The glare hurt my eyes. We were forbidden to cross the perimeter of sharpened stones.

I wore a brief wisp of yellow silk, fastened at the left shoulder, my only garment. Two bracelets were on my right wrist. I did not mind the silk. Indeed, I was grateful for it. It had only been permitted to me a few days ago. Too, of course, as I have indicated, the weather was warm. I brushed back my hair. I have brown hair, and brown eyes. My hair was now long. It was now below the small of my back. This is not untypical. Many of the others had hair even longer.

I looked, again, at the wall, so smooth and sheer. It had a lovely pattern in its marbling, but this pattern, through the glare of the sun, could not be seen to its advantage. I looked up, again, at the lofty, formidable height of the wall. The wall seemed very smooth. Surely no purchase could be gained there. And the wall was very high. And there were the knives at its summit.

Behind me, in the interior of the garden, I could hear the soft splashing of the fountain. It was set among the trees, and its spill fed into the pool.

I looked again at the wall.

I heard voices, coming from the house. As swiftly as I could, wincing, hurting myself on the stones, I withdrew from the wall. It was my intention to circle about, through the shrubbery, and the tiny, lovely trees of the garden, to the vicinity of the fountain.

Two

It is difficult to comprehend such realities.

I had screamed, of course, but I had had no assurance that I would be heard.

Indeed, I suspected that I would not be heard, or, if heard, that I would be merely ignored. I suspected, immediately, that my own will, my own feelings, and desires, were no longer of importance, at least to others. And even more profoundly, more frighteningly, I suddenly suspected that I myself, objectively, had now become unimportant. I realized that I might have value, of course, in some sense or other, for I found myself, and in a certain fashion, in this place, but this is not the same sort of thing as being important. I was no longer *important*. That is a strange feeling. It is not, of course, and I want you to understand this, that I had ever been important in any of the usual senses of "important," such as being powerful, or rich, or well-known. That is not it at all. No, it was rather in another sense of "important" that I suspected or, I think, better, realized, that I was no longer important. I had now become unimportant, rather as a flower is unimportant, or a dog.

It is difficult to comprehend such realities, the darkness, the collar, the chains.

I had screamed, of course, but, almost immediately, I stopped, more fearing that I might be heard, than not heard.

I crouched there, shuddering. I tried to collect my wits.

My neck hurt, for I had jerked, frightened, against the collar, turning it, abrasively, on my neck.

I do not think that I had realized fully, in the first instant, or so, though I must have been aware of it on some level, that it was on me.

Perhaps I had, in that first instant, refused to admit the recognition to my full consciousness, or had immediately forced it from my consciousness. Perhaps I had simply put it from my mind, rejecting the very possibility, refusing to believe anything so improbable. And in consequence I had hurt myself, unnecessarily, foolishly.

I felt it, in the darkness. It fitted closely, and was heavy. I could not begin to slip it. A ring was attached to it, and a chain was attached to this ring, running, as I discovered, to another ring, fastened to a plate, apparently bolted into the wall.

My wrists were also confined. I wore metal cuffs, joined by some inches of chain. My ankles, by metal anklets, linked by a bit of chain, were similarly secured.

I crouched in the darkness, terrified.

I felt the collar again. It was closed by means of a heavy lock, part of the collar itself. It would thus, presumably, respond to a key. The cuffs and anklets, on the other hand, were quite different. They had apparently been simply closed about my limbs, closed by some considerable force, perhaps that of a machine, or even, perhaps, unthinkably primitive though it might seem, by the blows of a hammer on an anvil. They were of flat, heavy, straplike metal. They had no hinges. Perhaps they had begun as partly opened circles into which my limbs had been thrust, circles which had then been, by some means, closed about my limbs, confining them. They did not have hinges. There was no sign of a place for the insertion of a key. They clasped me well. It would be impossible to remove them without tools. I could thus be freed from the collar, and the wall, quite simply, by means of the key. I could not be rid so simply, of course, of my other bonds. This suggested to me that I might be, in the near future, removed from this place, but that no similar indulgence might be expected with respect to my other bonds. I wondered who held the key to my collar. I suspected that it might be merely one of many keys, or, perhaps, a key to many similar locks. It would doubtless be held by a subordinate, or agent. The key to a collar such as mine, I suspected, would not be likely to be held personally by anyone of importance. The will by the rule of which, by the decision of which, I, and perhaps others, might be confined would doubtless be remote from the instrumentalities by means of which the dictates of that will would be enacted. As far as I knew I did not have any enemies, and I did not believe that I had ever, really, truly offended anyone. I suspected, accordingly, that what had happened to me was in its nature not personal, at all, but was, rather, objective and, in its way, perhaps quite impersonal. Accordingly, although I did not doubt that I was here because of something about me, perhaps because of some properties or other, and thusly, doubtlessly, for some reason, I did not think that the matter really had anything to do with me in a truly personal sense. I suspected it had to do rather with a kind, or a sort, of which kind, or sort, I was presumably an example.

What had become of me?

What was I now?

I dared not conjecture, but knew.

The place where I was damp, and cold. I did not wish to be there. I did not want to be in such a place. I heard water dripping from somewhere, probably from the ceiling. I felt about, in the darkness. Near me, as I brushed aside straw, I discovered two shallow, bowl-like depressions in the floor. My fingers touched water in one. In the other there was something like a bit of damp meal, surely no more than a handful, and a curl of something, like a damp crust.

I lay back down, in the damp straw, on my right side. I pulled up my knees, and put my head on the back of my left hand.

I would certainly not drink from such a source, nor eat from such a place.

I pulled a little at the chain, that attached to the collar on my neck. I could feel the force, small as it was, transmitted through the chain, to the collar, the collar then drawing against the back of my neck.

Once footsteps passed, in what I supposed must be a corridor outside. I lay there, very quietly, not daring to move. I saw, for a moment, as the footsteps passed, a crack of light beneath the door. Until that time I did not know the location of the door. The light was some form of natural light, that of a candle, a lamp, a lantern, I did not know. As it passed I saw some of the straw on my side of the door. The door, as one could tell from the light, it revealing the thickness of the beams, was a heavy one. Also, along its bottom, reinforcing that portion of the door, one could detect a heavy, bolted band. It seemed likely, too, of course, that the door might be reinforced similarly at other points. These things, the light, the nature of the door, seemed to fit in well with the primitive confinements in which I found myself.

I then, trembling, put my head down again.

Perhaps, I thought, I should have called out, as someone, or something, had passed.

Of course, that is what must be done!

But when the steps returned, I was again absolutely quiet, terrified. As the steps passed, I did not even breathe. I remained absolutely still. I was frightened, even, that the metal on my body, in which I was so helpless, might make some tiny sound. I did not want, even by so small a sound, to attract attention to myself. It was not that I doubted that whoever, or whatever, was out there was well aware of where I was, and how I was. It was merely that I did not want to draw attention to myself. I would later be taught ways in which it is suitable to draw attention to oneself, and ways in which it is not suitable to draw attention to oneself. On this occasion I am confident that my instincts were quite correct. Indeed, they have seldom, if ever, betrayed me.

I gasped with relief, as the steps passed.

To be sure, but a moment later, I again castigated myself, at having neglected this opportunity of inquiry or protest. Indeed, shortly after the steps had passed, I scrambled to my knees! I must be angry! I must pound upon the door! I must call out! I must insist upon attention! I must demand to see someone! I must demand release! I must bluster and threaten! I must attempt to confuse my jailers, and terrify them into compliance with my will! If necessary, I must appeal to undoubted legalities!

But I could not pound upon the door, of course. I could not even reach the door. I had not been chained in such a way as to make that possible. And I did not doubt but what that was no accident.

I struggled to my feet, bent over. I could not stand fully upright, because of the chain on my neck. I put my hand up. It touched the ceiling. I had not realized the ceiling was that low. I then lay down, again. I was alarmed, and dismayed. The area in which I was confined was not so much a cell, as something else. It was more in the nature of a kennel.

My mood, or fit, of indignation, or resolve, of protest, of momentary righteousness, of transitory belligerence, such a futile bellicosity, soon passed. Save for the sounds of a bit of chain it had been silent. I supposed I had thought I owed it to my background, or my conditioning program. To be sure, I suspected that neither of these was likely to be particularly germane, or helpful, with respect to my current plight, or, more likely, condition. It was not merely that it seems somehow inappropriate, or silly, and likely to be ineffective, to adopt a posture of belligerence when has a chain on one's neck, and cannot even stand upright. It was rather that, given my current situation, chained and confined as I was, it seemed to me that any such pleas, or demands, or such, would be absurd. Doubtless decisions had already been made, pertinent to me. Matters, in effect, like those of nature, had doubtless already been set in motion. If there had been a time when such threats, or protests, might have been effective, it was doubtless long past. Too, I did not doubt, somehow, but what I was not the only one, such as myself, in this place. The chains, the ring, the depressions in the floor, the apparently small, close, nature of the area of my confinement, the incomprehensibility of my being here, except perhaps as one of a group, perhaps similar to myself, all suggested this. Let others, if they wish, I thought, adopt such postures. For myself, not only did I not find them congenial, given my nature, but, too, I was afraid, distinctly, that they might not be found acceptable, unless perhaps, very briefly, at the beginning, as a source for amusement. Too, I considered the nature of legalities. One tends, if naive, to think of those legalities with which one is most familiar as being somehow the only ones possible. This view, of course, is quite mistaken. This is not to deny that all civilizations, and cultures, have their customs and legalities. It is only to remark that they need not be the same. Indeed, the legalities with which I was most familiar, as they stood in contradiction to nature, constituted, I supposed, in their way, an aberration of legalities. They were, at the least, uncharacteristic of most cultures, and historically untypical. To be sure, if the intent is to contradict nature rather than fulfill her, there was doubtless much point to them. Thusly, that they produced human pain and social chaos, with all the miseries attendant thereupon, would not be seen as an objection to them but rather as the predictable result of their excellence in the light of their objectives. But not all legalities, of course, need have such objectives. As I lay there in the darkness, in my chains, and considered the factuality and simplicity of my predicament, and the apparently practical and routine aspects of my helplessness and incarceration, I suspected that my current situation was not at all likely to be in violation of legalities. Rather I suspected it was in full and conscious accord with them. I suspected that I was now, or soon would be, enmeshed in legalities.

To be sure, these would be different legalities from those with which I was most familiar. These would be, I suspected, legalities founded not on politics, but biology.

I was now very hungry. But I would not, of course, drink from a depression in a floor, nor soil my lips with whatever edible grime might be found in an adjacent depression.

I was cold, and helpless.

If it would be stupid, or absurd, as I suspected, if not dangerous, to pretend to a belligerent stance, to protest, or threaten, or to appeal to legalities, the purport of which might well be aligned precisely against one, then perhaps, I thought, one might appeal to the pity, the mercies, of one's captors. Could one not plead with them, armed in all the vulnerable panoply of one's tears, of one's utter helplessness and need? Could one not beg them for mercy? Might one not even consider, in such a desperate predicament, the almost unthinkable option of kneeling before them, and lifting one's hands to them? Might one not, in such desperate straits, dare even to assume that posture, one so natural, so apt, to supplication? And might not one even cry, or pretend to? Surely they could not resist so piteous a spectacle. Surely, considering one's weakness, and the presumed power of one's captors, this would be an endeavor more likely of success than the utterance of empty threats, of meaningless protests, the enunciation of futile demands.

I would not drink here, nor eat here.

I did not think, really, given the fact that I was here, the presumed methodicality of my arrival in this place, the presumably routine manner of my incarceration, the nature of my cell, or kennel, suggesting that it was not unique, that my presence here would not be its first occupancy nor its last, the unlikelihood that there was anything special about me, the probability that I was only one of several such as myself, that my pleas would move my captors.

I changed my position several times.

It is hard to comprehend such realities, the darkness, the dampness, the stones, the walls, the wet straw, its smell, the collar, the chains, the not being clothed.

There was some sense of security, oddly, just being on the chain.

I did not speculate that I might have gone insane. The chain was too real.

In time I went to my belly and put my mouth down, and lapped the water in the shallow depression beside me. Then, a little later, I reached into the other shallow depression and withdrew the damp crust there, and fed on it. Too, in a moment, I addressed myself to the small bit of meal in the same container. Later, with my finger, I carefully, methodically, wiped out the inside of the depression, that I might not miss whatever last, tiny, wet particles of meal might adhere there. They had suddenly become very precious. As I licked these gratefully from my finger, these few particles, such tiny, damp things, I realized that what I was fed, and when I was fed, and in what amounts, and, indeed, literally, even if I *was* fed, was now up to another. This is a very frightening thing to understand.

I lapped again a bit of water, and then wiped my mouth with the back of my hand.

I rolled to my back.

I looked up, into the darkness.

I bent my knees. I put my chained wrists over my head. I could feel the chain there, behind me, leading up to the ring on the wall from my collar.

I was not strong, or powerful. I was not strong, even, let alone powerful, for the sort of creature I was. What, I wondered, then, could be the meaning of the chains I wore. Perhaps in them, I speculated, was a lesson. Oh, to be sure, they confined me. They kept me in a place. I could not rush at the door, if it were opened. I could not run. I could not use my hands freely. They might keep me from being something of a nuisance, I supposed, particularly at the beginning, if I were so inclined, or became difficult or hysterical. But their primary reason I suspected had less to do with security than something else. That they were on me, that I was in them, and helplessly so, I suspected, might be intended, particularly at this time, to be instructive. Let me begin to be familiarized with chains, let me begin to become accustomed to them. Let me learn, too, in this graphic, profound fashion, what I had become, what I now was. I supposed that later, too, such as I might find ourselves chained. But then, I supposed, apart from practical matters, such as security, and mnemonic considerations, and such, that that might be regarded as much a matter of appropriateness as anything else. I, and perhaps others, were such as to be appropriately chained.

That was the sort we were. To be sure, beyond such things, there is no doubt as to the effectiveness of chains. They hold us, perfectly.

I rolled to my side.

I considered the simple, meager fare. What was I, I wondered, that such stuff had been deemed suitable for me. Too, I again considered the chains. What was I, I wondered, that I wore such?

I dared not conjecture, but knew.

I drew up my legs, and put my hands on my shoulders, huddling, making myself small in the damp straw.

I was cold.

The corridor was quiet outside.

I lay very quietly.

One feels some comfort, and security, perhaps oddly enough, in such a situation, being on one's chain.

Three

I had looked again at the wall.
I had heard voices, coming from the house. As swiftly as I could, wincing, hurting myself on the stones, I had withdrawn from the wall. It was my intention to circle about, through the shrubbery, and the trees of the garden, to the vicinity of the fountain.
"Stop," I heard, a man's voice.
Instantly I stopped, my heart sinking. I turned, of course, immediately, and fell to my knees, putting my head down to the lavender grass, as was its color here, in this portion of the garden, the palms of my hands down, too, on the grass, beside my head.
It was a man's voice that had spoken.
I did not dare look, of course, upon he who had addressed me.
I had not received permission to do so.
But how could it have been a man's voice?
How could it be, a man's voice, here, in the garden, at this time of day?
Normally we vacate the garden when men enter it to work, as, for example, its gardeners. We are not for the eyes of such as those. And normally, if there are to be guests, if we are to entertain, information to that effect is issued to us hours in advance. We must, after all, have time to prepare ourselves. One must bathe. One must do one's hair. There are silks, perfumes and jewelries to be considered. One must be made up, and so on. On the other hand, ironically, our appearance, achieved at such cost, with so much labor, and so much attention to detail, seems most often taken for granted by our guests. Often they scarcely seem to notice us, as we serve. To be certain, we are taught,

in such situations, to be self-effacing, and to serve deferentially. Such things can be changed, of course, at so little as a word, or the snapping of fingers.

How could there be a man here, in the garden, at this time of day? I kept my head down to the grass.

I had not been given permission to raise it.

Sometimes when men are to enter the garden, suddenly, or with little notice, such as guardsmen, say, in the line of duty, as in inspections or searches, a bar is rung, and we must find our body veils, and kneel, head down, and cover ourselves with them. Such veils are opaque. We are not, after all, for the eyes of just anyone.

But I was not now concealed in my body veil!

Who could this man be?

I was in light silk. It was extremely brief, and was, for most practical purposes, diaphanous. Certainly it left little doubt as to my lineaments.

Four

I do not know how long I lay in the darkness. Sometimes I slept.
I did not know what time it was, what day.
Indeed, I suspected that I would not be familiar even with the calendar.
Once or twice some meal, and another crust, was placed in the shallow depression beside me. This was done while I slept. No longer did I permit it to linger there. I devoured it, gratefully, eagerly.
But for a long time now there had been nothing more in the depression. The depression for the water, like a sunken bowl, was replenished from a slender, flat trickle of water. I could feel it with my finger. It was little more than a dampness. That trickle, I assumed, had its origin elsewhere in the darkness. It derived, doubtless, from the water which, as I could hear, slowly, drop by drop, fell into the chamber, perhaps from the ceiling, perhaps from some pipe or ledge. The water bowl did have a tiny run-off which might carry excess fluid away, presumably toward some drain, but the amount of water was so small in the bowl, and took such time to accumulate, that the run-off was not used. I learned to conserve the water, my tongue even licking the rough bottom of the depression.
But there had been no more meal, or crusts, of late, in the food depression.
I was ravening.
I wondered if my captors had forgotten about me. I wondered if I had been left here to die.
I mustered the courage to call out, piteously. "I am hungry," I called. "Please feed me. Please! I am hungry!"

But I doubted that anyone heard. There seemed to be no one about.

I pulled on the chains. They held me well.

How helpless I was!

I was ravening. I was ready to do anything, just to eat.

Then, again, perhaps a day later, when I awakened, I found a bit of meal, and a crust, in the depression. It might have been the rarest of viands. I fell upon them, like a starving little animal. For a day or two then such slender provender made its appearance in the depression. I knew that I had lost weight. This would doubtless make some difference with respect to my curves. But, more importantly, I think, I was learning to make do with what was given to me, and to be appreciative for it, whatever it might be. Too, of course, I had learned, and more keenly, and profoundly, than before, that I did not have control over my own food. I had learned that even for such a thing I was now dependent on another.

I awakened suddenly.

I thought that I heard a sound, outside.

I became instantly alert, frightened. There was a sound, outside! It came, I thought, from somewhere down the corridor, to the left.

I rose up, hurriedly, to my knees. I was wild, frightened. My chains made a noise.

I heard a door, heavy, grating, opening somewhere, away, to the left. I heard a voice. My heart almost stopped. I do not know what I expected. Perhaps I had feared that it would be merely an animal sound, not so much a voice, as a barking or growling. But it was a human voice.

I felt my body, quickly. I was frightened. I was unclothed. How much more slender seemed my body now!

I was frightened.

It was, you see, a man's voice.

I heard doors opened, on different sides of the corridor, it seemed, getting closer. I heard, now, more than one man's voice. Their tones seemed imperative, as though they would brook no question or delay. The voices themselves, though clearly male, and human, seemed unlike those of men with whom I was familiar. I am not sure, precisely, in what the differences consisted. It may be merely that they spoke somewhat more loudly than the men I was accustomed to, for such things often vary culturally. But I think it was more than some possible difference in mere volume. Too, I do not think it had to do merely with an accent, though they surely had such, an accent which appeared distinctively, oddly, in words they uttered in various languages, languages some of which I could recognize, though I could not speak them, as the doors were opened, and which, on the other hand, seemed so natural, so apt, in their discourse among themselves. No, it was not really so much a matter of volume, or of accent, as of something else. Perhaps it was the lack of diffidence, the lack of apology, in their speech, which struck me. Perhaps it was this sort of simple, natural assurance which most struck me. Too, in their tones, intelligent, clear, confident, forceful, it was not difficult to detect a simple, unpretentious aspect of command. Indeed, in the tones of several, perhaps their leaders, there seemed something which might best be characterized as a sort of natural, unassuming imperiousness. This made me terribly uncomfortable. How dare they speak like that? Who did they think they were? Men? Did they think they were men? That is, of course, "men" in a sense long since prohibited to, or abandoned by, the males with which I was familiar. And could they be really such men? And, if so, what consequences might that entail for one such as myself? How could one such as I, given what I was, possibly relate to such creatures? In what modalities, on what conditions, would it be possible to do so?

I put my hands about my body, again. I was much more slender now. I could tell, even in the darkness. I had not been much fed.

The doors, opening, were coming closer now. They were heavy doors, doubtless like that on my chamber. That could be told from the sound of their opening.

Beneath my door now, visible in the crack between those heavy beams and the reinforcing iron band and the floor was a light. It was doubtless a dim light, but it seemed very bright to me, as I had been long in the darkness.

I heard a door across the way and a little to the left opened. I heard an imperious voice. Again I recognized the language, but could not speak it.

Then, a few moments later, I heard a key, large, and heavy, turning in the lock to my door.

I put up my chained wrists, suddenly, frantically, wildly, and, as I could, on one side and then the other, fixed my hair.

As the door opened I covered myself as well as I could.

I winced against the light, and could not face it. It was only a lantern held high in the threshold, but I was temporarily blinded. I looked away, my hands over my body.

"Be absolutely silent," said a voice, a man's voice.

I would not have dared to make a sound.

"I see that you do not need to be instructed to kneel," he said.

I trembled.

"You already know what posture to assume in the presence of a male," he said. "Excellent."

I squirmed a little, being so before a man. I fought the sensations within me.

He laughed.

I blushed.

"Put your head to the floor," he said.

I obeyed, immediately. There were tears in my eyes, from the light, you understand.

He entered the chamber.

The lantern, now in the care of another fellow, remained mercifully by the door. It was easy to tell its position, as its light was clear, even through my closed eyelids.

The fellow crouched down beside me. "Remain still," he said. "Do not look at me."

With the pain of the light I would not have wished to look at anything.

He threw my hair forward. I felt a key thrust into the lock on my collar, and then, in a moment, for the first time in how long I knew not, that confining metal band, close-fitting, sturdy and inflexible, with its chain, attached to the ring on the wall, was no longer on my neck. I was no longer chained to the wall!

I kept my head down, of course. I did not move. I did not look at him. I did not make a sound.

I then felt his hand in my hair. I winced as he drew me up, forcibly, to all fours. He also, almost at the same time, keeping me on all fours, pushed my head down. I was then on all fours, with my head facing the floor. He did not do these things gently. I was handled, and positioned, as though I might be no more than an animal.

"You will keep this position," he said, "until you receive permission to change it. Now, go to the corridor, where you will be appropriately placed, aligned and instructed."

I shuddered.

"Keep your head down," he said. "Do not look at us."

I fell, so frightened I was, trying to comply, caught up in the chains. I lay there for an instant, in terror, unable to move, feeling so exposed to him. My whole back felt terribly vulnerable. I was afraid, even then, even knowing as little as I did at the time, that he might not be pleased, and that I might be struck, or kicked. But he saw fit, at that time, at least, to show me patience. I regained the position and, slowly, carefully, my limbs trembling, crawled from the chamber. One may hasten on all fours, so chained, but it is much easier, of course, to move in a measured manner, bit by bit. It is not difficult, incidentally, to crawl on all fours in chains, even those such as I wore. It is just a matter of moving within their limitations.

I was to be appropriately placed, aligned, and instructed.

Outside the chamber I could see little but the stone flagging of the corridor hall. I was aware of the proximity of two or three men. I did not look up. They wore heavy bootlike sandals. One of them reached down and took me by the upper left arm, and guided me to a position in the center of the corridor. My body was then aligned with the long axis of the corridor. With respect to the interior of my chamber, I was facing left.

I heard other doors opening behind me, one by one, and heard the voices, in various languages.

I remained as I was, not daring to change my position in the least degree.

I was yet, it seemed, to be instructed.

I realized then, only fully comprehending it for the first time, one takes such things so for granted, that the voice which had addressed me had done so in my own language.

Other doors opened, farther down the hall, behind me.

Patterns of light moved about on the stones, the consequence, I suppose, of the movements of lanterns.

He had had an accent, of course. Whereas it is surely possible to speak a language which one has not learned in one's childhood without an accent, it is, as one might suppose, unusual. One's speech generally tends to retain a foreign flavor. Sometimes that the tongue one speaks is not native to one is revealed by so little as an occasional slip in pronunciation, say, the shifting treatment of a consonant, perhaps under conditions of stress, such as anger, or fear. He had made no attempt, as far as I could tell, to disguise an accent. That his speech might be intelligible to me was, perhaps, quite sufficient for him. I could not place the language these men spoke among themselves. It was no language I knew, nor even one I could recognize. Yet, oddly, it seemed sometimes reminiscent of other languages, which, to one degree or another, if only by sound, I was familiar with. At times I even thought I detected a word I knew. To be sure, similar sounds need not mean similar words. A given sound might have many meanings, and quite different meanings.

I kept my head down.

My eyes were now becoming adjusted to the light.

The only source of light in the corridor, as far as I could tell, was that carried by various men, which source I supposed was lanterns. Without that light the corridor, as far as I could tell, would have been totally dark. The corridor itself, I supposed, would be sealed off by some door or gate. Even if I had been able to get loose from my collar, that by means of which I had been fastened to the wall of my chamber, even if I had been able, somehow, to get through the heavy door which kept me in my chamber, I would, I supposed, have soon encountered another barrier, that which, presumably, closed the corridor. Too, as the corridor was in utter darkness, as soon as a lantern was lifted in it, I would have been rendered temporarily blind, and totally at the mercy of whoever had entered.

From the point of view of most, I suppose, the corridor would have counted as being, at best, only dimly lighted, but, as such things tend to be relative, it seemed, by contrast, well illuminated to me.

I was aware of a fellow standing near me. He had the heavy bootlike sandals, as did the others. Other than the sandals, his legs were bare. He wore a tunic, or something like that. I did not understand his mode of dress. It was totally unlike things with which I was familiar. I did not think I knew this place. This place, I thought, is very different from what I am used to. His legs were sturdy. I found them frightening, and disturbing. What place is this, I asked myself. It is so different from places with which I am familiar. I am not in my own culture, I thought. This is not my culture, I thought. This is a different culture. This may be a *quite* different culture. Things may be quite *different* here.

And my speculations, as I would soon learn, would prove correct, profoundly correct.

It would be a world quite different from that with which I was familiar.

Then the man moved away.

But another, in a short time, paused near me.

I was much aware of him, but, of course, I kept my head down. He was, it seemed, like the other, large and strong. I found his presence disturbing, as I had found that of the other.

The culture here, though quite different from my own, I thought, seems all of a piece. Things seem to fit, the nature of my incarceration, the simplicity of things, the architecture, the mode of dress, the iron on my wrists and ankles.

I kept my head down.

What place was this? How had I come here? Surely I did not belong here! But then I trembled. Perhaps, I thought, the thought terrifying me, this *is* where I belong. Perhaps I was not where I belonged before. *Perhaps this is exactly where I belong.*

The fellow beside me moved away.

The last door had now apparently been opened. I heard no more of them being opened.

I lifted my head the tiniest bit. I saw small ankles before me, joined by chain, as mine were. I was only one in a line. It was then, I conjectured, as I had suspected. I was here as a result of selections, based upon some criterion or other. The matter was objective, not personal. It was not that I had offended someone and that my plight had been accordingly engineered for someone's amusement, or that it constituted perhaps, in its way, some sweet tidbit of revenge, one perhaps of many such, the subjects of which, left here, might later be dismissed from mind, and, in time, forgotten. No, the matter was impersonal. My position here was not a consequence of who I was, but, rather, of something else, perhaps of *what* I was. The primary reason I was here was, I supposed, because I was of a certain sort, or kind. But what sort, or kind, could that be? I did not know. I looked at the ankles before me, and the anklets, so close about them. Some of the links of chain between the anklets rested on the stones. I supposed that the metal on my own ankles, though I had not seen it in the light, was the same, or similar. Certainly there would be no reason for it to be different. No, there was nothing unique or special about me, or, at least, nothing any more unique or special than characterized the others in the line. It extended before me and, doubtless, behind me. How many were in it I did not know. There had been several doors opening and closing. Perhaps, I conjectured, there might be fifty of us in this line. There were several in front of me, and doubtless several, given the doors opening and closing, behind me. I thought I might be about two thirds of the way back in the line. Those before me and behind me, as nearly as I could tell, from the languages which had been addressed to them, did not speak my language, or, indeed, one another's language. Our placement in line, I suspected, might not be a matter of chance. I did not think that we had a language in common, as yet.

I heard the tread of those heavy sandals approaching. I put down my head, even lower. Then they passed.

I, and doubtless the others, had been forbidden to look upon our captors. This was very unsettling to me. I wondered why this was. Yet I was, also, afraid to look upon them. I did not know what I would see. Why do they not wish us to look upon them, I wondered. Can their aspect be so terrible, or hideous, I wondered. Perhaps they are disfigured, I thought. Perhaps they are not truly human, I feared. Perhaps they are animals! Or, perhaps, to them, I am an animal! I did not want to be eaten! But I did not think they were animals. And I doubted that I would have been brought here to be eaten. Certainly I had not been fattened. Rather, given the meager diet to which I had been subjected, my figure had been excellently trimmed. This suggested an entirely different theory as to what might be one of my major values in such a place. To be sure, terribly frightened, I thrust this very thought immediately from my head. It was too terrible to even consider.

I then heard, the sound frightening me, from back, near what must be the end of the line, the sound of several coils of chain thrown to the flooring.

"Steady," said a voice near me.

I heard other utterances, too, before me, and behind me, soft, soothing utterances, in other languages. Their import was perhaps similar.

"Steady, little vulo," said the voice.

I was very still. I did not know what a "vulo" was, of course.

I could hear the chain approaching, slowly, pausing briefly by each item in the line, its links moving against one another. Too, shortly after each pause, there was a clear click, as of the meshing and fastening of metal. After a time, it was quite close, only a few feet behind me.

I considered leaping up, running.

But I would only have fallen, miserably.

I was shackled.

Too, where would one run?

Most importantly, I knew that I would not have dared to leap up and run, even if I were not where and as I was. Only a fool, I thought, and understood, even at the time, would be so stupid as to disobey men such as these, in even the smallest way.

I looked to my right, and before me. I could see the shadow there, on the floor, of the man who had spoken to me, it flung before him by some source of illumination, presumably a lantern such as I had seen earlier. He was clearly in a tunic, of some sort. Even in the shadow he seemed large, formidable. He, personally, was behind me, and to my left. He was carrying something in his right hand, which I could see in the shadow, coils of something, the coils stretched out, distorted somewhat, like the silhouette itself. I did not know what the coils might be. I suppose it was obvious but I did not even consider it at the time. Too, if I had known more of where I was, I would have found his mere location, behind me and to my left, a source of considerable apprehension.

"Steady, little tasta," he said, soothingly. I did not know what a "tasta" might be. I had heard the expression 'tasta', and 'vulo', and others, used elsewhere by these men along the side of the line, ingredient among locutions in various languages. Such words, 'vulo' and 'tasta', I gathered, were words in their own language. We, of course, would not know their meaning.

Suddenly I heard, beside me, the rattle of a chain, and before I could think of reacting, had I even dared, a metal collar had been placed about my neck and snapped shut. It, like the collar in the chamber, fitted closely. This was one collar, apparently, of a large number of such collars, for I could see the lower loops of a long chain, one interspersed with such collars, before me. In a moment what was before me was also in a collar. Then the chain and collars were being taken forward, again. The fellow who had been behind me now passed me, on my left. I suddenly then saw the lower loops of what he had been carrying. There was no mistaking it now, no way to misinterpret its appearance. I gasped, and almost fainted.

It was a whip!

After a time two new chains were brought forward, each attached, in turn, down the line, so that, in the end, one long chain was formed.

We waited, those of us already attended to, heads down, on all fours.

Then the last of us, the first in the line, was on the chain.

We were all on the chain.

They then began to speak to us, in various languages. In mine I heard, "Kneel in the following fashion, keeping your head down. Kneel back on your heels, with your knees widely spread. Keep your back straight. Hold your shoulders back. Keep your hands back, and to the sides. The chain on your manacles is to be tight against your waist."

I gathered that our "instruction," now that we had been "placed and aligned," had begun.

Men passed down the line, adjusting positions here and there. When one approached me I drew my hands back as far as I could, to the sides, at my waist, given the length of chain that joined my metal wristlets. I could feel the links of the chain deeply in my flesh. I forced my knees as far apart as I could manage.

"Good," said the man, and continued on, down the line.

In time it seemed that we were all in the position desired.

Again the voices spoke, in diverse languages. In my own language, I heard, "Your heads are bowed in submission. Your bellies are under the chain."

I did not raise my head, of course. I had not been given permission to do so. I looked down. The chain was tight against my waist. There were even marks of the links there. My belly, I had been told, was beneath the chain. What could that possibly mean?

We were left there for a time, in that fashion, kneeling, unattended to, our necks fastened together by the chain.

The men had withdrawn somewhat, I would guess to the end of the line. Their voices now came from behind me. They sounded as though they were several yards away. Perhaps they were at the end of the hall. I could hear them conversing, in their own language, whatever it might be, that language I could not place, that language which seemed so unfamiliar as a whole, and yet in which I detected, or seemed to detect, from time to time, like an image suddenly springing into focus, a familiar sound, perhaps even a word I knew.

I knelt as I had been positioned, my head down, the chain pulled back, taut, at my waist. This rounded, and emphasized, my belly. It called attention to it. There was my belly, with its rounded softness, and, over it, the chain, its links now warmed by my own flesh, but still, though flesh-warmed links of steel, inflexible and merciless. My belly, I had been informed, was beneath the chain.

I did not dare to move.

What did it mean, that my belly was beneath the chain?

I would later become extremely familiar with such positions, but they were, at the time, quite new to me, and somewhat frightening. What most frightened me about them was the way they made me feel. It was not merely that, in them, I felt profoundly stirred. In them, helplessly, vulnerably, I also sensed a personal rightness. I knew that in some sense I belonged in them. This was in contradiction to my entire upbringing, background, education, and conditioning. Could such things have been wrong?

Let us return to the position which had been dictated to us, there in the corridor. It was, of course, a lovely one. There is no doubt about that. But you must understand that much more was involved here. It was not merely that the line of us, the fifty of us, or so, were well revealed in this position, excellently and uncompromisingly exhibited, but there was involved here more profound meaningfulnesses. Let us consider merely two or three aspects of the position. That our shoulders must be well back accentuates, of course, our figure. This calls to our attention, and to that of others, our unique, special and beautiful nature, that it is not to be hidden, or denied, or betrayed, but openly acknowledged, even celebrated. We must be, unapologetically, what we are. The symbolism of kneeling, itself, is doubtless obvious. So, too, perhaps, at least upon reflection, may be the symbolism of the opening of our knees, and what it tells about what we are. But I was not fully aware of this at the time. I was aware only that I felt terribly vulnerable. This makes clear our vulnerability. My own thighs felt inflamed at this exposure. Had someone so much as touched me with the tip of his finger I think I might have screamed. But there are various positions, kneeling and otherwise, and each has many significances.

Why were we now kneeling here, unattended to? Had we been forgotten? Must we wait, as though we might be nothing? I could hear the men speaking. Were they discussing us? Were they commenting on us? Might I, or some of the others, be being spoken of, in particular? Were they consulting records, were they checking off items on a list, or perhaps making entries?

We knelt, becoming more and more sensitive to our position, absorbing more and more deeply into our very beings and bellies its nature.

We knelt, chained, unclothed, fastened together by the neck, in a primitive corridor, heavy doors to the sides, doors to damp, straw-strewn cells or kennels, from which we had been removed. We knelt, forbidden to look up, forbidden to speak.

We waited.

Obviously we were not important.

We waited, neglected.

That we could be kept in this way, and as long as others wished, became clear to us.

Who were these men, that they could treat us in such fashion?

What could we be to them?

We had not even been permitted to look upon them. I was afraid to learn what they looked like, but I wanted to know. I did not think they were animals. I thought they were human. I wondered if they were fully human. Why did they not permit us to look upon them? Could they, for some reason or another, be so terrible to look upon? Who were they? Or, what were they? They seemed men, to be sure, but they did not seem men in the sense, or in the ways, in which I had grown accustomed to think of men. In some senses they seemed quite different. Who, or what, were they? I wanted to know, desperately. But, too, I was afraid to learn.

We knelt there, learning our unimportance, understanding more and more clearly our vulnerability and helplessness, and experiencing sensations, unusual and troubling sensations, sensations which were very deep and profound.

Then the men were amongst us again, and one stood quite close to me, a bit to the left, before me.

He was perhaps a yard from me.

The chain on my neck extended to the collar in front of me. I could feel its weight, and I could feel, at the back of the collar I wore, the weight of the chain there, leading back to the collar behind me.

I could see the heavy bootlike sandals.

He was to the left of the chain before me, almost at the shoulder of the preceding item on the chain.

My head was down. I dared not look up.

I began to tremble.

But I held position as well as I could.

He was close!

In whose power were we?

I heard voices before me, down the line, in order, approaching, and heard, shortly thereafter, one after the other, gasps, and soft cries.

I kept my head down.

I was terribly frightened, and terribly aware of the presence of the man before me.

"You may lift your heads," I heard. "You may look upon us."

I lifted my head and gasped. I cried out, softly, an inarticulate, unrestrainable sound, one of incredible relief, even of joy, one consequent upon the release of incredible tension, one consequent upon the discharge of an almost unbearable emotion.

He was human!

He smiled and put his finger to his lips, a gesture that warned me that I was not to speak, a gesture with which I was familiar, from my own cultural background. I did not know if it were native to his as well.

I heard the voices continuing behind me, and, down the line, more gasps, and cries.

I looked up at the man near me. He was not now looking at me, but, rather, looking back, behind me, down the line.

Perhaps I was not important enough to be looked at.

But I looked at him, wildly, drinking in all that I could. He was strikingly handsome. It took my breath away, to look upon him. But this handsomeness, you must understand, was one of strong, powerful features. It was not the mild, pleasant configuration which in some localities, such as those with which I was more familiar, those more germane to my own antecedents, was often mistaken for that quality. There was a ruggedness in the features. He was handsome undoubtedly, even strikingly so, as I have indicated, but this was in a simple, direct, very masculine way. He had seemed kind. He had smiled, he had put his finger to his lips, warning me to silence. He was a large, strong, supple man. He had large hands. He had sturdy legs. The legs disturbed me, for they were strong, and, in the tunic, brief, coarse, and brown, much revealed. He wore the heavy bootlike sandals that I had noted before. These, with their heavy thongs, or cords, came high on the calf. This footwear somehow frightened me. It seemed to have a look of menace or brutality.

I was unutterably relieved that he was not looking at me.

I had never seen such a man!

I had not known such a man could exist!

I did not know what I could do, or would do, if he so much as looked at me. I wondered, though I attempted to prevent the thought from occurring, sensing its immediate and inevitable appearance, what it might be to be in his arms. I tried to put such a thought from me, to banish it to the secret depths from which it had emerged, but I could not do so. It was more powerful than I. It was irresistible. I shuddered. I knew that, in his arms, I would be utterly helpless. Indeed, if he had even so much as looked upon me, I feared I might have begun to whimper, beggingly. Could this be I? What was I? What had been done to me? How was it that I could be so transformed, and so helpless, given merely the sight of such a man?

But then, frightened, I looked wildly ahead, and about. So, too, it seemed, were the others. I looked at the other men. Again I gasped, startled. Again I was shocked. Again I could not believe what I saw. The fellow before me was not unusual, it seemed, though, given my previous acquaintance with men, surely I would have thought him quite unusual, if not unique. The other men, too, in their way, were strong, handsome fellows, and that, too, in an almost indefinable, powerful masculine way. This much disturbed me. They were dressed similarly to the fellow near me. They, too, wore tunics, some of them sleeveless, and, invariably, the same sort of sandals, sandals which might have withstood marches. Where was I, I wondered, that such men could exist?

Again I looked up at the man near me.

Then, suddenly, he looked down, at me.

I averted my eyes, in terror.

Never before anything had I felt myself so much what, irreducibly, now undeniably, I was.

I trembled.

It might have been not a man, but a beast or a god, or an animal, a cougar, or a lion, in human form.

The only relation in which I could stand to such a thing was clear to me.

Some other men passed by me, going to one part of the line or another. Some of them carried leather quirts. Others carried whips.

They then began, along the line, and behind me, to talk to us. They did so quietly, soothingly.

The fellow near me crouched down beside me. He turned my head, gently, to face him. I looked into his eyes. He put his left hand behind the back of my neck, over the metal collar, and the fingers of his right hand lightly over my lips. I was not to speak.

"You have no name," he informed me.

I did not understand this, but his fingers were lightly over my lips.

He then stood up, and looked down at me. My eyes were lifted to his.

"Do you wish to be fed?" he asked.

I looked up at him, frightened.

"You may speak," he said.

"Yes," I whispered.

"Do you wish to live?" he asked.

"Yes," I said.

Then he looked at me, frankly, appraisingly, unabashedly. I had never been looked at like that in my life.

It seemed he would regard every inch of me.

I could not even understand such a look.

Or did something in me understand it only too well?

Suddenly, piteously, I rose up from my heels, and, still kneeling, of course, lifted my hands to him. Tears coursed from my eyes. I wept. I could not control myself. I could scarcely speak. But he seemed kind. He must understand. I knelt before him, in helpless petition. "Mercy," I wept. "I pray you for mercy!" I clasped my hands together, praying him for mercy. I lifted my hands to him thusly clasped, in desperate prayer, piteously. "Please!" I wept. "Please!"

He looked down at me.

"Please, I beg you," I wept. "Mercy! I beg mercy! Show me mercy! I beg it! I beg it!"

His expression did not change.

Then I felt unutterably stupid. I put down my hands, and my head. I sank back to my heels, my hands, in their metal wristlets, on my thighs.

I looked up at him, and then put down my head again.

"I am not to be shown mercy, am I?" I whispered.

"Not in the sense I suspect you have in mind," he said. "On the other hand, if you prove superb, truly superb, you might eventually be shown a certain mercy, at least in the sense of being permitted to live."

I shuddered.

"Position," he said, gently.

I struggled back to the position which I had originally held.

How stupid I felt. How stupid I had been!

I was merely one on a chain. I had not been brought here, doubtless at some trouble and expense, to be shown mercy.

How could I have acted as I did?

I was stupid.

I hoped I was not stupid.

I hoped that he did not think I was stupid.

Once again I felt his eyes upon me. Once again, I was being subjected to that calm, appraising scrutiny which had, but a moment before, so unnerved me.

"Please," I begged him.

He seemed to be regarding me as might one who is practiced in such appraisals, one who, in effect, might be noting points. But surely I should not be looked at in such a way. Surely only an animal might be looked at in such a way. But surely I was not an animal!

My hands crept up from my sides, that I might, however inadequately, cover myself.

"No," he said, gently.

His tone, in its kindliness, its patience, suggested that he did not think me stupid, in spite of my earlier outburst. This, for some reason, gladdened me.

Then I knelt as I had before, tears coursing down my cheeks, open, exposed, to his scrutiny.

It was thus that he would have me before him, and thus it was that I would be before him.

Before men such as these I understood that I would be choiceless in such matters.

"You are supposedly quite vital," he said. "Is it true?"

"I do not know," I said. I did not even understand the question. Or, perhaps, rather, I somehow, in some part of me, understood it only too well.

Would he now think me stupid? I hoped not. I did not think I was stupid.

He then continued his scrutiny.

Somehow I wanted, desperately, doubtless dreadfully, for him to be pleased, genuinely pleased, with what he saw.

Was I "vital"?

What could that possibly mean?

How would I know if I were vital or not?

Had he touched me, I think I would have cried out, in helplessness.

I could not help it if I was vital! It was not my fault! I could not help it!

And at that time, of course, I did not understand how such things could be brought about, even in those initially inert or anesthetic, how such things could be, and would be, suspected, discovered, revealed, and released, and then nurtured, and enhanced, and developed and trained, until they, beginning as perhaps no more than almost unfocused restlessnesses, could, and would, become fervent, soft, insistent claims, and then, in time, implacably, inexorably, desperate, irresistible, pitiless needs, needs overriding and overwhelming, needs over which one had no control, needs in whose chains one is utterly helpless.

I knelt there, then, as they would have me kneel. No longer did I dare to look at him. I kept my head down. Then, in a moment, he had apparently finished his examination, or, I feared, assessment. I did not know what might have been the results of his examination. He said something to another fellow. I did not know whether or not I was the subject of their discourse. Their tones, on the other hand, seemed approving. Both seemed pleased. To be sure, I did not know for certain whether or not I was the subject of their discourse. But it seemed to me likely that I was.

I suspected then, if I was not mistaken, to my unspeakable relief, that I might have been found at least initially acceptable.

I hoped that he who was nearest to me did not think I was stupid.

I did not want him to think that.

I was supposedly intelligent. I was, or had been, a good student. To be sure, the learning for which I might be held accountable here, if such learning there was to be, would doubtless be somewhat different from that to which I had been accustomed. The collar on my neck suggested that, and the chains on my limbs.

I heard voices, ahead of me, and, too, some behind me.

"You may lift your head," he said. His fellow had went further back, behind me.

I lifted my head.

The metal shackle on my neck had been put on from behind. There is variation in such things. Most often, particularly with items such as we, new to such things, and naive, it is done in that fashion, I suppose, to minimize the tendency to bolt. At other times, however, it is done from the beginning, particularly with individuals who realize clearly and fully what is going on, so that they may, in full specificity and anticipation, with full intellectual and emotional understanding, see it approach, one by one, and then find themselves, in turn, no different from others, secured within its obdurate clasp. The first, you see, might be frightened at its sight and, in their naiveté, be tempted to bolt; the second, on the other hand, might be terrified at its sight, but realizes that there is no escape.

I heard the voices before and behind me.

It was not for no reason that I had been permitted to lift my head.

Here and there before me, and, I suppose, behind me, one or another of the men were thrusting whips to the lips of the items in the line. He who was nearest to me had such a device hooked on his belt. I looked on, disbelievingly. Then the fellow nearest me removed that effective, supple tool from his belt. I began to tremble. "Do not be afraid," he said, soothingly.

I watched the device, as he loosened the coils a little, arranging them, in almost hypnotic fascination.

"It will take but a moment," he said. "Do not be frightened."

The coils were then but an inch from my lips. I looked up at him.

"It was foolish of me to beg for mercy," I whispered. "I am sorry."

"You will learn to beg, in rational contexts, even more piteously," he said. "Indeed, it will be important for you, to learn how to beg well. I do not mean merely that you will be taught to beg prettily, on your knees, and such things. I mean rather that upon certain occasions the only thing which might stand between you and the loss of your nose and ears, or life, may be the sincerity and excellence with which you can perform certain placatory behaviors."

"I do not want you to think I am stupid," I said.

He looked down at me. I could not read his expression.

"I am not stupid," I said.

"We shall see," he said.

I heard words. I saw a whip thrust to the lips of the item before me in the line.

A whip, too, was within an inch of my own lips.

I drew back my head a little, and looked up at him.

He did nothing.

I did not know what to do. What was I supposed to do? I knew what I should do, what would be appropriate, what I wanted to do.

"I do not know what to do," I said.

"What a shy, timid thing you are," he said.

"The others are speaking to us," I said. "You are not speaking to me. You are not telling me what to do."

"What do you think you should do?" he asked.

"I don't know," I said.

"What do you want to do?" he asked.

"No, no!" I said.

"You will kiss, and lick, the whip," he said, "lovingly, lingeringly."

I looked up at him, in terror.

"Do you understand?" he asked.

"Yes," I said.

"First," he said, "the whip will come to you, and then, second, you will come to the whip."

"I understand," I said.

Surely I must resist this! I could feel the chain at my belly. I squirmed a little on my knees.

He held the whip gently to my lips. He could, I realized, have done this in a very different manner. He might have done it with brutality. He might, in effect, have struck me, perhaps bruising my lips, perhaps bloodying my mouth, forcing the soft inner surfaces of the lips back against the teeth. I might have tasted leather and my own blood. But he was very gentle. With incredible feelings, which I could scarcely comprehend, I kissed the whip, and then, slowly, licked it.

He then removed the whip from my lips and held it a few inches before me.

I was now, I gathered, to come to the whip!

It is one thing, of course, to have such an implement forced upon you, giving you, in effect, no choice in the matter. It is quite another to expect you, of your own will, to approach it, and subject it to such intimate, tender ministrations. What did he think I was? I would do no such thing!

I fought with myself. Part of me decried the very thought of coming to the whip. And part of me, some deep, fearful part, longed to do so.

The deeper part of me was stronger.

I leaned forward a little, and reached out with my lips for the whip. In ecstasy, I kissed it. I kissed it lovingly and lingeringly. I think that I had never been so happy, or so fulfilled, as in those moments. Then, with my tongue, again and again, softly, tenderly, lovingly, I licked it. I could taste the leather. I feared only the moment when it would be taken from me.

Then the implement was drawn back.

I looked up into the eyes of he who held the whip. I now knew what, in my heart, I was.

He who had been nearest to me now stepped away. I, and, I gather, the others, were now, again, left kneeling, but now our heads might be up.

We knelt there.

We were now being given time to ourselves, I suppose, kneeling there, the chain at our belly, that we might understand, and appreciate, the momentousness, at least from our point of view, of what had occurred. Let us now, kneeling there, the chain at our belly, realize what we had done; let us now understand, and appreciate, how we might now be utterly different from what we had been before.

I had kissed his whip, in giddy ecstasy!

I was prepared to give myself to him, to love him!

Had he so much as snapped his fingers I would have done anything!

I heard, again, voices behind me. One or another of the men were coming down the line, approaching from behind. I did not look back. It is not so easy to do, held in the collar, both from before and behind. Too, I did not know if it were permitted. This seemed a place in which it might be well to be very clear on what was permitted, and what was not.

Then, out of the corner of my eye, coming from behind, I saw the coils of another whip. Then two men were rather before me, to the left of the chain. I looked up. Joy transfigured my countenance for one, with his whip, was he who had earlier been nearest to me, he to whose whip I had pressed timidly, then fervently, my moist lips, which whip, too, I had subjected to the tender, eager servile caresses of my tongue. But it was the other fellow's whip which was now held before me! It was not that of he who had hitherto been nearest to me! I looked up, dismayed, startled, at he who had been nearest to me. Surely it was his whip, and his whip alone, which I must kiss! He looked down at me. There seemed, for a moment, a sternness in his gaze. This terrified me. Quickly I put my head forward a little, as I could, in the chain and collar, and kissed, and licked, obediently, tears welling in my eyes, the other's whip. The two men then, paying me no more attention, went forward on the chain and, in turn, each of those before me kissed what, too, for them, must have been a second whip. I knelt there. I looked after he who had been nearest to me. I choked back a sob.

In a few moments we again received instructions.

"To all fours," I heard.

I, and the others, went forward to all fours.

We then waited there, on all fours, in the line. My tears fell to the stone flagging. My knees felt how hard it was, and my hands and toes.

It had a rough texture. The corridor, it now seemed, was damp and cold. Too, it seemed dim now. The light from the lanterns flickered about. I became even more aware of my chains.

I sobbed.

I had kissed his whip. I had thought that it had meant everything, but it had meant nothing. But, of course, in meaning nothing, it had, in its way, in a sense more grievous and fearful than I had understood at the time, meant everything. The kissing of the whip had been impersonal. I was, apparently, in this place, one for whom it was appropriate to kiss the whip. That was the kind of which I was, whatever kind, in this place, that might be. The kissing of the whip had been impersonal. It made no difference whose whip it was. It could have been any whip. That was the lesson of the "second whip."

After a time the men returned and, here and there, took positions along the line.

He who had been nearest to me was now near to me again. This was doubtless because he could speak my language. He was a bit before me, and to my left. I looked up at him. What emotions I felt! I had kissed his whip! He put his finger over his lips, cautioning me to silence. The whip was now partly uncoiled, in his right hand.

I put my head down.

The chain attached to the ring on the front of my collar looped forward, and up, to the side of the item before me. The chain attached to the ring on the back of my collar, as the link turned, and given my position, lay diagonally over my back, behind my left shoulder, whence it descended, to loop up, to the front ring of the collar behind me.

We waited.

I felt the coils of his whip touch my back lightly. It seemed an idle movement, prompted perhaps by no impulse more profound than might tempt one, in passing time, to doodle on a sheet of paper with some writing implement, but, of course, any such touch shook me profoundly.

I looked up at him.

Again, with a gesture, I was cautioned to silence.

Did he not know what that touch did to me?

I put my head down again. There was a tiny sound of chain. I assumed that we, those of us in the line, would be soon removed from this place.
I did not know what awaited me.
Then, again, I felt the touch of the whip. This time, however, I did not sense that its movement was a completely idle one, little more, if anything, than doodling. Rather, it seemed somewhat more curious, more directed, as though it might have some object of inquiry in mind. It moved, gently, inquisitively, along the side of my body. I gasped. There was a sound of chain. I almost fell. I recovered my position. I shuddered. I moaned, a tiny, helpless sound. I looked up at him, wildly.
"You do not have permission to speak," he said.
I put my head down, again.
Then I felt the leather again, in its gentle, exploratory fashion, here and there, touch my body.
I did not dare to protest, of course. I was one, I gathered, to whom such things might be done.
"Ohh!" I said, suddenly.
"You may prove satisfactory," he mused. "You may survive."
At that moment words were again spoken, farther ahead in the line. But there need not be exact translations for us all, for the import of these words was clear enough, from the actions of those first in the line, who understood, and from the movements of the whips in the hands of the men, gesturing forward.
I heard the slack in the chains being taken up. I saw those before me, farther down the line, begin to move.
"Keep your head down," he said.
I could not forget the feel of the whip, its touch, upon my body.
He who had been nearest to me was now back somewhere, back beside the line, behind me.
I heard chains moving ahead of me. Neck chains, and those on small wrists and ankles.
I had felt the gentle touch of the whip.
It seemed my body was on fire.
Then I felt the chain grow taut before me, and draw on the ring on the front of my collar, and I, too, on all fours, joined that procession

moving down the corridor, and, in turn, so, too, did those behind me.

I crawled in chains, at the feet of men.

The corridor was long.

I could not forget the touch of the leather. I had succumbed, physiologically, emotionally, to its touch.

What could that mean?

What had become of me?

What lay ahead of me?

"Harta!" called a man. "Harta!"

Did he expect us to understand him? That must be a word in his language. Certainly it was not one in mine.

"Harta!" he called.

How could we possibly know what that meant?

There was suddenly, from well behind me, yards back, back down the line, a sharp, cruel crack, almost as clear and terrible, in the narrow corridor, as the report of a rifle. I, and several of the others, cried out, with misery and terror. But I do not think that anyone had been struck. I do not think that I had ever heard that sound before, or certainly not in such a way, or place, but there was no mistaking it. Something in me, immediately, without reconnoitering, without complex reflection, recognized it. To such as I that sound was very meaningful. We recognized it, and understood it, instantaneously. We did not have to be told what it was.

We hurried forward, sobbing.

From time to time, as we moved down the corridor, we heard that sound again, from here and there along the line. Once it came from behind me, and to my left, only a few feet away. I screamed in terror and fell. My neck chain dragged forward on the collar. It cut at the back of my neck. What was behind me moved half beside me, sobbing. Instantly as there was again that terrible sound I struggled to my hands and knees, hurrying forward.

"Harta!" I heard. "Harta!"

But we were hurrying! How could we go more swiftly?

Again came the terrible crack of that snapping coil!

Gasping, crying out, sobbing, we moved even more swiftly!

We were terrified by the very sound of those supple implements.

Surely they could not be used upon us!

Surely these men, these leonine males, like gods and beasts, did not regard us as being subject to such attentions! But somehow I suspected that these men, these unusual males, these incredible males, our striking, magnificent captors, were not likely to be patient with us. We were a kind, I gathered, on which such men were not likely to lavish patience.

But what kind could that be?

Of what kind was I now, or had I been, and now was explicitly, openly?

I dared not conjecture, but knew.

Somewhat behind me, to the side, I heard again that terrible sound, that sharp, fearful crack of leather.

I sobbed.

I hurried.

Five

I was kneeling in the garden, on the lavender grass, as it was in that part of the garden, my head down, the palms of my hands on the grass.

I had earlier crossed the perimeter of small, sharpened stones, a foot or so deep, about ten feet wide, which lined the interior wall of the garden. I had gone to the interior wall, the marbled wall, and touched it, and looked upward, to its height, and the incurved blades at the top. It had hurt, of course, to so approach the wall, because of the sharpened stones, and one's being barefoot, but I had wanted to do so. The garden was within the city itself. On the other side of the wall there was, I thought, a street. One could hear people talking, calling out to one another. One could hear vendors hawking their wares. One could hear wagons passing, drawn by four-legged tharlarion, ponderous draft creatures of this world. But not all the draft creatures of this world have four legs. Some have two legs. Sometimes, too, I could hear the snarl of animals, doubtless leashed. Too, sometimes one could detect the tramp of men, and, sometimes, too, they sang as they marched. Sometimes there were altercations outside the wall. Once I had heard the clash of metal. At other times there was the laughter of children, running, sporting in games, games which might be common, I suppose, to children anywhere. Occasionally heralds, or criers, would pass by, calling out news or announcements. Many on this world, you see, cannot read. Thus the importance of the heralds, the criers, and such. Many things are advertised, too, in such a way, by calling out bargains, the fruits in season, the markets, the cost of cloth, and such. Too, one may hear men, or, often, boys, for it costs less to hire them, calling out the pleasures of various taverns, and the delights that may be found within. I should not have gone to the wall, of course. We are forbidden, even, to step upon the perimeter of sharpened stones, that lining its interior side. But I had wanted to do so. I had wanted to look closely upon, and even to touch, the ascendant surface of that looming confinement, so beautiful, and yet so practical, and formidable. Did I expect to find within it a chink, or a secret door? No, I am not so stupid. I think I wanted to touch, and to understand, if only a little better, that which held me in this place. I have always wanted to touch, and to understand. The wall, in its way, aside from its height and thickness, its weight, its formidableness, its rearing terribleness, was mysterious to me. Perhaps better I might say that it, in its way, symbolized a mystery for me. What was I doing here? Certainly I was not one of the finest flowers in the garden. There seemed nothing so unique, or different, or precious about me. I did not think myself such that I might be selected out from hundreds to be brought here. There seemed to me no special reason why I should have been brought here. I did not know why I was here. Too, my curiosity was roused by the transition which had taken place in my fortunes, so abruptly, and with how I had been brought here, so secretly. One does not, commonly, go from what I was, within my kind, to one of the gardens. Usually one is either selected out almost immediately for the gardens, almost from the beginning, or, later, after one has attained various intermediate levels or degrees. One seldom goes, so to speak, in one moment, from straw mats and clay bowls to silk and gold. Betwixt there are many things, sheets of copper, plates of bronze, ingots of iron, tablets of silver, such things. To be sure, one may be seen, and have a fancy taken to one. There is little predictability in such things. Too, it must be admitted that one is sometimes brought secretly to such a place. I do not mean, of course, merely one who is not of my kind, that is, as yet, legally, or officially, but who will doubtless soon be of my kind, legally, and officially, but those who, to begin with, when acquired, are of my kind. Yes, even some of the latter are brought to such places secretly. Just as they may be acquired secretly. What the garden contains, you see, its contents, and their value, need not be for everyone to know. But I did not think I had been brought here merely in the light of such familiar, comprehensible considerations. Of course, I did not know. It may have been that someone noticed the turn of an ankle, the movement of a hand, the fall of one's hair on the back, the hints whispered by a tunic, an expression, such things. I did not know. Could things be that simple? Perhaps they were that simple. I hoped so. But I was uneasy. I was not sure of it. Could I be different from the others, in some sense I did not understand? I thought, somehow, I might be. To be sure, I served here, as the others, and was subject to the same perfections of keeping as they. In this sense I was no different from them. Many of them seemed jealous of me, and resented me, for no reason I understood, but such things are natural, I gather, in such a place. But I did not think they really thought it strange that one such as I should be here, nor did the guards seem to think so. These all took me for granted, much as it is common to take for granted those in the gardens, saving perhaps one or another who might enjoy greater or lesser favor now and then. I was, from the point of view of the others, and the guards, as far as I could tell, only another adornment here, only another flower. Doubtless there was no more to it. I had touched the wall, and looked up to its height, and the knives. I did not want to be within the garden. To be sure, there are doubtless worse places to be. Many doubtless long for the garden, its plenty, its security, its beauty. It is doubtless safer here than on the other side of the wall. One could tell that at times from the alarms, the running of feet, the cries, one heard outside. At such times we looked at one another, in fear. Muchly then were we pleased to be within the garden. We were sometimes frightened that the portals of the house might be breached, that the hinges of barred gates might be broken from the stone, that the garden might be entered, and we might be found, helpless in the garden, like luscious fruit in an orchard whose supposedly impregnable walls have been rent. These fears were not as ungrounded as one might suppose. Times were hard in the city, I gathered, though I did not understand much of what was occurring. Sometimes something like anarchy seemed to reign in the streets. Certain gardens, we had gathered, had been breached, and plundered, their contents taken away, to what places and for what purposes who knew. But our house, I understood, was immune from such ravages. Our house, it seemed, enjoyed some special status. It stood high, it seemed, in the favor of those who controlled the city. We had been, until now, at least, exempted from exactions, confiscations, taxations, and such. To be sure, it was in its way an uneasy existence for us, in the garden, for we could hear what occasionally went on in the streets, on the other side of the wall, and we had gathered, from remarks of guards, overheard, and such, that not every house in the city, with such a garden, had been spared rude, abrupt attentions. In the garden we were pampered and soft. We need only please and be beautiful. We had silks, perfumes, cosmetics, and jewelry. Let such things be our concern. We were ignorant, almost entirely so, of what went on outside. Indeed, that was appropriate for us. It was not ours to be informed. That is not the sort we were. Sometimes, when there were harsh sounds in the street outside, I looked at some of the others, and saw them regarding one another, fear in their eyes, drawing their silks more closely about themselves. There was a world on the other side of the wall, a world quite different from that to which they were accustomed. It was a harsh, violent, impatient, exacting world. Were they to find themselves within it I did not doubt but what they would discover their lives considerably transformed. I myself, however, did not wish to remain in the garden. I had seen a world much more real outside the wall. It was in that world that I wished to be, even with its cruelties and dangers. It was not that I was dissatisfied with my condition, you understand, because I had come to understand what I was, and to rejoice in it. It was, rather, that I wished to be what I was *outside* the wall, not within the wall, not within the garden. Indeed, within the wall, I could not fully realize my natural condition, not to its fullest extent, what I was. One required for that a full world, with its thousands of ramifications and perils. I would have preferred a rag, if permitted that, outside the wall, to the silks and jewels of a favorite within.

I had heard voices coming from the house. I had then, swiftly, as swiftly as I could, given the stones, withdrawn from the wall. It had hurt to do so, cruelly, but it would be far worse to be discovered there, as the wall is forbidden. Indeed, it is forbidden even to enter upon the expanse of stones inside it, at its foot. Oh, I should not have gone to it, of course. It is forbidden. I had looked about, however. I had done my best to make sure that I had not been observed.

I had been sure that I had not been observed.

It had been my intention to circle about, through the shrubbery, and the tiny, lovely trees in the garden, to the vicinity of the fountain.

But I had scarcely entered upon the grass when I had heard a man's voice. "Stop," he had said.

I had knelt, of course, immediately, and put my head down to the grass, the palms of my hands, too, on the grass.

How could it be a man, here, at this time of day?

I did not raise my head. I had not received permission to do so.

I did not break position.

I had not received permission to do so.

I was in light silk. It was extremely brief, and was, for most practical purposes, diaphanous. Certainly it left little doubt as to my lineaments.

I knelt before him, my head down to the grass, my palms on the grass.

Who was he?

What could he want?

Six

"On your belly," had said a man.
I complied.
It is unthinkable on this world that such a command not be obeyed instantly, or, at least, that one such as I not obey it instantly.
And so I lay on my belly, on the colorful tiles, in one of the sales rooms in the pens.
Too, of course, one does not simply sprawl on one's belly. There are ways, diverse ways, of assuming this position. We are taught them. Other women, women unlike us, one supposes, do not know them. They, too, of course, can be taught. In this house, such a command, unqualified, requires that the head be turned to the left and the arms be placed down, beside the body, the palms up. A slightly different command requires the crossing of the wrists behind the back and the crossing of the ankles, as well. This is sometimes used when one is to be bound. If one receives permission to look up, or is commanded to do so, which is frightening, the hands are normally placed to the sides, at the shoulders, and one then lifts one's upper body. The belly itself, of course, remains in contact with the surface on which one lies, the grass, the dirt, the gravel, the deck, the floor, the tiles, whatever the surface may be. But there are numerous variations in such things, as there are in ways to kneel, ways to hurry, ways to serve, ways to crawl to the furs, and such. There are even ways in which the whip, if called for, is to be brought. In our training, as you might suppose, we learn many things. In time our training, extending even to the tiniest nuances of attitude, and to the smallest movements and gestures, is internalized, indeed, in such a way that we are no longer, or seldom,

even aware of it, it having become, in effect, the way we are. There is a world of difference between us and certain other women, women unlike us, as you might suppose, but what is perhaps less obvious, and what might be pointed out, is that there are considerable differences amongst us, even those such as I, as well. Consider merely the matter of training. One of us who is trained will normally, other things being equal, be appraised more highly than one who is not; one who is superbly trained will normally, other things being equal, be appraised more highly than one who is merely well trained, and so on. I refer, of course, to appraisals in a practical, factual manner, having to do, for example, with what men will *pay* for us.

"She bellies well," observed a man.

"Has she been long in the pens?" inquired another.

"Not long," said he who had first spoken.

"Has she made progress?" asked a fellow.

"She has made excellent progress," said another.

"Can she understand what we are saying?" asked another.

"Yes," said another.

"She is quite intelligent then," asked one of the men. I did not recognize his voice. I did not think I knew him. I had not, of course, looked boldly about. Too, when one is on one's belly, with the head turned to the side, one is scarcely in a position to study the countenances about one. Too, even if one is standing, or working, or serving, one seldom meets the eyes of such men directly.

"Considering her origin, and what she is, she is extremely intelligent," said a man.

"Good," said the fellow who had spoken before, him I did not recognize. But, to be sure, he was with three or four others who, too, I did not know, or doubted that I knew. They were from outside the house. I was sure of that.

"She is absolutely ignorant of the political situation?" asked the fellow I did not know.

"Yes," said a man.

"She is from the world, Earth," pointed out another.

"There is such a place?" asked a man, one of those I did not know.

"Yes," he was assured.

"It is an excellent source of stock," said another.

"And she has only recently arrived on our world," asked one of those I did not know.

"Recently enough," he heard.

"She has been in the pens?" asked another, one of those I did not know.

"She has not been outside them since her arrival," said a man.

That was true. I had little, if any, idea of the nature of the world to which I had been brought.

"Are you interested in her?" asked one of the men I knew, one from the house.

"Have her stand, and turn," said a man.

I heard the snapping of fingers.

Quickly I rose to my feet, and turned, before them.

"Interesting," said a man.

"Clasp your hands behind the back of your head," said a fellow from the house.

I complied.

"Arch your back," said another.

My left foot was now slightly advanced. I was bent backwards, my back arched. My hands were clasped behind the back of my head.

"Yes," said another. "Interesting."

"Belly," said the fellow who had first spoken to me.

Instantly I returned to my belly, as I had been before, my head turned to the left, my arms back, down at my sides, my hands turned so that my palms, their softness, faced up, exposed.

The new fellows, those who were strangers in the house, I gathered, were not to be shown more, not without having requested it, it seemed, not without having, in effect, committed themselves to some degree, in virtue of the expression of some explicit, rather more tangible, interest. Those of the house were skilled in what they were doing.

"Perhaps we should look at others," said one of the fellows I did not know.

"We have items from various cities, and from villages and districts, brought in from time to time, requisitioned, and such," said the fellow from the house. "We have an excellent item from Besnit, blond, whose hair comes to her ankles."

"It must be an outworlder," said a stranger, impatiently, he who seemed to be first among those I did not know.

"That was my understanding," agreed the fellow from the house.

"But there must be other outworlders," said one of the strangers, rather lightly.

"Yes, we still have several," said a fellow from the house. "As you recall, you looked upon them last night, by lamplight, while they slept, in their kennels. This one, as I understand it, was your choice."

I lay there. I had not realized that I, and the others, had been looked upon last night, while we slept. There is, of course, no way to prevent that.

"You have seen the papers," said one of the fellows of the house to someone. "You have seen the reports. You have spoken to the teachers, and trainers."

"They have other outworlders," said the cautious fellow, one of the strangers.

"We do not have as many as we did," said a fellow of the house. "They tend to be distributed about. We get only our share. Too, of those we receive, we normally have orders for several. Some we ship without training, to other houses and such. You must understand that, over the past few years, as their value has come to be more generally recognized, such items have become more popular."

"And more expensive," observed a stranger, irritably.

"Sometimes," it was admitted.

"Are you sure you want an outworlder?" asked one of the fellows of the house.

"Yes," he was told.

"Given your specifications," said the fellow from the house, first among those of the house, "I really think this item is your likely choice."

There was a silence.

"You must understand," said the fellow from the house, first among them, "that your specifications are not easy to fulfill. If an item is reasonably skillful in the language it is not likely to be ignorant of the world, and, if it is ignorant of the world, it is less likely to be adept with the language."

"This one is intelligent?"

"Quite so, subject of course, as made clear, to her origin, and what she is."

"Let us consider others," said the cautious fellow.

"We have seen them. We have examined their papers, and such," said the stranger who, I took it, was first among them.

"We have several items in stock," said the fellow from the house, who was first among those of the house. "You may examine them, if you wish, more so than you have already done. Nonetheless I really think that this item is the one best for your purposes. It should well satisfy your needs. I conjecture that it should do quite nicely." He added, "I am quite familiar with our current inventory."

"You could examine items at another house," said another fellow of the house.

There was silence.

"Are you interested only in an item which satisfies the criteria you have made clear to me?" asked he who was first of those of the house.

"I do not understand," said a man.

"I might, with your permission," said the first fellow, "mention that this particular item has certain qualities to recommend it, should you be interested in them, beyond being intelligent, an outworlder, having developed, in a short time, a modest command of the language, and being ignorant of political intricacies."

"Other qualities?" asked a fellow.

"Other than those which are quite evident to your senses, other than those which you could detect by merely laying eyes upon her," said the fellow from the house, first among those of the house.

There was laughter.

I lay there, before them.

"Are such things also of interest to you?" asked he who was first among those of the house, first, at any rate, among those present.

"Are they not always of interest?" asked a fellow.

There was more laughter.

"More importantly," said one of the strangers, "should she not be such as to appear plausibly to have been purchased for the typical reasons for which such an item might be obtained?"

"Yes," mused another man.

"I assure you," said the fellow from the house, "that she could be excellently, and judiciously, purchased for just such typical reasons."

"She fulfills such criteria, independently?"

"Assuredly," said the fellow from the house.

"Let her perform," said he who, I took it, was first among the strangers.

"Prepare," said he who was first among those of the house.

I rose lightly to my feet, and turned, and, head down, put my hand to my left shoulder. I was unclothed, of course, but had I been silked the disrobing loop would have been at the left shoulder. I had learned how to remove the silk gracefully. Now, of course, I must merely pretend to do so. I moved my hand as though loosening the disrobing loop, and then, gracefully, stepped away from the silk which had supposedly fallen about my ankles. I then, facing the strangers, the newcomers, knelt before them, in a position of obeisance, my head down to the floor, the palms of my hands on the floor, too.

"She looks well in such a position," said a man.

"They all do," said another.

I had known, of course, for years, even before puberty, that such deferences, obeisances, and such, were owed to men, but I had never expected, except perhaps in dreams, to find myself in my present position, one in which I was subject to, and must behave in accordance with, such appropriatenesses.

"Begin," said he who was first among those of the house.

I rose to my feet, and, obedient to the injunction under which I had been placed, began to move. I moved first before one man and then another. I began, of course, with he whom I immediately sensed was first among the strangers. I sensed this from his position, central and prominent among them, and from the nature of his gaze upon me, which I could meet only for an instant. I moved before the men, first before one and then before another, approaching, withdrawing, sometimes as if unwilling, or shy, sometimes almost as if daring to be insolent or rebellious, but not quite, or not really, of course, for if such things are misunderstood one may quickly feel the lash. It is more as though a token challenge were offered but one which is clearly understood as, and is presented as, no more than that, for one knows that even such tokens may be swept away, and crushed, and one may find oneself suddenly upon one's knees, in one's place, cringing in terror, in the rightful servitude of one's nature. And then there is a sensuousness which can be taunting, in effect, a challenge to one's conquest, and a sensuousness which is taunting in another respect, an invitation to partake of proffered raptures. And there are the movements of petition, of pleading, of begging. There are movements of these, and of many other sorts. Some of these movements I had been taught. Others, in effect, were known to me from long ago. I had, in secrecy, practiced them, before mirrors, when alone. I had found them somehow in the piteous recesses of my needs, had drawn them forth as though from an ancient knowledge. I had wondered how it was sometimes that I could have known such things. Had I moved thusly long ago, in a former life, before a prince of some royal house on the Nile, before some caliph in his cool, white palace abutting the slow waters of the Tigris, in the house of some oligarch overlooking the Tiber? Or were these things locked in the very cells of my body, in the mysteries of genes and chromosomes, a part of my nature, selected for, over thousands of generations? Perhaps, thusly, such as I had, at times, writhed naked and piteous at the feet of some primitive hunter, before his fire, that he would not use the heavy stone in his hand, that I might be permitted to live. How I would have been prepared to accept, and relish, eagerly, gratefully, the harsh terms which he might decree! And here, too, it seemed, in this place, new revelations had come to me of my nature. Here, away from my own world, with its confusions, its lies, its contradictions, its asceticism, its hatred, its envy, its resentment, its pervasive negativities, it seemed as though for the first time I could be what I truly was, without pretending to be something else. Here for the first time I felt I could be me, not some other. Had I so moved in Thebes or Memphis, or Damascus, or Baghdad, or Athens or Rome? I did not know. But if I had, here, in this place, such possibilities seemed much more real to me. It was as though I were suddenly in touch with a thousand possible lives, ones which I might have lived, ones which, surely, I could have lived. Or if these things lurked in the beauties of a biological heritage, here, at any rate, it seemed such an inheritance, such a heritage, might, at last, be spread forth in the light, a treasure no longer concealed, denied, in dank vaults, but put forth to gleam in public view, to be honestly what it was, to be admired, to be prized, to be used.

Oh, there are many such movements, and they must flow into one another well.

"Ah!" said a man.

I then transposed into floor movements, as these are often the climactic episodes of such a performance.

I made certain, of course, that I concluded my performance before he who was first among the strangers. It would not do at all to have finished it elsewhere. Sometimes an item such as I, struck with love, or careless, may move cumulatively, so to speak, and most meaningfully, before one who is not first in such a group. Such an error, however, despite its understandability, the desire to display oneself before, to call oneself to the attention of, and to attract him in whose power one wishes to be, can be very dangerous. Such things can lead among the men to rivalries, to fallings out, even to duels and bloodshed. And for one such as I they might lead at best to the thonging of the wrists and the waiting at the post, for the lash.

I heard exclamations from the men, the sudden intakes of breath, tiny sounds of surprise, murmurs of approval. These things coursed through the group, some even from those in the house. Such as I, you see, do have some power, but the ultimate power, of course, is not ours.

Then I lay on my back, the performance concluded. My left knee was up, and drawn further back than my right knee, which was also raised. My hands were down beside me, at my sides. The palms were up, as is proper. The vulnerability of the palms is a part of the symbolisms involved. My head was turned to the right, and I looked toward he who was first among the strangers. Then having done this, I turned my head back, and looked up. I could see the pitting of ceiling above me. My hair was about. My body was covered with a sheen of sweat. I was breathing heavily.

"She is quite beautiful," said a man.

"She has become even more so, since she came here," said he who was first of those present, he who was of the staff of the house.

I lay there, feeling their eyes upon me.

I had found the way in which I was regarded by these men, almost from the beginning, as soon as I became aware of such things, almost from my first moments after having crawled from the corridor in line, with the others, chained by the neck, to the first processing area, to be startling, or, at least, very surprising. You see, I had never thought of myself, really, on my old world, as having been beautiful. I had thought of myself as perhaps pretty, at best. I did have, I suppose, delicate, some said, exquisite, features. But my body, you see, would be all wrong for my own culture. It approximates, very closely, that of the statistically normal female. For example, it is not unusually large, unusually tall or unusually thin. It is not unusually long-legged, and it does not, as it might if it were almost breastless, seem to be, in effect, that of a stripling youth. It is, rather, for most practical purposes, only the body of a normal woman, as women are, only that. Agencies would not select me, for example, as a model, or, at least, one fulfilling the normal stereotypes of the model. For example, I could never slip a chain on my waist, fastening me perhaps to a beam. It would hold me quite effectively. The nature of my body would keep me its prisoner. And so I had never thought of myself as beautiful. But here I found, in this culture, that the standard of beauty is set by what women really are, in the helplessness of their hormonal richness, rather than, for some reason, the way boys often are, in their adolescence, before they achieve the girth and strength of their manhood. So, to be sure, I might not have worn certain narrow, stiltlike garments as well as a model but I had learned, initially to my surprise, and later to my dismay, and terror, and later, yet, rather to my contentment, and even joy, that I might, in a bit of silk, or in a bracelet and a pair of bangles, seem to be such that in me men might take great interest. Most of those who had been on my chain were, like myself, normally figured females. There had been only two of the "model" sort and they, it seems, had been brought here for a specialty market. The men did not regard them with much interest. As I began to understand how I, and my sort, those with normal figures, were viewed on this world, I began to feel sorry for the "models," whom, at one time, I would, absurdly, have envied from afar. How difficult it must be for them, given their previous experiences, to recognize, and adjust to, the simple tolerance, if not contempt, in which they now find themselves held. But there is surely hope for them here, as there was, too, for us, on the old world. As we once were on the old world, so, too, here they are encouraged to put aside all thoughts of their "faults" and "plainness," or what counts as such here, and compensate with qualities of personality, attentiveness, and character. But I do not feel too sorry for them. For, just as there doubtless were men, true men, on the old world, though on such a world they must guard the secrecy of their manhood, who would prize the normal female, she made for arms, and crying out, and yielding, so, too, there must be on this world men, and doubtless true men, who find the tall, breastless "model type" of interest. Two such, for example, were brought here. They were on my chain. But it is nice to find out that one is such that, in a given culture, one is regarded as beautiful. Too, I think the culture is more normal than that from which I was extracted, as it seems that beauty might most plausibly be found within the normal parameters of womanhood, rather than, say, at its fringes. For what it is worth, as an economic sidelight on such matters, normally figured women, assuming, of course, that they are attractive and beautiful, tend, by far, to bring the highest prices. To speak plainly, men on this world, statistically, will *pay* more for them. Perhaps another remark or two might be made here. Whereas I am short, as are most women, I am not fat. My figure, which is small, has been "optimized," so to speak, at least from the point of view of these men, within its own parameters. I have had no control over this. It has been seen to. It is a matter of diet, exercise, proper rest, and such. In the house these things are, in effect, taken care of for me. I am told that outside the house, however, items such as I, depending on their situation, are often assigned more personal responsibility in such matters, subject, of course, to supervision and discipline. They are expected, outside the house, just as within the house, it seems, to keep the latitudes of their bodies within certain prescribed parameters. If they become lax in such matters, they are punished. A second point is that one of the men, as I have indicated, spoke of me as having become even more beautiful since my arrival here. I think this is true, as mirrors, and guards, have testified. The truest beauty, of course, comes from within, and, I suppose, from many sources. It may be, for example, a function of the lessening of inhibitions, and the removal of anxieties and internal contradictions. It may come from contentment, from happiness, from fulfillment, from joy, from such things. Such things cannot help but transform one's expressions, one's movements, one's entire attitude and behavior. The beauty of the outside begins its journey from within. And, lastly, it is only fair to mention, beyond such things, the subtleties of silking, of perfumes, of cosmetics, of adornment, and such. We are expected to know such things, and to utilize them to achieve desired effects. At times I had trembled, seeing what was revealed in the mirror, and understanding the only way in which such a thing could be understood by a man, and yet knowing, too, that that was I, that tasteless, brazen, garish, dramatic, provocative thing, in one of my authentic modalities. And then, too, such things could be applied with sensitivity and taste, and sometimes, if one wished, so subtly that only I perhaps might guess what enhancements had been applied. And at other times we were permitted only a rag or a bit of silk and taught so to stand, to sit or kneel that even so, without cosmetics, with no more perhaps than our hair combed, we would be beautiful. There were mirrors in most of the training areas. These accustomed us to be acutely conscious of how we might appear to others. This is very helpful, particularly in the early phases of training, before so many things, such as good posture and graceful movement become second nature to us. Sometimes I, and others, were placed before the mirror, in a rag, or silk, and told to stand there, or kneel there, or sit there, and see ourselves as we were. I would look into the mirror, and see myself as I was. I was now very different from what I had once been. I was now quite different. And so I had come to a place where I had found myself to be beautiful, even extraordinarily so. I looked into the mirror. I saw there one who was beautiful. This much pleased me. But, too, sometimes, I was frightened. I saw there in the mirror before me not merely one who was beautiful, but one's whose beauty was only in one sense hers. In another sense, it was not hers, just as she herself was no longer hers, but another's.

I lay before the men, suitably. I was looking up at the ceiling. My hair was about my shoulders. I was still trying to regain my breath, from the exertion of my performance. My breasts heaved.

"Is she hot?" asked a man.

"It is so certified, by the house," said one of the strangers. I gathered this information had been obtained from my papers.

"We have had to warn the guards away from her," said one of the fellows from the house.

I kept my eyes up, on the ceiling.

"Already she has learned to beg," said a man.

"She has been instructed to keep her hands within the bars of her kennel," said another.

"In a few weeks," said one of the fellows from the house, "she will be utterly unable to help herself."

One of the fellows from the house walked over to me. "Put your knees down," he said.

Immediately I complied. He then kicked one of my ankles to the side, so that I lay with my legs open.

I kept my eyes on the ceiling.

He who was apparently the leader of the strangers came and stood near me.

I looked up, but then looked away, quickly. I dared not meet his eyes.

He stepped away from me.

I moaned, a little.

"Are you interested?" asked the one who was first of those present, of the house.

"We will take her," said the leader of those not from the house.

Seven

I did not break position.
I had not received permission to do so.
I continued to kneel before him, on the lavender grass, my head down to the grass, my palms upon it, as well.
The position is a common one, of obeisance.
I could hear some birds, among the trees. I could also hear, a few yards away, the fountain.
I sensed that his eyes were upon me.
I was in light silk. It was extremely brief, and was, for most practical purposes, diaphanous. Certainly it left little doubt as to my lineaments.
I knelt before him, in an attitude suitable for one such as I before one such as he, a male, that of obeisance.
I did not know who he might be, or what he might want.
Too, had he seen me near the wall?
"It is the rest period," he said.
"Yes," I said.
I had heard voices from within the house but I had thought them the voices of the one who was first amongst us and the assistants of that one. Some of us, in a place such as this, are usually subject to others of us. I was surprised, and frightened, when I had heard the voices, for it was unusual to hear such during the rest period. The rest period, I knew, was not over, or should not yet be over. If I had thought it even close to the time for the rest period to be over, I would not, of course, have been in the vicinity of the wall. That is, you see, not permitted.
"Why are you not on your mat?" he asked.

"I was not tired," I said.
"You wanted to walk in the garden?" he asked.
"Yes," I said.
"It is the heat of the day," he said.
"Yes," I said.
"Why were you not in the shade?" he asked.
"I do not know," I said.
"One such as you must be careful," he said.
"Yes," I said. I did not fully understand him. I was frightened.
"You should guard your complexion," he said.
"Yes!" I agreed, relieved.
"It would not do to become sunburned, to become reddened, or blistered."
"No," I said.
"Or worse," he said.
"No," I said, trembling.
How was it that he was here, a man, now? Who was he?
"You might then be less pleasing," he said.
"Yes," I said.
"You are new in the garden," he said.
"Yes," I said. How could he have known that? I was sure he was not of the staff. Certainly I did not recognize his voice.
Could I be of interest to him?
Other, of course, than in the way in which one of my kind might be found of interest by any man?
"Position," he said.
So said, so simply, I straightened my back, and knelt up, straight, but back on my heels, my knees widely spread, for this was in accord with my kind within a kind, the palms of my hands on my thighs. I kept my head bowed, however. This sort of thing, I had learned, tends to depend on the city, and the man. It is safest to keep it bowed, unless one knows that it is to be held otherwise.
"You may lift your head," he said.
No, I did not know him. I did not recognize him. He was a strong, powerful man, of which here, in this place, on this world, there seemed no dearth. He was tall. He wore a street tunic, a fillet of wool holding back long, dark hair, a wallet. He did not appear to be armed. I was

small, and soft, before him. I did not doubt but he, as one of his kind, would well know the handling of one such as I, one of my kind.

"What is your name?" he asked.

"I have had many names," I said. It was true. A name for the purposes of training, a name for the purpose of kennels, and so on.

"You have an accent," he said.

"Yes," I said.

"What are you called in the gardens?" he asked.

"'Gail'," I said.

He smiled. "An excellent name," he said.

I put down my head, but raised it again, remembering that I had been given permission to lift it, a permission which suggested that it might be well to keep it lifted, unless otherwise instructed. Still, he had not commanded me to meet his eyes. Accordingly, gratefully, I tended to keep my eyes averted from his. It can be difficult for one such as I to meet the gaze of such a man.

"For one such as you," he added. I was silent.

"That is an Earth name," he said.

"Yes," I said.

He then was aware of at least a portion of what is called the "second knowledge." He might, thusly, be of high caste.

"You were originally from such a place?" he asked.

"Yes," I said.

"But now you are only from here, aren't you?" he said.

"Yes," I said. It seemed that nothing could be more true than that.

He drew a sheet of paper from his wallet. On it was a design, or a word, or name.

"Can you read this?" he asked.

"No," I said.

"You cannot read?" he said.

"No," I said.

I was illiterate on this world. I had not been taught to read or write any of its languages. Such skills were not deemed needful for one such as I.

He turned the paper over.

"Do you recognize this sign?" he asked.

"Yes," I said. "It is the sign of the city." It was a simple mark. I had seen it before, even within the house, on documents and such.

My mind raced. I did not know what, really, I was doing here, in the garden, or why I had been brought here. To be sure, perhaps I had been brought here, really, no differently from others, nor for purposes essentially different from theirs. That was possible. But I was not sure of it. The "flowers" here were of astounding quality and I was not at all sure that I, even given the fact that I might be of interest, even of remarkable interest, on this world, really belonged among them, at least on purely aesthetic grounds. Similarly I was not versed in song, I was not skilled with lute or lyre, I did not even know the special dances of the gardens. It is one thing to writhe naked before guards, one's body obedient to the slightest tremor of the flute, and quite another, for example, to swirl in a belt of jewels on the dancing floor of one of the golden taverns, reached only from the high bridges. But then, perhaps, they are not really so different after all. But, in any event, I had not had special training, or, at least, no training more special than any one such as I would have, who is not intended to be, and sold as, a dancer.

Why should he be asking me these things?

Of course I could not read! Could he not simply look upon my lineaments, and my silk, and know that? Of course some of the flowers could read. That was true. But I could not! Would he not know that? Of course I could recognize that one sign. Was it not well known?

What did he want?

He returned the sheet of paper to his wallet.

I looked up at him. I wanted to read his eyes.

"Have you been near the wall?" he asked, offhandedly.

I must have turned white.

I was now sure that he had seen! He must not tell. He must not tell!

"Brand," he said, idly.

I knelt up, from my heels, and, still kneeling, turned to my right. I drew up the silk on my left side, with the fingers of both hands, to the waist, as one does, this exposing the tiny, graceful mark there, high on my left thigh, just under the hip.

"A lovely flank," he remarked.

Many times before had I received such compliments. My flanks, I had gathered, were of interest to men, and other portions of my body, as well, and the whole, the whole.

But then I sensed it was the brand he was regarding.

"Yes," he said, looking at it.

But surely it could mean nothing to him. It was, as I understood it, in its variations, the most common mark on this world for one such as I. It was only the common mark, nothing special, or different.

"Yes," he said, again. He seemed satisfied.

He was not surprised, of course, that the mark was on me. It would have been utterly improbable that that mark, or some equivalent sign, would not have been upon me, and most likely in that place. That is the most common site for such a mark. Merchant practice, and social custom, tend to standardize such things.

I, too, regarded the mark. It is expected, indeed, in such a situation, that we, too, will regard it, as it is exposed on the flank, the silk lifted to the waist with the fingers of two hands. We are to turn our eyes downward and to the left, and look upon it, seeing it once again, understanding it once again.

I looked at him, and he was looking at me, a slight smile about his lips.

I looked down, again, to the mark. What could be his interest in it? Surely one such as he, large, tall, strong, vigorous, of this world, one in whose demeanor I sensed an unconfused unity and will, one in whose loins I sensed considerable power, would have seen such a thing many times before, and would have seen such as I many times before. I did not think he would be unfamiliar with my kind, the uses to which we might be put, our diverse values, and such.

Perhaps he had only wanted me to expose my flank to him. After all, cannot it be pleasant, or amusing, for them to observe us, while we, under command, perhaps reluctantly, perhaps in tears, reveal ourselves to them? Perhaps it was only in I that he was interested, as he might be interested in any of my kind, he what he was, we what we are. But, no! He had been concerned with the brand. But what could it have meant to him? It was only the common mark. It was a small, tasteful, beautiful mark, of course. I had no doubt it much enhanced my beauty. Too, of course, it had its symbolic aspects, in its design, and its reality, that it marked me. Indeed, sometimes, even thinking of it, I had screamed softly with passion. More than once I had, in my former places, bared it to a guard, in mute petition, calling thusly to his attention what I was and what I wanted from him, and what I hoped for from him, and what I needed from him, thusly pleading without words that he might deign to take pity upon me. But often they would not so spare my pride and would have me at their feet, licking and kissing, and begging explicitly. Then they would either take pity on me, or not, as it pleased them. Sometimes, of course, we would be denied human speech. At such times we must make known our needs by other means, such things as moans and whimpers, and tears. But the primary purpose of the mark, one supposes, is not to be understood naively in such terms as its simple factual enhancement of our beauty, nor even in terms of how it makes us, those who wear it, feel, but rather, more simply, in virtue of more mundane considerations, such as its capacity to implement certain practical concerns of property, and merchant, law. By its means, you see, we may conveniently be identified, and recognized.

But he had, I was sure, been interested in the particular brand I wore. This was hard to understand, of course, as it was merely one of the numerous variations on the common mark. There were doubtless many in the city, even thousands, I supposed, who wore the same, or a very similar, mark.

I looked up at him again, and then, sensing that I might do so, lowered the silk. I then returned to my former position, kneeling back on my heels, facing him, not meeting his eyes.

He had seemed satisfied, regarding the brand. It had seemed to mean something to him. I did not understand it. But surely he could not be interested in me, save as one such as he might be expected to be interested, if only as a passing whim, in one such as I.

"In what house were you first processed?" he asked. I looked at him, frightened.

"You have not been near the wall, have you?" he asked.

"Please," I wept.

He regarded me.

Tears formed in my eyes. "I do not know in what house I was first processed," I said. It was true.

"What was the name of he who over you first held total rights?" he asked.

"I do not know!" I said. I didn't.

"In what city," asked he, "were you marked?"

"It was done in the pens," I said, "shortly after my arrival here. I was not permitted out of the pens. I did not know where I was."

"You heard none speak the name of the city?"

"No," I said.

He nodded. This response, it seemed, was the one which he had expected.

"What were the names of those who trained you, who taught you?" he asked.

"They did not speak their names before us," I said. He smiled. That, too, it seemed he had expected. I remembered one especially, one whom I had never forgotten, he who was the first of the men of this world I had seen clearly, when permitted to look up, in the corridor. I, a woman from another world, a world not his, I, a woman removed from, torn from, my own world and brought as a mere captive, or less, to his, kneeling naked at his feet, fearfully, in chains, had looked up at him. I had quailed before him. I had not known such men could exist. It was he who, of all men on this world, I had first seen. It was he to whom I had thought that I might have been important. His whip had been thrust to my lips. The ceremony, so meaningful, in timid compliance, had been performed. I remembered him. It was he to whose whip my lips had first been pressed. I had thought that I might have been important to him. Then, when I had kissed the second whip, I had realized that I was not. I was no more to him than another on the chain. I had often, in my training, piteously, tried to call myself to his attention, but he had paid me little heed. It was only too clear that I was nothing to him. Sometimes he even seemed to regard me, unaccountably, with rage. Never did he touch me, save to improve a posture, or to position me more appropriately. At such times he would handle me roughly, even severely, certainly more so than was necessary. He was not patient with me, as he might have been with the others. Surely, for some reason, he did not like me. I shook beneath his touch. I could hardly stand when he was near. Sometimes when I begged him, he would spurn me with his foot. Sometimes he would merely turn away, leaving me behind, on my knees, scorned, rejected. At other times he would throw me to another. I had never forgotten him. It had been he, of all on this world, on whom I had first, in my chains, from my knees, fully looked. It had been he to whose whip my lips had first been pressed. I could still remember the taste of its leather. I did not even know his name.

"How were you taken from the pens?" he asked.

"I do not know," I said. "I was drugged. As the drug began to take effect, I was hooded, and shackled."

"How were you transported?" he asked.

Why was he asking such questions? What difference could it make to him, or to anyone?

"I am confused," I said. "I was kept drugged. It was now doubtless mixed with my food. I think there was a ship, I think there was a wagon, for a long time. I could not see out of the wagon. It was metal, and locked. The roads were rough. I was kept closely chained in the wagon, and hooded. I could hear little. People seldom spoke in my presence. It was sometimes hot in the wagon. It was sometimes cold. I was in it for a long time. We may eventually have been in mountains. There seemed steepnesses which were being ascended. I know very little of these things. I was unhooded only to be fed and watered. I could hear the locks opening and closing. Mostly I slept. I could not stay awake. I was sometimes slapped awake, to be fed and watered, and was then allowed, once again, mercifully, greedily, to subside into unconsciousness. Then I seem to remember being bound hand and foot, and then being unchained. Never, it seems, was I without bonds. Did they fear I might escape? I did not know where I was being taken or what would be done with me. Could I be of some importance? Surely not! One such as I is not important. But why were such precautions taken with me? I could see nothing for they would not remove my hood. I was then wrapped in several folds of a blanket, it tied about me at several places, the ankles, knees, belly, breasts and neck. Were it not for this precaution I fear I might have died of exposure. I was then placed in some sort of basket. I could feel the fiber through the blanket. I was fastened in the basket by straps, at my ankles and neck. The basket swayed frighteningly. I was muchly grateful for the straps which held me in place. The wind whistled through the chinks between the fibers. Muchly, too, then, was I grateful for the protection of the blanket. The basket, it seemed, clearly, was being borne through the air. At the time I did not understand how that could be. I had thought it must be part of the drug, part of the dreams. Sometimes I heard weird, wild, birdlike screams. Sometimes I was frightened. But mostly I slept."

"How long was it, after you left the pens," he asked, "that you were transported, or think that you were transported, in one or another of these possible modalities?"

"I do not know," I said.

"Days?" he asked.

"Yes, I think so," I said.

"Several days?" he asked.

"Yes," I said. "I would think so."

"Weeks?" he asked.

"Possibly," I said.

"I would suppose it would be hard to tell, in the state of consciousness you were in," he said.

"Yes," I said. Surely he knew how helpless we were in the grip of such substances.

What could be his interest in these things?

"There seems to have been a great deal of caution, or secrecy, in your transport," he remarked.

"I knew nothing else, at the time," I said.

"But that is clear to you now, is it not?" he asked.

"I gather so," I said, "from what I now know." This was true. Normally there was little concealment, or secrecy, involved in our movements. We tended to be moved about, and shipped, usually, quite openly. Most often, it seemed, we were moved about in wagons covered with blue and yellow silk, our ankles chained to a central bar aligned with the long axis of the wagon bed, a bar which can be lifted up and down, and locked in place. Sometimes we are moved in special ships, constructed for us, with narrow, slatted tiers, on which we lie down, chained, closed off from one another with narrowly meshed steel screens. Sometimes, on flatbed wagons, we are chained to frameworks, or kept in metal containers, roped in place, or in sacks, tied, too, in place. There are, too, of course, simple cage wagons, in which, as what we are, we may be viewed behind the bars. There are many ways in which we may be moved. Indeed, it is not unusual for us, even, in brief tunics, chained together, by neck, or wrist, to trek the roads, afoot, under the surveillance of mounted guards astride saddle tharlarion. If others should approach, say, a caravan, we commonly yield the road, kneeling beside it, facing it, in obeisance, until the dust, the bells, passes.

I suddenly looked at him, in agony. He must not tell about the wall, that I had been near it!

Surely he would not tell!

"Stand," he said. I complied.

I was regarded then, as such men regard one such as I.

"Disrobe," he said.

My hand moved to the loop at my left shoulder, and I drew upon the loop, and, in a moment, stepped from the silk.

He gestured to the grass, permissively.

I sat back, on the grass, leaning back, on the palms of my hands.

In this fashion one's hands are rather behind one, and rather held in place, by one's own weight.

This position is one we are taught. In it, as is clear to us, we are more vulnerable.

He crouched beside me.

I was frightened.

I looked behind me, and upward, to the wall. I feared that I might see the back of a guard there. Although where we were was hidden from the house, by the shrubbery, it would have been an ill-disguised location for an assignation in the garden, being easily visible, as most parts of the garden are, from the wall. To be sure, the guards were supposed to keep their eyes away, unless suspicions were legitimately aroused, from the interior of the garden. Indeed, at certain times, they were not even allowed on the wall. This was, however, the rest period. They might well be on the wall now. Too, we had sometimes seen them observing us, and not merely when it was time for us to swim, or bathe, in the pool, or to try on silks, or for some of us to learn dances, but even when we might be taking our exercise, strolling in the garden, before the one who was first amongst us, though we pretended not to notice. It is interesting how our behavior changes, and so remarkably, when we find ourselves under the eyes of a man. It is as though we must suddenly become more beautiful. I think this is true even of women quite other than we. I think that they, too, thusly, in their hearts, know to whom they belong.

"You are frightened," he said.

I looked at him.

He put his fingers gently over my lips. "You are not going to cry out, are you?" he asked.

I regarded him, in terror.

He lifted my right foot a little up from the grass, a few inches, with his left hand. My ankle was helpless in his grasp. He rubbed his index finger across the ball of the foot and then, his finger bright with a spot of blood, placed it to my lips. I tasted the tiny bit of blood. My foot was cut, of course, from the sharp stones. I had exercised too little caution in fleeing from the wall.

He then did know, of course, that I had been at the wall. Indeed, he had doubtless, perhaps to his amusement, seen me there. What power in the garden did this give him over me! But who such as he needed any further power over one such as I? Did not, if not he, then his kind, already possess absolute power over one such as I!

"You are not going to cry out, are you?" he asked.

I moved my head, wildly, not so much in negativity, as in helplessness, and frustration.

"I am known in the house," he assured me.

But that did not entitle him, surely, to enter the garden! To be with one of us, as he was!

"Very well," he said. He reached down, beside me, to my discarded silk, and folded it several times. It was so light that even with several folds, it was not bulky. These layers of silk, folded neatly into a flat rectangle, he thrust crosswise in my mouth. Partly now they were back, between my teeth, my teeth closed on them, and partly, in front, those folds, they protruded from my mouth. I could feel them, between my lips. They extended an inch or so beyond my lips.

"You may recline," he informed me.

I lay back, terrified.

Did he not know this was the garden? Did he not understand the danger?

"It is said," he remarked, "that one such as you might be hot."

Why had he phrased that in such a fashion? Those such as I might well be "hot"! That was not unusual. Indeed, we had better be, if we knew what was good for us! If we were not sufficiently hot, or sufficiently pleasing, we could expect to be whipped, or worse! We were not the sort of women who could use our favors, or the coolness of our responses, to achieve our own ends. Those weapons, if weapons they were, were no longer at our disposal. We had been disarmed. If wars were involved here, women such as I had clearly lost them. We had been defeated, utterly. We were now the helpless, obedient conquests of men. But, more importantly, we were, it seems, women like us, selected with various parameters in mind, such as intelligence, beauty, and heat. Then, too, we were placed in a situation where reservations, qualifications, inhibitions, compromises, and such, were simply not permitted. And our natural heats, which are in all of us, were brought forth, and encouraged, and even trained. They were fanned into flame, until we found ourselves their victims and prisoners, frequently, helplessly, profoundly, periodically, recurrently dependent upon men for their quenching. And in this place I had been muchly kept from satisfaction. I had often begged to be put forth for use, to lie chained between the tables for the use of guests, to be fastened even to a bench in the garden, my use a gratuity for those who worked there, or to be sent, gratefully, ecstatically, back-braceleted, a sheet over me, to the quarters of guards, but the one who was first amongst us, who seemed to hate me, for no reason I could understand, had, almost invariably, to my pain and my misery, to my suffering, denied me these things.

I looked back, wildly, frightened, to the height of the wall, above and behind me. I feared a guard might make his rounds, that he might see!

Then he who was with me touched me, gently.

I reared half up, helplessly, a wild cry stifled by the wet silk I clenched between my teeth. He placed his hand over my mouth. Then he removed it. I had been unable to help myself. I looked up at him, piteously, tears in my eyes. I lay back, but whimpered, pleadingly. I lifted my body to him, beggingly. I looked wildly up at him, half in astonishment, half in supplication.

He seemed pleased. "Yes," he said, rather as he had when he had noted the lovely mark, incised on my thigh. It would not come off, of course. It had been put there, in me, over a period of a few seconds, with a white-hot iron.

I tried, helplessly, to press my body against his hand.

What cared I now for my questions, what mattered it if I understood him or not, if I fathomed his presence here, or what he wanted, or even if his interest in me might, frighteningly, be more than that of one such as he who had, in a garden, encountered one such as I.

I whimpered piteously, begging him, looking up at him, my teeth clenched on the silk, my body lifted.
I writhed, touched.
Again I lifted my body, begging.
But I was not touched. Tears welled in my eyes. Surely I was not to be tortured!
I whimpered, pleadingly.
I knew what could be done with me. He must not torture me! He must not torture me!
I looked up at him. All was in his hands.
I sobbed gratefully, entered.
I clutched him. On my left ankle were golden bangles. On my left upper arm, there was a golden armlet. On my right wrist were two narrow golden bracelets. They made a tiny sound as I clutched him.
I did not think he would take long with me.
Surely he would know the dangers of the garden.
I clutched him. I held to him, fiercely, with all my small strength.
He would be soon done with me.
I was only a girl in a garden.
I held to him, fiercely.
I wanted to savor every sensation, every feeling, every tiny movement. I was grateful, such as I was, for whatever crumbs might be thrown to me.
I looked at him, pleadingly, over the sopped gag in my mouth.
My eyes begged him not to stop.
I wanted more, more! I could not help myself!
Then I suddenly feared he might cry out. Sometimes such men, in their joy, in their ecstasy, roar like beasts! His cry might bring down the guards upon us!
I looked at him, frightened, my teeth clenched on the silk. He must not cry out!
I shook my head, wildly.
But he paid me no heed. His eyes were fierce. I might have been nothing in his grip!
Then I began to feel my own helplessness.
I knew that I was but a moment from being again conquered.
How piteously I looked up at him, and how well, I am sure, he read my helplessness.

He paused.
I tried not to move.
I tried not to feel.
I looked at him.
He must not tell that I was near the wall! He must not tell that I was near the wall!
I had been quiet and obedient.
I had not cried out.
I had not called for guards.
Was I not pleasing him?
He must not tell that I had been by the wall!
What more could I do?
He must be quiet.
He must not make noise.
This place was not safe.
How long had we lain together?
Did he not know that we could be seen from the wall?
I feared that guards might see!
The rest period must be nearly over.
Others will be coming into the garden.
What if the one who was first amongst us should come to the garden?
What if we should be discovered?
But it was the helplessness which precedes the yielding.
All was in his hands.
I moaned.
I looked up at him.
He had brought me to the point where he could do with me what he wanted.
I was now his.
How it must amuse them, and please them, I thought, to have such power over us! But I clung to him in my helplessness. He could do with me what he wished. All was in his hands.
Oh, let him be merciful! Let him be merciful!
How they can wring from us our surrender!
Let him be kind! Oh, please, be kind! Please be kind!
He looked down at me, I fastened in his arms.
With my eyes I begged him, piteously.

I wondered suddenly if he had come to steal me, or one like me. To pluck a flower, to seize, and make away with, a luscious fruit of the garden? But such things are almost impossible to do. To be sure, sometimes a flower would disappear, but then so, too, usually, would have a guard, or member of the staff. That was dangerous, but possible. But he was not of the house, or of the staff, or the guards, I was sure of that. How, thusly, without the knowledge of the house, without the keys, the passwords, perhaps even friends within, could he hope to get me over the wall, or through the gate, past the guards? How could he even hope to ascend the wall himself, with the incurved knives at the summit? But he had said he was known in the house. Could that be true? If that were so, then I supposed that he might, quite unlike one such as I, simply take his leave. Perhaps, waiting, he had wandered into the garden, to pass the time. He might then have seen me by the wall, and, perhaps taken with my beauty, as some men were, decided, on a whim, to accost and enjoy me.

How hateful he was!

But now I was his.

Helplessly!

He had brought me to this point.

He could now do with me what he wanted.

But I knew in my heart that I had wanted him perhaps a thousand times more than he had wanted me.

He was a man of this world, and the sight of one can wrench out our insides.

We are made for such men.

He moved slightly.

I whimpered, begging.

I sensed whispers of the yielding, tiny whispers, becoming more insistent.

Already I was within the throes of the helplessness, that helplessness which precedes the yielding, which heralds its proximity, which warns of its imminence, that helplessness which sometimes seems to hold one fixed in place, where one, as though chained to a wall, knows that there is no escape, which sometimes seems to place one on a brink, bound hand and foot, in the utmost delicacy of balance, at the mercy of so little as the whisper of another's breath.

I bit on the silk.

He moved, slightly.
I whimpered, gratefully, eagerly.
I looked up at him.
No heed did he pay me.
I clutched him.
How could I be brought more closely to the yielding?
I wanted it!
My eyes begged it.
I thought I heard voices from the house. I groaned.
Was this some torture to which he was subjecting me?
It may as well have been, so helpless I was, so much at his mercy.
To be sure, I was nothing, only a girl in a garden.

I had, of course, in chains, and in ropes, learned what such as he could do to me, how they could bring me again and again, gently, surely, cruelly, as it might amuse them, to such a point, to such a delicate, exact point, to the very threshold of release, to the very edge of ecstasy, to where I was only the cry of a nerve away, begging, and then, if they wished, simply abandon me there, letting me try to cling there, in place, until, protesting, suffering, weeping I would slip back, only after a time, if it might again amuse them, sometimes with so little as a few deft touches, to be forced to begin again the same ascent. Considering such power held over us by men, it is perhaps clearer now why women such as I strive desperately to be pleasing. Not all instruments of torture are of iron; not all implements of discipline are of leather. An analogue may be noted, of course, between such torture and the treatment often inflicted upon the males of my old world by women of my old world, in pursuit of their own purposes. But such matters need not concern us here. Rather they lie between the women of my old world and the men, or males, of that world. Here, as you might suppose, such techniques are not at the disposal of women such as I. The prerogatives of such torture, if it is to be inflicted, lie not in our hands but in those of men. We have been vanquished. I would not have it otherwise.

I heard again the sounds of voices, from the house. The rest period must be over!

I looked wildly, frantically, at he in whose arms I was captive.

He looked down upon me.

It was as though I was helpless, chained to the wall, at his mercy. It was as though I were on the ledge, bound hand and foot.

He moved, slightly.

And then suddenly there was a different helplessness, one which seemed for an instant to recognize, and then flee in terror before what could not be stopped. And then it was as though it stood to the side in awe.

I clutched him!

It was the yielding, and that of one of my kind!

Again and again I wept and sobbed.

No longer did I then, in those moments, care for the danger, or whether I cried out, or if he cried out, or about the guards, or who might enter the garden! Nothing mattered, nothing was real but the feeling, the sensations, the moment!

I only then became aware of the might of him, too, as though molten, charged and flooding, within me.

I held to him.

He looked down at me.

My surrender, I gather, had been found satisfactory.

I did not want him to let me go, but, too, I was terrified now. We were in the garden!

I tried to pull back, a little bit. Did he not know the danger?

He pulled the wet silk from my mouth. He lifted it a little, to the side, and the folds fell out, and he dropped it to the grass, beside us.

I was helpless, of course, pinioned. And then, again, he had both his arms about me.

I could not now understand his expression, as he looked down upon me.

"In the house, where you first trained," he said, "did those there speak as I do?"

What had this to do with anything? Did he not understand the danger?

I could not move. I was helpless in his arms.

I wanted to flee, and yet, too, I wanted to remain there, held. He had had me, and now was interrogating me. What was his intent regarding me? How much at his mercy I was! Clearly his interest in me was more than a fancy of a moment, a whim in a garden. I was frightened. He had put me to his pleasure almost casually because I was there, a matter of convenience. But his primary interest in me, I was certain, went well beyond the gratification and entertainment, slyly stolen, he might derive from one of a garden's casually encountered, exquisitely figured, frightened, helplessly responsive flowers. I had been put to his pleasure almost as a matter of course. Now that he had done with me, he returned to his questions. Well then was I reminded of my own triviality and meaninglessness.

How helpless we are!

"They spoke the language," I said. Here when one spoke of "the language" it was well understood what language was meant. Of course, those where I was trained spoke "the language." They were not barbarians. It was I who was the barbarian.

"No," he said. "I mean their accents."

"They spoke the language differently," I said.

"Did you recognize their accents?" he asked.

"No," I said.

To be sure, I had heard such accents here and there, after having left the pens, and had heard them even, sometimes, though rarely, outside the wall, but I did not know what accents they might be. Indeed, I had heard a variety of diverse accents on this world.

My fears flooded back, again, upon me. What could be his interest in such matters?

"Turn your head from side to side," he said.

I obeyed, held, frightened.

"Your earrings are pretty," he said.

They were tiny, and of gold. They matched the bangles, the armlet, the bracelets.

"They contrast very nicely with the darkness of your hair," he said.

I looked up at him, pleadingly.

I did not understand him.

Of course he knew I was a pierced-ear girl, with all that that, on this world, implied. He would have known that before he had ordered me to disrobe.

He must release me!

No, he must continue to hold me, if only for a moment!

No, no, he must release me!

We were in the garden!

Did he not realize the danger?

"Were your ears pierced when you came to our world," he asked.

"No," I said.

"They were pierced in the pens?" he asked.

"No," I whispered.

There was, at the pens in which I was first trained, I had learned, an additional charge for that, as there would have been for the piercing of the septum, permitting the insertion of a nose ring.

"Where were they pierced?" he asked.

"Not there!" I said.

He looked down at me.

"I do not know what you want," I wept. "I am not special," I protested. "I am not different from thousands of others."

He drew back a little, and surveyed me. "Do not underestimate yourself," he said. "You would bring a quite good price."

I regarded him, in anguish.

"But, essentially," he said, "what you say is true. You are, in your essentials, in what you are, no different from thousands of others."

"Please let me go!" I begged.

"But that would have been to have been expected," he said.

"Please," I begged.

He looked up.

"Please!" I begged, squirming, twisting.

"Ah!" he said, suddenly.

But I had not meant to excite him!

But then again I felt him surgent within me and found myself again, even as I heard approaching voices, put to his purposes.

I then clung again to him, sobbing, helpless.

Did he not know the danger?

He looked at me, suddenly, fiercely. "Are you *Janice*?" he asked.

"I am Gail!" I said. "Gail!"

"Have you ever been called *Janice*?" he asked.

"No!" I said.

"Are you lying?" he said.

"No!" I said.

"Do you know the penalties for one such as you who lies?" he asked.

"Yes!" I moaned.

"But you are not lying?"

"No!" I said.

"Do you know a girl, one of your sort, who is called 'Janice'?"

"No!" I wept. I had been told how I must respond to such questions, if they were asked.

"Have you ever been to the city of Treve?" he asked.

"No! No!" I said. I had been warned of the possibility of such questions. I had been instructed as to how to respond. To be sure, it had not seemed likely to me, nor, I think, to those who had instructed me, that I would ever find myself in a situation in which I might be expected to respond to such inquiries. How could such matters be of interest to anyone? Why should such information be regarded as sensitive, or confidential? These things made no sense to me. I understood nothing of them. Perhaps those who had instructed me were mad. I knew nothing of interest or importance to anyone. I was not important. I was not special. I was no different from thousands of others, save, perhaps, in being such that I might, in certain situations, bring a higher price than certain others.

I looked up at him.

Let him not concern himself with such things!

I was only what I was, nothing more.

But might not that suffice, for the little that it might be worth?

I, his, in his arms, was in the garden. I was confused, frightened at his questions. But, too, I was shaken, with my sensations and myself. I had found myself, one such as I, once again put deliberately, and with perfection, to the pleasure of one such as he. My station, my condition, was unmistakable. I had been reminded, clearly, in no uncertain terms, of what I was. I lifted my lips timidly to his, gratefully, hoping to be permitted to touch them.

How hard they seemed, how soft mine!

Then eagerly, helplessly, gratefully, for there was time, there must be time, did I, my head lifted, kiss again and again at his lips, his face, his shoulders, his body.

Then I heard a voice, that of the one who was first amongst us, near, almost at hand.

I uttered a tiny cry of misery, and tried to pull back, but I was held in place, close to that mighty chest.

I heard a shrill cry of rage.

I turned my head to the right and beheld, in terror, she who was first amongst us!

But he did not fling me from him or leap up. Rather, to my terror, my misery, he held me there, helpless, unable to move, naked in his arms.

He then released me, and he stood up. I scurried to my silk and clutched it, and, kneeling, trembling, terrified, held it closely about me.

He turned, rather in irritation, it seemed, to regard those who had come upon us, she who was first amongst us, carrying a long, supple switch of leather, and her two assistants, both large women.

In one hand he held, loosely, his tunic, and the belt, with his wallet.

The three women who had come upon us were silked, of course, but rather differently, and more richly, than I had been, as was to be expected, as they were much higher in this place, in the garden, than I. My silk, that now clutched about me, with its irregular mottling of dampnesses, from where it had been held in my mouth, where it had served as my gag, stifling my cries, keeping me silenced, that silk bearing even in places the imprint of my teeth, where it had been desperately bitten upon, clenched between them, as I had become more and more helpless, even to becoming uncontrollable, was no more than a brief, diaphanous tunic. But, as mine, their silks, though not diaphanous, were in their way excellently revealing, as such things are intended to be. She who was first amongst us wore a sleeveless silken vest, scarlet, against which her beauty protested. It was tied shut with a tiny string, the ends of which are loose, that they might, with a casual tug, be freed, the vest then ready to be slipped away, to the back. Her two assistants wore scarlet halters, fastened in front with accessible hooks. She who was first amongst us, doubtless because of her standing, had, in her belly silk, low upon her hips, been permitted the rather modest Harfaxian drape, in which the silk is a rectangle, which fastens at the left hip. In this fashion the right leg is concealed. To be sure, the left, as the wearer moves, is revealed. Indeed, her left side, is, in effect, bared to the vest. It was fastened at the left hip with a golden clasp. Her two assistants had been shown no such indulgence. Their belly silks, low on their hips, consisted each of two narrow rectangles. This is more common. These silks, in their case, were hemmed over a belly cord, which was fastened at the left hip. The cord must be tied in such a way that it may be easily tugged loose. Most men here, as on my old world, are right-handed. Such silks, however, are not always hemmed over the cord, or belt. Often they must be merely thrust, before and behind, over the cord, or belt. In this case they may be even more easily removed. Like myself the three of them were ornamented. They, too, wore bangles, and bracelets, and each, too, had an armlet. But they, unlike I, had necklaces, some with pendants. The beads of these, and the pendants, hung sometimes to their bared midriffs, moving against them, touching them. We were all pierced-ear girls, as it is said. I wore, as I have mentioned, tiny golden rings in my ears. Those were what I had been permitted. She who was first amongst us wore more elaborate adornments, which, in wire and tiny plates, hung down beside her cheeks. Her two assistants had in their ears large golden loops. All wore talmits, it should be mentioned, those fillets about the head indicative of authority. She who was first amongst us wore as fillet a narrow, golden band. It had a jewel, a ruby, set in its center. Her assistants had common fillets, of scarlet silk. One additional adornment, or mark, did we all have. We were all collared. Have I neglected to mention that I was collared? Perhaps. One takes such things so much for granted. It is customary for such as we to be collared, of course. We all wore golden collars, or, actually, collars plated with gold. These collars lock behind the back of the neck. We cannot remove them. We are quite helpless in them, I assure you. They are not uncomfortable. Often one even forgets that one is wearing one. But one may always be reminded, of course. The brands, which we all wore, of course, mark us as what we are. That is useful, as I have suggested, for legal, and commercial, purposes. The collar, commonly, identifies the house, or he who holds absolute rights over us. Both the brand and the collar are in their diverse ways, identifications, but the collar, as you can understand, is somewhat more specific. Collars can change, of course. But the brand does not. It remains.

"What are you doing here?" demanded she who was first amongst us, Aynur, of the tall, long-haired fellow to whose lips, to whose face, to whose shoulders and body, but a moment before, I had been pressing kisses, only, in terror, hearing her approach, to try to draw back, but not being permitted to do so, rather being held exactly in place, exactly where I was, naked in his arms.

"What?" she screamed. "What?"

I, kneeling, terrified, clutched the bit of silk against me. What, under the circumstances, a pathetic, insignificant defense it constituted for my modesty!

"What?" she screamed.

I was frightened. Aynur had a vile temper, but I had never seen her this way before. She seemed beside herself with rage. I trusted that she had not seen me kissing the stranger. That would not do at all! She must not have seen that! I must have been simply taken and used, without my consent, totally against my will, you understand. I must pretend to have found the whole matter distasteful. I must pretend to have experienced no interest, or gratification. Our passion, in theory, at least in the gardens, is to be regulated, reserved exclusively for he who holds total rights over us. But I do not know who actually believes such a thing. They make us, totally, the properties of men, and such that we can change hands and collars in a moment, and then act as though our exclusive passion must accompany, in effect, a bill of sale. It is absurd. Certainly the girls in the taverns and brothels are not expected to fulfill such a myth. Even in the gardens are we not sometimes placed at the disposal of others, as he who holds total rights over us, perhaps in his astuteness, or liberality, may decree? And if we have not been pleasing, and if we have not well responded, as may be determined objectively, from the effects of such responses on our bodies, may we not be severely punished, or even slain? Are we not, too, for example, often used in our way to further the fortunes of those who hold total rights over us, as our beauty might contribute, say, to the decor of the banqueting hall, and our activities, such as our serving and entertaining, sometimes on a chain between the tables, to the quality of the banquet itself? And is it not expected that we will writhe gratefully, and well, on the chain, and authentically, which matter may be checked? No, asking us not to feel, not to be what we are, is too much. Rather one might as well scold helpless, oil-drenched straw for bursting gratefully into flame at the touch of the torch. We are at the mercy of all men, as what we are. Do not blame us. But I must pretend, of course, that I had felt nothing. One must pretend to subscribe to the myth. That is important. I trusted that Aynur had not seen me kissing him, and as I had, as what I was! Perhaps Aynur believes the myth, I thought. I hoped, desperately, that Aynur might believe the myth.

"What?" she screamed. He did not respond to her.

"I shall call the guards!" she hissed.

I was puzzled, of course, that she had not yet done so. Aynur cast a look of hatred toward me. I knew she did not like me, but this look was terrifying. I had never seen her look like that at anyone. I put my eyes down, swiftly, in terror. I felt very small and vulnerable, there on the grass in the garden, the silk clutched before me.

"The garden is private," said Aynur to the stranger. "You did not have permission to enter! You should not be here!"

Again he did not respond to her.

"You have no right to be here," she said to the stranger. There seemed indignation, outrage, fury, in her voice.

He merely regarded her.

I could hear the fountain in the garden.

The rest period was over.

But the other flowers had apparently not received permission to reenter the garden. Or, perhaps, wisely, they had refrained from doing so.

I did not understand Aynur's manner. She had discovered a stranger in the garden. She had not fled away. How did she know he had not come to pick fruit, to pluck flowers? How did she know that he might not leap at her, and seize her, and gag her, and bind her, hand and foot, and carry her to the wall? How did she know that she might not, bound hand and foot, squirming, in a net, or bound on a rope, be hauled by confederates to the top of the wall, thence to be hurled to a great cushion of straw below, heaped in a wagon bed, to plunge beneath it, to be held there, invisible, by another confederate, the wagon then trundling away? I did not understand her manner. She had not fled. She had not called the guards.

Of course, she must know the man!

I lifted my head a little and, for a moment, met her eyes. But she then again faced the stranger. He was the center of her fury, her rage. I had, in the moment that our eyes had met, seen that I was a secondary consideration. I had seen that I was not important. I had also seen, in that look, that I could be attended to later.

The stranger did not seem frightened of Aynur.

Perhaps, as he had said, he might be known in the house. But that would not, presumably, uninvited, have given him permission to enter the garden, to partake, unlicensed, of its delights, such as they might be.

That he had no such permission seemed clear in Aynur's attitude.

Did she wish that it had been she, instead, who had been found in the garden?

Why had I not resisted?

Why had I not called out for the guards?

Surely Aynur would wish to know that.

She must not learn that I had been near the wall!

That is why I had not resisted, why I had not cried out, of course, because I had been near the wall. It was that which had, in this place, given him, a stranger here, such power over me, not that such as he did not, independently, in a sense, have absolute power over one such as I.

But I knew that this was false, of course. I had disrobed quickly enough. I had obeyed quickly enough. I had wanted his hands upon me. I had wanted to be in his arms. Such as I belong to such as he. And the garden is lonely, with only the flowers, so beautiful, but meaningless and incomplete in themselves, and the glimpse, occasionally, of a guard. Too seldom did we, in this house, entertain, and, amongst the flowers, too seldom was I included amongst the entertainers. When Aynur made her choices, we all hopefully, beautifully, excitingly arrayed, silked, perfumed, bedecked, made-up, before her, I had been almost always rejected, told to remove my things and report back to my mat. I did not think that I was so much worse than the other flowers. Surely I might have sufficed for the bearing of trays or the pouring of wine. Some men had found me, I recalled, not unattractive. It was almost sometimes, I thought, as though I were not a flower, or at least not a flower in the same simple, innocent sense as the others, but that I might be something rather different. It was almost as though I were here less as a flower than merely as something else, something to be kept in the garden. It was almost as though I were hidden here. To be sure, we are all kept in the garden. In a sense, we are all hidden here, not for the eyes of all, but for those of he who holds absolute rights over us, and such others as he might permit. But these thoughts were foolish. I was only another flower, neither more nor less. I had not been put forth more because Aynur disliked me. So, too, evidently, did several of the others. This, I think, was perhaps because some resented the possibility that I might, in chains upon a sales block, guided by the deft touches of the whip, responding helplessly, bring a high price, perhaps one even challenging theirs. Another reason may have been in virtue of my origins. I was the only girl of my world in the garden. We are not always popular with others such as we, of this world. Too, I had wanted, and desperately needed, his touch, because of what I am, and was, though I had fought it, and not understood it so clearly, even before I came to this world. Too, I had never even been touched by he who held absolute rights over me. I did not know if the others had or not. Indeed, I had never even seen him, for, when I had been brought to the house, and stripped and displayed, he, or perhaps merely some agent, had viewed me from behind a screen. On those times I had served in the house, at suppers, or banquets, only his subordinates had been present. Only his name was known to me.

I looked at the stranger.

But he paid me no attention.

He must not tell that I had been near the wall. He must not let her know that I had, of my own will, kissed him, perhaps once or twice.

I looked at the two women with Aynur. They were Tima and Tana, her assistants. Those names are extremely common on this world, for women such as we. There must be thousands with such names. Both had doubtless, over time, in their sojourn in the collar, had many names. Even I, who had not been so long on this world, had had various names. We learn to answer quickly enough to whatever name is put on us. We do not have names in our own right, of course, given what we are, no more than, say, tarsk and sleen. Both Tima and Tana were large women. Either alone might have overpowered me easily. Tana looked at me and smiled. I looked down, frightened. At her right hip, over the belly cord, hung a pair of bracelets, small, sturdy, pretty bracelets. They were joined together with three links of steel.

"What have you to say for yourself?" demanded Aynur, angrily, of the stranger.

Her behavior, her attitude, her demeanor, her apparent indignation, her virulence, her rage, as I have suggested, puzzled me. I did not understand it, at all. Too, of course, it frightened me, terribly. What could it mean? What could be the explanation for these things? It was almost as though she might have been somehow, personally, insulted or betrayed.

"Well!" she demanded.

"Have you received permission to speak?" he inquired, quietly.

Tima, on Aynur's right, gasped. Tana, on Aynur's left, made a tiny noise, of fear.

His eyes regarded Tima and she flung herself to her knees in the grass, head down to the grass, palms of her hands on it, in obeisance, as I had been earlier. As his eyes fell then on Tana she, losing no time, assumed the same position. The two small, sturdy, pretty bracelets, hanging at her right hip, made a tiny noise, striking together, as she assumed the position. They then hung from the cord a little before her right hip. Both Tima and Tana were large women, but before such a man, and before others, even less than he, they were small.

His eyes then fell upon Aynur. He regarded her, evenly. For the briefest moment, as though in futility and rage, she met his eyes. Then, shaken, uttering a cry of misery, and rage, her eyes brimming with tears, she removed her eyes from his. Then she was before him, as the others, her head down to the grass, her palms upon it, too, in obeisance. The golden fillet, with its ruby, was at the grass. Beside her right hand, discarded, was her dreaded leather switch. I trusted that she had not dallied too long in her obedience. Men such as he tend not to be patient with such as we.

He looked down at me, and I looked away, clutching the silk about myself.

"May I speak?" begged Aynur.

"All three, position!" snapped he.

The three women, instantly, assumed the common position, kneeling, back on heels, back straight, knees wide, palms of hands down on the thighs.

"You may raise your heads," he said.

They might now regard him. It had been permitted to them. It pleased me, of course, to see them thusly, as any of us, even they, might be before one such as he. But then I looked down. They had been knelt before a man in a common posture of submission. Given their position in the garden, and the considerable authority they held here, over me, and the others, I did not think it would be wise for me to permit myself to be detected remarking this in any obvious manner. Too, of course, I could be immediately put in the same posture.

"May I speak?" begged Aynur, in tears, in rage.

"No," he said.

Tears of frustration ran down her cheeks.

He then looked down at me, and I looked down.

I did not fully understand that look. It was not simply a look at a girl he had used, a bemused glance at an instrument, now unimportant, which had served his purpose.

I was not special, I told myself. I was not different from thousands of others.

I made as though to draw my wet silk hastily over my body.

"You have not received permission to silk yourself," he said.

Quickly I put down the silk. I was still kneeling.

"Tunic," he said, handing it to me.

I stood obediently, and shook out the tunic, and kissed it, as one is trained to do. I then helped him into it.

"Belt and wallet," he said.

These, too, I kissed, and, putting my arms about him, trying to touch him as little as possible, for the others were watching, affixed the belt, with wallet, in place.

But the nearness to him made me tremble, he a man, and one of this world.

He pointed to the grass, to one side, and I knelt there, one such as I at the feet of one such as he.

He kicked his sandals to one side, a few feet away. Then he regarded Aynur. She looked at him, almost in protest, disbelievingly. He then pointed to the sandals, and snapped his fingers.

Aynur dropped to all fours and crawled to the first sandal, picked it up in her teeth, and brought it to him, and dropped it at his feet. She then fetched the second sandal, in the same manner. She then looked up at him, but he merely indicated, with a gesture, that she should return to her place, which she did, kneeling between Tima and Tana.

Aynur, she who was first amongst us, Aynur, in her rich silk, and ornaments, Aynur, in her golden talmit, with the affixed ruby, had fetched sandals, and before such as Tima and Tana, not to mention before one such as my own lowly self! On this world hierarchy exists, and status, and rank, and distance. Such things, always real, are not here concealed. Here they are in the open. The people of this world do not deign to conceal that each is not the same as every other, and not merely is this true of those such as I. Such articulations, of course, so healthy with respect to maintaining social stability, constitute an institutional counterpart to the richnesses of difference in an articulated, ordered, holistic nature. On this world, for better or for worse, order seems most often preferred to chaos, and truth to fiction.

Aynur had been made to fetch sandals, and before Tima and Tana, and such as I!

It is not that the important thing here was the fetching of the sandals themselves. Not at all.

Indeed, I myself would have been pleased to fetch such sandals, and lovingly. It is a way of pleasing, and showing what we are. It is a way of beautifully serving. To be sure, such an act can be used for disciplinary purposes, forcing us to understand clearly what we are, that we should bring the sandals so.

But it is one thing of course for one such as I to be permitted to bring sandals to one such as he in, say, the privacy of our precious intimacy, or before peers, where I might find myself honored before others, I and not they accorded this permission, or even in a public place, such as the baths, or the vestibule of the gymnasium, where no one perhaps but I, treasuring it, and relishing it, thinks anything of it, but it is quite another for one such as Aynur to be forced to do so in a situation such as this, before such as we. Indeed, I suspected that Aynur, had she been alone with him, had she not been before us, had she not had her talmit, had her hair been loose, had she been naked, save perhaps for her collar and some ornaments, might have begged prettily, and quite abjectly, upon her knees, for the permission to render him such a service. But this, of course, was not such an occasion.

Tears ran down Aynur's cheeks, she kneeling between Tima and Tana.

The worst, of course, was not that she, who was first amongst us, had been forced to behave as though she might be the least amongst us. No, rather, the worst was that she, having fetched the sandals, had then been merely returned to her place. It had been hers merely to fetch the sandals. She would not, it seemed, be permitted to place them upon his feet. He would not, it seemed, have her so much as touch him.

He then regarded me, imperiously. But I was not special! I was not important!

He pointed to the sandals, at his feet. He snapped his fingers.

I hurried to kneel before him. I picked up one sandal, looked up at him, lowered my head, kissed the sandal, looked up at him again, and then bent to put the sandal on his foot, which I did, carefully tying the thongs. I then did the same with the other sandal. We are taught to do this in this fashion. One commonly, unless otherwise instructed, places the right sandal first, then the left. I did it in that fashion, of course. Two of the first things we are taught are the bathing and dressing of a man. I completed my ministrations by kissing his feet, of course, each in turn, and then backing a bit away, and kneeling, in common position. We may thusly await further instructions, if any may be forthcoming.

Aynur sobbed in fury.

This frightened me. It was not my fault that I had been ordered to tie his sandals! I had not, in fear of her, at least as far as I was aware, put myself in the way of being subjected to such commands. I had not, as far as I knew, at least clearly, attempted to call myself again to his attention. I had not attempted, or had I, to solicit such commands? There are, of course, ways in which women such as I, subtly, wordlessly, with a tiny movement of the body, a seemingly inadvertent placement of ourselves, a lifting of the bosom, a catching of the breath, the shyest of glances, the tiniest movement of a lip, can petition, and even beg. Had I done such a thing, naturally, without even being fully aware of it? I might have done so, I knew. It would not have been unusual in the sort that I was. We are such, even helplessly, you see.

Her eyes seemed to bore into me. Tart, she seemed to say, slut! But I could not help it if he had chosen me to tie his sandals! Tart, tart, slut, slut, her eyes seemed to say. Perhaps I had done something. I feared I had. It would have been only too natural! But then I was sure that even though I might have in some subtle way solicited permission to perform this service for him, which on a very deep level I desired to do, it would, in any event have been required of me.

Aynur, I recalled, had dallied, if only for the briefest moment, in assuming before him the position of obeisance. Such things are not likely to be forgotten, or overlooked. Instant obedience is expected of us. And these men, as I have suggested, do not tend to be patient.

Grievous at his hands was the punishment of the lovely, imperious Aynur, who was first amongst us in the garden. She had not been permitted speech. She must, before us, like a low girl, publicly fetch sandals. And then, the sandals fetched, she had been returned to her place, denied the opportunity to place them upon his feet. How mocked, how scorned, how reduced, was lofty Aynur, in her golden fillet, with the ruby!

Aynur wept in frustration and rage. Her small fists were clenched on her thighs. I had never seen her like this, almost beside herself. She was, after all, it seemed, in spite of her authority, in spite of her power, like us, only a woman.

She must remain positioned.

His will had been made clear.

She would obey.

Aynur looked at me in fury. I trembled. In part of me I was not at all pleased to have been made use of in this way, to have been used, in effect, as an instrument for her punishment. That would certainly, in one sense, not give me an enviable position in the garden. But, of course, in another sense, I was terribly pleased that it had been I, and not she, or not Tima, or Tana, whom he had selected out for the kissing and tying of his sandals. Only I, who only a few days ago had first been permitted silk in the garden! This pleased my vanity no small bit! Too, in a sense, it would surely elevate my status among the flowers, if they came to know of it. Might they not envy me this distinction, though, too, recognizing only too clearly the perils which it might entail?

Then I became conscious that I was once again beneath the gaze of the stranger.

I hoped, in fear, that I had pleased him. Certainly he had not been stinting in taking his will of me.

I flushed, too, recalling how I had been given no choice but to yield as what I was, and how with what authority he had made me his, and the spasmodic raptures which had accompanied my seizure and conquest.

He continued to regard me.

I trembled.

He must not tell that I was near the wall!

He smiled. I suspected then that he must have guessed my fears. How trivial such things might appear to him, the alarms of a small, curvaceous animal, but how momentous they were to me! He could leave, but I must remain in the garden!

He continued to regard me.

Many were the questions he had asked me.

I had been frightened by these questions, as to what might be their purport, or significance.

Why did he ask me if I were "Janice," or had ever known a slave named "Janice," or if I had ever been in Treve?

I had, of course, responded negatively, as I had been instructed to do. But such questions, it had been thought, by myself, and others, I supposed, would never be asked of me. But now they had been asked of me.

What did this mean?

But I was not special. I was not important. I was only another girl, only another flower, nothing more, in her collar, in a garden.

Then I could no longer meet that gaze. I put down my head, frightened.

He then took his leave of the garden.

This left me alone with Aynur, and Tima and Tana.

In a moment or two, perhaps when she was sure he was gone, Aynur leaped, enraged, to her feet. Tima and Tana, too, rose to their feet. Aynur looked after his route of departure, apparently a quite open one, through the inner gate, leading to the house, then doubtless through our quarters, then through the other gates, sealing off our quarters, and thence to the main portions of the house, and, eventually, out the main portal. He would then be outside the house, in the street. I had been brought here hooded, so I had never seen the city, which, I gathered, was a large one, nor even the street outside, which seemed to be a busy one, particularly in the early morning. Many of the flowers, incidentally, were quite as ignorant, and sheltered, as I. We wondered what the world might be like on the other side of the wall. To be sure, we were sometimes frightened. Sometimes we heard cries of pain, of such as we, and the sound of a lash. Sometimes we heard lamentations, of such as we, and the sounds of chains, and the cracking of whips. Sometimes we heard even, to angry cries, and the cracking of whips, cries of weariness, and misery, and effort, of such as we, cries mingling with the sounds of the tightening and slackening, and tightening, of harness, the groaning of heavily laden wagons, the creaking of large wooden wheels turning slowly on pavement. At such times you may well understand how it was that we within the wall, in the garden, in our delicate, pampered beauty, our light silks, our golden collars, might exchange frightened glances. Our lives would have been quite different, it seemed clear, if we were on the other side of the wall. Sometimes even I was grateful for the guards, and for the height and sturdiness of that massive wall within which we were sheltered. Only too obviously might there be perils, and fearful severities, outside the wall. I was not insensitive to such things. Indeed, I was much afraid of them. But still, on the whole, even so, I wanted to be out of the garden. Better to squirm in a tavern, better to trudge behind an army as one of its collared camp followers, better to be harnessed to a peasant's plow, wary of his lash, than to languish in the garden! If I were a flower, let me blossom in the fields, or among paving stones, not in the garden. I wanted to be outside, where I could see, and, yes, be seen, where I could actively and visibly be what I was, serving and loving. Better a steel collar in the street than one of gold in the garden!

"I shall call the guards!" wept Aynur. But she did not do so.

It might be mentioned that Aynur, and Tima and Tana, despite their authority, and their importance, in the garden, were less than the least of the guards. They, too, in the final analysis, you see, were only "flowers." More importantly, they were females, and the guards were males.

I wondered why Aynur did not call the guards.

She must, I conjectured, know the man.

Suddenly Aynur pointed to the dreaded switch at her feet and Tana knelt down, quickly, and retrieved the switch, and, then, head down, humbly, with both hands, lifted it up to Aynur, who seized it away from her. Tana then rose to her feet. All three then faced me.

My silk was on the grass, by my right knee.

"Position," said Aynur. "Head up!"

I now knelt before them, as Aynur had commanded, positioned, my head up.

I was distressed, but dared not reveal my feelings.

Surely it was not before such as they that I should be so kneeling. It was not that such postures were not suitable for me. They were eminently suitable for me. Indeed, they were quite correct for me. Indeed, I belonged in them. But not before such as they.

"It seems that Gail has been naughty," said Aynur.

"No!" I said.

"What?" asked Aynur.

"I have not been naughty!" I said.

"Who has not been naughty?" asked Aynur.

"Gail has not been naughty!" I said.

"You may now explain what occurred," said Aynur.

"I was in the garden," I began.

"During the rest period?"

"Yes."

"What were you doing in the garden during the rest period?" asked Aynur. "Why were you not on your mat?"

"I was not tired!" I said. "I wanted to walk in the garden!"

"But it was the rest period," she said.

I was silent.

It was not forbidden to be in the garden during the rest period. She would know that. But it would not do to remind her of it.

"There are ways to keep you in the vicinity of your mat, you know," she said.

"Yes," I said.

There was, near my mat, as there were also near other mats, a heavy ring, set in the floor. It would be easy to chain me to that, presumably by an ankle ring.

"Did you expect to meet someone in the garden?" she asked.

"No!" I said.

Even objectively, of course, such meetings would be difficult and dangerous to arrange. We had no direct contact with the outside, and, for most practical purposes, those outside had no direct contact with us. And there was the wall, of course, and the knives at the top. Who, unsolicited, could simply come through the house, and enter the garden? But it seems that one had. He had said he was "known in the house." It seemed likely. It is not the case that the gardens are without politics, nor that intrigue is not rampant within them, but these things are usually amongst the flowers themselves. As flowers, as far as outside contacts might occur, we were almost entirely at the mercy of others, guards and such. Sometimes there were attempts from outside houses to reach suspected flowers within. For example, let us suppose that a woman, not like one of us, is suspected of being held in a given garden. One might then attempt to ascertain this. Too, might she not attempt bribe guards, or such, promising rich rewards for her release? But let her not be apprehended in such an intrigue, lest her lofty status vanish by morning, and she find herself in the garden then no more than another such as we. Then the matter would take on another complexion. It would become, in all probability, then, not a difference between captivity and freedom, but a mere changing of collars. In all intrigues within the garden, involving the outside, a guard, or staff member, is almost always involved. They are necessary as intermediaries. But such things are terribly dangerous. Too, of course, there can be internal liaisons, and such. A flower, for example, much taken with a handsome guard, upon whom she has spied, might, risking all, place herself in his way, letting her needs and feelings be known. Too, of course, such liaisons might be initiated by a guard or staff member, for such are not as ignorant of the contents of a garden as is sometimes supposed. But, then again, there is terrible risk in such matters.

"Go on," said Aynur.

"I was not tired," I said. "I wanted to walk. I went into the garden."

"You did not know anyone was there?"

"No!" I said. "I thought the garden was empty."

"But it was not, it seems," said Aynur.

"No!" I said.

"There was a man there?"

"Yes!" I said.

"Were you surprised?" asked Aynur.

"Yes!" I said. "I was shocked! I was terrified! I was horrified! A man there! In the garden!"

"What did you do?"

"I did not know what to do," I said.

"It seems that you managed to do something," said Aynur. Tana laughed.

"I had no choice!" I protested.

"You could not help yourself," suggested Aynur.

"I was seized!" I said. "I was helpless!"

"Perhaps you were beaten," said Aynur, "but you do not appear to have been beaten. Perhaps you were bound, hand and foot, but there do not appear to be rope marks on your wrists or ankles, or at your belly."

"I was overpowered!" I protested. I supposed that this was, in a sense, true. I had been overpowered by his authority, by my consternation, by my not knowing who he was, or his license to be here, by the hold he had over me, having seen me by the wall, by my own desperate, crying needs.

"Doubtless you resisted?" said Aynur.

"Yes!" I cried. "But I was too weak. He was so much stronger than I!"

"Why did you not summon guards?" asked Aynur.

Why had *she* not, I wondered, summoned guards?

"Why did you not call out?" inquired Aynur.

"I was gagged!" I said, relievedly. "See? The silk is wet! It was put in my mouth!"

"It does not appear to have been wrested from you," observed Aynur. "It does not seem to have been torn from your body."

"The disrobing loop was drawn!" I said.

"Who drew the loop?" asked Aynur.

"He!" I lied. "He!"

"And you were gagged with the silk?"

"Yes!"

"Why did you not cry out before the silk was removed?" asked Aynur.

I looked at her, frightened.

"It could not very well be in your mouth and on your body at the same time," she said.

"He seized me from behind," I said. "He held me back against him, his left hand over my mouth. With his right hand he drew the loop. As I struggled the silk fell. He then flung me to my back on the grass, and put the silk in my mouth!"

"It was tied in place?"

"No," I admitted.

"You did not attempt to eject it?"

"I did not dare to do so," I said.

"When we came upon you," she said, "the silk was not in your mouth."

"It had become dislodged," I said.

"And you did not then cry out?"

"I was afraid," I said. This would be plausible. At least I hoped so. Such a man, of course, could have snapped my neck with one hand.

"It seems then that you are in this matter fully guiltless," said Aynur.

"Yes!" I said, relieved.

"But he did put you to his purposes?" she asked.

"Yes," I admitted.

There seemed no point in denying this.

We had, I recalled, been discovered naked in one another's arms. Indeed, I recalled that I had been held for a time, naked in his arms, even after Aynur and the others had discovered us. I feared that he might have made it quite clear, even flagrantly so, to my shame and terror, what had been going on. I could only hope that I could convince Aynur that I was in these things only an unwilling, innocent victim. She must believe that!

"Poor Gail," said Aynur.

I looked at her, gratefully.

"You felt nothing?" asked Aynur.

"No!" I said. "My passion, such as it might be, is reserved exclusively for he who holds total rights over me!"

I hoped that Aynur would believe the myth.

Aynur walked around, behind me.

"Kneel up a little," she said. "And put the tops of your toes flat on the grass."

I must obey.

"Ah!" said Aynur.

I trembled.

"The bottoms of our feet," said Aynur, "are to be soft, and caressable. That is why we must consider the surfaces upon which we tread. That is the meaning of the lotions and creams with which they are treated."

I did not respond.

"But the bottoms of your feet have been roughened. They are cut, and bloody. You have been near the wall."

I did not speak.

"And apparently," she said, "you were too stupid to have trod softly."

She then walked around me again, so that she was, again, before me.

I had been alarmed at the sounds of voices. That was why I had hurried, foolishly, from the perimeter of sharpened stones. That is why my feet had been cut.

"You did not respond to the man who was here?" asked Aynur.

"No!" I said.

"How then do you explain the condition of your body, when you were found?" asked Aynur.

"I may have felt, a little," I whispered.

It would do little good, I feared, to attempt to deny, to an observer as astute as Aynur, what would have been obvious. There are so many signs, the dilation of the pupils, the helplessness, the sheen of sweat, the oils, the smells, the mottling of the body, the erection of the nipples, such things.

"You have felt the whip, and iron on your wrists," said Aynur.

"Yes," I said.

"Do you still claim to have felt little?" she asked.

"No," I whispered.

Women such as I, of course, and Aynur, and so many others, inside the walls, and outside of them, are the most responsive of all women. We are not permitted, for example, dignity and inhibitions. Such are incompatible with the collar. We know what is expected of us, and what we must be like. And we are trained. And we are under discipline. Too, we are, I suspect, selected with heat in mind. It is presumably one of the properties which those whose business it is to acquire us keep in mind. Such a consideration may, in many cases, make the difference with respect to whether or not we are to be acquired. Such a property is apparently important, for example, when want lists are compared with inventories.

"Do you think I cannot recognize a hot little tart when I see one?" asked Aynur.

"I do not know," I murmured.

"Do you think I have not read your papers?" she asked.

"I do not know," I said. I could not read them, of course. I did not even know what they said. There was apparently some remark on them pertinent to my heat. He whose whip I had first kissed, in the corridor long ago, he who had later treated me with such cruelty, spurning me, throwing me to others, he whom, in the long nights in the kennels, I had never forgotten, had told me that I was supposedly quite "vital." The matter had been confirmed in the pens, of course. I had wept with misery and shame for hours afterward. But the proper endorsements had been included, I had gathered, on my papers. Aynur, it seemed, could read.

"You were at the wall," said Aynur.

"Yes," I admitted.

"Although it may have been difficult for you to wholly refrain from feeling," said Aynur, "you undoubtedly did your best."

"Oh, yes, yes!" I said.

"And you remained totally inactive," said Aynur.

"As inactive as possible," I whispered.

"Then you did not, for example, kiss him?"

"Of course not!" I said.

Tima and Tana broke into laughter. I looked at them, frightened.

"You saw?" I asked.

"Yes!" said Aynur, in fury.

My heart sank.

I had not known how long they had been watching. Apparently it had been long enough. I had heard a voice. That of Aynur. And then, a moment later, she had cried out in fury. I had then, in terror, tried to pull back, but he had not permitted me to extricate myself. He had held me where I was, against him, in his arms, naked.

"Slut!" cried Aynur.

"He ordered me to kiss him!" I cried.

"And you did so reluctantly?" she screamed.

"Yes, yes!" I cried.

"Liar! Liar!" she wept.

I was terrified. I almost lost position.

"Naked, collared tart!" she cried.

Did not Aynur wear a collar, too? Did her collar not fit as well as mine? Did it not proclaim its message on her neck, as mine did on mine? Was it not well fixed there, and was she not as incapable of removing it as I was of removing mine?

"Naked collared slut!" cried Aynur.

Was there such a difference between us? Was she so loftily garbed? Was she not in her way almost as naked as I? Was there truly so much more to her attire than mine, other than the necklaces, and the jewelry, the earrings, and such, richer than mine? Was there so much, for example, to the silk she wore, the open skirt, held only at the left hip by a single, easily detached golden clasp, one which might be flicked away with a finger, to the scarlet silken vest, against which her beauty strained, tied at the front with a scarlet string, one which could be undone with a single tug?

"Naked collared lying little slut!" cried Aynur.

She chastised me as might have a woman other than we! Surely she knew my condition, and nature. I did not think it was much other than hers. I had surely sensed that Aynur was frustrated in the garden, and that she was, at least latently, highly and powerfully, and significantly and helplessly, sexed. Perhaps she had sensed the same of me, though I was smaller, and so much more vulnerable. Perhaps that was why we had not cared for one another. Perhaps that was why she hated me.

"Lying slut!" wept Aynur.

I had then been seen kissing the fellow in the garden. I had been unable to help myself. I recalled that I, conquered as such as he can do to such as I, had done so, willingly, eagerly, gratefully, helplessly, passionately, uncontrollably.

"Slut! Slut!" cried Aynur.

Did she wish that it had been she who had been caught in the garden?

"Slut! Slut!" she cried.

Would she have behaved so differently from me?

"Slut!" she wept.

I did not think she was so different from me, in what we were, but here, in the garden, in the articulated structure of this world, we were separated by a chasm of almost infinite proportions. She was first amongst us, and I was the newest and, surely, the least of the flowers.

"Slut!" she screamed, beside herself with rage.

She raised the switch and I cringed.

But the blow did not fall.

Aynur had lowered the switch.

Then she said, quietly, her voice unnaturally calm, "Bracelet her."

Tana, seizing me by the hair, threw me forward on my belly, on the grass. Then she and Tima, one on each side, crouched beside me. Tima jerked my hands behind my back, and held them there. I heard the clink of the bracelets being removed from Tana's belly cord, where they had been over the cord, near her right hip. Then, with two rather clear, definitive little snaps, tiny, but quite decisive little noises, the bracelets were locked upon me. Tima and Tana then remained where they were, one on each side of me. I lay there on my belly, on the grass, my hands pinioned behind me.

The quietness which had been in Aynur's voice, and that unnatural calm of it, had terrified me more than her rage.

"Get her on her feet," said Aynur, quietly.

I, by Tima and Tana, one on each side of me, by the upper arms, was drawn to my feet, and held there.

Aynur slipped the base loop of the switch over her left wrist. The base loop, in certain adjustments, supplies additional control and leverage to the user of the implement. It also, of course, assures greater security in its retention. Too, by its means, obviously, the switch may be conveniently suspended, for example, over a hook or peg, or, say, as Aynur now had it, over a wrist, freeing the hands. Aynur bent down and picked up the silk and, neatly, carefully, very methodically, very deliberately, folded it, until it was again in the shape of a small, soft, layered rectangle, some three inches by five inches, as it had been earlier, when the stranger had placed it in my mouth.

Aynur looked at me.

I tried desperately to read her eyes.

I could not do so.

Then she thrust the silk crosswise in my mouth.

I bit down upon it.

I could still not read her eyes.

I was again gagged.

Aynur then turned about and went toward the house. "Bring her along," she said, over her shoulder.

I, biting down on the silk, terrified, tears in my eyes, my upper arms helpless in the grip of Tima and Tana, my wrists behind me, locked in bracelets, stumbling, was conducted toward the house.

Eight

I had stirred groggily.

For a moment I had expected to awaken in a former place, in a former dwelling, in a once familiar room, as I had so often before.

I lay on my stomach.

I would feel the sheets, and, with the tips of my fingers, beneath them, the familiar mattress.

Everything would be the same.

But it seemed that something hard was beneath me, not the mattress, but a surface less yielding, more severe.

I kept my eyes closed. There was light. It was rather painful. How foolish I was! I had forgotten to draw the shade last night.

Various were the memories, or seeming memories, which mingled in my confused, sluggish consciousness.

I did not know what was dream, and what was reality, if aught.

I had had the strangest dream.

I had dreamed I had somehow found myself on an alien world, one on which such as I had their purposes.

I must awaken.

What a strange dream it had been!

I could remember chains, and the cracking of whips, and others like myself.

I could remember kneeling in a dimly lit corridor, chained by the neck with others, manacled and shackled. I could remember my pressing my lips fervently, obediently, to the whip of a male unlike any I had ever known or had believed could exist. And there had been others, too, such as he. No dearth of such was there upon that world!

I stirred, uneasily.

And there was on that world an unfamiliar language in which such as I must develop a facility posthaste.

Oh, we strove desperately to learn that language! You may be sure of that! It was not we who held the whips.

Under such conditions, you must understand, such as we learn quickly.

The dream seemed very real, I thought, the lengthy training sessions, the kennels, and such.

Tears had formed in my eyes as I had thought of he whose whip I had, in what must be the dream, first kissed. But how cruel he had been to me, after his first kindness, his first patience! How he had rejected me, and mocked and scorned me, how I had felt his foot, or the back of his hand, how he had thrust me to the tiles, how he would order me, angrily, to another, or even hurl me impatiently, sometimes in chains, to such a one!

But how much it seemed I had learned there, in that place, in my training! And how seldom were we even clothed, save perhaps to instruct us how to bedeck ourselves in certain garments, and how provocatively, gracefully, to remove them. I had learned much about myself there, it seemed. And I had learned, too, to my dismay, and shame, what men could do to me, and what I could become in their arms. And then I began to want this. How frightful the dream! How embarrassing, how terrifying, to learn that one cannot help oneself, that one is astonishingly, helplessly vital! And how miserable and embarrassed I had been when I had learned that this information, of such intimacy and delicacy, and secrecy, had been publicly recorded on papers pertinent to me.

The light seemed bright. Even through my closed eyelids it hurt.

Had I forgotten to draw the shade?

I must awaken.

Then I remembered, too, being summoned to a room. There had been men there, of the house and not of the house. I had performed. I had been discussed. Arrangements had been made. I must drink something. I had begun to lose consciousness even as I was hooded. I had lain back, within the hood, on the floor. I was dimly aware of my limbs being placed in certain positions, and then being chained. It was almost as though it were being done to another. I remembered trembling a little, and sensing the chains, and hearing them, and realizing that it was I who wore them, and not another, and then I had lost consciousness. There had then been a nightmare, it seemed, of transitions. Once it seemed, as I determined by touch, I was lying in a low, narrow, mesh-walled space, as on a slatted bunk. There were terrible smells. There was a motion, as of a ship. There were cries and moans, as of others like myself, about me. Because of the motion and the smells I feared I might vomit in the hood. But then, again, I lost consciousness. Then later there had been a wagon, one of metal, in which I was hooded and closely chained. Sometimes it was hot. Sometimes it was cold. When it was cold I held about myself, when I was conscious, as best I could, the single blanket I had been given. Then I would lapse again into unconsciousness. I was awakened, sometimes, and unhooded, and slapped awake, or awake enough, to take drink and sustenance. Then I would again drift into sleep. Some drug perhaps, in this dream, was mixed with my food or drink. I did not know where I was. I did not know where I was going. Indeed, in one sense I did not even know who I was. I felt myself somehow bereft of identity. I knew that I was no longer what I had been. That sort of thing had been left on a former, vanished world. That sort of thing was all behind me. Who was I? What was I? What was I to be? Such things it seemed, here, on this world, were not up to me. They would be decided by others. The wagon had left smooth roads. It had seemed, irregularly, but with frequency, to ascend, jolting and rocking. Within I was much bruised. Once it had nearly tipped. Eventually it, days, perhaps weeks later, must have reached its destination, wherever that might have been. I was bound hand and foot, and then, so secured, was relieved of the wagon chains. I was wrapped closely in a blanket, which was then tied closely about me. This blanket was not the same as that which had been in the wagon. That blanket, it seemed, would be burned, and the wagon's interior scrubbed clean. There would be few, if any, traces, of my occupancy left in the wagon. I take it that even those of scent were, to the extent possible, to be eliminated. Perhaps such might have been of use to some sort of tracking animal. I did not understand the point of such precautions. It seemed for some reason that my passage here was to be as though it had not occurred. I was then removed, so bound and so enveloped, from the wagon; I was carried for a time, over a shoulder, my head to the rear, which somehow seemed, vaguely, to be the way I should be carried, however shameful or embarrassing I might find it to be; and I was then, at the end of this peregrination, placed on some sort of wooden platform. It was hard, even through the blanket. A little later I was placed in some sort of large, heavy basket, in which I was fastened down by two straps, one at my ankles and the other at my neck. The basket must have been something like a yard square. I must accordingly, bound, tied in the blanket, strapped in place, keep my legs drawn up. I was still hooded.

What a strange dream!

It seemed the basket flew!

Sometimes it seemed I heard the smiting of air, as though in the beating of giant wings. At other times I heard great birdlike cries, from above and ahead, or to one side or the other. And then I would lose consciousness again.

I decided that I must awaken, and in my own bed, on my own world.

The light seemed too bright, through my closed eyelids. I must, foolishly, have forgotten to draw the shade last night.

I was on my stomach. I pressed down with my finger tips, to feel the sheets and, beneath them, the familiar mattress.

But it seemed that something hard was beneath me, not the mattress, but a surface less yielding, more severe.

I kept my eyes closed. There was light. It was rather painful. How foolish I was! I had forgotten to draw the shade last night.

But the light did not seem to be coming from the proper direction. It should be coming more from behind me, to my left, where, as I was lying, or thought myself to be lying, my window would be. But it was not. It was coming rather from before me, and my left. I must have somehow, in my sleep, twisted about. I felt disoriented.

Everything did not seem to be the same. Many things seemed different.

I then, as I became more certain, but not altogether certain, that I was awakening, or awakened, became quite afraid.

I was not yet ready to open my eyes.

I remembered one thing quite clearly from my dream. I had been banded. It had been put on me. I had worn, almost from the first, a light, gleaming, about-a-half-inch-high, close-fitting steel collar. It locked in the back.

Not opening my eyes, frightened, I moved my fingers upward, little by little, toward my throat. Then, with my finger tips, I touched my throat. It was bare!

Again I felt my throat.

No band was there.

I did not wear such a circlet. I was in no neck ring, or such device. My throat was bare. No closed curve of steel, locked, inflexible, enclasped it.

I was not collared.

It would be hard then to describe my emotions.

Should they not have been of elation, of joy, of relief? Perhaps. But instead, perhaps oddly, as I lay there, somehow half between waking and sleep, I perceived a sudden poignance, as of irreparable loss. As of isolation. As of loneliness. I felt a wave, cold and cruel, of misery, rising within me, a forlorn, agonizing cry of alienation, of anguish. It seemed that I had suddenly become meaningless, or nothing. But then, in an instant, how pleased I tried to be, as I should be, of course. I attempted, instantly, to govern my emotions, to marshal them, and break them, and align them in accordance with the dictates to which I had been subjected all my life.

Yes, how relieved I was!

How wonderful was everything now!

It had been, you see, a dream!

There was nothing to worry about.

It was over now.

I might, now, even open my eyes.

But the surface on which I lay did not seem soft, nor did the material beneath my finger tips seem to have the texture of cotton sheets. The light, too, was wrong. I must have twisted about in my sleep. Something seemed wrong.

Memories of the dream recurred, the movements, the metal wagon, the chains, the hood, the basket, the wind through its coarse, sturdy fibers.

My head, it seemed for the first time in days, seemed clear. I now experienced, it seemed for the first time in days, a consciousness I recognized as familiar, as my own, neither confused nor disordered. I did not have a headache. I did not know how long I had slept. It might have been a long while.

But the surface seemed wrong, the direction of the light seemed wrong.

Somehow I must be disoriented.

I opened my eyes, and gasped, shaken. I began to tremble, uncontrollably.

I lay upon stone.

That was what was beneath my finger tips. There were no sheets. There was no mattress.

I lay upon stone!

I rose to all fours.

I seemed to be in a sort of cave, carved into the living rock of a mountain, or cliff.

I looked to the opening of where I was housed, for it was from thence that came the illumination.

There was no window there. Rather there was a large aperture. It was regular in form. It was like a portal. Surely it was not a natural opening. It was in shape something between a semicircle and an inverted "U." It was flat at the bottom, rather squared at the sides and rounded at the top. It was some six or seven feet high and some seven or eight feet wide. It was barred. The bars were heavy, some two or three inches in thickness. They were reinforced laterally with heavy crosspieces, an inch or so high, every foot or so.

My consciousness, suddenly, was very vivid, very acute. I seemed to be in a tiny brown tunic. How had this come about? It was no more than a rag.

I would never have donned such a garment!

I would never have permitted myself to be seen so, so bared, so displayed, so exposed in such a scandalous garment!

It was frayed, and torn. It was terribly brief. It was terribly thin. It had no nether closure. And it was all I wore!

I was outraged!

I might have torn it from me, but it was all I had.

Who had dared to put me in this garment?

Surely I had not done so!

A sense of acute embarrassment, and then of fury, overcame me! What right had someone to do this, to take such liberties, to so garb me, in so little, so pathetically, and so revealingly, and publicly, to so dress me, to so demean, insult and shame me, so deliberately, so grievously!

How could such a thing have been dared?

Who did they think I was?

What did they think I was?

I realized, of course, too, suddenly, the thought almost making me giddy and frightened, that whoever had done so must have seen me bared, fully. Whoever it was must, I surmised, surely have been male. Surely it was the sort of garment that only a man would put a woman in, or perhaps observe a woman being put in, under his direction. I wondered if he had liked what he saw. I felt vulnerable. Had I been violated while unconscious?

Things began to flood back to me.

Certain things now became very real.

It occurred to me that I was no longer the sort of woman who could be "violated." An animal could be put to use, but surely it could not be "violated."

It could be done with me as others might please.

And suddenly, it tending to shock me, in my confusion, the thought rose up irresistibly within me that I should, more properly, not be distressed by the rag I wore, but rather I should rejoice that I had been granted this gift, the indulgence, the lenience, of even so minuscule a scrap of clothing! It served to give me at least a little cover. Was I entitled to any? No, I had not the least right to such, or to anything. Surely I should be heartfeltedly grateful for even so little! Surely it need not have been granted me. Had I not, in the pens, as it had seemed to me in my dreams, if dreams they were, often pleaded for so little as a thread of silk?

What was I?

What had I become?

Something within me seemed to know.

The drug had now worn off. But it had induced a sense of confusion, an uncertainty as to what occurred and what had not occurred, what had been dream and what had not been dream.

Had I dreamed the house, the pens, the chains, the wagon, the strange passage through cold, windy skies?

Was I dreaming now? Was I delirious? Was I mad?

Muchly had I been disoriented by the substance to which I had been subjected.

Was I still, unwittingly, its victim?

But it did not seem so.

The stone, the close-set bars, the long, looming, tiered vistas beyond them, seemed very real.

I sought something to prove, or disprove, my fears.

Where was I?

Was I no longer what I had been, as I suspected? Had my reality, as I suspected, been transformed radically, utterly?

I must know!

I knelt back. I again felt my throat. No collar was there! Madly, feverishly, I pulled up the skirt of the tiny brown tunic, to bare my left leg to the waist. Yes! Yes! Yes! There it was, the tiny, lovely mark, incised into my thigh, just below the hip. I wore it, in my body! It marked me! There was no mistaking that small, beautiful sign. How beautiful it was! How well it marked me! It was my *brand*. It was truly there! I had been *branded*!

I again went to all fours, shaking, almost collapsing, now laughing, now weeping! I was overcome with elation, with joy, with relief. These emotions, from the depths of me, burst upward, like light and lava, like the throwing open of shades and the risings of suns, like floods, like tides, like treasures, like hurricanes, like fire, powerful, irresistible, precious! No longer did I suffer the sense of loss. No longer was I isolated, or wandering alone, apart from myself, not knowing myself, lost from myself. Forgotten then was the cry of alienation, of anguish. I had not been returned to my former condition of meaninglessness, that of nothingness, in which I, denied to my real self, it forbidden to me, must pretend to false identities, must conform to uncongenial stereotypes imposed upon me from the outside. Here I was free to be what I was! Here I might feel, truly feel! Here one need not live as if indoors, sheltered from sunlight and rain, here one might look upon truth as it was in itself, not as it might be distorted in the labyrinths of prescribed protocols, here one might touch real things, like grass and the bark of trees.

Then, quickly, I knelt back, and, hastily, furtively looking about, thrust down the brief skirt of the tunic. What if someone should see? We have our modesty! I smoothed it down, with something like the dignity which, I seemed to recall from my training, we were not permitted.

I looked about.

I was here, truly here, wherever it might be.

The nightmare of the journey was apparently over.

It was now clear to me, as it had been when I was first subjected to the substance, in some house faraway, that I had been drugged. Now, however, as nearly as I could determine, the disordering, sedative effects of whatever substance had been administered to me had worn off. The dosage, apparently, for some time, had not been renewed. Too, I was now no longer hooded, or even chained. Indeed, even my collar had been removed. I had no idea, of course, as to where I might be. It did not seem to me that the drug would have been necessary. Surely the hood would have been enough, and the metal wagon, and such. Indeed, it seemed to me that I might as well have been transported openly, for all I, given my ignorance of this world, might have been able to determine of my whereabouts. Why, then, had such precautions been taken with me? Men had not even spoken to me, and only occasionally in my vicinity. I had heard some things, some phrases, some scraps of discourse, when half-conscious, struggling with the haze of the drug, but very little, and nothing that told me what I most wanted to know, where I was being taken, and why. What was to be my fate? What was to be done with me? To what purposes was I to be applied? Why should I not at least be permitted to know where I was? What difference would it make, I wondered, if one such as I knew where she was?

But such as I, I have learned, are commonly kept in ignorance.

But I was here now, wherever it might be.

Then, interestingly, I became afraid. I was here, and in the power of others, whom I knew not. Surely there was, after all, something to be said for the tepid world from which I had been extracted. Would it not have been better then to have awakened between my own sheets, in my own bed, as I had so many times before, in those familiar surroundings? Was that world not, for all its lies, its hypocritical cant, its ludicrous, wearying pretenses, its tedious self-congratulatory self-righteousness, and such, a more secure place, a safer place? The dangers there, it seemed, were for the most part at least comfortingly slow, and invisible, such as minute quantities of poison in food, significant only over time, and lethal gases accumulating in the atmosphere, molecule by molecule. Indeed, the men of my world, in their self-concern, preoccupied with their own affairs, doubtless of great moment, seemed prepared to let their world die. I did not think, on the other hand, that the men of this world would allow their world to be destroyed. Nature, and its truths, were too important to them. And so my feelings were understandably somewhat ambivalent. Doubtless I would have been safer in my tepid, gray, polluted world, conforming to its values, being careful not to question, or to feel, or discover or know, but I, somehow, perhaps unaccountably, was not discontent to be where I was. I had no doubt that there were dangers here as, in fact, there were on my old world, but the dangers here, I suspected, at least for the most part, would be intelligible. As intelligible as the teeth of the lion, as the point of a weapon. Too, the question, I reminded myself, was somewhat academic. I was not on my old world. I was, whether I liked it or not, and for better or for worse, here.

I had quickly determined earlier that the tiny brown tunic was all that I wore. I had felt a momentary wave of embarrassment, and surely of irritation, even fury.

There had been that much of my old world left in me at that time.

But now I felt gratitude.

To be sure I was clearly dressed for the pleasure of men.

What beasts are men, what commandeering, controlling, imperious beasts!

But I did not mind. I was suddenly pleased to be beautiful, and to have my beauty displayed. If one is beautiful, why should one not be proud of it? Even if men force one, for their pleasure, to show it! And are we not pleased to be so displayed, to be seen as they will have us seen? Are we not then in the order of nature, as men will have us? Must one hide one's beauty because of the envy of the ugly? But here, I thought, men would not permit one to do so, even if one wished. But what beautiful woman would wish to do so? I was pleased now, even brazenly so, to be beautiful. But I did recognize its dangers, for it excites and stimulates men. We are, after all, their natural prey. On a world such as this a beautiful woman, or at least one such as I, is in no doubt as to her desirability, her vulnerability, and, I fear, her peril.

I had however learned, in the pens, that not all women on this world were such as I. But I did not know, at that time, if they were numerous or not. I had seen, at that time, only two. I had seen them, disdainful and resplendent, in the pens. How daintily, how haughtily, how fastidiously, they had picked their way about! I shall speak briefly of them later.

But even such women I suspected, in a world such as this, were at risk.

In any event, the men here, I thought, know how to dress women, or at least my sort of women, when it pleased them to dress them.

I was not collared.

I wondered if I had been freed.

Yes, I have used the expression 'freed'.

I do not see, now, how I could escape its use.

I have hitherto been reluctant, as you may have noticed, perhaps even foolishly, to speak explicitly of my status, and condition, on this world, which remains so to this moment, but I suppose it has been evident to the reader—if this is permitted to come to the attention of a reader. I am writing this in English, of course, for I can neither read nor write Gorean. Nor does it seem likely they will permit me to learn. It seems they prefer for me to be kept as I am, illiterate. That is common with women or, better, considering our status, *girls*, such as I.

Perhaps it has been evident that my status on this world is something with which the reader is likely to be unfamiliar, perhaps even something that he would find it hard to understand.

One does not know.

But I suppose, by now, it is evident to all that I am a *kajira*, or *sa-fora*. But of course it is not evident! How could it be? Forgive me. You do not know these words. Aside from the words, of course, my condition, my status, is doubtless clear to you. Would it not be clear from the speaking of chains, and collars, and such? You may find it objectionable. I do not. I love it. In it I find my fulfillment, my happiness, my joy! Perhaps you think what I am is degrading, and perhaps it is, but, if so, it is a delicious, precious, joyful degradation which I treasure, and in which I thrive and prosper, and one I would not, at the expense of my very life, have otherwise.

It is a thing of softness, heat, devotion, obedience, service, beauty, and love.

In it I am happy, and fulfilled, completely, perfectly, totally as a total woman, as I could be in no other way.

In brief, the word *sa-fora* means "Chain Daughter" or "Daughter of the Chain". The word *kajira*, on the other hand, is by far the most common expression in Gorean for what I am, which is, as you have doubtless surmised, a female slave. Yes, *slave*. The male form is *kajirus*. The plural of the first word is *kajirae*, and of the second *kajiri*. As *kajira* is the most common expression in Gorean for a slave who is female, I suppose it might, in English, be most simply, and most accurately translated, as "slave girl." In a collar, you see, understandably, all women are "girls." Almost all slaves on Gor are female. There are, of course, male slaves, but most are laborers, working in the fields, in quarries, in mines, on roads, and such, in chains and under whips. Some women keep male silk slaves, but they are rare. The Gorean view is that slavery is appropriate for the female, and not for the male. A saying, a saying of men, of course, has it that all women are slaves, only that some are not yet in the collar. I know now, of course, as I did not earlier, that there are many free women on Gor, and, indeed, that most women on Gor are free. An exception seems to be a city called Tharna. I do not know why that is the case.

I now return to my narrative.

Could I have been freed?

To be sure, the mark was still on my thigh. But that, of course, was only to be expected.

I looked to the heavy bars at the portal.

They did not suggest to me that I had been freed.

Too, I smoothed down the skirt of the tiny tunic. It was so brief! It was little more than a rag! That garment did not suggest, either, that I had been freed. As mentioned, it had no nether closure. This is common with slave garb. The delicious, moist intimacies of the slave are commonly left unshielded. She is to be open, and know herself open, to the master; this reality contributes to her sense of vulnerability, and informs, enhances, suffuses, and considerably deepens the rich emotionality of her nature. She is to be ready for the master at any time of the day or night, and in any place or manner which he may indicate. This helps her to keep in mind what she is. I had only twice, in my training, in my costuming, and silking, and such, worn a garment with a nether closure. The first was no more than a long, narrow silken rectangle thrust over a belly cord in front, taken down between the legs, drawn up snugly, and then thrust over the same cord in the back. The other, more elaborate, was a "Turian camisk." It is rather like an inverted "T," where the bar of the "T" has beveled edges. The foot of the "T" ties about the neck and the staff of the "T" goes before one, and then, between the legs, is drawn up snugly behind and tied closed in front where the beveled edges of the bar of the "T," wrapped about the body, have been brought forward, meeting at the waist. It may also have side ties, if permitted, strings that tie behind the back, to better conceal, in one sense, and, in another, better reveal the figure. We must know how to put on such a garment, for example, and well, if one is thrown to us. This Turian camisk differs from the common camisk. The latter is little more than a rectangle of cloth with an opening for the head in the center. It is worn over the head and tied at the waist, normally with one or more loops of binding fiber. The common camisk, of course, has no nether closure. Nether closures, as I have suggested, are seldom permitted to women such as I. We are expected, almost always, you see, to be immediately available to those who hold total rights over us.

And well does this help us understand what we are!

I smoothed down the skirt of the tunic even more firmly, more deliberately. One must be careful how one moves in such a brief tunic, of course. One is taught how to move gracefully in such a garment. Too, one learns how to do little things, such as, crouching down, to retrieve fallen objects.

I was pleased, of course, despite its brevity, to have been accorded a tunic. I knew I might not have received that much. Too, I knew, somewhat to my chagrin, that it could be ordered from me with so little as a snapping of fingers. I did try again to feel a bit indignant at the tunic, for a moment or two, it being all I wore, and so brief, and little more than a rag, but, to be honest, I was much pleased with it. Yes, I was pleased to wear such things. They set me off well. I knew that men found me exciting in them. I did not object to this. I was a woman. Too, if it must be known, such garments excited me, too. I found them arousing. I loved to wear them.

I was not collared.

Could I have been freed?

The garment did not suggest so, nor the bars at the portal. I had best behave as I had been taught, I thought, at least until it might be clear that I had been freed. I shuddered. Twice, in training, I had felt the lash, each time a single stroke. I did not care to have that experience repeated.

Could I have been freed?

Then I laughed at the absurdity of the thought. These were not men like those of my world. Men such as these would never free one such as I. They preferred us as we were, theirs.

On this world I was what I was. That was that.

I then rose, and went to the barred portal. I stood there, and held to the bars. Outside it, breathtakingly beautiful, I could see mountains, many of them snow-capped.

I was in awe.

I had not realized this world could be so beautiful.

To be sure, what had I seen of it, really, other than pens, some rooms, some kennels, a glimpse, when unhooded, of the interior of a closed-sided cage wagon, such things?

I looked up. There was a narrow, rectangular slot in the ceiling through which, it seemed, the bars, lifting, as a gate, might rise. There was doubtless a system of weights and counterweights. The bars would not swing outward. That was well, for I could see, from where I stood, grasping the bars, that there was a narrow ledge outside the bars. It was surely no more than a yard wide. I feared, from the valley below, and the mountains across the way, that the drop from the ledge might be precipitate. I crouched down to see if I might be able to lift the bars. I seized one of the crosspieces with both hands. I tried to lift the gate. I could not begin to do so. I had not really expected the gate to open, but I had thought I might be able to lift it a little, assuming some counterweights were engaged, at least an inch or so, until it was stopped by some device, say, some lock, or bolt or holding bar. But I could not move it, even an inch. If there were counterweights engaged then more than my strength was needed to activate them.

I turned about and examined the room, or cave, in which I was incarcerated. It was in depth some twenty feet long, in width some fifteen feet wide, in height some eight or ten feet high. Surely it was no kennel. It seemed to me large, even for a cell. I did not think it had been designed for the keeping of such as I. It could, in easy effectiveness, have held several men. The walls, and ceiling, were rough and irregular. The area was carved out of living rock. I had looked to the back. I had thought there might be some other entrance, perhaps a small iron door at the back, but there was not. In some cells, designed for such as we, there are, inserted within a larger door, or gate, a small door or gate. Whereas the larger door or gate may be opened, and men may enter the cell standing, if they wish, such as we are usually entered into the cell and summoned forth from it through the smaller door or gate. We thus enter on all fours and emerge on all fours, or, if it is wished, on our belly. This sort of thing is thought useful in reminding us of our status. It is also harder, obviously, to bolt through such an opening. Also, on all fours, or on our belly, as we emerge, it makes it easier to put us on a leash. But such has to do, of course, with cells. I was more familiar with kennels. These are usually quite small. They do not permit one to stand upright in them. They usually have barred gates. In this way, we, behind them, are always visible to our keepers. Toward the back there was a bit of straw and, I was pleased to see, a blanket. It was heavy and black. It would doubtless be warm. There were also three vessels in the cell. Two of these were of a simple yellowishly glazed clay, fragile and chipped about the edges. They had perhaps been discarded from some kitchen. The other was of a heavier, whitish porcelaintype substance. The yellowish vessels were to one side and the whitish porcelaintype vessel was to the other. I walked to the back, to examine them. Of the two to one side, the yellowish vessels, one was a flattish bowl, which contained a crust and some meal; too, within it I was pleased to see what I thought were some slices of dried fruit; such things are often included in our diet; they are precious to us; in the other vessel, of the two to one side, the left, as I faced them, my back to the bars, a taller, craterlike vessel, there was water. On the other side of the room, to the right, as I faced the back of the cell, was the larger, whitish porcelaintype vessel. I was grateful for its presence. Such things are not always permitted to us.

I wondered where I was.

I walked back to the bars, and, through them, gazed again, enraptured, at the beauty of the mountains.

Then, more curious about my surroundings, I grasped the bars. I pressed my face to the bars. I could not put my head between them. They were too closely set. I pressed the side of my face against them, first to the left, and then to the right, trying to see to the left and right. I could see, through them, only a bit of the ledge, narrow, extending to each side. I pressed my body against the bars. I felt their hardness against my softness. This disquieted me. It made me uneasy. But I then pressed myself even more closely against the bars. Their hardness, suddenly, seemed powerful, and delicious. It made me feel weak. I felt so helpless behind them. They were so stern and hard, so uncompromising, so unyielding. And I was within them. Herein I think I found figures, or images, or symbols, of what I was not certain. There was the hardness of the bars, and my softness, things so utterly different, and yet somehow, subtly, meaningfully complementary. And then, too, there were the bars and, within them, utterly helpless, was my softness. How mighty were the bars! How strong they were, and perfect! I pressed my cheek and body against them, happily, joyfully, gratefully, knowing that I could never break them.

I then drew back a little, but kept my grasp on the bars. This room, or cave, I conjectured, had not really been designed for such as I. It was so large, and strong. But it would hold one such as I quite as effectively as one such as they. I, though much smaller than they, no more than they, could even dream of slipping between the bars. They were too closely set.

I could see little from where I was, other than the ledge, and the mountains across the way. I thought it quite possible, however, that my cell was not the only one in this mountain, along that narrow path. That did not seem likely. It was, presumably, one of several along the path. Indeed, there might be other such paths cut in the mountain, above this one, with other cells, and perhaps, to be sure, below me, as well, where I could not see. I considered calling out. But I did not call out. It is perhaps just as well. Women such as I, you see, are subject to discipline. I did not know if I might call out or not. I had not received any explicit permission to speak. In my training I had twice, for days at a time, been refused permission to speak. One must then do as best one can, with gestures, with whimpers, and such, to make one's needs known, that one desires food, that one begs permission to relieve oneself, and so on.

Yes, this cell would hold men, as well as such as I. Too, I thought, it would hold animals, even large animals. I wondered if animals were ever kept in it. Animals other than, of course, the sort that I was. I looked back to the porcelaintype container, near the back wall, to the right. I was glad it was there. I would be expected to use it. One is taught, I, and animals, too, of other sorts, to use such things, corners of cells, boxes, drains, and such. I, of course, was "cell broken." If no receptacle were there, and I need not "wait," sometimes in misery, until conducted by keepers to a suitable place for the discharge of such homely functions, I knew enough to use the back, right-hand corner of the area. It is not pleasant to have one's face nearly thrust into one's wastes and then, on all fours, be dragged by the hair to the back, right-hand corner of an area, where the keeper points meaningfully to the appropriate place of deposition. One learns quickly, of course. One trains well.

I looked out toward the mountains.

I grasped the bars.

Here, on this world, I was an animal. I must obey. I was branded. I could be collared. I could be bought and sold. It could be done with me as others pleased.

I had been brought here, to this world, to this fate.

The mountains across the way were very beautiful.

I wondered where I was.

I was not unhappy.

I put one hand through the bars, reaching out, idly, toward the mountains. How beautiful they were. I drew my hand back, and held to the bars. I had not seen a guard, or keeper. I drew back a little and pulled down on the short skirt of the tunic. This made it tighter for a moment on my body. This movement, drawing the skirt down as I had, conjoined with a shy expression, and an attitude of timidity, can be quite provocative. One does this as an act of seeming modesty but, of course, it accentuates one's figure. In such a way may the secret riches of a country be hinted at and an invitation issued to its conquest. I had thought of this, incidentally, even on my old world, but I had never done it there. I did not have the appropriate garmenture there, except, in effect, in my dreams. Too, there I had been a person, and not an animal. Too, to whom there might such an invitation be meaningfully offered? Doubtless there must have been some there who could have taken me in hand, but I had not met them. I had not been touched, as far as I knew, since I had left the house in which I had been trained. The drug, or drugs, had muchly suppressed my needs. Now, however, the effects of the drug, or drugs, had worn off. I was awake, and fully conscious. Indeed, I was even hungry. I was prepared to kneel behind the bars and put my hands through, begging. I did not think I would have to beg too hard. I had been popular with the guards at the house. They had, at least, made frequent use of me. Such as I, incidentally, often compete for the touch of men. Perhaps we should share, but each of us wants what she can get, and so we behave in such a manner as to obtain all we can. Our bitterest rivalries then are commonly with our "sisters." In these competitions, as they had occurred in the house, in training, I had enjoyed what was apparently an unusual success. Aside from my possible independent interest to men, I do not doubt but what this success was largely due to my swift progress in readiness, need and heat, which progress was sure, profound and irreversible. Indeed, toward the end, primarily, I think, because of my ignited appetite and heat, my inability to control my responsiveness, my inability to help myself in the arms of men, I was getting what was regarded as far more than my fair share of attention. This compromised to some extent, it seems, the training of others. It did not endear me, of course, either, to my fellow trainees. Sometimes I was struck. Twice I was beaten. At any rate, to my dismay, shortly before I was removed from the house, the guards had actually been warned away from me. No longer, it seems, was I to be permitted, with my smells and heat, the promise of my responsiveness, my possible beauty, my anxious petitions, to seduce them from their duties. Too, I was ready, it seemed, to leave the house. And there were, after all, fires to be stoked in other bellies. Others, too, must be readied for departure. It is not that I was totally neglected, of course, which neglect would have produced utter anguish, but rather that my use was then restricted, or rationed. But, to be honest, not all the guards observed the schedules, the warnings, the cautions. More than once, late at night, while others slept, I was awakened by a soft tapping on the bars and summoned forth from the kennel, to serve there before it, in the light of a dark lantern, thence to be returned to the kennel. Gratefully had I crawled forth; reluctantly had I crawled back.

I clung to the bars.

I smiled.

There would be men here, doubtless, in this place, similar to those whom I had known in the house.

I recalled how the guards had been warned away from me, late in my training, in the house. In its way that, at least in the memory, pleased me. They had not been subjected to such restrictions with respect to any of the others in my group. I was the only one! How special that made me feel! Oh, how I had wanted the guards! How prettily I had begged! And, if not soon satisfied, how rather desperate and plaintive had become my petitions. I could recall having been on my belly more than once, kissing their feet, weeping, imploring their touch. But on the whole I had not had to beg very hard. "Temptress," had said more than one of me. I had in heat desired them, and they, in their power had put me often to their uses. Oh, yes, I had been needful and beautiful! Too, I had been quick in learning. I had mastered my lessons well. Certainly I was at least one of the best of the students. The guards had been warned away from me! Was it my fault if I might look well, kneeling at their feet? Was I to blame, if they found me of interest, perhaps even disquieting, or distracting? They did not have to spend additional time with me! It had been their choice! I laughed. How popular I had been with them, with perhaps one exception, he whose whip I had first kissed, he who had treated me with such cruelty. But what did he matter? Who cared for him! How special I was! Toward the end they had even warned the guards away from me. They must not be distracted by my plaints and beauty. I was already ready, hot in my shackles. Were there not others to be trained, as well?

I did not doubt but what I would be well able to please what men might be in this place.

Had I not been evaluated, and purchased for this place?

Was I not trained?

Often, on my old world, I had been unsure as to how to relate to men, how to behave with them, I mean, really. I was familiar, of course, with the protocols of neuterism, the silly, self-contradictory tenets of unisex, invented by those apparently as innocent of logic as glands, and the pathetic absurdities of "personism," such things, the fictions, the lies, the pretenses, the many tiny, brittle crusts concealing the smoldering depths of difference, of reality, of sexuality within one. But how tiresome it had been, and how frustrating, pretending to be only a surface, with no interior, no inner reality. Were those who preached such stupidities, I wondered, only such a thing themselves, a one-dimensional surface, or were they simply lying. Could there be very different sorts of human beings? Were some, in effect, hollow? If so, perhaps it was natural for them to suppose that others must be as empty as they. But I did not think that human beings were one-dimensional or hollow, even those who spoke in such a fashion. I thought that we were all very real. Some of us, however, might fear to inquire into this reality. Some of us might feel it was safer to pretend it did not exist, to deny it.

It seemed now to be late afternoon.

I clasped the bars.

On my old world I had been unsure as to how to relate to men, how to behave with them. Many had been the uncertainties, the confusions, in such matters. We had seemed, such as I, and men, on that world, to have no clear identities. We were strangers, and ambiguities, to one another. It was almost as though we had no reality of our own. It was almost as though we were only images, only projections, only shadows, only vapors. But here, on this world, such as I, at least, had an identity, an explicit, verifiable identity, an explicit, verifiable reality. I was here something, something very real, something as real as the living rock about me, as real as the bars of my cell. Here, on this world, there was no puzzle as to how such as I were to relate to men. Here there were no uncertainties. Here the doubts were dissipated. Here the confusions had vanished. On this world I would kneel before men. I would serve them. I would please them to the best of my ability, in any way they might desire.

I clung to the bars.

I pressed my left cheek against them. I thought of the men of this world. How else could a woman such as I relate to such men? I suspected they would find me pleasing. I was sure I could please them. I now knew how to relate to men. I now knew what to do. I had been trained. The uncertainties, the ambiguities, were gone.

I did not think I would have difficulty pleasing the men here. Too, I had had no difficulty in pleasing the men in the house, with but one exception. Why had he hated me? Was he angry that I could not help but be what I was?

The guards in the house, late in my training, had been warned away from me. That did not seem to me likely to happen here. Presumably that had been a special situation, where the resources of instruction must be rationally distributed, where there were others who must be trained, and such. But these were not, presumably, pens. If I were popular here I did not think it likely that men would be warned away from me. There would be no point to it. Rather, I would be merely the more frequently used. If any were to be upset about such a matter, it would presumably be others such as I, but, in that case, let them look out for themselves! I was quite ready to compete, you see, in any such contests!

How scandalous, I thought, that I should have such thoughts. What had I become? But I knew.

Yes, I was sure I could please men!

I leaned against the bars, dreamily. I would, at any rate, do my best. I knew that I had always wanted to please men, and serve them. That had seemed to me in the order of nature, and to be fitting and right. But now, suddenly, remarkably, I had found myself on a world where, literally, I must do so. On this world, I had no choice in the matter. I was subject to discipline. I did not wish to be punished. I did not wish to be killed.

I held to the bars.

I looked out, at the narrow ledge, the beautiful mountains, the vast, bright, late-afternoon cloudy sky over the mountains.

How beautiful was this world!

To be sure, I was not important. I was less than nothing within it.

I thought of my old world, and its buildings, its streets, its roads, its signs, its crowding, its people, so many of them so wonderful, so precious, so many of them so miserable and sad, their mode of dress, now seemingly so unnatural, or eccentric, the vanities, the hostilities, the offensive, disgusting mindlessness of its materialism, the abuse of serious intellect and genuine feeling, the sense of emptiness and alienation, the destructive, pathetic search of so many for toxic stimulants, the banal electronic gaudiness, the unwillingness to look within, or ahead, the culture of selfishness, comfort and distraction. I was not then so disappointed to be where I was. In my old world I had been told I was important, as one tells everyone in that world, but I had not been, of course. Here I knew I was not important, but hoped that I might, sometime, mean at least a little to someone. One need not be important, you see, not at all, for that to be the case.

But how terrible was this world!

In it I had once actually been put in a collar, a steel collar, which I could not remove!

How I had treasured it!

Oh, there were dangers here, doubtless. And I did not know how many, or of what sorts. How ignorant I was!

But I did not think I was discontent, really, to be here. I did not even mind the cell, really. Such as I must expect to be kept in such places. Surely it would not do, to let us run around as we might please.

I thought of some of my friends, on my old world. We had, of course, gone about together. I had had classes with some of them. But it was interesting how I now thought of them. I did not think of them now so much as they had been, on the bus, in classes, in the library, in labs, wandering about with me in the wide, smooth halls, and corridors, and courts of one or another of an endless list of shopping malls, patronizing garish restaurants whose claim to fame was the speed with which inferior food could be served, and such, but rather how they might be now, if they, like myself, had been brought to this world. How would three rows of thonged bells look, jingling on the left ankle of a bare-footed Sandra? Wouldn't Jean look well, in a common camisk, carrying a vessel of water, balanced with one hand on her head, as we had been trained to do? And surely Priscilla would be fetching in a tiny bit of yellow silk, all she would wear. And Sally, plump, cuddly little Sally, so excitable, so talkative, so self-depreciating, so cynical with respect to the value of her own charms, let her wardrobe for the time be merely a collar, and her place only the tiles at a man's feet. Let her kneel there in terror and discover that her previous assessments of her desirability, her attractions, were quite in error, and that, in such matters, much depends on the health of men, their naturalness and their power. I now thought of my friends, you see, rather in the categories of my new world. I wondered what prices they might bring, on a sales block. Certainly all were lovely; certainly all would look well in collars. It was my speculation that they would all, all of them, my lovely friends, my dearest friends, bring excellent prices.

Men would want them all.

But what if I had to compete for the favor of a master with them? That would be different. It would then be every girl for herself.

I heard, suddenly, from far off, out of sight, to my right, a shrill, birdlike cry.

I grasped the bars and pressed myself against them, looking up, and to the right. I saw nothing.

The cry had seemed birdlike, but, even far off, it was too mighty to have had such a source.

Then, a moment later, closer, I heard the same cry.

Again I pressed myself to the bars. I could see nothing, only the sky, the clouds.

I wondered what had made the sound.

My thoughts then wandered to some of the men I had known on my old world. I wondered, too, what they might look like, clad not in the enclosed, hampering, eccentric garments prescribed for them by their culture, but in freer, more natural garb, such as tunics, and, as I had sometimes seen in the house, robes, and cloaks, of various sorts, things which might, in a moment, be cast aside, beautifully and boldly freeing the body for activity, for the race, for wrestling, for bathing, for the use of weapons, for the command of such as I. But whereas it seemed natural to think of the women of my world, or some of them, clad as I was, it seemed somehow foolish, or improbable, to think of the men of my world in the garmenture of the men of this world. It did not seem appropriate for them. I doubted that they could wear it honestly, if they could wear it well. I thought that they, given what they were, might be unworthy of such garments. But perhaps I am unfair to the men of my old world. Doubtless on that world, somewhere, there must be true men. And I did not think, truly, that the men of my old world were really so different from the men here. The major differences, I was sure, were not biological, but cultural. I had been given a drink in the pens, for example, the intent of which, as I understood it, was to prevent conception. This suggested surely that the men here were cross-fertile with women such as I, and, thus, presumably, that we, despite the seeming considerable differences between us, were actually of the same species. The differences between the men of this world, so self-confident, so audacious, so lordly, so natural, so strong, so free, and those of my old world, so little like them, then, I assumed, must be, at least primarily, differences of acculturation. On my old world nature had been feared. It must be denied, or distorted. Civilization was the foe of nature. On this world nature had been accepted, and celebrated. It was neither distorted nor denied. Here, civilization and nature were in harmony. Here, it was not the task of civilization to disparage, condemn, and fight nature, with all the pathological consequences of such an endeavor, but rather to fulfill and express her, in her richness and variety, to enhance her and bedeck her with the glories of customs, practices and institutions.

I suddenly then heard again, this time so much closer and terrible, from somewhere to the right, perhaps no more than a hundred yards away, that dreadful shrill birdlike cry or scream. I was startled. I was terrified. I stood behind the bars, unable even to move. Then I suddenly gasped with fear. My hands were clenched on the bars. Moving from the right toward the left, some yards above the level of the ledge, some seventy or so yards out from it, I saw a gigantic hawklike creature, a monstrous, titanic bird, of incredible dimension. It must have had a wingspan of some forty feet in breadth! It is difficult to convey the terribleness, the size, the speed, the savagery, the power, the ferocity, the clearly predatory, clearly carnivorous nature of such a thing! But the most incredible thing, to my mind, was that I saw, in the moment or two it was in my visual field, that this monster was harnessed and saddled, and, astride it, was a helmeted figure, that of a man!

I almost fainted behind the bars.

How grateful for the bars was I then!

The figure astride the winged monster had not looked toward the mountain, the ledge, the cell.

What had lain in this direction had apparently not concerned him.

Indeed, what could be of importance here, what worth considering?

I clung to the bars. My holding to them kept me from falling.

Such men existed here!

I felt giddy.

Men who could master such things!

I staggered back from the bars. My fingers went to my throat. Surely there must be a collar there! But there was not. I pulled down, frightened, on the edges of my brief skirt. I wanted then, somehow, to more cover myself. But, of course, the gesture, given the brevity of the tunic, was futile. I felt my thigh, through the tunic. The tiny mark was there, identifying me for any who might have an interest in the matter, as the sort I was. I put my finger tips then again to my throat. It was now bare. But I did not think that it would be long, in a place such as this, where there were such men, without a collar.

Suddenly certain of my memories, or seeming memories, of my journey here, made more sense. I, sometime ago, hooded, had been bound hand and foot, wrapped in a blanket, and strapped, apparently, in some sort of basket. I had felt as though it were borne through the air. I had thought I had heard great snapping sounds, doubtless now the beating of wings, and certain cries, doubtless, now, of such a creature, or of one somewhat like it, utilized for draft purposes.

I was terrified of that gigantic bird.

And I was property in this place, where there were such things, and men who could master them.

I was afraid.

I did not wish to be fed to such a thing.

But surely it was unlikely that I had been purchased and brought here, apparently from so far away, for such a purpose.

But then, perhaps strangely, perhaps unaccountably, I became excited, sexually.

I returned again to the bars, and, again, grasped them.

I thought again of my friends. I wondered if they ever thought of me. I wondered if they wondered, sometimes, what had become of me. I was not the same I knew. I was now much different. What would they think, I wondered, if they could see me now, in such a rag, in such a place, captive, and more than captive, animal and property, behind bars. Never would they suspect, I speculated, that their friend was now other than they had known her, that she was now quite different, that she was now subject to the collar, that she was branded. Would they be able to grasp now that she must obey, that she must please and serve? No, they could presumably not grasp such things. But I understood them quite well. How thrilled I was to be here, and, too, to be what I was. I had seen the great bird, in all its magnificent power and savagery. And I had seen its rider, too, paying me no attention, so careless of the cells. How exotic was this world! How beautiful it was! How exciting it was! How thrilling it was! How different it was! And I was here, and as what I was. I pressed myself against the bars, trembling. I wondered then again if my friends could have understood something of what it was to be a woman such as I, on a world such as this. Perhaps, I thought. They, too, are women.

What would it be like, I suddenly wondered, to compete with them? Surely they were lovely, all of them. What if they, too, were here?

Would we not, suddenly, find ourselves divided against one another? Yes, I thought. We would. We would all strive to be the best, the most pleasing! Alone together, in our silks and collars, in our locked, barred, lovely quarters, we might still be friends, chatting, gossiping, sharing intimacies. But before men how could we be other than competitive slaves? And how would this affect us, when we were again alone? "He likes me more!" "No, he does not!" "Did you see how he looked at me?" "I did not notice." "I want that silken scarf!" "No, it is mine to wear!" "Oh, you knelt prettily in your serving!" "I knelt as I must!" "No!" "Yes!" "Collar meat!" "Collar meat!" "Slave!" "Slave!" "It is I who will be taught to dance!" "But as a slave!" "Of course, little fool, what do you think we are?" "It was I who was called to the furs of the Master the night before last!" "But not last night!" "The Master was distracted!" "You are supposed to be the distraction!" "I can do better!" "You had better, or you will be lashed, slave!"

There must be other women such as I, I suddenly thought, in this place! Surely I could not be the only one! There had been sixty women, as it had turned out, in my group in the pens, divided into ten groups of six each, each group under a whip master, the groups sometimes training together, sometimes separately, under the tutelage of various others, some coming and going, switching about, teaching different matters, others concerned to teach specific subjects, and so on. We had all been from Earth. As soon as we had begun to learn our new language, we could, of course, as permitted, converse. We thus learned much about one another. Too, there had been five of us who spoke English as a native language, and some others who knew it as a second, or third, language. We had been separated from one another, however, on the chain in the corridor, and early in our training. Of the five who spoke English natively, two were from America, I one of them, two were from England, and one was from Australia. Among the other Earth languages represented amongst us were French, German, Dutch, Italian, Greek, Spanish, Mandarin Chinese, Cantonese Chinese, and Japanese. But those in the pens, which were apparently large, were mostly native to this world. We of Earth constituted a small minority amongst them. We regarded the girls of this world as incredibly beautiful, from what we saw of them, but we did not really regard ourselves as so inferior to them, particularly as our training progressed. One becomes more beautiful, of course, with the training, not simply as one learns to move, to care for one's appearance, and such, but, I think, even more importantly, as one begins to find oneself in one's natural place in the order of nature, as one's tensions and confusions are reduced, as one begins to discover what one really is, as one becomes gradually truer to oneself, and so on. Beauty, as is well known, begins within. Some of our teachers were girls of this world, of the same sort as we. They, too, had their collars; they, too, were subject to discipline. Our lessons were varied. Some were in homely domestic matters, such as the making of bread and the sewing and laundering of garments. Others were, from our point of view, at least those of the Western girls, more exotic, such as the proper fashion in which to bathe a man, one of the first things we were taught, and the proper use of the tongue. The latter skill is useful, for example, if one's hands are tied behind one's back. But I mention these things primarily to make it clear that there were large numbers of us in the pens. Too, sometimes new girls would be brought in, naive, ignorant, cringing, terrified, in their chains, as we had once been, and other girls, more trained, would be taken away, presumably to other places of incarceration, perhaps where they might await their display and sale. How superior we felt to the new girls being brought in, and how frightened we were, too, fearing the time when we, like the more thoroughly trained girls, might be removed from the security of the pens, to what fates we could scarcely conjecture, in an unfamiliar, foreign world. No, I did not think I would be the only woman such as I in this place. There was clearly a place and role for my kind on this world. I did not doubt but what we were numerous. To be sure, I did not think that my kind, in origin, from Earth, would be common here. We, I gathered, were quite rare, though it seems not as rare as once we were. Some men, we gathered, actually preferred us. A market for our kind, it seems, though perhaps a small one, had, over the years, opened up. Our predecessors here, it seems, had proved that we could be of interest, and, I gather, of considerable interest.

Not all women here, of course, were such as I. I have mentioned that I had seen two, earlier. They had toured, with guides and guards, some of the cleaner, more respectable areas in the pens. They were apparently esteemed visitors. They had been richly robed, even veiled. Perhaps they were part owners of the enterprise. I did not know. We were not told such things. Before them we prostrated ourselves, in our nudity and collars, to the very belly. We were less than dirt before them; we were animals, things to be despised and held in contempt, things unworthy the notice of such lofty creatures. I recall wondering, however, as one passed me, and I saw the regal, swirling hem of that sparkling robe, if the concealed ankle within it would look well clasped in slave steel; I supposed that it would wear a shackle well; why not, was she not a woman? When they had passed, and I dared, I lifted my head a little from the damp stone and looked after them, they, in their layered veils, in their cumbersome splendor, in their glorious, elaborate ornateness! How perfect, how superior, how arrogant they were! But were they truly so different from us? I doubted it. Let them be stripped, I thought, angrily, and knelt down, and collared, and feel a stroke or two of the lash! I conjectured then that they, as quickly as we, would hasten to obey, and strive desperately to be found pleasing.

Did they not know that men were their natural masters, and that they might, as easily as we, if men chose, find themselves in chains and collars?

But surely legally, and socially, institutionally, culturally, we were not such as they. They were not such as we. Between us lay a mighty chasm.

I shall later, briefly, recount what happened when one of these women turned back, to stand before me. I suspect she had noted, or sensed, that I had dared to lift my head and look after them. Perhaps she had suspected what might have been my thoughts, thoughts inappropriate in a slave. To be sure, perhaps it had merely been something about me which had annoyed her, scarcely noticed, in passing. Perhaps, in my eagerness and curiosity to see them, for I had not seen free women of this world before, I had allowed some imperfection in my position, say, with respect to the angle of my body, the backs of my hands beside me, resting on the stone, the touching of the stone with my forehead? But then, again, perhaps it was merely a whim on her part, or a tactical device, randomly applied, to assess the quality of our training. I do not know, nor do I think it is important. In any event, for whatever reason, she had suddenly turned back, and I had not yet lowered my head. I had been caught by surprise! I gasped in misery, and quickly put my head down. But it was too late. An imperfection had been detected in my position! Too, my curiosity had been evident, and curiosity, it is said, is not becoming in such as we. Yet I wonder who, on this wide world, is likely to be more zestfully and earnestly inquisitive, more delightfully curious, than we! That is natural for women as a whole and it is certainly natural for us, who are the most female of all women. I shall briefly speak of this later, as it may shed some light on an aspect of Gorean society.

But it was not such women here, of course, that I was concerned with. They doubtless had their own world. Rather was I concerned with women here who might be such as I! It was those with whom I must compete!

How strange, I thought, what I had become!

I wondered what my friends, Sandra, and Jean, and Priscilla, and Sally, might have thought if they saw me at a man's feet, clad as I was, tendering there the ministrations of one of my kind.

They, too, of course, if were they here, would soon enough hurry to do so!

There were the chains, the whips.

But what if they, secure in my old world, locked in that gloom, held within those walls, should see me so? I wondered if they would be startled, or shocked, or scandalized, or dismayed. And what if they saw how willingly, how eagerly, how joyfully I did this! But I thought, rather, that they, somehow, if only after a moment or two, beneath the immediate, superficial crusts of their conditioning, on some deep level, would feel something quite different, not shock, not scandal, not dismay, but something genuinely different, perhaps at first even frighteningly so, a tremor of understanding, an unspeakable thrill of recognition. I suspected then they would feel envy at the openness, the naturalness, of this, the beauty, the rightness, of it. Was this truly so strange to them? It is not so hard to understand. Had they not often been, if only in their dreams, in such a place? I could conceive of them being here, each of us in our collar, glancing shyly, one to the other, looking down, happily, scarcely daring to meet one another's eyes. We had no choice, you must understand, given what we are. Might we not even meet, perhaps while on errands, or laundering at a stream or public basin, and discuss those who held total rights over us? In their hearts, if they knew, I did not doubt but what they would envy me, how free I was here, and what I could do. Too, was it not natural that we should belong to such men! But they, such men, of course, in one sense, would take us apart quite from one another. Our group, as it had been, would be broken up. We would find ourselves separated, each from the other, each of us now with a different destiny and fate, each of us having now to relate to a man, and a different man, hopefully, and what might these men have in common, other than the fact that we were theirs, that they held total rights over us?

But my friends were not here.

How strange, I thought, what I had become.

Yet, too, I knew it was what, in my heart, I had always been.

It was now growing dark.

The air, too, seemed to be getting chilly. I was glad there was a blanket behind me, in the cell.

I missed my friends. I wished they might know my freedom, and joy, but, too, of course, there were terrors here, and dangers. I shuddered, recalling the great bird in flight, the anonymous, helmeted warrior in its saddle. Such a man, I feared, might not be easy to please. Too, such as he doubtless owned whips. I was excited by the fullness and beauty of life, and I felt it more intensely here, even in this barren mountain cell, behind these bars, than I had ever felt it on my old world.

I felt wanton, and excited, and alive!

Too, in spite of my brand, my tunic, the cell, the bars, I felt free, more free than I had ever felt before.

There were women here who would doubtless know more than I, not merely about this world and its ways, but about the pleasing of men. I was only just out of the pens. And one's learning, one's training, I had been given to understand, is never to be regarded as finished, as complete. And men, too, are so different!

But I did not fear the other women!

I was sure I could compete with them.

In the pens I had been popular.

Let the other women be jealous of me! I had certainly encountered no little evidence of that sort of thing in my training. I did not care. Let them dislike me! I did not care! Perhaps they would not help me. Then I would not help them! Perhaps they would not tell me their secrets. Then I would not tell them mine, if I should discover any! Or we might bargain, and trade in such matters. Such things, you see, can be terribly important for women such as we. How amusing the men sometimes find us! What monsters they are!

But on this world I could not help but feel irremediably, profoundly, unutterably female.

Never on my old world had I been so conscious of my sex, and how important, and wonderful, and beautiful it was. It was so special, and glorious, and tender, and different from that of a man. For the first time in my life, on this world, I had rejoiced in being a woman. Gone now was the absurdity of the asserted irrelevance of the most basic fact about my being. Gone now were the acculturated insanities of pretenses to identity. Here I reveled in my differences from men, accepting what I was, for the first time, with joy.

I held the bars.

Oh, I did not fear to compete with the other women. I could compete for favor, and attention, and gifts, such as bit of food thrown to me where I was chained beneath a table, as we sometimes were in training, while the guards feasted, or the rough caress of a male hand, such things. I could compete! I had been popular! I did not fear the others! I thought again then of Sandra, and Jean, and Priscilla and Sally. They were pretty. They would bring high prices. What if we were in the same house? I could conceive of that. I had thought of it before. But then we would be slaves, all of us. I did not doubt again then that in such a situation, we in silk and collars, and such, we, even we, who had been friends, would quickly find ourselves pitted against one another. Before, you see, there had been no male to divide us, to come between us. Now, however, there would be a male, and one, presumably, of a sort appropriate to this world. How we would then compete! How each of us would strive to be first, the favorite! How we would fight for his attention, for his touch, for the opportunity to be chained at the foot of his couch! How jealous, how resentful, we might come to be of one another! How we might even come in time to hate one another! With what trepidation and watchfulness might we wait kneeling to see who was to be braceleted that night and sent to the quarters of the rights holder. With what fury we might, from within our sheets, twisting upon our sleeping mats, look upon another mat nearby, but one which was unoccupied, one which was empty.

But I did not expect, of course, to be competing with my friends, for which I was just as pleased, because I did not doubt but what they, suitably trained, and on this world, as I was, would be formidable competitors, highly intelligent, and tantalizingly and deliciously seductive, nor, indeed, did I expect to be competing even with women of my old world. I did not think it likely that there would be any such, or many such, here. Here, on this world, it seemed likely I would have to compete, if with anyone, with women of this world.

It was now almost dark.

Yes, it would be, doubtless, with women of this world that I must compete.

I would do so well, I was sure. I was trained. I had been popular with the guards, with the exception of he whose whip I had first kissed, he whom I had most zealously, even to the point of anguish, desired to please.

I did not fear the property women of this world!

I would show them what a property girl from Earth could do!

But then I was afraid. If the other women did not like me, if they were not kind to me, if they did not help me, might my life then to some extent be endangered? And what if they lied about me, perhaps telling the men I had stolen a pastry, or something? I did not wish to be whipped, or killed. Perhaps I must pretend to be their friend? That might be safer. And then, in secret, I might woo the men? Would the women suspect? Yes, for they, too, were women! Too, they could certainly tell from the reactions of the men to me. But what if I were not fully pleasing, and authentically so, to the men, even before the other women, at all times? Would I not then, again, be in danger of being whipped, or slain? Yes!

For a moment, in misery, I did not know what to do!

Then I asked myself, who held the power, ultimately? It was the men, of course. And for what purpose had I been brought to this world? What, now, was the meaning of my existence? To be pleasing, and serve men! That was now what I was for. The men then must protect me from the other women. Naturally the other women would be my rivals. That was only to be expected. My best tactic for survival then would be to ignore the women, to disregard them, in effect, and set myself to please the men as best I could, letting the results fall out as they might. I must not defeat myself. I must let myself be superb. I must strive for excellence. Too, I wanted to please the men not just for the sake of my safety, or survival, or that I might be better treated or fed, or have a better kennel, or for the sake of my vanity, or because of a sense of power, exerted over rivals, but because, ultimately, of what we were, they men, I a woman. I wanted to be myself on this world. It was the first world I had found on which such a thing was possible.

I wondered if women such as I, from Earth, might not prove to be of interest to many men here, or, at least, to some of them. We had been brought here from a sexual desert, thirsting and starving; we had not known that men such as these existed; we had never been permitted before to be ourselves.

I held to the bars.

It was now dusk.

I then put my elbows on one of the crosspieces, my forearms outside the bars, my hands grasping them above my head, and laid my left cheek against them.

I had then, having resolved these matters in my mind, felt dreamily confident.

Yes, there would doubtless be rivals.

But I did not care! Let them beware! I did not fear them! They would be nothing to me! I was excellent, I knew. I had been popular in the pens. Too, a girl must look out for herself! Too, I had desperate, peremptory needs, which required satisfaction. Too, I wanted to be excellent, to be superb!

There was nothing to fear.

Suddenly from my right emergent out of the dusk so quick so fierce so fast so large its head perhaps two feet in width the head large triangular its eyes blazing lunging toward the bars big the thing a hideous noise bars body pressing scratching I leaping back, screaming, it biting at the bars the fangs white grinding on the metal the snout thrusting against them the snarling, it couldn't get through, the growling the snarling I falling back twisting crying out then terrified on my hands and knees seeing it long thick like a gigantic furred thing snakelike lizardlike the thing it had six legs its snout then pushing under the bottom crosspiece of the gate, trying to pry it up, to get at me I screaming!

I had been unable to lift the gate, even an inch.

But I saw the snout of that terrible triangular head, perhaps two feet wide at the base, push it up three or four inches and then it struck against some bolt, some bar or holding lever. It could not crawl under the gate. I could not get under it either. It then in frustration pressed its snout against the bars, filling the cave behind me with the waves of its enraged growling. I went to my stomach and put my hands over my ears. I shut my eyes. I shuddered. I could hear the gate creak as the beast pressed its weight against it. I wept. The entire cell reverberated with the sounds of the beast's fury. But it could not get through. When the sound stopped I uncovered my ears and opened my eyes. It was gone. I could not control the movements of my body. I was trembling reflexively. I could not have stood up had I wished to do so. I had never seen such a thing. And, even so, given the darkness, I had not had much of a look at it anyway. It had been little more than a dark, ferocious, gigantic shape trying to get at me. I sobbed. The bars had held! For a time I could not bring myself to approach the bars. I think it might have taken ropes or chains to pull me to them, or the snapping of the fingers of a rights holder. But they had held. How grateful I was to them! In time, as I was able to control my body, I rose, shaking, trembling, to all fours and crawled toward the bars, taking care not to come too close to them. I looked to the left and right. I saw no further sign of it.

I had thought there had been nothing to fear.

Unable to walk I crawled back, on all fours, to the rear of the cell.

I looked back toward the bars.

They had held.

It was now dark. I shivered. It was chilly now in the cell, as doubtless it would be in these mountains, at night, even during a summer. I found the blanket. I wrapped myself in it, and knelt there, looking toward the bars.

The blanket, I knew, might be used to give my scent to a tracking animal, but I did not care!

What choice had I?

I must use it. I needed it. I was cold. I did not think I had much choice. I did not want to freeze.

Too, there had been the other blanket, that in which I had been wrapped in the basket. That was probably kept somewhere. I could only hope that it had, in the meantime, been used for other girls. Too, my scent was doubtless in the cell, as well, from where I had lain, or stepped. On this world I had not been permitted footwear. It is said that it need not be wasted on animals. It is also said that this helps us to understand that we are animals. It also serves nicely to contrast us with our betters, free women. But, too, I think, it makes us easier to track, given the oils and moisture, the residue, of our barefooted passage.

Too, as I was frightened, as well as cold, the blanket gave me some sense of sheltering, of protection, of warmth, or security.

These things can be precious to a girl.

Too, clothed as I was, if clothed one may say, I would be forced to use the blanket. Those who had placed me in this cell doubtless knew that. How we are controlled and managed! My scent then would be redolent in the dark folds of the heavy cloth, but nonetheless I must wrap it about me. What choice had I?

I must use it. I did not want to freeze.

I did not care!

I gave no thought to escape. On such a world where would one escape to?

On this world I later learned, as I had already conjectured, there is no escape for one such as I. We are slaves, and will remain slaves, unless it is decided otherwise by our masters. And on this world there is a well-known saying that only a fool frees a slave girl. I think that it is true. Who so fortunate as to own one of us would have it otherwise? To be sure, we may be sold or traded.

I had never seen a mammalian creature, if it was mammalian, like that. It was long-bodied, large and terrible. It may have weighed fifteen hundred pounds. It had had, I was sure, six legs.

I had not imagined such things could exist.

My mistake, I was sure, had been that I had had a portion of my body, my elbows and forearms, outside of the bars. I was confident that was what I had done wrong, for, you see, I was reasonably sure that my cell, in such a mountain, would not be the only one. There might, on various trails, be a hundred such cells in the mountain. And surely some of these might have occupants. But I had not heard the beast threaten, or attack, the bars of other cells.

How did I know that it was not some wild creature of the mountains, come to the ledges, hunting for prey?

There were various reasons for supposing that unlikely, even if it had not been for one item. Presumably, if that were the case, the ledges would be within its territory, and it would have learned by now that it could not enter the cells. It might have investigated them, perhaps even testing them, to see if they were locked, but it would not be likely to have been so agitated or enraged. Too, there must be men about here, at least sometimes, men with weapons, doubtless hunters, and such, and it did not seem such a beast, so dangerous, so formidable, would be permitted to traverse this area with either regularity or impunity. Surely it would be driven away, or killed.

So, even had it not been for one item, one might plausibly have doubted that it was merely a wild thing, come to the ledges in hunger, seeking food.

The one item which seemed to put the matter beyond all doubt was the fact that the beast was collared. The collar was at least a foot in width, with a dangling ring, and covered with spikes. Such a collar would doubtless protect its throat against its own kind and other such beasts. The fact that it had made its appearance after dark suggested that it had been released as a guard beast, to patrol the ledges at night. I shuddered, thinking what might be the fate of one such as I found outside the cell at night. We were not permitted, I gathered, even to have part of our body outside the bars. I was sure that was what must have triggered the beast's frenzy.

I had thought there had been nothing to fear.

But there were such beasts on this world.

Doubtless they could be trained to kill us, or hunt us down. I did not doubt but what they would be indefatigable, efficient, tenacious hunters.

What escape could there be for such as I?

Was it not enough that I was dressed as I was, that I was branded, that I might be collared!

My scent was doubtless already within the blanket about my shoulders, or in the other, that in which I had been wrapped, in the basket. It was, doubtless, even in the cell itself!

I sobbed.

I thought of such beasts.

Perhaps they helped to preserve order here.

I did not wish to be fed to one!

But then I had presumably not been brought here, with such secrecy, over such a distance, merely to be fed to such a beast, no more than to that gigantic, carnivorous, hawklike creature, that titanic bird I had seen. No, that would make no sense. It would not be, presumably, for such a purpose that I had been evaluated, and acquired. But for what purpose *had* I been evaluated and acquired? I did not think it would be merely for the usual purposes for which one such as I might be obtained, say, being purchased off a sales block or being obtained in barter or trade. They had been very particular in their requirements, requirements which, incidentally, might be difficult to satisfy conjointly, not being likely to be found combined in any single item of merchandise. They had wanted an Earth female who would have an adequate, or better, facility in their language, that of the rights holders, but who would be, in effect, almost completely ignorant of this world and its ways. She was to know nothing, it seemed, of its cities or countries, its geography, its history, its politics, such things. Indeed, they had wanted one who had, as yet, it seems, never even been out of the pens.

I groped about in the cell and touched with my finger the rim of the shallow bowl of water. I did not know if, in this place, at this time, I was permitted to use my hands to feed myself or not. At times we had been permitted to do so in the pens, and, at other times, we had not been permitted to do so. I did not know what the case was here. It is well, of course, not to be too sanguine in assuming permissions which one might not have. Many were the times in which I, and my fellow trainees, had eaten and drunk on our bellies, or on all fours. Sometimes we must kneel, thrusting our faces into feeding troughs, our hands braceleted behind us. Sometimes, when we had been chained under the tables of feasting guards and food was thrown to us, we might use our hands and, at other times, we might not. Many times had I, whimpering, been hand fed, putting my face to a guard's knee. Many times had I picked up morsels thrown to the floor with my teeth. And I did not know what the case might be here. So I went to my belly and drank, lapping the water. Given what I was, that seemed safest to me. The water was stale, and cold. I did not know how long it had stood in the bowl. I fed, too, similarly, on the meal, and the crust. The slices of dried fruit I would save for later. It is not so much that I feared I might be being spied upon, or I feared that oils, or traces, of food, or such, might be found on my fingers. It was not even so much that I feared I might be challenged, later, on the matter, and my reactions, my expressions, my body, in their subtlest nuances and movements, read, to determine whether or not I was lying. It was

rather, more simply, because I did not know whether or not I had the permission.
 Let those who are such as I understand this. Let others not.
 Too, let those who have been under discipline understand this. Let others not.
 Then, from my belly, I had drunk and fed. The pieces of dried fruit I would save for later.
 I wrapped myself, kneeling, in the blanket.
 It was quite cold in the cell now.
 I was very grateful for the blanket.
 I realized it could be taken away from me. I hoped it would not be. I did not want to lie on that stone floor, in the cold, my knees drawn up, my arms about myself, shivering, in only the tunic. Indeed, the tunic, too, I realized, could be taken from me.
 What lay in store for me?
 What did they want of me?
 What was I supposed to do?
 I did not know.
 I had thought there was nothing to fear.
 I had been mistaken.
 I put my hand out, in the darkness, and felt the rough, granular texture of the enclosing wall, of rock.
 In the cell were three vessels, one for food, one for water, and, a larger one, to my left, as I knelt within the blanket facing the bars, for wastes. The smaller vessels may have been discards from some kitchen. Both were chipped at the edges. The food bowl was cracked. The larger bowl, for wastes, was of some porcelaintype substance. None of these vessels was made of metal. There was no metal within the cell, you see, which might be used as a tool for, say, excavation. I had not even been given a spoon, not that such might have been availing. What could it have done other than scratch futilely at the enclosing stone?
 I knelt there in the darkness, the blanket clutched about me.
 I did not know where I was, or what was expected of me.
 I was helpless in the cell. I was well kept here. I was totally in the power of others.
 It was dark, and cold.
 What was wanted of me?

I suddenly became very afraid.

I felt then within me a sudden body's urgency and cast aside the blanket and groped awkwardly toward the larger of the three vessels.

In a few moments I had returned to my place.

I had reached the vessel in time. That is important. One does not wish to be punished.

I had learned to use such things, and drains, in the pens. If nothing like that is provided one waits, or, if permitted, uses the back right-hand corner of the enclosure, as one faces the rear of the enclosure.

One of the early lessons one learns in the pens is that one is not permitted dignity or privacy. I recalled the guard from the pen who had been, for some reason, unlike the others, so cruel to me, he whose whip I had first kissed. Several times it had been he who, it seemed in anger, had elected to "walk me." Several times I must squat at the drains and relieve myself before him.

Though I was a slave I found this shameful, and embarrassing. Not before him, of all, he who was so precious and special to me, he who figured in my most helplessly lascivious and submissive dreams, he whose whip I had first kissed on this rude, beautiful world! Why did he hate me so? Why did he make me do this? Why did he wish to so grievously shame and humiliate me? Is this how he wanted to think of me, or remember me, as a foul, pathetic, meaningless little animal relieving herself upon command before him?

One cleans oneself, if permitted to do so, and this permission, because of hygienic considerations is seldom, if ever, denied, with what might be available. In this cell, as was presumably intended, I had done it with straw and water. That is not that uncommon. The straw is left in the vessel. We are trained to clean ourselves well, incidentally. If we do not, we are whipped.

The slave is not a free woman; she must keep herself, as best she can, fresh, rested, clean, and attractive.

I now sat back in the cell, my back against the wall, wrapped in the blanket.

The blanket was warm, but, within it, I felt very bare, in the skimpy tunic.

Within the blanket, with the finger tips of my left hand, I felt under the skirt of the tunic. The tiny mark was there, my brand. Within the blanket I felt very soft, and vulnerable. Within the blanket I touched my throat. No collar was there.

I suddenly pressed back against the wall.

For the moment I dared not breathe.

The shape which had so terrified me but a bit ago was again at the bars. It was like a darkness among darknesses. It was standing there. I smelled it, too, now, a heavy beast smell. I heard its breathing. It thrust its snout against the bars. I heard a low, rumbling, warning growl. I pressed back even further. Then it was gone, padded away.

I gasped, shaken.

When I was sure it was gone I went again to my belly, and to the food bowl. I put my head down and, delicately, bit off part of one of the pieces of dried fruit. I then ate it, treasuring it, even that small part, bit by bit, little by little, particle by particle. Then for a long time I fed there, bit by bit finishing the first of the three pieces, and then the second, similarly, and then the third. Such things, the slices of fruit, are very precious. I had saved them for last. When I was finished, I rose, to all fours.

I had relished the fruit, dry as it was.

I was grateful that it had been given to me.

I then turned about and, for a time, on all fours, the blanket about me, faced the bars.

I heard a howling, far off. I did not know if it were the wind, or some beast.

I was suddenly frightened, and lonely.

I hoped the men would be kind here. I would do my best not to displease them.

Surely they would be kind! They must be kind! Had I not been fed, had I not been given a blanket? Surely that was a kindness. My scent could always be taken otherwise. Had there not been three slices of dried fruit in the bowl?

But I had seen the great bird, I had seen the prowling beast, that fearsome guardian of narrow ledges.

I feared that men here might be strict with such as I, with their slaves.

Afterwards I lay down and slept.

Nine

I lay on my stomach on the floor of the mountain cell, my head toward the back of the cell, my legs widely spread, my arms extended outward and upward. It is difficult to rise quickly from such a position. I was counting slowly, aloud, to one thousand. One begins to count when one hears the gate lower and lock. One does not know if, or how long, someone might watch, and listen, to see if the directive is honored. So one counts aloud, and slowly. When one reaches one thousand one may rise, and fetch the food and water bowls, and the clean wastes vessel, from just within the bars, where they have been left. One knows when to place them before the bars because there is a signal, the ringing of a suspended bar, from somewhere outside. At the signal one puts the empty bowls and the wastes vessel near the bars, and then assumes the indicated position, one of prone helplessness, facing the back of the cell. I had received these directives on the morning after my first night in the cell. They were issued to me in a female voice, belonging to a person I did not see, from somewhere outside the cell. I had, accordingly, as yet, seen nothing of my jailers. I did not know if the voice I had heard was that of one who was free, or one who was bond, as I did not doubt but what I was, in spite of the bareness of my throat. It seemed to me most likely that she would have been bond, as it did not seem likely that free females, in a world such as this, would be involved in tasks so lowly as the care of prisoners. From what I had seen of free females in the pens, to be sure, only two of them, in its more respectable areas, and from what I had gathered from remarks of guards, rough jokes, and such, they were a haughty, exquisite, frustrated, pampered, imperious lot. I had also been warned by more than one guard that I should watch my step with particular care among such creatures, as they enjoyed being incredibly cruel, petty and vindictive towards those such as I, who, doubtless for reasons of their own, they regarded with utter contempt and hatred. "How different they are from us!" I had once breathed in the pens. "Not so different," said one of the guards. "Naked, on their knees, in a collar," said another, "they are not other than you."

I was pleased that he had said this for I myself, earlier, had boldly speculated much to the same point, but I did not, of course, explicitly profess this concurrence of our views. It is one thing for a man to say such a thing; it would be quite another for a slave. I did not think he would beat me, but I did not know. So I remained silent. I was pleased, of course. He grinned at me, so I suppose I did not conceal that as well as I might have. In any event he did not beat me.

But how contemptuous, and how regal, they had appeared, and so beautifully robed and veiled! Many I was told, wore platforms of a sort on their feet, perhaps as much as eight to ten inches high, which would increase their apparent height, and, of course protect their slippers from being soiled, for example, in muddy streets, or, certainly, in the damp pens. The two I had seen, however, had been in "street slippers." Such, I suspect might provide better footing in the pens, for in places the stones are damp, even wet. One is very much aware of that when one is barefoot. How serene and beautiful they seemed, in their veils and robes!

I had briefly, once, inadvertently, met the eyes of one.

It had happened in the pens when I had looked after the free women, as they had passed me. One, the first, had turned, and caught me with my head lifted. In that instant I saw her body stiffen with rage, and, over the colors of her veils, I saw her eyes were cold, and filled with hatred. I returned instantly to my belly, fully, arms down and back, the backs of my hands on the stone, my forehead against the stone. I trembled, and tried not to move. I was terrified. She came back and stood before me. I lay before her, prone and helpless, as what I was, a prostrated slave. I was nothing. She was mightiness, and beauty. I lay before her, miserably, trembling, helpless, hoping that she would not have me beaten. She remained standing before me, for some time. I dared not move. I scarcely dared to breathe. One of the guards attempted to distract her, calling her attention to a new model of a pleasure rack. But still she remained standing before me, looking down at me, I suppose. Then he said, "She is only an ignorant Earth slut." "But she is learning," said another. I was grateful to the guards. Had I not been so popular I wondered if they would have been as generous. I saw that they were trying to protect me. But I was frightened, too, that they might deem such protection necessary. What might she have done to me if she pleased?

"Kneel," she snapped.

I scrambled to my knees before her, less gracefully, I fear, than I might have, but I was frightened of her. I sensed in her great hatred, and contempt.

"Split your knees," she said, fiercely, "more widely!"

I complied, instantly.

Tears ran down my cheeks. It is one thing to kneel so before a man, and quite another before a woman.

"She is an Earth slut?" said the woman.

"Yes," she was told.

"I would have thought so," she said. "They are all worthless, and stupid," she said.

I dared not move.

"Yes, she is from Earth," she said, musingly, acidly. "One can tell, of course. See how plain, and ugly, she is. How lacking in grace and poise! Just to look at her, you would know she is from Earth. Yes! It is easy to tell! The women of Earth are such inferior goods! What true man could possibly be interested in them? In the markets it is no wonder they are jokes. How lacking they are! Earth is such a thin, unlikely, impoverished soil for slaves. I shall never understand why they bother noosing these sluts. One can harvest nothing there of interest, only pathetic mediocrities, at best, with good fortune, perhaps a girl of merely average attractiveness. Earth women are shabby stock, third-rate merchandise, inferior goods. At best such things could be only pot-and-kettle girls, low slaves, cleaning slaves, laundresses, and such. I do not see what men see in them. They cannot begin to compare to a Gorean woman. See, for example, this ignorant, presumptuous little slut, this meaningless little piece of slave suet trembling in her collar! I think she might well profit from a bout with the tongs and hot irons!"

"We have some new male slaves in Pen 2 of the Ba-Ta Section," said another to her, he whose whip I had first kissed.

The woman turned, to see who had addressed her, and suddenly, for a moment, she seemed taken aback. I think she had not seen him well before. He whose whip I had first kissed was, in his unassuming way, a powerful, handsome Gorean male. I thought him the most handsome of all the guards. He was the most attractive man I had ever seen. I was weak when near him. It was his whip which I had first kissed on this world. It was from such a man that a woman might beg the collar! Why was he so cruel to me? I wanted only to please him, and as the slave I was. Her attitude immediately changed.

"Oh?" she said, archly.

"I do not know if you would be interested," he said. "They are male silk slaves, pleasantly featured, symmetrically proportioned, charming fellows, gentle, sensitive, unthreatening. They are well trained to be a woman's slave."

"Ah!" she said, as though interested.

I did not move a muscle. I knelt almost rigidly, my knees spread. I had not dared to meet her eyes. It can be deemed presumptuous for a slave to directly meet the eyes of a free person, unless the permission is clear.

Suddenly she had forgotten about me!

"They are the sort," he said, "with whom a lady might chat of her day, her doings and thoughts, with whom she might exchange gossip, and gratefully share delicate confidences. They are well trained to be a woman's slave. They would look well in their silk at your slave ring. You could be proud of them as they hurry about your errands, keep your quarters and serve your friends."

"They are not masculine, are they?" she inquired. "I find masculinity so offensive and vulgar," she said.

The liar, the liar, I thought. Even within her garments I sensed her naked body palpitating in his presence!

What possible interest could she be to such a man, other than perhaps to be seized, stripped and caged, for an eventual sale?

"You need have no fear," he said. "They have been selected for their nature, which is that to be a woman's slave."

I sensed that she, as any hormonally normal woman, would despise such creatures.

"By all means," she said, "let us look at them."

"Follow me, if you would," said he.

The woman had then turned away. I was grateful that she had been distracted! I had been forgotten!

The guard, it seemed, was interested in displaying the goods of the house.

I turned my head a little and saw her following the guard, he whose whip I had first kissed, from the area. He did not even look back at her. Doubtless I should have rejoiced at this development, facilitating as it did my escape from what might have been a most unpleasant situation. How fortunate that he, in the line of his duty, he so impatient and efficient, had recalled to her the presumed itinerary of her schedule. I was pleased that this, doubtless by some fortuitous coincidence, had occurred to him. But I had felt, too, a sudden uncontrollable wave of hatred and jealousy for her, she being permitted to follow him as she did. She followed him quickly enough, and meekly enough, I thought. This might have been noted, too, by the guards.

The woman with her accompanied her.

Then they were gone.

"I wonder what she would look like on a block," said one of the guards. "Not bad, I would guess," said another. "Do you think she could dance?" asked another. "Yes," said another. "It is instinctive in a woman," said another. "Certainly she could be taught," said another. "She needs a collar, and a taste of the whip," said another. "That is what they all need," said another, "a collar, and a taste of the whip."

Then the guards looked at me.

I knelt before them as well as I could.

"Do not mind what she said," said one of the guards.

"No," said another.

"You are beautiful," said another.

"We will decide who is beautiful and who is not," said another.

"And you are beautiful, very beautiful," said another.

"Yes," said another.

"May I speak?" I asked.

"No," I was told.

"We know her," said one of the guards.

"She was abandoned by her intended companion, who had become enamored with a lovely Earth-girl slave," said another.

Perhaps I should not have been, but I was pleased to hear this. Her projected companion had preferred one such as I, an Earth-girl slave, to one such as she! Inferior goods, indeed!

I wondered if the slave had simply been taken, or purchased, by the fellow, whether she wished it or not, or if she had smiled, and posed, and, finding him of great interest, had proffered herself as a slave, promising him delights beyond the interests, or ken, of a free woman.

We can do such things, you know.

In any event, good for her!

"If the women of Earth were not hot, desirable and beautiful, if they were not superb slave goods, truly superb slave goods, they would not be brought to Gor," said another.

"True," said another.

I wanted to express my gratitude, my elation, at their words. I wanted to ask them a thousand questions!

"May I speak, may I speak?" I begged.

"No," I was told.

So I was silent.

A bar then rang out, which summoned us again to our training.

I was jealous that the free woman was alone with the guard, but I had no fear that he would bother her. It was not as though she were a slave, alone with him, naked, in her collar, who might be simply thrown back against the bars, and lifted up, and then, her feet off the ground, her back against the bars, made use of, for her major purpose, the pleasuring of a master.

We were then marched to the training room, our hands clasped behind the back of our necks. This lifts the breasts and allows us to feel the collar.

I had had my first experience of the warfare between the free woman and the slave girl.

I would not forget it.

* * * *

As I had reached the count of one thousand I rose and went to the bars, and looked out. I could see nothing much different from before, the mountains, the ledge, the clouds.

I picked up the food and water bowls, each replenished, the one, to my pleasure, even to three tiny pieces of dried fruit, called a larma, and put them in their place, to the left, at the back of the cell. I then, too, took the wastes vessel, now cleaned, and put it back, and to the right. I had speculated, by the sounds I had heard, that there had been two carts outside the bars, one of which followed the other, the wastes cart coming first, the food-and-water cart second. I supposed, but I did not know, that there were two women involved with the carts, one for each. I had heard, of course, only one woman, and, for most practical purposes, had only heard her once, when, unseen, she had issued my directives. To be sure, she did speak, in response to a pleading question from me on the day following her issuance of my directives, as I lay in the position indicated, facing the back of the cell, one additional word, "No." I did not know whether or not there was a man in the vicinity. I supposed that there might be, as the bars had been lifted easily. I had tried the bars some days ago, to lift them even an inch or so, before they would strike the bolt, or locking device, but had been unable to do so. The beast, that with six legs, had lifted them with its snout some three or four inches before they had struck the bolt or locking device. The strength of two women, combined, did not seem to me likely to be able to accomplish the task, or, at any rate, as smoothly as it had been done. To be sure, there might be a lever or some such device outside which was unknown to me which would have put the task within even my strength, unaided. Perhaps, too, there was some way in which weights could be engaged from the outside, by means of which the task could be easily accomplished. One would not then need the strength of a man, or of the titanic beast I had seen. But I had not heard the use of such a lever, or the specific engagement of such weights. Another reason I thought there might be a man about is that the authority accorded to women usually derives from men and, in the final analysis, is backed by men. Too, might not two women such as I, performing their lowly labors, be being supervised by a man? Perhaps they were even chained to their carts. I might thrust aside a woman or women, but it was unlikely I could accomplish this with a man, nor was it likely I could elude a man, as my body, for whatever reason, had not been designed by nature to permit this, nor was it likely that I could hope to escape his grip once it had closed on me. To be sure, on the ledge, in the vicinity of the cells, perhaps there was no need of the actual presence of men. Where would one go? And there was the beast. And men would be somewhere.

I went back to the bars, to look out.

I still did not know if I might use my hands to feed myself. That information had not been included in what might count as my "orientation," that issued to me on the morning after my first night in the cell. Indeed, my "orientation" had consisted only in directives, and a spelling out, so to speak, of the rules of my incarceration. On the second day, lying prone on the floor, arms and legs spread, facing the back, I had begged permission to speak. There were so many things I wanted to know, where I was, and such, not just such small things as whether or not I might use my hands to feed myself. "May I speak?" I had begged. "No," I had been told. So then I must be silent. I had been told "No," in no uncertain terms. She who had spoken then, I had gathered, did have severe authority over me. I must obey her, as though she might be a man. Behind her, you see, would be the power of such, the power of men.

I stood behind the bars.

As you have doubtless gathered by now, one such as I is usually expected to request permission to speak, before being allowed to speak, and, as you may also have gathered, this permission is not always forthcoming.

In such a case, of course, one must remain silent.

This homely device is, of course, a great convenience to the master, and, too, of course, there are very few things which so clearly help us to keep in mind our condition.

This was now my fifth day in the cell.

At various times in the past days I had seen one or more of the gigantic birds, coming or going, aflight over the valley between my location and the mountains in the distance. Sometimes there seemed great speed in the flights, moving to the left, at other times the birds smote the air with leisurely precision. Sometimes formations left the area. Twice I had heard drums and rushed to the bars to see perhaps twenty such winged monsters aflight, the second stroke of the wings keeping the cadence of the drums. Once, a large formation, consisting of perhaps two hundred such creatures, wheeled about in diverse aerial maneuvers, sometimes in abrupt, breath-taking turns, and ascents and descents, sometimes breaking into smaller groups and then reuniting, as though converging on aerial prey, to piercing whistles, and sometimes in more sedate, stately evolutions, responsive to an almost ceremonial skirl of shrill pipes. It was then as though there were a parade ground in the sky itself. Sometimes I would see birds leaving or returning to whose harness were slung baskets, sometimes open, sometimes closed. I did not doubt but what I had been brought here in such a conveyance. Too, of course, I could not but wonder if others such as I, coming and going, might be cargo in such containers. Once I saw some ten birds returning in straggling formation, some struggling to remain aflight. Some riders drooped in the saddles. Others, bandaged, seemed clearly wounded. Some were tied upright in the saddle, proudly unwilling, perhaps, to bow to exhaustion or wounds. On some birds there were two riders. Some of these men lacked weapons, helmets and shields. I could see the long hair of some of them, flying in the wind.

What manner of place could this be, I wondered. Perhaps there was agriculture in the valley below, which I could not see. Perhaps there was grazing there, and herding. Perhaps animals could be kept there, down in the valley, or even back among the mountains, in lofty, remote meadows, in which summer pasturage might be found. But what I could see from the cell suggested to me that the economy of this place exceeded what might be attributed to the pastoral simplicities of the herdsman and the bucolic labors of the tiller of the soil. More than once, sometimes in twos and threes, sometimes in tens and twenties, I had seen riders returning with bulging saddle bags, and sacks tied behind the saddle, and about the pommels, and with golden vessels, and candelabra, flashing in the light, slung from the saddles on cords. Sometimes, too, they returned with items of a different sort, living, luscious, excellently curved, stripped items, tied at the sides of the saddles, fastened there hand and foot to rings, or, literally, thrown over the saddle itself, belly up, their hands fastened back over their heads and down to a ring on the left side of the saddle, their feet fastened to a ring on the right side of the saddle. I was exceedingly excited by the sight of these captures. I wondered how many would be kept, and how many would be disposed of, doubtless like the gold and silver, in various markets. I wondered how many were women such as I and how many might, perhaps only days ago, have worn the heavy, complex, gorgeous, ornate robes and veils of the free women of this world. In a tunic such as mine, and branded, and subject to the whip, I did not doubt but what the latter would find that a considerable change had occurred in their life. Stripped as they were, the lot of them, the men would have little difficulty in assessing their quality. I wondered how the former free women might feel, for I assumed there must be some such among them. Some perhaps might be humiliated to learn that their objective value was now less than that of some of the women whom they had previously despised, of which sort they were now only another specimen. And some, perhaps, might be disconcerted to find that they now actually possessed an objective value, and one exceeding, on the same terms, and in the same dimension, at least some of those whom they had formerly regarded with such contempt. But I did not think that they would object to learning that they might have value. They were, after all, women. I bit my lip, wondering how I might compare with them. We might all, you see, be stood by a wall, and assessed. On my old world, you see, I had been priceless, so to speak, and thus worth nothing. On this world, on the other hand, I knew that I had a value, a particular, practical value, based on what men would pay for me. This value, of course, as I recognized, would be likely to fluctuate with various market conditions.

No, this place was not some typical primitive community, sustained by some herds, by some gardens, by some fields, and such. Rather I thought that it was in its way more than that. It was, in its way, a lair of eagles.

I considered myself.

How clever, and marvelous and special, I had regarded myself on my old world. Then I had been removed from it, and brought here. Here I had found myself put in my place, not my political place, but my true place.

Truly my life had changed.

I had had little doubt, from shortly after my arrival on this world, what, in one sense, I was doing here. That had been made clear to me in the pens. I had learned to cook and clean, to sew and launder, and to perform numerous domestic tasks. Too, of course, for such domestic tasks are well within the scope of any woman, I had learned to please and serve, and, I think, with great skill, given my brief time on this world, in more significant modalities, innumerable modalities, sensuous and intimate. I had learned to move, and stand, and kneel. I had learned to apply the perfumes and cosmetics of this world. I had learned to wear silk and iron. And I had learned to please men, *truly please them*. How different this was from my old world!

And so my life had changed.

I had been brought here, and had found myself put in my place. Here I found myself an animal, a property, subject in all things to the will of others.

But what was I doing in this particular place, here in the mountains?

I had been brought here secretly.

I had not been brought here as these others I had seen, tied at the side of a saddle, balancing another tied at the other side, or thrown over a saddle, bound there on my back, helplessly, in effect, displayed, as other booty, wrists and ankles fastened to rings.

I was not even *of* this world.

I was not a peasant lass, surprised in a field, nor a rich woman, one indigenous to this world, stolen from her boudoir. Surely I was not booty in the sense of these. I had been paid for.

What was I doing here?

Surely I had been brought here at least in part for the typical purposes of one such as I. That, at least, had seemed clear from the attitudes and interests of those to whose scrutiny I had been subjected, the strangers, my apparent purchasers, those who had assessed me in the pens, I performing before them, nude, clad only in my collar.

But I did not think I had been brought here merely for the typical purposes of one such as I.

Surely there was more to it than that.

I thought of these things, standing by the bars.

I was a woman from faraway, from a quite different world, a world of banality, glitter and hypocrisy, a world fearful of authenticity and truth, one afraid to understand and feel.

How special and wonderful, and clever, I had thought myself, on my old world. Then one, or more, it seems, on that very world, my old world, had seen me, and had made a decision. I had been brought here. No more was I now than an animal, and a property. Had I done anything, I wondered, to occasion that decision. Perhaps I had brushed against someone, the wrong person, and had permitted a tiny sound of irritation to escape me. Perhaps a mere expression of transitory annoyance had crossed my features. Perhaps something in my demeanor had hinted at an attitude of too much self-satisfaction or complacency, or had suggested some pretense to a fraudulent superiority or had tended to convey some subtle contempt. Perhaps the decision had then been made, and I had been brought here, perhaps to the amusement of one or more, to be what I now was, nothing, and at the mercy of the rights holders. But perhaps, too, all I had had to do with my presence here was to have been what I was, a female of interest to one or more appraisers, one fulfilling, perhaps excellently, certain criteria. I had perhaps been discovered, noted, followed, and reviewed, attention being paid not so much to what I was then, as to what I might, with suitable training, become. How, I wondered, did those who concerned themselves with such things, to whom they were doubtless a matter of business, assess such potentialities? Did they imagine me naked, or how I might look in silk, moving sensuously, or kneeling, in chains, such things? And how did they know about my secret heats, and the frustrations, I had attempted to conceal so zealously from the world? Were such things betrayed, without my knowledge, to those who could see them, in certain tiny movements, in subtle expressions? How had they seen me—as an appealing property, one as yet unowned, as an animal, isolated and meaningless, one, as yet, lacking its master?

How bored I had been on my old world!

How little things had meant!

How dissatisfied and frustrated I had been!

I had been a tiny fragment, adrift, purposeless, moved with the waves and wind.

Then the decision had been made.

I had been brought here. I had now learned to wear silk and iron.

I was terrified, in a way, to be here.

But now I was no longer adrift, no more than the bars of the cell. No longer was I detached from the truths and ways of nature. Here I would be, whether I wished it or not, what I ultimately and most profoundly was, a female, in the fullest sense of the word.

And I was not discontent.

Suddenly another great bird smote its way over the valley, this time moving to the right, returning apparently to its source of origin.

This one did not bear apparent booty, but bore, rather, it seemed, on long straps, dispatch cases. The rider was not armored. The bird was smaller than many, and with shorter wings. Such are most adept, I would learn, in evasive maneuvers.

What manner of men were here, I wondered. What manner of men here would own properties such as I? To whom would I, personally, belong? I wanted to belong to one man, to serve him perfectly and wholeheartedly in all ways, and, hopefully, to be his only property of my sort. But men such as these, I feared, might have several such as I. Could such a man be content with but one of us? What if his whim, or mood, should change? I would try to be such, of course, that my rights holder would feel no need for another, indeed, I would try to be such that he would not even think of another. And are we not expensive? Would this not be an argument for a rights holder not keeping more than one of us, at least at a time? But men here, it seemed, from what I had seen from the cell, might not pay for their women, or, at least, all of them. Apparently they took them rather as it pleased them.

I shuddered.

I recalled the booty I had seen, booty other than I, and booty such as I.

How terrified I was of the men I had seen, masters of such monsters as the mighty birds I had seen!

I was pleased that I had learned how to wear silk and iron.

This place, I feared, was a lair of eagles.

Ten

I screamed suddenly, startled, at the pounding of the pipe between the bars, and at the snarling at the beast. I had not been looking. I had been taken totally unawares. I had not expected either sound. I scrambled to the back of the cell and pressed myself, my body and the palms of my hands, against the stone there. It was as though I would try to press through the rock itself. I looked back over my shoulder, wildly. I saw shadows there. "Please, no!" I cried in my native language. Then I realized in misery that such a lapse might earn me a beating. I saw the beast there, the low, large, long, heavy beast, the six-legged monster, with the triangular viperlike head. It was just outside the bars. At its side stood a corpulent, massive male, in a half tunic, with a heavy leather belt, and leather wristlets. In his left hand he held the beast, on a short leash. The metal pipe with which he had struck the bars he threw behind him, on a shoulder strap. It was the sort of thing with which he might have subdued even a man. From his belt there hung a ring of keys and a whip. I heard the beast snuffling and growling. I heard the ring of keys, jangling, removed from the belt. He went to the side, as I could see, turning half about, past the right side of the door, as one faces outward. I heard him then, out of sight, to the right of the door. He opened, it seemed, a panel of some sort. I heard a key thrust in a lock, and turned. The locking mechanism, you see, is not visible from the cell. It is somewhere outside, and, I conjectured, protected in a paneled niche. I was to some extent familiar with these things from the cell's having been opened several times before, in the morning. To be sure, I had then, warned by the signal bar, been prone at the back of the cell, helplessly spread-eagled. He had, however, as yet, not demanded any such accommodation. I crouched now at the back of the cell, turned about, looking. I saw him re-emerge into view, the keys back on his belt. He looked through the bars and, for an instant, our eyes met, and then I looked away, unable to meet his eyes. I saw him transfer the leash to his right hand and reach down and, with his left hand, in one motion, with a sound of sliding metal, lift the gate. I gasped. This had apparently required considerable force, but it had been done easily. I suspected then that he, or another such as he, might have been with the woman, or women, earlier. The beast put its head down and moved forward, a quick, stealthy step, little more than the movement of one paw. I groaned. I trusted it was under effective discipline. I hoped the man could hold it, if it were not. But I had no assurance of that. It was larger and heavier than he, by far, and had the leverage of six clawed legs. I hoped the leash would not break. I heard the growling of the animal. I flung a pleading, helpless glance at its keeper, and perhaps mine. I did not dare meet the eyes of the animal, for fear I might trigger some attack response. It could have torn me in pieces. It could have bitten me in two. Briefly again, fleetingly, in terror, begging him to control the animal, my eyes met those of the massive male, and then, again, I looked down. He was a man not untypical of this world, in his size and strength. But, too, even more typical of this world, one could read in his eyes the absence of vacillation and confusion, the undivided nature of his character, the firmness, simplicity and unilaterality of his will. He did not belong to a world in which men, through deceit and trickery, and lies, and insidious, hypocritical conditioning programs, had been bled and weakened. On this world, at least where women such as I were concerned, men had kept their power. They had not surrendered their manhood, their natural dominance. In his eyes, you see, I saw the firmness of his character, the strength of his will, which was as iron. In his eyes, in a sense, you see, I saw, unpretentious and untroubled, the severity, the simplicity, the strictness, the rigor, the uncompromising relentlessness of nature.

I knelt before him then, with my back straight, but my head down. I spread my knees very widely.

I wanted to beg him for permission to speak, but I was afraid to do so. I wanted to beg his forgiveness for having cried out in my native language. After all, it would not be his language, and his language must now be my language. Our language must become that of the rights holders.

I heard the animal growl, a low, rumbling noise, and sensed it move forward another step.

I looked up, again, and then, frightened, knelt forward, putting my head to the stone flooring, my palms, too, down on the stone, in a common attitude of obeisance.

I trembled.

"Look up," said he, in his language.

I looked up, frightened, crouching before him then on all fours. I did this immediately. He was the sort of man, like so many on this world, whom a woman obeys instantly.

Two gestures then did he make, in quick succession, the first indicating the left shoulder where, had I been tunicked in that fashion, there would have been a disrobing loop, and the second indicating, fingers spread, palm down, the floor. Instantly I drew the tunic over my head, stripping myself before him, and turned about, and put myself to my belly, legs and arms spread widely, spread-eagled.

I lay there thusly for some moments, regarded.

Then I sobbed as I felt the snout of the beast, prodding, rude, inquisitive, cold, pushing about my body.

"Do not move," he said.

As if I could have moved!

"May I speak? May I speak!" I begged.

"No," he said.

I sobbed, silenced.

"He is not really taking your scent," he said. "He is only curious about you."

I trembled, under the investigation of the beast. I smelled its fetid breath.

"Later," he said, "once you have been named, you will be introduced to our pets in the sleen pens."

I did not understand this at the time, but it would later become all too clear. The name is, of course, important, as it serves, in conjunction with other signals, to direct and target a hunt.

I did understand, of course, that I did not have, as of now, a name. I might as well have been then, I realized, in a collar. Any possible

doubts as to my status had been dissipated. My brand was as meaningful as ever. It remained in full effect.
I felt his hand on my body.
I lifted it a little, to him, placatingly.
"Kajira," he chuckled.
That is one of the words in the language of the rights holders for women such as I. Indeed, as I have suggested, it is by far the most common word in their language for women such as I. The first words I had been taught on this world were "La kajira." —"I am a kajira." —"I am a slave girl."
He took the tunic I had discarded and folded it in small squares.
I had not been given permission to speak, and had thus not been permitted to beg forgiveness for having cried out in my native tongue. On the other hand, it seemed he had chosen to overlook my outburst.
I had, at any rate, not been kicked or cuffed.
I assumed he would have known, even before coming to the cell, that I was not from this world. And my outburst, under the circumstances, his sudden appearance, the noise, the beast, and such, certainly would have been an innocent enough one, a natural enough one.
To be sure, eventually, even such outbursts, I had little doubt, would be uttered in the language of the rights holders, that language, too, later, having become mine.
The men of this world are terribly strict with us, but few of them are cruel. Their pleasure is found in the manifold perfections of our service, intimate and otherwise, and in our devotion and love, not in our distress or pain. These men keep their animals under perfect discipline, as is their way, but they also, on the whole, treat them well.
I felt his eyes upon me.
"Kneel, and face me," he said.
Swiftly I complied.
He placed the folded tunic in my mouth, deeply back, between my teeth, crosswise, and I, as I knew was expected, closed my teeth upon it.
He then stood up, and I, kneeling before him, looked up at him.
"You are a pretty one," he said.
I looked at him, gratefully. Had I not been pretty, I supposed, I would not have been brought here. I gathered they tended to select

"pretty ones." They liked that sort. Interestingly, on my own world, as I have indicated, I had never really thought of myself as being particularly attractive, at least generally, particularly as I had regarded my body as erring, so to speak, in approximating closely the statistical norms for a human female. Here, however, it seemed that the normal woman, well curved and luscious, was, for whatever reason, esteemed more highly than her more boyish, sticklike sisters. I did not mind this, of course. It pleased my vanity. On the other hand, my desirability, such as it was, I recognized, might place me in danger. "I would like to have you in my shackles," a guard had once told me. "I, too," had said another. "And I," had laughed another. I had been frightened. Many men, it seemed, and men such as these, such fierce, strong men, men like predators, like carnivores, might want me in their shackles!

"You are from the slave world?" he asked. I looked at him, puzzled.

"From the place called "Earth"?" he said. I nodded.

"Are there others like you there?" he asked. Tears brimmed in my eyes. I nodded.

He laughed. He then snapped his fingers and indicated that I should rise and leave the cell, going to the right, as one faced outwards.

I leaped to my feet and, going far to the right, stopped only by the stone, put as much distance between me and the six-legged beast as possible.

Then I was outside the cell!

It was breathtakingly beautiful. The air was bracing. I bit down on the folded tunic between my teeth. The wind blew through my hair.

I looked down to the left, and groaned, for there was a precipitate drop there, some forty or fifty feet to another trail below, and below that another such drop to another trail, and thence to another. Similarly, above me, I could see what seemed to be similar ledges, three or four of them, receding. There must have been more than a dozen such trails and ledges, several below, some above. Too, I could see several openings in the mountain, most of them barred. This was, in effect, I gathered, a place of imprisonment. I stepped back, dizzy for a moment, from the edge of the trail, and touched the rock to my right. I gasped; hundreds of yards ahead of me, where the trail led, past several barred cells, and approached by a narrow, ascending trail, there was a startling, lofty, sheer edifice that seemed to rear up from the mountains itself, its towers lost among clouds. It was walled. It was some sort of fortress or citadel. I looked again to the left. I could see the valley below now, or part of it. It was, I was sure, cultivated. Then I looked back, and trembled. The jailer was there, and the fearsome beast, held on its leash. Behind the jailer and the beast I could see the ledge trail going back around the mountain. To my right I saw the panel box, locked now, within which must lie the locking mechanism to the cell. The panel box itself, not to mention the mechanism within, could not be reached from within the cell. Other than this there was only the steepness, the side of the mountain, there on the right, rising up, and, on the left, below the ledge, the drop, forty or fifty feet, to the ledge and trail below. The rock ledge felt very hard, and granular, beneath my bare feet. It was chilly on the ledge. I looked back, again, at the jailer, and the beast.

Though I was out of the cell no leather or chain had been put on my neck.

The beast was leashed, but not I.

I had, incidentally, in the pens, been taught to walk gracefully, and to kneel, and pose, and such, in a leash. We are sometimes taken out in such fashions. There are also wrist leashes, usually worn on the right wrist of a right-handed girl, or on the left wrist of a left-handed girl, and ankle leashes, similarly oriented.

The point of the leash, of course, is seldom to hold or control a woman, for we are rational, and know we must obey, but rather to make it clear whose property she is, and to display her. Similarly, when a woman is leashed her status is made clear to her. Too, it might be mentioned that the leash has a profoundly erotic effect upon the female, as its meaning, and its symbolism of her domination, is profoundly arousing to her.

In this respect it is rather like the collar itself.

It does, of course, as a simple matter of undeniable fact, and this is something which should be openly acknowledged, have its custodial aspect. In it she is held. She is its prisoner. She is on her leash.

But I was not now leashed.

It was not necessary for one such as I, I thought then, to be leashed, perhaps for a free woman, or a new girl, or a naive girl, or an ignorant girl, but not for one such as I, who had some understanding of the world on which she found herself, and what she was upon it.

But I would soon learn how wrong I was!

I would soon learn how much that simple device, the leash, had to teach me!

He was looking at me.

I straightened my body. We are not free women; we may not be slovenly or slatternly. We must stand and walk with excellent posture. I lifted and smoothed my hair a little, and moved it back, about my head. We have our vanity. His grin showed me that he saw me as a slave. I saw that he would expect perfect obedience of me, and was well aware that he would receive it.

No, a leash would not be necessary.

I understood the world on which I found myself, and what I was upon it.

How naive I was! How much I had still to learn!

Ahead of me was the trail and the looming fortress or citadel in the distance. Wisps of cloud hung about the cold trail, and the turrets, or towers, of the structure in the distance.

He drew down the gate of the cell. It locked automatically. He then gestured ahead. As soon as he did this the beast uttered a menacing growl and tugged forward. I swiftly, stumbling, turned, and hurried along the narrow ledge in the direction indicated.

The tunic was clamped between my teeth.

I looked into the cells as we passed them. Most were empty. Some, however, were occupied. In some were sullen men, clad in the remnants of what might once have been uniforms. Their wrists and ankles were chained. In others there were unchained men, some men sitting cross-legged, playing some game with bits of cloth. Others stood near the bars, but kept their hands well within the bars.

"Hello, little tasta," called one of the men to me.

I hurried on.

A tasta is a kind of small, sweet candy, usually sold at fairs. It is commonly mounted on a stick. Some men use it as a slang expression for one such as I. Another such is 'vulo'. The vulo is a small, soft, usually white, pigeonlike bird. It is the most common form of domestic fowl kept on this world. It is prized for its meat and eggs. It is notoriously incapable of eluding hawks and other forms of predatory birds, by which it can easily be torn to pieces.

I passed another cell containing such men.

"Is she to be given to us?" one of them called out.

Again, frightened, I hurried on.

It occurred to me that I might, of course, being what I was, be thrown among them, for their gratification or amusement.

Not every cell which was occupied, however, contained men.

Some contained women such as I, who looked fearfully out, often from the back of the cell, through the bars. Their fear frightened me as I thought they might know more of this place than I. Some of these were clad in tunics such as I had been, invariably brief and revealing, the sort of garments in which men might choose to clothe women such as I. Others were clad in what appeared to be rags, some little more than castoffs, which might have been soiled even, from use in the kitchen, others in rags which, I think, were actually scandalous ta-teeras, artfully arranged rags, intended to well display the women placed in them. I was sure these women were such as I because their throats were encircled by collars, mostly of the common variety, those closely fitting, of narrow steel. But two, at least, wore the looser collars of rounded metal, the Turian collar. To be sure, it, too, cannot be slipped.

Some women in certain other cells, on the other hand, were not collared. They were, however, stripped. Too, they were in sirik, chained hand and foot, and neck.

The sirik is a common custodial device for a female, and is quite flexible in its possibilities. The common arrangement is a collar with dangling chain, to which are attached two smaller chains, the first with wrist rings, the second, at the termination of the dangling chain, with ankle rings. Women are very beautiful in it. I had learned to wear it attractively in the pens.

As the women were not collared I conjectured that they might be free.

"Do not look upon us, slut!" cried one. Quickly I looked away.

I wondered how she felt, locked in slave steel. Doubtless she was awaiting, or being held for, her processing. Such takes place, of course, at the convenience of the rights holders. Sometimes a captive is held in incarceration for days, being given time to reflect deeply and fully on what is to become of her. I did not think she would be as imperious should her thigh come to wear, as I suspected it might soon do, a mark like mine, identical in import if not in actual design.

In another cell I saw four women in rags of white silk. As they wore collars I gathered that they were women such as I. The combination of the collars and the white silk suggested that they might be virgin slaves. A "white-silk girl" is a virgin; one who is not a virgin is sometimes referred to as a "red-silk girl." This need not refer, literally, of course, to the color of their garmenture. White-silk slaves, as you might suppose, are very rare. There is apparently a market for such. The most expensive of such slaves, as I understand it, are those which have been raised from infancy in seclusion, kept literally in ignorance of the existence of men. Then, when they are of a suitable age, they are purchased, unbeknownst to themselves, by unseen buyers. Later they are drugged and removed from their familiar surroundings, to awaken in new surroundings, of the buyer's choosing.

It is in those surroundings, those of the buyer's choosing, that they will learn that they are women, and that there are men.

I felt the hot breath of the beast on the back of my calves, and sensed the hot mouth, the teeth, at my heels. I whimpered in dismay, and hurried on.

The trail became steeper and my breath became shorter. The pace I was keeping began to hurt my feet.

I heard a fellow laugh, from within one of the cells, as I hurried past. Momentarily I was angry. Surely there was little dignity in my progress!

I supposed, however, if I proved capable of sustaining a more rapid pace, that that would be expected of me. I cast a glance back over my shoulder at the jailer. He gestured ahead, and held the beast back, by the leash and collar.

Again I hurried forward.

The soles of my feet felt raw. My legs began to ache. I moaned. I tried to draw breath in, wildly, through my nostrils, even about the rag in my mouth. Tears formed in my eyes.

I did not see how I could, given this elevation, and the ascent, maintain this pace.

And one of the prisoners had laughed at me!

I would show them!

Imperceptibly then, so subtly they would not even notice, I determined to slow my pace, ever so subtly, so subtly that they would never notice!

I could thus, in my way, fool them. I could thus, in my way, dally.

I had not been punished for having inadvertently cried out in my native language. I had been given a tunic and blanket in the cell. There had been slices of fruit in the food bowl. There had been straw in the cell, for my comfort and cleanliness! Even a vessel for wastes had been provided! Could it be that these men were weak, or, if not weak, that they were tolerant, understanding, and kindly?

Then it would surely be easy to fool them.

I need be only a clever girl.

I heard the slightest sound behind me and turned about, moving, and looked over my shoulder. My heart almost stopped! He had removed the whip from his belt and shaken out its coils. I then, despite the difficulty and the pain, weeping, in terror, increased my pace even beyond what it had been before. I feared to feel the whip. I knew that a man such as he behind me, a man of this world, would not hesitate for an instant to use it on a woman such as I.

I wept, hurrying up the trail, the beast at my heels, the jailer at its side.

"Hurry, little kajira," I heard from one of the cells.

I sobbed!

There was laughter, that of more than one man, from the cell.

I hurried forward, pressed to even greater haste. I could feel the breath of the beast behind me, on my legs. I heard it strain forward, its claws scraping on the stone. It nipped at my heels.

I moaned. I wept.

How could I go more swiftly?

The whip suddenly, like a shot, cracked behind me.

I went more swiftly!

I heard laughter from a cell, from some men, crowded behind the bars. I caught only a glimpse of them. Were they so much more than I?

"Give her to us!" called a man.

Yes, they were far more than I.

I feared being thrown to them.

The whip cracked again.

I stumbled, frightened, I regained my balance, I hurried on again, crying. In my fear I had almost lost the tunic from my mouth. I thrust it firmly back in my mouth. I hoped it would not be disarranged.

I did not wish to be beaten.

Women such as I, on this world, are much at the mercy of men!

There was suddenly, to my left, out from the ledge, a piercing scream, a great smiting sound, and, on my right, on the cliff, as though flung there, twisting, a vast moving, wheeling shadow. A torrent of air threw me against the side of the cliff. I saw the fur on the beast blown as if by hurricanelike winds to its right, and the jailer, too, must brace himself not to be hurled to the side. I held the tunic in my mouth with both hands, crouching down. Then the gigantic bird had turned abruptly, wheeling about, and was making its way, it seemed, to the very heights, the very pinnacles, lofty and cloud-obscured, of the citadel itself. The rider, now in the distance, moving swiftly, looking back, lifted his arm to the jailer, and the jailer, grinning, raised his whip in salute. Such men, it seemed, must have their jokes.

The jailer looked at me, and I leaped up, and continued my journey up the trail.

The joke had had nothing to do with me. I had been incidental to the interests of such men.

It seemed that I was being permitted to go more slowly now. Perhaps the jailer was contemplating some revenge on the prankster. He chuckled, perhaps in his ruminations, I almost now forgotten, having come to some suitable resolution. I was grateful for this respite. Then he suddenly made a sound of annoyance, as though abruptly recalling to himself his business, which, I gathered, had to do with the delivery of a kajira. Again the whip cracked and I again addressed myself to my hasty ascent. The sound of the whip, too, seemed to stimulate the beast. It snapped at my heels. It seemed I must now try to attain even greater speeds! I wanted to cry out, to remonstrate with him, to beg him for a little indulgence, but I could not do so, for the gag.

Perhaps that was the point of the gag, I thought, a kindness in its way, that not being able to protest or plead I need not be lashed for having dared to do so.

What manner of men could these be, in this place?

What hope had I of mercy?

Could they be so much the masters?

One does not, of course, remove such an obstruction without permission. That would be a serious offense.

"Kajira!" called more than one man, in a given cell, as we passed them, seemingly to alert those in cells farther down the trail as to our passage. "Kajira!" I heard, behind me. Then the same cry I heard ahead, and it was then, from thence, relayed forward, again, and again. Men came to the bars, to watch. They pressed against the bars, but they did not put their hands through. Perhaps they did not wish them torn off by the beast! In the pens we kajirae, kneeling or crouching down, had sometimes put our hands through the bars of our kennels, trying to touch a guard, to call ourselves, whimperingly, to his attention, but this experience suggested, uneasily, a quite different sort of possibility, one in which such as I might have to tread a passage with care, lest we fall within the grasp of fearsome, dangerous inmates. Would we not be in our way rather like food, dangled almost within the reach of starving men?

"Give her to us!" called a man.

But the whip cracked again, and again I sped forward. Then we were past the cells!

I continued to climb upward. We were now on the trail leading up to the citadel.

The cliff rose sheer on my right, the drop, precipitous, was to my left. Behind me was the beast, so fearful, and the man, so powerful, with his whip in hand.

The whip cracked again.

I was being herded!

My feet were sore. I struggled to breathe. My body ached. Again I felt the teeth of the beast at my heels.

I was not even of this world! How dare they treat me in this fashion? How dare they do this to me!

I had been taken from my own world!

I had been brought here!

Then I recalled that I was now a kajira, and that anything might be done to me.

I fell and, frantically, struggled to regain my feet. "Hurry, kajira," said the man, sternly, restraining the snarling beast. I sped forward, again.

I wept.

There was no dignity here.

I was being herded! I was now being driven upward, like a pig, toward what I knew not!

Then, gasping, trying to hold the gag in my mouth, I sank to my knees before part of the stone mountain, a sheer wall of stone, at the end of the trail. There was the mountain there, rearing upward, and, high above, perhaps a hundred feet above, seeming to rise out of the rock itself, were the walls of the citadel. I could go no further. There was no place to go now, unless it were back. I looked back, frantically, at the beast and jailer. The beast viewed me balefully. Surely it must understand one could go no further! The jailer took from his wallet, slung at his belt, a whistle, on which he blew a succession of piercing notes. The notes, some simply, some in combinations, were linked, I would learn, with the alphabet of the language. The notes were spelling out, in the language, a phrase or password. These phrases change daily, and sometimes oftener. I heard a responding whistle from above, also with a succession of notes. The original signal and its response constituted the exchange of a sign and countersign. The beast, whose hearing was doubtless acute, seemed discomfited by these sounds. It twisted about, growling.

I heard a grinding sound from above and saw a wooden platform, in which there was a rectangular aperture, slide out from the wall.

Through this aperture there soon appeared a dangling rope, with one or more things attached to it, which, perhaps released from the cylinder of a windlass, began, swinging, to descend rapidly toward us. In a few moments the rope was within his reach. There was something on it like a stirrup, and, above that, something like a canvas bag. The jailer motioned that I should approach him. I did so, timidly. He opened the bag, the bottom portion of which was sacklike, but had two apertures in it. He indicated that I should step into the bag, putting my feet through the apertures, and I did so, one foot at a time. He then pulled the bag up, I standing, until it was snugly on me. Next he closed the bag about me, my hands and arms inside, and buckled it about me, tightly. Lastly he buckled it shut about my neck. I could now walk, my legs through the leg holes, but only to the extent permitted by the rope on the bag. Within the bag I was helpless. I looked at the jailer, frightened, and at the beast, and, upward, toward the platform so far above me. Clearly I wanted to speak. The jailer fixed the folded tunic in my mouth, more carefully. I was not to speak. I looked at him, pathetically, over this gag. But he paid me no attention. He stepped away from me, going to the beast. He freed it from the leash, putting the leash at his belt. He then returned to the rope and pulled on it, twice. I now saw the rope begin to move upward. I shook my head wildly, whimpering. I did not dare release the gag, of course. I had, for example, no way of retrieving it if it fell. Too, I did not know what would be done with me if I should even let it fall, let alone eject it. Too, it was my only clothing in this place, and that made it inordinately precious to me. Too, I did not want to be punished. Too, these were not men of Earth. If I lost my clothing, I did not know when, or if, it might be replaced. I suddenly felt my toes lift from the stone. I tried to reach down with my toes to touch the stone, but they could not do so. The rope now, with my weight on it, was taut. I felt myself ascending. I saw the jailer, below me, put his foot in the stirrup, his left foot, and at the same time grasp the rope with his left hand, above his head; and then the rope, too, bore his weight. The bag was attached to a ring on the rope by means of its own ring, a ring which could open and close. In this way, even if a girl, in her ascent, should squirm or struggle, the bag, ideally, remains affixed to the rope. I trusted, of course, that these rings would hold. Too, I hoped the rope would hold our weight. The beast, below, looked upward. Then I saw it prowl away, perhaps returning to its lair, or perhaps to its patrol of the ledges. The bag swung a little on the rope, but the weight of the jailer, below me, muchly steadied it, preventing what might otherwise have been a most frightening swaying of that stout strand. From the stirrup, incidentally, a sword may be used. The stirrup is commonly attached to the rope below the sack for two reasons, first, in order to facilitate its defense, and, secondly, to enable it to be steadied, or even held, or supported, if necessary. I kept my legs still, not wanting to put stress on the rings which held the sack in place. Foot by foot the rope moved upward. I was soon some yards above level of the trail. The rope swung a little, moving upward. I was absolutely helpless. I felt no tearing of canvas, no breaking, or pulling away, of stout threads, one by one, from straps. I looked up at the rope above me. I detected no unraveling of strands. It seemed the rings and the ropes might hold. I grew more confident. I had not been this high before, at least unhooded. I saw ranges beyond ranges of mountains, some snowcapped, extending into the distance. I put my arms about myself, inside the sack. I bit down on the tunic. The air was bracing.

The mountains were very beautiful. In a few moments I could hear the cranking of a windlass. I looked down as I could. The jailer, below me, his foot in the stirrup, his left hand on the rope, was seemingly contemplating the mountains. That seemed remarkable to me, for he was no more than a brute of a man. In a sense we both perhaps felt small before them, and both found them awesome and beautiful. I looked up. I could see the platform now, so close, a few feet above me, and the aperture through which I would be lifted. I could not see the windlass. The rope ascended through the aperture and went over a pulley, attached to what was apparently a tripodlike arrangement of beams. Above the platform the walls of the citadel reared up, toward the clouds. Perhaps we might feel small before the mountains, in their vast, mute grandeur, but men, here, had made themselves a part of this, making for themselves a lair, an aerie, in this very magnificence, like eagles.

I was drawn upward through the rectangular aperture and found myself suspended, a bit below the pulley, some ten feet above the platform. I dangled there. The jailer had stepped from the stirrup to the platform as the stirrup had cleared the aperture. Greetings were exchanged between the jailer and some men on the platform. These men were in scarlet tunics. Doubtless it was a livery, or uniforms, of some sort. They were, I gathered, guards, or soldiers, of some sort. I heard the windlass and felt myself being lowered. When I reached the vicinity of the aperture the jailer reached out and drew the sack, by the rope, back over the platform. With difficulty I got my feet under me. The rope descended another yard or so. He then, I standing, and the slackness of the rope facilitating it, opened the ring on the sack, and freed it of the rope ring. I was now free of the rope. I knelt, as was proper, for I was in the presence of men. I did edge back from the opening. From the platform I could see the mountains. The jailer looked at them, too, for a moment. Those on the platform, on the other hand, paid them little attention. To them they were doubtless quite familiar. I looked up at the jailer, and then looked down. He and I might both have noted the beauty of the mountains on the ascent, achieving in that moment a sort of brief parity, suspended as we were on the rope, between the land and the sky, between worlds, in a sort of aesthetic void, an artificial stasis, but we had now come to the platform, to its solid beams. He stood. I knelt. Once again worlds of difference loomed between us. I was a kajira. He was a free man.

"This is the one who was purchased?" asked one of the soldiers.

I gathered that these men seldom purchased their women.

"Yes," said the jailer.

"For what purpose?" asked a soldier.

I listened, eagerly.

"I do not know," said the jailer.

Could it be that he did not know?

Another of the soldiers crouched beside me, and took me by the hair, pulling my head back, sharply, that they might better observe my features. We may be handled in such a fashion, as, on my old world, might be, say, horses. Do not blame them for this. Do not think anything of it. On this world, as I have mentioned, we, women such as I, are animals.

"Not bad," said he who held my head back.

"No," said another.

"When you buy them," said another, "you can at least see what you are getting."

"Fully," agreed another.

Some of the men laughed.

This was, I suppose, a vulgar joke, but there were no free women present, who might be offended, or scandalized. My presence did not count. I was kajira.

Women, of course, are commonly examined nude before being purchased. Men like to see what they are getting, all of it. It is said that only a fool would buy a woman clothed. That is doubtless true.

I was no stranger to this sort of thing.

Before I had been sold I had been so examined in great detail, even to the extent of performing what was almost a choreography before my prospective buyers, that my features, expressions, attitudes, movements, charms, if any, and such, might be the better assessed.

One theory for the revealing garb in which kajirae are commonly kept is that in a primitive, warlike, barbarous world, a world in which slavery is common, and beautiful women are regarded as a familiar form of booty, such garb tends to make them the desiderated objects of capture, seizure and theft, this being thought, in its way, to constitute something of a protection for the free women, in their cumbersome, concealing robes and veils. But there are, doubtless, several reasons for the distinctive forms of garb in which kajirae are placed. One commonly mentioned reason is that it draws a clear distinction in a profoundly stratified society between our lowliness, marked by our rags, or brief tunics, and such, and the loftiness of free women, expressed in the complexity, richness and ornateness of their habiliments. It is not likely then that we will be confused with our betters. The most significant reasons, however, I suspect, have to do with the gratifications of men, who enjoy dressing us, if at all, for their pleasure, and with the informative, mnemonic, and stimulatory effects achieved on the slave herself. It is hard to be dressed in certain fashions without comprehending very clearly and meaningfully that one is beautiful and desirable—*and owned*. These comprehensions, in turn, enhance sexual responsiveness. The garmenture of the slave, then, has its effect not only on those who see her, but on the slave herself. With respect to the first reason, that of protecting free women, I think there may be something to it. For example, if stalking, or careful hunting is involved, or if an escape must be made quickly, then the robes of concealment, as they are often called, might give some pause to a hunter. Who would wish to risk his life for a woman only to discover later in his camp, after her unveiling, that better than she might have been purchased for a few coppers from an itinerant peddler? Would he not feel much a fool? To be sure, he might be lucky. He might have his rope on a prize. But, even so, would that not be mere luck, and, in a sense, would he not then be merely a lucky fool? Certainly professional slavers on this world would customarily exercise great care in such matters, perhaps even having recourse to elaborate techniques of inquiry and espionage. It is rumored they sometimes work in conjunction with free women who manage baths, and such, patronized by free women. In the conquest of cities, of course, or in elaborate raids, in which perhaps outlying villas, or cylinders, are struck, by several men, one may take more time, sorting out captures into field girls, kitchen-and-laundry girls, kettle-and-mat girls, tower slaves, pleasure slaves, and such. In the capture of a city a woman may be disrobed, or ordered to disrobe, on the spot. One then may decide whether or not to put her on his rope or, in some cases, to bind her and then insert a nose ring, to which a leash cord may be attached. Sometimes a given warrior may have several women hurrying behind him, their leash cords grasped in his fist. When a conquering force is disciplined, the women are sometimes merely bound helplessly, and marked, and then left where they may be easily found later, in collections, for return to the original captor. The marks are various. Sometimes the names, or signs, are written on her body. Sometimes a token is affixed to her, as, say, a tag-bearing wire thrust through an ear lobe and then twisted shut, to preclude dislodgment. Women of my world, of course, for the most part, are not veiled. In this way those of this world who come to my world, doubtless for various purposes, but amongst them, it seems, though perhaps only incidentally, to acquire women for this world, women who will become such as I, encounter little difficulty in making their assessments. Doubtless it pleases them to do this at their leisure, and quite openly. How convenient all this is for them! Are the goods not, so to speak, publicly displayed?

What sort of culture, I wondered, allows its women to be so exhibited, to be displayed so brazenly, so publicly and conveniently, for the inspection of men? And what of the women? Have they, in their haughty displays, no inkling of how they appear to men? Do they wish to insult men? Do they wish to disturb and taunt men? Do they wish, in their frustration, to challenge men? Or do they long on some level to be taken in hand, and be done with as men please? Do they long on some level for the iron and the chain?

I remembered with chagrin how I had on my old world obtained gratification from teasing boys. Now I belonged to men.

The soldier released my hair, and my head came forward. I kept it lowered.

The platform on which I knelt was some twenty feet square, and the aperture within it was some four feet by five feet. It had slid out from the side of the citadel. It was large enough that one of the great birds could have landed on it. The tripodlike arrangement of beams which, with its pulley, facilitated the movement of the rope, could be set up or taken down. Above the track of the platform, swung back now, was a double gate. It was such that the platform, if the tripod of beams was not set up, could be extended or withdrawn without reference to it. In each of the double gates was a smaller opening which was now shut, through which only one person at a time might pass. Given these arrangements several permutations were possible, the most obvious being the gates shut and the platform withdrawn, the gates shut and the platform extended, and the gates open with the platform extended or withdrawn. I would not wish to have been on the platform if the gates were closed and the platform was withdrawn. I suddenly whimpered, for the platform began to move back, into the citadel. I did not dare rise, of course. I did look up and saw, as I passed under the wall, heavy and menacing, in a large, oblong overhead slot, the downward-pointing spikes of a great, barred barrier. One would not wish to have been beneath those spikes had they descended. Just behind that area was the inner threshold, which would be closed by the gates. With a rumble the platform stopped. It stopped well within the gate. This allowed the gates, if and when they would be closed, clearance of the tripod, that associated with the windlass. In this fashion the tripod might, if one wished, be kept in its braces. I then saw, rattling and heavy, the barred gate, with the spikes, descend. The spikes descended into sockets in a stone sill. I could now see the windlass. It was within the gate itself. The gates were then closed.

I knelt on the drawn-back platform. The gates were twice barred, with heavy beams. They slid slowly across the inner faces of the gate. They must have weighed hundreds of pounds. They were now secure within their monstrous iron brackets.

The gates were now closed, now barred. The gates were heavy and high. They must have been a foot thick. The exterior surfaces had been sheathed with nailed copper sheets, the intention of which, one supposes, was to resist fire.

I looked at the great gates.

How helpless I felt, kneeling on the platform, my upper body pinioned helplessly within that stout canvas sheath. It was so tightly buckled upon me that I could scarcely move my hands and arms within it. Too, it was buckled closely about my neck.

The beams of the platform were rough and heavy. They felt splintery beneath my knees and where the upper sides of my toes, as I knelt, now rested upon them. The bottoms of my feet burned from the ascent to the lower level. Here and there on the platform were deep gouges, where weapons might have struck, or the talons of the great birds.

I did not know where I was!
I had not asked to be brought here!
What was I doing here?

This was not even my world!

I was afraid.

How faraway then seemed my own world, and my past.

"I will tell them that you are here," said one of the soldiers.

We were then, it seemed, expected.

This understanding did not ease my apprehensions.

What was I doing here?

Why could I not be as other girls, routinely processed, auctioned summarily off a block to the highest bidder, and then led, braceleted, barefoot, frightened, hopeful, to the domicile of my buyer, and new master?

How was it that I was so different?

We waited on the drawn-in platform.

It seemed we waited a long time.

It was hot in the sack, my hands and arms closely confined within it, but, on my bared legs I could feel the cool air of the mountains. The mountain air, too, moved my hair a little. I shook my head a little, to move the hair away from my eyes. Confined as I was I could not reach it with my hands.

"Steady, little vulo," said one of the men.

He brushed the hair back from my face with his large hand. I looked up at him, gratefully, and then again put my head down. Masters are often kind to us, for we are so much theirs, and so helpless. But they are always the masters.

I was grateful for his small kindness.

A touch, a smile, a candy, a pastry, mean much to us.

We are kajirae.

On my old world I had lacked an identity. Perhaps we all did. On my old world roles and masks made do for identities, for realities. We were all told we were real, of course, but when we inquired as to what we were, *really*, we were met with evasive answers; I suppose we were just supposed to know; when we went to touch those supposed realities, our hands passed through them. They weren't really there. And if they were truly us, then we, too, were not there. But we knew we were real somehow, something beyond the masks, the roles. Not everyone wants to disappear behind a mask, or even to hide behind one. It seemed we were all waiting. Young, we were supposed to wait. Reality was around the corner. Existence and truth must be postponed yet another day. And so we waited, and distracted ourselves with sweets and lies. But where was the end of this? Were the older ones real either? Could it be that the older ones, too, were waiting? Were they embarrassed to admit this? Were the parents real? Had they learned, in their longer lives, secrets they refused to reveal? It is a terrible thing to look behind a mask and see nothing. The masks can be voracious. How many scream, trapped within a mask? How many do not scream, unaware that they have become the mask, that now there is nothing left but the mask?

We awaited the return of the soldier.

How could I be here?

Was it not madness that I was here? But I was here.

Here, however, I had a reality. I had an identity. There were no problems with that matter here. No longer need I wait in some windy place, on some lonely bridge or busy street corner, hoping to meet myself. That rendezvous had now occurred. Here, at last, I was something, *really*. Here I had an identity. It was an identity as real as that of a dog or pig. I was a *kajira*.

I looked up. Then I looked down.

"Bring her," said the soldier to the jailer.

He stood some ten or twelve feet from us.

I felt myself drawn to my feet. The jailer did this. It was done by means of the ring on the back of the sack, that by means of which I had been attached to the ring on the rope. I stumbled a little. I feared to fall. My hands and arms pinioned I would have no way of breaking the fall. I did not lose the tunic. It was now muchly dampened, and must bear within it tooth marks.

The jailer snapped a light leash to a small ring on the sack straps, just below my chin.

This development affected me with apprehension.

I had not been leashed below, outside, on the ledge.

Was a leash necessary?

Surely not!

But what manner of place was this? What was I to see? This leashing was surely not for purposes of display, not here, not now, but now, I understood, of girl management, of girl control! Or perhaps girl instruction! I knew a female could learn much on a leash. And where was I to be taken? I was suddenly very much frightened. I was suddenly so much more in their power.

I was leashed!

Did they think I was a new girl? But here, in this place, I was a new girl! I was an ignorant slave here, one unaware of her surroundings and their nature. Might I run, or bolt? Might I, in some imminent situation, overcome with terror, attempt irrationally, unable to help myself, to flee? But even if I wished to do so, and dared to do so, I could not. I was leashed.

Or was it to teach me something that I was leashed? Did I not yet know myself slave enough?

Apparently they would see to it that I would learn.

Had I not been leashed on the ledge, that I might be the more startled, the more apprehensive, the more conscious of it here? Where was I to be taken? What was to be done with me?

The soldier turned about, and strode away. The jailer followed him, and I followed him, on the leash.

If I were to precede him I supposed that he might have used the stout leash with which he had restrained the six-legged animal, it secured to the ring on the back of the sack.

Leashes are often held partly coiled on this world, the leash otherwise being somewhat long. The length permits the leash to also serve as, in effect, binding fiber. One usually prefers to be led rather than to lead. When one leads, as, say, if it might be the wish of the rights holder to so display one, one might, if one does not, for example, walk well, feel the free end of the leash only-too soon, as a lash. That is another advantage of the long leash, of course, that one, if the rights holder wishes, may be punished while still upon it. I preferred to be led. I hastened to keep up with the soldier and jailer, the leash in the grasp of the latter. They moved quickly. One is customarily expected to follow at an appropriate distance, that constituting an attractive, lovely interval, but it is not always easy to maintain such an interval, for various reasons, such as crowding, or the rapidity of the leash holder's pace. Two or three times I was jerked forward, and nearly fell. The leash was often taut. I was conducted through several narrow passageways. Sometimes portions of these were barred, and signs and countersigns were given. Twice we passed women such as I, but in collars. As the men passed, they went immediately to their knees, performing obeisance. Both wore brief tunics, the skirt of one being slit to the waist on both sides. There seemed few in these narrow passages, or streets. I did see one child. I would have had to kneel before it, as before any free person. It regarded us idly. It had apparently seen many women such as I, so conducted. Then the leash jerked taut again and I nearly lost my footing. I hastened on. I did not think it would be difficult to defend such passageways.

In what seemed but a matter of moments we had come to a large, heavy door, almost a gate. A panel was slid back, a sign and countersign exchanged, and the door opened. Within was a high, vaulted room, apparently a guard station. Inside there were some tables and benches, several men, in scarlet livery, and some chains dangling from the ceiling. It seemed clearances were to be obtained here. One of the men fastened me, by the ring on the back of the sack, to another ring, on one of the dangling chains. These dangling chains were such that they could be drawn upward. The keeper, or jailer, looped the leash coils about my neck, rather closely, tucking in the loose end to hold them in place. He then went to one of the tables, accompanied by the soldier. Two men then, by means of the rings and the chain to which I was now attached, hoisted me upward, foot by foot, until I was suspended some thirty feet above the floor, some two thirds of the way to the ceiling. At this point the chain was secured. I swung there, waiting, while the jailer completed business at one of the tables. There were papers in his wallet which he presented. I supposed they were my papers. One feels terribly helpless, suspended thusly. One is not in contact with the floor, or ground. One has no leverage. One cannot bolt, or run. Indeed, from such a height, even if one is not gagged, it is not practical to communicate. One waits, isolated. One waits, at the pleasure of others.

The jailer, and the soldier with him, were still before one of the tables.

I squirmed a little, but then noticed one of the guards looking upward, so, frightened, I stopped. I had gathered some inkling in the pens as to how I, or, indeed, I suppose, any kajira, struggling, or even moving a little, might be viewed by a strong man. I then kept as quiet as I could. It was hot near the ceiling. I bit down on the gag. I was afraid of dropping it. The leash coils were about my neck, looped there rather closely, the free end of the leash tucked in, to hold the coils in place. I saw, far below, over to one side, briefly tunicked, entering with a pitcher, unobtrusively, as was appropriate, a woman such as I. She glanced up, but then looked away. I gathered that she had seen more than one woman, perhaps even free women, suspended thusly in this place, in the custody of the sack and chain. The chains suggested that that might not be uncommon in this place. The custodial arrangement, as you might imagine, was quite effective. On the other hand, I would suppose that it was primarily designed with free women, prisoners, or new kajirae, in mind, women who might not yet fully understand the meaning of their collars. I did not think the security of this arrangement was necessary for such as I. I might be a new kajira but the pens in which I had been trained had been efficient. Not long on this world, I has already learned something of discipline. The kajira who had entered with the pitcher was collared, of course. I could see the collar. It was flat, narrow, about a half inch in height, and closely fitting, a common collar. She was blond. I saw this with some contempt, and perhaps a bit of jealousy. This may have been something lingering from my old world, for, on this world, brunettes seem to be favored, it being claimed, truly or not, that they are much more easily aroused, and much more helpless, and passionate, in the furs. But, to be sure, blond hair, genuinely blond hair, is rare on this world, except for certain areas, as it is on my old world. This rarity, of course, as would be expected, tends to increase its marketability somewhat, except in more northern markets, where it is common. The hair of kajirae who are up for sale, incidentally, is never dyed, or, if dyed, that is made clear to the buyers. A buyer who regards himself as defrauded can be, as I understand it, extremely disagreeable. With respect to heat it is my supposition that blondes, at least if properly managed and disciplined, are also responsive and passionate. Indeed, they had better be. Frigidity is not permitted to kajirae. We are not free women. If it is pertinent I might mention that in the pens I saw blondes on their bellies, tears in their eyes, begging the touch of guards, just as brunettes and redheads. These things really depend not on the color of hair, but on the individual woman. I might note, in passing, that in many slave markets, the single, most prized color of hair seems to be auburn. That hair color is highly prized in a kajira. An itinerant vendor, then, if desiring to defraud buyers and raise the price of a kajira, is more likely to have her hair dyed auburn than blond.

At the table there seemed some puzzle as to my disposition, one which the jailer, as far as I could tell, could not really dispel.

I noted, to my irritation, that the fellow who had been looking up at me was now eyeing the blonde. But surely I was more attractive than she! She was pouring some liquid from the pitcher into one of the vessels on the table. And I think that she, the vixen, was not that unaware of his scrutiny! He was suddenly standing quite near to her and she looked up, into his eyes, only inches from him. Then she hurried away, through a beaded side-entrance, and he, in a moment, followed her.

I squirmed in the sack. That fellow had been handsome. It might be pleasant to be in his arms! He was not an ugly, repulsive, callous giant like the jailer. Perhaps I should have moved a tiny bit more before him, as though inadvertently, you understand.

I whimpered a little, not so much as to make it clear that I was trying to attract attention to myself. Indeed, I was not trying to attract attention to myself! I had just made a little noise, you see, not really meaning it.

When I sensed that one of the fellows was looking up I moved my legs a little, putting them together, and then separating them, and pointing the toes a little, and bending my legs back, a little. I had pretty legs, I was sure. I did not think this display, even though totally inadvertent, would be lost on such men. And I could always pretend that they had misunderstood. To be sure, such defenses, in a kajira, are not likely to prove effective. Indeed, what would such men be likely to care, really, whether they had understood me or not?

"What is her name?" asked the fellow below me.

My heart leaped.

"She does not have a name," said the jailer.

I was muchly pleased. He had expressed interest. The name is important. One commonly keeps track of a girl by her name. It is useful in putting in a call for her, in having her sent to one, and so on. But I did not, as of now, I had just learned, have a name.

Perhaps it was just as well, I thought. These men, or some of them, were the masters of monstrous beasts. I did not doubt then but what they would be excellent, and severe, masters of other sorts of beasts, as well, for example, curvaceous little beasts, such as I.

How fortunate then!

If I did not have a name, it would be more difficult to put in a call for me. I needed then have less fear of being summoned to the furs of such brutes! But I wanted a name, though I knew it would be only a slave name, put on me for the convenience and pleasure of masters. How else could I be summoned, or have it written on a shard drawn at random from an urn? I had not been caressed in days! Surely someone must have mercy on a kajira! I supposed the name, as I was an Earth girl, would be an Earth-girl name. They are regarded as slave names. Sometimes they are put on a Gorean girl as a punishment. I did not mind, of course. I hoped it would be a pretty name. Surely it would be one which, to a Gorean master, would say "slave."

The business at the table had now, apparently, been successfully terminated.

We were apparently cleared to proceed.

I was lowered, foot by foot, to the floor. Then I had my feet under me. I was now among the men. I seemed very small among them. Suddenly I felt rather frightened. No longer was I secure in a protected elevation. To be sure, that security, and that elevation, that protection, that sanctuary, had been wholly at the discretion of others. They might accord it to me, or terminate it, instantly, as they pleased.

The leash was then unlooped from about my throat. It was then securely in the hand of the jailer. I was then freed of the chain.

Briefly then my jailer and the soldier, his guide in this place, conferred.

One of the guards, a handsome fellow, he who had looked up at me, and asked my name, regarded me. I looked away, and tossed my head.

Let him understand that!

What cared I for him!

But he slapped his thigh in amusement.

Had I not yet learned my collar?

I feared suddenly that he might one day make me pay dearly for that expression, that gesture.

But my jailer, preceded by the soldier, now, again, continued on his way.

On the leash I swiftly followed him.

I heard laughter behind me.

Those men might remember me, I feared.

We passed through a portal, once again one less like a common door than a stout gate.

I followed, leashed.

Within was a long, dimly lit tunnel, with several opened gates within it, some of bars, some of metal-sheathed wood, with tiny apertures some eight to ten feet above the floor. These were tiny ports, used, I would learn, for the missiles of the crossbow. They are manned by platforms which are a part of the interior surface of the doors. I did not notice them at the time but there were other ports overhead from which missiles might be fired toward the doors, should foes achieve the dubious success of reaching them. I think there was no place in that corridor, or perhaps generally in the fortifications as a whole, which could not be reached by missile fire from at least two directions. Noxious materials might be emitted from such vents, as well, such as pitch, acids, and heated oil.

When we went through the next gate, we were suddenly plunged in darkness, absolute darkness.

For several minutes we made our way through a number of labyrinthine passages, occasionally stopping at various gates, which, after an exchange of signs and countersigns, were opened for us. I think there were side passages, too, for I occasionally sensed a difference in the air. If one did not know the passages, I supposed one might, lost and helpless, wander about in them for days. Once I silently screamed, and bit down, fiercely, on the gag, that I might not lose it, and wept in terror, for I felt my thigh brushed by the thick, greasy fur of a large, curious animal, one, I think, like that I had encountered earlier on the ledge. I do not know how many of them were in the passage. Though I could not see them I could often smell them. They were silent. Once I heard claws scraping on the stone. There was no reflection of light from their eyes for in those passages there was no light to be reflected. The soldier, and the jailer, continued to move with assurance. I did not know if they had memorized the passages or not. Perhaps they guided themselves by touch, or by some irregularities in the flooring. My own passage was guided by the leash. Had I not been leashed I would have had to be led in some other way. A common slave-girl leading position is to grasp her by the hair and hold her head at your hip. Needless to say, we prefer the leash.

Perhaps this is the reason for the leash, I thought, that I not be lost in the tunnel, or injure myself against the walls, or flee in terror, madly, upon the discovery that the tunnel is shared by beasts, whose function is doubtless to protect it from any to whom its passage might be prohibited. Such utilities were intelligible, and plausible.

These things were doubtless true, but I would learn, as well, that the leash had additional purposes, later to become clear to me.

Several times I lost my balance, and must struggle, stumbling, to regain it. This was not easy to do, as I could not make use of my hands and arms, they being so tightly confined against my body, within the sack, it strapped so tightly about me. One is not only helpless in such an arrangement, but one is very sensitive to one's helplessness. One feels very vulnerable. You follow the leash as best you can. Twice I actually fell, bruising myself in the darkness on the stone flooring. Then the leash would pull against the sack ring, under my chin, and I must needs rise up, and again follow.

My legs were tired. The bottoms of my feet were sore, mainly from the ledge.

It had been, so far, a lengthy, wearing, mysterious peregrination. Surely we must be near its end.

In the darkness, I had sensed that we were often climbing.

I did not know how high we might be.

We then passed through another door, and emerged, at last, into a lighted passage, though it was lighted but dimly, with two torches, one at each end of the passage. The light was not bright, but it hurt my eyes. We paused, all of us, waiting for a bit, to allow our eyes to adjust to it.

Then I shrank back, to the end of the leash.

We had come, on the other side of the door, a few feet from the door, to a deep, narrow, moatlike depression. This extended in the corridor, from side to side, for the width of the corridor, perhaps for some five to seven yards, until it terminated several feet before the farther door, at the end of the passage. Bridging this moatlike depression, running parallel to the sides of the corridor, there lay a narrow, retractable metal beam or plank, perhaps two inches in width.

I shook my head negatively, wildly, beggingly, piteously.

Even were I not confined as I was, I would not have dared to essay that narrow span, that long, terrifyingly narrow beam. At best, unconfined, under duress, I might have tried to inch across it on my belly, trying to balance upon it, clinging desperately to it.

I began to tremble.

I feared I could not long remain on my feet, so weak and frightened I was.

I looked at the soldier, the jailer.

My eyes must have been wild with fear. I whimpered in terror. My legs buckled under me. I slipped down to the stone. I could not stand. I could not even begin to rise to my feet. I knelt down, and put my head to the stone. I could not speak a word, for the gag which I clenched between my teeth. But my mien, doubtless, was pathetic.

I could not even stand.

The jailer may have expected some such response from me. Perhaps he had brought other kajirae to this place.

In any event he did not remonstrate with me, or order me to my feet, or lash me with the strap of the leash.

Perhaps he had not expected more of me. Would a Gorean girl have been different? I did not think so.

He roared with laughter, which much unsettled me.

This was, it seemed, a joke of Masters?

Of course, I suddenly realized, he had not expected me to negotiate that barrier. Perhaps some women might have managed it, even in constraints as I was, but I was not one of them.

The soldier, I saw, made his way swiftly across the bridge.

This startled me.

The jailer then reached down and, to my misery, I helpless, scooped me up, and threw me over his shoulder. I bit down on the gag, that I might not scream with fear, and lose it in the moatlike depression. He carried me with my head to the rear, as women such as I are often carried. We are helpless in this carry, and cannot see to what we are being carried. I held my breath until we reached the other side. He moved across that narrow bridge swiftly and surely, as had the soldier. I saw, in the bottom of the depression, some forty feet below, numerous upward-pointing knives. Perhaps the bridge was wide enough and sturdy enough for those accustomed to such things, but it seemed terribly narrow to me, with the drop beneath, let alone the knives. Men, I knew, in carnivals, or circuses, traversed even narrower and far less steady surfaces. But I did not think those surfaces were likely to be suspended over knives. I then kept my eyes closed until we reached the other side. The bridge shook, and vibrated, with a ringing noise, as we crossed it.

"Wait here," said the soldier.

I was then put to my knees to one side. The jailer lifted a chain from the side wall. It was attached to a ring there and was itself terminated with another ring. He clipped the ring on the back of my sack to that ring. I was thus, in the sack, kneeling, fastened to the wall.

We waited.

"Do you like our little bridge?" he asked.

I shook my head, negatively.

"There are far worse things in this place," he said.

I regarded him, frightened.

"You are going to be a good little kajira, are you not?" he said.

I nodded my head.

"I wonder why you were purchased," he said, looking down at me.

I looked up at him. I did not know.

"To be sure," he said, "you are pretty."

I put my head down, quickly. One is sometimes wary when one hears one so spoken of, too, by such a man. The buckles of the sack were within his reach, of course. It was I who could not reach them.

"We are in the vicinity of one of the high terraces," he said.

I thought I detected a freshness of air, and a draft from beneath the door.

"You have not been a kajira long, have you?" he asked.

I shook my head, negatively.

"You are familiar with gag signals, are you not?" he asked.

I whimpered once. When a woman is gagged, one whimper means "Yes," and two, "No."

"That is better," he said.

I hoped he would not cuff me.

"You wish to use them then, do you not?" he said.

I whimpered once. Of course! Of course!

"Good," he said. "Have you been a kajira long?"

I whimpered twice.

"You have much to learn," he said.

I whimpered once.

"Within," he said, "you will find yourself in the presence of an officer. Do you understand?"

I whimpered once. I did not really understand, fully, the import of what he was saying but I gathered enough to understand that he within, or he on the other side of that door, he before whom I might soon expect to appear, was of some importance in this place.

This was, as you might suppose, a piece of very frightening intelligence for me.

"You do wish to live, do you not?" asked the jailer.

I whimpered once, earnestly, fervently. Tears sprang to my eyes.

"Good," he said.

We continued to wait.

"You do not know why you were purchased, do you?" he asked.

I whimpered twice. I looked at him, pleadingly.

"I do not know either," he said. "Perhaps it is merely because you are pretty."

I looked down, frightened.

"You are pretty," he said.

I whimpered a little, not in response, but rather in fear.

I could hardly move in the sack. By means of it I was tethered to the wall.

He looked down at me.

I was within his power.

But he did not unbuckle the sack. I wondered if I might be in some way special. I had certainly not been regarded as special in the pens, except perhaps insofar as I might have been thought to have been of "special interest" to strong men, or, in their rude humor, "specially delicious" as a "tasta" or "pudding."

I looked at the door, fearfully.

I wondered what lay beyond it.

Behind that door then, I would guess from some several yards behind it, there sounded a gong.

I looked up, wildly, frightened.

"Steady," he said "It will be a few Ehn."

He then unclipped the leash ring from the ring on the straps, under my chin. He then, over the straps, pushed my chin up, and fastened the leash, by means of its own clip and ring, about my neck, a portion of the leash thus serving as its own collar. The loop fitted closely about my neck. Perhaps there was something like a half inch of play in the loop. He jerked the loop open, as far as it would go, to its limit, where it was stopped by the ring and guard. I then had something like an inch of play within the loop. I could not, of course, hope to slip such a tether.

"Note," he said.

He then gave a slight tug on the leash and I looked up at him in terror. Whereas the loop might widen to the point where I might have as much as a full inch between my throat and the leather, no limit, other than my throat itself, was imposed on its closure. As the leash was now arranged, it constituted a choke collar. This was quite different from the earlier arrangement, when the ring had been attached to the sack straps.

"Do you like a choke collar?" he asked.

I whimpered twice.

"They are commonly used for dangerous male slaves," he said, "sometimes for new girls, sometimes for arrogant free women, that they may immediately cease to be arrogant, sometimes for ignorant girls, sometimes for stupid girls. Sometimes women use them for controlling other women, for they have less strength."

I looked up at him. Such a collar terrified me.

"Do you think it necessary for one such as you?"

I whimpered twice.

"No," he said. "I do not think so, either. But I thought it useful that you should feel it, and understand that it can be used on you here."

I trembled.

I was not totally unfamiliar with choke collars, for they had occasionally been used in my training, in the pens. I did fear them. I shall elaborate on this matter briefly, at a later point.

"Good," he said, "I see that you are an intelligent kajira, and that you understand. But have no fear, or no more than is necessary. I will now make a simple adjustment."

He fixed the ring differently.

"There," he said.

He then jerked the leash. But now it did not close on my throat. It had been adjusted, to be a normal collar.

I looked at him, gratefully.

I still could not slip it, of course.

"That is better, is it not?" he asked.
I whimpered once.
"You do not now fear the leash, do you?" he asked.
I whimpered twice.
"You are mistaken," he said.
I regarded him, puzzled. What was there to fear from a common leash?
He then freed the ring at the back of the sack from the chain on the wall.
No longer was I attached to the wall.
I felt him unbuckling the sack.
I whimpered, begging him to speak to me.
"You are perhaps concerned about the gong," he said.
I whimpered once.
"That was the first signal," he said.
When the sack fell free from about my upper body I was put to all fours. My upper body suddenly felt cold. It had been uncomfortably warm in its tight canvas enclosure, from the pressure of my limbs held so closely to my body and the general heat and constraint of the sack. It had been covered with a sheen of perspiration, from its confinement and my exertions. Now it felt cold, from the air of the corridor. He then had me crawl forward, until my legs, too, were free of the sack. He then folded the sack and put it to one side. He then picked up the leash, looping its long end in three or four coils.
We then waited, again.
He was to my left. I was naked. I was on all fours. The tunic, in its small, neat folds, was gripped between my teeth.
The leash, in his hand, looped down, and then up, to my neck.
I regarded the closed door.
"Remember that you would like to live," said the jailer.
I whimpered, once.
He looked down upon me, as such men often look, and appropriately, upon women such as I.
"You are a pretty little she-sleen," he said.
At that time, though I was familiar with sleen, or at least the one who had patrolled the ledge, I did not know the word.
There are many varieties of sleen, incidentally, adapted to diverse environments; the most formidable, as far as I know, is the forest sleen.

There is also a sand sleen, a snow sleen, even some aquatic varieties, types of sea sleen, and so on. They vary greatly in size, as well. Some sleen are quite small and silken, and sinuously graceful, no larger than domestic cats. They are sometimes kept as pets.

It was easy enough to understand, of course, that a "pretty little she-sleen" must be some sort of domestic animal. I was on all fours. I was to be, apparently, marched forward, through the door, on all fours, leashed. How could it be made more clear to me that I was an animal?

At that time I did not know of the habit of some masters, usually imposed as a punishment, to refuse an upright posture to their girls, and to refuse them, as well, the use of human language. They must go about on all fours, or their bellies, and communicate, as they can, by whimpers, moans, and such. They are naked, save for their collars. They are not permitted to use their hands to feed themselves, and so on. Needless to say, they also serve in this modality. There are various Gorean expressions for this; one is the "discipline of the she-tarsk." A tarsk is a piglike animal. The boars are tusked, and can be quite large. They are also territorial and fierce. Many hunters have lost their lives in their pursuit. The sows are smaller and lack tusks. The male keeps them in his group, or, so to speak, in his harem.

"Do you understand the leash?" he asked.

I whimpered once.

"I wonder," he said.

He then, suddenly, without warning, jerked the leash upward, and its leather was tight under my chin and I was jerked up to my knees, and I looked at him wildly, helplessly held in place; he then, with ease, with flicks of the leash, flung me to one side and the other, bruising me on the stone and the walls, and then put me to my back, and his booted sandal was on my belly; I looked up at him, in terror; the stone was hard beneath me; and then, with snaps of the leash and the sides of his feet, and gestures, he rolled me about on the stone, from one side to the other; and then he flung me to my belly; how hard was the stone! I shuddered, lying before him, on my belly, in his power. How well I had been controlled by the leash, even though my hands were free! I lay there prone, trembling, sweating on the stone, the tunic tight between my teeth; he then put his foot on my back, holding me down, pressing me to the stone, and, leaning forward, pulled up the leash, the leather again under my chin; my head then was painfully back; always, as a practiced leash master, he avoided exerting pressure on the throat; that can be extremely dangerous; the pressure of a collar, of whatever sort of collar, is to be always high, under the chin, or at the back or sides of the neck; happily, he had adjusted the collar so that it was no longer a choke collar; else I might have been slain; most collars, of course, as mine now was, given the adjustment he had made, are not choke collars; such collars, as suggested, can be extremely dangerous; indeed, most masters eschew them; too, they commonly train their girls to such a point of perfection that there is no need for such a device; too, of course, the girls will go to great lengths in diligence and perfection of service to avoid having such a device put on them; also, as a matter of fact, other devices are as much or more effective in girl training, even things as simple as bracelets and a switch; but even if a choke collar is used, the slave knows that she has nothing to fear from it, unless she is in the least bit recalcitrant or disobedient; then, of course, there is much to fear from it; he then, with the free end of the leash, which was long, tied my hands behind my back, and then crossed my ankles, and pulled them up, painfully behind me, and tied them to my wrists. I reared up a little, but was helpless. I then lay, subdued, on my belly, before him, my wrists tied behind me, my ankles pulled up and tied to my wrists.

How I had been intimidated, controlled and mastered!

"Do you understand the leash now," he asked, "a little better?"

I whimpered once, fervently.

I now understood the leash, and its power, as I had never understood it before.

And as he had adjusted it, it had been only a common leash. How terrifying then would be a choke leash!

I had received additional training.

I gathered that he had thought I needed it.

Certainly I would be a better kajira for it.

Another device which can be used for training, display, control, or such, is the slave harness, to which a leash may be attached. This does not touch the throat. Such a harness, well cinched on the slave, can be extremely attractive. There are usually two rings on such a harness, for the attachment of a leash; one is on the front of the harness and the other is on the back.

He then unbound my hands and feet, and gestured that I should once again go to all fours.

I did so, the leash still on me.

I would be taken through the door leashed, on all fours. I was a slave, an animal. And thus I would be presented, as an animal, before whoever might be on the other side of that door. The leash was a common leash. I did not require a choke collar.

"Soon, little tasta," he said. "Soon."

We waited.

My knees, and the palms of my hands, were sore, from the stone. My body, too, was bruised from my leash training.

I had a clearer notion now of what I was.

I was more of a kajira now than I had been this morning.

This was, I think, a kindness on the part of the jailer. He wanted me to live.

Then I started as, from behind that door, from somewhere well behind it, once again, sounded the gong.

Then the door opened.

"Proceed, little tasta," said the jailer.

I then, on my leash, crawled toward the opening.

Eleven

As soon as I crawled through the opening I felt fresh air, and my hair was blown back somewhat by the wind.

I found myself on the stone flagging of a large, circular terracelike structure, perhaps some forty yards in diameter. It was apparently the roof of a bastion or tower of some sort. About its edges, facing outwards, were defensive works, some movable, some roofed. Above it, supported by beams, casting a pattern of almost intangible shadows, seeming to stir on the flagging, were numerous, swaying strands of fine wire.

The sky was very bright, and very blue. In it billowing clouds scudded like speeding fleets. The air of this world is very clear, and rich.

At the far side of the large area, away from the door, near the outer circumference of the circle, was a stone dais, reached by some three steps, on the top of which was a thronelike chair.

I crawled forward, slightly in advance of the jailer, who, the leash in his hand, was to my left.

"Stop," he said, softly.

I stopped.

There were only a few individuals on the terrace, and these were on, or near, the dais.

Their eyes were upon me.

I put down my head.

I wondered what was wanted of me.

The jailer then, to my surprise, removed the leash from my neck.

Perhaps he had received some sign from the dais to do so. I did not know.

I stayed there, on all fours, my head down.

What did they want of me?

I wondered if I were worthy enough to have been brought here.

Was I good enough? Would I prove to be satisfactory? My experience in the pens had suggested that I might do. I had been popular there, with most, if not with all, if not with one, in particular.

I trusted that those who had made this decision, to bring me here, knew their business. I hoped they knew their business. I did not want to die!

And there would be other women here, doubtless, women of this world. How would they view me? I gathered that they might view me as negligible, as far less than they, even if their own fair throats were enclosed in collars.

There was one woman besides myself on the terrace. She wore scarlet silk. She was well bejeweled. She was not veiled. Her face, like mine, was bared. Any might look upon it, as they pleased. She was on her knees, to the left of the thronelike chair. She was chained to it by the neck. On the other side of the thronelike chair, lying there, stretched out, indolently, its large, triangular head down on its paws, was one of the six-legged beasts, one such as that I had met on the ledges. It was chained to the right side of the thronelike chair. As the beast was at the right hand of the thronelike chair and the woman only at the left, that signified, in this world, that she was less than it.

On the thronelike chair reclined a richly robed figure. His shoulders were of great breadth. His robes were largely of scarlet, lined with purple. He was strikingly handsome, and had large hands. On his feet were golden sandals; on his forehead was a golden circlet.

He gestured that I should rise, and I did so. I then stood some fifty feet, or so, before the dais.

He then indicated that I might remove the tunic from between my teeth. Gratefully I did so. I then held it in my right hand. It was very damp.

He then said something to one of the men standing near him. Among them was the soldier who had brought us here, but it was not he to whom he spoke.

I stood very well, naked before him. How different this was, the thought crossed my mind, from my old world. How far I was from the shops, the malls. I wondered how my old companions, Jean, and

Priscilla, and Sandra, and Sally, might stand before such men, masters of women.

I think he was pleased with me. I was sure that he had commented favorably concerning me to his fellow on the dais. The woman to his left, she kneeling, chained by the neck to his chair, had not seemed much pleased. That was surely a point in my favor. She would not like me. I was sure of that. She was, even now, regarding me angrily. I did not like her, either. Let her watch out for herself, and her place on a chain! I hated her!

I considered the eyes of the men.

I stood even straighter, more gracefully.

"Slut," said the woman.

I pretended not to hear. I gathered that she must be a high slave, and that she had a general permission to speak. To be sure, such a permission may be instantly revoked, at so little as a word. If men do not wish to hear us, we must be silent.

It seemed to me now that I could feel the interest of the men, reaching toward me, almost like heat, in waves of desire.

I now felt less frightened. I was now more confident that the slavers who had taken me may have known their business after all, at least as far as externals were concerned. I was such, it seemed, as might quite plausibly appear upon a slave block. And I wondered if only I, at that time, had known the "internals," so to speak, of these matters, that I was such as would be fittingly placed on such a block, indeed, that I was such that I, in a sense, belonged on such a block. Could they have known that, as well, from some clues I was not even fully aware of? It seemed possible. How skilled were they? Doubtless quite skilled. And certainly determinations, made with merciless thoroughness in the pens, had clarified such matters beyond all doubt. And entries pertinent to these matters, I gathered, and had gathered originally to my dismay, for I had regarded such things as my closely guarded secrets, now appeared explicitly on my papers.

The man before me, regarding me, spoke again to some of those about him.

The collars were removed from the monstrous beast on his right, which yawned, and rose to its feet, and from the woman, on his left, who remained kneeling, close to the arm of the thronelike chair.

I was not too pleased to see that the beast was loose.

The others, however, did not seem alarmed.

The man then motioned to me, that I should approach. Timidly I began to do so. Then, suddenly, I stopped. I flung my hands before my face. I screamed. I could not move! The beast, descending lightly from the dais, had bounded toward me. It was now behind me, having circled about.

I took down my hands from before my face. I opened my eyes. I was still alive!

I heard some laughter. My terror had seemed to amuse them!

"Stupid girl," said the woman.

There is a considerable difference between the killing charge of such a beast, direct, ferocious, energetic, savage, violent, ravening, once, after exploratory sallies, it initiates it, and this approach. But I knew nothing of these things. And I think that even one who is familiar with this world would find it quite alarming to be approached, even as I had been, by such an animal.

"Do not be afraid," said the fellow on the thronelike chair.

I cast him a grateful glance.

"He will not kill you unless I tell him to do so," he said.

I nodded, numbly.

"She knows little, I think, of our world," said the jailer.

I saw glances exchanged amongst some of the men near the chair.

"She is stupid," said the woman.

I wondered then if the releasing of the beast, perhaps anticipating its curiosity, and its likely inquiry, had been a test of sorts, one assessing my familiarity with this world and its ways.

I shuddered.

I sensed the breath of the beast on my calves.

"Come closer," invited the man on the dais.

I stopped, warned by his eyes, a few feet before the dais.

"Put aside the tunic," he said, "and turn about, fully, slowly."

I complied.

Then I was again facing him.

"Are you trained?" he asked.

"To some extent, Master," I said. I suspected he must know this.

"Do you know where you were trained?" he asked.

"No, Master," I said.

"Do you know where you are now?" he asked.

"No, Master," I said.

"It is my understanding," said he, "that you can move in fashions which may not be entirely without interest."

I looked at him, frightened.

"But that is not inappropriate for what you are," he said.

"No, Master," I said.

"Move," said he.

And swiftly then did I comply, much as I had done in the house from which I had been sold, before the agents, or buyers.

"Ah!" said a man.

One learns to display oneself, and well, as the merchandise one is. Much of what I did I had learned in the pens, but much, too, comes from within one. Some movements I had done as long ago as my old world, in the secrecy of my bedroom, before the mirror. Sometimes in the midst of such presentations, in effect, the dance of a woman as a woman, as herself, her true self, so brazen, so forward, so honest, and yet, too, so pathetic, so vulnerable, so needful, and, above all, so totally and unutterably different from a man, I had abruptly wheeled away, weeping, crying out, in shame, frightened, miserable and confused that I, only one such as I, might be so desirable, so beautiful, and, for my world, so exquisitely and forbiddenly feminine, but then, later, I had returned to them, determinedly, unabashedly, accepting at last, even angrily, what I was in truth, and should be, a woman, a total woman, in all her moving, exciting variety, in all her richness, in all her vulnerability, in all her marvelousness.

"Excellent!" said a man.

How pleased I was!

It is dangerous, of course, to appear as a woman before strong men.

But here I had no choice. I must be what I was.

My performance must be concluded with "floor movements."

"Excellent!" said a man. "Excellent!" said another. Some of the men struck their left shoulders in commendation. I saw that the woman in scarlet silk, she kneeling at the left side of the thronelike chair, she who had been but moments before chained to it, was looking upon me with great anger.

"Excellent!" called another man.

I then lay before the dais, supine, gasping for breath, covered with sweat, even in the coolness of the elevation and wind. I turned my head to the right. I looked toward the thronelike chair.

"Excellent, excellent," said men.

But I could not read the expression of the occupant of the thronelike chair.

I went then to my stomach and lifted myself up, on my hands, and regarded him.

Had I done well enough? Would I be acceptable?

Those about the chair looked at its occupant. He regarded me. I looked down, and to the right, unable to meet his eyes.

"Let her be fed," he said.

I sank to my belly. I was no longer capable of sustaining my weight on my arms. I lay before the dais, trembling. I was to be fed. I would then, at least for a time, be kept. He had not then, it seemed, been totally dissatisfied. It seemed then that, at least for a time, I would be permitted to live. This decision, I had sensed, had been welcomed by those about the dais, with doubtless one exception.

The woman in scarlet silk rose somewhat angrily. She had a narrow steel collar on her neck, which had been covered by the earlier higher, heavier collar, that to which her chain had been attached. I was quite pleased to see that she was collared. She too then was only a slave! She went to the side, to a small table within one of the roofed defense works. There she shook some meal from a cloth sack into a shallow pan. She then, from an earthen pitcher, poured some water into the pan. She then shook the pan, mixing the ingredients. She held the pan in her left hand. From the table, she picked up, to my dismay, a long, supple switch. I did not care to see it in her possession. She now approached me, the pan in her left hand, the switch in her right. She put the pan down, on the stone flagging, before the dais, a bit to the right of its center, as I faced it. She pointed to the pan with the switch. I rose to all fours and crawled to the pan. I put down my head.

"What do you think of her, my dear Dorna?" asked the man in the chair.

"She is worthless," said the woman.

"Perhaps not entirely without worth," he said.

"She is worthy only to comb the hair of a true woman, if that," she said.

The fellow chuckled.

"Give her to me, as a slave's slave," she wheedled, "that I may do with her as I please."

"I do not think you will be displeased with her disposition," he said.

"Oh?" she asked, interested.

"You will see," he said.

This exchange alarmed me somewhat.

"Continue to feed," said the woman to me.

I continued to feed. It was slave gruel.

Whereas the food was certainly food, and true food, though plain fare, the function of this feeding, of course, was primarily symbolic or ceremonial. I was feeding as a certain sort of thing in a certain sort of way, on a certain sort of provender. I was under no delusions as to what I was, or how I fed, or on what I fed. Another lesson implicit in this matter, which might be noted, was that I was dependent on others for my food, not only with respect to its quality, quantity and nature, but even with respect to whether I would be fed or not. In this, of course, all slaves, even the highest, are similarly dependent. The people of this world are rich in traditions and symbolic behaviors, which are very meaningful and important to them. There are many such behaviors, traditions, ceremonies, and such, and there is, apparently, a considerable variety in such matters from place to place.

I sensed a man moving about, behind me.

"Keep your head down," said she who had been called Dorna.

There was some laughter.

I continued to feed.

One is, of course, vulnerable, so feeding. More than once in the pens I had been caught at such a pan.

Then the man who had been behind me had ascended the dais. He had entered recently, apparently. He conferred with the occupant of the chair. He then left. He had paid me, as far could tell, little, or no, attention. Indeed, he may have scarcely noticed me. I was not important. I was only a kajira, feeding at the foot of the dais.

"Lick the pan," said Dorna.

I did so. I was angry with her. She held the switch. Had my performance not been of interest? Could she have done better? Were her curves likely to be of more interest to men than mine? But it was I who was feeding, and she who held the switch. But I could set myself to please the men! Take away her switch! Let us compete as equals!

"Lift your head," said Dorna. "How silly you look!"

There were crumbs of meal about my mouth and lips.

"Bring some meat," said the occupant of the chair.

Dorna, with an angry swirl of her silks, spun away, to return to the small table under the roofed defense work.

I wondered that the fellow accepted, with such apparent tolerance, what appeared an obvious manifestation of annoyance on the part of the slave, if not of actual insolence. Did she not fear her silks would be removed and that she might be tied to a ring and whipped? I supposed she must have felt the whip at one time or another. She did move well, of course. That suggested that she was not totally unfamiliar with the whip. We must move well. We are not free women. If we do not move well, men, and their whips, see to it that we soon do. And whatever might have been her peripheral tokens of irritation or exasperation she did obey with alacrity. Yes, I thought, she undoubtedly knew something of the whip. Yet, too, undeniably, her behavior seemed to leave something to be desired. Perhaps she presumed too much on the status of a high slave, which status, it seemed, must be hers. Or perhaps she had been a high free woman, and her master, or masters, allowed her to act as she did, finding some amusement in the absurdity of it, she not understanding the joke, knowing they could in an instant bring her to her knees as a humbled, abject, servile, weeping slave. But, in any event, she was accustomed, it seemed, to being treated with some indulgence, perhaps even with permissiveness. How else would she have dared to exploit such latitudes of tolerance as seemed to be accorded to her? To be sure, she was a high slave. But are not such, in the final analysis, owned every bit as much as we? And is not one man's high slave no more to another than the least of his bond maids, laboring shackled in his stables, her use a perquisite for rude grooms, and is it not the case that even for the very same man she who is this evening a high slave may be tomorrow the least of his properties in the scullery?

Dorna returned with a small dish in which there were some tiny bits of meat.

She handed this to the occupant of the great chair.

He regarded me, and I looked up at him, from all fours, from the floor below the dais.

"She has pretty hair," he said.

"Mine is better," said the woman.

We were both dark brunettes. Indeed, our hair was almost the same color. Perhaps hers was a little darker. I suddenly realized that our complexions must, too, be similar. I then suspected, naturally enough, immediately, that perhaps we were both of the "type" in which the personage in the chair might have an interest. Some men, it seems, are interested in certain "types" of women. On this world men have little difficulty in finding the types in which they might be interested. Here there are many markets, some of them even specialty markets, catering to particular tastes. One may accordingly, at one's convenience, browse through various markets, seeking wares to one's liking. A fellow, sooner or later, is almost certain to find an item, fastened to one ring or another, which will conform to his particular taste. Too, as an option, "want lists" may be circulated. Some women of Earth, I suspect, owe their very presence on this world, their very brand and collar, to the fact that they happened to satisfy, unbeknownst to themselves, in virtue of some particular configuration of properties, features and such, to a greater or lesser degree, the requirements of such a list. To be sure, these are doubtless delivered to specific customers. If there is a consolation or advantage in this it is that they are almost certain to find that they are exactly, or almost exactly, what someone wants. I did think that my figure might be superior to hers, at least from the point of view of what seemed to be the common preferences of men of this world.

The occupant of the chair tossed one of the pieces of meat to the floor.

I went to it, on all fours, and put down my head, and picked it up.

The next tidbit of meat he tossed to the first step of the dais, where I retrieved it.

I looked up at him, the palms of my hands on the first step of the dais, my knees on the flagging below the dais.

He tossed the next piece of meat to the second step.

Obediently I took it. He was drawing me upward.

The next tidbit he threw to the floor of the dais, before his chair. I crawled to the floor of the dais and put down my head and picked up the bit of meat. I was grateful for it. I had not had meat since the pens. I looked up at him. My hair fell before my shoulders. I was nude. My neck was innocent of a collar. On my thigh there was, of course, the brand. Once or twice in the pens I had been given a candy, a hard candy, and once, a part of a pastry. I did not hope for such items here, of course, at least at this time. He now held the next piece of meat between his fingers. I was to approach him, and take it from his hand. I crawled to him, and knelt before him, and dared to put my hands upon his left knee. Dorna, the high slave, was a little before me, and to my right. She was standing beside the arm of the thronelike chair, at his left. I put my head forward, delicately, to take the piece of meat, but he drew back his hand a little. I then drew back my head a little, and looked up at him.

"You are from the world called 'Earth'?" he said.

"Yes, Master," I said.

"What have you learned of our world?" he asked.

"Very little, Master," I said.

"But you have learned how to obey, have you not?" he asked.

"Yes, Master," I said.

"Are the women of your world obedient?" he asked.

"Doubtless some, Master," I said.

"But you were not," he said.

"No, Master," I said.

"But you have now learned to obey, have you not?" he asked.

"Yes, Master," I said.

"And you now obey very well, do you not?"

"Yes, Master," I said.

"Instantaneously, and unquestioningly?" he said.

"Yes, Master," I said.

He then put the bit of meat into my mouth.

I took it, gratefully. I finished it. I looked up at him. I hoped that he found me of interest. Women such as I, on this world, must please men. It is what we are for.

"Do not concern yourself with her," said Dorna. "She is totally unworthy of your attention. She is nothing, only a slut from Earth."

The broad-shouldered, large-handed man looked down upon me. How tiny I felt before him. He had been referred to as an "officer" by the jailer. Those large hands, I suspected, were not unpracticed in the techniques of weaponry. Certainly they seemed rough, and strong. I feared to sense what they might feel like on my body.

At his least touch I knew I would respond to him as what I was, a kajira.

Then I put my head down, quickly, for I sensed that he understood this, as well. Indeed, he could doubtless read women such as myself with ease. He had undoubtedly subjugated many of us in his time, reducing us to helpless, spasmodic, begging slaves.

"She has no status, even as a slave," said Dorna. "Put her from your mind. She is only from Earth. She is entirely worthless."

The fellow smiled at the insistence of the slave.

"They are the coldest of the cold," said Dorna.

Two or three of the men about burst into laughter at this remark. They had experienced, and perhaps even owned, I gathered, women such as I, from Earth. Indeed, perhaps they kept one or more in their domiciles now. I doubted that we were brought to this world because we were cold. If anything, for another reason. I kept my head down. I reddened.

"Sometimes women learn heat in a collar," said a man.

"I have heard that of a slave named 'Dorna,'" said another. There was laughter. Dorna looked away, angrily.

"Are you 'cold,' little kajira?" asked the man.

"I do not think so, Master," I said.

I wondered if some women did not, indeed, learn their heat in a collar.

"They are the hottest of the hot," said a man.

"It depends on the particular woman," said a man.

That, I supposed, was true.

I did not believe, of course, that the women of my world were cold. Certainly, at least, they did not seem to be once they had come to this world. To be sure, there were doubtless many reasons for this. On this world we found ourselves in a true world, a biologically natural world, a world in which nature was fulfilled, and celebrated, not outlawed, denied, and denounced. Here a natural sexuality was acceptable. Indeed, it was required of us. Here, for example, we need not pretend to subscribe to the pathologies of identicalism, neuterism and personism. Here we found ourselves in the order of nature where, biologically, we belonged. And here, too, at last, after having lived for years in a sexual desert, unhappy, frustrated, deprived and starved, we find ourselves in a land of plenty. How eagerly we eat! How joyously we drink! But, too, of course, we have little choice in these matters. Heat is here required of us. Just as total passion and complete surrender were, in effect, forbidden to us on our old world, here they are, quite precisely, required of us. Do we have reservations, or scruples? Are there lingering vestiges of the barbaric conditioning programs to which we, even as innocent children, were subjected? Such reservations, such scruples, such vestiges, may be quickly removed with the lash.

"They are all cold," insisted Dorna.

The fellow in the chair reached out and I watched his hand, with apprehension. Then he placed it on my body.

I gasped, and drew back. I trembled. I closed my eyes. I whimpered.

I tried to hold myself still. He must remove his hand! He must! He must!

"She would be hot in her chains," laughed a man.

In another moment I felt I must thrust myself against him, again and again, desperately, kissing and whimpering.

Then, mercifully, he removed his hand from my body.

I looked up at him and, my eyes wide, licked and kissed his hand.

"They are all meaningless, hot-bellied sluts!" said Dorna. "That is all they are good for, rolling about, kicking, screaming, moaning, gasping, begging, in the furs!"

"They have many uses," said a fellow.

"Yes," laughed another.

"Slave belly!" snapped Dorna.

"I thought you said they were all cold," said a man.

"No," said Dorna. "It is rather that they are all trivially, meaninglessly hot."

"They are the hottest of the hot," said another man.

"It depends on the individual woman," repeated another.

Again that seemed to me true.

"They are the lowest of the low!" said Dorna.

"That is true," said a man.

"Yes," agreed another.

"Are you the lowest of the low?" asked the man.

"I do not know, Master," I said.

"You are," he assured me.

"Yes, Master," I said. If I had had any doubt as to how I had stood on this world before, I had none now.

Dorna laughed.

The fellow in the chair still held, in the palm of his left hand, some tidbits of meat.

He took one of these between the thumb and forefinger of his right hand and held it out to me.

I took it, and ate it.

I looked up at him. I wondered if he would again touch me.

I took the next piece of meat.

"You take your food from men," he said.

"Yes, Master," I said.

He then held another piece.

"See her being fed by hand!" said Dorna to those about.

I took the next piece of meat.

"Feed, little Earth beast!" laughed Dorna.

Suddenly the occupant of the chair turned toward Dorna and regarded her.

She turned white.

Her switch was taken from her.

Then the proud Dorna knelt beside me and, putting forth her head, angrily, in fury, was fed as I.

"You take your food from men," the occupant of the chair informed the proud woman kneeling beside me.

"Yes, Master," she said. That admission, I conjectured, had cost her much.

About us some men laughed, and some smote their left shoulders in approval.

In order that the matter be lost on no one, the occupant of the chair, of the last three pieces of meat, casting each to the floor of the dais, cast the first to the six-legged beast, which lapped it up instantly with its tongue, scarcely a scrap to such a maw, the second to me and the third to Dorna. Dorna and I, then, on all fours, from where we had retrieved that largesse which had been granted to us, cast to the floor of the dais, looked up at he who occupied the chair.

"May I rise, Master?" she asked.

Though a high slave it seemed she thought it wise, under the circumstances, to request this permission.

"Yes," he said.

She leaped to her feet.

I remained on all fours, before the chair.

Dorna was regarding me with fury. She was not pleased to have been knelt beside me, and fed as I was, nor to have to have pursued a bit of meat thrown to the floor, just as I had, as one might expect of a low girl. And there were others about. It was not as though she were naked, and alone with him.

I saw that she was very angry with me. Surely she must blame me for her humiliation. Too, I suspected she might, for some reason, be jealous of me. Was it my fault if I might be more beautiful or desirable than she? Did she resent the interest of the men in me? Did she fear that I might turn the head of the fellow in the chair? Might that be it? Did she fear that she might cease to be his preferred slave, if, indeed, she was that? I did not think that she was likely to have been a bred slave, except insofar as every woman, being a woman, is a bred slave. Perhaps she had once been a high free woman. But now, of course, somehow, it seemed that she had come into the collar. Perhaps her life now was quite different from what it had once been. Perhaps once she had even possessed some sort of authority, perhaps even over certain men. But now, it seemed, she must obey men, strive to please them and hope to be fed. Perhaps she hated me because I was from Earth. It was not that uncommon for women of this world to hate us, I had gathered. Perhaps they regarded us rivals, or something? Perhaps we were resented because many men of this world seemed to prize us, though, to be sure, they kept us under strict discipline, as perfect slaves.

They wanted us that way, and saw to it that that would be the way we would be kept.

Little on Earth prepares a woman for Gor.

"Return to the foot of the dais, and stand," said the man in the chair.

I backed down the steps of the dais, on all fours, and then, at its foot, rose to my feet.

"Bring slave wine," he said.

My heart leaped.

Dorna, angrily, descended the steps of the dais behind the thronelike chair and went again to the table beneath the roofed defense work.

I was pleased.

I looked down, shyly.

I had been given slave wine in the pens, of course, but it was not mine to call that to their attention. Indeed, the matter was undoubtedly noted on my papers. Perhaps these men merely wished to make sure of the matter. Or perhaps they merely wished to have me drink slave wine before them, either for their amusement, or because of the effects of this act, which were not only practical but symbolic. The effect of slave wines, at least those now in general use, seems to be indefinite, but they are commonly renewed annually, perhaps largely for symbolic purposes. One removes the effects of such wine by drinking a "releaser." The wines themselves could be sweetened, but are normally served bitter, which taste, as I understand it, is closer to that of the original root, the sip root, from which they are ultimately derived. The "releaser" or, at least, the wine in which it is mixed, the "breeding wine" or "second wine," is sweet. The breeding of slaves, like that of most domestic animals, is carefully supervised. Slave breeding usually takes place in silence, at least as far as speech is concerned. Similarly the slaves are normally hooded. They are not to know one another. This is thought useful in reducing, or precluding, certain possible emotional complications. The breeding takes place under the supervision of masters, or their agents, with endorsements being recorded on proper papers. I was pleased, of course, because, just as I took my feeding to be an indication that I was to be kept, if only for a time, so, too, I would interpret my being given slave wine as constituting something of a reassurance of my desirability, something in the nature of an indication that I might have been found, these men looking upon me, not without promise as a kajira, even though I was a woman of Earth.

Dorna handed me the goblet.

I could be every bit as good as a woman of this world, I was sure!

I did not even look at Dorna.

Who needed to look upon her?

I stood naked before the dais, and looked up at he who sat in the thronelike chair.

What could a woman of my world be before such men but their slave?

And they would have it so! Choiceless we would serve, docile, obedient, fearful, overwhelmed. They were our masters. Did they care what was in our secret hearts? Did they know we wished to be taken in hand, commanded, prized? Did they know we wished to be objects of such desire, that we wanted to be sought, tenaciously and powerfully, and relished? Did they know they had appeared in a thousand secret dreams, as our masters? Did they know that we were born for them, that we would be forever incomplete without them? I asked only, choicelessly, to love and serve such men.

"Drink the wine, slut!" hissed Dorna.

I did not look at her, but at the man in the chair. I felt suddenly very strong, and very powerful, though I was so small and weak. I had aroused the interest of these men as a kajira. I was sure of that. Let Dorna fear then for her place on a chain! I would happily, eagerly, compete with her for the privilege of kneeling before such men!

I lifted the wine a little upward and toward the man in the chair. I then looked at him over the rim of the goblet. My eyes spoke to him, I think eloquently, over the rim of the goblet, telling him doubtless what he knew, that before him there stood a slave.

I then drank. It was terribly bitter. I shook with the bitterness. I clutched the goblet with both hands.

"Do not spill any," warned Dorna.

Tears came to my eyes.

"Hurry, slave," said Dorna. "More quickly!"

I lifted the goblet again.

It seemed more bitter than that I had had in the pens.

"Hurry," said Dorna.

I could hardly take a sip.

"Hurry," she insisted.

I looked to her for mercy, but in her eyes there was none.

"Drink, slut," she said.

Then I tried to rush the fluid, that I might be finished before I could fully taste it.

It was mostly gone then and I held to the goblet, and shuddered, and coughed.

There was laughter.

In the cup there now remained only a tiny bit. I could even see the bottom of the goblet through what remained.

I looked again to Dorna, but she was merciless.

"Finish it," said she. "Drain the cup. Drink it to the last drop."

I finished the liquid, to the last drop. Dorna swept the goblet from my hand and took it away. I stood before the men, half bent over. I could still taste the bitterness, palpably, like tiny, foul damp grains in my mouth, on my tongue, my lips. I put my hands over my face, as much to wipe away my tears as anything. I trembled. Then I took down my hands and straightened up. I looked about a little. I sensed now that the men looked upon me somewhat differently. Now doubtless I was more what they wanted, or, perhaps, actually, merely more assuredly so. Was I not now, even more obviously than before, a plaything or a possession, something that might figure in the most casual of gratifications, something which now might be utilized even in amusement or sport, with no fear whatsoever of any inconvenient consequences?

I looked up at the man in the chair.

I now felt no more than a cringing, vulnerable slave.

"Let her be collared," he said.

I gasped, and put my hand to my throat.

"There are various collars," said Dorna.

"A common collar will do," said he.

I would not have expected to have worn other than a common collar, of course. There are many sorts of collars. The most familiar are the "common collar," which, in its varieties, tends to be flat and closely fitting, and the "Turian collar," which, in its varieties, is more rounded, and barlike, and fits more loosely. Both lock behind the back of the neck. Dorna wore a "common collar." Some other types of collars are decorative collars, holding collars, training collars and punishment collars.

"A used collar?" said Dorna.

"Certainly," said he.

I now realized that I was not as special or important as I had thought I might be, or had hoped I might be.

"We have them with a variety of names," she said.

I had expected, naturally, to be named. It is useful, after all, for a slave to have a name. It makes it easier to refer to her, to summon her, and so on. But I would have expected a master to have considered me with some care, as he might another form of animal, and to have then selected a name for me which, at least to his fancy, seemed to him fitting or suitable, a name which might then, sooner or later, be inscribed on a collar. To be sure, not all collars have the slave's name on them. Some apparently say things as simple as "I am the slave of so-and-so," "I belong to so-and-so," "I am the property of so-and-so," or "Return me to so-and-so," such things. An advantage of having the girl's name on the collar is in tracing her. After all, a rich man might own a hundred or more women. A typical collar might read, "My name is Tula. I am the slave of so-and-so." But it seemed now that I would not be considered, and named, with a collar, a new collar, a personal collar, eventually following the naming, as one might hope, being suitably inscribed, but that my name, whatever it was to be, would be the result of what already appeared on a collar. The collar would not be a function of the name, so to speak, but the name, it seemed, would be a function of the collar, of some name already on a collar!

"What do you suggest?" he asked. He seemed amused.

"She is from Earth," said she.

"So?" said he.

"I then suggest," said she, "one with an Earth-slut name on it."

"Would you do that to her?" he asked.

"Surely no harm could come of it," she said.

A man laughed. I felt uneasy.

"Still," said the fellow in the thronelike chair, "she seems to have learned at least a little about our world, and, for her time here, seems unusually adept at our language. Indeed she seems, subject to what she is, and her antecedents, quite intelligent. That is clear even from her papers. Perhaps then we should be kinder to her. Perhaps we should not do that to her."

"Oh, no, Master," said Dorna, quickly. "She is from that place and so that should be made clear in her name. Let her wear a name that makes clear her origin, so that men will know the treatment she deserves, and how to deal with her."

"Do you so hate those from that place?" inquired the man in the chair.

"Were it not for one such," she cried, "I would not be here in diaphanous silk with a collar on my neck!"

"One from such a place enslaved you?" asked he.

"No," she said, "but were it not for him I might now be tatrix in my city!"

"Your schemes failed," said a man.

"One from Earth brought your plans to naught," said another.

"Your city is now quite different from what it once was," said the man in the chair.

"You are quite fortunate to be here, and in a collar," said another man.

"Rejoice that you live," said another.

I understood nothing of this.

"But we are now considering this little kajira," said the man in the chair, returning his attention to me.

Dorna looked down at me, in fury.

I was frightened, and, unbidden, I knelt.

"She kneels well," said a man.

I knelt in position, of course.

I looked up at the man in the chair. I wondered if he would send for me this evening.

I trembled, even thinking of it.

Dorna, I think, was not unaware of the fact that I fell well within the regard of him in the great chair.

"You think that a collar with an Earth-girl name would be suitable?" he asked Dorna.

"Suitable, and appropriate, Master," she said, in honeyed tones.

This made me apprehensive, particularly when I recalled her remarks to the effect that this would let men know how I was to be treated, and such.

"Shall we give her an Earth-girl name?" asked he in the chair of the men standing about.

"Do so, Captain," said one of them, smacking his lips.

"Yes, Captain!" approved another.

Many Earth-girl names I would discover, understandably enough, I suppose, have an exotic flavor to the men of this world. They tend to find them sexually stimulating. They are also, like certain names of this world, regarded as slave names. I am not fully certain why that is. It may be because they tend to be unfamiliar names to the men of this world. It may be because they are found on women brought to this world to be slaves. It may be because we are often sold under such names, we then wearing them as slave names, put on us for the convenience of masters. To be sure, it may be for another reason, a simpler reason, the simple reason that we make excellent slaves. There are some names, of course, which are common to both this world and my old world, which suggests interesting questions of etiology. Similarly there are some names on this world which are on free women but which are also, often, found on slaves. One such is 'Dina'. It is not unusual for a name of this world, incidentally, to be put on an Earth girl brought here. This is not entirely unnatural, of course, as such names are often beautiful, and, naturally, more familiar to the masters. Too, such names sometimes help the new slave to make the transition to her new status and condition. Indeed, they sometimes help to free her of her inhibitions and increase her sexual responsiveness. In other cases, it seems clear that wearing an Earth-girl name, whether one which was once her own, now put on her as a slave name, or another Earth-girl name, now also, of course, only a slave name, can have similar effects on a girl from my world, she now recognizing herself as, and being, in effect, embonded fauna in an alien environment, singled out, and marked, as such, by the name. The contrast between the familiarity of the name, like a tie to an old world, and the new reality in which she finds herself can be both astonishing and stimulating. An interesting variation on this sort of thing is the giving of Earth-girl names to women of this world. This is a way of informing them, I gather, that great heat is now expected of them and that they are now, at best, to regard themselves as the lowest of slaves. To be sure, in time, as we learn our collars and condition, I think that names make little difference. Many names, of diverse sorts, are stimulating and beautiful. And, of course, perhaps most importantly, we are well aware that any name we wear, whatever it may be, is, when all is said and done, a slave name.

"Very well," said he in the chair. "Choose some collar with an Earth-girl name."

"Yes, Master!" said Dorna, eagerly. She hurried back to the roofed defense work. I gathered that there might be several collars there, some of which bore names which either were, or might be regarded as, Earth-girl names.

In a moment or two Dorna had returned to the dais with a collar. The collar was a common collar, flat, bandlike, gleaming, not unattractive, now closed. Looped about it was a string, on which there were two tiny keys. She showed the collar to the fellow in the chair. "Excellent," he said. She then showed the collar to others about the dais. "Quite suitable," said one fellow. "Indeed," added another. She then hurried down the steps, and showed it to others. One man laughed. "Good," said another. "Quite good," smiled another. "Superb," said another. "Excellent," said another. She then hurried back to the dais and the man in the chair opened the collar and slipped off the keys and string. He handed the keys to one of the fellows near the dais. I gathered that he would put them somewhere, or would turn them over to someone. I did not know where they would be kept. The collar was then returned to Dorna and she came down the steps of the dais and stood near me, where I knelt.

I looked upon the collar.

I would wear it.

I looked up at the man in the chair.

"You now have a name," he said. "It is that which is on the collar."

"Yes, Master," I said.

I did not, of course, at that point, know my name, only that I had one.

"Read it!" said Dorna, holding the collar before me.

"I cannot," I said. The script was unintelligible to me.

"She is illiterate," said the man in the chair.

"It is on her papers," said another.

"Stupid illiterate slave!" said Dorna. The man in the chair looked at me.

"You belong to the city," he said. "The collar is a state collar."

That I had not counted on! I did not even understand what it might be, to belong to a polity, a city, a state. Who then owned me, the polity, it seemed, the city, the state. But who did I serve? What did I do? I would doubtless learn.

"Prepare her for her collaring," said the man.

"Down on all fours, slut," said Dorna to me.

I immediately obeyed.

Dorna walked about me, in front of me, and handed the collar, opened, as it was, to the jailer, he who had brought me here, to the terrace. He was just a little behind me, and to my left.

Dorna then crouched down, and, combing it a little with her fingers, brought my hair forward, before my shoulders. She then arranged it. It hung down before me. My neck was muchly bared.

Dorna then rose to her feet and stood a bit before me and to my right.

"Is she prepared for collaring?" asked the man in the chair.

"She is," said Dorna.

"Tenrik," said the man in the chair.

"Yes," said the jailer.

"Are you prepared to collar her?" asked the man in the chair.

"Yes, Captain," said the jailer, whose name I now understood to be 'Tenrik'. We, of course, do not address free men by their names but as "Master." Similarly, we address free women as "Mistress."

"Collar her," said the man in the chair.

I was then collared.

I was naked on all fours, before the dais, on a barbaric world, a collared slave girl.

I heard Dorna laugh. Was she so much more than I? Did she not, too, wear a collar?

"She is pretty in a collar," said a man.

"They all are," said another.

Dorna turned away, angrily.

"Has she been collared?" asked the man in the chair.

"Yes, Captain," said Tenrik.

I gathered that this must be part of the ritual of the collaring, as there could be little doubt, now, about the light, inflexible, gleaming circlet gracing my throat.

"Kneel," said the man in the chair to me.

I knelt, in position. I knew I was beautiful in this position, collared. I had seen myself in mirrors, in the pens.

"Remove the collar," said the man.

I looked up at him, puzzled.

I could not read his eyes.

But one does not wait for a command to be repeated. I tried to remove the collar. I could not do so, of course, as it was of inflexible steel, and securely locked.

Dorna laughed. I threw her an angry glance. Let her remove her collar, if she could!

"Can you remove the collar?" asked the man in the chair.

"No, Master," I said.

"Do not forget it," he said.

"No, Master," I said.

"You are pretty," he said.

"Thank you, Master," I said.

"Take her to the ring," he said, gesturing to his left.

I looked up at him, startled, but had scarcely time to react for I was seized by the hair, by the jailer, and, half scrambling, half dragged, was conducted to the side, to a ring. There I was knelt down and my wrists were tied together and fastened to the ring. I looked wildly over my shoulder. The jailer was there, and was shaking out the five strands of a broad-bladed slave whip. "Masters?" I cried. Another man brought my hair well forward, again, as it had been for my collaring. "Please, no, Masters!" I cried.

"Do you think we are weak?" asked a man.

"No, Masters!" I said. "No, no, Masters!"

I had seen the six-legged creatures. I had seen the great birds. I had seen the warriors go forth. I had seen them return, sometimes with loot, with booty, at their saddles, silver and gold, and women.

Then the lash fell and I shook and sobbed. I had felt the whip before, twice in the pens, a stroke each time. I was not at all eager for a repetition of that experience.

Again the lash fell.

In the pens it had been a single-bladed lash.

Again I felt the leather.

I went to my belly, unable to remain on my knees. I could not believe what I felt.

I had heard of this whip before, the broad-bladed, five-stranded lash, designed for use on such as I, but never before had I felt it. It is to be clearly distinguished from many other forms of whip, in particular, from the "snake," a terrible whip used sometimes on men, beneath the blows of which even a strong man might die. The five-stranded lash, that to whose attentions I was now, to my dismay, to my misery, being formally introduced punishes terribly, but inflicts no permanent damage. It is designed to hurt, not injure. Indeed, it does not even mark the subject, which might reduce her value.

Again the lash fell.

"Please stop!" I begged.

What had I done? I had done nothing as far as I knew!

"Please stop, Masters!" I cried. How naturally I had called out to them as "Masters"! Of course, I knew by now who were the natural masters, and, indeed, on this world, even the legal masters. On this world the fundamental biological realities of dominance and submission, thematic throughout nature, had not been falsified. Indeed, they were recognized by, and acknowledged within, and confirmed within, the very institutions of this world. But even had it not been for my understanding of what I was, an understanding going back even to my native world, one which I had achieved, but had scarcely admitted to myself, long before I had been brought here, and one which I now understood even in terms of actual, significant, pertinent legalities of my condition and status, I would, I believe, in that moment, have called out to them as "Masters." I would think that any woman, even the most anesthetic, even the most stupid, even the most naive, even the most defensive, even the most resistant, even the most brainwashed, would have cried out so. In such moments shams dissipate. In such moments fundamental profound realities obtrude. I think that in such moments almost any woman would be likely to see through the illusions to which she has been subjected, through the lies that she has been taught, through the puppetry of her conditioning program. Behind the fabrications and prevarications of political facades lurks the *Realpolitik*, so to speak, of nature. And on this world, at least with respect to women such as I, the facades do not exist. We are put on our knees. We are collared. We are in our place. We obey. We serve.

Again the lash fell.

I writhed on my belly on the flagging. The stones felt cold, a considerable contrast with the flames that danced on my back. The feeding in the cell, and the watering there, that I had been fed and watered, and even that I had been given some bits of precious fruit were, it seemed, quite meaningless. So, too, surely had been the blanket, and even the wastes vessel! Had I understood such things as evidence of a special status, of special treatment, of special consideration, either of myself personally, or, more generally, of my sort of woman in this place? Had I interpreted such things as signs of lenience or tolerance? Had I understood them as signs of weakness or even, say, of a sort of soft kindness which I might be able, cleverly, in time, to exploit to my advantage? Let now, then, a stupid slave be disabused of such illusions!

Again the lash, like lightning, flashed downward. Again I wept. No longer could I cry out. I was helpless. I could do nothing for myself. I was completely dependent on others. I was in the hands of the masters.

Four times more the lash fell.

I then lay at the ring, on my belly, my crossed wrists stretched toward the ring, to which they were fastened. I tried to breathe. Tears had run down my cheeks. The flagging was wet from them. The bonds on my wrists, too, from earlier, were moistened by the tears. In one place the back of my wrist was wet where a tear had slipped between the cords.

The whip was being put away.

I lay there.

I suddenly realized that in all likelihood there had been nothing whatsoever personal in the beating. I had not, for example, at least as far as I knew, been displeasing, nor had I offended anyone, unless it be the other kajira. I had not done anything, at least as far as I knew, in any normal sense, to provoke, or merit, the beating. To be sure, reasons are not required for beating a slave. If the master wishes, they may be beaten simply at his whim. They are, after all, slaves. Similarly, as far as I could tell, these men bore me no ill will. I was, from their point of view, only a domestic animal. The beating then, in all likelihood, had not been punitive or even, really, disciplinary. Similarly it did not seem to be arbitrary. Rather it had been, it seems, ritualistic or institutional, and, presumably, by intent, instructive. It had been painful, but surely brief, strictly considered. I had not been informed of its purpose. I had not had to beg for the beating. I had not had to denounce myself before or during the beating. I had not had to count the strokes aloud, and so on.

The cords binding my wrists were freed from the ring, and then the cords were removed from my wrists.

I still lay at the ring.

I did not know if I could move.

The purpose of the beating I am sure, and thereby the intent, the rationale, of its inclusion in my induction here, so to speak, was neither unprecedented nor unusual. It was to help me understand certain things very clearly from the very beginning, that I was subject to the whip, that the men in this place were fully capable of using it on me, and that, if they saw fit, or felt so disposed, would do so. As I have suggested this lesson is neither unprecedented nor unusual. It is often thought to be a valuable lesson for a girl, particularly when she is brought into a new house.

Then I cried out as the jailer pulled me up to all fours by the hair and then, his fist in my hair, hurried me back to the dais.

I was now on all fours, at the foot of the dais. I looked up, through my hair, it muchly before my face now, and my tears, at he in the great chair.

"Do you wish to be beaten again?" he asked.

"No, Master! No, Master!" I said.

"Kneel," said he.

I obeyed.

"To whom do you belong?" he asked.

"To the state, Master," I said. To be sure, I did not know what state.

"Are you important?" he asked.

"No, Master," I said.

"Put your head to the floor," he said. "Clasp your hands behind the back of your neck."

I wept, and obeyed.

"Tenrik," said the fellow in the chair.

"Yes, Captain," said Tenrik.

I cried out.

Dorna laughed.

"Keep your hands clasped behind the back of your neck," warned Tenrik.

"Yes, Master," I wept.

My eyes widened.

"Oh!" I said.

"Steady," said Tenrik. "Clasp your hands."

"Yes, Master," I said.
"You feel that?" asked Tenrik.
"Yes, Master!" I said. "Yes, Master!"
I tried to hold myself still.
"Steady," said Tenrik.
"Yes, Master," I whimpered.
"Permit her to squirm," said the man in the chair.
"You may move," said Tenrik.
I began then, gratefully, to move, almost beside myself. I began to gasp.
"She is a pretty little thing," said the fellow in the chair.
"Yes," said one of the men near him.
"Oh!" I said.
"See the Earth slut!" said Dorna.
I began to cry out, softly, helplessly.
"Listen to her!" laughed Dorna.
I tried to stifle my cries.
"See her move," said a man.
"She cannot help herself," said a man.
"No," said another.
"A kajira," said a man.
"Yes," said another.
"She is pretty in her collar," said another.
"They all are," another reminded him.
"True," agreed the other.
Dorna made an angry noise.
There was laughter.
But no one paid her much attention.
"Oh!" I said.
"A quite pretty kajira," said another.
"Yes," agreed another.
"Oh!" I cried.
"There!" laughed a man. "She is over the brink!"
"She cannot return now," said another.
"She has gone too far. Tenrik has her now. She is lost!"
"No," said another. "She is on the verge."
"Please," I begged. "Please!"
"See?" said the man.

"Yes," said the other.
"Please, Master!" I begged.
"Captain?" asked Tenrik.
"Very well," said the man in the chair.
"Ohhh!" I cried.
"Now she is lost," said one of the men.
"Yes," said another.
"Ha!" cried Tenrik, a sudden cry, more that of a beast than a man.

I cried out. His hands were on me like iron. I could not have been held more helplessly in the vise of a branding rack. It seemed I was struck again and again.

Then I was left whimpering on the floor before the dais.

"Good," said Tenrik, appreciatively, now on his feet, his voice husky.

"You find the kajira satisfactory?" asked the man in the chair.

"Even in such a way, in such a time," said Tenrik. "It may only be conjectured to what lengths she might be brought, given different circumstances, and more time."

"Do you think she will soon reach the point where she is totally helpless?" asked the man in the chair.

"Yes," said Tenrik.

I lay before the dais. It was with bitterness, and chagrin, I heard myself so discussed. It was done so publicly, so candidly. Did they not know I was present? Did they not know others were present? I was being discussed as publicly, as candidly, as though I might be an animal. Then I realized again, of course, that I *was* an animal. I trembled. I already felt that I was, in such modalities, helpless. I was startled to learn I might become even more so. What then could I do? What then would I be? I had learned in the pens that I had an unusual potentiality for vitality, that somehow beneath the encrustations of a subtle, pervasive, insidious conditioning program, one to which I had been mercilessly subjected from childhood on, beneath, and in spite of, all the antibiological values, all the instilled inhibitions, reservations, hesitations and guilts, there lurked a primitive, powerful, natural, healthy responsiveness. This conditioning program, and its effects, now, bit by bit, fragment by shattered fragment, had been broken away from me. In its ruins I had emerged, like a beautiful thing, innocent from the sea. To be sure, I had emerged as something real, not mythical, something which found itself in a very real world, a world in which I learned I was a certain sort of thing, vulnerable, precious and beautiful, and not at all the same as certain other sorts of things which were quite as real as I, and the world, but quite different, as well.

"How worthless she is!" said Dorna.

"Not altogether," said a man.

There was laughter.

"Look at her body," said a man.

I knelt, covering my body as I could. It was muchly flushed. I covered my breasts. I did not want them to see the erection of my nipples. I was gentle. They were tender. I kept my head down.

"Position," said the man in the chair.

I must obey, instantly.

I knelt now with my back straight, back on my heels. My hands, now, were down on my thighs. My knees were spread. I kept my head down.

"Head up," said the man in the chair.

I lifted my head. There were tears in my eyes.

I knelt, collared, before masters.

"See her," said a man, considering the condition of my body.

"Yes," said another.

"She is a new slave?" asked a man.

"She is just out of the pens," said a fellow.

"We had her on her first retail sale," said another.

"Her brand was still smoking," laughed another. It was a saying.

"She was delivered, hooded, only a few days ago," said another.

"It is hard to believe that she is new to her collar," said a man.

"It is so certified," remarked another.

"I have seen her papers," said a fellow.

I knew I had papers but, of course, I could not read them. Such papers, as I understood it, begin with a girl's arrival in the pens. That is when her meaningful existence, her slave existence, begins. Nothing before that counts. There is no interest in our origins, save that we are of Earth, nor in our history or background. Such things have no relevance, or importance. They are all behind us. We are no longer free women. What interests them is merely that we are slaves, and our slave properties. A number of things are commonly found on the papers, which may be more or less detailed, for example, our brand type, a number of measurements, the sorts of training we have received, and such. There is also, usually, a place for sales endorsements, for when a girl changes hands. There is also a "remarks section," where miscellaneous information may be recorded.

"And already, so soon," said another, "she cannot help herself."

"She is hot," said another. "*Slave* hot."

"Superb," added another.

I blushed, even more.

"Yes," said one of the men, considering me, "a hot slave."

How could they speak of me so?

But, of course, I was an *animal*!

"Consider what she will be when the slave fires have been truly lit in her belly," said another.

"See," said a fellow, "she is afraid!"

"But see, as well," said another, "she is intrigued."

"Yes," said another. "She wants it. She wants it."

"And helplessly, desperately!" said another.

"Yes!" laughed another.

I tried not to meet the eyes of any of the men.

Could they so read me?

And could there be more? Could I be more helplessly theirs than I was now?

And what were "slave fires"?

I dared not speculate.

"She might easily be a silver-tarsk girl," said a fellow.

I did not understand the allusion, but gathered that a silver tarsk was a coin, and might be a good price for me.

Not only could my face and body, my beauty, if beauty it be, my dispositions, my talents, my capacities, my intelligence, my feelings, my emotions, my service, my pleasure, be sold! My *heat*, too, could be sold. It, too, could be put up for sale!

Men could *buy* it!

It could be purchased with the rest of me.

It is all of her, you see, the whole slave, that is *sold*.

"See her!" laughed a fellow.

My entire body, I fear, was a rage of subsiding arousal, and scarlet shame.

Could I help it if my body was so alive, and so much at their mercy? Too, had they not done much, the men of this world, to bring me to this helplessness?

They had not permitted me to hide from myself! They had forced me to be myself!

—*slave*.

"She is an Earth slut," said Dorna. "That is the way Earth sluts are. They are all like that!"

"I do not object," said a man.

"Nor I," said another.

There was laughter.

I wondered what I was supposed to do. Should I have tried to be unresponsive and frigid, and thus, in some absurd or perverted sense, have attempted to uphold the honor of the women of Earth? And it was not merely that in the pens many of my inhibitions had been forcibly removed from me and that my natural sexuality had been freed and encouraged, permitted to grow, to thrive and blossom, but that my reflexes had actually been honed, so to speak, to greater sensitivity. I was now no stranger to arousal and responsiveness. I had even received training. Besides, I was a kajira! If I proved to be displeasing, I could be punished severely, even slain.

And so I knelt before them, naked, in a position of submission and subservience, a collared slave girl.

I had a name, but I did not know it.

"A hot, curvaceous slut," said a man.

I knelt before them.

My body was no longer my own, but belonged now to the masters.

I must obey. I must serve.

How far away now was my old world, how far away now were the boutiques, the shops, the malls!

I wondered how my old friends, Jean, and Sandra, and Priscilla and Sally, would have looked, kneeling as I was. Doubtless much the same.

"See the whipped slave!" laughed Dorna. "See the utilized slave! See the Earth-slut slave!"

I stared ahead. I did not look at her.

"How are you, kajira?" inquired Dorna.

"I will obey! I will try to be pleasing!" I said.

"Do women kneel thusly, before masters, on your world?" inquired Dorna.

"Some, perhaps," I said. "I do not know!"

"Did you?" asked Dorna.

"No," I said.

"What is wrong with the men of your world?" she asked. "Are they not men?"

"I do not know!" I said.

"You did not kneel before men," she said.

"No," I said.

"But now you do," said Dorna.

"Yes," I said.

"Yes, what?" she snapped.

"Yes, Mistress?" I asked.

"Yes!" she said.

"Yes, Mistress," I said. I must then, it seems, address her as 'Mistress'. She was not free, of course. It was rather that I was so much less than she. I did not think she was "first girl" over me. I would have dreaded that. It seemed rather that I was a low slave, and she a high slave. And, perhaps she wished to be addressed as 'Mistress' by me because I was from Earth. She seemed to hate Earth, and those from Earth. I had gathered one from Earth might once have been involved in some shift in her fortunes. Now, of course, she had one before her who was from that world, and only a helpless kajira. I trusted that the men might protect me from her. After all, it was they who were the masters of us both.

"Earth slave!" sneered Dorna.

"Yes, Mistress," I whispered, frightened.

It was true that that was what I was, and all that I was.

Dorna turned about and hurried up the steps of the dais. I did not care for the expression I detected on her countenance the moment before she turned away. Then she was at the left side of the great chair, which it seemed was where she belonged, and there she turned about, and was now facing me, looking down at me. But she addressed herself to the man in the chair. "She is the lowest of the low, is she not! Master?" asked Dorna.

"Yes," said the man.

Dorna then leaned down, confidentially to him, and whispered something.

He smiled.

She then hurried down the stairs and, going behind me, seized my hair and held it up over my head, knotted securely in her grip, with both hands. I winced. She turned my head to the right and held it back, exposing the left side of my head to the chair. She then, retaining her grip on my hair with her right hand, with her left, with the tips of her fingers, her palm up, indicated, and lifted slightly, the lobe of my left ear. It was almost as though she might be a slaver, or a slaver's man, calling attention to some feature which might be of interest to a buyer. I did not understand what she was doing. "Pretty?" she asked. "Yes," said the man in the chair. Then she returned both hands to my hair and, still holding it up, over my head, twisted my head to the left, and back, thus exposing now the right side of my head to the chair. She kept her left hand in my hair, and I whimpered, at the tightness of her grip, and then displayed, in the fashion she had earlier, the right side of my head, indicating, and lifting, slightly, the lobe of my right ear. "Pretty?" she asked, again. "Yes," said the man in the chair. She returned both hands to my hair and held my head back, forcibly, cruelly, before the dais. "Let her ears be pierced!" she cried.

I heard cries of protest, of dismay, from several of the men about.

She held my head back, painfully, as she had before.

"Let her ears be pierced!" she cried.

"Yes!" suddenly said one of the men, almost inaudibly.

"She is very pretty," said a man.

"Why not?" suggested another.

"Can you imagine what she would look like, thusly?" said another.

"Excellent," said another man.

"She is only from Earth," said another.

"Yes," said another.

"Let her ears be pierced!" urged another.

"Yes!" said another, eagerly.

There was a silence.

"Yes," smiled the man in the chair, musingly, looking down upon me, with such a look of power, of possessiveness, of mastery and desire, that even held as I was I almost fainted. "Yes," he said musingly, "let her ears be pierced."

"Excellent!" cried Dorna, releasing my hair and stepping away from me, looking down at me with triumph.

"Excellent," said more than one man. I heard the striking of shoulders behind me. It is done with the flat of the hand, the left shoulder with the right hand.

I understood very little of this. I had not had my ears pierced on Earth, but I had considered it from time to time. I had not had the courage to do so. I suppose I regarded it as too barbaric, too sensuous. After all, I was not then owned. Such an act, too, it seemed to me, would be to make too public certain secrets of one. It would have seemed to me, in effect, to acknowledge one's inner realities, to call attention to what lay within one, to proclaim one's inner self publicly, to offer oneself for bondage, to beg, in a way, the collar. I certainly had no objection to having my ears pierced. Did this mean that I was so obviously a slave? I assumed, of course, they had in mind some natural sort of piercing, and not some grotesque mutilation. But I did not think that was involved here. The men of this world, with all their barbaric animal heat, with all their ardor, and power and mastery, loved and desired women, and relished them, and prized them. The last thing they would want to do would be to decrease the beauty or value of a woman. Even their strictest and most severe devices of punishment and discipline were designed with the protection of such features in mind. Indeed, if anything, these men insisted on the women making themselves, and keeping themselves, as desirable, attractive and beautiful as possible. That is the way they want us and, if necessary, even to the imposition of punishments and disciplines, that is the way they will see to it that we remain. To be sure, I was so poor a woman of Earth that I did not mind being desirable and beautiful. Indeed, I was eager to be such that I would bring a high price on a slave block. Indeed, as I am a slave, even on Earth I had wanted to be such, desirable and beautiful, and such as would bring a good price from lustful, bidding masters. But what distressed me now was the sense I gathered of the response of the men to the suggestion that my ears be pierced. I realized now, only too clearly, that this primitive, barbaric, homely little detail, seemingly so tiny in itself, the piercing of the ears, making possible the affixing of certain forms of ornaments, seemed, for some reason, quite momentous to them. I gathered that once my ears were pierced there would then be, at least from their point of view, something quite different about me.

"Come here," said the man in the chair. I regarded him, but he was looking at Dorna.

"Master?" she said.

He pointed to the floor of the dais, before the chair.

Frightened, she hurried there, and knelt before him. He drew her more closely to him, she still kneeling, and he bent forward. He took her head in his hands and brushed back her hair. "Master?" she said, uncertainly. He turned her head to one side, and then to the other.

"Pretty," he said.

"No!" she said. "No!"

He turned to one of the men to the side. "Let her ears be pierced," he said.

"No!" cried Dorna. "No!" She leaped to her feet and turned about, fleeing, stumbling down the steps of the dais and then, at its foot, half bent over, turned about, facing the man in the chair. "No!" she cried. "No!"

He regarded her.

"No, please, no!" she said. She did not seem so haughty then, so arrogant, so imperious, so hard. She seemed then only what she was, a female, in the hands of men.

He did not speak, but continued to regard her.

She then drew herself up, proudly, as though she might be other than what she was. "Never!" she said. "Never!"

"Perhaps," he said, "you would prefer to go to the ring." She took a step backward, aghast.

"I am Dorna," she said.

"That may be changed," he said.

"I am a high slave!" she protested.

"That, too, may be changed," he said.

"No!" she said.

"Does Dorna want to go to the ring?" he asked.

"No!" she said, shuddering.

"What?" he inquired.

"Dorna does not want to go to the ring," she whispered.

"You seemed to find it amusing when the Earth slave was at the ring," he said.

"Be kind," she begged.

"But then she is only an Earth slave," said the man.

"Yes! Yes!" said Dorna.

"But you would doubtless wriggle at the ring, as well as she," he said.

I did not want to meet the eyes of any of them. I was frightened, kneeling before the dais. Dorna and I were the only two women on the terrace. We were both slaves.

"Please, no, Master!" said Dorna. I noted she called him "Master."

"Perhaps you would enjoy being at the ring, and then being publicly utilized, as was she," said the man in the chair.

"No, Master!" cried Dorna.

"Your silk can be taken from you," said the man in the chair.

"Please, no, Master!" she said.

"Perhaps it could be given to the Earth slave."

"No, Master, please!" said Dorna. She cast me a wild glance. I saw she was genuinely frightened.

"The Earth girl might be made a high slave and you a low slave," he said.

"Please, no, Master!" she said.

"The word 'Master' sounds well on your tongue," he said.

"Yes, Master!" she said. "Thank you, Master!"

"I think you do not use it frequently enough," he said.

"Forgive me, Master!" she said. "I will try to improve my behavior, Master!"

"Does Dorna want to keep her silk?" he asked.

"Yes, Master!" she said.

He regarded her.

"Dorna wants to keep her silk!" she cried. She clutched the silk about her, desperately.

"But perhaps I have a better idea," he mused.

"Master?" she asked.

"Perhaps you should be returned to Tharna in chains," he said.

At this Dorna turned white and flung herself to her knees at the foot of the dais.

"Oh, no, Master!" she cried.

"They might enjoy seeing you again," he said.

She began to weep and tremble. She looked small, and piteous, and female, at the foot of the dais.

"Look up," he said.

She did, through wild tears.

"They might enjoy having you again within their walls," he mused.

"No," she sobbed.

"I wonder what it might be, after the procession through the streets, you naked, in chains, on a chain neck-tether, conducted through the jeering crowds, goaded by spear points, hastened by whips, and after the public humiliations, would it be torture and the spear? Presumably not, as that is too simple. Too, that is too honorable. And you are now merely bond. Perhaps then you might be nailed to the great gate or to the public boards. It can take days to die in such a fashion. There is little bleeding. Or, more quickly, you might be cast to sleen, or fed to starving urts, or be flung to the fangs of dry, thirsting leech plants."

"No," she whispered. "Please, no."

"You might be spared," he said. "You might be enclosed in a cage, suspended in the piazza. Others might then learn from your fate a lesson. You might be put in a dozen chains and flung into the deepest dungeon in the city. Perhaps then, eventually, you would be forgotten, save perhaps by a warden and some urts. You might even be kept chained in the public tarsk pens, in the mud, for years, there to compete naked, mocked by all, for your swill."

She put her head down, trembling.

"To be sure," said he, "as you are only a slave, it might be amusing for them to keep you chained to a ring in the lowest brothel in the city, your use free to any and all.

"Lift your head," he said, sharply.

She looked up. Tears streamed down her face.

"Your face is bared," he said.

She sobbed.

"The faces of slaves should be bared," he said, "that their tiniest expressions may be read."

Again she wept.

"No longer," said he, "can you hide behind a mask of silver, or gold."

"No, Master," she wept.

"Your face is bared," he said, "as is fitting for the face of a slave."

"Yes, Master," she said.

"But there is another possibility," he mused, "an interesting one, one other than merely returning you in chains to Tharna."

"Master?" she asked, frightened.

"You could be returned to he from whom you were stolen," he said.

"No!" she screamed, in terror. "No! No!" She suddenly, wildly, crawled up the steps of the dais, and flung herself to her belly before the man in the chair. She pressed her lips again and again to his feet, fervently, in terror, covering them with frantic kisses. "No," she begged. "Please, no, Master!"

"Do you not know how to kiss a man's feet?" he inquired.

She sobbed, and then delicately, humbly, softly, submissively, devotedly, with much care, with great attentiveness, with exquisite sensuousness, with her tongue as well as lips, addressed her ministrations to his feet and sandals.

"Better," said he.

I was frightened at the terror exhibited by the slave. The mere thought of being returned to some former master, from whom, I gathered, she had been stolen, was apparently more dreadful to her, more fearful to her, than the assemblage of fates which had just been outlined before her, those possibly consequent upon her being returned to Tharna, some city into the power of which, it seemed, she would be ill-advised to fall.

"I would think you might enjoy being returned to your former master," said the man in the chair, "he who first captured you, and put the collar on you."

"No! No!" she said.

"He is rumored to be one of the finest swordsmen in the world," said the man.

She sobbed, and continued to kiss his feet.

"Did he not slay a retinue of one hundred men before he reached the curtains of your palanquin, to tear them aside?"

She did not raise her head, but trembled.

"It was he who first removed the mask from you," he said.

"Yes," she whispered, shuddering.

"And did you not, even as a free woman, kneel in the dust beside the palanquin, your mask taken from you, and kiss and lick the blood from his sword?"

"Yes," she said.

"I wonder that he was interested in you," said the man.

"Master?" she asked, lifting her head a little.

"His sword could have won him many women, women whose attractions he would presumably have had little difficulty in detecting," he said.

I assumed he meant women such as I—slaves, suitably clad, lightly and revealingly, women of whose charms there could be little doubt.

"Could he have known that you were as beautiful as you are?" he asked.

"Thank you, Master," she said.

"It would not seem so," he said.

"But doubtless he was pleased to see that you were beautiful," he said.

"Perhaps, Master," she said.

"But he must originally have had you in mind for some other purpose," he said. "He must have had some use in mind for you."

"Master?" she asked.

"But the first use was doubtless merely that you would follow him naked, and collared, bearing his shield."

"That was the second use," she said.

"Of course," he said.

"I would think," he said, "that you would have enjoyed belonging to him."

"No!" she said, in terror.

I was frightened to think of such a master, one who inspired such terror. I shuddered. What manner of man might he be? As slaves, of course, it is appropriate, and not at all unusual, for us to retain a healthy fear of our masters, particularly if we suspect we may have been in some detail remiss or may have been in some respect less than perfectly pleasing, for we are, after all, their slaves. We are totally dependent on them in all things, and they have absolute power over us. More simply put, they are master.

"For you two would seem to have much in common," he said.

"Do not return me to him," she wept.

"But you would seem much the same as he."
"No, no!" she said.
"No?" he said.
"No," she said. "I am a female."
"You now understand that?" he asked.
"Yes," she said.
"It seems he knows how to keep a slave," said the man.
She shuddered.
"What did he want you for, other than the usual purposes of a slave?" he asked.
"I do not know," she said.
"Perhaps we are too lenient with you here," he mused.
"No, no," she whispered.
To be sure, it did not seem likely to me that this was a place in which men might be criticized for being too lenient with their slaves.
"I wonder what we should do with you," he said.
"Do not return me to him, I beg it!" she wept.
I saw she was terrified. I thought of the master she feared. From her reactions even I, who did not even know him, began to tremble. From her fear I was afraid. I was afraid even to think of such a man. Then I thought that perhaps I now better understood the men in this place, that they might steal from such a man. To be sure, I did not know the whole story. Perhaps her former owner, he under discussion, was ignorant of the identity of her thief. Or perhaps the men here had merely purchased her, or captured her later, from another. Between the man she feared and this place she might have changed hands a dozen times, as any property.
"I wonder what I should do with you," he said.
"Keep me!" she begged.
She did not request her freedom, of course. How insulting and absurd would have been such a request of men such as these. We wore our collars and would continue to wear them. They liked us in our collars, and found us precious in them. It would be as absurd and meaningless for us to be freed on this world as it would be for a dog or horse to be freed on my former world. It is said that only a fool frees a slave girl. It is true.
"Keep me, Master," she begged. "Keep me, Master."

She then, lowering her head again, began again, beggingly, pleadingly, submissively, with tears, desperately zealous to placate and please him, to lick and kiss his feet. She did this quite well, I thought. My fear did not prevent me from observing her carefully. I was only a collared Earth-girl kajira. One might even have said, as one had, as the saying has it, that my brand was still smoking. Surely it was fresh. I had much to learn. Knowing suitable placatory behaviors, sometimes necessary to pacify and appease these impatient men, these demanding and powerful masters, is something very much in a girl's best interest. Indeed, being able to please and placate a male can sometimes mean the difference between life and death, between being ordered to the furs, there to be incontestably ravished and subjugated, there, gratefully, to be totally conquered—and being hurled to ravening sleen.

She lifted her head to him, timidly, after a time, doubtless anxious to examine his visage for some clue, however faint, as to his mood, seeking there some trace, however tiny, which might hint at what was to be done with her.

I myself could not determine what he might be thinking.

"Have my ears pierced, Master!" suddenly said Dorna.

"What?" he asked.

She rose to her knees, begging, before him. "I beg to have my ears pierced, Master!" she said. "I beg it!" She turned her head before him, to one side and then to the other. She displayed herself, desperately, pleadingly. She indicated her ear lobes. "Let my beauty, if beauty it be," said she, "be enhanced with earrings!"

There was laughter behind her, but Dorna paid no attention to it.

"Are you not curious to know what I might look like in earrings, Master?" she asked.

"Do you not fear that such might enflame your belly?" he asked.

"Let it then be enflamed!" she said.

"You do not care how much of a slave you become?" he asked.

"No, Master!" she said.

"Perhaps I could have your ears pierced, and have you put in earrings, and then have you returned to your former master," he mused.

"Oh, please, no!" she wept.

She sank down, again, to her belly.

"It is interesting to ponder what might be done with you," he said.

"I am Master's slave," she said. "It will be done with me as Master pleases."

Dorna then, clearly, was not a state slave. He in the chair was clearly her master. I did not even know his name. He was an officer in this city, it seemed, a captain, or perhaps even a high captain.

"Do you think you have been pleasing?" he asked.

She lifted her head, tears in her eyes. "I have not been pleasing," she said. "Forgive me, Master. Let me begin again. I beg to be permitted to begin again. Let me prove to Master how good a slave I can be."

"Kneel," he said.

She rose to her knees before him.

"Speak," said he.

"I beg to have my ears pierced," she said.

He regarded her.

"Dorna begs to have her ears pierced," she said. "Dorna, who is Master's humble and abject slave, begs to have her ears pierced."

"But it has already been decided," said he, "that Dorna will have her ears pierced."

"Yes, Master," she said.

"Dorna does not wish," said he, "to be returned to her former master?"

"No, Master!" she said.

"What does Dorna wish?" asked he.

"To be kept by Master!" she said.

"I see," he said.

"Let me prove to you that I am a new slave," she begged. "Let me prove to you that I am not totally worthless in your collar!"

"Perhaps I shall make the decision tonight," he said, "after your ears have been pierced."

"Yes, Master!" she exclaimed.

"I am curious," he said, "to see what you will look like in earrings."

"Yes, Master," she said.

"See Dorna on her knees," said a man.

"See her beg," said another.

"I would like to see her in earrings," said another.

"She belongs in them," said another.

"A bared face and earrings," laughed one, "is a far cry from a mask of silver or gold."

"She might make an interesting slave," speculated another, "a common slave, I mean."

"Yes," said another.

"I beg to be pleasing to Master," said Dorna.

"Hear Dorna begging to be pleasing to a man," said a man.

"Doubtless she did not foresee this when she fled Tharna," said a man.

"No," laughed another.

Doubtless Dorna could not have helped, on one level or another, to have been aware of the comments of the men. But if she was aware of them, she gave little, if any, indication of it. Her primary attention was clearly on he in whose power she lay totally, as a helpless slave.

"Do you think you are capable of being pleasing?" he asked.

"Yes, Master," she said.

"And you wish to be kept?"

"Yes, Master!"

"At least for a time?"

"Yes, Master!" she said.

"Tonight," said he, "I will give you an opportunity to please me."

"Thank you, Master," she said.

"Your performance tonight will help me decide," he said, "as to whether or not there is any point in keeping you among my women."

"Yes, Master," she said.

"You understand?"

"Yes, Master."

"Do you think you will do well?" he asked.

"I shall do my best to be pleasing in all ways," she said.

"You will endeavor to prove acceptable?" he asked.

"Yes, Master," she said.

"But I require more than mere acceptability in the performances of my women," he said.

"That is well known amongst us, Master," she said.

"It will be a test, will it not be?" he asked.

"Yes, Master," she said.

"What level do you think you must attain to pass this test?" he inquired.

"I know that I must be superb!" she sobbed.

"And do you think you can attain such a level?" he asked.

"I will do my best, Master," she said.

He then spoke to one of the fellows near the great chair, the same to whom he had given the keys to my collar. "Take this slave away," he said, indicating Dorna. "Send her to me tonight, bathed and perfumed, in earrings, with but a single veil."

"Yes, Captain," said the man. "Slave," said he to Dorna, indicating a location near the wall, where a flat trap had now been thrown back, revealing a stairwell. "Yes, Master," said Dorna to the man. Then she put her head down and, quickly, kissed each of the feet of the man in the chair. "Thank you, Master!" she said. Then she leaped up, and hurried to the stairwell, preceding the man down. She would not dally, nor make him wait. She was a slave.

Attention was then returned to me, and, instantly, frightened, I adjusted my position, so that I knelt with perfection. Under the gaze of he in the chair I subtly, frightened, widened my knees, slightly. One feels terribly vulnerable kneeling before men in the common position. It makes it so clear that one is a slave, and, too, so clear, the sort of slave one is.

I did not know where I was. I did not know my name. I did not know why I had been purchased. I did recall that he in the chair had speculated to Dorna, before his displeasure had been incurred, that she would not be displeased with my disposition. That did not reassure me. To be sure, perhaps it meant only that I was not to be entered into his household. I was, I had learned, a property of the state in this place, whatever place it might be. Dorna was now no longer on the terrace. She would thus, not immediately, at least, learn my disposition. To be sure, sometime or another it might well come within her purview. Perhaps then, I thought, swallowing hard, she might not be displeased to learn it. I had thought of her immediately as a rival, and doubtless she had thought of me in this fashion, as well, even though I might be a new slave. Indeed, even in the pens I had looked upon the others, and doubtless they upon me, or most of them, as rivals. But I suppose this is natural enough for women, even on my world. Even those who seem most hostile to men also seem, perhaps paradoxically, to desire to be pleasing to them. Perhaps this is an implicit recognition, even in such unlikely quarters, that men are the masters. But the matter is clear on this world, at least with women such as I, and she, Dorna. Here it is obvious that we are the slaves and men the masters, and that we are to please the masters. In this fashion it is not only the case that kajirae within the same house are likely to find themselves in rivalry, but that in the culture as a whole, wherever we are, on whatever chain, fastened to whatever wall, running whatever errand, heeling whatever masters, we tend to have a sense of such things. For example, we commonly strive on the sales block to bring the highest prices. I do not think this is merely because we wish to be purchased by more affluent masters, which suggests that our life may be easier, but because of the personal vanities involved. Each wishes to be the most precious, the most costly. This is perhaps not so different from my old world, except that here women do not vend themselves, and take their own profit, but are rather vended by others, who take the profit on them. How many women, I wonder, marry truly for love, and only love? Do we not consider many other matters—the finances of our potential spouse, his education, his family connections, his position in society, the likely location of his domicile, the presumed trajectory of his career, the prestige of the match, and such? But here, as I have suggested, we do not sell ourselves, reaping our own profits. No, here we are sold by others, and it is these others who will reap the profits. It is they who will make the money. It is ours, rather, to be fully pleasing, and see that we obey with perfection.

"She kneels well," said a man, observing me.
"She is from Earth," said another.
"Yes," said another.
"That is a land," said one.
"Where is it?" asked another.
"To the south," said a fellow.
"No," said another. "It is a world."
"A world?"
"Yes, a different world."
"Are you certain?"
"Yes."
"Do not be foolish," said another.
"No," said another. "He is right."

"Tarns can fly there?" asked one.

"No," said another, "it is reached in ships."

"Slave ships?" said one.

"Perhaps, among others," said a man.

"Tarns do not care to leave the sight of land," said another, as though reminding his peer of something.

"Of course," said the fellow.

"If it is another world," said a fellow, "how can ships sail there?"

"They are special ships," he was informed. "They float on clouds, as other ships on water."

"Oh," said the man.

I had occasionally heard conversations of this sort in the pens, particularly among the lower guards. The men of this world, I had gathered, differed considerably among themselves in their sophistication and information. Some seemed quite aware of the nature of my world, its civilizations, its views as to the correct relations among the sexes, and so on, and others seemed astonishingly ill-informed and naive. I suspected that the man in the chair, and certainly the higher officers and guards in the pens, were quite cognizant of most of the pertinent realities of my world of origin. This world seemed one of technological paradox. I had been brought here by a technology which currently, at least in certain dimensions, exceeded that of my old world. And yet here many men, if not most, seemed unclear as to its nature, if not completely ignorant of its very existence. How astonishingly paradoxical seemed my situation! Here on this world, where men seemed so proud, so untamed, so unbroken, so free, so mighty, so hot-blooded, on this world seemingly so primitive, so splendid and barbaric, on this world of leather, and silk and iron, not of plastics and synthetic fibers, of heat and love, not of tepidity and hypocrisy, of ardor and skill, not of boredom and gadgetry, on this world where men had mastered monsters and seemed ready, at a word, to adjudicate disputes with edged weapons, I knelt before a dais, naked and collared, as a barbarian slave girl. Yet I could not have been brought here except in virtue of an obviously advanced technology. It was almost as though I had been somehow magically flung into the past, into a world quite different from my own, a world whose ways I must speedily learn and in which I must learn, if I would survive, to be obedient and pleasing. But there was no magic here, no enchanted rings or sorcerer's wands.

Things here were quite real, as real as the stone flagging beneath my knees, as real as the mark in my left thigh. A sophisticated technology may have brought me here but I knelt here, literally knelt, and on my throat was a steel collar. Clearly, or, at least, so it seemed, the technology was not the property of all the men of this world but, at best, of some of them. Too, it might be furnished, I supposed, by others, say, allies or confederates, not of this world itself. That, too, I supposed, was a possibility.

"But what matters it," asked a man, "the place from which she came, and whether it is a land, and where it might be, to the south, or elsewhere, or a world, and wherever it might be?"

"It matters naught," said another man.

"It is enough," said another, "that it be a suitable orchard from which slave fruit may be plucked, a suitable field from which may be harvested crops of slaves, a place of suitable herds, from which may be selected slave meat."

"True," said another.

"Women from Earth make good slaves," said another.

"Excellent slaves," said another.

"Yes," said another.

I supposed there were reasons for this. Yet, I think, ultimately, the matter has to do not with geographies but with biology, not with origins but with nature. If we made good slaves it did not have ultimately to do with the fact that we were from Earth, even given its terrible conditioning programs, but that we were women. Ultimately, there are women, and there are men.

"A pretty kajira," said one.

"Yes," said another.

"Yes," agreed another.

I knelt there, helplessly. I was very conscious of my nudity, my collar, my brand.

"Yes," said another.

How helpless one is!

"Yes," said yet another.

I was very much afraid. Men on this world, you see, had not surrendered their sovereignty.

"She is quite desirable," said another.

"Yes," said another.

This frightened me, but I was pleased, as well. What woman does not wish to hear that she is desirable?

But women here must fear. Men here, you see, had not surrendered their sovereignty!

They had power, and women, at least those such as I, did not.

They could do with us as they pleased. We were slave. They were master.

Some of the men walked about me. I did not dare to meet their eyes. A kajira knows when she is being appraised, frankly and openly, from the top of her head to the tip of her toes.

"Lovely hair," said one.

"Note the perfection of the figure," said another.

And thus did they assess the property and animal before them.

"Superb," said one.

"Yes," said another.

"It is a shame that one had to pay for her," said another.

"True," said another.

They preferred, it seemed, to take their women, perhaps to stalk them with stealth, as game, then to spring the nets or snares at some time of their choosing, some moment of unsuspected ripeness, or to seize them in capture strike, or to take them by theft, perhaps roping and gagging them in their own beds, there to enjoy them, and then to hood them and carry them off, bound hand and foot, to this aerie, or at sword point, in open challenge, or even to obtain them in raids and war, perhaps as incidental loot or perhaps, even, as the principal object of such endeavors, for women on this world, you see, even free women, not just women such as I, count as an accustomed and legitimate form of loot or booty, as much, or more, than gold and silver, and fine cloth, and such things. Indeed, wars have been fought to obtain us. These are often referred to as "slave wars."

The men stepped back.

Many seemed interested in me. I wondered if I would be sent to any of them. I wondered if he in the chair might sometime, recalling me, have me sent to him, perhaps, as he had suggested with Dorna, in earrings and a single veil, if that. I would surely try to please him. But I feared the feel of such hands on me. I feared I might begin to spasm at the first sight of him.

You must understand. We are totally theirs.

I lifted my eyes, timidly, to he in the great chair. But he had now turned to others. He was conversing with them. Their business, I gathered, had nothing to do with me. A wave of irritation coursed through me. I had been much the center of attention, but now, it seemed, I was forgotten. It was strange to be kneeling so conspicuously before the dais, but neglected. One was, of course, familiar with the studied inconspicuousness of the serving slave, for I had learned it in the pens. One serves humbly, self-effacingly, eyes cast downward. When not serving one kneels deferentially, silently, well back, and to the side, of the low tables. When then one is summoned to further service, by perhaps so little as a glance or a snapping of fingers, one leaps up and hurries forward, perhaps then, on one's knees, to clear, or perhaps to fetch and then serve, again kneeling, the tiny cups of strong coffees, or black wines, the shallow silver bowls of white and yellow sherbet.

And so I knelt there, in correct position, naked and collared.

My thoughts wandered back to my old world, to my life there, to my classes and classmates, to the shops, the malls, to my friends, Jean, and Priscilla, and Sandra, and Sally.

I could feel my hair blown about my shoulders by the wind sweeping across the terrace. It was now a bit before my face. I did not break position to adjust it.

My back stung from the lash.

On my neck was a steel collar. I could not remove it.

"Slave," said the man in the chair.

"Yes, Master!" I said, eagerly.

Once again I felt eyes upon me.

"As you have doubtless surmised," said he, "your disposition has been decided."

"Yes, Master," I said. He was the sort of man whom I think even a free woman might have found herself drawn to address as "Master."

"Perhaps you have guessed what it is to be?" he said.

"No, Master," I said.

But naturally my mind raced ahead. I had learned in the pens that I was unusually beautiful and desirable. Similarly I had trained quickly and exceedingly well. Too, though I was often terrified, I, on the whole, loved my new life. In it I and my sex had for the first time in my life become truly meaningful. No longer was the most important thing I was to be regarded as an inconsequential accident, as a mere irrelevancy. Rather its significance was recognized and, by strong men, would be uncompromisingly enjoyed and exploited. I had found my life and my meaning in bondage. I had, in this far place, for the first time in my life, come home to myself. I had once in the pens jested with a guard, confiding to him that it seemed I was "born for the collar." I have not forgotten his reply. He said, simply, "So, too, are all women." But with respect to my disposition I was sure, given my beauty and desirability, and my talents, even such as they were now, that it would be a lofty one. I was thinking in terms of the high slave, one of great value, one who might even expect sandals, to say nothing of costly, if revealing, silks, and perhaps even a golden collar. Had not the female, Dorna, a high slave, clearly exhibited jealousy of me? Perhaps I would be first girl in the slave quarters. I might even be given a talmit and a quirt, that my authority might be clear. I might receive further training. I might be displayed with pride to a master's acquaintances, or perhaps, as a state slave, to foreign diplomats or merchants. I would not need to fear the lash like a common girl. I might be often called to the couch of high men, to kneel there, belled and perfumed, and kiss the coverlets, and then, bidden, to insinuate myself sinuously into their arms.

"Beware, slave," said the man in the chair, "of making a false step."

"Master?" I asked.

"Hood her," he said.

Someone behind me, whom I did not see, placed a hood over my head and drew it down, over my features. It was then buckled shut, under my chin.

In a moment then I was lifted in someone's arms, perhaps those of the jailer, and carried about. In a moment or so I was disoriented in the hood.

Some hoods are cruel but this was a simple, common hood, one which did not even contain a gag, part of its structure. Hoods are, of course, far more effective than the common blindfold. Sometimes we must kneel in hoods for hours, forbidden to move. We do not even know at such times whether we are under surveillance or not. Can we move with impunity, for no one is watching? Or is someone watching, and, if we move, we will be punished, terribly? We do not know. We kneel in the hood, unmoving, docile and obedient. There are many purposes for hoods. Sometimes we are put in them and handed about. I had worn one almost constantly in my journey to this place. Accordingly I had no idea how I had come here or what place this was. I have indicated, too, that such devices are frequently used in the matings of slaves.

I was now set down, on my feet. I seemed to be standing on some sort of board. My hands were free, of course. But I had not received any permission to remove the hood.

"Walk forward," said a voice.

The board seemed wide enough. It must have been twelve or fourteen inches in width. I felt its edges once or twice with one or the other of my feet.

"She walks well," said a man.

I had, of course, been taught in the pens how to walk. I continued to walk forward. I was a little uneasy, as the board seemed to move a bit under my weight. "Masters?" I called.

"Continue," said a man.

"Stop!" he said.

Naturally I stopped.

"Remove the hood," said the voice.

I unbuckled the hood, and drew it from my head.

I screamed and staggered, and put out my hands, wildly.

Below me yawned an immense drop, one of hundreds of feet, with jagged rocks below.

In an instant, with rapid steps, sure-footedly, the jailer had reached me, lifted me up, turned about and returned me, trembling, wild-eyed, to the foot of the dais.

"Beware of making a false step," said he in the chair.

"Yes, Master! Yes, Master!" I cried from my belly, a terrified slave girl.

I had learned a lesson. This was not a place where, nor were these men among whom, false steps would be wise.

The jailer, with some difficulty, pried my fingers from the hood, and handed it behind me to someone.

"Tenrik," said the man in the chair.

"Captain," said the jailer.

"Bind her, hand and foot," he said.

My hands were pulled behind me and my wrists crossed. In a moment, with a dispatch and effectiveness that could only have been the result of long experience in such things, the knots had been jerked tight. Then my ankles were crossed, and, with a separate bit of cord, lashed together.

"Carry her to the wall," said the man in the chair.

The jailer then lifted me up and carried me in his arms to the wall, on which he stood, I in his arms. The wind blew fiercely there. I whimpered piteously, terrified.

"Look down, slave girl," called the man in the chair.

"Please, no, Master!" I cried.

"Must a command be repeated?" he inquired.

"No, Master!" I wept.

I turned my head and, moaning, looked down. The rocks were hundreds of feet below.

"It is enough," he said.

I closed my eyes, and put my head back, tightly, against the chest of the jailer, trembling.

"You realize you could be easily hurled to the rocks below?" inquired the man in the chair.

"Yes, Master!" I said, not even opening my eyes.

"Sleen come there at night, looking for bodies," said the man in the chair.

"Yes, Master," I said, keeping my eyes shut.

I was then carried down from the wall and deposited, again, before the dais. I lay on my side. How welcome was the stone flagging of the terrace floor!

I looked up, fearfully, at the man in the chair.

"You understand something now of what it might be to be a slave in this place?" asked the man in the chair.

"Yes, Master!" I said.

"You will try to be a good slave, will you not?" he inquired.

"Yes, Master!" I cried. "Yes, Master!"

I lay there, on my side, bound. They then attended to other business. I was sure that they were through with me now, at least for all practical purposes. Why then was I not carried away, or conducted somewhere?

Somehow, now, I was no longer so certain that my disposition, apparently already determined, would be as lofty and certain as I had hitherto conjectured.

I did not even want to go near the wall again, not even to the parapet. The board I had trod earlier was wide and, objectively, it was easy to tread, even hooded as I was. Certainly the folks of this world seem to have little fear of such narrow places. They are accustomed to them. They think little more of treading them than I might have of treading a sidewalk on my old world. Much depends on what is familiar to one, what one grows used to. Many of the "high bridges" in a city such as this would be regarded as quite alarming, at least initially, by most of those of Earth, as they might range from a foot to four or five feet wide, and arch over frightful drops, sometimes to a maze of bridges below, but these people, who have grown up with them, seldom give them a thought. The point of the high bridges seems to be twofold, first, they are lovely in their traceries against the sky and between the cylinderlike buildings, and such things are important to these people, who seem to have an unusually developed aesthetic sense and, second, they have military value, inasmuch as they are easy to defend. Each of these cylinders, in its way, can constitute a stronghold, a fortress or keep. To me, of course, traversing these bridges, particularly in the beginning, constituted a nightmare of terror. I would sometimes crawl on them, scarcely able to move. I would sometimes go to great lengths to avoid them, even though I must then hasten, gasping, running, on my errands, the message tube tied about my neck, my hands braceleted behind me, that I might not have been thought to have dallied. I am still uneasy on such bridges. My fears sometimes occasion amusement among the masters. But my fears, I have been told, are not unprecedented, and, indeed, are not unusual among girls of my sort, girls from my world, brought here as slaves. But fortunately insouciance and thoughtlessness on the high bridges, common to those of this world, are not required of us. It is other things which are required of us.

I lay there on the flagging, on my side, helpless, bound hand and foot, for some time, while business was conducted. I could see the tiny tunic to one side, where it had been dropped. I made no effort to call attention to myself. It would be done with me as others pleased. I was slave. I did, at one point, see one of the men looking down at me.

I pointed my toes a little, even with my ankles bound, and sucked in my waist, that the line of my legs, and the nature of my figure might be accentuated. I do not think that this was particularly because I realized that the means at my disposal to improve my life and condition here were largely limited to my beauty, heat, and service, but, rather, simply, because, under the eyes of a man, such a man as one of these, I could not help myself but behave as a slave, and perform as a slave, and present myself as the slave I was. He laughed, and I blushed, and, shamed, looked away.

Shortly thereafter the fellow who had conducted Dorna away, she preceding him with alacrity, returned to the terrace. With him was a grimy fellow in a leather apron with a tiny kit of tools.

Seeing he who had conducted Dorna away I thought immediately of her. Tonight, I recalled, she was to serve as the slave *she was*. Perhaps even now she was preparing herself, or, perhaps, as she was a high slave, she was being prepared by lesser slaves, for her "test."

I was certain she would strive humbly and zealously to pass that test. I gathered it would not go well with her if she failed.

Somewhere else, I gathered, at another time, she had been a free woman and, it seems, an important personage. They had even spoken of a mask of silver, or gold, or such. Here, of course, her face was naked, and she was only another slave.

The man with the fellow who had returned to the terrace was, as I would later learn to recognize at a glance by his garb, a member of the leather workers. In many of the Gorean cities there is a caste structure which is significant not only socially but politically. The leather workers are a "low caste." The high castes are normally accounted five in number—the Warriors, the Builders, the Physicians, the Scribes, and the Initiates. The Initiates are sometimes thought of as the highest of the five high castes, and the Warriors as the least of the five high castes. In actual fact, the Warriors commonly produce the administrators and ubars for a city. It is not easy in a world such as this to deprive those who are skilled with weapons their share of authority. If it is not given to them, they will take it. There are some ambiguities in the caste structure. For example, some rank the Merchants as a high caste, and some do not; and some rank the Slavers with the Merchants, and some see them as a separate caste, and so on. It is usually a very serious thing to lose caste in this society. To be sure, not everyone has caste.

Priest-Kings, for example, whoever they may be, have no caste. They are said to be "above caste." Similarly, outlaws and slaves have no caste. Outlaws are thought to have relinquished caste, and, in a sense, thus, to be "out of caste," and slaves, of course, as animals, are "below caste," or, perhaps better, "aside from caste" or "apart from caste." To be sure, I think there are others who also lack caste, really. Some may not have been raised "in caste," some may decline or flee their castes before the initiations, and so on. Similarly, there are entire groups of people, as I understand it, barbarians, savages, and such, whose social arrangements are not based on caste. Very little on this world, and, I suppose, on others, is simple.

"Dorna is now a pierced-ear girl?" asked he in the chair of the fellow who had returned to the terrace.

"Yes, Captain," said the fellow.

The man in the chair smiled. There was laughter from the men about. Some smote their left shoulders in approval. I had gathered earlier that the piercing of the ears was regarded on this world as somehow rather significant. That surmise was now confirmed.

"Slave," said he in the chair to me.

"Yes, Master," I said.

I looked up at him from my side, where I lay. He had not ordered me to kneel. It seemed it was his will that I should retain my low position. It is difficult, of course, to get to one's knees, bound as I was, but it can be done. If ordered to do so one strives to do so as quickly and gracefully as possible. We are expected to obey unhesitantly and swiftly, subject, of course, to the proviso that we should do so as well, as beautifully, as possible. These people have, as I have suggested, a highly developed aesthetic sense. They require beauty in their slaves, both in appearance and movement.

"Dorna," said he, "has been a slave longer than you so it is fitting that it would be her ears which would first be pierced."

"Yes, Master," I said.

"Accordingly," he said, "even though she is a high slave and you are a low slave, you are, at this moment, as your ears have not been pierced, a thousand times higher than she."

"Yes, Master," I said. I was, of course, puzzled by this. One thing seemed clear, once again, the apparent cultural momentousness of ear piercing on this world.

"But," said he, "as soon as your ears are pierced, you will be, again, a thousand times lower than she."

"Yes, Master," I said.

He then turned to the fellow in the apron. "Pierce her ears," he said.

I could not resist, of course, bound as I was.

The leather worker put his tiny kit of tools down beside me, and, undoing a string, opened it, and spread it out.

"Kneel her," he said.

A fellow seized me by the hair and pulled me up, painfully, to a kneeling position.

"Spread your knees," he said.

I obeyed.

"Hold her head," said the leather worker to the fellow who had knelt me.

He crouched behind me and fastened his hands in my hair, tightly. I could not move my head in the slightest without great pain. It hurt even as he held me. "Take her arms, you, and you," said the leather worker to two other fellows. "Hold her down, on her knees." The two fellows addressed then, one on each side of me, seized an arm. I was then held in place, bound hand and foot, down, on my knees, one man holding my head, by the hair, another holding my left arm, and another my right. Their grips were tight. I had little doubt that marks would be left on my arms. To me, of course, these precautions seemed not only unnecessary, but excessive. I did not much fear having my ears pierced. I gathered, however, that on this world many women might. Perhaps they would shriek and struggle, however futilely. I began to sense then, even more, how momentous ear piercing was on this world. This made me uneasy. If I had truly understood the meaning of ear piercing on this world perhaps I, too, I supposed, might have regarded it with horror, and striven to resist, however meaninglessly, however stupidly, however unavailingly and ineffectually. But I doubted it. As a slave it seemed to me fitting that my ears would be pierced, and that men would do with me as they wished. It was not lost on me, of course, that I was knelt. This was to make it clear, I gathered, that ear piercing was something that was done to slaves. Too, the fellow who had pulled me up to my knees had told me to spread my knees. Thus, I would be kneeling as a certain sort of slave, when this was done to me. I would thus, I suppose, associate these two things, my ear piercing and the sort of slave I was.

I saw the leather worker with a bright, long needle.

I felt my left ear lobe drawn downward, taut. It was then pierced. There must have been a drop of blood, as the worker rubbed the ear with his thumb. He then inserted a tiny object, like a droplet with a steel pin, through the wound and, on the other side of the ear lobe, snapped on a tiny disk. These operations were then, with suitable adjustments, repeated with respect to the right ear lobe, even to the wiping away of what must have been another drop of blood. I was then released and allowed to lie on my back. The leather worker was then wiping his needle and returning it to his kit, which he then did up, as it had been. There had been very little pain, though I had felt a prick each time, and I could now feel the tiny rods through my ear lobes. It was a strange feeling. My ear lobes felt a little sore. This soreness, I realized, would quickly pass.

"You are now a pierced-ear girl," the fellow in the apron informed me, grinning.

"Yes, Master," I said.

I sensed, frightened, he liked me that way.

"You are not to disturb this work," said the man in the chair.

"No, Master," I said. I gathered that some women, doubtless women of this world, might, perhaps in hysteria, try to tear such things from their ears.

The man in the apron stood up, and caught a coin in one hand, tossed to him by the fellow who had conducted him hither. The man in the apron then bowed, and, with another look at me, lying on my back, bound, on the flagging, took his leave.

One of the men looked down at me. "Pierced-ear girl," he sneered.

I turned my head away. I did not dare to look at him.

I suddenly sensed a new, pervasive, remarkable interest in me. I sensed powerful heat. It was almost like waves of flame. I lay there, small and helpless, a naked, bound slave at the mercy of masters. Was there now so much that was now so different about me?

"Tenrik," said the man in the chair, sharply.

"Yes, Captain!" said the jailer.

"This is not the time for us to amuse ourselves with a slave," said the man in the chair.

"No, Captain," said Tenrik.

In that moment it seemed that order was restored.

Whereas the remark had been ostensively addressed to Tenrik it had obviously not been intended for him, or for him in particular, but, by means of him, so to speak, had been a remark addressed to all.

I gathered from the remark, of course, that there might well be times when such as I might be given up for the amusement of men, but that this was not such a time.

Too, I gathered that there was discipline in this place, and here I do not speak of such things as the correctives and admonitives, however sure, strict and severe, to which an errant slave might find herself subjected, but of sterner stuff, the discipline of the military, that of the Warrior, that discipline necessary for the raid, the engagement, that required for decisive and coordinated action in highly dangerous circumstances, and, even, too, that other sort of discipline, the long, slow, staying sort of discipline, that which might be required for weeks and months, even years, that tenacity, that sturdiness, needed for the sometimes seemingly endless rigors and privations of campaigns, and wars.

I rose a bit, on my elbows, my wrists tied behind me.

I looked about a bit. Some of the men were still regarding me. But they would not act, not now.

I was safe now, at least for a time.

I looked away from the eyes of a man, frightened. His eyes might as well have been those of a lion.

But I was safe now.

The eyes of others, too, were as those of lions.

I shuddered.

How fearful it must be for any woman to be among such men, let alone one such as I, a slave!

I felt as though I might be a delicacy, one which, had it not been for a word from he in the chair, would by now have been seized and devoured. But on this world there were doubtless many such delicacies, silked and perfumed, combed and belled, deliciously curved, trained, eager to please. Might they not be encountered in any tavern? Indeed, I had at one time thought that I might be sent to such a tavern. Girls such as I, from my world, are apparently popular purchases with tavern keepers.

I lay there before the dais, helpless, but now, apparently, quite safe.

But I felt somehow angry, somehow vaguely dissatisfied, even irritated.

What sort of girl was I?

How pleased I was that I was now safe!

They could not touch me now!

But my belly seemed aflame. My ears had been pierced! I had some sense now as to what that might mean to men such as these. I could feel the tiny rods in my ear lobes.

But I was safe now. How pleased I was!

But I was somehow angry.

I went to my back, lying on my crossed wrists, they below the small of my back. This arched my body somewhat, lifting my belly up, having my head a bit down. I breathed quickly, deeply, prominently, two or three times, and moved my shoulders a little, twisting them, and lifted my knees a bit. I did this though I knew the eyes of several were upon me. How foolish this was, for would it not call attention to the slave at their feet? But surely this was all quite innocent, and quite unintentional, or, at least, must be seemingly so. What woman would dare to stir thusly before such men, even in all innocence, in all inadvertence, almost like a restless, frustrated, yearning, begging slave, one attempting to call attention to herself, surely only one naive, or one reckless, or one oblivious to, or heedless of, what she might be doing. Did she not understand how such things might be viewed? Had she not considered the danger of provoking them, of even in some subtle way perhaps igniting their heats and needs? How foolish must such a woman be! Might not such movements, all innocent and unintentional as they might be, be misconstrued? Might they not even be understood as slave movements? I glanced to one of the men. I am not sure then precisely what happened. I think an expression of irritation, or of annoyance, may have crossed my features, perhaps fleetingly, ending perhaps in a tiny smile, perhaps in an as-if-triumphant little smile, as I turned my head away. I was safe from him. He could not have me now! This was all subtle, you understand. Even now I am not quite certain of everything that occurred in that moment, or half moment. What I think I may have done was to convey, or seem to convey, my contempt for them, subtly, challengingly, that I had not been seized and ravished and, at the same time, slyly, vaunt my immunity from their predations. I was, I suppose, in my way, taunting them. This was, of course, a mistake. It was not one I would make again.

"Slut!" cried a man.

"Oh!" I cried in pain, kicked.

"Throw her to sleen!" called another.

"No, please, Masters!" I wept. "Oh! Oh!" I cried, twice more kicked.

"Take that, slave!" cried another.

"Oh!" I wept.

"And that!" cried another.

"And that!" cried yet another.

"Oh! Oh!" I wept.

"Bring the whip!" cried a man.

"No, Masters!" I begged.

"I have it," cried another.

"Please, no, Masters!" I begged.

Down came the lash!

"What have I done?" I cried.

"Stupid slave!" cried a man.

"Lying slave!" cried another.

Again and again the lash fell.

"Forgive me, Masters!" I cried, writhing bound under the lash. "Forgive me! Forgive me, Masters!"

"It is enough," announced the man in the chair. "She is new to her collar, and yet naive."

"She must learn quickly," snarled a man.

"Kneel, slave," said the man in the chair.

I struggled to my knees and knelt before the dais. I put my head down to the floor before the first step of the dais.

"You are a pathetic spectacle, Earth girl," said he in the great chair.

"Forgive me, Master," I said. "Forgive me, Master!"

"In the future," said he, "you will be concerned to be more pleasing, will you not?"

"Yes, Master," I said. "Yes, Master!"

"Tenrik," said the man in the chair.

"Yes, Captain," said huge Tenrik.

"Lift up the state slave," said he.

Tenrik lifted me up, in his arms. My weight was as nothing to him.

"She is to be sent below, into the keeping of the pit master."

"The Tarsk?" asked a man.

"What a waste," said a man.

"It seems a pity," said one of the men, oddly enough the one who had just used the whip on me.

"This one is pretty," said a man. "And I think she will learn quickly to serve. Choose another."

"This one has not been particularly purchased because she is pretty," said the man in the chair, "though I do not expect the Tarsk will object to her particular configuration of visage and curves."

"I should think not," said a man.

"The Tarsk is a lucky beast," said a fellow.

"She has been purchased primarily for her ignorance," said the man in the chair.

"She is not as ignorant now as she was a few moments ago," said a man.

"No," laughed another.

"What are her duties?" asked a man.

"She will be one of the pit slaves," said the man in the chair, "kenneled like the others, serving like them, as the Tarsk directs."

"Beyond that, what are her special duties?" asked a man.

"These have been made clear to the Tarsk," said the man in the chair.

"I see," said the fellow.

"The Tarsk will see to it that she performs them," said the man in the chair.

"And doubtless others as well," said a man.

"Yes," smiled the man in the chair.

There was laughter.

"The descent is cleared, to the depths," said the man in the chair.

I understood very little, if anything of this. I was miserable. I lay on the stones. I was a bound, lashed slave. I knew only that I must strive to be more pleasing to the masters. I would so strive! I would so strive! Please Masters, I thought, I will try to be better! Please, Masters, do not lash me further! I will obey! I will try to be more pleasing!

A hood was put over my head and buckled shut under my chin.

Why was this done?

The jailer turned about with me in his arms. He walked about for a bit, turning this way and that, at one angle or another, proceeding for one distance or another. Sometimes he reversed himself. At other times he spun about, accomplishing various numbers of rotations and partial rotations. I was totally disoriented. I no longer knew where I was with respect to the dais, even whether near it or not. I might have been somewhere near the center of the surface; I might have been at an edge; I did not know.

I heard a lifting of stone, almost at our feet, one or more of the tiles, or flaggings, apparently having been moved. I then heard what sounded like a wooden trap being lifted, one which had perhaps been hidden beneath the flaggings.

The jailer set me down on stone.

I felt a rope passed before me and then under my arms, the loose ends behind me. It was drawn back, tight against me.

"What of her tunic?" asked a man. I had put the tunic aside, a few feet before the dais, shortly after I had come to the surface of the tower. It had been the desire of the man in the great chair that the slave be bared. Too, he had had her turn before him, slowly. In this fashion may a woman be assessed. Later she had "performed." In this way a woman may be even better assessed. There are many names for this sort of performance. It is sometimes called the "dance of the displayed slave," though it is not really a dance; sometimes it is called "block movements" or "circle movements," from the fact that such movements are sometimes called for on the sales block or within the exhibition circle; sometimes they are called "cage movements," from the necessity of performing them upon request in the exhibition cages, and so on. If the man "calls" the movements, the activity is sometimes spoken of as putting the girl "through her paces," and so on. Perhaps the easiest way of thinking about them is to think of them simply as display movements or exhibition movements. Their most obvious purpose is to help make clear the beauty of a slave, by displaying it in a variety of movements, attitudes, and poses.

"It will be given to another," said a man.

"The Tarsk will now decide whether or not she is to be permitted clothing," said another man.

"True," laughed another.

I was moved slightly, and my feet suddenly slipped downward. I drew my feet back up, quickly. My body was thrust forward a bit. Again my feet slipped downward. I whimpered. I pulled my feet back a little. I could feel something like wood against my lower right calf. The hood was unbuckled, but not removed from me. I felt the rope which had passed before my body and then under my arms tighten even more. As it pulled inward against me both the ends, behind me, must have been in the hands of one man. I felt a hand reach to the hood, to its top, which would doubtless draw it away. I was then suddenly, without warning, thrust forward, and, as I cried out with alarm, I descended, in which descent the hood, by my motion downward and the grip on the hood, was removed from me, which descent, after a yard or so, was arrested by the rope. I looked up, wildly. I could see, putting my head back, through a trap above me, the sky, the two ends of the rope behind me, and some of the men. I did not have the least idea where the trap opened on the surface. I was within some sort of sectioned metal tube, perhaps a yard in diameter. I could see riveted seams here and there. Had I been free I might have controlled my descent in such a device but I was bound. "Masters!" I cried. I saw one of the ends of the rope released and it whipped downward under my left arm, across my body, half turning me, back under my right arm and upward. "Please, no!" I shrieked. I was descending in the tube and the rectangle of sky above me shrunk and disappeared, and, in a moment, even the dimness of light was gone, and I spun about, turning, crying out in misery, spiraling downward through the darkness. The descent had been cleared, I had heard, to the "depths." Thus, it seemed, there might be different levels accessible from this tube. Its major purpose presumably had to do with the rapid, perhaps secret deployment of troops among levels. Too, obviously it might serve for an emergency evacuation of the surface. It was more protected and less susceptible to fire than ladders and stairwells. It gave a possibility, too, for the immediate securing of loot. Suppose a pursuit was hard-pressed. Might not treasures be safely herein committed? Perhaps a captive free woman dared entertain hopes of rescue, but she then finds herself, clad only in her slave bracelets, whirling helplessly downward, toward what fate she knows not, in the very bowels of the city. Too, most easily by means of ropes, the tube might be ascended, and, in such a way, defenders might appear unexpectedly on any given level. Even the surface might be regained.

"Masters! Masters!" I wept.

I plunged, and spun and slid downward. I was in utter darkness. The tube tended to spiral. Sometimes the descent was relatively slow, and sometimes it was more precipitous. After a little I was gasping, buffeted and weeping, seemingly struck from one side to another. I tried to catch my breath. I wept. I do not know how long the descent took. Doubtless it did not take long, but sometimes it seemed as though it would never end. There was the darkness, the movement, the terror. It is difficult to judge time in such matters. Then I felt myself plunge into a stout, yielding, reticulated surface. Closely meshed cords were now all about me. They were tight. I swung back and forth. The device had been closed, it seemed, by my weight.

Twelve

I swung back and forth.

About me the cords were tight. It was dank in this place, and utterly dark.

I lay very quietly in the cords, moving only a little to change my position, to twist a bit to my side, to ease the attitude of my bound limbs.

I could see so little that I might as well have been hooded.

I thought I heard, several feet below me, a movement, as though in water.

I was apparently in a net of some sort. With my thigh, and my shoulder, pressing against it, and with my fingers, behind me, I tried to ascertain its nature. It was a stout net. Its cords were perhaps a half inch in thickness. It would doubtless have served to confine something much larger, much heavier and stronger than I. On the other hand, the cords were not coarse. I, or things such as I, would not be likely to be burned or cut in it, even if we struggled. It was not woven of those terrible ropes, sometimes used in punishment ties, in which a disobedient slave might find herself swathed from head to foot, ropes within which, in misery, she scarcely dares to move. Its mesh was apparently woven in a regular pattern, either of diamonds or squares, I suppose, depending on one's axis of viewing it. The sides of these regular diamonds, or aligned squares, were some four inches in length. This mesh was thus capable not only of holding things of my size, and larger, but also things which might be considerably smaller. The softness of the cords doubtless had to do with the fact that some of the net's catches might be expected to be such as I. I did not think particular consideration would be shown, say, to male prisoners. Our prettiness, obviously, tends to figure in our value. We are seldom, if ever, marked unless there is a purpose to it, as, say, when we are put under the hot iron and branded, say, for purposes of identification. It is thought to be stupid to gratuitously mark a slave. Such things may lower her value. Even the dreaded five-bladed slave whip is designed in such a way as to avoid marking the slave in any permanent fashion. One need not fear any lessening in discipline, of course, for there is, well within the parameters of protecting the master's investment, more than enough, far more than enough, I assure you, and from personal experience, which may be done with us. Perhaps a brief remark on nets might be order. Obviously there are several kinds, and they serve several purposes. I was now enclosed, it seemed, in a general-purpose net, one of a sort which might serve many purposes, perhaps even the transfer of supplies from one side of a chasm to another, or cargo from one ship to another. In a net of the sort in which I was now enclosed, it is easy to inspect the contents, to see what is held. This is different from many slave nets, which are often so closely woven that one can scarcely put one's fingers through the mesh. The point of such nets seems to be to impress on the slave her helplessness, and, as well, to excite the curiosity of passers-by, say, prospective buyers or such, as to the nature of its contents. Similarly some auctioneers like to bring women to the block clothed, which vesture may then, as the bidding intensifies, be progressively removed. There is also a variety of capture nets, designed with different animals in mind. I confine myself to those which are designed to net slaves. To be sure, they function quite effectively with free women, as well, who, it must be noted, unless surprised in their boudoir or bath, are often impeded by the cumbersome robes of concealment. Interestingly the very robes which are supposed to discourage predation upon them render them more vulnerable to it. Accordingly, ironically, in a given situation, a lightly clad slave, in her fleetness, might elude a captor to whom a free woman would fall easily. And when the "free woman" is capable of matching the slave's flight, she, too, perhaps being then bedecked in a less inhibiting garmenture, it will be too late for her, for, by that time, she, too, will be a slave. The nets I have in mind then are capture nets designed for the taking of slaves, or, perhaps better, more generally, women. They are light, easily cast and weighted. They are commonly circular, with a diameter of some eight to ten feet. The cords are commonly of silk and the mesh is normally fastened in diamonds or squares, some two inches, or so, in width. They swirl, twisting, through the air. It is like a sudden, odd cloud come between you and the sun. One is first aware of the reticulated shadow which seems to descend and then one has it all about one. One is suddenly caught. Usually one is running, and, in an instant, one falls, tangled, helpless. Sometimes one leaps up, only to find it all about one. One tries to tear it away. One forces it in one direction to be the more helplessly grasped by it in another. Then, commonly, one falls, or one's feet may be kicked away, from beneath one. One looks up through the mesh and sees one's captor. In an instant then one may find the net secured about one, tied closed. One is its prisoner. Or one may be pulled from the net, and braceleted, or secured as the captor wishes. It is up to him, as you are then his. I have suggested that the slave, given her garmenture, is more likely to elude a captor than a free woman, which is surely true, but it is necessary to add that it is, of course, a relative matter, and one of degree. Neither the slave nor the free woman has much hope once, in a suitable situation, the hunter-has decided upon her. We are smaller than men. We are weaker than they, we are less swift than they. It is thus that we find our place, and have our place, in the design of nature, whatever may be her mysterious purposes. Nets are, of course, but one way of acquiring women. Looped ropes, for example, are extremely common. Bolas are not unknown, too. Indeed, in the southern hemisphere, I understand that they are extremely common. I think I would fear to be taken by such a thing, it whipping about my legs, pinning them together. More cruelly the woman is sometimes stunned by a throwing stick, a method which is used, I have heard, in a place called the delta of the Vosk. The Vosk, I gather, is a body of flowing water, a stream, or river. Similarly, chains, hoods, and such, too, have their purposes.

I lay very still in the net.

It was damp, and cold, in this place.

The free woman does have one advantage, of course, over the slave, in eluding capture, which is that she is not a domestic animal. For example, let us suppose that a given city has fallen, and that effective resistance within it is at an end. In such a situation, where a male might expect to continue the pursuit of a free woman, who is, after all, at that point, still a free person, he might not wish to tire himself pursuing a slave. He might simply, rather, instruct her to halt, and command her to him, ordering her to present herself for his chains, or his bracelets or binding fiber, and thong and nose ring. The slave might then, if she is wise, hurry obediently to her new master. Has she not been commanded? Does she dally at the wall, against which she has been trapped? Does she hesitate in the room, within which she has been cornered? Is she not a slave? Must a command be repeated? She kneels at his feet, putting her head down, humbly licking and kissing his feet, perhaps his dusty, ash-stained, bloody boots, in timid, tender obeisance. Does she not now have a new master? And is it not he? Must she not hasten to her place at his feet, summoned even as might be another form of domestic animal, perhaps by a mere word, or whistle? She dares not disobey. She knows what might be the penalties for such. She is a domestic animal. She now, merely, has a new master. She kneels before him, submitted. She accepts, unquestioningly, as she must, her new bonds.

I heard again a movement below me, something like a twisting, a stirring, in water. It was, I conjectured, several feet below me.

I conjectured that I might be suspended over what might be the sump of a fortress.

I did not know.

Perhaps, rather, it was some sort of pool or reservoir.

I did not know.

Certainly it must be deep beneath the fortress, or city.

I twisted a little. My ankles were bound, tightly, to one another. My wrists were still secured behind my back. I was helpless. I had no hope of freeing myself. When men such as those of this world tie a woman, she remains tied. I had learned that weeks ago, in the pens.

One of my first lessons in the pen was to have been bound hand and foot, and then ordered to free myself. I had then, while watched, twisted and struggled for more than an Ahn. Then at last I had wept, in futility, "Forgive me, Masters! I cannot free myself!"

"Do not forget it," said a guard.

"No, Master," I wept.

I had then expected to be freed, but they had left me as I was, helplessly bound, past the time of the evening meal and throughout the night. They freed me in the morning and I was permitted to relieve myself and crawl on all fours, as I could, my muscles and limbs stiff and aching, with the other girls, hungry, to my pan of morning gruel.

What was I doing here, I wondered.

I was to be a pit slave, it seemed, whatever that might be.

The "pit master" was spoken of as "the Tarsk." I did not understand the allusion.

Given the length of my descent, from which my body was still sore, I must be far beneath the fortress, indeed, or perhaps far beneath the city, as the descent had often seemed an oblique one. I could be hundreds of yards from the vertical axis of the tower.

The "pit" or "pits," I thought, must be near here. Surely I was at least in their vicinity.

It was dark here, and cold.

What was I doing here?

Why had I been purchased, and by men who, it seemed, seldom bothered to purchase women, preferring, it seemed, to acquire them in other manners?

Why did they wish a girl here who was ignorant, or muchly so?

I did not want to be here.

I was supposedly beautiful. But of what use would be my beauty, if beauty it was, in this place, in the pits?

Too, I was supposedly quite vital, unusually so, it seemed, even for this world. My vitality, my sexuality, had, of course, been disparaged, belittled, denied, and starved on my own world. I had kept it concealed, hidden. I had even tried to be ashamed of it. How strange was my world, one on which one was expected to pretend to numbness and insensitivity, one on which one was conditioned to be ashamed of health. Women who had feelings such as mine for men were to be denounced with all the epithets available to the anesthetic, to the perverted, to the freaks and frustrates. Did we really constitute such dangers, I wondered, to the pervasiveness and mightiness of their eccentric conditioning programs? Was it not enough for them to exercise an almost perfect control over media and education? Did they fear a tiny whisper of truth so much? Was it truly so dangerous? Must all reflection, all inquiry, all thought be suppressed? Was it truly required that the "free marketplace of ideas" be closed, except in name? What a tiny, small thing were the genetic codes of an organism! One could scarcely detect the traces of such things with the most awesome instruments. What a frail straw was truth! So a blade of grass grew between the paving stones, one tiny, green blade of grass among the stones? Did they fear that so much? Grass is so beautiful. It did not seem to me that feelings such as mine were really so threatening to prescribed "movements." Did it really make it so difficult for them to continue to present their particular interest as though it were the general interest? Surely I was not stopping them from doing that. Could they not even find little truths amusing, they so weak and tiny, lost among all the glittering, massive lies? Who could fear them? They were so tiny, those little truths. But perhaps they were right. Perhaps even little truths were dangerous. A match may be seen from far off in the darkness. The tiniest of sparks might imperil a mountain of straw. So, too, perhaps even a modest truth, no stranger to eons of history, might undermine the myths of a world. Did the moons of Jupiter not shatter the crystalline spheres? Destroy telescopes then, for they might see the truth. They see too far, and too clearly. They look too deeply into reality. Did not a handful of fossils overturn a world? Let men then not examine the earth beneath their feet, for they might learn on what it is that they truly stand. How insidious the modest, recurrent elements of a healthy organism, the components of a natural biological development. How subtle, how insistent and quiet, and yet how tenacious a foe of promulgated perversions are the whims of nature, that she should choose to be so constituted. But nature cannot read. Thus she does not know what she is supposed to be. She is content to let others read her, if they dare. How odd if we should truly be the end of history, if our tiny grasp of things, our demands flung into the void, should be the finality of the universe. Are we, familiar with the rise and fall of empires, who have witnessed the building of the pyramids and walked the streets of Babylon and Nineveh, who have heard the tread of the legions and watched the armada set forth, to take our moment, our brief afternoon, to be the summit and meaning of eternity?

And so I was supposedly quite vital, unusually so, it seemed, even for this world. I was a palimpsest, with texts concealed beneath texts. On this world what had been written on me on my world, to obscure the underlying truths, had been scraped off, the dross scraped away to reveal the suspected, now-revealed, infinitely more precious message beneath.

How liberating it was for me to come to this world, where I might, at last, be myself, as I truly was!

To be sure, vitality is expected in a slave. In markets, we may even be tested for it. It is not only, you see, that a profound sexuality, an acute sexual sensitivity, an uncontrollable responsiveness, is permitted in a slave; it is required in her. It is one of the things for which we are purchased. We are slaves, you see. We are not free women.

But of what use would my vitality, if such it might be, be in this place?

I wanted to feel the arms of a guard upon me. I wanted to lie, moaning, in his arms. But instead I lay cold, and bound, in a net.

I twisted, and sobbed.

"There *is* someone there!" announced a voice, a woman's voice, from somewhere to my right, in the darkness.

"Yes," I said, startled.

I heard the creak of a chain, to the right.

"I knew something descended into the net," she said. "I thought I heard it."

I turned, as I could, in the net, toward the voice. "It was I," I said.

"You are in the power of these brutes as well?" she asked.

I was silent. I did not know who was there in the darkness. I heard the chain creak once more.

"You are in the power of these creatures as well?" she asked.

"Totally," I said.

"Are you chained?" she asked.

"I am bound," I said, "hand and foot."

"They bind us well, do they not?" she inquired.

"Yes!" I said.

"I am imprisoned," she informed me.

That intelligence seemed strange to me, as it seemed her voice was quite near me. To be sure, I could not see in the darkness.

"I am soon to be free!" she assured me.

I was not certain as to how to interpret this remark, issuing from the darkness, from this unknown source.

"How I despise these fools!" said the voice.

To such a remark, of course, I did not dare reply.

"How poorly they treat us!" she cried.

I did not dare respond.

"Have they treated you well?" she asked.
"I have been whipped," I said. Indeed, I had been twice whipped.
"Poor thing!" she cried. "You must be of low caste!"
I was silent.
"They would not dare to whip me!" she announced.
I thought the speaker might profit from a whipping.
"You have an unusual accent," she said, suddenly.
"I am from far away," I said, evasively.
"Are you clothed?" she asked.
"Please!" I protested.
"The beasts!" she said.
"Where are we?" I asked.
"In the pits," she said. "I think somewhere beneath the keep, somewhere beneath the fortress. I truly do not know. This place is a labyrinth!"
"What ransom are they asking for you?" she asked, suddenly.
I was silent.
"It will not be as high as mine," she informed me.
"You are from far off?" she asked.
"Yes," I said.
"Do you know in what city we are?" I asked.
"No," she said. "I was brought here, my features wrapped in my own veils!"
I decided I should not dare to speak further to her, even in what seemed to be our common predicament.
"How were you brought here?" she asked.
"My features, too, were obscured," I said. Need she know that I had, in much of my journey, worn a slave hood?
I was becoming very uneasy with our conversation.
"None of these beasts have so much as glimpsed my features," she averred.
I could make no such claim, of course. I was, and had been, public to men; I belonged to them; I was subject to their regard and whim; I had been exposed as frequently and routinely, and, I suppose, as naturally and as appropriately, as any other sort of domestic animal. Indeed, but a bit before, I had performed for men, before the dais, providing them not only with a glimpse of my beauty, if beauty it was, but with an authentic, detailed, lengthy, provocative display of it, an

exhibition designed to leave little to conjecture concerning at least the externals of whatever interest I might hold for them. It seemed I could have done little more unless I had stood chained on a sales platform, to be literally handled as the curved, tender little beast I was, or had perhaps been conducted behind the purple screen to be tested in a more intimate fashion. In such exhibitions, in such performances, movement, grace and rhythm are, of course, quite important. It is the moving, living, breathing, vital woman which is of interest. One must not only look beautiful, you see, but one must *be* beautiful.

"Such, I gather," said she, "has not been the case with you."

"No," I said.

"Men have looked, then, upon your face?" she asked.

"Yes," I said.

"They would not dare to look upon mine!" she said.

I was silent.

"And have they seen more than that?" she asked.

"I am naked," I admitted.

"Poor thing!" she cried. But I think she was pleased to have been concretely apprised of this intelligence.

"You, too, are at their mercy!" I exclaimed, trying to sit up in the net.

"No, no!" she cried. I heard a rattling, as though of bars. I thought she must, then, be clutching them, and shaking them. She seemed frustrated. I heard the bars shaken again. I heard, too, the creaking of the chain from the right. Below me, too, if I was not mistaken, I heard again, a stirring, in the water. Something below, perhaps, had surfaced, or approached, hearing the sounds above.

"I am of high caste!" she cried. "I should not be here thusly, so held, so humiliated!"

I was silent.

I lay back in the net, bound.

"Men are fools!" she cried.

It was she, of course, and not they, who seemed to be in some sort of confinement.

"They are fools!" she wept.

The men I had seen on this world did not seem to me to be fools. Indeed, they seemed to be anything but fools. By the force and intellect in them I had often felt awed. They did make many men of my old world now, in this perspective, seem fools. Here men seemed assured of themselves. They had not been confused, and bled, and subverted, and crippled, by a sick society. Here they had never surrendered their natural dominance. Here, for the first time, I had begun to understand what true men might be like, in all their splendor, in all their natural, bestial magnificence.

"How I hate men!" she cried. "How I despise them!"

I would certainly not respond to this. Indeed, what if she were a spy, set to examine me, perhaps even, cruelly, to trap me into some insolent inadvertence, trying to tease from me some careless, thoughtless, prideful, idly arrogant remark? Too, of course, more importantly, I did not, in fact, hate the men I had found here, nor did I despise them. If anything, I tended to admire them, and feel grateful toward them. Too, they tended to excite me, as a female, as few men of my old world had. To be sure, I did regard them with a healthy respect, even fear. They were, after all, the masters.

"But what could one such as you, of low caste," said the voice, "know of one of my sensitivity and nature? How could one such as you understand the feelings of one such as I?"

"Only with great difficulty, if at all, doubtless," said I, perhaps somewhat testily.

"But have no fear," said she. "I will be patient with you. We are, after all, despite the discrepancies in our caste, sisters in sorrow, in misery and grief."

I was silent.

"We have in common our precious freedom," she said.

I did not respond to this. To be sure, I was confident that she was in some sort of confinement, and I lay bound and naked, in a net. But I did not doubt she had in mind some more serious sense of freedom, and one that made me uneasy. From things she had said, I had little doubt but what she was, in a sense important on this world, "free." On the other hand, in a sense also important on this world, and doubtlessly more profoundly important, I was not "free." It was not merely that I had a collar on my neck, close-fitting and locked as it might be, and a brand on my thigh, lovely and unmistakable, put there deeply and clearly for all to see. Nor was it even that my nature was such as to put me helplessly, lovingly, and appropriately at a man's feet. It was rather that in the full legalities of a world, in the full sanction of the totality of its customs, practices and institutions, in the fullness of its very reality, I was not free. I was an animal, a property, a slave.

I had had little, if anything, to do with free women. I had encountered two of them earlier, in the pens, and not pleasantly. I have briefly, as I recall, recounted the nature of that interlude elsewhere. I did know that an impassable gulf separated me from such lofty creatures, an unbridgeable chasm, one of the same immeasurability that separated the lowliest of domestic animals, which slaves were, from the heights and glories of the free person.

"What is your caste?" she asked.

I was silent.

"Mine is the Merchants," she said.

"That is not a high caste, is it?" I asked. I had heard conflicting things about the Merchants.

"It certainly is!" she cried.

I was silent.

"I would take you to be of the leather workers," she speculated.

I did not respond.

"Or perhaps, less," she said, "you are one of those boorish lasses from the fields, that you are of the Peasants."

Again I did not respond.

"That is doubtless it," she said, seemingly satisfied.

The Peasants were generally regarded as the lowest of the castes, though why that should be I have never been able to determine. That caste is sometimes referred to as "the ox on which the Home Stone rests." I am not clear as to what a Home Stone is, but I have gathered that it, whatever it might be, is regarded as being of great importance on this world. So, if that is the case, and the Peasants is indeed the caste upon which the Home Stone rests, then it would seem, at least in my understanding, to be a very important caste. In any event, it would seem to me that the Peasants is surely one of, if not the, most significant of the castes of this world. So much depends upon them! Too, I am sure they do not regard themselves as being the lowest of the castes. In fact, I doubt that any caste regards itself as being the lowest of the castes. It would seem somewhat unlikely that any caste would be likely to accept that distinction. Perhaps many castes regard themselves as equivalent or, at least, as each being the best in diverse ways. For example, the leather workers would presumably be better at working leather than the metal workers, and the metal workers would presumably be better at working metal than the leather workers, and so on. One needs, or wants, it seems, all the castes.

"Yes," she said, "you are of the Peasants."

I was silent.

I trusted she would not fall into the clutches of peasants. I understand that they are not always tolerant of the laziness and insolence of arrogant, urban free women. They enjoy using them, when they obtain them as slaves, in the fields. I wondered how the woman in the darkness would feel, sweating, harnessed naked to a plow, subject to a whip, or crawling, perhaps hastened by the jabbing of a pointed stick, into a dark, low log kennel at night. But perhaps she would be permitted to sleep chained at her master's feet, within reach, at his discretion. But I feared it might be dangerous to speak to this person. To be sure, we were both in the darkness. But she was free. I was not free.

"Do not be sensitive that you are only of the Peasants," said the woman. "There is much to be said for the caste."

"Yes," I said. "Those who eat are often thought to owe it a debt of gratitude."

"Surely," she agreed.

That seemed to me quite generous on her part.

"You were doubtless picked up on a country road," she said, "perhaps ravished in the nearest ditch."

"Perhaps," I said.

"I myself was the victim of an elaborate plot, an intricate stratagem to secure a highborn prize for ransom."

"Oh?" said I.

"As you are merely of the Peasants," said she, "you must fear, terribly."

"Why is that?" I asked, not that I was not afraid. I was a slave.

"They may not hold you for ransom, you see," she said.

I was silent.

"I hesitate to call this to your attention, but you must face the possibility, my dear," she said. "These men are brutes, powerful brutes! They may have another fate in store for you, one we dare not even think of!"

"What?" I asked.

"How obtuse you are, my dear," she said.

I did not speak.

"You are of low caste," she said. "Surely you can guess."

I was silent.

"The collar!" she whispered.

I was silent. I was relieved, muchly. I had feared, from her tone of voice, and such, that she might have had something else, something dreadful, in mind, such as being thrown to a six-legged carnivore of the sort which I had encountered on the ledge, or on the surface of the tower. But I did not think I would have to fear such a thing unless I proved to be displeasing, and I had no intention of being displeasing, at least if I could help it. Not only was I determined to be pleasing, if only as a matter of simple prudential consideration, that I might not be whipped or slain, but I genuinely, authentically, sincerely *wanted* to be pleasing. Something in me, from the time of puberty onward, had wanted to serve men, and love them, helplessly, and fully. Yes, I admit it, and on this world the admission costs me naught! I want to please men! Denounce me if you will but I am such! But, too, perhaps you know not men such as are on this world! In their presence I find myself docile, submissive, and obedient. Let their free women rant at them, contradict them, and attempt to make them miserable, for whatever strange reasons might prompt them to do so, but before them, before such men, I am only, and can be only, a slave.

"Yes," whispered the voice in the darkness, "the collar!"

But I already wore a collar! I could feel it, even now, on my neck. It was a state collar, I had been informed. I was not eager to be owned by a state, of course. I would have preferred to be owned by a given man, a private individual. I wanted to be a treasure to a man, and to love and serve him, with all my heart. Perhaps if I were very pleasing, he would not beat me, or sell me.

"Because of my rumored beauty," said she, "there was no dearth of ardent fellows who would compete to be my swain. Many gifts I had from them. And I gave nothing! One lesser known begged me to attend a rendezvous in a jeweler's shop, one which had but recently opened its doors in the city, that I might there pick for myself the finest of a dozen ruby necklaces, which he would then purchase for me. And as he would be a secret swain, one who accosted me from time to time amasked, purportedly that the elevation of his birth not be betrayed, the rendezvous was to be clandestine. My curiosity was piqued, naturally. And when he showed me a sample of the sort of necklaces in question, I feared my head was turned."

"What happened?" I asked.

"I would meet him at the new shop, that very afternoon, secretly," she said. "I did not even have my palanquin borne there, but descended from it at a park, ordering my bearers to await me. I then made my way afoot, by circuitous, devious paths, though it was more than a quarter of a pasang, to the shop."

I did not think that that was very far, though, to be sure, I was not really familiar with linear measurements on this world.

"In a rear room in the shop, shut away from the sunlight and bustle of the street, he met me amasked, I veiled. In this room, in the lovely light of golden lamps, were the dozen necklaces displayed. I know the worth of such objects. I was muchly impressed. I selected the largest, and finest, of course."

"Please, continue," said I.

"It contained more than a hundred rubies," she said.

"Please," I said.

"'May I place it about your neck?' he asked. I saw no harm in this, it being done, of course, over my robes and veils. And he did so. It would have been hard for me to do it myself, you understand."

"Of course," I said.

"There was a mirror in the room, and I could see him behind me, as well as sense him there, as he put the necklace about my neck, and closed its clasps. I had never been necklaced by a man before. There seemed something unsettling in it, somehow, the tiny click of the clasps, and such."

I was silent.

"I continued to gaze into the mirror. How beautiful I seemed! And how strikingly lovely, too, was the necklace, in its numerous, softly shining strands. And he was still close behind me, quite close. I felt uneasy. I could not understand this feeling. A soft sound, a gasp, I fear, escaped me. He was so near. I even felt weak. 'It is pretty,' I informed him, lightly. 'It pleases me that it pleases you,' said he. His voice sounded very deep, very strong. He was close behind me. Then he put his hands on my upper arms. I saw him holding me, thusly, in the mirror. I wavered in weakness. Perhaps the room was close. I knew that if he chose, I was in his power. But it was unthinkable, of course, that he might press his advantage, perhaps even to the alarming extent of touching his lips to my shoulder. He was a gentleman, surely. Yet he seemed very close, and very strong. Should a gentleman seem such? It did not seem so. He made me feel uneasy. I resolved not to like this sensation. I decided that I would teach him to respect a woman. He would be reminded of the behavior which was expected of him. I would put him in his place. I would taunt, and torment, him. 'Perhaps you would care to be rewarded for your gift,' I said. 'Perhaps you would like me, for a moment, to lower my veil,' I said, 'that you might glimpse my features.' 'Dare I hope for so much?' he said. 'No,' I said. 'And unhand me!' I said, sternly, sharply. Instantly he removed his hands from my arms, and stepped back. I thought that a fleeting smile crossed his features, but I must have been mistaken. I again regarded myself in the mirror. I was truly quite beautiful. 'I will leave now,' I said. 'Of course,' said he."

"You did not thank him for the necklace?" I asked.

"No," she said. "Such things are owed to such as I from such as he."

"And you did not, even for an instant, lower your veil?" I asked.

"Certainly not," she said, angrily. "What do you think I am?"

I was silent.

"I am a free woman," she said.

"Yes," I said.

"I went then through the shop, to the street outside. Fortunately, a public palanquin was nearby, no more than a few yards away. I was pleased. Thus I need not walk, and perhaps soil my slippers in the public streets. With a gesture, my swain summoned it for me. He gave a coin to the first bearer. I somewhat impatiently awaited my swain's hand, that he might graciously assist me into the palanquin. He did so. I then reclined within the palanquin, adjusting my robes and veils about me. I would not so much as glance at my scorned swain. Let him suffer, tormenting himself as to how he might have displeased me. I had the necklace, and so it did not matter whether or not, really, I saw him again. The transaction had been a profitable one from my point of view. On the other hand, I did find the buffoon of interest. And he must be rich, for he had afforded such a necklace. And, indeed, who knew what further largesse one might obtain from such as he, particularly if one handled such matters cleverly, what further rare and precious encouragements such as he might lavish upon me, to woo my favor? My favor, I assure you, would not be easily won, if at all. Let the necklace be but the first of a succession, I thought, of ever richer and more hopefully, more desperately proffered gifts, the first of many similarly tendered inducements. In such a way, I might make clear to him, he might hope to add some weight, some charm, perhaps even some persuasiveness, to his entreaties. And his mask suggested he must be highborn, perhaps one of the highest born in the city. There would then be, I speculated, even should I deign to permit the relationship to develop, no difficulty, or impediment, with respect to caste. One must be careful about such things, you know. Surely he had tried to conceal his identity, that the shame of my rejection, which he surely must have realized he might risk, not be too publicly broadcast. He would come back, of course, for doubtless he was smitten by me, as a man may be by a highborn free woman. After all, I was not one of those curvaceous, scarcely clad little sluts whose job it is to attend, and with perfection, to a man's baser instincts. Such meaningless slime is easily come by. It may be purchased cheaply in any city, even at many a crossroads."

"Yes," I said. Many of us were doubtless not expensive. I did not even know how expensive I might have been, had it not been for some special characteristics pertaining to me, in particular, my newness to the world, and my consequent ignorance, conjoined with an adeptness in the language unusual for so new a slave. To be sure, I was supposedly quite pretty, and I was certainly, sometimes to my chagrin, extremely helplessly sexually responsive. Such things, too, might have improved my price. I did not know, of course, what I had cost. I did not think I had come too cheaply, but, too, perhaps, my price had not been too dear. I really did not know.

It had been conjectured, above, that I might easily be a "silver-tarsk girl," but I did not really understand what that might be. The "silver tarsk," I supposed, was a coin, and being a "silver-tarsk girl" would presumably mean that I might be expected to bring as much as a "silver tarsk" to whoever sold me, but all this was not that illuminating as I had no clear idea of the values involved. I had gathered, however, that it would be a good price for one such as I. And this price, I gathered, had much to do with what was coming to be in me, I feared, an easily aroused, quickly ignited, uncontrollable, unrestrainable passion. And my beauty, too, if beauty it was, I supposed, would not be likely to reduce my price either. I trust that the reader, if this ever finds a reader, or readers, will not be shocked by this sort of thing. Just as men will buy one animal for speed, perhaps for racing, and another for strength, perhaps for draft purposes, they will buy another for beauty and passion, for the purposes of their compartments and furs. To some extent this still disturbed me, but I recognized my helplessness in these matters. It was not only that I knew I must well please a master, and heatedly respond to him, if I did not wish to put my life in jeopardy, for I was owned, but that I could not have helped myself. Men had done this to me. I was now theirs. Let those who can understand these things understand them. Let those who cannot understand them not do so. What other choice have they?

"And it did not matter," said she, "what his caste might be, assuming it was high, for I was of the Merchants, one of the highest of castes, there being none higher, I insist on that, saving perhaps that of the Initiates."

I knew little or nothing of the Initiates, but I had heard that such as I were not allowed in their temples, lest we profane them. Normally, if our masters attended their services, we would be chained, or penned, outside, along with other animals.

"So," said she, "whatever his caste, assuming it was high, of course, it would be practical for us to contemplate a companionship, and if his caste should be *thought* higher than mine, however mistakenly, I could, in such a relationship, be *thought* to raise caste. Why should I not, in virtue of my beauty, attain to the highest of castes, assuming the Merchants was not already regarded, correctly, of course, as such—yes, to the very highest of castes, saving only that of the Initiates, of course."

It seemed clear to me that she did not really believe, whatever might be her protestations, that the Merchants was a high caste. She would be only too eager, it seemed, to "raise caste." What had love to do with such things, I wondered. Why should she wish to raise caste? Surely that was not truly important. Caste considerations seemed to me artificial, and rather meaningless, except as they tended to reflect sets of related occupations. Suppose there was something to caste. Why should she feel herself entitled to raise caste? What was special about her? Why should a Merchant's daughter aspire to a higher caste? With what justification? Why should she be permitted to raise caste? Why should she not look for love in her own caste, or in a lower caste? Why should she not look for love wherever she found it, regardless of caste? But then I was not Gorean. She was a free woman, of course; she could bargain, plan and plot to improve her position in society. How different from a slave. The slave's position in society is fixed, as fixed as the collar on her neck. She cannot sell herself, but is sold. She must serve the humblest master with the same heat, devotion and perfection as the administrator of a city. In fact, I have sometimes wondered if the existence of kajirae on this world does not contribute to its stability. The man who has everything from a woman is not likely to be dissatisfied, cruel and viciously ambitious. He tends to be happy, and happy men are not likely, on the whole, and absent serious provocations, to disrupt society. And the slave, of course, hopes to find her love master, whom she desires in the fullness of her femininity to serve submissively, diligently, gratefully, and joyously, he who will care for her, and love her, and treasure her as a slave of slaves. It is to his whip she wishes to be subject. In all their tenderness he will never let her forget whose collar she wears, and she loves him for it, his strength, and his gift to her, fully and uncompromisingly mastering her.

I wondered if in the free woman, so haughty there in the darkness, there was any femininity, or a woman.

She seemed to have no sense as to what it might be to be a woman. Doubtless her ransom would be paid, and she would never learn.

Had she no slave in the cellars of her heart?

Had she no concept as to where her true happiness might lie?

"Yes," she said, "to the very highest of castes—saving only that of the Initiates, of course."

The Initiates, as I understood it, were celibate, or putatively so.

"Oh, yes! He would come back!" she said. "He was smitten with me! But I would not so much as glance at him now, I reclining in my palanquin. Let him tremble. Let him suffer! The palanquin seemed a sturdy sort. It was he, of course, who would close its shutters. 'Doubtless you will bring a high ransom,' he said. 'What?' I said, turning quickly toward him. The doors of the palanquin swung shut. I heard two bolts slide into place. It suddenly seemed extremely quiet in the palanquin. I rose to my knees and pounded on the door. I could hear my pounding very clearly but could hear little or nothing from the outside. I was suddenly extremely frightened. The palanquin lifted. It began to move. I lost my balance. I wept. I recovered my balance. I cried out. I scrambled about the palanquin, pounding on the sides, the ceiling, the surface of the couch. It continued to move. I did not know to whence it was being borne. I was wild inside it, like a trapped animal. I called to the bearers. It seemed they could not, or would not, hear me. I screamed, my cry wild in the palanquin, reverberating within it, hurting my ears. But such a cry, I suddenly suspected, might not even be audible outside the palanquin. I tore away the hangings inside the palanquin. Behind them was iron. It was doubtless layered, insulated, and baffled. Outside, visible from the outside, would be the lacquered wood of the palanquin, it giving no hint as to what was inside. I lunged, and pressed, against the shutters of the door. They were, too, beneath the silk, torn away, of iron. Their construction was doubtless the same as, or comparable to, the construction of the sides. They were closed, and locked. I put my fingers to the margins of the shutters. They were fitted closely into heavy linings of leather. I could not begin to move them. I flung aside the cushions of the palanquin. I tore aside the coverlets. I thrust back the mattress. The flooring, too, was of iron. I tore the silk from the ceiling. It, too, was of iron. In it, as in the walls, were tiny baffles, doubtless such as to admit air, but soften, or preclude, the exit of sound waves. I knelt on the floor, pressing upward. I could budge nothing. I screamed again. I called out. I threatened. I promised rewards! I cajoled! The palanquin continued to move. It turned from time to time. Perhaps we were in less-traveled streets now, side streets. I grew hoarse with calling out. I could now scarcely speak. The finger tips of my gloves, and the palms of them, were worn and soiled from pressing the hard surfaces about me. My gloves were expensive. They would be ruined. They were even torn at the knuckles. And my knuckles within them, and the sides of my fists within them, hurt, from my pounding on the sides, the floor and ceiling of the palanquin. It turned again, and continued to move. I thrust down the mattress and the coverlets, twisted as they were, and knelt on them, and pounded them, in frustration, in futile rage. I then, exhausted and miserable, threw myself to my stomach upon them, weeping."

"Go on," I said.

"I was in an iron box," she said, "being carried away."

"You were helpless," I said.

"For the first time in my life," she said. "The palanquin was apparently later placed on a wagon, doubtless covered over, and thusly was I removed from the city. I eventually fell asleep and, doubtless Ahn later, I awakened. The palanquin must have been removed from the wagon. The doors opened, and a voice said, 'Come forth.' I crept to the edge of the palanquin, to the threshold. It was dark outside. I was in some sort of ruined barn. I could see through its sides, and roof. We were somewhere in the country. The moons were full. A rope was dropped over my head and drawn closely about my neck. By its means I was drawn from the palanquin. One man then stood behind me, he who held the rope by means of which I was kept in place. I was then, other than for the fellow behind me, standing before my captors. There were, altogether, six or seven of them. He who had lured me to the shop was there, and still masked. It was he who was most prominently before me. It was he, it seemed, who was first among them. 'What is the meaning of this?' I demanded. 'You cannot get away with this!' I cried. 'You will pay for this!' I cried. 'Release me!' I demanded. 'Keep your mouth shut,' he said. He said that to me, a free woman! 'I will do as I please!' I said. 'Do you wish to keep your clothing?' asked one of the men. Another laughed. 'I am a free woman,' I whispered. The fellow in the mask, whom I had foolishly taken as a smitten swain, seemed to be regarding my figure, in the moonlight. Shadows fell across me from the ruins of the barn. Doubtless he was free and could respect me, as I was free, as well. But it made me uneasy, to see him look at me, regarding me in the moonlight, in the shadows, from head to toe. 'Whatever the ransom you wish,' I assured him, 'it will be paid, promptly.' 'Let us strip her,' said one of the brutes, 'and have her serve us, keeping her as a slave, until the ransom is paid. None will know. And she, in her vanity, will never speak of what was done to her.' I could not move, for the rope on my neck. 'No,' said another, 'and if she dared to do so, she would doubtless be remanded to the pens, for sale outside the city.' I trembled. You can well imagine my terror, at the thought of being at the mercy of such beasts! Can you imagine? I, a free woman, to be kept as a slave? I am not such! The thought of it was unconscionable! I wavered. I almost fainted at the thought. 'You see,' said one of them, 'she desires so to serve!' 'No, no!' I cried. They laughed. How could they so misunderstand my responses? 'You would oil, juice and gush, naked, your beauty in chains,' said another. 'No!' I cried. 'You would hasten to serve, once having felt the lash,' said another. I almost swooned. 'No, no,' I murmured, scarcely able to speak. 'Interesting,' mused their leader. Did he, too, misunderstand my responses? 'I am a free woman!' I cried. But then I drew back, in terror, for he in the mask, their leader, had produced a knife. But I did not want to press back against he behind me, either. I stood where I was, frightened, the rope on my neck. Then I did shrink back, for the knife approached me. 'Please!' I protested. I felt its point move through my robes, their layers. Its point was at my lower abdomen. Then, with a quick lateral motion, I crying out a little, it opened a slit in my robes, perhaps a mere hort or two in width. 'Keep your hands to your sides,' said the leader of my captors. The knife, its point, was within my robes. Then it directed itself toward me. I felt the point press lightly, twice, against my lower abdomen. 'Please!' I wept. The point came forward a little. I pressed back, against the captor behind me, literally against him. I was pinned against him, by the point of the knife. My head was up, from the rope on my neck. 'Does she have a belly?' asked one of the men. 'Oh!' I said. I winced. 'It would seem so,' said their leader, he in the mask. The men laughed. 'Is it a pretty one?' asked a man. 'Let us see,' said another. 'Hands at your sides!' I was sternly warned by the leader. I felt the knife turn within my robes, its blade upward. From the manner in which it had earlier parted my robes I knew it was extremely sharp. With one upward diagonal movement I had little doubt it could part my garments, with one stroke revealing me from my lower belly to my throat. I sobbed. I tensed. The knife was removed from my garments, and sheathed. I quickly put my hands over the tiny rent in my robes, and then adjusted them, that it would be covered. One of the men uttered a sound, as of disappointment. 'Hands to your sides,' my captor reminded me. I put my hands again to my sides. The rent was now well concealed, as I had adjusted the robes. 'The value of a slave can only be adequately ascertained when she is utterly bared,' said my captor, 'but the value of a free woman, one for whom a ransom is requested, is often the better preserved the more her modesty is respected.' 'True,' said a man. Unaccountably I was angry. 'Keep your hands to your sides,' said my captor, again. I complied. I then felt a broad band of leather put about me. It was quite snug, and it was buckled behind me. Within it, my arms were helpless. It also had, as I later learned, a ring in the back, by means of which I might be attached to various objects, such as other rings or stanchions. I then stood before them, in this confinement. The rope was still on my neck. 'What ransom shall we ask for you?' inquired my captor. 'I am priceless,' I said. 'Nonetheless,' said he, the beast, 'we shall think in terms of a finite amount.' 'Armies will search for me!' I said. One of the men laughed. 'But doubtless there will be a search,' said another. 'Have no fear, lady,' said my captor. 'We have a place in mind for you, an excellent place, one for your safekeeping, where no one will ever find you.'"

At this point she desisted in her discourse and I heard, in the darkness, an angry, futile rattling of bars. I also detected, again, the creaking of a chain, as though some object, suspended on it, might be swinging back and forth. I did not know in what sort of incarceration she was, of course, but I did not doubt, from what I knew of this world, that it would be effective. I also heard a churning below us, in the water. The sound must have excited the curiosity of something down there.

"He then put his hands to my head," she continued, "I helpless before him, confined in the broad band of leather, held in place by the rope on my neck. His hands were at my veil! 'No!' I cried. His hand removed the pins. He held the veil in place. 'No!' I begged. I was helpless! He could face-strip me at his pleasure! 'You did not care, as I recall,' he said, 'to lower your veil, that even for an instant your features might be glimpsed.' 'No!' I sobbed. These words reminded me, of course, of my own, in the shop. I was terrified. His hands were on my veil. He could remove it, in any fashion he might wish, at any time he might wish. 'If you do not wish your veil lowered,' said he, 'then let it be raised.' He then lifted my veil upward and bound it about my face. In moments, with the veil and other cloths, I was blindfolded. A cloth, too, over the veil, was drawn back between my teeth, deeply, and tied, within my hood, behind the back of my neck. I was thusly gagged. My hood then, too, was drawn forward, over my features, and tied beneath my chin. The rope remained on my neck. I was lifted from my feet, and sat upon the wooden floor. To my horror my hose and slippers were removed. 'She has pretty feet,' said a man. 'Like a slave,' said another. 'Yes,' said another. I drew back my feet, but a man crossed them, the right over the left. They were then lashed together, with the hose. 'The slippers are rich, and intricately embroidered,' said the leader. 'Doubtless there is not another such pair in the city. They will be easily recognized. They will serve as token that she is within our power.' Then said the leader to me, 'One whimper means "Yes," and two whimpers means "No." Do you understand?' I whimpered once. There is apparently a code in such things."

This was true. Such a convention was, as far as I knew, commonly observed on this world. At any rate I, who had been fitted with, and subjected to, and had learned to endure, a considerable variety of gags, and mouth bonds, in my training, was familiar with it. It had been taught me as early as my first gag. I understood, of course, that such things might well not be familiar to free women. To be sure, they are not stupid, no more than other women, and can be taught them quickly. Most slaves, after all, doubtless, were once free women. One interesting form of gag is being "gagged by the master's will," in which the woman is simply forbidden to speak, except, of course, for whimpers, in response to direct questions. One may also be "bound by the master's will," in which case one must keep one's limbs in a given position, perhaps wrists crossed, at the back of one's head, as though they were literally bound, forbidden to separate them without permission. I do not know why one whimper is used for "Yes," and two for "No." It is probably because one usually thinks of such responses, for whatever reason, in terms of "Yes" and "No," rather than of "No" and "Yes." It does not seem to be correlated with the greater frequency of affirmative to negative responses to questions. For example, "Do you wish a blanket in your cell?" is likely to elicit a piteously affirmative response, whereas "Do you wish to be lashed?" is likely to elicit one which is earnestly negative.

"The rope was removed from my neck," she said. "I was then lifted in the arms of someone. 'We expect you to be cooperative,' I was informed by the leader. His voice was from before me, so it was not he in whose arms I was held. 'If you are not cooperative, or choose to be troublesome,' he continued, 'your clothing will be removed, and you will be lashed, as though you might be a slave. Do you understand?' I assumed he was bluffing, but with such a man, with such men, such beasts and brutes, I could not be sure. I whimpered once. 'Take her away,' said the leader. I sobbed, and whimpered, and struggled, but it was to no avail. I was later placed in a trunk of some sort, I think. I heard the latches fastened. Indeed, I thought I heard, as well, the closing of four heavy padlocks. This was placed on a cart. Several times I was transferred from one container or vehicle to another. I was ungagged only in darkness and then to be fed and watered. More than once I was aerially transported."

I, too, at least once, had been so transported. Well I recalled my helplessness, the whistling of the wind, the swaying of the basket. It would be by air, it seemed, in one fashion or another, one would most likely arrive at this place, this apparently remote aerie. She had claimed to be clothed. I supposed it true, but in the darkness I did not know. She must be fortunate. Certainly most of the women I had seen brought here, when I was in the cell in the side of the mountain, had been brought here as stripped, or scantily clad, captives. Slaving, it seemed, was a part of the business of this place. On this world, as I have indicated, women count as loot. Perhaps the women were then transported beyond the mountains, to far markets.

"Often did I recall," said she, "how they had spoken of having a place in mind for me, one for my safekeeping, one in which no one would ever find me!"

I heard her shake the bars in the darkness.

"Oh, yes!" she cried. "Here I am surely theirs! Here I need not fear rescue!"

I thought it true.

"Where is the ruby necklace?" I inquired. I thought it must be very pretty, and of great value.

"They left it on me, the sleen," she cried, "until I arrived here. It was their joke, I think, that I should wear, for all to see, hung about my neck, when I arrived here, what I had sought so avidly, so greedily, that with which they had baited their trap, that by means of which I had been snared, that in virtue of which I had come so simply into their power! But, their joke finished, it was removed from me before I was put here."

"You do not know where it is?" I asked.

"No," she said. "Perhaps it is now once again at its work. Perhaps, even now, it is being used to snare another.

"They are clever wretches!" she cried, suddenly. Again I heard the movement of what must be bars, shaken. She wept.

It seemed, indeed, she had been deftly, and cleverly, taken. The men here, it seemed, were not unskillful in diverse endeavors. Many businesses might be herein practiced. Certainly her acquisition, the arrangements, her transportation and such, spoke of a tried methodology, of some sort of experience or acumen in such matters. I gathered that she was rich. Her ransom, I speculated, would be considerable. It would doubtless be far more than she, or, I supposed, almost any woman, would be likely to bring on a sales block. If that were not the case, it seemed unlikely that the men here would be holding her for ransom. Rather, they would simply sell her, perhaps individually, or in a lot, with others. She was, it seemed, a free woman. I myself, on the other hand, was the sort of woman who is most appropriately owned. I had known this, even on my old world. And here, on this world, I was owned. To be sure, I would have preferred a private master. You might think, incidentally, that all of us would prefer to choose our own master, and not merely a private master, but an individual master, but that is not true. I think I would have preferred to choose my own master, but that is perhaps only because I remembered one from long ago, one before whom I had knelt even before my body had grown used to bonds of iron, one whom I had never forgotten, one whom I had failed to please, one whose whip I had kissed. But some of us, at least, would prefer not to choose our own master, but, rather, to have one imposed upon us, whom we must then, in the fullness of our bondage, willing or not, strive to please. Indeed, had I not met a particular man, one I well remembered, I, myself, might have preferred this latter alternative. I did, of course, hope to have a kind master, or, at least, one as kindly as was compatible with the clear, strict relationship in which we stood to one another. I wanted to win the love of my master, whoever he might be. I asked only the opportunity to serve and love. I was waiting to serve and love. But, in any event, it is not we who choose the masters. It is the masters who choose us.

"Hist!" she said, suddenly. "Someone is coming!"

I sat up, as I could, in the net, my hands bound behind me, my ankles crossed and tied. The net swung.

I heard nothing.

I saw nothing.

I was very still. I strained to hear. If she had truly heard something, her senses must have become considerably sharpened in this environment. To be sure, she might have learned, somehow, to detect and interpret the slightest of sounds in such a place. I did hear a stirring in the waters somewhere beneath. I had heard that sound before.

Then I thought I did hear something.

Something was approaching!

I became suddenly conscious, terribly so, of my helplessness and vulnerability. It was not merely that I was naked and bound, and helplessly the prisoner of a net. It was rather the institutionalized helplessness and vulnerability, so complete, perfect and uncompromising, that was symbolized by my brand and collar. I was a slave.

I thought I saw a light, dim, far off.

What would be done with me?

I recalled that the man in the chair had speculated that Dorna, the high slave, would not be displeased with my disposition. That recollection did not hearten me.

Closer grew the light.

"He is coming," whispered the woman from the darkness. I heard the slight creak of the chain.

It seemed to me that at least two were in the passage, but it may be, I thought, that only one counted.

Of what use, I asked myself, would be my beauty, if beauty it was, or the helplessness of my sexual reflexes, taken as a matter of course in a slave, in a place such as this?

But doubtless I would be assigned my duties!

The light came closer.

I did not even know my name! I had a name. One had been given to me by masters. But I did not know what it was. It was on my collar. I knew that. But I did not know what it was. Indeed, I could not even read.

Now I could hear tiny sounds, unusual sounds, in the approaching passage.

I shuddered, waiting, bound in the net.

I recalled the girl from the surface, a slave, who had been whipped and sent, plunging, into the depths. She was terrified. I had no doubt she would do her best to be found pleasing.

The light was now closer, and I could determine, clearly, that there were two figures in the passage. The first was a woman, in a brief tunic. No more than a rag. She was excellently curved. She was doubtless a slave. She carried a torch. I was not sure what was behind her.

I did not even know, for certain, if it were human or not. It seemed a large, broad thing, but it had tiny legs. It walked bent over. I did not know if it could straighten itself or not. It less walked than shambled. It moved with small steps.

I blinked against the light. It was now bright, contrasting with the precedent darkness.

The woman continued to approach.

The thing, whatever it was, with its small steps, its lurching gait, came shuffling, shambling, behind her, snuffing, sniffing, and grunting. It was not, I surmised, human.

The woman stopped.

She now stood a few feet from me, behind a low wall. This wall was apparently circular. My net, I now discovered, was suspended almost over the center of what appeared to be a large, circular, well-like enclosure. The enclosure was perhaps some sixty-five to seventy feet in diameter. The water, several yards below, was very dark. I saw that my net had some ropes attached to it, which extended to a wall behind the walkway where the woman stood, behind what appeared to be the exterior wall of the well-like structure. I heard a creak of chain to my right, and I looked there, quickly. It was from that direction that I had heard the voice of the free woman earlier. I gasped. There, a few feet to my right, there hung, suspended from a heavy chain, fixed in the ceiling, a narrow, conical-topped, cylindrical cage. It was perhaps some six feet in height, and some two to three feet in diameter. In this cage, standing within it, veiled, in robes of concealment, was a woman. The arrangement of the veils suggested that they were merely tied about her features, and not pinned. Her robes of concealment seemed soiled and, at the hems, were torn. Her small hands grasped the bars of the cage. It was these she had, it seemed, futilely tested from time to time. She did not have gloves, which must have cost her modesty somewhat, but I did not find this surprising. From time to time, her wrists might have been corded before her, or behind her, and men on this world seldom, as I understand it, put bonds over such things as gloves or hose. They prefer on the whole, it seems, to place bonds upon, and to check and test their knots, the arrangement and such, on the bared limbs themselves. In this approach one obtains greater security, of course, as layers between the bonds and the flesh are avoided. I recalled her slippers had been, by her own account, taken from her to be used as evidence of her capture. Too, as I recalled, her ankles had been bound with her own hose. That sort of thing is not unusual. Indeed, the guards in the pens had said that free women were eager to oblige their captors, for they carried about with them, for the convenience of the captors, their own bonds, one stocking for the ankles, the other for the wrists. The free woman pulled her feet back, a little, more under her robes. She was doubtless terribly distressed that her feet were not covered. She was not, after all, a slave. Slaves, I might mention, are often kept barefooted.

"What is that on your neck?" suddenly cried the free woman. "I see it through the cordage of the net! It is glinting! It is a collar! You are a slave, a slave!"

I was too frightened to answer her. I had not told her that I was not a slave, of course. On the other hand, I had not corrected her misapprehension as to the matter. I hoped this would not count as lying. We can be punished terribly for lying.

"Lying slave!" she screamed.

"No, Mistress!" I cried. "Please, no!"

"Oh, you are a well-curved slave!" she cried, angrily. I hoped she would not hold this against me. What could it matter to her, a free woman, if I might bring a good price on the block?

"Deceptive, deceitful slave!" she cried.

"No, Mistress!" I said.

"Well-curved, lying slave!" she screamed.

"Forgive me, Mistress!" I begged.

"Beat her! Beat her!" she called toward the walkway, that behind the wall.

"Please, no, Masters!" I called over my shoulder.

"Deceitful, deceptive, well-curved, lying slave!" screamed the free woman.

"Forgive me, Mistress!" I wept.

"See her ears!" suddenly cried the free woman. "They are pierced!"

The torchlight, doubtless, had reflected from the tiny objects, dropletlike, with their steel pins, which were fastened in my ear lobes. The tiny pins, studlike, had snapped into small disks on the other side. I did not think that these things were intended to be so much ornaments in themselves as devices by means of which to guarantee that the penetrant channels wrought in my body by the worker's needle could not, even in the healing of the flesh, close. They must remain open, held open by the tiny posts about which the wounds would heal, which posts could later be removed, their work done. And thus it was that portions of my body were made such that they would be ready later, at a master's convenience, should he so desire, for the affixing of ornamentation. Even so, of course, the devices made it rather clear that my ears were pierced, as they were.

"Beat her!" screamed the free woman.

"Please, no, Mistress!" I begged.

Then I turned back, blinking against the light, for I felt myself, in the net, by means of ropes, being lowered, and being drawn toward the wall.

I did not want to be beaten!

The net neared the wall. The light was very bright.

"Close your eyes," said the woman with the torch.

I closed my eyes, gratefully, against the light. But, too, of course, I was frightened. The light hurt my eyes. But, too, I wanted to see. But, of course, I had no choice. I had been commanded. I must obey. I am a slave.

I felt the net drawn over the low wall and then I was on the walkway, supine in the net, behind the wall. I could sense the torch, reddish, through my closed eyelids. Its radiated warmth was welcome. I lay on the stones. I heard a sniffing and a shuffling, a grunt. I shuddered, my eyes closed. I felt the toils of the net being drawn aside.

"Let us see what the object looks like," said a slurring voice, scarcely human in sound. "Oh, it is a pretty object."

I felt something large, almost pawlike, brush back my hair. I felt my head turned, from left to right, and back.

"Its ears are pierced," said the slurring voice.

"Yes," said the woman.

They had apparently now determined by actual inspection, at close range, that my ears were indeed pierced, that the objects in view were not otherwise affixed, held in place by, say, clips, or tiny plates, tightened with tiny screws.

"A pierced-ear girl," slurred the voice.

"Yes," said the woman.

"You are a pierced-ear girl," said the voice.

"Yes, Master," I whispered, my eyes closed.
"You are so low?" it asked.
"Yes, Master," I whispered.
"You may open your eyes," said the woman.

I opened my eyes, blinking against the light. I could see her fairly well, standing over me, the torch lifted. She was a brunette, and indeed shapely, and beautiful. She wore a ta-teera, a slave rag. On her neck was a collar. It was narrow, and close-fitting, like mine; this is the sort of collar found most frequently on this world's numerous kajirae; most of us wear it. I could not well see the features of the large, shaggy head which hung over me, as the light was behind it. I knew it could speak. But I did not know if it were human or not. I was sure, whatever it was, it was free. It was the woman behind it, in the collar, the torch lifted, who was slave.

"Untie her ankles," said the voice, and the thing straightened itself a little.

The woman placed the torch in a holder on the nearby wall, near the exit of the passage.

She then crouched down, near my feet. The large, bent thing stood before the torch. I could see only the misshapen shadow, like something between a boulder and an animal.

"You need not look upon his face," she whispered to me, "unless commanded to do so."

"Mistress?" I asked.

"He does not care to have his face gazed upon," she said.

"Is he a beast in the service of the pit master?" I asked.

"He is the pit master," she whispered. "All here who are slave are as though his. In the pits his word is law for us. He is to be obeyed with perfection in all things, instantly, unquestioningly, with no appeal. He is here, in this place, as master."

"'Master'," I whispered, frightened.

"Yes," she said. "That is the power he has here, total power over us, in all ways, the power of the master! We are his, fully, to do with as he pleases."

"The state is my master," I whispered.

"Here," said she, "he is as the state."

I trembled.

"This is his world," she said, "the pits, the darkness. He has power here not only over such as we, but over the prisoners, as well."

"Prisoners?" I asked.

"Of course," she said. "And thus is order kept in this place."

"Is he human?" I asked.

"Yes," she said.

"What are you saying there?" asked the slurring voice, almost like that of a beast.

"Nothing, Master," she said.

"Nothing?" asked he.

"It is only the meaningless drivel of a slave," she averred.

"What have you said to her?" asked he.

"Only little things," she said. "She may desire to live."

"Are you untying her ankles?" asked he.

"I bend to my task, Master," she said.

She knelt by my ankles, bending forward. Her small fingers struggled with the knots. They would not be easy to undo. They had been jerked tight by a man.

"Wait," said he.

"Master?" she asked.

"Does she appear to you sensitive, extremely feminine, even high strung?"

I looked up at the slave, startled.

"Yes, Master," responded the slave, after a moment, thoughtfully.

"Are her ankles still tightly bound?" he asked.

"Alas, yes, Master," said the slave, frightened.

"Desist in your efforts to free her, for the moment," said he.

"Yes, Master," said the slave.

"You are a newcomer to our world, are you not?" it asked.

"Is she not of the Peasants?" called the free woman from her cage, angrily, suspended over the dark waters.

But none paid her attention.

"Yes, Master," I said.

"But you have learned to call men 'Master'?"

"Yes, Master," I said.

"This world is very different from yours, is it not?" he asked.

"Yes, Master," I said.

"But you are learning to fit in, are you not?" he asked.

"Yes, Master!" I said.

"And you belong in a world such as this, do you not?" he asked.

"I fear so, Master," I whispered. It made no sound.

"Yes, Master," I said.

"And as what you are?"

"Yes, Master," I said. It was true.

"Your ankles are tightly tied, are they not?" he asked.

I moved them, a tiny bit. How helpless I was! How tight the cords were!

"Yes, Master," I said.

"Before her ankles are untied," he said, "let her look upon my face."

"Yes, Master," said the slave at my ankles.

I half reared up, my hands bound behind me.

"Courage," whispered the slave, rising to her feet. She went to the torch behind the beastlike figure and removed it from the holder. He approached me, his face in darkness. I moved back a little. I could feel the toils of the net beneath me. How terrifying to be a slave! How helpless we are! His face was now close to mine. The woman then brought the torch forward, so that it was, lifted, a little behind me, near the wall. In this fashion were the features of the pit master illuminated.

I screamed, and tried to scramble back, bound as I was. His hand, on a bound ankle, drew me forward, over the net, on the stones. I twisted and thrashed for a moment, and then, in misery, in disbelief, looking up, past the torch, toward the recesses of the ceiling, lay still. I felt his heavy, pawlike hand. It moved about. I shuddered. "She has smooth skin," he said. He then put a hand to my hair and, by my hair, drew me up, sitting, before him. In my hair his hand was tight. I did not complain. A slave is not a free woman. She does not expect to be handled gently. I did not wish to be cuffed. I kept my eyes closed, desperately. He drew my head forward, closer to his. I could feel the heat of his breath on my face. I sobbed. I gasped. Burning tears forced themselves from between my tightly pressed eyelids. "Open your eyes, it said. I could tell that it was not pleased. His hand was now cruelly tight in my hair. I was well held. My ankles fought the cords on them. My hands were tied behind my back. I could not press him away, or even try to do so. I could not leap up. I could not run. He tightened his grip yet more on my hair and, instantly, sobbing, I ceased to struggle. I held as still as I could. The least movement would have caused me excruciating agony.

"Courage!" whispered the female slave.

"Must a command be repeated?" he inquired.

"No, Master!" I whispered.

I then opened my eyes and now, for the first time, confirming the horror of my earlier, briefest glimpse, looked fully upon the features of the pit master.

It was in the power of this thing that I was!

A convulsive shudder overcame me.

I lost consciousness.

Thirteen

I awakened, kicked.
"Awaken," said a voice, "weak-stomached slut."
"I am awake, Master!" I wept.
"Oh!" I cried, again kicked.
I lay on the walkway, on the toils of the net, on my stomach. I was still bound, as I had been.
"Kneel," said he.
"Master!" I begged.
But he did not qualify, or rescind, his order.
I struggled to comply. Twice I fell, groaning. I feared I might be beaten. Masters are seldom patient with us.
"Master!" I begged, again.
But he was silent.
Again I struggled to comply.
Then, sore, and gasping, I was successful!
A frightened slave girl now knelt before him, naked, and bound hand and foot.
It was I.
I dared not look again on that monstrous head, with its hideous features. The female slave, standing nearby with the torch, had said I need not look upon it, unless commanded to do so.
I kept my eyes down.
He was standing before me.
I could see his sandals.
I bent forward, from the waist, and, putting my head down, pressed my lips to his sandals, licking and kissing them.

And thus did I, a slave girl on an exotic world, seek to placate he who was to me in this place as master.

"Do the women of your world seek to placate thusly the men of their world?" he asked.

"Doubtless some, Master," I said.

"But it is done rarely?" he asked.

"I do not know, Master," I said.

"But it is not done rarely on this world," he said.

"No, Master," I said.

"And you are now of this world," he said.

"Yes, Master," I said.

"You lick and kiss well," he said.

"Thank you, Master," I said. I loved to render such obeisance to men. It seemed, somehow, so very real, and fulfilling to me. In such a humble act I acknowledged, and honored, not only the maleness of a given individual, of a given master, but, in a sense, all maleness, and the might of the mastery, and expressed, lovingly, in joy and tenderness, my femaleness. There is something profoundly symbolic in this simple act. I find it very moving. To be sure, it can be performed under many quite different circumstances and conditions. Sometimes one performs it in timidity, or even terror. Sometimes one may perform it as a way of pleading, even, for one's life. And this thing to which I now addressed these attentions, I knew, might not even be human. It seemed to me, in effect, a monster. But it seemed to me, still, this way of rendering obeisance, to be a way of expressing even to it, even to what was perhaps some sort of monster, that I was a slave, and desired to be pleasing. I was, after all, subject to its domination, as I would have been to an individual master, one who had, say, bought me off a block.

He bent down and lifted me up, and then sat me back, my back against the retaining wall, separating the well-like enclosure from the walkway.

"Can you untie her ankles?" he asked the female slave.

"I do not think so," she whispered. She had struggled futilely with the knots. They were, it seemed, beyond her strength.

The shape then bent down and, with its great hands, undid the knots. He did this easily.

I was then lifted to my feet. I stood unsteadily.

"We will show her the pool," said the creature.

I did not look at him. I kept my eyes away from his visage.

"Yes, Master," said the slave with the torch.

The three of us stood then near the wall. I was still unsteady. The walkway went all about the well-like enclosure. I could see other passages opening from it, here and there.

"Beat her!" called the free woman from the cage.

The pit master regarded her. The slave with the torch lifted it higher.

"She told me she was a free woman!" said the free woman.

"Did you tell her that?" asked the creature.

"No!" I said, frightened. "I did not tell her that!"

"Do you think you are a free woman?" he asked.

"No, Master!" I said.

"What are you?"

"A slave, Master!" I cried.

"Anything else?" he asked.

"No, Master," I said, "only a slave, only that!"

"Did you let her believe you to be a free woman?" asked the creature.

"Yes, Master," I moaned.

"See!" cried the free woman.

"You should have informed her instantly that you were only a slave," he said.

"Yes, Master," I said.

"She told me she was of the Peasants!" said the free woman.

"No!" I cried. "I never said that!"

"You permitted her to believe it?" asked the pit master.

"Yes, Master," I whispered.

"You should not have done that," he said.

"I am new to your world, Master!" I said.

"You must learn our ways more quickly," he said.

"Yes, Master," I said.

"You must be punished," he said.

"Yes, Master," I said.

"And was she never even of the Peasants?" asked the free woman.

"No," said the pit master. "She has always been casteless."

"She was not even once of the lowest of castes?" inquired the free woman, puzzled.

"She has always been casteless, completely," said the pit master.

I could sense that this puzzled the free woman.

"As an animal?" asked the free woman.

"Yes," said the pit master.

I thought of the women of my world. Certainly the vast majority of us did not have caste. How natural then that we should be put in collars! And even if we had caste our castes would doubtless not be respected by these men. They would simply take them from us, making us their slaves. There had been two girls from India, beauties both, in my training group. Certainly they had not found themselves regarded any differently, or treated any differently, from the rest of us, whether from Germany, or Japan, or the United States, or elsewhere. Their caste had been taken from them. They, too, as we, were now only slaves. They learned to lick and kiss the whip as quickly, as delicately, as the rest of us. And, indeed, the vast majority of female slaves on this world would surely be native to this world, and would, thus, presumably, have once had caste. But, in being enslaved, they were stripped of their caste. In the end, it seemed, there were no castes, only men, and women.

"She is a barbarian?" asked the woman.

"Yes," said the pit master. He spoke to her, I supposed, because she was free.

"I knew that!" she said. "I could tell from her accent, which is terrible."

"She speaks well," said the pit master.

I undoubtedly did have an accent. On the other hand, I gathered that I spoke the language quite well, considering my limited time on this world. One might mention that the language, as far as I can tell, is spoken with a great variety of accents. For example, the men in the pens spoke quite differently from those I had encountered on the surface of the tower. Too, there seemed to be class differences even in given areas. I had heard my accent spoken of, incidentally, as a "slave accent," of which there were apparently several. On the other hand, the free woman had apparently not taken it as such. Perhaps if she had seen me in a slave tunic, kneeling before her, she might have done so. I supposed it would be impossible for me to ever completely eradicate the "slave accent" from my speech. I had not, for example, learned the language as a child. Too, there were certain words, and combinations of words, in this language I found it impossible to pronounce like a native speaker. Too, if I grew excited, or confused, I would surely betray myself by some slip. Too, some utterance in my native tongue might escape me in dreaming. And there were numerous other ways, too, physical and otherwise, in which my origins might be betrayed, such as a vaccination mark and two tiny fillings. The latter, for example, would surely be discovered when a possible buyer checked the condition of my teeth. Too, I would be ignorant of thousands of things which would be common knowledge to natives of this world. Too, I would never have an opportunity to learn many of these things, secret sayings and such, for it is forbidden to teach them to slaves. The important thing, of course, is not the accent, or what one knows, but what one is. Even the most informed and sophisticated woman of this world, you see, once she is enslaved, becomes instantly, doubtless to her horror, no more than a property, an animal, that which must serve, that which may be done with as the master pleases.

"Fellow," said the free woman.

"Yes?" said the pit master.

"What nonsense was it," asked the free woman, "your talk about another 'world,' or such?"

"It is no nonsense," said the pit master. "She comes from another world."

"I have heard of such things," said the free woman. "Are they true?"

"Yes," said the pit master. He then put his hand in my hair and forced me forward, more in the light of the torch. I literally now felt the height of the wall against my thighs. I did not like standing so close to it. A small pressure could have forced me over the wall, tumbling to the dark waters below. To be sure, his hand was in my hair, holding me. I felt very helpless. My hands were still tied tightly behind my back. "Here is the proof," he said. By his grasp on my hair he pressed me further forward, more tightly against the wall, and then, holding me there, he pulled my head back by the hair, to better show my collar. "A barbarian slave girl," he said.

"Beat her!" cried the free woman. "Beat her!" She wrung her hands. "How she humiliated me," she cried, "letting me think her free, letting me think she held caste! How demeaned I have been, speaking to one who was only bond!"

He pulled my head back, further.

I whimpered.

He held me there, thusly. And thus was I exhibited naked, and bound and collared, in the torchlight, in that dark place, before another woman, I only a barbarian slave.

"Insolent slave!" cried the free woman. "Insolent slave!"

The cage actually moved on its chain, so incensed she was.

"I was speaking to a barbarian slave!" cried the free woman, in misery, dismayed, furious.

I had not known what I should have done! I had been frightened, and bound, in the darkness. But of course I should have known what I should have done! Certainly I had been fearful enough in the darkness, filled with enough trepidation concerning her presumptions. Did I not know the differences between such as I and such as she? Was I not such that I would at best be privileged to serve her deferentially at table—briefly tunicked, were men present, were she a thoughtful hostess, for their pleasure—my head down, not meeting her eyes, not even daring to speak to her? Or perhaps one such as she might have me serve garbed in a long, sleeveless, demurely white serving gown, my hair bound back, that I not be too distractive to the males, save perhaps for the collar on my neck. She would not wish to remove the collar, of course, but, too, she must know its effect on males, that it says that she who wears it is *kajira*, in effect, *theirs*. Most slave garments, incidentally, are sleeveless. I am not sure why that is, but it seems to be another way of drawing a distinction between slave and free. I suppose it has to do with the baring of flesh, which is regarded not only as acceptable for a slave, but, in the case of an animal, which she is, appropriate. It is also a way of helping the slave keep in mind that she is a slave. The contrast with the robes of concealment is obvious. I think, incidentally, that the robes of concealment must be terribly uncomfortable in the summer. In hot weather free women often wear sliplike garments in the privacy of their own quarters. In slavers' raids they are not unoften surprised and discommoded in such a state of charming dishabille. Their appearance is so fetching in such garments that they are sometimes permitted to retain them until caged in the hunting camp. They might also be presented in such garments in their sale—at the *beginning*, I should say, of their sale. One might mention, in passing, that Gorean men find the *entire* female sexually stimulating, not just, say, the legs, the bosom, the derrière, and so on. They can also be excited by the throat, a wrist, and certainly the arms, and so on. Too, perhaps surprisingly, from the point of view of at least some men of Earth, they are interested in what is going on inside of her, as well, in her internal world, so to speak, in her thoughts, her feelings, her emotions, and such. These women are properties, you see, and men, as is well known, take a great interest in their properties. Why not, they belong to them; they own them. I think it is indisputable that the average Gorean master knows a great deal more about his slave or slaves, inside and out, so to speak, than the average husband does of his wife. How many husbands, for example, will kneel their wife down naked and have her talk to him for two or three hours at a time? One, of course, learns a great deal about a woman in this way, and very quickly. The whole slave is bared to the master, not just her lovely body. She cannot help this, this exposure of her so fully, for she must keep talking. She will reveal more and more of herself, regardless of her wishes. One cannot help that. The speaking, too, of course, may be directed by questions and commands, and, if necessary, with blows of the switch. A woman under this regimen, so fiercely dominated, cannot keep shut the doors of her heart. She must open them, sooner or later, whether she wishes to or not. She finds that she is helpless. She must bare more and more of herself to the master. He will have it no other way, and thus he learns her, and she, before him, on her knees, knows herself learned. Too, this practice has its effect on the slave as, by its means, she finds herself, despite what she may initially will, becoming more and more his. After as little as a few days, subject to this enforced and prolonged intimacy, she begins to find the master irresistible, and she longs to give herself to him. But he may starve her for physical contact until one day he snaps the whip and permits her to crawl to his feet, as she fervently wishes to do, and beg to serve him. She wears his collar. Will he not permit her to please him? She begs him to effectuate the mastery, as though he had not already done so, and put her to his pleasure.

"She is new to our world," said the pit master, somewhat angrily.

"She should know better!" screamed the free woman.

"True," said the pit master.

"She is stupid!" cried the woman. "She is stupid!"

"She is extremely intelligent," said the pit master, "considering what she is, a slave." He had doubtless been expecting me here, and had doubtless been apprised of the contents of my papers. I was glad to learn that I might be thought to be intelligent, if only for a slave. Such things, I had learned, considerably improve a girl's price. The men on this world relish intelligent women. We make, it is said, the best slaves. How they make us serve and obey!

More is expected, you see, of an intelligent slave. Demands are placed on her intelligence. It is challenged, and exploited. She is in the beginning perhaps its lamenting victim, for she is treated with such impatient severity and so much is expected of her, but is soon, as she grows, blossoms and thrives in her bondage, and as her master is more pleased with her, the joyful recipient of its attendant benefactions. Intelligent, she derives more from the uncompromising completeness of her state and the deliciousness of her domination. She is expected, you see, to serve with sensitivities, delicacies, diligences and subtleties beyond the ken of simpler women. Our intelligence, interestingly, makes us more the properties of our masters, just as one will demand, and have, more from an intelligent animal than from one less intelligent; we are more easily controlled in a thousand ways by as little as a glance or gesture, because we grasp what is required; our bodies, too, tend to be more sensitive, and this puts us the more at the mercy of our masters, and any disciplines he may choose to impose upon us; if we attempt to conceal our intelligence, in order to have less expected of us, we are whipped; our service is to be perfect, and well beyond that of a less intelligent woman; too, our faults or shortcomings are dealt with more severely, for we should know better. Too, for what it is worth, intelligent women are commonly better looking than less intelligent women, a feature which is not without its appeal to masters, and one which makes them more likely candidates for the slavers' ropes and irons; too, they also tend to be more helplessly responsive in the arms of a master. They tend, as well, to be more in touch with their inner selves and secret needs, and less the victims of negativistic conditioning programs. The intelligent woman often knows what she is missing and what she wants, whereas the less intelligent woman is often little more than the troubled, unwitting victim of the prescriptions and pathologies of a negativistic culture within which she is, unbeknownst to herself, imprisoned.

"I am a helpless free woman," said the free woman, wheedlingly, "and you are a free man. I have been insulted. I must depend upon you to see that my honor is suitably satisfied."

"The barbarian slave will be suitably punished," he said.

"Excellent!" she said.

The pit master, in spite of the power which he doubtless held in this place, even over prisoners, as I had been informed, seemed concerned to treat the free woman with respect. This, I gathered, might be cultural, or perhaps he, somehow, oddly, despite his grotesque appearance, might be sensitive to some subtle canons of gentility. I had noted that the guards in the pens had similarly shown great deference to free women. To be sure, those free women might have been important, and they were certainly not prisoners. This deference, it might be mentioned, had not precluded, later, and the next day, the women gone, a number of rude jokes pertaining to them, nor some rather explicit speculations as to what they might look like, chained naked to a floor ring. The respect commonly shown to free women on this world is not, of course, accorded to slaves. It would never have occurred to the pit master, or to other men of this world, to treat me as other than what I was, a slave. How different we are from free women! And yet, interestingly, how artificial, and how fragile, and how culturally precarious, is the distinction between the free woman and the slave. Do the free women understand that that distinction is not part of nature, like dominance and submission, but that it depends merely on the will of men? Do they not understand that their lofty status requires the permission of males, and, in a sense, depends upon the whims of males? There is a thin line, and a short distance, between the free woman and the slave, a line as thin as slave silk, a distance as short as the three links joining slave bracelets.

"What of my ransom?" called the free woman. "Has it arrived?"

"No," said the pit master.

"Surely it is overdue!" she cried, grasping the bars of the cage.

"I do not know," said the pit master.

"Well, inquire!" she cried.

The pit master was silent. I did not think he was pleased. He removed his hand from my hair. Instantly I knelt, head down, near him.

"Inquire!" demanded the free woman. The pit master was silent.

"Expedite the matter!" she cried, shaking the bars. He was silent.

"Please, my handsome fellow," she wheedled.

"Lift the torch, higher," said the pit master, slowly, as though curious, to the lovely brunet slave beside him.

As none were paying me attention I dared to look up. Should the pit master turn to regard me I would instantly look down, and away. I did not wish to appear insolent, meeting his eyes. Too, I was not eager to behold again that visage.

The ceiling flickered wildly in the illumination of the torch.

Suddenly the pit master, that shambling creature, who had apparently been curious to look more closely upon something, uttered an angry noise.

The slave with the torch gasped.

She, too, it seemed, had noted something.

The free woman in the cage stepped back a little.

The pit master pointed toward the bottom of the cage. The cage, as the net had had, had various ropes attached to it. By these ropes, I surmised, once it was lowered on its chain, perhaps by some sort of windlass, it might be drawn toward the walkway.

"What is wrong?" asked the free woman.

I gathered that she might, from her words, have some conception as to what might be wrong.

"Remove the cloth," said he, "from the latch."

"No!" she wept. "Please!"

But she obeyed. The cage, apparently, opened and closed from the bottom, gated by a hinged plate. She had tied something, probably a strip of cloth from the bottom of her robes, which were ragged now, in such a way as to prevent the release of the floor. A cord, coiled on the walkway, ran to the latch. By drawing on this cord it seemed the latch could be released. She stood in the cage, over the water. In her hand was the piece of cloth.

The pit master reached to the cord which controlled the latch.

"Please, no!" she cried.

"How," asked the pit master, "is a female prisoner who is a free woman to address her jailer?"

"As 'Sir'!" she cried.

"You seem, hitherto, to have omitted that courtesy," he observed.

"'Sir,' 'Sir,' 'Sir'!" she wept.

"You must understand," he said, "that in this place you are mine."

"Yes, Sir!" she wept.

"Hold to the bars," he said.

Desperately, weeping, she clung to them. I gathered that she might have experienced something of this sort before.

He jerked the cord and it sprang the latch, and the bottom plate of the cage, she screaming with terror, I, too, crying out in terror, dropped down, on its hinge. She slipped partly through the opening, and then scrambled back within the cage, clinging to the bars, her feet trying to find some purchase there.

The cloth she had held floated down to the water.

Instantly I heard a rushing, a stirring in the water, a turmoil there, and the ripping of cloth, and an angry squealing.

I could not see what was there.

The free woman was screaming.

I almost fainted.

The pit master then went to a wheel set in the wall and, turning it, bit by bit, foot by foot, lowered the cage toward the water.

"Sir, Sir!" screamed the free woman, as the cage, foot by foot, descended.

"Show the slave the pool," said the pit master.

"Up, slave, to the wall," said the brunette with the torch.

I rose up. I could hardly stand, so frightened I was. I did not want to approach the wall too closely. I was afraid of falling. My hands were bound behind me. What if I should lose my balance? How could I protect myself?

"Closer!" said the brunet slave.

I came closer to the wall, looked, gasped, cried out in terror, and shrank back.

The free woman was hysterical in the cage.

"Look!" commanded the brunet slave.

I came forward, again, and looked. In the water, swirling about, were several dark, sleek shapes. I had never seen anything like them.

They seemed like some form of rodent, but they were far too large. They were not like the six-legged creatures I had seen before, that on the ledge, that on the surface of the tower.

"Urts," said the female slave with the torch.

I saw some of these things now, their fur wet, their ears back against the sides of their heads, leaping upward, trying to reach the cage.

Then the cage stopped descending.

The free woman tried to draw herself higher into the cage.

I could see in the torchlight, a moment before it broke the surface, one of the beasts, swimming rapidly upward. Then it left the water, rushing upward from it, erupting from it, and I saw its full body, shedding water, its neck extended, its jaws open, its forepaws down against its body, streamlining its shape, its hind legs extended, it leaping upward, then yards above the surface of the torn, dark pool, and then it seemed to pause in the air, and then, snarling, just short of the cage, it dropped back into the pool. Water splashed up. It drenched the cage, the feet of the free woman. I felt it even on my body, where I stood. Other beasts, too, now essayed the leap. They, gathering force, swimming swiftly in ever widening, preparatory circles just under the water, would plunge down, yards from the cage, and then ascend rapidly, spearing upward, snapping, from the water. Then, in rage, in frustration, they would drop back in the water. Closer and closer they came. The brunet slave held the torch back that its flame might not be extinguished by the drenching water. One of the beasts caught a bottom circling bar of iron in its teeth. It swung for a moment from the cage. Its forepaws fought for purchase at the cage, but the claws scratched futilely on the dangling solid gate, forcing it back on its hinges. The free woman screamed. It snapped at the free woman, in this action losing its hold on the cage. Again she screamed, the thing just below her. Then, snarling and squealing, it fell back into the water. Its jaws had been no more than inches from the feet of the free woman. Another beast leaped upward, falling just short of her, its snout actually within the opened cage. Some beasts did not leap upward but remained patiently, tensely quiescent in a wide circle in the water, a circle ranging about the cage. They lay there, almost flat in the water, mostly submerged. One could see their nostrils, their eyes, the top of their glistening heads, the ears back against the sides of the heads. Their bodies were oriented in such a way as to face the center of the circle. The free woman could climb no higher in the cage. She clung within it, sobbing and hysterical, like a small, wet, trembling, terrified bird. Up leapt another of the beasts and it caught a hem of her ragged robes in its teeth and tore a strip from them, which it bore with it back to the dark pool. Again she screamed. I could now see a flash of calf within her robes. It was not a poorly turned calf. I thought she might be acceptable as a slave. Again and again she screamed. Then the pit master, slowly, reversed the wheel and, bit by bit, raised the cage, until it was level with the wall. The free woman clung within it, her feet drawn up. The pit master left the wheel and took the cord. He snapped it up, and the cage floor, flung up, snapped into place. To be sure, so little as another tug, like the first, would once again release it.

"Release the bars," he said to the free woman. "Stand on the floor of the cage, in its center, your hands closely at your sides."

Trembling, she obeyed.

I saw the cord taut between the hand of the pit master and the latch.

The slightest tug on the cord would spring the latch, dropping the floor of the cage, which was its gate, plunging her helplessly to the cold, dark waters below, to the jaws of the waiting beasts.

"You are never again," said he, "to impede, or attempt to impede, the operation of the latch."

"Yes, Sir," she whispered.

"The cage must be such," said he, "that at any time, perhaps even when you sleep, the latch may be released. Do you understand?"

"Yes, Sir," she said, weakly.

How helpless she was! How vulnerable must be one in such a confinement!

"Understand, too," said he, "that the cage is designed for naked, shackled, shaved-headed slave girls."

The nudity of the imprisoned slave, I supposed, aside from the usual purposes of such, such as to protect clothing from being soiled, to help her keep in mind that she is a slave, and such, is to prevent the possible use of clothing to secure the latch. The shaved-headedness of them, aside from the usual purpose of such, which is punishment, would doubtless be to prevent the attempt on their part to secure the gate by means of their hair. Shaved-headedness, of course, is not always a punishment. It is sometimes done for hygienic purposes, as on slave ships, and for safety purposes, as in factories. Too, a girl's head may be shaved simply to obtain the hair, which may then be sold. For example, our shorn hair may be sold to jobbers who deal with the manufacturers of artillery and siege equipment. Our "pelting," as it is sometimes referred to in the trade, is apparently considerably superior to hempen strands for use as catapult cordage. Slave girls, it might be mentioned, normally have long hair, as it is very beautiful, and much may be done with it, both cosmetically, so to speak, and in the furs. Too, we may even be bound with it. The shackling in such a cage, of course, aside from its common purposes, such as showing that the female is a slave, enhancing her beauty, and such, would make it difficult or impossible for her to prevent her slipping through the opening of the cage. This would particularly be the case if her hands were shackled behind her and her ankles were shackled closely together.

"I am kept in a slave cage?" she said.

"Yes," said he.

"I am a free woman," she said. "I protest!"

"Your protest is noted, and overruled," he said.

"May I remove my arms from my sides?" she asked.

"No," he said.

She continued to stand in the center of the cage, her arms at her sides. The cord was still taut between his hand and the latch.

"We have been until now indulgent with you," he said. "But you have abused our lenience. If you should dare again to attempt to interfere with the possible functioning of the cage you will find yourself within it as though you might be a slave girl. You will be shackled within it, naked, and with your head shaved. Do you understand?"

"Yes, Sir," she said.

"You may remove your hands from your sides," he said.

Swiftly, gratefully, she seized the bars, putting her arms about them. It seemed she scarcely dared to stand on the floor of the cage, that constituting, too, its gate.

"You are gloveless," he said. "Your hands have been stripped."

"Yes, Sir," she said.

"And your feet have been stripped," he said.

"Yes, Sir," she said.

"And your face, too, as you doubtless realize," said he, "might be stripped, your features revealed to all and sundry."

"Yes, Sir," she said.

"And you realize that your body, too, might be stripped," he said, "utterly."

"Yes, Sir," she said.

"You understand all this?" he asked.

"Yes, Sir," she moaned.

"Be good," he said to her.

"Yes," she whispered.

"Yes, what?" asked he.

"Yes, Sir," she said.

He went then again to the wheel, at the wall, and, turning the crank, began to raise the cage. She moaned. As the cage rose the various ropes, and the cord extending to the latch, uncoiled from their respective places. And still there were many coils left. He now raised the cage to a point much higher than it had been at first. It hung now, swinging on its chain, but a foot or two below the lofty vaulted ceiling. The torch hardly reached so high. If the latch were sprung now she would plunge perhaps twenty yards before striking the surface of the pool.

"Sir!" called the free woman, from high above. "Sir! Please, Sir!" There was a ring to her voice, from the stone of the chamber.

The pit master looked up at the cage. The brunet slave lifted the torch a little higher.

As the demonstration, or whatever it might have been, for the benefit of the free woman, and perhaps, too, for my benefit, seemed to have been concluded, I knelt. Indeed, it was hard to stand. I was shaken. I was trembling. Too, of course, in the presence of a free person, or persons, this is an appropriate, and common, posture for slaves. When a free person enters a room, unless we are serving another, or something of such a sort, we commonly kneel. Even if we are naked in the furs, we will commonly kneel, perhaps then merely to be thrown back upon them.

And so, unbidden, I knelt, a slave.

"How progress negotiations pertinent to my ransom?" she called down.

"I do not even know if there are such negotiations," he said.

"What?" she cried.
"I have no information pertaining to such," said he.
"Surely I have not been forgotten!" she cried.
"I do not know," said he.
"Surely negotiations proceed!" she exclaimed.
"Perhaps," he said.
"In this very city!" she said.
"No," said he. "Such negotiations, if there are such, would be conducted elsewhere, perhaps even thousands of pasangs away." This was, I gathered, a great distance.
"Is it not known that I am here?" she begged.
"No," said he. "It is not known that you are here."
"How long must I stay here?" called the free woman.
"I do not know," said he. "Perhaps for years, perhaps forever."

The free woman, far above us, cried out with dismay. I heard the bars shaken. I heard her weeping.

I put my head down, swiftly, for I was now illuminated by the torch.

"Stand," said he.

I struggled to my feet, as quickly as I could. If one knows what is wise for one, one obeys the men of this world instantly, and as perfectly as possible.

He took the rope which had bound my ankles and looped it about my bound wrists, behind me.

"Bend over, at the waist," said he.

I did so, and he took the double strand of the rope looped about my wrists and brought it forward, between my legs, and then looped it up and, separating the strands, passed one over my collar and then tied it to the other. In this fashion was my head held down. This is a not uncommon tie. It may also function to keep a kneeling girl's head down. It is useful in learning deference. A similar tie, but one which immobilizes the slave, utilizes a short tether running from her bound ankles to the front of her collar. In these ways any pressure which might be exerted is exerted at the back of the neck. The front of the throat is, of course, as you are doubtless well aware, easily damaged and is to be carefully protected. Similar precautions occur with several other forms of domestic animal, as well, not merely slaves. In my training, in the pens, I had occasionally been put in a choke collar. In it, I assure you that I obeyed instantly, obedient to its slightest pressure. On the other hand, such things, I think, should seldom, if ever, be used with slaves, particularly with female slaves, who tend to be beautiful, delicate and sensitive. Their use, I think, if they are used at all, should be reserved for fierce animals, such as the six-legged beasts I had seen, or perhaps for powerful warriors, or brawny, recalcitrant male slaves in the quarries or mines, captives or animals whose control may require such fierce devices. We do not need them! We know who is master. Our leash training, I assure you, may be accomplished readily with the common leash and collar, and a whip or switch. Indeed, I believe it can be more quickly and efficiently completed, as, less terrified of our lives, except to the extent that we might be found displeasing, we are, in a normal leash and collar, freer to concentrate our attention more fully on our lessons. If you are concerned with such things, do not fear. The whip or switch, I assure you, gives you more than ample control over us.

"Oh!" I said, for he had seized the rope running from my hands, tied behind my back, to the front of my collar, and, by means of it, threw me forcefully, stumbling, toward the passageway. Within it I stopped, gasping. He and the slave were still behind me, on the walkway about the retaining wall. I could tell their position from the torchlight. I could no longer see the cage, suspended at the top of the chamber.

"May I speak, Master?" asked the slave with the torch.

"Yes," said he.

"Do you think her ransom will be paid?" she asked.

"Let us hope so, for her sake," said he, "for I have not found her pleasing."

"Yes, Master," she said.

He then entered the passageway, shambling within, followed by the beautiful brunette, holding the torch. Her hair was long and loose. Not even a string had been given to her to dress it. It flowed about her shoulders, and behind her even to the small of her back. I envied her such hair. I had no doubt she would bring a high price. Was the coinage of beautiful women so plentiful here, in this city of raiders and warriors, I wondered, that even specimens such as she, such gems as she, who might be the centerpiece of a collection elsewhere, who might be brought to the block at the climax of an auction, labored here in the darknesses beneath the city as though she might be the lowest of slaves, subservient in a gloomy labyrinth supervised by a monster. But she could not be the lowest of slaves for I was surely lower than she. My ears were even pierced, which was, it seemed, a matter of great moment on this world. Too, I need not pity her too much, nor with fear and loathing bemoan the uniqueness of her fate, for the monster to whom she addressed the title "Master" was none other than that to which my own service and deference were due. I began, bent over, to tremble in terror. What manner of place was this? How could it be that my hands were tied behind my back, how could it be that I could not straighten up, that my head was held down, how could it be that there was a collar on my neck! How far away were the malls! But, yet, too, how vanished here were the confusions, the anomie, the pretenses, the trivialities, the meaninglessnesses, the nonrealities of my former life! In this very real place, on this far world, I found myself, for the first time in my life, very real. I was now something quite real. No longer was there doubt about my existence or my meaning. No, that was all behind me. I was now something quite real, as unimportant as it might be. I now had an identity, as lowly as it might be. It was as clear, certain, inflexible, and undeniable as the collar on my neck.

The monster, or whatever it might have been, entered the passage, the slave behind him. He paused at a panel set in the stone, unlocked it, opened it, and revealed several levers, one of which he moved. Lines of bars emerged from the walls about the pool and, diagonally, descended, fitting into sockets in the retaining wall. This sealed off the area of the pool. He moved a second lever, and I saw bars descend, closing our passage. From the sound I thought that other passages might have been sealed, as well. I could not see from where I was. As there were several levers it seemed possible that passages might be sealed off selectively, or, perhaps, as I thought might be the case now, at the same time. The panel box was perhaps a master control for the adjacent passages. If all the passages were sealed off, and the side bars engaged, as they were now, that would isolate the walkway. I could still see the walkway beyond the bars in the torchlight. Another lever was depressed. I did not, at the time, understand its function, but, in a moment or two, its effect had become clear. It must have opened some access between the pool and the walkway, for I heard a scratching and sniffing and then saw, to my horror, on the other side of the bars of the passage gate, reflected in the torchlight, the blazing eyes of one of the large rodentlike creatures. There were other bodies, too, behind it. I saw snouts pressed against the bars. These things then might, if one wished, be introduced into various passages, depending on the opening and shutting of the gates. I also learned, later, that access to nesting areas was similarly provided. This was, of course, but one area in the "pits," of many different sorts of areas, and, I might mention, neither the best nor the worst. They constitute almost a city beneath a city. I think regiments might lie concealed within them, and I have little doubt they could, passage by passage, be tenaciously defended. I would come to know certain portions of them very well, but in many portions I would not be permitted. I was, after all, a slave.

"Precede us," said the pit master.

"Yes, Master," I said.

"Turn left here," he would say, "and right, there, and now left again," and so on.

I was soon bewildered and lost, but, nude, head down and bound, I must precede them.

"Harta!" said he. "Faster!"

I hurried, even more, as I could.

Mostly I could see little but the floor of the passage at my feet, and the shadows, my own before me, and his, a misshapen, gliding thing, half on the floor, half on the wall, to the right of mine.

"Left here," he would say. "Right here!"

"Yes, Master!" I would cry.

I was aware, too, as we passed them, of gates here and there, some barred, beyond which I could see the darkness of a further corridor, and some of plain iron, secured with bolts and padlocks, leading perhaps, too, to further passages. Sometimes I trod not on stone but on perforated plate or grillwork. What, if anything, or of what depth, might lie beneath most such platings or grillwork I did not know. Beneath one such flooring, however, far below, I heard moving water. Beneath another I thought I heard, far off, a sort of roaring. I did not know the cause of the sound. It may have been that of wind or water, oddly magnified and distorted in the tunnels, or, perhaps, that of some beast or beasts.

"Hold!" said the monster behind me, sharply.

Instantly I stopped.

I screamed!

From either side of the passage, with a swift, loud, rattling sound, there had suddenly sprung forth a set of sharpened metal projections.

The closest of these was only inches from me.

I sank faintly to my knees, sick, unable to stand.

"On your feet," I heard.

I struggled to my feet. I could see the torchlight reflected on the points.

"In the pits," said he, "there are numerous such devices. Some you will learn. Others you will be kept ignorant of, even within passages with which you will be familiar. Will they be set, or not? It will be in your interests to confine your movements to prescribed routes at specified times. Do you understand?"

"Yes, Master," I said.

"It is well that you obeyed promptly," he said.

"Yes, Master," I said. "Thank you, Master."

We are, of course, trained to instant obedience. The value of such training, of course, is easy to see in matters as obvious as that recently noted. What may not be as immediately obvious is its similar value in avoiding what may be even greater dangers, such as displeasing the master. We are not first here, at least women such as I. It is the men, they, who are the masters.

He went to the side of the wall, as I could see from the shadow, but I could not detect what he did. The points receded into the walls.

"Precede us," he said.

"Yes, Master," I said.

"Harta! Harta!"

"Yes, Master!" I wept.

Sometimes, too, we crossed chasmlike gaps in the passages. We did this on narrow, metal bridges. These bridges were not such as the earlier "bridge," that which had led toward the surface of the turret, or tower, which had been little more than a flat rail. These bridges, while frightening, were considerably less harrowing. They must have ranged from twelve to eighteen inches in width. In the torchlight I picked my way carefully across them. I did not dally, for fear of the monster behind me. I feared him more than the bridge. The bridges were locked in place on pegs. For one possessing the means, they could be freed and drawn away, to one side or the other, or even plunged into the opening below. I did not know how deep these openings were. Given the narrowness of the bridges a single man, armed, could have defended them against several foes, for they could approach him only singly. The monster behind me, and the lovely slave with the torch, crossed them easily. I was from Earth, however, and was uneasy on such passages, as routine or secure they might have been for those of this world.

I could not rid my mind of the sudden appearance of the rattling projections. Such devices, I supposed, might be common in places such as these. I had heard, too, of such things as blades and pits. Naturally then I was terrified that I must hurry ahead. Yet I reminded myself that I was not a free person, but only a domestic animal and thus, presumably, as long as I was docile, and obedient, and perfect in my service, and fully pleasing, I might hope to be spared. I do not here, incidentally, discuss the nature of slave traps, as they constitute a different object of discourse. Some of these are rather benign devices, with no object more in mind than to discommode a free woman until the hunters arrive and collect her. Others, with coiled wire, with springs and steel teeth, generally designed for the capture of escaped male slaves can be quite cruel. Smaller, lighter versions of such traps exist for escaped female slaves. Within some of these devices, surrounded by the wire and blades, one cannot move without cutting oneself to pieces. I had once, in training, been carefully entered into one, and then left there, standing, for more than an hour. It helped to impress upon me, as did a thousand other considerations, physical and social, the hopelessness of escape for a female slave.

We crossed another such bridge.

"Hold," said the pit master.

Instantly I stopped, gasping, looking wildly about me. But he merely unlocked the bridge from its pegs behind us, drew it on our side of the opening, and locked it there, so that it could not be slid back, without being unlocked, from our side.

A few yards ahead I saw what appeared to be the opening to a large, cavernlike room. It was, it seemed, illuminated by lamps. We paused at its entrance. Yes, the light within it was from lamps, two of them, set on wall brackets. The lovely brunet slave extinguished her torch, thrusting it into a vat of sand near the entrance. The room seemed primitive. The walls were of simple stone, like those of the passages. Within it, to one side, were some cupboards. Near its center was a roughly hewn table, with rude benches. There was a pitcher, and a trencher, and some clay vessels on the table. To one side there lay some boxes, and sacks. On the wall, near the boxes, there hung some ropes, some chains, and shackles. There were some switches there, too, and a whip. I could see, too, some rings here and there, on the walls, and on the floor. Two dangled from the ceiling. At one wall, chained in place, at our arrival they had been reclining or sitting, they were now kneeling in obeisance, were five women. There were some blankets by them. This it pleased me to see. To the left, in an oblique extension of the same wall, I could see several small, barred gates. These, it seemed, were kennels, carved into the rock. Behind the bars, two in chains, I could see three women. There was a brunette and two blondes. All were kneeling at the bars, heads down, in an attitude of obeisance. In these three cells, or kennels, the three occupied cells, or kennels, I was certain that I detected blankets. Again I was pleased. Further to the left, at the side wall there, rather back, and out of the way, some piled on others, were several small, stout slave cages. These were empty. They were, I conjectured, being stored here.

"Kneel," said the pit master.

I knelt and, my head down, saw my face not inches from a stout ring in the floor.

"You may lift your heads," said the pit master to the women who were, I gathered, his charges.

I then became aware that they might be kneeling upright, surveying me, appraising me, judging me, while I knelt before the ring, my head still fastened down.

"This is a new girl," said the pit master, in that slurring voice, almost like a natural force, water or lava, issuing from some aperture.

"May we speak, Master?" asked one of the women at the wall. She, like the others, was fastened to it by two chains, independently, one on her neck, one on her left ankle.

"Yes," said he.

"What is her name?" asked one.

"What is your name?" inquired the pit master.

"I do not know!" I said.

"Is it on your collar?" asked he.

He had not, it seemed, read the collar. He had, however, certainly carefully ascertained the piercing of my ears, which had apparently been of considerable interest to him, and he had, as I had lain helplessly bound before him on the walkway, with his large, rude boorish hands, or paws, if that is what they might better be termed, so heavy and hairy, and rather thoroughly, determined, traced and assessed my curves, "slave curves" as they are often called. But he had not, it seemed, read the collar. I supposed that my name was not all that important, or even if I had a name. After all, who cares what might be the name of a dog or horse? But, too, perhaps he could not read!

"Yes," I said. "I think so!"

"What is it?" he asked.

"I do not know!" I said.

"You were not told?"

"No," I said.

"You saw it?"

"Yes," I said.

"You cannot read?"

"No," I said.

"She is illiterate!" said one of the slaves.

"How insulting that she should be put with us!" said another.

"Beware," said the pit master.

"Forgive me, Master," she said, quickly.

"What was her caste?" asked one of the women.

"She never had one," said the pit master. "She has always been casteless."

"Ai!" said the woman, softly, in disbelief.

"So unutterably low?" asked another woman.

"Yes," said the pit master.

"What was her Home Stone?" asked a woman.

"She comes from a world without Home Stones," said the pit master.

I sensed that this information was met with disbelief. It was not my fault if I came from a world without Home Stones, whatever they might be!

"She is not from our world?" asked one of the women. It was one of those who were kenneled, the brunette. She was just within the bars, kneeling there. In her kennel, as in most, one, even a woman, cannot stand upright. I could see the shadows of the bars on her face and body. Her hands were on the bars of the kennel gate. I gathered that this was permitted.

"No," said the pit master.

"Master jests with his girls," said one of the women, reproachfully, one at the wall, in her chains.

"No," he said.

"I knew such a slave once," said one of the women at the wall. "She was sold in the same auction as I. She brought a high price."

"They often do," said another woman, bitterly.

"Some men like them," said another. "They look for them in the markets."

"In some cities they are popular," said another.

"It is only a matter of supply and demand," said another. "There are so few of them."

"They are rare," said another. "But their numbers increase."

"More must be being brought in," said another.

"Yes," said another.

"Who would want a barbarian girl?" asked one of the women.

"There is obviously a market for them," said one of the others.

"I understand that men are quite strict with them," said one of the women.

"Yes," said another.

I trembled.

"What is that beneath her hair?" inquired one.

The pit master gathered together my hair gently, and lifted it, and held it, bunched, behind my head. I could feel the stress on the hundreds of tiny hairs at the sides of my head, taut, drawn back, but he did not hurt me.

"Yes!" said one of the women. "See! See!"

"Her ears are pierced?" asked another.

"Yes," said the pit master.

"Not only a barbarian, but a pierced-ear girl!" exclaimed another.

"Yes!" said another.

"Do not keep such a slut with us!" cried one of the slaves.

"No!" cried another.

"No!" protested yet another, one from the kennels.

"I think I shall summon the leather worker," said the pit master.

"Master?" said one of the women, frightened.

"That the ears of all of you may be pierced, that adornments may be hung from them."

"No, Master!" cried more than one of the women.

"Forgive us, Master!" cried others.

They shrank back, those at the wall to the very rings to which they were chained, those in the kennels back in the kennels, well behind the bars.

I remained at the ring. I had been put there.

I was confident, though I may have been mistaken, of course, that the reaction to the threat of the pit master had not been one of unmitigated scandal and horror. I thought I detected something else which was involved. The feelings of the women, I gathered, were not unmixed. To be sure, I did not doubt but what on one level they feared and dreaded the very notion of the piercing of their ears but, too, on another level, a much deeper level, I think they were deeply fascinated, and deeply stirred, by the idea. I think they found it disturbingly exciting, and arousing. I sensed this, seeing how some knelt back trembling, quivering, against the wall, and others lifted their fingers to their ear lobes, as though, even now, they might feel adornments fixed there. Their feelings with respect to the piercing of their ears seemed to me, in short, profoundly ambivalent. Did they sense, tremblingly, how exciting they might seem to men if they were so adorned, how much this might increase the desire which they might provoke in masters? And were they not, all, slaves? Did they not want to be exciting, beautiful, and desirable? Did they dare to conceive of themselves, however, being that exciting, that beautiful, that desirable? Did they not understand the perils and terrors which might be consequent upon such a thing, upon being so fiercely coveted, so fiercely sought, so fiercely desired? Were they prepared, in their hearts, to be such, to have so much demanded of them? Did they dare to be such, the first to be summoned forth from captive herds, the first to be assessed, the first to be chained? Were they not such as to be the first to be thrown to the furs? Were they not such that the whips snapped most fiercely about them? How could they dare to be such? Would they not swoon in terror, understanding how men might view them? Did they truly dare to be such as to be fiercely thrust to the surface of the sales block, to hear the men screaming with need, vying to own them?

"Prepare the new girl some gruel," said the pit master.

"Yes, Master," said the brunette, she who had held the torch.

The monster crouched down, near me. He undid the rope which ran from my bound wrists to my collar and brought it forward, between my legs, in front of me. I whimpered as his hand touched the interior of my left thigh. I felt stirred. How needful is a slave! I kept my head down. I trembled. I muchly feared him. He then, the rope now before me, threaded it beneath the ring, again over my collar, once more under the ring, and then tied its circuit closed. It was now looped twice about the collar and ring. I could lift my head a little more, but not much. My collar, the double strand of rope taut, was about a foot from the ring. I then felt him undo my bound wrists. These he brought before me and bound them there, tightly, crossed, before my body. My heart began to sink. I could hear the brunet slave, to one side, pouring some meal into a dish or bowl.

"Master?" I begged.

I feared that it needed now only that my hair be thrown forward, before my shoulders.

It was done.

I moaned.

I heard the brunet slave, behind me, at the table, pouring some water into a bowl.

"Would you prefer to be beaten tomorrow?" he asked me.

"No, Master," I said. I wanted to get it over with.

He went behind me, doubtless to the wall. In a few moments he returned. I saw, on the flooring before me, the shadow of the whip, in his hand.

I watched the shadow, waiting for the lash to rise. When it descended I would shut my eyes. I was pleased that I could see the shadow. Sometimes we do not know when the blows will fall. It is so much harder then! Too, if we do not know the number of blows! It is most merciful when we know the number of blows and they are delivered with predictable periodicity. Sometimes we must, as we can, count the blows. Sometimes, too, we must, as we can, if we can, state the reasons for the blows, if there are reasons for them. There are many ways, of course, in which discourse can figure in such episodes. "Why are you being beaten?" "That I do not forget that I am a slave." Sometimes, too, we must beg for our punishment. It is terrifying to crawl to a man, the whip in one's teeth.

But I saw the whip put down on the stone beside me.

I nearly fainted. Was I not to be beaten? The free woman would never know, of course! But I recalled that the monster had assured the free woman that I would be punished. Again my heart sank. The men of this world do not give their word lightly. There would be no escape for me. I would be punished.

But what was the delay?

I felt his hands on me and he turned me to my side, and then put me to my back, my head by the ring, tied to it by the collar. He bent over me. No, he must not, I thought. Please, no! I pressed up at him a little, weakly, with my bound hands. I could not have forced him away, of course, nor would I have had the courage to try. My gesture was no more than a tiny, futile, almost inadvertent protest. I hoped I would not be beaten for it. I even drew my fingers back a little. I turned my head to the side, in order that I not look upon his features. I was at his mercy. He could do with me as he wished. I belonged, I had learned, to the state, and in this place, I had learned, he was as the state. In this place then he was to me as master, with all privileges, rights, and powers, I helpless and nothing before them, that that entailed on this world. In this place, for all practical purposes, I was his. In this place, for all practical purposes, I belonged to him. He held my head, lifted it a little, and turned it back toward him. I kept my eyes closed. I heard a snuffling, grunting sound. It was as though a beast bent over me. I could feel its breath upon me. Why did it not begin? How merciless would it be? Let it pity me! I was only a slave! Then it made a little noise, as of satisfied curiosity.

I did not understand this.

I heard the brunet slave now stirring the water and meal together.

The monster then put me back on my knees, my head down, near the ring. A strand of hair, out of place, he brushed forward. Now again my hair was before my body.

"Her gruel is ready," said the brunette.

I did not understand why he had, a moment ago, put me to my back.

He had been, it seemed, curious about something.

"It is best," he said to me, "that you not eat first."

"Yes, Master," I said. I might not, otherwise, be able to retain the provender, even as simple and bland as it might be.

I saw, in the shadow, the whip, now once again in his hand.

"This slave," said he, to the other women in the room, "has been errant. She, in a darkness, did not reveal her condition, bond, to a free woman. She permitted the free woman, in ignorance, to speak freely to her. She permitted her not only to think that she was free, but even of a given caste."

The women at the wall looked at one another.

I suddenly realized why I had been put on my back. He had read my collar. He, then, could read. He knew my name, that which I had been given, that on my collar, which, perhaps, had been worn by many others before me! I recalled that some of the guards in the pens did not care to administer a formal whipping to a woman, as opposed to some admonitory blows now and then, until they knew her name, assuming she had been given one. Punishment on this world is often construed in a somewhat personal fashion, as something passing from a particular master to a particular slave. This has a way of making it more meaningful to the slave. Too, of course, knowing the name, if the slave has one, makes it easier, particularly in a situation such as the pens, to keep track of things, to inform others, and such, for the punishment for later infractions may be considerably more severe if it seems the slave has failed to profit from her earlier discipline, and so on. I did not know my name. But he knew it.

"Why did she do that?" asked one of the women by the wall.

"Why did you do that?" asked the pit master.

"I was afraid!" I said. "I did not know better! I should have known better! I should have known better!"

"You did not think that you were the same as she," said the pit master.

"No!" I assured him.

"You understand clearly that you are only a slave, an animal, and nothing more?"

"Yes, Master!" I said.

"She is a new slave," said the pit master to the women in the room.

"Let her learn her collar!" said one of the women.

I felt the coil of the whip touch my back. I shuddered.

I was indeed a new slave. I had undoubtedly much to learn. But I did not think that I was really a stranger to the collar. I had, I was confident, as all women, an instinctive grasp of its import. I felt that I had, thus, in a sense, understood it even before it was on me. Had I not considered it in countless thoughts? Had I not worn it in a thousand dreams? To be sure, it doubtless had many meanings, rich and complex, subtle and deep, which only gradually, bit by bit, as they were revealed to me, I might come to understand, and love.

"Perhaps, Master," said the slave who had borne the torch, "as she is a new slave, and did not know better, one might, this time, omit her punishment."

There was a silence.

"Forgive me, Master!" she said, and knelt, her head to the stones, her beautiful hair upon them.

"You will know better next time, will you not?" asked the pit master.

"Yes, Master!" I said.

"How many blows should you receive?" he asked.

If one suggests too few, one is almost certain to receive far more than one might otherwise receive. If one suggests too many, perhaps in the hope of receiving less, one may find that one receives precisely what one has requested. The master usually has some number in mind which seems appropriate to him. You will never receive less than that number, but you may very well, particularly if you try to manage matters cleverly, receive far more.

"However many Master wishes," I said. It was a response I had learned in the pens. One is a slave. One does not play games with the master. All depends on him. All depends on his will. One is a slave.

I saw the shadow of the whip lift, and I closed my eyes.

I received ten lashes.

I lay there by the ring for several minutes afterward. I was on my belly. My cheeks were wet with tears, even the stone by the ring. I hurt. I sobbed. Yet he had not been cruel with me. The blows had been sharp, but clean. They had been mercifully arranged on my body, even predictably so. Too, they had been timed. It is particularly frightening when, as a part of the punishment, one does not know where the blow will fall, or when. Too, mercifully, though he saw to it that I was well punished, he had not used his man's strength on me. Only on the tenth stroke, which, before its delivery, he informed me was the last, did he let me glimpse even a particle of the strength with which a stroke, if he so chose, might be delivered. I had screamed, so struck. Then I had not even been able to scream. I had knelt there, wide-eyed, in disbelief. Then, an instant later, I had sunk to my belly. "Mercy, Master!" I wept. "Mercy, Master, please, mercy!" But the beating, of course, was done, for the tenth blow was the last. But still, hysterical, I wept. "Please, do not strike me again, Master! Please, Master, do not strike me again!" I realized then what, even with so small a portion of his strength, might be done to me. I had been well punished by the first nine strokes, I assure you, but that tenth stroke told me more than the first nine. It said, in effect, "Beware, let this be the tiniest hint of what might be done to you." And so now, minutes later, I lay at the ring. I choked back tears. I had now well learned my lesson. I was only a punished slave. But the lesson I had learned extended, of course, as doubtless it was intended it should, far beyond the occasion of the moment. It had to do with more than the mere triviality of my having failed, in my confusion and fear, to make my condition clear to a free woman in the darkness. It had also informed me that I was not only subject to punishment, but, when appropriate, would be punished. This reinforced, too, my understanding of my condition, which was bond, and its obvious concomitant, that of being subject to masters, fully, in all things. Lastly, I had been taught something more of the whip. I now understood, better than I had before, what it might do to me. I now feared it, terribly. I was afraid, now, even to look upon it.

"Kneel, barbarian," said the brunette, not unkindly. I struggled to my knees, my hands bound before me, my neck still tied to the ring.

"Feed, barbarian," she said, placing a shallow bowl of gruel before me.

I put down my head, and, not using my hands, fed.

I ate, hungrily, obediently.

But, too, from time to time, head down, pausing in my feeding, from licking at the sides of the bowl, the gruel about my mouth, I trembled. Beyond the leather, I knew, even to the tiny extent that I now understood it, there were other things, things far more frightening and effective, to which I might be subjected, if it were the will of men. I moaned, and returned to my feeding. I ate eagerly, gratefully. Tears fell into the gruel. My punishment, I realized, however informative and momentous from my point of view, had doubtless been, from the point of view of the pit master, relatively light and perfunctory. My offense, it seemed, happily, had not been regarded as particularly heinous, particularly in a new slave. Indeed, I was even being permitted to feed.

"Oh!" I said, suddenly, startled. I stiffened. "Master?" I said.

My fingers twisted, startled, my hands bound before me.

"Master?" I asked.

"You may continue to feed, if you wish," he said.

"Oh!" I said. But I could not feed, of course! The rope on my collar pulled against the ring.

He moved my hair about, away from my ears. "Pierced-ear girl," he murmured.

"Oh!" I said.

His grip on me then was like iron.

"Master!" I said.

How absurd then suddenly seemed my earlier fear, when he had put me to my back! By what right might I have expected such a dignity! But how absurd even was this thought, for a slave! Is it likely that we would be thrown on our backs for our dignity? No. Slaves are not permitted dignity. That is for free women. Rather, on our backs, if our masters desire, our subtlest nuances of expression, our helplessness, our fear, our joy, our yielding, our vulnerability, what we hope for, what we beg for, may be read! They may with their triumphant gaze ravish our helplessly bared features, surveying the myriad subtleties of our flushed countenances, taking account of our tremblings, our raptures and terrors, scrutinizing us in our misery, our ecstasy and helplessness, delighting in our tumult, we face-stripped, unveiled, before them, imprisoned in their arms, their slaves.

He made a low, growling, bestial noise.

Should I fight him, as I could?

What would it matter, in the end?

And might I not be beaten for the slightest show of resistance, unless, in its futility, he found it amusing.

I whimpered.

Could he read in me my signs of growing helplessness?

I was refined, I was delicate, I was sensitive! How could this be being done to me? But then I recalled that I was a slave.

I uttered a small, helpless cry, one of weakness, but one, too, in its way, of petition.
Please do not desist, Master!
But, of course, he would not desist.
I rejoiced that in his heart, as in the hearts of such men, there was no mercy.
"See the slave!" cried one of the women at the wall.
And so progressed my subjugation.
"Master!" I wept.
And thusly was I humiliated, and thusly was I disgraced, and debased and degraded.
Soon I began to lose control!
"Oh!" I said. "Oh!"
His victory was at hand.
Soon I knew I would be naught but a yielded slave.
"Master!" I cried.
"Ah," said he. He was then like a lion in feeding, blood running from its jaws.
I then yielded to him my utter submission, my total surrender.
I could not help myself.
I was slave.
And thusly was I, a mere slave, again conquered.
I lay for a time at the ring.
He went to one of the small slave cages to the left and pulled it somewhat forward and to the right, until it was a bit to the left of the unoccupied kennels. He then went to the table and busied himself there, with some papers, perhaps mine. The brunet slave came and crouched down beside me. She carried a wet cloth and wiped the gruel from my face and, I fear, some from my hair, as well, as I had sometimes, gasping, squirming, twisting, writhing, thrust my head too low, too near the dish. "You have a good belly," she said. "It is a hot belly. It is an excellent belly for a slave." "Thank you, Mistress," I whispered. I had known, of course, that I could be easily aroused, and that I was unusually responsive, and, in moments, could become even helplessly so. To be sure, such reflexes, and such, are expected in a slave. She may be beaten if she is inadequate. They are even trained into her. We are not free women. Also, interestingly, as earlier suggested, sexual responsiveness in the slave is openly regarded

as a desirable property, like intelligence and beauty. These three things all considerably improve her price. In a slave sexual vitality, uncontrollable responsiveness, then, is not regarded as a source of embarrassment, scandal, or shame. Nor are sexual inertness and frigidity regarded as virtues, or as concomitants thereof. We are not free women. Similarly, and naturally enough, our vitality is not something to be hidden, except, of course, from free women. Indeed, we must accustom ourselves to hearing it candidly discussed, particularly in situations in which our sale may be in question. Too, naturally, it is one of the properties which, if we are on the auction block, we must expect to hear proclaimed to the buyers.

As earlier suggested, it is the whole slave, all of her, every bit of her, that is for sale.

It is the whole slave, all of her, every bit of her, the whole she of her, that men want, and *buy*.

I lay at the ring.

He had permitted me to retain no particle of dignity. To be sure, I was not entitled to any, as I was a slave. No choice had been mine. He had had all from me. To be sure, I must yield it at so little as the snapping of fingers. I was a slave.

Would the brunette regard me with reproach? I did not meet her eyes. She rose to her feet and went to one side.

I heard, from one side, the gentle sound of some links of chain.

Surely I must reproach myself, but I could not bring myself to do so. It was not merely that I was a slave, and thus will-less in such matters, and that I must obey, and with perfection, and such, but rather that I felt a fulfillment, a calmness, a contentment.

I felt metal anklets, linked, being snapped about my ankles.

"The knots, Master," said the brunette.

The pit master rose from the table and undid the ropes tying my hands before my body.

Metal wristlets, linked, were snapped about my wrists. These wristlets, by a length of chain, were attached to the anklets.

The rope tying my collar to the ring was undone.

I felt a metal collar clasped about my neck, over the kajira collar. This collar was attached to the same chain that ran from the linkage of the anklets to the linkage of the wristlets. My ankles, wrists, and neck, then, were on a common chain. I was in sirik.

I knelt as the pit master checked the locks. Then he returned to his work at the table.

I looked up at the brunette.

How I had yielded to the beast!

But I saw no reproach in her eyes.

How grateful I was!

She must understand how helpless I was! Not only that I was a legal slave, but that I was, undeniably, in my body, my mind, my needs, a rightful slave, a full and natural slave.

It is what I am, I thought. I cannot help myself! Be kind to me!

But in her eyes there was not the least reproach. I was grateful for this, for resentment, pettiness, jealousy, and competition are common among slaves. In a sense, are we not all rivals for the favor of masters?

"May I speak, Mistress?" I whispered.

"Of course," she said.

"Do you know my name?" I whispered.

"Yes," she said. "It is on your collar." She might have just seen it. She might have noted it, earlier, even when the pit master, seemingly idly curious, before beating me, he not having concerned himself with the matter before, examined the collar. She could read then. I could not read. How low I was!

"It is a state collar, is it not?" I asked.

"Yes," she said.

"Do not tell me my name," I said.

"No one then, truly, has told it to you yet?" she asked.

"No," I said.

"Have no fear," she said. "I have no wish to be thrown to sleen."

A girl's name, you see, if one is permitted to her, is given to her by men. It is, thus, from men that she must first hear it spoken. If there should be some inadvertence or error in these matters, she will be given a new name, one she will hear first from masters. A girl, such as the brunette, who knew my name would be careful not to be the first to speak it to me. Afterwards, of course, it does not matter. The name is then as familiar and common as that of any animal.

"Cage her," said the pit master.

"On all fours," said the brunette.

I went to all fours, in my chains.

The brunette went to the small cage and opened the gate. She indicated the entrance. "Enter the cage," she said.

I crawled to the cage and entered it.

The gate was shut behind me.

I turned about, on my knees, inside. I put my head down, in the collar, when the pit master came to check the closure of the cage. Then he went back to the table. I then lifted my head. I knelt there, behind the bars. The cage had a floor and ceiling of solid iron. The four sides, on the other hand, were open, save for the bars. The bars were stout and closely set. They must have been an inch in diameter and some three inches apart. I put my face against them. I grasped two of them. There was a tiny clink of chain from the linkage on my wristlets, they touching the bars. I looked up at the brunette. One cannot begin to stand upright in such a cage, nor can one extend one's body fully within it. Within it one must kneel, or sit, or lie, one's body curled up.

"Mistress," I said.

"Yes," she said.

"Why am I here?"

"For the same reason as the rest of us," she said. "It is the will of men."

"But what am I to do?" I asked.

"What you are told," she said.

"Are there others here?" I asked.

"Others?"

"Men," I said.

"Yes," she said.

I regarded her, plaintively.

"Guards," she said.

"Am I available to them?" I asked.

"At the discretion of the pit master," she said.

I briefly closed my eyes.

"But these are not their quarters. They do report here from time to time. Doubtless they will be pleased to learn of your addition to our number."

"That is what I am here for," I asked, "for the guards?"

"Your availability to them is incidental," she said. "The pits are, in effect, in this area, a prison, and one in which, for the most part, the lowest and most dangerous prisoners are kept."

I shuddered.

"There is little danger," she said, "if you watch your step."

I swallowed, hard.

"I do not know what will be your precise duties," she said, "but I would expect that you, as the rest of us, will be given some corridors, within which you will discharge assigned tasks."

"Tasks?" I asked.

"Bringing food to the prisoners, replenishing cisterns, emptying wastes buckets, carrying fresh straw, cleaning cells, that sort of thing. One cannot expect the guards to do that."

"No," I said.

"In many cities," she said, "such work is performed by free women of low caste, but here it is done by slaves. Do you know why?"

"No," I said.

"That a token be conveyed to the prisoners of the contempt in which they are held."

"I see," I said. I rather doubted that this token was likely to be interpreted by the prisoners in the same fashion that the judiciary of the city, or the free women of the city, whatever city this might be, had anticipated. It was my guess that a male prisoner might more enjoy a glimpse of a slave than the lengthy scrutiny of a free woman. To be sure, it might be different if the free woman were a prisoner or criminal, sentenced to the prison for a time, to serve there, perhaps denied her veil, perhaps being forced to reveal her ankles or even calves to the prisoners. They might enjoy that. But I recalled the pleased howling and catcalls of the prisoners above, those I had passed on my journey along the ledge. They had seemed vital and strong. I had felt myself relished, even to my terror. To be sure, I was not serving them. Also, there surely seemed a paradox here, for free men, outside of the prisons, and such, apparently delighted in being served by slaves, and the strongest and most powerful, it seemed, would have it no other way. It must be the principle of the thing then, I supposed, that in the prison it was imposed upon them, presumably as some sort of insult or disparagement, while in their freedom, on the other hand, it was something they would themselves relish and require.

"Too," she said, "you may upon occasion be used to torment and taunt them, that they may, in their misery and frustration, the better understand their helplessness."

"I see," I whispered.

"Their time in the pits," she said, "is not intended to be pleasant."

"I see," I said.

"It is a form of torture," she said.

"I understand," I said.

"In all things," she said, "remember to be pleasing to the pit master."

"Yes, Mistress," I said.

"For you may be given not only to the guards," she said, "but to the prisoners."

"Yes, Mistress," I said.

"They might tear you to pieces," she said.

"Yes, Mistress," I said.

"I trust that you will rest well," she said.

"Thank you, Mistress," I said.

"How is your back?" she asked.

"It hurts," I said.

"Mistress!" I said.

"Yes?" she said.

"The free woman said that my accent was terrible. Is it terrible?"

"How vain you are!" she smiled.

"Please," I said.

"Speak," she said.

"I am a barbarian," I said. "I come from a world I call "Earth." I and several others were brought here to be slaves. I do not know the city to which I was first brought, nor where I am now. I do not even know my name. I do know that I am a slave."

"You speak very well," she said.

"My accent is not terrible?" I asked.

"No," she said. "But it is, at least at this point, a slave accent."

"Yes, Mistress," I said.

"But accents," she said, "do not matter, you must understand, whether or not you have one, or of whatever sort it might be. What matters is what you are, that you are a slave. Most slaves, you see, such as myself, do not have accents, or at least in any ordinary sense. But we are total slaves, I assure you, just as you are, and will remain, others things being the same, even should you be able, masters permitting it, to lose your accent."

"I understand," I said.
"Mistress," I said.
"Yes?" she said.
"Is the pit master truly human?" I asked.
"Of course," she said. "He cannot help that he was born as he was."
I looked down.
"He is afraid to go to the surface," she said, "in spite of his intelligence, and his great strength, for there even children mock and ridicule him. It is better that he is here."
"He makes me sick to look upon him," I whispered.
"Then do not look upon him," she said.
"He must make you sick as well," I said.
"No," she said.
"Why do they call him "the Tarsk"?" I asked.
"I would suppose that would be obvious," she said.
"What is a tarsk?" I asked.
"You have never seen one?" she asked.
"No," I said.
"It is a form of beast," she said. "To be sure, I do not think he really looks like a tarsk. I think they call him that not so much because he looks like a tarsk, really, as because, in some ways, in what they take to be his ugliness, he reminds them of a tarsk."
"He is hideous," I said.
"I am not sure of that," she said.
"No, he is hideous, hideous!" I said.
"One grows used to him."
"Never!" I said.
"What manner of man is he?" I asked.
"He is actually a gentle creature," she said, "save when aroused. To be sure, he is strict."
"You must loathe him," I said.
"No," she said.
"You must fear him," I said.
"Of course," she said.
"You seem to have some sort of special relationship to him," I said.

It was she who had carried the torch and assisted him, she who had fed me, and such.

"He sleeps me at his feet," she said.

I shuddered.

"You will not compete with me for his favor?" she smiled.

"No, no, no!" I said, shuddering.

"You yielded well," she smiled.

"I could not help myself," I said. "I am a slave. Any man can make me yield!"

"Any man?" she asked.

"Yes!"

"Even one you resent or loathe?"

"Yes!"

"Even one you dislike, or despise, or hate?"

"Yes!" I wept.

"And yield fully, even against your will, unreservedly, unstintingly, unable to help yourself?"

"Yes!" I sobbed. "I cannot help myself! I am helpless in their arms! You must understand such things!"

"Yes," she said. "I understand them quite well."

A tear ran against the bar, against which was pressed my right cheek.

"You are beautifully vital," she said.

"Are you not, too, a slave?" I asked, my eyes burning with tears.

"Men must find you a very beautiful, and very valuable, property," she said. "You would undoubtedly bring a high price in the market."

"Are you not, too, a slave!" I wept.

"Yes," she said. "I, too, am a slave."

I put my head down a little. I could feel the two bars against my forehead. My hands, chained, continued to grasp the bars.

"Do you think you are the only one whose belly has screamed in the darkness for a man's touch?" she asked. "The only one that has desired to kneel? The only one that has desired to serve, and love, and with her whole being, holding back nothing? The only one that has cried out, and squirmed gratefully under the haughty, audacious touch of one who owns you?"

I looked up, regarding her, tears in my eyes.

"And we would not be other than as we are," she said.

"No," I said. "We would not be other than as we are."
"We are slaves," she whispered.
"Yes," I whispered.
"It is time now for you to rest," she said.
"I am afraid!" I whispered.
"There is much to fear when one is a slave," she said.
"Yes, Mistress," I said.
Then she had turned away.

I knelt in sirik, in the cage, grasping the bars, looking after her.

The "Tarsk," the pit master, or, to use his more exact title, the depth warden, was still at the table. His small legs were under him on the bench. His large upper body, swollen and disproportionate, boulder-like, leaned forward, over the table. He had put aside the papers, which may have been mine, and was now, by the light of a small lamp, perusing a scroll. It was doubtless late.

I sat down in the cage, my knees drawn up. The sirik fitted me very well. My measurements might have been sent down from above, earlier. I looked about. I was well exposed to view, on four sides, given the construction of the cage. To be sure, I might have been even better revealed, had it not been for the bars, which were thick and closely set. There are a great many varieties of slave cages, with respect to the number of occupants for which they are designed, and, within such parameters, with respect to shape, size, and materials. I was in a fairly standard, common-model, single-girl cage, one involving a design compromise between display and security, security not from the point of view of containing the occupant, which a lighter cage would be fully effective in doing, but security against being broken into by thieves. At one end of the spectrum one has cages which are designed primarily for display, cages within which the woman is held as helplessly as a kitten but which are not thought to afford adequate resistance to men equipped with suitable tools. Cages of this sort are usually used temporarily, as during daylight hours in enclosed courts, and such, when slavers' men are about. At the other end of the spectrum are heavy cages in which the bars may be two inches in diameter and spaced but an inch or so apart, in which the occupant can be barely discerned. Cages of the sort in which I was currently kept are sometimes spoken of as "tantalizers," for a great deal of the woman is displayed, surely enough to arouse interest, but, because of the bars, perhaps not enough to make a satisfactory determination. The slaver then, of course, agrees to draw the occupant forth for more careful examination. In this way, a girl's charms, she now drawn forth from the cage and displayed, are assured their due consideration. It is easy to insufficiently attend to, or even neglect, or dismiss, these charms when she is merely one of a number of others, chained, say, in a sales barn or on a cement shelf in an open market. But let the buyer now, his interest aroused, his attention focused, examine the occupant. What now of her visage, and hair, of the delicacy of her throat, the slightness of her wrists, the trimness of her ankles, the smallness of her hands and feet, and her slave curves? And thus might an excellent buy, perhaps one even fit to be a love slave, be brought to his attention, a buy which, otherwise, might have passed tragically unnoticed. To be sure, he might only be buying for investment purposes, or perhaps he merely wishes to pick up a gift for a friend. There are also, of course, a large number of other incarceratory devices, such as slave chests, or boxes, and slave sacks. These, of course, are not designed to display the slave, but are intended for other purposes, in particular, punishment or transportation. The sort of cage in which I was held is also suitable, incidentally, for transportation. There was no need, of course, that I be chained in the cage. That was only, I supposed, to help me keep in mind that I was a slave. I had no blanket. The others had blankets. I hoped I might be given one later. I was a new girl. There were three women in the kennels, the brunette and the two blondes, and, at the wall, there were five women, each chained there by the neck and left ankle. Two of the kenneled women were chained, the brunette and one of the blondes. I hoped that I might, in time, be adjudged not only worthy of a blanket, but even of a kennel, for there were five such, and two were empty. I did not expect to be given such luxuries now. I was a new girl. I was not certain that I wanted to be chained at the wall, for I feared the other women there. I was a barbarian, and my ears were pierced.

I lay down in the cage, curling up.

I saw the slave who had borne the torch, and who had locked me in sirik, putting out the two wall lamps. This left only the tiny lamp on the table, recently lit, where the monster read. I could see the glint of the lamplight on the bars of the kennels, and on some chains hanging on the wall. On the wall, too, I saw, briefly, for I quickly looked away, hanging on its peg, the whip. How placid it seemed, how quiet now. Yet its very sight filled me with fear. I was subject to it. The brunette removed furs from a chest and spread them near the table. From the same chest she removed a coil of chain, and put it carefully, presumably not to disturb the monster, by a ring, toward the foot of the furs. She then lay down upon the furs, toward their bottom. High status had she amongst us, certainly! She was the only one amongst us, for example—of me, and the women in the kennels, and those at the wall—who had *clothing*. And she was at the foot of his furs, not that I envied her *that* privilege! It was not as though he were one of those powerful, handsome brutes, as many I had seen here, before whom a slave might faint with weakness and desire.

He moved the scroll a little, rolling shut what he had read, unrolling, opening, a new vista of ideas.

The slave at the foot of his furs, I thought, might be asleep.

I rose to my hands and knees in the cage. The chain from my collar dangled to my wrists, and went thence to my ankles. There were so many things I wanted to know. I did not know under what city I might be, I did not even know the name of the world on which I found myself. I did not even know my own name. I wanted to call out to the brute at the table. But I did not dare to do so.

Then I lay down again.

I glanced toward the wall. One of the women there, sneeringly, with her blanket about her, formed words toward me. I could dimly make them out in the tiny light. "Pierced-ear girl!" she had said. I looked away. I knew I might have to fear her, or the others. They might not only treat me badly, as I might expect, being a barbarian, a new girl, and such. But they might trick me in such ways that I might be beaten.

I moved a little in the cage. There was a tiny clink of chain.

I saw the beast put down the scroll and push the lamp a little to one side. He did not extinguish it. He turned about on the bench, and sat there, for a time, regarding the brunette. The light, as he had placed it, fell softly upon her. I think she was asleep. He then slid from the bench and, bent over, the great body on those tiny legs, went to the ring and chain. He attached the chain to the ring, with a click. The brunette stirred in her sleep. He then took her left ankle in his hand and she stirred again, and uttered a tiny moan, and a little, inarticulate cry, still asleep. But then, with its clear, firm, definite click, the ankle ring was upon her, fastening her to the ring. I do not think she awakened during this. But, I suspect, too, in some way, on some level, she was aware that she was chained. Is not even a free woman aware of such a thing, on some level, when, as she sleeps, she is chained to her own bed? Does this enter into her dream? Does she dream it so, fearfully? Surely its very possibility is to be rejected from consciousness with all the force of rationality! Surely it was only a dream! How amusing! But she awakens and finds herself chained. As the woman was sleeping the chain was first set to the ring and thence to her body, that the tether will be in place as soon as the restraint snaps about her ankle. Had she been awake, the procedure would presumably have been reversed. When the woman is awake the usual procedure is to put the first bond on her body, so that she will know it on her, that she is bound or shackled, and then to attach it, she now aware that she is subject to your will in this matter, to whatever one pleases.

The brute then returned to his reading, putting the lamp where it had been before, as though nothing had happened.

But the brunette was now chained!

I lay on my back in the sirik. I could feel the chain from my collar, running over my body, to the wrists. Then it continued, over my belly, and against the interior of my right thigh, until it flowed to my ankles. I moaned and turned to my side.

I tried to come to grips with my chains, and the bars, and my reality. How could I begin to understand what had been done with me? How could I begin to understand what I had become, what I now was? How could I begin to cope with this turn in my life?

I lay on the small, square iron floor of a confinement.

Here was a becaged slave. Could she be I?

Here was a slave, behind bars, in this tiny prison, naked and chained. Surely she could not be I!

She wore a slave collar, and was branded. Surely she could not be I!

But it was I!

I sobbed, afraid. I must do as I was told. I must obey. I must fear the whip.

Then, trembling, frightened, I recalled the use to which the monster had put me.

Oh, he had well had his will with me!

I recalled the feelings, uneasily. Even now they made me squirm.

My ears were pierced.

I reddened in the darkness, heated and sweating. How I had yielded to him, as such a slave!

He had made me his!

I had been conquered and enraptured, destroyed and renewed, rent in fragments and made whole, freed and enslaved, broken and created.

And in the end, overwhelmed, struggling to comprehend, I had found myself more a slave than ever. The strongest chains, you see, are not those of iron, nor the strongest bonds those of steel. How frail are such things compared to the chains of desire, the bonds of need! Even now, as fulfilled as I had been, I could sense a growing restlessness in my body. To be sure, it can be dangerous to be too importunate. One can be whipped for it. But what men can do to a woman, had surely, in me, been at least begun. How natural it is, once one understands these things, to fall to one's knees, begging plaintively.

I knew myself, as I lay there, to be wholly a slave. It was what I should be, and was.

How fortunate I was to have been made what I was!

How few women have been made what they are!

I had been named, but did not know my name.

In time the beast, the monster, closed the scroll, tying it shut with a string.

He lowered the lamp a little, but left it on the table. There was only a little light now in the chamber. His shadow seemed wild, deformed, exaggerated, on the walls. He glanced once toward me, but I pretended to be asleep. The other slaves, I think, were asleep. I saw him crouch near the brunette and then he took her by the upper arms, and pulled her to a sitting position. She made a little cry, half in her sleep. There was a rustle of chain. I saw her arms raise as her tunic was drawn up, over her head, and then discarded. He then pulled her by the upper arms, the chain leaving its coil by the ring, toward the center of the furs. Then her arms were about him, to my horror. But she was a slave. She must obey! I heard him grunt, in satisfaction. She uttered a tiny cry. I did not know if she were fully awake or not. But then I saw her, to my dismay, press her lips to that monstrous visage. Had she been commanded to do so? I did not know. I had heard no command. Once, in training, I had had to lavish loving kisses on a discarded sandal. To be sure, it had been appropriate to do so, and I had been pleased to do it, for it had been a man's sandal. Too, I would have begged to have done it, even at that stage of my training, and would have done it gratefully, had it been the sandal of he whose whip I had first kissed, but, alas, it had not been. I could see the two of them, together, in the dimness, in the flickering glow of the tiny lamp. She was held tightly in his arms. Escape would have been impossible for her, even had she not been chained. But, too, it seemed she pressed her beauty, even eagerly, against that grotesque body. Her curves were superb, even for those of a slave. I did not doubt her value in a market. She had been seized in her sleep, and drawn to him. He had wished her. Nothing more need be said. We are at the convenience of the master, fully, wherever, however, and whenever he may please.

I lay very quietly in the cage. I did not want to stir, and move the chain.

I could hear them together, some feet away, on the furs. They made tiny sounds. I sometimes heard the movement of the chain.

It was she, it seemed, who was slept at his feet, but, as the whim might seize him, I was sure he might have availed himself of any of the women in this place, state slaves, but here, in this place, as his own slaves. He might have drawn forth one of the blondes from her kennel, he might have utilized one of the women at the wall, perhaps she who had sneered at me, she as lowly, and as much at his mercy, as any other, or, indeed, he might have opened my cage and drawn me forth, as well, the new girl, the barbarian, to use me as he saw fit, perhaps on a blanket, perhaps on the stone floor itself.

In time he put her from him and she found her tunic and put it on, pulling it down, over her head. She then crept to the foot of the furs and lay there.

I saw her reach up, as though to touch his foot, but then she drew her hand back.

Doubtless she had a name. But I did not know it. I did not know that of the others, either. I did not even know my own name!

I lay very quietly, in my chains, in the cage.

How small it was!

I was no more than any of the women here, no more than a slave. Indeed, in a way, I was less than they, for I was a barbarian, and my ears were pierced.

But I felt strangely excited, and moved, and stirred.

Whereas I was terrified to be exactly where I was, to be here, in this specific place, in the depths below the fortress, or city, at the mercy of some misshapen beast, I was not at all discontented that I had been brought to this world, nor was I discontented, though I grasped its perils, to be a slave. Even in the little I had seen of it I had found myself falling in love with this world, with its honesty, its truth and beauty. Surely a brand and collar is a small price to pay for being permitted to come here, to tread such soils, to breathe such air. And here, too, I had learned to be alive, and to feel and experience, with a keenness, and with depths and heights, I would never have believed possible on my old world. Too, here, in this place, I had, for the first time in my life, come to understand my own most profound reality, that which had been concealed beneath the veneers of civilization, that which had called out to me in secret moments, crying out even in my dreams. I had been told I must live a lie. I had been told I must pretend to be what I was not. But here I had learned I must live the truth, and must be true to myself.

Here I was given no alternative but to be what I was.

I was grateful, and joyful.

But what mattered such reflections? What matters it whether I am pleased, or fulfilled, or satisfied? It matters not at all. I am a slave, and must serve.

I am choiceless. My will means nothing. How delicious this is to me! I am excited, and thrilled, and stimulated in all my senses, to understand the uncompromising domination to which I am subject. I am owned and must obey, and with perfection! I would not have it otherwise. But even if I wished, I could not have it otherwise. On my neck is a Gorean collar.

Even if I screamed and cried out, and struggled, and wept, and pulled futilely against my chains, and beat on the bars of my cage, nothing would be changed, save that I would be whipped to silence.

It had been done to me.

I was here.

On my neck was a Gorean collar.

The brunet slave lay quietly at the foot of the furs, the chain running from her left ankle to the ring. I think she was asleep. I am sure the others were, as well. The monster, bent over, picked up the tiny lamp, its flame long lowered, from the table, and, moving slowly, went to the kennels which, one by one, lifting the lamp a little, he checked. From where I was I could not see two of the women in the kennels. They must have been toward the back of the kennel. I could see the shadows of the bars on the kennel walls, from the lamplight. I did see the figure of one of the women, the chained, kenneled brunette. The shadows of the bars fell across her body, the shadows moving with the movement of the tiny lamp. Then the monster shambled toward the wall. I saw the tiny lamp lifted and saw, at the wall, the women there, the five of them, chained. They lay in various attitudes. Three lay upon their blankets, doubled. The bodies of two of them were partly covered with a fold of blanket, the belly of one, the calves of another. One of the women, she using her blanket doubled, lifted her head a little, blinking, but then put it down again, on the blanket. Such nocturnal checks are not unusual in the pens, of course. I had awakened once or twice in the pens, early in my training, to see the light of a lamp on the walls, the shadows cast there by the bars. But then, after a time, one tends to sleep through such things. One knows, of course, that one's presence in the kennel is likely to be verified during the night. Too, one knows, as a slave, that one is not permitted modesty, not even in one's sleep, that one's beauty may be looked in upon, that as one lies there, exposed, behind the bars, it may be subjected to the consideration and scrutiny of men, as they please. We are, in our way, public. Sometimes even buyers, I have heard, scrutinize us in our sleep. I think those who had purchased me from the pens, for this place, may have so regarded me, once or twice, in my sleep. It is said that sometimes slavers enter the boudoir of a free woman and scrutinize her in her sleep, in this considering what value, if any, she might hold as a slave. How does she move in her sleep, how does she twist, or turn, what tiny noises does she make? Perhaps her movements, and her tiny cries, and such, suggest needs, and latencies, of interest. He regards her. Yes, she is a slave. She needs only the brand, the collar. Should he take her then, or should he merely enter her name on the list, to be picked up later, at one's convenience? I would suppose that men might sometimes find it pleasant, to look in upon us, in our helplessness, and our sleep. Sometimes, too, we might find that we had, even in our sleep, all unbeknownst to ourselves, aroused their desire. Sometimes, indeed, the guard had awakened me, by a gentle tapping on the bars. He had then brought me forth, to serve him. Sometimes, of course, I would suppose that he had planned this earlier, looking forward to the time when he might draw me forth. But, at other times, I am reasonably confident that my use was merely a matter of the interest of the moment. But sometimes, too, I had waited, anxiously, for him, to plead in whispers for his attention, not wanting to awaken the others. Sometimes my plea would be granted. At other times it would be denied. I had heard there were guards in the pits, or depths. Doubtless they had their rounds to make, of the cells or whatever incarceratory devices might be found in this place. I did not think they would check this area. This was the place of the pit master. He would doubtless strictly control the gratifications of the women here, as much as, or perhaps even more so than, their food and bonds. I saw the pit master turn toward me. I was very frightened. He terrified me. But I, too, one of his charges, as much as the others, would doubtless be looked in upon. I pretended to be asleep. I heard him approach the cage. I was sure, then, he was quite close to me. Through my closed eyelids I was aware of the lamp. But he did not turn away! For better than a minute he stood there. Then, frightened, I rose to my knees in the cage and, facing him, put my head down to the tiny iron floor, performing obeisance.

"Why did you pretend to be asleep?" he asked.

"Forgive me, Master," I said. He was silent.

"I was afraid," I said. "Forgive me!"

"How is your belly?" he asked.

"My back, Master?" I asked. I thought I must have misunderstood him.

"Your belly," he said.

"Master?" I asked. Then I said, "It is all right, Master. Thank you, Master."

"You have a hot belly," he said, "particularly for one so new to the collar."

I kept my head down. I was silent.

"You may be easily controlled by it," he said. "It puts you much at our mercy."

"Yes, Master," I said.

"In the beginning," he said, "I think I will permit you to be touched by men only infrequently."

"As Master wishes," I whispered.

"We shall see how you serve."

"Yes, Master," I said.

"Lift your head," he said.

I did so, but I did not look at him.

"Lift your hair, and turn your head from side to side."

I put my chained hands to my hair, and lifted it, and turned my head from side to side.

"Pierced-ear girl," he murmured.

Then he said, "You may lower your hands."

With a movement of my head, I tossed my hair down, about my shoulders. I adjusted it a little, with my hands, they close together. I kept my head up. I had not received permission to lower it. I did not, of course, look upon him.

"You are pretty," he said.

"Am I pretty?" he asked.

"No," I said.

"Am I handsome?" he asked.

"No," I said. "Forgive me, Master."

"For speaking the truth?"

"The opinion of a slave is worthless," I said.

"Why do you say that?" he asked.

"I do not wish to offend Master," I said.

"Do you think, because you have been put in a collar, you become less intelligent?"

"No," I said.

"Slavery has many effects on a woman," he said, "It softens her, it enhances her beauty, it gives her a profound sense of herself, it fulfills her, it increases, considerably, her sexual responsiveness, it increases a thousandfold her capacities to love, but one effect it does not have, it does not reduce her intelligence."

"Yes, Master," I said.

"Why should it?" he asked.

"I do not know, Master," I said.

"It does not."

"Yes, Master," I said.

"There is a sense," he said, "in which the opinion of a slave is worthless, and another sense in which it might not be worthless. The sense in which it might not be worthless is the sense in which it might be true, or insightful, or helpful, such things. But in that sense the opinion of an urt or sleen, or any other form of animal, might not be worthless. It might be true, or insightful, or helpful, such things. The sense in which the opinion of a slave, or other form of animal, is worthless is the sense in which it is just that, the opinion of a slave, or animal. Do you understand?"

"Yes, Master," I said. My thoughts, like my feelings, did not count. They were only those of a slave.

How these men, these brutes on this world who had never relinquished their manhood, dominated us! How totally, how uncompromisingly, they dominated us! How deliciously they dominated us!

"Intelligent women," he said, "make excellent slaves."

"Yes, Master," I said.

"They understand what has been done to them, what they then are, how they must be, and so on."

"Yes, Master," I whispered.

"And they are quick to grasp the impossibility of escape, and the irreversibility, by their own efforts, of what has been done to them."

"Yes, Master," I said. But did he not understand how much more there was to it than this? Did he not understand the need for the master, the longing for him, the yearning for him? Did he not understand the need to serve, and love, selflessly?

"You look quite well in chains."

"Thank you, Master."

"You belong in them."

"Yes, Master."

"You know that, don't you?" he asked.

"Yes, Master," I whispered. I was such a woman. Even had it not been for such things as the desire to serve and love wholly, with no thought of self, only with thought for the happiness of the master, I would have belonged in chains. I knew that. I had been petty, and vain, and selfish, and doubtless, to some extent, still was. I had little doubt that if I had been permitted to retain my freedom I would have abused it, almost certainly so in my old world. How fitting then, I recognized, that men, in their arrogance, not wishing to accept such insult and folly on my part, had simply made me a slave, had simply branded me and put me in a collar. I now wore chains. I was now subject to the whip. I would obey, and be pleasing. These things had been decided by men.

"Master!" I begged.

"Yes?" he said.

"For what reason have I been brought here?"

"Here?" he asked.

"To this city, this place," I said.

"To this particular city, and this particular place?" he said.

"Yes, Master," I said.

"You will learn in time," he said.

"Master!" I begged.

"Yes?" said he.

"I do not know my name," I said.

"It is on the collar," he said. He indicated that I should more closely approach the bars. I put my right cheek against them, my eyes closed. I felt his pawlike hand slide the kajira collar up, beneath the sirik collar. "There it is," he said, lifting the lamp a bit. "It is there, your name, on the collar, which you cannot remove from your neck."

Of course I could not remove the kajira collar! Such collars are not made to be removed by a girl. They are locked. The lock is at the back of the neck. Such collars are light, close-fitting, and attractive. They are pretty. One does not slip them.

I knew that the name was on the collar, and that, thus, in a sense, my name was on me, clearly and obdurately, for anyone to see, anyone who might be literate and care to peruse the collar. In this way a girl may be more easily recognized, and remembered, or identified or traced, or such. She is denied the refuge of a gracious and sheltering anonymity.

And of course I could not remove the sirik collar either. It was locked on me, as well.

The brute knew this. He was merely reminding me of my helplessness. It was doubtless an excellent lesson to be administered to a slave, and particularly, I supposed, to one such as I, an Earth-girl slave.

"It was shown to me," I said, "but I cannot read. I am illiterate! It was never told to me."

"Even if you could read," he said, "you could not see it now, for it is on your collar."

"Please, Master," I said, my eyes closed. "I would know my name."

I must, I knew, hear my name first from the lips of a man.

"Do you beg to know the slave's name?" he asked.

"Yes, Master," I said. "I beg to know the slave's name."

"It is a barbarian name," he said, "short, luscious, and splendidly fitting for a slave."

"Yes, Master," I said.

He was silent.

"I beg to know the slave's name," I said.

"It is 'Janice'," he said.

"Yes, Master," I said.

"What is your name?" he asked.

"'Janice'," I said.

"That is the sort of name beneath which a slave squirms well," he said.

"Yes, Master," I said. I felt the chain from my wrists between my thighs. Thence it ran back to my shackled ankles.

"Who are you?" he asked.

"I am Janice, Master," I said.

"Go to sleep now," he said, "Janice."

"Yes, Master," I said.

In a bit he had returned to his furs. He blew out the tiny flame of the lamp.

We were then in the utter darkness.

I lay there for a time, and then lifted the chain on my wrists a little. I pressed my lips to it, and then to the manacles on my wrists, one after the other. I was ignorant of many things, but now, at least, I was no longer ignorant of my own name. I now knew who I was. I was Janice.

I then fell asleep.

Fourteen

"How free slaves are!" she cried, delightedly.

"Shhh, Mistress," I cautioned her.

"You must not call me 'Mistress'!" she whispered.

"Forgive me," I said. Such things, from training, and from force of habit, sometimes slip out.

"And do not ask for my forgiveness," she whispered. "Please! Someone might hear! Think of me only as a slave in your charge."

"I will try," I said. We had come from the bazaar with its sights and sounds, and booths and stalls, and the crowding, and the music. I much enjoyed that part of the city. We were now climbing steps to the upper terraces and courts. From there one may obtain a grand view of the mountains.

"I am so grateful to you!" she said.

I held her leash, preceding her. Her hands were braceleted behind her.

"It was your idea," I said. "I only conveyed your pleas to the depth warden. Had I not done so, in some failure to comply with your request, I might have risked serious discipline."

"Nonetheless, I am grateful!" she exclaimed. "You need not, I am sure, have conveyed my pleas. You might even have managed somehow to escape punishment for the inadvertence. Since my care was put in your keeping I have not even seen the depth warden. He might never have known. You might have pretended to misunderstand, or forget, or you might have denied that such pleas were made."

"In such a matter," I said, "your word would be taken over mine."

"How vulnerable are slaves!" she marveled.

"Yes," I said, climbing upward. "We are vulnerable."

"But you could have conveyed my pleas in such a manner as to have had them discounted, or rejected as haughty demands, or such."

I was silent.

"You must have enjoined them upon the depth warden with sympathy."

I supposed that was possible. She had been so pathetic.

"Oh!" she suddenly exclaimed, in pain.

"Do you wish to pause?" I asked.

"No," she said, looking at me, wincing, lifting one foot a little.

"Your feet are not yet toughened," I said. She was barefoot, of course. This was in accord with her guise.

"Do you wish to wait?" I asked.

"Someone is coming," she said.

Coming down the stairs was a man.

"Come, slave!" I said. "Do not dawdle!"

With a little cry of pain she followed me up the stairs, the leash straight between us. Little consideration is shown to slaves. The fellow glanced at us, sizing us up, as men do, as slave meat, in passing. We looked down. Had he stopped, we would have knelt.

"Is your foot all right?" I asked.

"Yes," she said.

I think that the very first day on which I had seen the free woman, several days ago, over the pool, had been the same day on which a transformation had begun to be wrought in her. There were doubtless several causes for this, not to mention a certain ripening of her understanding, of how she was fully, truly, even though a prisoner, at the mercy of men. Specifically, I think it was useful to have had to explicitly, frequently, and humbly address the depth warden as "Sir," which practice apparently, in its present authentic form, began on that day, to know that she was not permitted to attempt to interfere with the latching of the cage, and might thus, at any moment, waking or sleeping, be plunged into the pool, to the creatures which frequented it, and, perhaps most significantly, to learn that she, though a free woman, was being housed in a slave cage. This latter comprehension, in itself, it seemed, had acted profoundly upon her consciousness. She had begun soon after that, as I had learned from the brunette, Fina, she preferred by the pit master, who slept at his feet, to kneel in the cage at the approach of the pit master, the depth warden, who commonly attended to her. Further, she began, aside from the courtesy expressed in the use of the expression "Sir," to address him with great deference, and to importune him, when she dared, in suitable humility. Too, as she now used the word "Sir" there could be no hint within it, as there might have been, as I understand it, before the day of her instruction at the pool, of irony or insult. Now no longer did she use it exaggeratedly, or pointedly, or sneeringly. It now emerged from her lips with sincerity, with understanding and respect. I recalled that once, in my training, one of the girls in my group had dared to say the word "Master" to one of the guards in such a fashion that it was clear she did not mean it, in such a fashion that it constituted, in effect, a sneer. She was punished, terribly, and, in an instant, was blubbering for mercy, contrite, and fiercely instructed, begging with the utmost terror and authenticity to he who was then to her as master for mercy. Such insults, of course, are not tolerated for an instant in a slave. We quickly learn that the masters are truly "Master."

"I am tired," she said, climbing the stairs. Too, I think her foot hurt her.

I looked up and down the broad stairs. They were empty now, save for us.

"Let us rest," I suggested.

She sat on the stairs.

"See," she said, proudly, "how I hold my legs together, and to the side. Is it not attractive?"

"Seeing you thus," I said, "I would think a man might be tempted to seize your ankles and part them."

"Oh?" she said, pleased.

"It is more modest to kneel," I said, kneeling on the broad step, my legs together.

"Should I be kneeling?" she asked.

"Yes," I said.

Immediately she knelt.

"As I hold the leash," I said, "you should be on a stair lower than I."

She descended one stair, happily.

"That is not how you kneel before men, is it?" she asked.

"You are inquisitive," I said.

"Is it?" she asked.

"No," I said. "I am a slave of a sort which, I expect, you, as a free woman, may never have heard of."

"You are a pleasure slave," she said, helpfully.

"You have heard of us?" I asked.

"Of course," she said. "My brother has two of you. He pits them against one another."

"The beast!" I exclaimed.

"He is well served," she said.

"Doubtless," I agreed.

"All the female slaves below are pleasure slaves," she said. "Fina told me."

"Fina is also a pleasure slave!" I said.

"Of course," she said.

"The pit master will have it no other way," I said.

"Of course not," she said. "He is a strong, powerful man."

"We are worked as though we might be field slaves!" I said.

"Oh, you are not worked so hard," she said.

I knelt back, smiling. "Perhaps not," I said.

"I think the pit master is kind," she said.

"You have not felt his lash," I said.

"It must be thrilling to be subject to the lash," she said.

"I do not care for the lash," I said. The thought of it even frightened me.

"But it must be thrilling," she said, "to know that you must please, and that you are subject to it."

I was silent.

"Is it not?" she asked.

"Yes," I said. Why must she, a free woman, pry so closely into these things? Too, what could one such as she understand of such matters?"

"But I think the pit master is kind," she said.

"Perhaps," I said.

"If he were not," she said, "he would not permit us to be here, or do this, would he?"

"No," I said. "I do not think so."

"So," she said, "that is not how you kneel before men, is it?"

"No," I said. "I am a pleasure slave. It is expected, accordingly, that I will kneel before men with my legs spread, unless, perhaps, free women are present."

"Like this?" she asked, eagerly.

I looked about, quickly, determining that none were about. It was warm, and late in the afternoon.

"No," I said. "More widely."

"Oh!" she said, softly, trembling.

"Yes," I said. "Like that."

"Thusly," she asked, "and before men!"

"Yes," I said, "or even more widely, depending on the master."

"Ai!" she whispered.

"Yes," I said.

One of her knees was now off the stair.

"How it must make you feel!" she breathed, delightedly.

"Yes," I said.

"How vulnerable you are!" she said.

"Yes," I said.

"It is very exciting," she said.

"It helps us to keep in mind that we are slaves, and the sort of slaves we are," I said.

"It is exciting," she said.

"'Exciting'?" I asked.

"Surely the intent of this exceeds mere mnemonics and instruction," she said, "such things as a mere desire to demonstrate to the slave her vulnerability."

"Perhaps," I said.

"Surely at least a portion of its intent is to arouse the slave, to make her feel receptive, and helpless, kneeling thusly before a male."

"I do not doubt," I said, "that something of that sort has entered into the thinking of the beasts, those who force us to assume such a position before them."

"Ah!" she said.

"It has its effect, too, upon the male," I assured her.

"I am so pleased to hear it!" she said.

She looked down at her knees. Her hands were braceleted behind her. Her leash went to my hand.

"Janice," she said.

"Yes?" I said.

"Do you like to kneel thusly before men?"

"Please!" I said.

"Please, tell me," she said.

"Must I speak?" I asked.

"I cannot order you to do so, not now," she said. "I am now naught but as a slave in your charge. That is the understanding, and the condition. But please, Janice! Please speak!"

"Yes," I said. "I do enjoy so kneeling before men. I find it sexually arousing. Too, I find it is right for me. I find that it is fitting and proper for me."

"It must make you feel very female," she said.

"Yes, it does," I said. "But it is all right for a woman to feel very female. There is nothing wrong with that."

"I am a female," she said. "I want to feel very female."

"But you are a free woman," I reminded her. She looked at me, agonized.

"There are two sexes," I said. "One is dominant, and one is not. Each should be true to itself. On this world, this basic truth has been recognized, and, in a portion of the social sphere, institutionalized."

"I want to be true to my sex," she whispered, "really true to it, fully true to it."

"Beware," I said. "You are a free woman."

She was silent.

"Freedom is precious," I said.

"I have had freedom," she said. "I know what it is like. Now I want love."

"I am a slave," I said. "And I have not found love." A poignant memory gripped me, but I turned away from it.

"What is wrong?" she asked.

"Nothing," I said. I need not speak the truth to her as she was to me now naught but as slave.

"I think you are a true slave, Janice," she said, softly.

"Yes," I said. "I am a true slave. I was a true slave even before I was brought here and collared."

"You love being a slave!" she said.

"It can be terrifying to be a slave!" I said.

"You love being a slave!" she said.

"Yes," I said. "I love being a slave!"

She looked down at her knees, so widely spread. She was "slave clad." One lovely thigh, her left, as she knelt, emerged from the brown rag which had been knotted about her waist. She wore a halter. We had improvised it from a twisted, matching piece of brown rag. In its simplicity and raggedness, it was surely believable as, and suitable for, a slave halter. It was I who had decided that she should be clothed in brief tatters. Too, it was I who had decided that her midriff would be bare, and considerably so. In these arrangements was expressed, doubtless, something of my view as to her condition, which was free. That is what I think of your condition, and what you really are, you free females! Take away your veils and robes, and we shall see what you are! There, see, you are no more than we, only more slaves! Yes, perhaps I had chanced to yield, to some extent, to the temptation to take a little vengeance on her, and, through her, on all free females. Too, how often does a slave get to dress a free woman, as the slave might choose to dress her? And how often will she have the opportunity to conduct one about, "slave clad," back-braceleted, and on a leash? What a turnabout is there! The pit master, when I had displayed her to him, had seemed startled. Certainly he had uttered a skeptical sound. Perhaps he had not realized before that the free woman was actually an attractive and desirable female, at least for a free woman, one who had not yet learned slave softness, slave helplessness. But he had let us leave the depths. She had not seemed to mind all this at all, but to find the whole matter delightful. Perhaps she would not have found it all so delightful if she had realized how she might now appear to men. Might she not then have been terrified? What free woman would dare to appear, as it is said, "slave desirable"?

Some days ago she had been removed from the slave cage over the pool and given a cell not far from our quarters. It was a comfortable cell, some eight feet in width and height, some ten feet in depth. Though there were rings within it, she was not chained to them. She had a pallet filled with straw, a dish for food, a vessel for water, and a wastes bucket. The luxury of the straw-filled pallet was doubtless an acknowledgment of her status as a free woman. One morning I had been ordered to fold my blanket early and emerge from my kennel. I had followed the pit master to the free woman's cell. I had been uneasy doing so, as I was afraid of her. Female slaves learn early on this world to fear free women who, for some reason, seem to bear them great malice and hatred. But it was a far different free woman I encountered in the cell than she I had recalled from the cage. She knelt at our first approach.

"I have heard nothing of your ransom, Lady," said the pit master to her.

She nodded.

I knelt behind the pit master, to his left. That is the common heeling position. I wore a typical slave tunic, brief and revealing.

"I congratulate you on the improvement in your behavior," he said.

"Thank you, Sir," she said.

"You understand," he said, "that we may, if we wish, put you back over the pool, and I assure you that that is not the worst sort of accommodation in the pits."

"Yes, Sir," she said. She bowed her head.

"Your behavior is particularly to be commended," he said, "as you are not bond."

She lifted her head, it seemed, as though puzzled.

"When one is bond," he said, "one has absolutely no choice—instant and unquestioning perfection of service is required."

"Sir?" she said.

"Janice!" he snapped.

"Master!" I cried, startled.

"Obeisance!" he said.

Instantly I knelt forward, the palms of my hands on the floor, my head to the floor.

"Lick and kiss," he said.

I scrambled forward and, head down, kissed and licked, swiftly, frightened, at his feet and sandals.

"Enough!" he said. "Back!"

I drew back, hastily. But he was no longer paying me attention.

"You see?" he asked the free woman.

"Yes, Sir," she said, trembling.

"You seem to have learned something of what it is to be in the keeping of men," he said.

"Yes, Sir," she said.

"Keep in mind," he said, "in the future, that you are still in their keeping, utterly."

"Sir?" she said.

"Though henceforth," said he, "more indirectly."

"I do not understand," she said.

"I am a free man," he said. "I have no intention continuing indefinitely to attend to you personally. It is not as though you were my slave, a girl whose hair I might comb, or in whose feeding and watering I might take some pleasure. Do you understand?"

"Yes, Sir," she said.

"Unfortunately," he said, "we do not have free women to attend to such matters in the depths."

"I understand," she said.

"This, Janice," said he, "is the Lady Constanzia, of the city of Besnit."

"Master," I whimpered, in misery.

"Lady Constanzia," said he, "the bond-maid, Janice."

"Janice," she said.

"Mistress," I said.

"You need not call her 'Mistress,'" said the depth warden. He then turned to the free woman. "Your care, for the most part, will be in her hands," he said. "Moreover, you will give her no trouble. And you will obey her."

"Yes, Sir," she said.

I marveled.

"Incidentally," said he, *females*—"

I was startled that he used the same expression to refer to us both. I supposed, of course, that we were both females, but, in a sense, within that genus, of two quite disparate species, one free, one slave. But, in another sense, of course, both of us were the same, both females, and were thus addressed, as only females, relative to his maleness.

"—you are to exchange little or no political or military information."

"I know little of such things," said the free woman.

And I knew myself, of course, almost totally ignorant of such matters, certainly on this world. Further, a limitation on our discourse had now been imposed, a limitation which would doubtless be respected. This was not a world on which such as we, she a prisoner, I a slave, would be likely to transgress such an injunction. Who would want to be thrown, for example, to those terrible creatures in the pool?

The pit master then turned about, and began to withdraw down the corridor. I had leapt up, and hurried to follow him. That was the first day on which I had begun the care of the free woman. That very night I took her her food and water. "Go to the back of the cell," I told her. She complied. She had not knelt, of course. I was not a man. Still, I was her keeper. I think she had not really known how she should behave with me. Nor, as a matter of fact, on the whole, did I. The pit master, however, had told me to have her kneel, and help her keep in mind that she was a prisoner. I had the key to the cell on a string. I put down the food and water, opened the cell, put the key back about my neck, and brought in the food.

"There are guards about," I informed her, though I supposed she must be aware of this.

"Yes," she said.

She did not seem particularly haughty or arrogant. A great transformation, it seemed, had come over her since the first time I had seen her, at the pool.

"Do not try to escape," I said. The door was, after all, now open.

"I will not," she said.

"You cannot escape," I said. "Escape is impossible for you."

"I know," she said.

"Kneel," I said.

She knelt.

I let her remain kneeling for a few moments, looking at me. I then came toward her and put the food down, on the floor, before her.

"Do not touch it yet," I said.

She drew back her hands.

I was standing before her.

She looked up at me.

"Remove your veil," I said.

She unwound the veil from her features, carefully, gently, where she had wrapped it about herself, and brushed back the hood of her robes of concealment.

She then looked up at me. She did not seem angry, or offended.

"You are the barbarian," she said.

"The one whom you had punished," I said.

"Yes," she said.

"I was whipped," I said.

"You have face-stripped me," she said.

"Doubtless you did not then expect to be where you are now."

"No," she said.

"I am the one," I said, "who speaks so terribly."

"You speak beautifully," she said.

"I have an accent," I said.

"Yes," she said. "You have an accent."

"A slave accent!" I said.

"It is a lovely accent," she said.

"But it is a slave accent!" I said.

"Yes," she said. "It is a slave accent."

"You think my accent is acceptable?" I asked.

"It is a beautiful accent," she said.

"I think you are trying to lie," I said.

"No," she said. "I am trying to accustom myself to telling the truth."

"Why?" I asked.

"It does not matter, does it?" she asked.

"No," I said. "I suppose not." She looked at the food. "But it is a slave accent," I said.

"Yes," she said. "It is a slave accent."

I did not think she had eaten since last night. She must be ravening.

"You may eat," I said.

She lost no time in addressing herself to the food, but, rather to my surprise, and irritation, she did so with delicacy. She had a certain breeding and refinement, it seemed, of a sort which one might not expect to find in my sort, in slaves. I supposed that if she were a slave, the signs in her manner of such breeding and refinement might be of interest to a master, not that they would make her any the less a slave. Similarly a high-caste accent, with all its elegance and refinement, would not make her any the less a slave either. Such learn to leap and obey as quickly as the rest of us.

"You eat with delicacy," I said.

Too, this refinement, this elegance, seemed so natural in her. Such, doubtless, was the effect of breeding.

"Your features are not unattractive," I said.

It had been in consequence of my orders that she must remove her veil, exposing her features. But this was not as momentous as it might seem. I was, after all, a woman. It was not as though I were a man, a brutal masculine captor, who had torn away her veil, that he might assess her promise for the collar. Too, many free women would think nothing of appearing unveiled before their serving slaves. Yet I was sure it would not have been lost upon her that she had had to remove her veil, that so precious thing to a free woman, at my command. But she had not seemed dismayed to remove it. Was she concerned, I wondered, to make clear to us the authenticity of her new understanding, that she must obey. Or, perhaps, did she find it appropriate, for some reason, that her features be bared?

She looked up at me, timidly.

"I am not lying," I said. "I am not a free woman. I am a slave. I can be punished terribly for lying."

She threw me a grateful glance.

"Am I pretty?" she asked.

"Yes," I said.

"Am I beautiful?" she asked.

"That would be a judgment," said I, "best made by masters." And then I added, maliciously, "—when you are stripped on a slave block."

"Am I beautiful?" she pressed.

"I would think so, yes," I said.

She put her hands to the throat of her robes, closing them more tightly. "Do you think I might," she asked, "be beautiful enough to be—to be a—a *slave?*"

"Shame," cried I, "free woman," scandalized.

"Please!" she begged.

"I would suppose so," I said. "I do not know."

She drew her robes yet more closely about her. She put her head down, trembling.

"Finish your food," I suggested.

She again addressed herself to her light repast.

"I thought of stealing some of your food," I said, "but I did not do so."

"Thank you," she whispered.

"The diet here has doubtless slimmed you," I said, "but I do not think they are planning on selling you. I think they are waiting for your ransom."

She kept her head down, eating.

It seemed as though she might have wished to raise her head, to speak, but she did not do so.

I knelt down, across from her.

I was sure she wished to speak to me, but she refrained from doing so.

In a bit she had finished the modest collation I had set before her. She pushed back the empty dish, the drained goblet. It had held only water.

"Doubtless," I said, "it is not what you were hitherto accustomed to."

"I am grateful to be fed," she said.

That seemed to me insightful on her part.

"Is this that on which you are fed?" she asked.

"It is better," I said. "Often we have only slave pellets and slave gruel."

"I am sorry," she said.

"We are slaves," I said.

I picked up the plate and goblet. I stood up.

"The provender of slaves," I said, "is designed to keep us healthy, trim, and vital, as the masters want us. It would be the same with other animals."

"Animals!" she breathed.

"Of course," I said. "But we get other things, too. The masters may feed us by hand, from their own plates, as we kneel by their tables, or throw us scraps, such things. Occasionally we may be given a candy, a pastry, such things. It depends on the master."

She nodded, frightened.

I turned to go.

"Please!" she said.

I turned back, to face her.

"Slaves are exercised, are they not?" she asked.

"We must exercise, yes," I said. Such is important for muscle tone, improvement of the figure, responsiveness, and such. We are not permitted to neglect such matters. Masters would not permit it."

"You are very clean," she said.

"We are not free women," I said. "We must wash frequently. We must keep ourselves pleasing, in so far as we can, for masters."

"I am miserable," she said.

I looked at her, puzzled.

"I have been cramped in for so long," she said.

"This cell is large," I said.

"I feel dirty," she said.

I shrugged.

"Look at me!" she said.

I regarded her.

"I'm filthy," she said.

"Yes," I admitted.

Her clothing, perhaps the very garments in which she had been originally captured, had, in her continual wearing of it, in her sleeping in it, in its contact with the floors of cages and cells, and such, become much soiled. It was thickly begrimed with weeks of wear and filth. Too, it was wrinkled, and faded, and torn. She was, in these things, a sorry sight.

How different was her appearance now, I thought, from what it must have been when she had long ago entered the fateful shop in Besnit.

"I must smell," she said.

"I am a slave," I said. "It would not be wise for me to notice."

"I must smell," she said.

"Yes, you do," I admitted.

She looked down, miserable.

"Do not be afraid," I said. "It is not as though you were a slave. You are a free woman. It is not as though you must, under discipline, groom yourself, attend to your appearance, keep your body clean, such things. Have no fear. Your neglect of such things, as you are a free woman, will not be punished."

"Perhaps," she said, softly, to herself, "I would that I were such that I might be punished for the neglect of such things."

"What?" I asked.

"Nothing!" she said. She shrank back, putting her finger tips to her lips, as though she might have chided them for what they, sweet, unwary guards, had permitted to pass their portal.

I stood there for a moment. I thought she might have wished to speak further. But she said nothing.

I then turned about, and went to the door of the cell.

"Janice!" she called.

I turned about again, and once more faced her.

"May I call you 'Janice'?"

"It is my name," I said.

"This morning," she said, falteringly, "you licked—and kissed—the feet of a man."

"Yes," I said.

"I have never licked and kissed the feet of a man," she said.

"You are a free woman," I said.

She regarded me.

"It is a not uncommon act for a slave," I said.

"It is surely very symbolic," she said.

"There are many symbolisms involved," I said. "It is not merely that it is a way in which a given woman makes clear her relation to a given man, that she is his slave, that he is her master. It is far more than this. It is, for example, a way in which our femininity avails itself of an opportunity to express, in the particular act with a particular master, something far broader and more profound, its deference toward, and its submission to, the very principle of masculinity. In this way its significance extends far beyond a particular couple. It has to do with men and women, and masculinity and femininity, and the order of nature itself."

I saw her tremble. I did not understand her agitation.

"Janice!" she cried.

But she did not speak.

"Janice," she then whispered.

"Yes," I said.

I saw that this would not be what she might first have thought to say. To be sure, it would perhaps be related.

"I fear a guard is coming!" I suddenly exclaimed. "Quickly, hide your face!"

She looked at me.

"Quickly, quickly!" I said.

Hurriedly she muffled her features in the veil, holding it in place with both small hands.

"No!" I said, suddenly. "He has gone another way! But I fear I must get back, quickly. I must return the key to the pit master."
She lowered her hands, and the veil.
"You were slow to veil yourself," I said. "He might have seen."
"Perhaps I should have let him see," she said.
"Do not be shameless!" I said.
"You are not veiled," she said.
"Nor should I be," I said. "I am naught but a slave."
"Do not go yet!" she begged.
"Stay on your knees," I said.
She remained on her knees.
"Janice!" she called.
"Yes?" I said.
"I would be exercised!" she said.
"It is difficult to exercise in the robes of concealment," I said.
"Perhaps something else might be devised," she said.
"Perhaps," I said.
"You must wash somewhere," she said.
"There is a cistern," I said.
"Might I not, too, be permitted to wash there."
"*Slaves* wash there," I said. "*Animals.*"
"I do not mind!" she said.
"Perhaps I could take you there when it is not being used," I said. "I would have to speak to the pit master."
"Please, please do!" she begged.
"Very well," I said.
"Janice!"
"Yes?"
"I want to be your friend!"
"There can be no friendship between us," I said. "You are free. I am a slave."
"I am not so different from you!" she said.
"I am far from free!" I laughed.
"That is not what I meant," she whispered.
I pondered this, but did not understand it.
She was a free woman.
I closed the door, and locked it, and put the key back about my neck.

"You may rise," I told her. The door was now securely locked. The lock was heavy, the bars were thick. She was well held within the cell.

I looked at her. She had remained on her knees.

Somewhat to my surprise the pit master had been agreeable to the free woman's desire to bathe, and he permitted me, the next day, when the cistern was free, to take her there. How joyously she bathed!

"Do you think now that I am beautiful enough to be a slave?" she had asked me later, happily, kneeling beside the cistern, throwing her washed hair behind her.

"Yes," I had told her. "I think you would look well in a collar."

She had laughed delightedly.

I eyed her pile of garments. How filthy they were!

"I shall launder these for you," I said.

"No!" she said. "I shall clean them!"

"You are a free woman," I said. "Free women, or at least such as you, do not attend to such matters."

"Please," she said. "I want to!"

"You want to work?" I said.

"Yes," she said. "Work me! Work me—*as a slave!*"

I regarded her, startled.

"You have been taught how to work, have you not?" she asked.

"Yes," I said. In my training I had been taught the performance of numerous servile tasks. I had, for example, by female slaves, been instructed in sewing, laundering, cleaning, cooking, the polishing of metal, and the grooming of leather. When one buys a woman, even a pleasure slave, one expects, as a foregone conclusion, that she will know how to do such things. Yes, even a pleasure slave, who might, in her more familiar modalities, drive a master mad with passion, may be expected, either out of his sight, or under his supervision, if he pleases, to make bread and repair a rent garment, such things.

"Show me how to launder," she begged, "—*as a slave!*"

"It is doubtless the same way in which free women of low caste launder," I said.

"Show me," she begged.

"Kneel beside the cistern," I said. "Knot your hair behind your head, that it not drag in the water. The garments must be soaked, and twisted, and kneaded, and beaten on the stone, again and again. One soaks the garments, one beats them. It is not easy work. It is hard work. It takes time. Begin."

She took her veil first, and submerged it in the water.

The next day, I came early to her cell. She had requested it. The pit master had given his permission. At my arrival she had knelt without being asked to do so, and had removed her veil.

"Greetings," I said.

"Greetings," said she.

"May I stand?" she asked.

"Yes," I said.

To my surprise she then removed her outer garments, putting them to one side. Then she stood before me in a light, silken, sliplike undergarment. It was quite brief. It was not, I thought, unlike a slave garment. I wondered if free women sometimes studied themselves in the mirror, in such garments. I recalled that I had, it now seemed long ago, wondering what I would look like if my wrists were roped, if there were a chain on my neck. She then, again, knelt.

"What if the guard should see?" I said.

"It does not matter," she said.

"Do not be foolish," I said. "Do you not know what the sight of you, as you are now, might do to a man!"

"What?" she asked.

"Do not ask," I warned her. "You are a free woman!" I dared not tell her the might of the desires of men such as these, of their mercilessness and their power.

"Janice," she said.

"Yes," I said.

"Exercise me," she said.

"Do not be foolish," I said.

"I know nothing of such things," she said. "Please!"

"In what way would you be exercised?" I asked.

"Exercise me," she said, "—as a slave."

I considered this matter. I supposed that her body might, indeed, cry out for some exercise. She had been long incarcerated. But why, I asked myself, did she wish to be exercised in a certain way, as a slave? Surely that was incomprehensible. On the other hand, I asked myself, how often does a slave have this power over a free woman? Indeed, would it not be amusing to exercise her—*and as a slave*?

"Stand!" I said. "Spread your legs widely! Put your arms out to the sides!"

I feared I was not easy with her. And yet the harder I was upon her the more eager, the more zealous, the more compliant, the more helpless and obedient, she was. Afterwards I took her to the cistern that she might wash her body and her garment.

After that she exercised regularly.

Once she asked me, "What are slave paces?"

"They are movements, attitudes, positions, poses, and such," I said, "designed to display a slave."

"Put me through them!" she begged.

"You, a free woman," I said, "ask to be put through *slave* paces?"

"Yes!" she said.

"You are mad!" I said.

"Please!" she begged.

"And that," I cried, a few minutes later, "is how a slave may be put through her paces."

"Yes, yes!" she had cried, wide-eyed, gasping, fighting for breath, drenched with sweat, lying before me on her belly, on the stone.

"To be sure," I said, "if you were really being put through your paces, you might expect certain things to be different. Presumably you would be naked and collared. I would be a man. I would have a whip or switch. There might very well be other men present, and so on."

"I understand," she whispered.

"Yet," I said, "perhaps now you have a sense of what might be involved."

"Yes," she whispered, in awe. "Thank you, Janice."

"Do you not now regret your request?" I asked.

"No," she said.

"Are you not now outraged and humiliated?" I asked.

"No," she said.

I had then left the cell, locking the door behind me. I looked back, once, at her. She still lay on the floor, in the tiny sliplike garment she had worn. She had lovely legs. She seemed in awe.

The next night she had wanted to know something of the intimate exercises of female slaves. I did not even know how she, a free woman, had heard of them. I described them to her.

"How helpless you are!" she breathed.

"Yes," I said. "We are helpless."

I had then again left the cell, locking the door behind me. When I looked back at her, she knelt. "I would put on again the veil and the robes of concealment," I said.

"Janice?" she said.

"The guard will be making his rounds," I said. "I do not think it would do to let him see you as you are."

"Why?" she asked.

"It is better, I think," I said, "that he not realize how beautiful you are."

"Why?" she asked.

"He might take you for a slave," I said.

"I see," she smiled.

"Do you not find that thought frightful," I asked.

"No," she said.

"Oh," I said.

"What if he did?" she asked.

"You do not know what it is to be the object of such inordinate, uncontrollable, raging desire," I said. "You do not realize what it is to be the object of such lust and passion, such as may be stimulated only by a woman in bondage."

She looked at me, startled.

"Men kill for us," I said.

"I see," she whispered, frightened.

"Wars have been fought for us," I said.

"I see," she said.

"To be sure," I said, "some men may prefer gold, but even gold is usually valued for its uses, one of which is to buy such as we."

"I understand," she whispered.

"Doubtless the bars would hold," I said.

"You could always stay back from them, so that he could not reach you. I do not think the pit master would permit him the key."

"But what if he could open the cell?"

"And took you for a slave?"

"Yes."

"Inquire not into such a dreadful possibility," I said.

"Janice!" she protested.

"You would doubtless be treated as what he had taken you to be, a slave," I said.

"What would he do?"

"I do not know," I said. "He might cuff you and throw you to the straw, where you might quickly learn what it is for a man to take his pleasure in you. And that would be but the beginning."

"I would have to serve him?"

"Utterly, lengthily," I said, "and as his least whim might dictate."

"But you are not behind bars," she said, "and you are not, surely, frequently and indiscriminately seized."

"There is a roster for my usage," I said. To be sure, in my view my usage was too closely restricted. It seemed there were two reasons for this, one, to make of me something of a prize for guards, a delight which they were accorded less frequently than they might wish, thus serving as an instrument in their control, and, two, to serve as an instrument in my own control. Needless to say, I did not approve of this second reason. There was little doubt, however, as to its effectiveness. There are many ways to control a girl. Among them, of course, is that, the control of her gratifications.

"In my city, Besnit," she said, "slave girls are numerous. One sees many of them. One thinks little of it. In most parts of the city they go about in relative safety."

"Doubtless many men in your city own their own," I said, "or have access to them, perhaps in taverns or brothels."

"Yes," she said. "But would it not be so, too, here, in the city above?"

"Yes," I said. I smiled. "There is no dearth of slave girls in this city." That was surely true. I had been startled by their number and beauty. This seemed to me an extremely rich city. It was only to be expected then, I supposed, particularly given the nature of the men on this world, that many of its riches would wear collars. I had been permitted, of course, from time to time, like the others, out of the pits. The city above was quite beautiful. It was like a lovely, lofty jewel set in the mountains.

"It would then be possible to be out of the cell, as a slave, and be in relative safety?"

"I suppose so," I said.

"As safe as a slave can ever be," she said.

"I suppose so," I said, "assuming she is suitably collared, and owned, and such."

"Are you ever permitted to go above?" she asked.

"Sometimes," I said.

"To the city?" she asked.

"Sometimes," I said.

"May I rise to my feet?" she begged.

I regarded her through the bars.

"Yes," I said.

She rose to her feet and hurried to the bars. She grasped them. "You have been so kind to me, Janice," she said. "You let me bathe, you let me clean my clothing, you have showed me how to exercise!"

"As a *slave*," I said.

"Yes!" she said.

"It is the pit master, the depth warden, really, ultimately," I said, "who permits such things."

She then knelt behind the bars, looking up at me.

I had not ordered her to kneel.

I looked down, into her eyes.

She was before me, she, a free woman, *on her knees*, before me, before a slave!

I did not understand this.

But it is not unpleasant for a slave to have a free woman before one, so.

There were tears in her eyes.

"Janice," she said.

"Yes," I said.

"I beg!" she said. "I beg!"

I supposed she might want a hard candy, or a bit of pastry. I thought the pit master might permit that.

Her behavior had been much improved of late.

"Yes?" I said.

"I long to see the sun, Janice," she said. "I want to see the sun!"

"I do not understand," I said.

"I want to go to the surface," she said. "Take me to the surface! I want to see the sun! I want to see the sun!"

"How can that be?" I asked. "This is not a trading city, some sort of multifaceted commercial metropolis. This is a city of thieves, of raiders and warriors. One does not have free women from foreign cities wandering about above."

"I have thought carefully about the matter!" she said. "I must needs be disguised!"

"As what?" I asked.

"As a female slave, of course!" she said. "I would then attract little attention. There must be many of them above."

"There are," I granted her.

"Please, Janice!" she said.

"There is no escape for you," I said.

"I know," she said.

"And there would be even less chance of escape," I said, "if you were clad as a slave."

"I know," she said.

"And your body would be muchly bared," I said, "and men could look upon you, even casually."

"Yes," she said.

"You find that acceptable?"

"Yes!"

"I do not think you understand," I said, "what it is to be looked upon by men, *as a slave*."

"Please!"

"You would not be permitted your veil," I said. "Your features would be bared, publicly."

"But no one would know me," she said. "Do you not see? They would not understand that they were looking upon a free woman, especially one such as the Lady Constanzia of Besnit! Some wear masks that their features not be recognized. But I, contrariwise, conceal my identity by going unveiled!"

"The depth warden would not hear of it," I said.

"Ask him for me, beg it of him, I beg of you. Please, Janice!"

"If the pit master should prove accommodating," I said, "are you prepared, actually, to go through with this?"

"Yes," she said. "Yes!"

"But we have no slave garment for you," I said.

"Surely something might be devised!" she said. "Anything will do!"

"Even a rag?" I asked.

"Yes!" she said.

That thought amused me—to put a free woman in a rag!

"You would have to wear a collar," I said.

"A collar!" she cried, softly. She put her hand to her throat, frightened.

"Yes," I said.

She stiffened.

"Never," she said. "Impossible!"

Clearly she understood the symbolism, the significance, of such a thing.

She was, after all, a free woman.

I, too, as a slave, understood the symbolism, the significance, of this. How momentously it marked the difference between us, between the slave and free!

"It would have to be," I said.

She seemed then to shake with ambivalence. Within her two women warred, I thought, one who wanted her to be as she was expected to be, the other who wanted her to be as she wanted to be.

"In this city an uncollared girl," I said, "would immediately attract attention, and suspicion." And I supposed that would hold for other towns and cities on this world, as well. Indeed, how could one be "slave clad" without a collar? Men expect to find collars on slaves.

"I would not dare take you to the surface without having a collar on you," I said.

"I do not know if I have that much courage—to go that far," she said.

I shrugged.

"Is that really necessary," she asked.

"Yes," I said.

"What sort of collar?" she said.

"A slave collar," I said, "the collar of a *slave*."

"Might there not be something else?" she asked. "Something which might resemble such a collar?"

"No," I said. "It would have to be a slave collar, an authentic slave collar."

She turned pale.

That is the end of that, I thought.

Then it seemed she came to some sort of resolution. And it seemed her entire body suddenly shuddered with delight, thrilled. A bridge, it seemed, had been crossed.

"Of course," she said. "Of course, I would have to be collared. Of course! Have me collared! And it must be the collar of a slave. Of course! Yes! Put me in a *slave* collar!"

"It would have to be an authentic slave collar," I said, "an actual slave collar."

"Of course," she said.

"And it would be on you, truly on you," I said.

"Of course," she said.

"You would be *in* it," I said.

"Of course," she said.

"It would have to be locked," I said, "and you would be unable to remove it."

I would take no chances with her, if it was not locked on her, if she were not well fastened within it.

It would perfect my custody of her.

If she were to escape my charge for even an Ahn I would be held responsible.

Too, it would be dreadfully dangerous if someone should, either routinely or on provocation, perhaps a guardsman, discover that it was not locked.

"Let it be locked!" she said. "Let me be helpless in it!"

"You want it to be locked?" I said.

"Yes," she said. "I want to be helpless in it!"

"You would be," I said.

"Yes," she said. "Yes!"

"There is one compensation for the degradation," I said, "though it is nothing in which you would be interested."

"What is that?" she asked.

"The slave collar is very pretty on a woman," I said. "The beasts who design them doubtless have that in mind. It much enhances the beauty, the attractiveness, and interest, of a woman."

"That is, of course, of no interest to me," she said.

"Certainly not," I said.

"But do you think I would be pretty in such a collar?"

"Strikingly so," I said. "You would be stunning in one."

"Oh?" she said.

"Yes," I said. "But, too, you must recognize its effect on men, for it says to them that you are such as belong to them, that you are lovely and helpless, that you are *kajira*, that you exist for their service and pleasure."

"Perhaps it has, too, its effect on the woman," she speculated.

"Yes, it does," I said, "clearly." But I thought it unnecessary, and perhaps improper, to elaborate on this, as she was a free woman.

"Such things are, of course, of no interest to me," she said.

"Of course not," I said. As she was a free woman, she could lie with impunity. I myself, if caught in a lie, could be switched mercilessly.

"Please, dear Janice," she said, earnestly. "Please convey my petition to the pit master!"

I regarded her. I did not really wish to risk the wrath of the pit master.

"I want to see the sun!" she wept.

Could there be more to it than that?

"I am not sure of this," I said.

"Please, Janice!" she wept.

"I will ask him," I said.

That night I had knelt before the pit master. "Master," I had asked, "may I speak?"

"Yes," he had said.

I conveyed to him the petition of the Lady Constanzia. I feared I might be cuffed.

"She wants to see the sun," I said.

"Undoubtedly," he said, "but she also wishes to have her body bared and to have it looked upon, it adorned in the rags of a slave."

"Master!" I cried, scandalized.

"Is it not what all women want?" he asked.

"I do not know, Master," I said.

"Is it not what you want?" he asked.

"Yes, Master," I said, boldly. Then I added, in a whisper, "But I am a slave."

"And so, too, are all women," he said.

I put my head down, trembling. I did not know if what he had said were true or not. Certainly some of the women who had been in my training group had denied it vehemently, particularly in the first day or two. But sometimes, at night, I heard them crying out with gratitude to masters in their sleep. Too, they had soon trained excellently. A little later I had often heard them conversing among themselves eagerly, looking forward to their sales, discussing what they hoped for in the way of masters.

"Master," I had asked, "may I again speak?"

"Yes," he had said.

"I do not know the reason for which I was brought here."

"You have not yet been informed," he said.

"Was I brought here to take care of the free woman, Lady Constanzia?" I asked.

"No," he said.

"For what, then?" I asked.

"You will learn, in time," he said.

"Master!" I begged.

"Curiosity," he said, "is not becoming in a kajira."

"Yes, Master," I whispered. "Forgive me, Master!"

Two days later, for the first time, I had knotted the rag about the hips of the Lady Constanzia and, as she had straightened her body, had cinched the halter on her.

"Oh!" she had said.

She was kneeling.

"Must it be so tight?" she asked.

"Yes," I said.

"Why?" she asked.

"To better display you," I said.

"I see," she said.

"Certainly you do not object?"

"No."

"When you walk, or move, try to do so with some care," I said.

"I will," she said.

The rag about her hips had, in its authenticity, no nether closure.

The female slave is commonly denied even a minimum of shielding for her delicious intimacies. She is to be vulnerable, and instantly available, with a minimum of inconvenience, to the attentions of the master.

"I am frightened," she said.

"Why?" I asked.

"I fear I do not even know how to walk," she said.
"Of course you know how to walk," I said.
"—*as a slave*," she said.
"It is just a matter of walking freely, and well, beautifully, attractively gracefully, with ease and loveliness, showing your joy in your bondage and womanhood, with vulnerable femininity."
"I am afraid," she said.
"You will have no difficulty," I said.
"It is so different," she said.
"Yes," I said.
"In the robes of concealment, we must walk sedately, with carefully measured tread, with dignity."

How else could one walk in such impediments, I wondered, so ornate and heavy, so confining and cumbersome? One is, of course, free.

How different were such garments from the usual scanty lightness of the slave's garmenture, usually a brief, revealing garmenture permitting her the luxurious freedom of her limbs, a garmenture in which she finds herself permitted a joyous and uninhibited freedom of movement. To be sure, she is in her collar.

"Do you think, truly," she asked, apprehensively, "that we can be successful in this?"
"Yes," I said.
"Do you think that anyone might take me, truly, for a slave?" she asked.
"Without the least difficulty," I said.
"I see," she said.
"Your movements, of course," I said, "as you have not been trained, and have not felt the whip, and such, will not have the grace and beauty of a more experienced girl, one who has been fully taught her collar." I recalled that my own posture, slovenly from Earth, had been corrected in the pens with the stroke of a switch. Men like their slaves to be beautiful before them. "But," I said, "I do not think that will matter. We will pass you off as a new slave. That will be all right. You will be seen, however, as fetchingly exciting, and doubtless men will see you in terms more of your potential, than your present, will see you in terms of what they can do with you and make of you."

"What they can do with me, and make of me?"

"Yes," I said.

"I see," she said.

I had then showed her the collar which had been kindly provided by the pit master. "The name on it, I am told," I said, "is 'Tuta'."

"You cannot read?" she asked.

"No," I said.

She took the collar and looked at it. "Yes," she said. "It says 'Tuta'."

"I am sorry it is such a name," I said. "I had hoped for something more aristocratic, more prestigious."

"It is fine," she said.

"I am told," I said, "that it is a common slave name."

"Yes," she said. "I have heard it many times. It is commonly worn by low girls."

"I am sorry," I said.

"Rather sensual sluts," she said.

"I am sorry," I said.

"The name reeks of sex and slavery," she said.

"Forgive me," I said.

"Like 'Fina' and 'Janice'," she said.

I put down my head.

"It was the choice of the pit master," I said.

"He is perceptive, and has excellent taste," she said.

I looked at her, startled.

"I love it," she said. "It is just right for me. It will do wonderfully well."

"Once you put on the collar," I said, "you will, for the purposes of our disguise, no longer be the Lady Constanzia, but only Tuta."

She put the collar about her neck, with the lock in front, and closed it. There was a small, solid click. Then, carefully, as it was a close-fitting collar, like most such collars, she turned it on her neck, so that the lock was at the back. This is the common way in which such collars are worn. She then smiled at me. "Now I am Tuta," she said.

"Yes," I said, "you are now Tuta."

"Is Tuta pretty?" she asked, timidly.

"Tuta is beautiful," I said.

She suffused with pleasure, basking in my commendation. She put down her head, blushing, her face and exposed limbs red with delight.

"Thank you," she whispered.

I stood up.

I looked down upon her.

She looked up, smiling, but a little frightened.

I thought I had probably been too indulgent with her. She was, after all, a free woman, and how often would a slave have such as she in her charge?

"Stand, Tuta," I said, suddenly, sharply, "and put your wrists behind your back, and lift your chin. You are to be braceleted and leashed."

* * * *

"Janice," said the free woman, the Lady Constanzia of Besnit, now disguised as Tuta, a slave.

"Yes," I said.

"I would not, as the sort of slave I am supposed to be, be kneeling thus, would I?"

We were kneeling on the broad steps leading to the upper terraces. Her knees were widely spread, as those of a pleasure slave.

"No," I said, "as you are presumably not to be understood as a pleasure slave."

She closed her knees, it seemed to me, reluctantly.

"But," I said, "any slave might kneel so, for example, as a placatory gesture, to avert a master's wrath, to interest a man, to plead with him that he might have mercy upon her, and give attention to her needs, and such."

"I see," she said.

"But it is only in the pleasure slave," I said, "that the position is commonly required."

"I understand," she said.

"Failure to kneel properly, for one such as I," I said, "is cause for discipline."

"Discipline?"

"The whip, or such," I said, "whatever the master pleases."

"I see," she whispered.

"Straighten your back," I said. "Lift your head."

She did so.

"You inspect your handiwork?" she inquired.

"Yes," I said.

"I am more exposed than most slaves," she said, "am I not?"

"Less so than those who are kept naked," I said. I regarded her.

I had knotted the brown rag low on her hips, so that their lovely flare might be the better noted.

"Is the halter too tight?" I asked.

"I do not object," she said.

This halter, improvised from a brown rag, like the skirt, was, in its simplicity and raggedness, as I have suggested, believable as, and suitable for, a slave halter. Too, if there were any doubts as to the matter, they surely would have been dispelled by the manner in which it was on her, by the height, tightness, and insolence with which it confined her, leaving little of the delights of her lineaments to speculation, the knots jerked tight with casual authority. Would she be clad as a slave? Then let her know how slaves might be clad, for the interest and delectation of men, we at the mercy of those delicious, masterful beasts.

"Am I attractive?" she asked.

"I would think so," I said.

"Do you think men might be interested in me?"

"Certainly," I said.

"Enough to pay good money for me?"

"Of course."

"Am I beautiful?" she asked.

"Yes, beautiful," I said.

"Am I truly beautiful?"

"Yes," I said, "you are truly beautiful. And you are also vain. Quite vain."

"But slaves are permitted vanity, are they not?" she inquired.

"Perhaps," I said. "But you are not a slave."

"Perhaps you are mistaken," she said. She smiled.

How irritating a free woman can be!

I looked away.

"I am clothed as a low slave, am I not?" she asked.

"Yes," I said.

"You enjoyed devising these garments, and putting me in them, didn't you?" she asked.

I turned, to look back upon her.

"Yes," I said, "free woman."

"A slave's vengeance on us?" she laughed.

"Perhaps," I said.

"Was I supposed to be dismayed, to be scandalized and shamed?" she asked.

"Perhaps," I said. "Were you?"

"No," she said.

"But when we came to the exit, at the height of the tunnels, you hung back," I said. "You were terrified. You feared to be drawn, as you are, into the light."

"Yes," she said. "I was afraid then!"

"Do you wish to return to the cell?" I had asked her.

"No!" she had wept.

"You will then, free woman," I had said to her, "emerge into the light, and as you are!"

I had then, she braceleted and helpless on the leash, unable to resist, drawn her forth, out into the light. Then she had stood there, just outside the opening to the tunnel, "slave clad," her head lifted, her eyes closed against the light, in the full light of the sun. She had seemed suddenly rapturous. It had been done. She stood there, outside of the tunnels. Her bared feet were on the warm stones. The light of the sun fell full upon her, illuminating and warming her. It was hot and bright on her muchly exposed body.

"I will show you the bazaar," I had said.

"These garments make me attractive, don't they?" she asked.

"You are attractive anyway," I said, "and would never be more so than if you were naked in your collar."

"But they do, too, make me attractive, in their way, do they not?" she asked.

"As all suitable slave garments," I said, "they stimulate and provoke interest."

"Yes!" she said.

"They conceal and hint," I said, "but, as slave garments, they are not permitted to deceive or falsify."

"I understand the distinction perfectly," she said.

"Even the relative modesty of a common slave tunic," I said, "tends to be stimulatory."

"Doubtless," she said.

"I have haltered your breasts high," I said, "the better to emphasize the line of your body, and the better to show you as one subject to bonds, but it is clear, from the way in which this is done, that deception is not involved. For example, it is quite clear what would be the case were they free to be gazed upon without interference, the halter having been, say, cut away. Too, the line in question is one of several quite natural ones. It would be similarly well revealed if your wrists were fastened to an overhead chain or if you were thrown on your back, head down, half over a couch."

"I see," she said.

"You would doubtless look delightful in a variety of slave garments," I said. "I think you would look quite fetching, for example, in a common slave tunic, sleeveless, brief and such."

"Yes," she said. "Let us come again and again to the surface. And garb me variously!"

"Perhaps," I said.

"But never forget," she said, "as you have garbed me now!"

"You do not object?" I asked.

"No!" she said. "I love it!"

"Perhaps," I said, somewhat maliciously, "the next time, if the pit master permits us a repetition of this adventure, I will march you through the streets as a bare-breasted slave, permitted only a string and slave strip."

She suddenly squirmed and jerked at the slave bracelets confining her hands behind her back. "Surely, Janice," she cried, "you would not!"

I laughed.

"You are teasing me!" she said.

"Yes," I said.

"Tell me more of slave garments!" she begged.

"Are you rested?" I asked.

"Yes," she said.

"We must be on our way," I said.

"Please!" she said.

"There are many varieties of slave garments," I said, "which have their various purposes and utilities, such as display of the slave, the mockery or humiliation of the slave, the assurance of her instant availability, punishment garments, confinement garments, and such."

"It is an entire world," she said.

"Yes," I said.

"But the important thing, really, about slave garments," I said, "whether they are the richest of gowns, with perhaps a slit in them through which a thigh must be revealed, or the tiniest of strings and slave strips, is that they are just that, *slave garments*. It is their meaning, primarily, which renders them provocative, that they are slave garments, that she who wears them is slave."

"Yes!" she said. "That is it!"

"We must be on our way," I said.

"I have seen some slaves in the streets naked," she said.

"Yes," I said. "We are subject to that."

"If I were a slave," she said, "I could be put in the street that way, couldn't I?"

"Of course," I said.

"You are so vulnerable," she said.

"Yes," I said.

She looked down at her knees. They were now pressed closely together.

"Have you heard, Janice," she asked, "anything of my ransom?"

"No," I said. "Alas, no."

"Perhaps I have been forgotten?" she said.

"No, I am sure that is not the case," I said. "You must keep up your hopes!"

"What do you know of my hopes?" she asked.

I did not understand this.

"Are you slaves dawdling?" asked a man's voice.

"No, Master!" I cried. "We were just leaving!" I leaped to my feet. "Up, lazy Tuta!" I said, angrily. I snapped the free woman's leash. She seemed startled at this but, responsive to my command, and doubtless, too, not failing to comprehend the leash signal, rose swiftly to her feet. "Does she not know how to respond?" asked the man. "What do you say?" he asked the free woman. "Yes, Mistress!" exclaimed the free woman. "She is new to her collar," I explained. "Do not be easy with her," said the man. "That is not how a slave is trained." "Yes, Master," I said. "Forgive us, Masters!" I said, for there were two men there, in tunics and cloaks. I then, head down, avoiding their eyes, as a slave normally does with unknown free men, turned about and led the free woman up the stairs. I think the men watched us ascend, and then, at their own pace, also ascended the stairs. We had ascended but two or three steps when I heard one of the men say something to the other. "A pair of juicy puddings," he said. "Yes," said the other.

In a few minutes, perhaps three or four, we came to the largest of the high terraces. There were many other high terraces in this part of the city, but none were as large, as spacious, as splendid, as this. I had a special reason for coming to this terrace.

"How glorious is the view!" exclaimed the free woman.

I recalled that she had told me that she had been brought here hooded in her own veils. I had had fastened upon me, doubtless appropriately, a simple slave hood.

I took her toward the balustrade, where we might look out.

"It is breathtakingly beautiful!" she exclaimed.

We drank in the sight of the snow-capped peaks, the darkness in the valleys, the patches of cloud in the bright sky. So small we were in the face of nature.

"Janice," said the free woman.

"Yes," I said.

"Do you remember what the man said on the stairs, as we left?"

"Do not concern yourself with the matter," I said.

"I am not sure I understood him," she said.

"Consider the beauty of the mountains," I said.

"Janice!" she protested.

"It is only a vulgar expression," I said, "like 'vulo' or 'tasta'."

"Those are not vulgar expressions," she said. "A vulo is a kind of bird, a tasta is a kind of candy, often mounted on a stick."

"They can be vulgar expressions when applied to slaves," I said.

"I see," she said.

"If you were a slave," I said, "you could understand how a man might speak of you as slave meat, or as his vulo, or his tasta, or his pudding, and so on, for that is, frankly, what you would be."

"Are you a juicy pudding, Janice?" she asked.

"I had best hope that I am," I said.

"Am I a juicy pudding?" she asked.

"Perhaps, if you were a slave," I said, "you might prove to be such."

"I see," she said.

"And you would best concern yourself to do your best to be such," I said.

"Of course," she said.

"Do not look now," I said, "but there is a fellow back a bit and to the right who has his eye on you. He may think you qualify as a juicy pudding right now."

"Like the men on the stairs!" she laughed.

"Yes," I said. "Don't look," I cautioned her.

"Do you think he would like me to be his juicy pudding?" she asked.

"It seems to me quite possible," I said.

"How wonderful!" she said.

"You might not think it so wonderful if you were roped and hooded, and carried off," I said.

"It would improve a girl's price, wouldn't it?" she asked.

"What?" I asked.

"Being a juicy pudding," she said.

"How vulgar you are," I said.

"Wouldn't it?" she asked.

"Undoubtedly," I said.

"How beautiful this place is!" she said.

"I have come here for a purpose," I said. "I want to check on something. I will, accordingly, take you to the side for a time, to the wall over there, and secure you there."

"Secure me?" she asked.

"Yes," I said. "To one of the slave rings. But I will be back shortly."

"May I inquire as to what you are going to do?" she asked.

"No," said I, "*Tuta.*"

"Yes, Mistress," she smiled.

We then turned away from the balustrade, to make our way across the large terrace. "Keep your eyes ahead!" I said. I had seen her glance about, doubtless trying to locate the fellow I had mentioned to her earlier. It had been a mistake, I supposed, to have called her attention to the matter. It was surely not necessary that she, as a free woman, know that she, looked upon as a slave, had been found of interest by a male. She now kept her eyes ahead. I think it cost her some effort to do so. But she was trying to be cooperative and, after all, it was I who held her leash. There was a three-tiered decorative basin on the terrace, on the way to the wall. The first, or uppermost, tier was some four feet above the surface of the terrace; the second, or middle, tier was about three feet above the surface of the terrace; the lowest tier, the third tier, was almost level with the surface of the terrace itself. "May I drink, Janice?" she asked. "Yes," I said. There had seemed something a little suspicious in her voice. I wondered if she truly wanted to drink, or if this were a stratagem to dally, perhaps to, as though inadvertently, steal a glance about, perhaps in the hope of seeing the fellow I had mentioned. But it was warm today. She stopped at the basin. She turned about. Yes, she was looking about, the vixen, over the surface of the water in the uppermost basin! "I cannot use one of the cups, or cup the water in my hands, Janice," she said. "Perhaps you will help me." Then she whispered, "Which one is he?" "The one over there," I said, "in the scarlet tunic, and cloak, looking this way." Quickly, flushing, she looked down. "He is handsome!" she whispered. "Remember you are collared," I whispered. She must be concerned about the propriety of her behavior! "Perhaps you will help me, Janice" she said, aloud. "No!" I said. What did she think? She seemed surprised by this, but then bent forward, to drink from the upper basin. "Oh!" she cried, jerked to the side by the leash. "What are you doing?" I asked her. "I was going to drink," she said. "I do not understand." "Kneel," I said, "and drink from the lowest basin. The upper basin is for citizens and folk of honor, the second basin is for resident aliens and common visitors, the third basin, the lowest basin, is for animals." She then knelt beside the third basin, the lowest basin, that which was almost level with the surface of the terrace itself, and, head down, her hands braceleted behind her, the leash running to her neck, drank.

When she had finished drinking, she looked up at me, from her knees. She seemed shaken. There seemed a sort of wonder in her eyes.

"It seems you have never drunk thusly before," I said, "from the lowest basin, as a slave."

"No," she said.

"Up," I said.

She stood.

"Is he still about?" she asked.

"I do not know," I said.

"Did he see me, drinking, as I did?"

"I do not know," I said.

"I would be terrified for a man to have seen me drinking in such a way," she said.

"Think nothing of it," I said. "It is a common way for slaves to drink at public fountains, basins, and such."

She did not raise her eyes. Her eyes seemed focused on the flagstones of the terrace, warm beneath her small, bared, white feet.

"There is a ring over there," I said. "We will use that one. It is in the shade."

The pressure of the leash collar on the back of her neck brought her quickly enough out of her thoughts.

In spite of my earlier injunction about keeping her eyes ahead, she now looked about much, over her shoulder and such. She was doubtless trying to ascertain whether or not the fellow in the scarlet tunic was about. It would have been difficult to tell. In this part of the terrace, more toward the wall, and shade, it was crowded. Some booths were set up on the terrace, for the sale of fruit and flowers.

"Oh!" said a voice, suddenly, angrily.

It was a female voice!

I saw a flurry of ornate robes.

My heart sank.

My charge, doubtless in her concern to survey the terrace for the scarlet-clad figure, had, it seemed, struck into a free woman of the city.

"A slave!" cried the figure in the robes of concealment, in horror. "I have been touched by a slave!"

My charge stood there, unsteadily, out of breath, from the buffeting, not quite comprehending what had occurred.

I had knelt, almost immediately. There were, after all, free persons about.

"Filthy slave! Filthy slave! Filthy slave!" screamed the figure in the robes of concealment.

This epithet, of course, although uttered repeatedly with great vehemence, was not literally correct. I had no doubt but what my charge was far cleaner at this moment than the free woman. Indeed, she almost sparkled. She had well bathed. It was only then that the rags of a slave had been knotted on her. There are, of course, filthy slaves, for example, those forbidden by a master to clean themselves, usually as a punishment, and slaves can be kept in filth, in tarsk sties and tharlarion manure bins, and such, also usually as a punishment, but this is not common. Among the Wagon Peoples of the southern plains, I am told, a slave who has not been fully pleasing may be tied overnight in a dung sack. I am also told that excellent order obtains among the kajirae of the Wagon Peoples. But then, as I understand it, excellent order obtains among all kajirae on this world. It is seen to by the masters. The most common device for improving a girl, of course, is the switch or whip. As I have suggested earlier, cleanliness and such things, are normally required of a slave, as they are not of a free woman. The free woman's cries, of course, one may suppose, were not intended to express an objective appraisal of my charge's current hygienic condition; rather they served as a way of ventilating what was apparently a considerable sense of outrage.

"I am not filthy!" cried my charge, a mistake, surely.

"Clumsy, collared she-urt!" screamed the offended woman. "Look," she cried to the bystanders. "She is standing! She is standing!"

"Kneel," I urged my charge. "Kneel!"

"Clumsy, insolent, collared she-sleen!" cried the offended woman.

"You struck into me as much as I into you!" said my charge. Woe, I thought. She has forgotten everything! Does she not know how she is clad, that she is in a collar, that she is leashed! Woe! She is acting like a free woman!

The free woman's eyes flashed above her veil.

Suddenly then I think that my charge realized her position and danger. I heard the bracelets pull suddenly against the close-set links which joined them. But she could not free her hands! They were confined behind her back! How helpless she was, helpless as a slave is helpless! Too, I think she became then much aware of how much she was exposed, of the softness, bareness, and vulnerability of her skin. She slowly sank to her knees.

"Bring me a switch!" cried the free woman. My charge cast me an alarmed glance.

"Beg her forgiveness!" I whispered to her.

"It was not my fault," she whispered to me.

"A switch!" cried the free woman.

"It was not all my fault," insisted my charge to me.

"A switch, a switch!" called the free woman.

"It was probably both your faults," I said. "Beg her forgiveness!"

"She is not begging mine," said my charge.

A lad brought a switch, probably from one of the booths. It was about three feet long, of leather, narrow, rodlike and supple.

The free woman seized it.

"Beg her forgiveness!" I said.

"Forgive me!" said my charge, suddenly, to the free woman. "Forgive me!"

"'Mistress', 'Mistress'," I urged.

"Forgive me, Mistress!" said my charge.

"You beg my forgiveness?" inquired the free woman, with mock interest, and solicitation.

"Yes, Mistress," my charge assured her.

"Oh, yes," said the free woman, maliciously, "you will beg my forgiveness, I assure you of that!"

"Please, Mistress!" I said. "She is in my charge! It was my fault. I did not watch her well enough!"

The free woman glared down at me.

"It was my fault," I said. "Beat me, instead!" I had, after all, felt the whip, and the switch. Too, it was horrifying to think that the Lady Constanzia might be struck. Such was not for such as she. She was a free woman!

"It was she who stood in my presence," she said, "it was she who dared to speak back, it was she who did not look where she was going!"

"Mistress, please," I begged.

"Be silent, collared slut!" said the woman with the switch.

"Yes, Mistress," I said, silenced.

She turned then to my charge.

"Does the stupid, clumsy girl beg my forgiveness," she asked, sweetly.

"Yes, Mistress," said my charge, timidly.

"We shall see!" cried the free woman.

I saw her arm raise. I closed my eyes.

"Wait," said a fellow's voice. "Do not mark her. She may have value on the block."

The free woman turned to him, angrily. But she lowered her arm. He seemed a fellow of some importance. On his left sleeve, toward the bottom, there was a blue chevron, a yellow one, and another blue. He must then, I thought, be of the Slavers, sometimes regarded as a subcaste of the Merchants, sometimes as an independent caste. He would, if of the Slavers, of course, be an excellent judge of woman flesh. "You are angry," he said to outraged woman. "You might lower her value."

"She is valueless," she snapped.

"She might bring something in a vending," he said. Then he turned to me. "She is new to her collar, isn't she?" he asked.

"Yes, Master!" I averred, gratefully.

Then he looked at the Lady Constanzia. "The more quickly you learn your collar the better for you, soft, tender little vulo," he said.

She nodded, frightened.

"What satisfaction am I granted here?" inquired the offended free woman, clutching the switch.

"To your belly, slave!" snapped the slaver to the Lady Constanzia.

Immediately she went to her belly. I almost threw myself to my belly, and I had not even been addressed. His voice was such as women understand. It was the sort of voice which a woman instinctively obeys.

Even the free woman, clutching her switch, shrank back in fear.

"To her slippers, stupid, clumsy girl," said the slaver, "and beg her forgiveness fittingly."

Immediately, terrified, the Lady Constanzia struggled forward and pressed her lips to the slippers of the free woman, kissing them again and again. "I am a stupid, clumsy girl," she said. "Forgive me, I beg of you, beautiful Mistress! Please, forgive me, beautiful Mistress!" The slippers, I supposed, might not be greatly unlike those which the Lady Constanzia herself had worn when free, even those which she might have worn on the afternoon of her abduction. Prisoners are seldom permitted slippers or hose. Her slippers had been used, I supposed, to make clear to someone that she was in the power of her captors. It is not unusual for a slave girl to address even a veiled free woman as "beautiful Mistress," incidentally. It is a way of trying to mollify and flatter them. Often, of course, one does not know if they are beautiful or not. They might be fortunate to bring a few coppers as a kettle-and-mat girl, but then, of course, what does that matter, as they are free.

"It is enough," said the free woman, drawing back. She handed the switch back to the lad who had brought it.

The slaver looked down upon the Lady Constanzia, who was prostrate before the free woman. I still held the Lady Constanzia's leash. "If you would live," he said to the Lady Constanzia, "learn your collar quickly, little vulo. Do you understand?"

The Lady Constanzia, frightened, perhaps hardly understanding what she had done, what had been done to her, or perhaps understanding it only too well, her head turned to the left, nodded affirmatively, vigorously.

"I thank you, Lady," said the slaver to the free woman, she in the ornate robes, who had been muchly offended, "on behalf of all property holders, for your understanding in this matter, for the lenience you have shown in this instance."

"It is nothing," she said, her voice shaking a little. She was, after all, even though free, a female in the presence of such a man.

"You are doubtless as beautiful as you are merciful," he said.

Her hand went, it seemed inadvertently, modestly, to her veil. Doubtless she wished to reassure herself that it was in place. But, it seemed, she disarranged it, slightly. But then, swiftly, she remedied this lapse. The slaver gave not the least indication that he might have noted her embarrassment.

"It is a lovely day," he said. "Might I be privileged to accompany you? In the lower gardens the veminia are in bloom."

"Of course," she said.

He then extended his arm and she placed her small, gloved hand upon it.

It is not unusual on this world, incidentally, for men to prize such things as flowers. Perhaps all men have this softer side to their nature. I do not know. At any rate, men here, or most men here, do not seem to fear this part of themselves or attempt, perhaps for some cultural reason, to conceal it. Perhaps, given their culture, in which are secured their natural rights, those of manhood and the mastery, they can afford to be whole men here, not cultural or political half-men, of one sort or another. It seemed paradoxical to me at first, of course, to discover that these men, with their great love of nature, would think nothing of keeping a cowering, cringing woman chained at their feet. Were we regarded, because of what we were, rightly, as being worthy of less consideration than the delicate petals of a tiny blossom? Did they know us that well? Was our nature so obvious to them? Did they know, too, I wondered, that we were the secret enemy? Did they understand the secret war? But did they understand, too, that we were the secret enemy who wishes to be subdued, and enslaved? Did they understand that we wished to lose the secret war, to be vanquished, totally, that we wished, conquered and humbled, to bend our necks to the collars of the victors, that we might then serve them as their helpless slaves? I had soon come to understand that these mysterious juxtapositions, these seeming paradoxes, this thing, the love of flowers, the subjugation of women, and such, is all of a piece. It is not simply because they know us, and know us well, our pettiness, our vanity, and such, that they put us to their feet. It is not simply because they know us, and know us well, as the enemy to be vanquished, that they put us to their feet. It is also, simply, in part, because of their adherence to nature, and their refusal to compromise it, that they put us to their feet, where we belong. They know that if we are not kept there we will destroy them. We despise and hate men too weak to keep us as slaves, for they then deny to us our own nature, and not only theirs to themselves. We want only to be owned, and to serve and love our masters. Is that too much to ask?

But then, suddenly, a wave of slave terror overcame me. I was a slave. It could be done with me as masters pleased! I was owned!

I watched the free woman withdraw, her tiny hand on the arm of the slaver.

Was she mad, I wondered. But perhaps she knew him. Perhaps he was well known in the city. Perhaps there was no danger. But surely she must understand the meaning of those three tiny chevrons on his left sleeve. Did she not know that he must have handled hundreds, perhaps thousands, like herself, in their chains and collars, appraising them, determining their order of sale, taking his profit on them?

They were now well across the terrace.

I wondered if she wondered, beneath her robes, and veil, walking across the terrace, what might be the feel of slave iron on her limbs, what it might be to feel the sawdust of the slave block beneath her bared feet, what it might be to hear the call of the auctioneer, proposing her for the consideration of buyers.

"They are gone now," I whispered to the Lady Constanzia. "Get up."

She rose to her knees, unsteadily, trembling. I did not think she could stand at the moment.

"I could have been beaten," she said.

"You are in a collar, and clad as a slave," I said.

"I could have been switched," she said. "As a slave!"

"Of course," I said. "I am only surprised that you were not."

"Why?" she asked.

"The switch," I said, "would not have marked you. Oh, it might have put stripes on you which might, for a day or so, have had some effect on your price, but the stripes would go away."

"Then why was I not beaten?" she asked.

"He might have been afraid that she did not know how to beat a slave," I said. "He might have been afraid that she, somehow, in her rage, might have actually injured you. Perhaps he was afraid that you might have been blinded, which would, assuredly, have lowered your price."

She shuddered.

"But, I think," I whispered, "that he, a slaver, suspected that you might not be truly bond, but something else, perhaps what you are, a mere prisoner. He might have thus intervened to prevent the indignity of you being beaten, as a mere slave."

"Do you think so?" she asked.

"Yes," I said. "Would the people of your city object to the switching or whipping of an errant slave?"

"No," she said. "If the slave is not fully pleasing, she is to be punished. Everyone knows that."

"And so," I said, "they would be unlikely to interfere."

"True," she said.

"And they would think little of the matter."

"That is true," she said. "They would think little or nothing of it. They might pause to jeer the girl, encouraging her to profit from her beating. That is all. It is just something that is done—and appropriately—*to slaves*. They must be instructed. They must be kept in line. They must learn to be pleasing."

"It is the same here," I said. "I have seen slaves publicly whipped three times in this city, once on a lower terrace, and twice in the bazaar.

And several times I have seen them hastened by a blow or two of a belt or switch."

She shuddered.

"They are slaves," I said.

"Of course," she said.

I looked at her.

"—As I might be taken to be," she said.

"Precisely," I said.

"And I might then be treated similarly."

"Certainly."

"And then I, too, might be whipped, as they, perhaps even on a mere whim—whipped—literally—*whipped*."

"Exactly," I said.

"Do you think any others might know that I am not bond?" she asked.

"I doubt it," I said. "Indeed, he may have thought you bond, but merely new to your collar."

"But you think he knew?"

"I think so," I said. "Presumably he is an experienced slaver."

"Do you think he had any doubts about you?" she asked.

"No," I said, reddening. "I do not think he had any doubts whatsoever about me."

"I could have been whipped," she said, wonderingly.

"Are you able to stand?" I asked.

"Yes," she said.

"You should have been switched," said a male voice, to the Lady Constanzia.

We both, startled, looked up, from our knees.

The Lady Constanzia gasped. Then, swiftly, she thrust down her head.

It was the fellow in the scarlet tunic, with the scarlet cloak, whom I had originally noted in the vicinity of the balustrade, where we had been looking upon the mountains.

"Lift your head, slave," said he to the Lady Constanzia.

She did so.

She kept her head up, but, after an instant, was careful not to meet his eyes. In her first glance she had grasped, with the immediate understanding a woman has of such things, the nature of his scrutiny.

She knelt very straight, frightened. She was being considered, as a female. He did not hurry. And he even walked about her. Then he was again before her. "A beautiful face," he commented to me. "Good slave curves. Excellent hair."

"Yes, Master," I said.

"You should have been switched," he said to the Lady Constanzia.

"Yes, Master," she said.

I was startled. That was the first time I had heard her use the word 'Master' to a man.

"Why weren't you?" he asked.

"I do not know, Master," she said.

He looked at me.

"I do not know, Master," I said.

"You were very fortunate," he said to the Lady Constanzia.

"Yes, Master," she said.

"I, myself, would not have been so lenient," he said.

"Yes, Master," she said, swallowing hard. He was such as would think nothing of beating her.

"Has she been whip-trained?" he asked me.

"No," I said.

"She must indeed be quite new to her collar," he said.

"Yes, Master," I said. He must then, I surmised, have been reasonably close, in the crowd, during the incident with the free woman.

"She nearly drank from the first basin," he said.

"Yes, Master," I admitted. He had been watching us then.

"It seems," he said, regretfully, "she is stupid."

"No, Master," I said. "It is only that she has much to learn about her collar."

"She is not totally stupid?" he asked.

"No, Master," I said.

"She has some intelligence then?" he asked, interested.

"Yes, Master," I said. "She is actually quite intelligent."

"Excellent," he said, pleased.

Then he looked at me, and snapped his fingers. "Collar," he said.

Instantly I, trained, leaped to my feet and stood quite close to him, uncomfortably close, and held my hands a little behind my body. I lifted my chin. He crooked a finger under my collar and pulled me closer to him, holding me in place. I could feel his finger against my neck, on the left side, between the steel of the collar and the flesh. I could also feel the collar drawn tighter against the back of my neck.

"It is a state collar," he said. "Your name is 'Janice'."

"Yes, Master," I whispered.

He released me, and I knelt.

He then regarded the Lady Constanzia. He snapped his fingers and said, "Collar!"

She rose uncertainly to her feet, and approached him. She had, of course, had my example from which to profit. She, to my surprise, however, stood closer to him than I would have expected, and more close to him than I had, originally. It seemed she was improving on my example. Was she then, in such matters, to be my teacher? She lifted her chin delicately. In response to the "collar command," the slave approaches the male, that he need not inconvenience himself by coming toward her. She then lifts her chin and places her hands behind her. It is thus that a girl renders herself vulnerable for the reading of her collar. In this case, of course, the Lady Constanzia's hands were already behind her, her small, lovely wrists closely linked together, well pinioned, in the steel of slave bracelets.

Still he put his finger under her collar, and, as she gasped, he pulled her even closer to him, indeed, quite close to him, "slave close," as the expression is. She could not move back, because of his hold on her. I was alarmed. She was a free woman! I could well conjecture her dismay, her discomfort, her fear, her wild sensations—she, *a free female*, being held so close to him, she half stripped, he fully dressed, so powerful, so masculine!

"'Tuta'," he read. "It is a good name for you, slave."

"Thank you, Master," she whispered.

"It is not a state collar," he said to me, "but, as she is in your custody, one gathers that she must be in the keeping of the state, for some reason, perhaps pending her sale."

I was silent.

He released the Lady Constanzia's collar. "Remain where you are," he said.

"Yes, Master," she said.

"Slave lips," he said to her.

She looked at him, wildly, in consternation.

"Purse your lips," I said to her.

She complied, frightened.

"Close your eyes," he said to her.

She did so.

She was then standing there, before him, her eyes closed, her lips pursed.

"Her lips are of interest," he said.

"Please, Master," I protested.

"I am going to taste your lips, Tuta," he said.

"Master!" I protested.

He did not immediately address himself, however, to the Lady Constanzia. Rather he stood there for a time, and let her stand there, for a time, her lips in the position he had commanded, her eyes closed, as he had ordered.

I heard a tiny clink of metal as she pulled a bit, futilely, against the bracelets which held her small hands confined behind her back.

Then, to my surprise, and dismay, I saw her lift her chin a little more, and stretch her neck a little, lifting her lips to him. How shameless! She was offering herself to him! Could the Lady Constanzia be a slave?

With a low, throaty laugh, almost a growl, he then enfolded her, she helpless, braceleted, in his arms and, indeed, tasted, and lengthily, and well, tasted the lips of the free woman, the Lady Constanzia!

After a time, perhaps even three or four Ehn, he released her, and she sank to her knees, before him. Then she looked straight ahead. Her eyes were wide. She was clearly shaken. She began to tremble. I feared she might collapse to the stones.

He crouched down beside her, briefly.

"Oh!" she said, suddenly.

"She is not in the iron belt," he observed.

"She has not had her slave wine, Master!" I said, quickly. "Please, I beg of you! Do not! Do not!"

He stood up.

"Have no fear," said he.

"May we leave?" I begged.

"Her lips are indeed of interest," he said to me. "To be sure, she was more kissed than kissing."

"Yes, Master," I said.

"Does she know how to use them?" he asked.

"No, Master," I said. "She is a new slave."
"But she is intelligent, you said?"
"Yes, Master."
"Then she can learn how to use them?"
"Of course, Master."
"Does she know the seven basic kisses of the slave?" he asked.
"No, Master," I said.
"Not even that?"
"No, Master," I said.

Naturally the number of "basic kisses" tends to vary with the nature of the analysis in question, much depending on how broadly or narrowly the notion of "basic" is understood, and the criteria for distinguishing between a "basic kiss" and a major variation thereof. If I may be permitted to exaggerate a point, for purposes of clarification, one might ask, are there two basic kisses with five hundred variations of each, four basic kisses with two hundred and fifty variations of each, five with two hundred variations of each, ten with one hundred variations of each, or, as some authorities might prefer, merely one thousand basic kisses? Or are there ten thousand, and so on? All authorities agree, of course, that the varieties of possible kisses, with respect to location, pressure, liquidity, duration, timing, and such, are infinite in number. The notion of "seven basic kisses," however, is, apparently, a common one. It deftly imposes some useful order on what might otherwise be a chaos. It is nothing against the value of a classificatory scheme that it is not the only one possible. As a last note, I might add that there does seem to be general agreement among authorities on the importance of a given number of types of kisses, and perhaps that is more important than whether one accounts a given kiss A to be a variation of B, or B to be a variation of A, and so on. There are apparently, incidentally, on this world, a number of manuals devoted to slave training. In most of these, as I understand it, seven is indeed given as the number of the "basic kisses." For what it is worth, that is the number which was impressed on me in the pens. I had had seven basic lessons on the matter, with variations taught within the lessons. There were also frequent review lessons later on. One does not, of course, forget such things. To be sure, much depends, as we were always being told, on the individual master. It is his will which, to us, is all. In our practices we were sometimes blindfolded.

I presume there were several reasons for that, for example, that we might learn how to concentrate on the tactual sensations involved, that we might be able to kiss well in the dark and, when we were using male slaves to practice on, that we should not become involved with them personally. When one kisses a man as a slave it is hard not to feel oneself as slave to him. I do not think the male slaves objected to being used in our training. Some who began by crying out in rage, perhaps new slaves, ended up moaning with pleasure. They, too, were generally blindfolded, except when we must kiss them upon their closed eyes. Later, as our skills improved, the guards permitted us, sans blindfolds, to practice upon them. And they were harsh taskmasters, I tell you! Diligently must we strive to please them! But we preferred their severities to the helplessness of the slaves for we knew that they were such as to whom we belonged, free men. Sometimes we felt the switch when we did not do well. I so wanted to kiss he whose whip I had first kissed, but he would never permit it. I wanted to kiss him as he had never been kissed before, but he would not permit it. How he scorned me! And perhaps rightly, for I was naught but a slave! After we had kissed the guards we were much aroused. Shamelessly, later, throbbing with need, we would beg their attentions from our kennels. Sometimes they were kind to us and sometimes they were not.

"She is quite ignorant then," said the fellow.

"Yes, Master," I said.

The Lady Constanzia, I am sure, did not appreciate my concurrence in this matter, but he was a free man, and I a slave, and his conjecture was, after all, obviously true.

"A pity," he said.

"Yes, Master," I said.

"Do you come often to this terrace?" he asked.

"We have not, in the past," I said.

"Will you in the future?" he asked.

"I do not know if we will be permitted abroad," I said.

"And if you are?" he asked.

"Perhaps then, Master," I said. I had wanted to come to this terrace for a particular reason. It gave access, by means of a bridge, to an area in which I had hoped I might obtain certain information. This was unknown, of course, to the Lady Constanzia. I had come here some times before, but things had not been satisfactory. One must be here, or rather at a place close by, at a certain time to learn what I wanted to know, if one could know it. The information I wanted, of course, like that which had been denied to me about the reason for my being in the pits, had been denied me. It was a simple enough bit of information, but a slave girl must be extremely careful about certain things. For example, asking a question outright, particularly of a stranger, can involve great risks. The stranger will presumably assume that you are supposed to be denied the information or you would have already obtained it from your master or keeper. To be sure, one may, kneeling, innocently request certain sorts of information, such as the directions to a shop or given street, or such, but to ask about something which is either sensitive or presumed to be generally known can be frowned upon. For example, a slave would not request information as to the departure or arrival times of sky caravans and such; and she would not, presumably, ask something of the simplicity of that which I wished to know. It would automatically be assumed that that information, for some reason, had been denied to her. One might, of course, merely be told that curiosity is not becoming in a kajira, which, I had learned, is something of a saying on this world, but, more likely, one might be cuffed or beaten, and then one might have one's hands bound behind one and one's question written on, say, the interior of one's thigh or on a breast, usually the left, as most masters are right-handed, where, when one returns to one's keeper or master, it will be clear that one has been disobedient, and attempted to obtain the denied information illicitly.

"Perhaps, then, I shall see you again," he said.

"Perhaps, Master," I said.

"You may leave," he said, suddenly, rather angrily.

"Thank you, Master," I said. I leaped up and the Lady Constanzia, not daring to look at the scarlet-clad stranger, rose, too, to her feet.

We turned about.

"Stop!" said he.

We stopped.

"Do not turn," said he. "Do not kneel."

We remained as we were, facing away from him, I with the leash, she with her hands braceleted behind her.

"When is she to be put up for sale?" he asked. His voice, in all its power, seemed almost to break. It seemed that within him, unaccountably, this question had cost him something. It was as though it had suddenly erupted within him. It seemed to have emerged out of a struggle, some internal conflict.

"I do not know, Master," I said.

"It does not matter, of course," he said, suddenly, angrily.

"Yes, Master," I said.

"Go!" he ordered.

"Yes, Master," I said. I swiftly then made my way toward my previous destination, a point on the wall of the terrace, which wall was, across an expanse of terrace, to the right of a bridge leading from the terrace, which bridge was, across an expanse of terrace, to the right of the balustrade.

I drew more heavily on the leash. The Lady Constanzia, clearly, was hanging back. I stopped and turned about. She then, too, turned about. We could see the scarlet-clad figure striding fiercely across the terrace, not looking back. He seemed angry. I conjectured that the Lady Constanzia had been trying, earlier, to glimpse his retreating figure over her shoulder.

"Do you think we will see him again?" she asked.

"I do not know," I said. "The cut of his clothes seems foreign to this city. He is probably here on some business."

"He will then be gone soon?"

"I would suppose so," I said.

"He kissed me," she said.

"Do not be upset," I said. "He thinks you are only a slave. He does not know you are a free woman."

"Do you think he likes me?" she asked.

"It is possible," I said, "that he might have found you of interest."

"Of interest?"

"Yes," I said.

"Of what sort of interest?" she asked.

"Of *slave* interest," I said.

"Ohh," she breathed.

"But half the men who look upon you, clad as you are," I said, "might not mind having a chain on you."

"Do you think so?" she asked, eagerly.

"Yes," I said. "But, too, they would probably all be of the opinion that you are short on whip-training."

"Do you think I am short on whip-training?" she asked.

"If you were a slave, certainly," I said. "But do not concern yourself with such matters, as you are a free woman."

Whip-training, incidentally, does not require that the pupil is struck, only that she is subject to that contingency. To be sure, it is difficult to get through whip-training without having felt the lash. On the whole, of course, the more intelligent the girl is, and the more quickly she trains, the less she is likely to feel the lash, and the stupider she is, or the more slowly or clumsily she trains, the more likely she is to feel it.

"I have never been kissed before like that," she said.

"You have never been kissed in a collar before," I said.

"It is not at all as one kisses a free woman," she said.

"I dare say," I admitted.

"I did not know a kiss could be like that," she said.

"They are brutes," I said. "What they are denied in the world of free women they arrogate to themselves in the world of slaves. It is there, in that world, that their natural dominance, liberated from the bondage of artificial constraints, flourishes unchecked. Beware, for in that world we belong to them. In that world we are totally theirs. In that world we must obey and serve them, utterly. In that world they use us as it pleases them, and have from us whatever they wish, in total perfection."

She shuddered.

"Rejoice," said I, "that you are a free woman."

"It is only in such a world, is it not," she asked, "that they can be true men?"

"Yes," I said.

"But then," she said, frightened, "it must be only in such a world that we could be true women."

"You are a free woman," I said. "Do not concern yourself with such matters. Do not think such thoughts."

The scarlet-clad figure had now left the terrace.

I then drew her to the wall.

"What are you doing?" she asked.

"Kneel here," I said, "your back to the wall."

"What are you going to do?" she asked.

"Exactly what I told you before," I said.

"Surely you were joking," she said.

"No," I said. "Must a command be repeated?" I inquired.

"No," she said.

She knelt down, with her back to the wall.

By means of the leash I chained her to a slave ring. Slave rings are common in public places on this world.

"I do not want to stay here," she said.

"I think you will find that you have little choice," I said.

"Janice!" she protested.

"I will be back shortly," I said.

I then hurried from her, toward the bridge. I did look back once, to see her there, looking after me, back-braceleted, kneeling at the ring, chained to it by the neck. It was doubtless the first time in the Lady Constanzia's life that she had been so situated. It is not unusual, of course, on this world, to find slaves so tethered, kneeling or sitting, awaiting the return of their masters. Indeed, on this world, there are many places in which slaves, as other animals, may not be taken.

In only a few moments I had come to the large, flat expanse over the bridge from the terrace. That was the object of my journey. On the left there was no balustrade. On the right there were numerous warehouses. This expanse was now empty. There were, near the warehouses, some boxes and bales, some covered with tarpaulins. There were some planks here and there, also near the warehouses, and some coils of rope. The sky was clear. The day was warm. I looked about. The expanse was now empty. It was not always empty. It was here I had hoped to find the answer to one of the questions which afflicted me. One day I hoped I might do so. But this, it seemed, was not the day.

I then returned, in haste, to the slave ring, to free the Lady Constanzia, for it was near the fifteenth bar. It would not do for me to return her late to the pits.

That night, when I brought her her food, she wanted, as she often did, to speak to me.

"You will take me again, to the surface, won't you?" she begged.

"I can ask the pit master," I said.

"Soon!" she begged.

"Perhaps," I said.

"Do you remember the fellow in the scarlet tunic and cloak, whom we met this afternoon?" she asked.

"Yes," I said.

"Do you recall that he kissed me?"

"Yes," I said.

"He kissed me," she said. "And I was in a collar." She was now, of course, in her cell, in the robes of concealment. She was, however, not veiled. It was too early for the guard's rounds.

"Surely you do not find it surprising that a female would be kissed when she is collared."

"No," she said, uncertainly.

"Nor surprising that you, personally, might be kissed, and, in particular, when you were wearing a collar?"

"I do not know," she said.

"I assure you," I said, "if we are concerned with probabilities or frequencies in such matters, a woman is far more likely to be kissed, and most often, when she is wearing a collar."

She nodded, numbly.

"But not kissed as a free woman is kissed," I said.

"No, of course not," she said, "rather, kissed as a slave is kissed."

"Yes," I said.

"And that is how I was kissed!"

"He did not know you were a free woman," I said.

"It was so possessive, so ruthless, so uncompromising, so merciless, so masterful," she said.

"He is a man," I explained.

"How can you resist such a kiss?" she asked.

"We are not permitted to do so," I said.

She trembled.

"What is wrong?" I asked.

"He kissed me," she said, "and I was in a collar."

"Yes, you were," I said.

"A *collar!*" she said.

"Yes," I said.

"A *slave collar,*" she said, "*the collar of a slave!*"

"Yes," I said.

"I am trying to understand my feelings," she said.

"I see," I said.

"I imagine such a man would have to be served very well," she said, lightly.

"I would think so," I said. "He seemed such a man."
"I feel uneasy, and frightened, and weak," she said.
"Do not be afraid," I said. "You will doubtless never see him again."
She threw me a look of anguish.
"On the other hand," I said, "it is possible, of course."
She seemed, then, to breathe more easily.
"He kissed me," she said. "Do you think he likes me?"
"He may have been merely trying you out," I said.
"Trying me out?"
"Yes."
"Do you think he might have been pleased?"
"I would not be surprised," I said.
"Do you think he likes me?" she asked.
"Perhaps he might find you of some slave interest," I said, "as might, incidentally, a great many men."
She smiled, shyly, pleased.
"Do you like him?" I asked.
"Of course not!" she cried. "Did you not see how he kept me on my knees before him?"
"Such a position is common for a slave before a free man," I said.
"But I am not a slave!" she said.
"He did not know that," I said.
"Surely one could tell!" she said.
"Not at all," I said.
I saw that this intelligence much pleased her.
"You think then that I could be taken for a slave?"
"Of course," I said, "and you were."
"Yes," she said.
"And you would make a lovely slave," I said.
"Do you think so?" she asked, eagerly.
"Yes," I said.
"Do you think I would bring a good price?"
"Of course," I said.
"And men might desire me?"
"Certainly," I said, "very much so. Even excruciatingly so."
I saw that this much pleased her.
"How dreadful!" she exclaimed.

"Not at all," I said.

"And did you not see how he demeaned me," she said suddenly, angrily, "how he walked about me, regarding me, examining me, inspecting me, as though I might be a slave!"

"He took you for a slave," I said.

"I?"

"Of course," I said.

"And he ordered me to him, that my collar might be read!"

"He probably wanted to know your name," I said.

"Do you think so?" she said, eagerly.

"Certainly," I said.

"He read your collar first!" she said.

"Certainly," I said. "I was the leash holder. But I think it is clear that his interest was in you, not in me. Indeed, I suspect he read my collar to learn more of you, for example, you would be the slave Tuta who was in the keeping of the state slave, Janice, and so on."

"Oh!" she said, excitedly. "But did you not see," she then said, angrily, "how he forced me to hold my lips, pursed, simply by his will, and I must keep my eyes closed, and wait, and wait, and then how he took me in his arms and kissed me, and how he kissed me!"

"Slaves may be kissed in such a fashion," I told her. Certainly her lips, although those of a free woman, had been as lengthily and patiently raped as those of a common slave in a master's possessive greed for her.

I doubted that free women were ever so kissed, unless perhaps they were but moments from the collar, such a kiss serving then as a token of the bondage that awaited them.

"I hate him," she said. "The beast, the arrogant brute, I hate him!"

"You hate him?" I asked.

"Yes!" she said. "Yes!"

"If you were actually a slave," I said, "it would not matter whether or not you hated him, or he you. You would serve with perfection in any case, as the slave you would then be."

"I suppose so," she said.

"Definitely," I said. "And if he was not pleased he would doubtless use the whip on you, and well."

"Do you think so?" she asked.

"Yes," I said. "Such men do not let women make fools of them."

"Janice," she said.

"Yes?" I said.

"Why did you ask me so silly a question, as to whether or not I might like him?"

"It was just a thought," I said.

"An absurd thought!" she said.

"Of course," I said.

"But why did you ask?"

"Just little things," I said.

"Such as?" she asked, testily.

"The way you spread your knees before him," I said.

"I did not!" she cried.

"Oh, yes, you did," I said. "It is one thing for me to kneel before a man thusly, for I am a pleasure slave. I may be punished if I do not do so. We are trained to kneel thus, brazenly and joyfully before men. But you needed not do so."

"I did not!" she said.

"Yes, you did," I said. "And as time went on, and particularly when he looked upon you, you spread them even more."

"Truly?" she asked.

"Yes," I said.

She put the tips of the fingers of her right hand before her mouth.

"But such things," I said, "might occur inadvertently, or without one's being aware of them, or without really paying them much attention, or one might forget about them promptly afterwards, as things that could not have happened."

She pressed her finger tips against her lips, as though fearing that she might speak.

"Did you know what you were doing?" I asked.

"I don't know," she said.

"Perhaps you were frightened?" I suggested.

"Yes," she said. "I was frightened."

"Such behaviors in a female can be consequent upon trepidation," I said.

"Undoubtedly," she said.

"Rather like the prone slave's timid lifting of her derrière, facing away from the master, at his feet, hoping thereby to distract him, perhaps from punitive intentions, with thoughts of pleasure.

"Oh!" she said.

"To divert wrath, to placate him, such things," I said.

"Undoubtedly," she whispered.

"But often such behaviors, the spreading of the knees, and such, are merely a way of presenting oneself, of offering oneself, of inviting attention, of begging for it."

"But I am a free woman!" she said.

"Even so, you are a female," I said.

"I have never thought of myself, so radically," she said.

"Perhaps you should, sometime," I said.

"There is a saying," she said. "It is that there are two sorts of female slaves, those who are collared, and those who are not yet collared."

"An interesting saying," I said.

"Do you think it is true?" she asked.

"I would not know," I said.

"What do you think?" she asked.

"It is true for me," I said. "I have always been a female slave, but it was not until I was brought to this world that I was collared."

"It is so easy for you," she said. "You know what you are."

"I must go now," I said.

"Ask the pit master if we may go again to the surface!" she begged.

"I will," I said.

"Janice!"

"Yes?"

"Surely my disguise as a slave might be more effective," she said, lightly, "if you were to instruct me, somewhat, in how a slave behaves, in the sort of things she is expected to know, and such."

"Perhaps you are right," I said. Certainly I might improve her deference procedures and her way of kneeling.

"Teach me the seven kisses."

I regarded her, startled.

"You are a free woman," I said.

"Please!" she begged.

"Perhaps," I said.

"And teach me to use my lips!" she said.

"There are many ways to use the lips," I said. "But you must understand, too, that there are many ways to use the hands, the feet, the hair,

and so on, indeed, in a sense, the slave is taught, in many ways, to use her entire body."
"Teach me!" she begged.
"I do not think the pit master would approve," I said. "Surely you would not wish me to ask him?"
"Of course not," she said, horrified.
"I did not think so," I said.
"It could be our secret," she said.
"It is better that you remain ignorant of these things," I said. "You are a free woman."
"Please, Janice," she said.
"It is knowledge more appropriate to slaves," I said.
"Please, please," she begged.
"I will think about it," I said.
"And surely," she said, "I ought to quaff slave wine!"
"It is terrible stuff," I said.
"But it might be dangerous on the surface," she said. "There might be ruffians."
"I think," I said, "rather, I will have you locked in an iron belt, the heaviest and most uncomfortable that may be procured."
"No," she said, "slave wine, slave wine!"
"You may be right," I said. "It would not do at all if some fellow on the surface, taking you for a mere slave, and insensitive to the civilities involved, should simply throw you to the stones and put you to his pleasure."
"Janice," she said.
"Yes?" I said.
"I knew what I was doing," she said.
"I thought so," I said.
"I know what I am," she whispered.
"Oh?" I asked.
"Yes," she whispered.
"Hurry, veil yourself," I said. "I hear the approach of the guard!"

Fifteen

"It is for this reason that you have been brought here," said the pit master.

I had followed him, to the lowest passages in the pits, and to what surely must have been one of the dankest corridors in that dismal place. There was damp straw on the floor of the corridor. Sometimes an urt, a small rodent, not like the large urts in the pool, scurried past. Water, here and there, dripped from the ceiling of the corridor. I could stand upright in the corridor, but most of the men of this world, I conjectured, could not have done so. The head of the pit master, for all his bulk, he like a bent-over bear, was lower even than my own. In such a place, in such a corridor, I think he, with his terrible strength, and almost like a four-footed animal, would have proved a terrible foe to almost any man, even those of this world. In this place there was a smell of dampness and stench. I was afraid to have come here. The pit master carried a tiny lamp. It cast long, strange shadows about. Fina, who usually accompanied him in the pits, had been left in our quarters, chained to her ring.

The pit master handed me the tiny lamp and, with five keys taken from his belt, undid the five locks on the iron door. He swung the door open and took back the lamp.

He motioned that I should follow him within.

Frightened, I crept within.

The ceiling within the cell was higher than that in the corridor. Within it a man, say, an interrogator, a guard, might stand upright.

"There," said the pit master, lifting the lamp.

I gasped.

Lying at the back wall of the cell was a crumpled heap. It rose slowly to all fours, blinking against the light. I was not sure it was human at first glance. Then I saw it was a man. It was an extremely large man. He was disheveled. His hair was matted and wild. He was heavily bearded. He wore rags. On each of his limbs, and on his neck, there was a heavy chain, each of these fastened to a different heavy ring in the wall behind him.

"This is to be your charge," he said. "You will add him to your other duties."

"Yes, Master," I said.

"You were purchased for this," he said, "even before he came into our keeping."

I nodded.

"But we did not expect to receive him as he is," said the pit master.

I did not understand this.

"He was betrayed into our hands," said the pit master, I thought with a note of regret.

"Ten sleen," said the pit master, "have been given his scent."

I was startled to hear this.

That is a terrible thing. The sleen is the tenacious, six-legged carnivore I had seen before, on the ledge, and on the surface of the tower. My own scent had been "taken" by two sleen, on the second day I had been in the pits. One is held down, naked, and the sleen, first one, and then the other, are ordered forward. They thrust their huge, cold snouts about one's body, learning one's scent. While they do this one's name is repeated, so that they will associate the name, which may then figure in a signal, with the scent. A hunt-and-kill order may then be issued, and the sleen will track down and tear to pieces the object of its hunt. The manner in which this operates, for my instruction, had been demonstrated. A gigantic haunch of meat was "named" and its scent given to the two sleen. It was then placed with other such slabs of meat. The signal given the two sleen rushed upon it and tore it to pieces, ignoring the other meat, to which they had not been given access. They are disciplined beasts. I had then crouched down naked, in my collar, at one wall. "You understand what may be done?" called the pit master. "Yes, Master!" I had cried. "Shall I give them the signal for you?" he asked. "Please, no, Master!" I had wept. "Do you wish to be set loose in the mountains, or in the city?" he asked. "No, Master!" I had wept, hysterically. "I want only to obey, and be pleasing!" He had then, with a word, sent the sleen back to their pens. I had later inquired of Fina if she, and the other girls, had been accorded this terrifying honor. "No," she had said. "That sort of thing is very seldom done." I had then understood, that, for some reason, I must, indeed, be special. "But do not think," Fina had said, "that our chances of escape are any better than yours." "No," I said. There was the collar, the brand, the garmenture, the close-knit nature of the society, such things. There was no escape for any of us, when we were slaves on this world. But it is one thing to realize the impossibility of escape and quite another to realize that one may be pursued by a merciless creature over whom one has no influence or control whatsoever. Such things do not care, for example, whether or not one has learned one's lesson, whether or not one is contrite, whether or not one is beautiful, and so on.

"Ten?" I said.

"Yes," he said.

That would be every sleen in the pit master's sleen pens.

"Who is he?" I asked.

"Curiosity is not becoming in a kajira," he said.

"Forgive me, Master," I said.

"He is '41,'" he said. "The prisoners in this corridor are referred to only by numbers."

"Yes, Master," I said.

"We are to meet someone here," said the pit master. "I think they are coming."

The prisoner had now changed his position. He was sitting there now, by the wall, cross-legged. His back was very straight. He seemed to stare into space.

I could hear movement in the passageway, outside.

I knelt.

Three men entered the cell. The first was the fellow who had occupied the great chair on the surface of the tower, to whom I had been presented several days ago. The other two I did not know. They were warriors. One carried a torch. After recognizing their leader, whom

I took to be an important person in this city, I kept my eyes straight ahead. As a slave, one must be wary of appearing presumptuous.

"Bring the torch closer," said the leader.

He looked carefully at the prisoner.

"Yes," said the leader. "It seems as reported."

The prisoner did not speak. He continued to gaze, seemingly unseeingly, into space.

"What is your name?" inquired the leader.

"I do not know," said the prisoner, slowly.

"It was the fall, from tarnback," said one of the warriors.

"From tarnback?" asked the prisoner, puzzled.

"No," said the leader. "You slipped, on rocks."

"We took him on the side of a mountain," said one of the warriors. "He slipped down, for several yards, a hundred or more. Then we got the ropes on him."

"Your name is '41'," said the leader.

"My name is '41'," said the prisoner, dully.

"Yes," said the leader.

"What is your caste?" asked the leader.

"I do not know," said the prisoner.

"You are in the garments of the Peasants," said the leader.

"I am of the Peasants," said the prisoner.

"Yes," said the leader. Then he straightened up, but continued to look down at the figure before him. "His own mother would not know him," he said.

"No," said one of the warriors.

"Is the girl proving satisfactory," asked the leader of the pit master.

"Yes," he said.

"Slave!" snapped the leader.

"Yes, Master!" I said, quickly.

"You have been told you will have duties here?"

"Yes, Master," I said.

"For most practical purposes you will be the only one to attend upon this prisoner," he said. "For most practical purposes you will be the only person he will know or see here."

"Yes, Master," I said.

"To be sure," he said, "there will be guards about."

"Yes, Master," I said.

"You understand the nature of this matter, the confidentiality of it, the privacy of this keeping, the isolation which is imperative?" the leader asked the pit master.

"Yes," said the pit master.

I understood very little, if anything, of what was occurring. I was, however, familiar with the normalities of the depths, and recognized that an unusual degree of caution, and certainly special measures, were being taken in connection with this prisoner. I gathered that he was of the Peasants as he, apparently, wore the rags of such garments. Too, he had acknowledged himself of that caste, as I had just heard. On the other hand, it seemed clear that he was no ordinary peasant. He must have some unusual importance or value. Possibly he possessed valuable information, information of great interest to these men. But, if he had such information, he did not seem to be aware of it. He did not, as far as I could tell, even know his own name. Indeed, I was not even certain that he had known his own caste for a moment, a matter apparently of considerable importance to most on this world. But then he had been reminded of it, it seemed, and had apparently recalled it. Why, I asked myself, would such a man be kept here, in this low corridor, in a five-lock cell, with five chains on his body? He was an extremely large man. He was doubtless very strong. Then I was afraid. Perhaps he was also extremely dangerous. Perhaps that was why, at least in part, he was the object of these special measures, these precautions. But he seemed gentle. It was almost as though he did not understand where he was, or the chains on him. There must be, I thought, something wrong with him. Perhaps he was simple. But he had had, I recalled, a fall.

"We named you 'Janice', as I recall," said the leader to me.

"Yes, Master," I said.

"Who are you?" he asked.

"Janice, Master," I said.

"Look up, Janice," he said.

I looked up.

"You are prettier than I had remembered," he said.

"Thank you, Master," I said.

"She is in a tunic," observed the leader to the pit master.

The pit master looked up.

"You show unusual consideration for pit slaves," said the leader.

"Sometimes, perhaps," said the pit master.

"But with respect to her duties here, in connection with this prisoner," said the leader, "she is to be bare-breasted, and is to be given, at most, a string and slave strip."

"It will be as you wish," said the pit master.

"And, tonight," said the leader, "see that she is thoroughly washed and combed, and made-up, and perfumed, and silked, and send her to my quarters."

"It will be as you wish," said the pit master.

Sixteen

The doors to his quarters, double doors, were opened before me, each by a deferential slave girl, her head down. They were briefly silked.

I had approached down a long, carpeted corridor. Flanking me, but a just a little behind, were two guards.

I wore rich silks, which muchly covered me. These were not altogether unlike the free woman's robes of concealment but the materials were not so inflexible and ornate. Far softer they were. Too, I had been veiled. The veil that I had been granted, however, was not of the sort commonly adorning free women, heavy and opaque, but was of light silk. Beneath it the lineaments of my features might be subtly discerned. The girl who was to be introduced into his apartments was not a free woman, but a meticulously adorned, exquisitely veiled slave.

I could see him within, reclining on a divan.

"Welcome, my dear," he called, and, with a gesture, invited me within.

The two slave girls closed the doors behind me, and slipped away. I was not followed into the room by the guards. I would suppose that they turned about, and returned to their duties, perhaps by the outer doors, those at the end of the hall.

Before the divan, but a bit to the right, as I faced it, was a low table, on which there were beverages and fruits, and tiny bowls and plates, filled with an assortment of viands. I felt momentarily giddy with the smell of the roasted meats, the breads and pastry.

We were not wholly alone in the room together for, to my right, back, near the divan, but not so close to it as the table, sitting on cushions, cross-legged, were three musicians.

I approached the figure on the divan, which wore lounging robes, and knelt before him, my head down.

"Kneel with your knees closed," he said, kindly. This seemed fitting, as I was dressed.

I closed my knees. I kept my head down.

He must have given some signal to the musicians, for they began to play, softly, in the background.

"You may serve," he said.

"Yes, Master," I said.

I then began, in the manners of this world, as I had learned them in the pens, to serve, deferentially, self-effacingly, proffering drink and food, sensitive to, and obedient to, his least inclination, his least word or glance. How different these things were from the provender of the pens, of the pits! There was no gruel here, no dried mush, no pellets. And I had not been fed since morning. I hated the silken veil then, despite its beauty, for it sealed my lips from food. I would have preferred, I assure you, primitivisms more typical of this world, such as the barbaric banquets of soldiers and guards, in which we must serve naked. There, at least, we might kneel and whimper, begging food. There, at least, we might hope, at least if we were found sufficiently pleasing, to be fed by hand or thrown scraps. But here I was ravening, and I dared not speak.

He dropped a tiny bone, sucked free of meat, onto a small, golden plate.

"You serve well, Earth woman," he said.

I handed him, at his gesture, a glistening napkin and he touched it to his lips.

I felt almost faint with hunger.

But these men, of course, do not spoil their slaves.

At his indication I held forth the tiny golden finger bowl, and he dipped his fingers within it, and then dried them on the napkin.

I replaced the finger bowl and the napkin on the small table. I then knelt before him.

The music was very soft, unobtrusive, in the background. The melodies of this world tend to be barbarically sensuous.

I sensed his eyes upon me, but did not look up.

The room was a large, rich room, with a smoothly tiled, glossy floor. Small rugs and cushions were here and there. There were numerous, rich hangings. In places slender pillars rose to graceful arches. At the walls, at places, there were ornate chests. Some screens with open grillwork were to one side. There were some side portals, with beaded hangings. It was through one of these that the slave girls had slipped away. In the left, rear part of the room there was a window. Outside it I could see lights in some of the tower buildings of the city. There was also an entryway in the back part of the room to what seemed to be an open porch. I could see more lights through this aperture, in the distance. Some of those lights, I think, may have been on the walls of the city itself.

I kept my head down.

I was well aware of myself as a slave.

I could see the coverings, and the cushions, at the foot of the divan.

The music was subtle, insistent.

I lifted my eyes, pleadingly, to the male, who was to me, though I belonged to the state, in this time and place, as Master.

"You may speak," he said.

I held the veil more closely about my features, as though this might the better conceal me. But, of course, as I instantly realized, this was foolish. I had seen it in the mirror. My features, my lips, could be discerned within it. It did seem to provide me with some protection from his gaze, but its actual effect, of course, was primarily symbolic, that there was a veil. If anything my gesture might, for an instant, have rendered my features more visible to him. I quickly lowered my hands, the veil, as it were, adjusted.

"I am hungry, Master," I said.

"Does the Earth woman beg food?" he asked.

"Yes, Master," I said.

He let me remain kneeling before him, my head down.

I could hear the music.

In it were reflected the nature and values of a complex civilization.

"Stand," said he, "and go there, and face me."

He had pointed to a place on the glossy tiles, some feet before the divan.

"Remove your veil," he said.

I obeyed, standing before him, a few feet before him. I removed the veil first from my features, opening it, and brushing it to the sides, and then, with almost the same gesture, I lifted it and put it back, behind me. It was then upon me, behind my neck, and before, resting over my shoulders. This veil, like many of the veils on this world, was quite large. It was some six feet in length and three to four feet in width. It was designed in such a way that it might be, if the wearer wishes, wrapped about the entire head, shoulders, and upper body. A smaller veil may be used, of course, with hooded robes of concealment. It is bound or pinned about the face, within the hood. Many robes of concealment are hooded. The hood may be either an integral part of the garment or an independent accessory. There is an entire lore of veils, having to do with their nature, opacity, style, coverage, and such. As with fans on my old world, in former centuries, much may be done with them by a clever woman. In typical, modest veiling, that called for by most proprieties, only the eyes and the upper part of the bridge of the nose are exposed. It was in that way that I had been veiled in my serving. When I had parted my veil, and brushed it back, and put it behind me, I could hear, in the music to my right, in a ripple of interest and approval, of delight and excitement, the musicians' reaction. I lifted and brushed back my hair, freeing it. I adjusted it, too, with a toss of my head. Perhaps it was a vain gesture. One of the musicians chuckled.

I then stood before he who was to me as Master.

"Let us see the collar on your neck," he said.

I adjusted the silks so that it would be clearly visible.

One of the musicians laughed.

I did not need to be reminded that I was collared.

The musicians, it seemed, were pleased. I was sure of that, from the music. To be sure, it was not they whom I must please, not at this moment, in this place.

I looked at the foot of the divan, at the cushions which were there.

I did not even know the name of he who reclined upon the divan. But what needed I to know, other than the fact that he was a free man, and I would address him as "Master"? He knew my name, of course, the only name I had, which had been put on me in this place, 'Janice'.

I was barefoot. There were bangles on my ankles.

"The Earth woman is hungry?"

"Yes, Master," I said.

"And would be fed?"

"Yes, Master."

"We shall see how you perform," he said.

"Master?" I asked.

"Do you know how to use your veil?" he asked.

"I do not understand," I said.

"Discard it then," he said.

I removed the veil from about my shoulders, and dropped it to the side. It floated to the glossy tiles, and lay there, lightly, crumpled.

"Remove your outer silks," he said.

I obeyed, and put them to the side.

The music rippled.

I wore now a skirt of filmy silk, which would swirl as I moved. It was open on the left. My midriff was muchly bared. My breasts were haltered high. Tiny straps came over my shoulders. In such garments one might serve at more decorous banquets, though, to be sure, most likely not if free women were present. When free women are present, one usually serves gowned, or tunicked. At less decorous banquets one might expect to serve differently, in a ta-teera, in rags, in a slave strip, naked, in such ways. I wore bracelets, an armlet, bangles. Too, I had been given earrings, golden rings.

"Do you know the name of this world?" he asked.

"Gor," I said.

"Do you know how to dance?" he asked.

"No!" I said.

"Surely they taught you something in the pens," he said.

"I am not a dancer!" I wept.

"Surely you know something of the basic steps," he said, "the walks, the glides, the presentations, the turns, the arm movements?"

"A little, Master," I said, in misery. To be sure, one is not likely to escape the pens without being taught such rudiments.

"You are going to dance for me, Earth woman," he said.

"I do not know how to dance!" I protested.

There was a tiny, skeptical skirl from one of the instruments.

"Beginning position!" he snapped.

There are several such. I swiftly flexed my knees, lifted my rib cage, and put my hands together, wrists crossed, over my head, the backs of my hands facing out, the palm of my right hand over the palm of my left hand.

He rose from the divan, as I stood thusly before the divan, so posed, and went to the side of the room. From one of the ornate chests he fetched forth a thick, single-bladed, snakelike slave whip. I watched him with terror as he approached. Then he stood to one side. Then, suddenly, at the side, he snapped the whip. The report was like the crack of a rifle. I nearly fainted. I sobbed.

"You are going to dance for me, Earth woman," he said, menacingly, "and as what you are, and what you are only, an Earth-girl slave before her Gorean master." He then snapped the whip again. "Do you understand?" he asked.

"Yes, Master!" I wept.

He then returned to the divan, on which he reclined, the whip on the silks beside him, inches from his grasp.

"Begin," he said.

I danced.

At one point he lifted his finger and the music stopped, and I stopped.

"Do you know the use of finger cymbals?" he asked.

"No, Master," I said.

"Continue," he said.

And so again the music began, and again I danced. Alas, I, so little trained in the art form, for an art form it is, was only too painfully aware of how far short my efforts must fall from those of a skilled performer. Could I do more than squirm, and writhe, and plead with my body, for mercy? But perhaps my desperation might amuse him? Perhaps he was merely interested in registering, with bemused tolerance, the inept, pathetic strivings of an Earth-girl slave to please him, hoping not to be beaten. Perhaps he was having me do this merely that he might at the end, for my clumsiness, lash me? Yet, too, I did not want to betray the dance. I loved it. It is so beautiful. I wanted, thusly, to suggest, within my limits, at least, something of the richness, the complexity, the profound sensuousness of such dance. Such dance can be a revelation to those who are unfamiliar with it, who have never seen it. Some never suspect how beautiful and exciting a woman can be until they see her in such dance. In few ways better than in such dance is it made more evident what an incredibly beautiful, marvelous, precious, wonderful thing a woman is. It is no wonder they want to get their chains on us. And, too, of course, I was frightened of him. I did want to display myself, and present myself, well before him. I did not want to be whipped. But, too, I confess, I wanted him to want me. I was stirred by him, powerfully, sexually, as I was by many men on this world, such men, and I wanted, thusly, to please him and excite him. He, as many men on this world, set fires in my belly. I danced before him. He helped himself, from time to time, to some of the food left on the table, a grape, a tiny viand, keeping his eyes on me. I must remember the hand and arm movements, the spins, the circles, the lifts, the thrusts! And then, at some point, perhaps when I was kneeling before him, moving my arms, and head and shoulders, I think I became one with the music and the dance. Startled I rose to my feet and began to move about the room. Were there hundreds present? Did they feast their eyes on this dancer? I went even to the musicians and moved, presenting myself as a slave, before them. Were they not, too, men, and thus such as before whom it was appropriate that I present myself, hoping for their approbation? In the eyes of the musicians I read something that I had not expected to find, that they were not displeased with the sight of the slave before them. How this made me hope, and how my heart was filled with a sudden surge of elation! But it was not these men whom I must most desperately strive to please. It was another. I returned, to move before him. Then, again, I whirled away, going about the divan, to the narrow window and danced before it. Doubtless there were none out there who saw me so move. The lights were beautiful. I then, in my dance, utilized the corners and surfaces of chests, and the walls of the room. I saw, beside the divan, a coil of chain. I danced away from it, terrified. Then it seemed I was alone with the dance, and my joy in it. And then, a moment later, wildly, it seemed again that I must dance for many. Did I hear the striking of the shoulders in applause, the pounding of goblets on low tables, the urgent cries of men? What power, I thought, must a dancer, a true dancer, exercise over men! How she must arouse them, how she must drive them mad with passion! But what power, ultimately, is hers, for she is in her collar? When the music stops is she not then, clearly, once again, only a slave at the feet of men? And is not the central, nonrepudiable message of this dance, in its entire concept, in its beauty, in its presentation of the female in all her marvelous sensuousness, that man is the master? This form of dance, on this world, is called "slave dance." That is perhaps partly because, on this world, it is permitted only to slaves, but I think it is more likely because, in it, the nature of woman is clearly manifested as slave. One might also mention that the dancer, in this form of dance, on this world, is commonly expected to satisfy the passions which she may have aroused. The submission which commonly figures in the finale of her dance, on this world, is not, I assure you, purely symbolic.

I danced out, onto the porch, overlooking the city, the lights. I now saw that some of the lights, indeed, were on the distant walls of the city. They were beacons. Their primary purpose is to guide in the warriors, mounted on the gigantic saddlebirds, to enable them to safely negotiate the defenses of stakes and wire on the walls. The stars were very beautiful. I looked up and gasped, for then, for the first time, I saw the three moons. I had learned there were three moons here but this was the first time I had seen them. One does not see the moons in the pens, or in the depths, and, if they were visible, I had not noticed them during the light of the day.

"Return, slave," I heard.

I swiftly whirled about, and re-entered the room. There were three moons here! But then, in a moment, I was, again, before he upon the divan.

He lifted his finger and the music stopped, and I, too, stopped.

There is one aspect to slave dance to which I have neglected to call explicit attention, but it is one which, I suspect, at least implicitly, is clear to all. Slave dance is arousing to the female who dances it. One cannot move as in slave dance without becoming sexually aroused. In this sense, a twofold effect occurs when we dance before masters. One has not only an arousal display but an arousal activity. And there is a reciprocal, mutually reinforcing, interaction between these things, as one understands that one is arousing, and he understands that you are also being aroused, and you know that he understands this, and so on. Indeed, slave dance can function as a cure for frigidity. It relieves inhibitions, improves confidence, and, I suppose, to some extent, literally stirs and stimulates organs. It is difficult for a body which has been trained in slave dance, for example, to be stiff and unresponsive. To be sure, there are many cures for frigidity. An obvious one is the condition of bondage itself. Another is the whip, and switch.

"Remove your upper silk," he said.

I undid the halter, and slipped it away.

I saw that I would, indeed, dance as an Earth-girl slave before her Gorean master.

For a time I danced in this fashion, and then, again, he lifted his finger and the music stopped, and, I, too, stopped.

I looked at the remains of the food on the low table. I was very hungry.

"Remove your silk," said he, "Earth woman."

My hands went to the hip band and undid the clasp there. I lifted the silk to the side. I dropped it to the tiles.

He indicated to the musicians that they should again play. This time, doubtless in virtue of some arrangement with, or signal conveyed to, the musicians, it was an extreme adagio melody to which I must move. I remained in place, so dancing, almost without movement.

He picked up the whip, and walked about me, scrutinizing the slave.

I was terribly afraid I would be struck.

Then he was again before me, back some five feet or so, that he might have an excellent view.

The whip, coiled, was in his right hand.

"Do the women of your world often dance thusly, naked before their males?" he asked.

"I do not know, Master," I said.

"Doubtless they will have them dance thusly, for they are men," he mused.

I was silent.

"And do they whip the women if they are not pleasing?" he asked.

"I do not know, Master," I said.

"You seem to know very little of your world," he said.

"It is very different from this world, Master," I said.

"But you know that you will be whipped, here on this world, Earth woman, if you are not pleasing, don't you?"

"Yes, Master!" I said.

With a motion of his wrist he flicked out the blade of the whip, uncoiling it. He observed it. The end of the blade, snakelike, narrow and tapering, was upon the tiles. He then, with another movement of his wrist, lifted it from the tiles.

"Please, do not whip me, Master," I begged. "I will try to be pleasing!"

"I am sure you will," said he, "Earth woman."

He then returned to the divan, and reclined thereupon. He indicated to the musicians that they might increase the tempo, which they did.

I danced.

How helpless we are!

How these men master us!

I wore my collar. It was narrow, close-fitting, locked. It was a state collar. On it was my name, that name which had been given to me, 'Janice'. I had been a free woman of Earth. I had then been brought to this world. I was now only a slave.

I danced.

How incredibly free and female I felt.

I danced.

I had been sent to his quarters.

I danced before him.

I wondered how I looked to him. I hoped desperately that he might find me pleasing. I wondered how women such as I looked to males. Well, I conjectured, in our collars, obeying, hoping to please, striving desperately to please. How exciting, how glorious, how joyful, how real, how meaningful it must be to be a male on a world such as this, I thought, a world in which they had such power, at least over such as I. Here, you see, they had kept their mastery, in the order of nature. Here males were men, and here females, at least those such as I, could be only women, *their women*. How was it, I wondered, that these men had never relinquished their nature, that they had never surrendered their manhood, that they had never betrayed their blood, that they had never permitted themselves to be diminished and reduced, destroyed and crippled? I did not know. But they had not. Did they sense the danger we might pose to them, if they were weak, or permissive, or lenient? Was that why they were as they were? Was that why they put us in collars and kept us at their feet, because they knew us so well? But how could we be women if they were not men? Or had they profited from some hideous illustration of nature gone awry, from the dismal instruction of some tragic lesson, from the clear example of some pathological mistake, one they would simply not permit to occur in their own world? Or, perhaps, it was merely that this world had developed as it had, drawing strength and meaning from nature, rather than trying to live, dry and rootless, apart from her? But, as I danced before him, I did not think merely how exciting, how glorious, how joyful, how real, how meaningful it must be to be a male on this world but also, despite its dangers, its terrors, how exciting, how glorious, how joyful, how real, how meaningful it was to be a woman on this world! I had never begun to feel so fulfilled on my old world as I had here. It was only on this world, it seemed, that I had, in my small, lowly way, begun to feel fully meaningful. It was here that someone, deeper and more real than names, had found herself.

I knew who she was.

It was fully fitting that she danced as she did, before such a man. It was not merely he who knew this, you see. It was I, as well.

"To the floor," said he, "Earth woman."

The Earth woman then, to the music, slowly and gracefully lowered herself to the floor, and there, to those sensuous strains, speaking so unabashedly to the blood of men and women, continued her dance.

He clapped his hands, ending the music.

I rose to all fours, before him, on the glossy tiles.

"You are not now closely silked," he said.

So I knelt now before him, my back straight, my head down, the palms of my hands down on my thighs, my knees properly, widely, spread.

I heard him speak to the musicians. I heard the clinking of what was doubtless a small sack of coins. One by one the three musicians left. One said, "A pretty slave." Another said, "Yes." He before whom I had performed said, "She has much to learn." "Doubtless she will be well taught," said the leader of the musicians. "I wish you well," said the officer to them. "We wish you well," said the leader of the musicians. They had then left.

I remained kneeling before the divan, head down.

I heard something strike the tiles before me. It was a tiny leg of roast fowl.

I looked up at him, knowing that I dare not yet break position.

I was ravenously hungry. I was starving.
But I could not yet reach for the food.
I had not yet received permission.
"You may feed," he said.
I bent forward, and snatched up the bit of meat, and, holding it in my right hand, steadying it with my left, with my head down, began to feed upon it.
"Janice is hungry," he observed.
In a few moments I looked up at him, hopefully. I felt a wing, another scrap from his plate, strike my body. It fell between my thighs. I seized it up. And so I was fed, on scraps from his meal, some tossed to me, as I have indicated, and others, later, I having been permitted to approach him on my knees, and kneel before him, fed to me by hand. In such a feeding, the slave, of course, is not permitted to use her hands. She takes the food in her mouth, delicately. Masters usually make the bites tiny. In this way it takes time to complete such a feeding. One utility of such modes of feeding is that it impresses clearly upon the slave who it is to whom she owes her food.
I ate eagerly and gratefully.
I looked again at him, hopefully.
But he had decided I had had enough.
"We must be concerned with your figure, mustn't we, sleek little animal?" he said.
"Yes, Master," I said.
He then poured some water from a small pitcher into a shallow bowl, and put the bowl upon the tiles. As he had not placed it on the table, nor handed it to me, I understood how I must drink. I knelt before the bowl, and, my hands on the floor, put down my head and drank. He then had me kneel straight, and, with the same napkin which he himself had used, wiped my lips. He then gave me the napkin that I might clean myself, my fingers and my body.
"The earrings are pretty," he said.
"Thank you, Master," I said.
He looked at the armlet, and the bracelets on my wrist.
I think he was pleased.
Then he looked to my ankle. "Bangles look well on your ankle, Earth woman," he said.
"Thank you, Master," I said.

"Do many women of your world wear bangles?" he asked.

"I do not know, Master," I said. I supposed that some might, in certain places, in certain cultures.

"Secretly, perhaps," he said.

"Perhaps, Master," I said. "I do not know."

"They are quite sensual," he said.

"Yes, Master," I said.

"Stand," he said.

I obeyed. I stood then before the divan.

He fetched the whip from the divan and, slowly, as he had before, walked about me. Few women on Earth, I suspect, have ever been looked at as these men look at a woman. It can be frightening to be looked upon in this fashion, but it can also be profoundly stirring, profoundly gratifying. I stood straight, with my head up. A slave is expected to be beautiful. She is expected to be worth owning. How reassuring, incidentally, that one is here recognized as being of sufficient interest and importance to be looked at, really looked at. One is here regarded as being worthy of attention, literally, and is actually accorded it. On my old world everyone, it seems, is regarded as being infinitely important but no one pays much attention to anyone else. How tragic, I thought, that so few of the women of Earth are ever truly looked at. It is not that they are invisible. It is only that no one pays them any attention.

I supposed that I might be a little more flushed now, from the food. My belly, doubtless, was a bit more rounded.

I felt the whip, coiled, move along my left flank, and then my waist. He was a bit to my left. He stood there. He lifted the whip to my lips. Quickly I kissed it. He then withdrew again to my left, and then to a bit behind me. I looked straight ahead, over the divan, to the wall behind. "Oh!" I suddenly said. My entire body jerked. "Steady," said he. He held the implement in place. I moaned. Then, slowly, he lowered it, sliding it downward, against the interior of my left thigh. I flexed my knees, and half sank down, trying to keep contact with it. Then it was gone. I stood straight again, but unsteadily. "Slave," he said. His remark was an observation, not a mode of address. They make us like this, I thought, angrily. And then they mock us for being so! But then I thought they did not make us this way. This was the way we were. It was only that they would not permit us to be other than we were. They did not permit us, so to speak, to lie. But then why would they mock us for what we were? We could not help what we were, that we were slaves!

He was then again before me. He lifted the coiled whip before him. He smelled the moist, hot, glossy leather, and looked at me, over the coil, and smiled.

I looked away, distraught.

"It seems," said he, "that the Earth woman is a ready slave."

I looked away. It was true.

"I thought that Earth women were supposed to pride themselves on their frigidity," he said.

"Not here, Master!" I said.

"They are not permitted frigidity here, are they?" he asked.

"No, Master," I said.

"It is not tolerated."

"No, Master," I said. Why did he torment me? I knew that frigidity was not permitted to female slaves, of whatever origin, that we could be beaten for it, that we could be slain for it. Too, why did he speak as he did? Surely he knew that I, a slave, whether an Earth woman or not, could not begin to resist men such as he, even if it were permitted. Too, surely he knew that I was a "hot slave." That information, like my eye and hair color, was on my papers. He would know that I was helpless under the caresses of men such as he, that I could not help myself, that I was the sort of woman, pleading, helpless, vulnerable and spasmodic, who must, to a master, yield the totality of herself, *sans* reservation, *sans* qualification. Many times had I surrendered wholly to them. They could completely conquer me.

"I wonder if you should be whipped," he said, musingly, lifting the whip.

"Please, no, Master," I said.

He held the whip before me, and I put forth my head and lips, and kissed it twice, quickly, fervently.

"Earth woman," he said.

"Yes, Master," I said.

"Slave," he said.

"Yes, Master," I whispered.

He regarded me.

I kept my eyes forward, not daring to meet his.

He then, to my relief, tossed the whip to one side. He lifted me up, sweeping me quickly from my feet. He then held me in his arms, looking down at me. I felt momentarily giddy. I was naked and collared. I felt very small in his arms. He was very strong. My weight was as nothing to him. I could see hair upon his chest, in the parting of the lounging robes. How different we are, I thought, my smallness and softness, and his lean, mighty frame, the breadth of the shoulders, the thickness of his arms. One has no contact with the floor. In one sense this is disconcerting, in another it is absolutely thrilling. One knows one can be carried, and placed where he wishes. His left arm was behind my back, his right beneath the backs of my knees. I dared to put my arms about his neck and kiss him, timidly.

"I melt in your arms, Master," I whispered. I hoped not to offend him.

He carried me to the rear portion of the divan, and placed me down upon it, on my back.

He then sat at the edge of the divan, the palm of his left hand on the divan, resting on it, across my body. His right hand was on his right knee.

"You did not dance badly," he said.

"Thank you, Master," I said.

"It is slave dance," he said.

"Yes, Master," I said.

"The Earth woman danced it well," he said.

"She is a slave, Master," I said.

"Is slave dance danced on your world?" he asked.

"Yes, Master," I said.

"Did you understand the meaning of slave dance on your old world?" he asked.

"I think so, Master," I said. Here, on this world, of course, there was no doubt as to what its meaning was.

"Do many women dance slave dance on your world?" he asked.

"Not many," I said.

"Why not?" he asked.

"They are afraid to be so beautiful before men," I said.

"They are afraid to be women?"

"Yes, Master," I said.

"Were you afraid?"

"Yes, Master," I said.
"That is unutterably stupid," he said.
"Yes, Master," I said.
He regarded me. "You are a woman, I assure you," he said.
"Yes, Master," I said.
"Do you object?" he asked.
"No, Master," I said.
"Do you want to be a woman?" he asked.
"I am a woman," I said.
"But do you want to be a woman?" he asked.
"Yes, Master," I said.
"How do you feel about being a woman?" he asked.
"'Feel'?" I said.
"Yes," he said.
"I love being a woman," I said.
"Good," he said.

Until I had been brought here I had not understood what a marvelous, glorious, wonderful thing it was to be a woman. To be sure, I had learned this, as perhaps one must, in bondage. A female slave, you see, is not permitted to deny her sex. Only here, for the first time in my life, had I found it possible to fulfill my sex. Indeed, here I had no choice in the matter. I must fulfill it, wholly and irreservedly. It was no wonder then that, in spite of the dangers in which I might stand, I was so joyful.

He rose from the edge of the divan and picked up the length of chain looped beside it. This chain was some seven feet in length. There was a lock clip at one end and a collar at the other. I lay there. He made me wait for the collar. By means of the lock clip he fastened the chain to a ring fixed in the divan, one near the floor, on the right, as one faced the divan. He then took the chain about the head of the divan and there, at one point, placed a link over a stout hook, part of an integral slide-ring mounted there. In this way, it was, in effect, as though the chain was mounted at the head of the divan, rather than at the side, the hook would carry the weight of the chain, preventing it from drawing against the collar, the length of chain between the hook and collar would rest on the divan, and the amount of play in the chain allotted to me, without opening the slide-ring, would be strictly controlled. Thus, I would be, in effect, on a short chain run from the head of the divan, but, ultimately, on a long chain, run from the side ring. This is a convenience in chaining for masters. One need not, then, locking and unlocking them, spend a great deal of time changing chains. The amount of chain allotted to me from the hook would be about three feet, and from the side ring, if the chain were freed of the hook, about seven feet. There were various rings and hooks about the divan, permitting a large degree of flexibility in custodial and pleasure arrangements. The slave is commonly prohibited from touching the slide-rings and, in any event, remains attached to the divan, by means of the longer chain. Also, of course, the slide-rings may not be available to her, depending on how she is secured, what she can reach, the number of chains, and so on. As an analogy, it would be quite easy for a girl to unbuckle certain sorts of leather wristlets and anklets, but if she is unable to reach the buckles, as, for example, if she is spread-eagled between rings, she is as helpless as if she were held by locked steel. Slide-rings, too, it might be mentioned, can be locked shut, either with their own locks, or, more commonly, with external clip locks. He then put the collar about my neck, and closed it. I was then chained by the neck to the divan, held about a yard from the slide-ring at the head of the divan, and held, ultimately, by the lock clip, to the side ring.

He stood beside the divan. He looked down upon me.

"You are not a trained dancer, of course," he said.

"No, Master," I said.

"Yet," said he, "I did not find your dance displeasing."

"The slave is grateful if she has not been found entirely displeasing," I whispered.

"I am now going to have you, Earth woman," he said.

"Yes, Master," I said.

I was well had and soon screamed my submission and my begging for more. His least touch, that of a master, set me on fire. Occasionally he tortured me, as it amused him, bringing me to the point of yielding, and then desisting, as I writhed, pleading, before him, lifting my body, begging for relief, for mercy. Four times he roared, laughing within me, as I clutched him. In the manner of these men with their slaves, almost in moments, I had been made wholly his. Numerous times, sweating in my collar, I yielded.

The minimalities, the tepidities, accepted by the men of Earth in their females were not, by men such as these, permitted to us.

They choose to own us, wholly.

Then, though I clutched him still, he wearied of me.

He undid the chain from the slide-ring at the head of the divan and thrust me from the divan to the floor. I looked up at him, above me, from the tiles.

"You will sleep there tonight," he said.

Tears came to my eyes.

"I may want you again, toward morning," he said.

I looked up at him.

"Turn about," he said, "so that you lie with your head toward the foot of the couch."

I rose to all fours, and turned about, and then lay down on the tiles, on my left side, so that I might face the divan. The chain was on my neck, holding me to the divan.

I drew my legs up.

He tossed me a sheet. I gratefully clutched it about me. I then lay there, huddled in the sheet, on the tiles, my head toward the bottom of the divan.

He was soon asleep.

I lay there for a long time, trying to understand my feelings.

But, too, it seemed, this last time, he had too soon finished with me.

He had wearied of me and then thrust me from him, before I had been completed.

I squirmed a little, and moaned softly.

He did not hear me, for he was asleep. And, if he had heard me, he might have ordered me to silence. Or perhaps kicked or beaten me.

I had seen two other girls as I had entered. They had then slipped away. I had no doubt that, in this place, they would be prize slaves, not ignorant girls from the pits. How I envied them, serving in their light silks in a place such as this. Might I not be able, sometime, to so serve, in some such place? Was I so inferior to them? Could I not serve wine, and tend to the cleaning, and polish silver, as well as they? How much better to be slave in a place such as this than in the pits! And how much better, too, I thought, might it be to be merely the slave of a quiet, simple man, not even a rich one, and serve him, and keep his compartments, and love him. I wondered why I had been brought here tonight. But I supposed that required, really, no explanation.

Tunics are not that efficient at concealing slave curves, even those of an Earth woman, nor are they intended to be. I wondered where the slave, Dorna, was, whom I had met on the surface of the tower. I wondered if she sometimes lay here, beside the divan, as I. I wondered if she was kenneled tonight. I did not think she would be pleased, if she learned who it was who now lay here, beside the divan.

I then fell asleep.

Toward dawn I awakened.

I lay there on the tiles. A bit of light crept into the room from the window and porch.

I heard him stirring.

I lay there, tensely. It would be he who would decide what was to be done.

He stood up, beside the divan. He lifted me in his arms, and turned me about, so that my head was toward the head of the divan. He then, with a rattle of chain, flung me upon it.

He must have slept well.

He was indeed refreshed!

But his day would doubtless be a busy one. He was an important man. He would have much planned. He had little time now for a slave. He was quick with me. But I had been restless during the night, it had almost been as though I had been waiting for him, hoping for him. My response was grateful, almost instantaneous. But then he was done with me. He thrust me from the surface of the divan, to my knees, beside it. I was grateful for whatever crumbs or morsels I had been thrown. He unlocked the collar from my throat. I was free now of the divan. "Fetch the street sandals," he said, indicating a pair of sandals across the room. I went to all fours and crawled to the sandals, and picked them up in my teeth, and, on all fours, brought them back to him, and dropped them at his feet. I had been taught to fetch sandals in the pens.

He looked down at me.

I knelt before him.

I picked up one of the sandals, and kissed it, and then, humbly, head down, placed it on his foot. I did the same with the second sandal.

I then looked up at him.

"You fetch, kiss, and tie sandals well, Earth woman," he said.

"Please do not call me an Earth woman, Master," I begged. "Surely, by now, it is clear what I have become, that I am only a Gorean slave girl!"

"But we will keep an Earth-girl name on you," he said.

"As Master pleases," I said.

"It may serve, from time to time, to remind you of your origins."

"Yes, Master," I said.

In a short time he was prepared to leave his compartments.

"Guards will come for you shortly," he said.

He carried some thongs, and motioned that I should lie upon my stomach in the vicinity of the double door. He crouched beside me and crossed my wrists. He jerked tight knots on them. He then crossed my ankles, and pulled them up, close to my wrists. In a moment, with a few quick movements, my ankles had been tied tightly together and fastened to my wrists. He then put me to my side. I looked up at him.

"Slave," said he.

"Yes, Master?" I said.

"You did not dance badly," he said, "and it is clear that you are familiar with slave movement." I supposed that slave movement, its subtlety, its grace, its sensuousness, was now a part of me, in part trained into me, in part naturally manifesting itself, in my current condition. I was no longer even aware of it, really. Slaves are not permitted to move with the rigidity, the awkwardness, of free women. Indeed, it is said that a skilled slaver can tell the difference between a free woman in the robes of concealment and a slave in them merely by having them walk about. Even so subtle a thing, you see, militates against a slave's possibility of escape. To be sure, a slave might escape one master, to fall into the hands of another. She might change her collar, so to speak. But then the new master, knowing her for an escaped slave, is likely to keep her in close chains, and treat her with great harshness and cruelty. Indeed, after he has pleasured himself with her for some weeks he may simply return her in chains to her former master, for her punishment.

"Master?" I asked.

"It was not merely for your ignorance that you were purchased," he said. "We also wanted one who was beautiful and desirable, and such things."

I was silent.

"You are a natural slave," he said, "and you have come along well. We are pleased."

"Then I, too, am pleased," I said, "Master."

"The peasant," he said.

"Yes, Master?" I said.

"He is in your keeping," he said.

"Yes, Master," I said. He was actually in the keeping of the pit master, the depth warden, of course, but it was I, it seemed, who would be attending to the servile trivialities of his keeping, his feeding, the emptying of his wastes bucket, and such.

"Do you recall how you are to appear before him?" he asked.

"Yes, Master," I said. "In a string and slave strip, if that."

"And how are you to move before him?" he asked.

"Master?" I asked.

"You are to move well before him," he said.

"I do not understand," I said.

"Surely I need not explain such things to a female slave," he said.

"Master?" I asked.

"He is to be tortured," he said.

I was silent.

"Let him, helpless in his chains, be mocked and taunted," he said, fiercely, "as might be a helpless male slave by an insolent slave girl."

I did not look up. My left cheek was upon the tiles. I saw only his feet.

"He is to suffer," he said. "He is to well understand the contempt in which we hold him, the insult we do him."

"Master?" I asked.

"He is my enemy," he said.

"Yes, Master," I said.

And so it seemed that I, a lowly slave, figured somehow, in no way I clearly understood, in some obscure affair of state. I now better understood, as well, my having been obtained. My beauty, if beauty it was, was intended to have its purpose in certain plans. It was, it seemed, to be as food exhibited to a starving man. And it seemed, too, that, from the point of view of those on this world, that some grievous insult was intended as well, first, doubtless, the general insult that he, a free man, would be attended by a mere slave, an insult common to those in the pits, and, second, that he, a free man, would be attended by such a slave, a mere pierced-ear girl, and one who would be clad in such a way before him, and behave in such a way before him, one whom he, to his misery, would be unable either to enjoy or punish. He must endure, even, it seemed, if they had their way, the provocations, the mockery, of a slave. How rich the joke! How delicious the insult! But I wondered, really, if the peasant, so simple, so huge, so remote, would even understand this sort of thing. Might it not all be lost upon him? I was not even certain he understood he was in chains, in the depths. Perhaps in his mind, he was in some simple hut, far off, perhaps in some small, fertile valley, tending his fields.

"You understand what is required?" he asked.

"Yes, Master," I said.

He turned away.

"Master!" I called to him.

He turned back to face me.

"What you did to me last night!" I cried. "What you made me do! What you made me feel!"

"It is nothing," he said.

"I do not even know Master's name," I said.

"Your name is 'Janice'," he said.

"Yes, Master," I said.

He then left.

A few minutes later one of the slave girls entered the room. The other was a little behind her.

They busied themselves, picking up, tidying.

One of them came over and looked down at me. "You are a well-tied little vulo," she said.

I did not respond.

"It stinks in here," said the other, lightly. "There must be a pit slave somewhere."

The two girls were not twins, but they were clearly a matched set. They were similar in height, figure, hair and eye color. They also wore matching tunics, brief, of yellow silk. I wondered if they had been sold as a matched set, or if the officer had matched them himself. I envied them their private collars. They were owned then not by the state but, presumably, by the officer himself. I wondered if they served his pleasure together. Many men, of course, own more than one woman. How they apply them, or mix them, is up to them.

"She is a pierced-ear girl," said the girl standing near me.

"I wish he wouldn't bring them here," said the other. "It lowers the quality of the compartments."

"You are an Earth slut, aren't you?" asked the girl near me.

I did not respond.

"Oh!" I cried, in pain, kicked.

"Aren't you?" she asked.

"Yes!" I said.

"'Yes', what?" she asked.

"Yes, Mistress!" I said.

"Speak when you are spoken to, slut," said the girl.

"Yes, Mistress," I said. "Forgive me, Mistress."

"Let us give her a switching," said the other girl.

"No, Mistress!" I begged. "Please, no, Mistress!"

"You will be a good little slave, won't you, Earth slut?" asked the first girl.

"Yes, Mistress!" I assured her.

"What do the masters see in such curvaceous little sluts?" asked the second girl.

"They are pretty little bundles of slave curves," said the first.

"That is doubtless it," said the second.

"But we are pretty, too!" insisted the first.

"Yes," agreed the second.

I did not think we were really so much different, either. Indeed, we were all rather similarly figured. Their yellow silk certainly did not do much to conceal their own "slave curves." What difference did it make, really, if I was from Earth and they were not? In the end were we not all the same, all women, all slaves?

There was a knock on the door.

"That will be the guard," said the first girl. "Bundle her silk!"

In a few moments I was standing, back-braceleted. A slave sheet was thrown over my head and body. It fell to my calves. It was held on me by a collar, fastened closely about my neck. To a ring on this collar a leash was attached.

The jewelry I had worn, the bracelets and the bangles, the armlet and the earrings, had been removed from me. They had been given, together with my silk, to the guard. He placed them in a pouch. These things would be returned to one place, and I to another.

I was then led from the compartments. I had been brought to them silked and veiled. I was taken away covered in a slave sheet. There would be few, thusly, who would be able to connect me with the officer.

Seventeeen

"What are you doing?" cried the pit master, with horror.

I turned about, startled, in the cell, that in which the peasant was confined.

"Obeying, Master!" I said, frightened.

"Down on all fours!" he cried.

Swiftly I went to all fours.

The peasant, sitting, cross-legged, by the wall, in his chains, looked at me, dully.

I heard the pit master draw his belt free of his tunic.

I moaned.

Down came the belt with a hiss and I cried out in misery, and went to my stomach, my eyes filled with tears.

I looked up at the peasant. He regarded me, impassively. I do not even know if he understood what was happening.

Twice more the belt struck me. I wept. I had not known the pit master could be so angry.

"Please, Master!" I wept.

"Who told you to behave in such a fashion?" said the pit master.

"The tall man," I said, "the officer, he whom I served last night!"

"And who gave you permission to appear before this prisoner clad as you are?" he asked.

"It was my understanding that I should so serve!" I said.

Certainly this had been expressed to me, and the pit master, as well, had heard words to this effect in the cell. I could recall that.

"Are you trying to torment this prisoner?" he asked.

"Master?" I asked.

"Beg his forgiveness," he said.

I crawled to the peasant on my stomach, over the stones. I was careful not to come within reach of those mighty hands. I did not think even the pit master would have cared to have come within their compass. I did not doubt but what the peasant could have torn my head from my shoulders.

"Forgive me, Master," I said, weakly.

I heard the snapping of the pit master's fingers. Quickly I backed away, on my stomach, from the peasant, and then rose up, on my knees, to kneel, head down, before the pit master.

"I have seen you move," said the pit master, his rage seemingly dissipated.

I looked up at him, frightened, and then looked away. It was still hard to look upon those grotesque, massive, twisted features, the irregular placement of the eyes, one larger than the other.

"You did not move as you might have, before him," he said.

"No," I admitted.

"It is one thing," said the pit master, "to appear bare-breasted, in a string and slave strip, before guards, before soldiers, before free men, serving their feasts, crawling at their feet, licking their thighs, dancing before them, and quite another before a prisoner. The free men may seize you upon a caprice and fling you down for their pleasure. They have whips. They may lash you to the furs. You may hope they will be kind enough to merely put you to their lengthy pleasures. It is not the same with a chained prisoner."

I hung my head.

"Yet," he said, "I know you. You did not move as you might have."

I was silent.

"Why?" he asked.

"I do not know," I said.

"I think you are not one of those petty, insolent sluts," said he, "who must have her wrists tied over her head and be whipped."

"Master?" I asked.

"You were told to torment him, weren't you?" he asked.

"Yes," I said.

"Did you do so?"

"Of course, Master!" I said.

"I know you, Earth slut," he said. "You could make a rock scream with need, but you did not do so."
"Forgive me, Master!" I said.
"You were reluctant, you were hesitant."
"Forgive me," I said.
"Were you afraid of him?"
"Yes," I said. "I am afraid of him."
"He is chained," he said.
"Yes, Master," I said.
"He cannot hurt you," he said.
"No, Master," I said.
"You might then have tormented him with impunity," he said.
"Yes, Master," I said.
"But you were reluctant to do so," he said. "You held back."
"Forgive me, Master," I said.
"Does it seem honorable to you," he asked, "to torment a helpless prisoner?"
"No, Master," I said.
"Do you think I would have permitted it?" he asked.
I looked up at him, startled. Then I looked down, in awe. "No, Master," I whispered, frightened, trembling, "you would not have permitted it."
Then I looked up at him, in misery. "Who am I to obey?" I cried. "The officer has told me one thing, and you tell me another! Whom am I to obey?"
"You will obey me," said the depth warden.
"But is he not higher than you?" I asked, timidly.
"Yes," he said. "He is higher than I, but you will obey me."
"Master?" I asked.
"For I am closer to you than he," he whispered.
I shuddered. I was indeed in the keeping of the depth warden. It was in his quarters that I had my kennel. It was on the wall of those quarters that hung the whip to which I was first subject. It was he within whose direct reach I was. I was in his power, at his mercy. He could do with me as he pleased. But I was frightened, too, because I now realized that the depth master was in direct violation of the

orders of his superior. He would manage the depths as he saw fit. His, then, was the responsibility.

"Whom do you obey?" asked the depth warden.

"You, Master!" I said.

The depth warden then turned to the peasant. "This is only a stupid slave, and I am only a stupid jailer," he said. "Forgive us. This will not happen again."

The peasant regarded us. I did not think he understood any of what had gone on.

"In the future," said the depth warden to me, "you will serve the prisoner with care and deference."

"Yes, Master," I said. "Master!" I said.

"Yes?" he said.

I put my head down and kissed his feet. "Thank you, Master," I said.

He then stepped away from me, and went to the door of the cell.

I, on my knees, gathered in the food and water bowl of the prisoner. I had come to the cell originally to fetch and replenish them.

The depth warden had stopped at the door of the cell. He was standing there, looking back at the prisoner.

"Is it time for the planting?" asked the prisoner.

"No," said the depth warden.

I may have been mistaken, but I thought that I detected the path of a tear on the cheek of the depth warden.

He turned to leave.

"Master!" I called.

He turned to face me.

"How shall I be dressed, to serve here?" I asked. I knew, of course, as did the depth warden, what had been the instructions of the officer.

"You will be tunicked," said the depth warden.

"Yes, Master," I said.

The depth warden then, indeed, was taking much responsibility upon himself.

"But do not fear, pretty Janice," he said. "The sight of you in a slave tunic will be torment enough for any man."

"Yes, Master," I said.

Eighteen

I was elated.

My heart pounded madly.

"The raiders are returning!" I heard. "The raiders are returning!"

"Kneel here, by the ring, quickly!" I said.

"Do you see him anywhere?" she asked, the free woman, who wore the collar on which was inscribed the name 'Tuta', a suitable slave name.

"He will doubtless be about, as before," I said. "It is the usual time. We have had our walk, and now is the time I put you here."

I looked up. I could see the tarns, in the distance, one by one, approaching. They are frightening, but very beautiful. There must have been more than a hundred. They would alight on the docking area, between the cliff and the warehouses. Numbers of citizens were moving even now across the terrace, and bridge, to the docking area. It is something like "festival," when a large raiding party returns. But the free woman, rising up on her toes, straining, had eyes only for those on the terrace, scanning them.

"Must a command be repeated?" I inquired.

"Please, Janice," she begged, looking about.

"It seems we must return to the depths," I said, angrily.

Quickly she knelt, her back toward the wall. Her wrists were pinioned behind her, in slave bracelets, as usual. Today she wore a simple brown slave tunic. It was a brief, sleeveless, pullover tunic with a deep V-neck. In virtue of such a tunic a free man has little difficulty in conjecturing the delights of a slave's figure. The skirt was also cut at the sides. This made it easier to spread the knees in kneeling.

As she was in my keeping, I had thought it only fitting that I wear a somewhat more modest tunic myself, one with a higher neckline, a lower hemline, but the pit master, this day, would not hear of it. He had taken his whip and hurled it across the room. I had then, on all fours, fetched it back to him, in my teeth, and, lifting my head, delivered it into his grasp.

"Do you beg to be clothed?" he asked.

"Yes, Master," I said, before him, on all fours.

"Who begs to be clothed?" he asked.

"Janice begs to be clothed," I said.

He shook out the blades of the whip.

"And how does Janice beg to be clothed?" he inquired.

"Janice begs to be clothed in any way that Master sees fit," I assured him.

He then threw an identical tunic to the floor.

I put my head down to his feet and kissed them, gratefully. "Thank you, Master," I said.

I had then donned the garment. So now the free woman and I were identically tunicked, in spite of the fact that it was I who held the leash. We might have been, I supposed, a matched set. Indeed, some viewers may have taken us for such a set. Slaves, incidentally, even on this world, where they are common, tend to attract masculine attention. There are few men who do not enjoy looking upon them. That is one reason that it is important for us to pay attention to our posture, and such. Strangers will reprimand us, and even strike us, if we do not hold ourselves well. In a sense, I suppose, we are part of the beauties of a city, an aspect of its scenic delights, part of the attractions of the area, as might be her flower trees and brightly plumaged birds.

This sort of thing may be difficult for those of Earth to understand. Perhaps they must content themselves to do the best they can with it.

The slave is a lovely animal—can those of Earth even understand this?—tender, vulnerable, graceful, *needful*—and she can think, and feel, and speak, and serve, and love! Surely then it is easy to understand how her presence might be thought to improve a cityscape, a villa, a beach.

What red-blooded male would object to viewing us? What truly virile male would object to owning one or more of us?

And suppose that we were not that rare. Think of the flower trees, the brightly plumaged birds!

Surely, in some way, we not only characterize, but adorn, a city.

One of the pleasures of fellows coming in from the country is to look upon the urban slaves, for which purpose they will stroll the avenues and loiter about in the plazas, the markets, and bazaars. We are apparently much different from the slaves they are used to, usually sturdy, large-boned girls, often of peasant stock, the sort which are most useful in the fields. And certainly few men will visit an unfamiliar city, on business or otherwise, without comparing the girls of that city with the girls of their own. Sometimes when important visitors arrive in a city, perhaps to negotiate trade agreements or contract alliances, many slaves are walked, or even sent on meaningless errands, to certain quarters, that they may be viewed. They are part of the display of the city, and are exhibited as an aspect of its wealth and abundance, intended to produce a favorable impression. Just as a city prides itself on the ebullience, variety, and colorfulness of its architecture, on its spacious plazas and broad avenues, on its numerous parks and gardens, so, too, it prides itself on the number and beauty of its slaves. Indeed, sometimes cities compete in such modalities, each seemingly eager to stimulate the admiration, if not excite the envy, of her neighbors. There is some speculation that this sort of thing has motivated more than one clandestine, intermunicipal slave raid. To be sure there is little need for covertness in these matters for there are many cities on this world, mostly small, but some quite large, and each city usually will have its quota of, or plenitude of, allies and enemies. Furthermore, there is no dearth of women, and on this world women, even free women, are regarded as legitimate and appropriate booty. A common recreation for a tarnsman, for example, particularly when not on duty, not on maneuvers or campaign, is to steal women from a "fair city," that is, one at war with, or on poor terms with, his own city. These women may be either slave or free. Most commonly, of course, they will be slaves, as they, often beautiful, are the commonly desiderated quarry of the net and rope, but, too, of course, doubtless, at least in part, because free women are more difficult to obtain, being more carefully sheltered, protected, and guarded. He brings the captives back to his city, where he may dispose of them as he wishes, often keeping them for a time, until, say, he tires of them, and then selling them. I might mention, briefly, in passing, what seems to be a variation on this custom. Spies in one city ascertain, by rumor, and such, who are supposedly the most beautiful *free* women of a city. One need not have recourse to rumors, of course, where slaves are concerned. One need only look. These women, then, the allegedly beautiful *free* women, preferably of high birth and considerable position, are regarded as prize game. They are "trophy catches." Tarnsmen draw lots and the winner sets out to obtain the particular woman. If he has "chain luck" he brings her back and presents her, stripped, to a committee of peers. They decide whether or not she is worthy to be a slave girl in their city. Is she desirable enough, beautiful enough, to wear a collar in that city? One would not wish her to reflect poorly on the city, of course. There seems, incidentally, to be a general view among hostile cities that the women of the enemy belong to them in some sense, that they are already in some sense their slaves—it is then just a matter of bringing them into their rightful collars. The committee of peers, so to speak, in the "trophy case," may either rule favorably or unfavorably on the catch. Let us suppose they rule unfavorably. The woman is then placed in a coarse, sacklike garment, usually a sul sack with holes cut in it for the head and arms, and returned scornfully, rejected, her wrists thonged behind her, to the vicinity of her city. Occasionally this is done with a stunningly beautiful woman, which is to say to the enemy, "even the most beautiful of your women is not worthy of a collar in a city such as ours." The effect on the woman, of course, is often pathetically unsettling. It is not unusual that such a woman will afterwards take to wandering the high bridges and lonely streets, the hem of her garments hitched above her ankles, perhaps that she not soil them, her veils disarranged a bit, perhaps by the wind. She then, so to speak, courts the collar, eager to reassure herself of her beauty, her desirability, her fittingness to be owned; she wants to prove to herself now that she does have some value, after all, as she had hitherto thought; had she been mistaken; had her arrogant surmise been no more than a little she-tarsk's vanity; too, now, after her experience, her abduction, her subjection to male domination, and such, she has some inkling of what it might be to be a slave; and she longs now, on some level, to belong to a man; she wants now, though she may not be fully aware of this, that she wants, and needs, a master; she wants now to be helplessly owned, and to serve and love. There are, of course, many differences among slaves, ranging from the preferred slave of a ubar, often a witty, literate, talented, highly educated, brilliant woman, though she, too, is at his feet, to the simplest kettle-and-mat wench, who, too, of course, is expected to be a throbbing, kicking, helpless delight in the furs, or blankets.

It might be noted, in passing, that when a woman has been embonded she is then understood as, and taken as, unmitigatedly, a slave. That is what she then is. For example, let us suppose that several women of a given city, say, A, are now slaves in a given city, say, B. Let us then further suppose that these women are recovered, so to speak, in a raid perhaps, or perhaps in war, perhaps in B's having fallen. The women will not now be freed. They will be kept as slaves, for that is what they now are. Did they not permit themselves to be captured? Well, then, let them remain in bondage! That is where they belong, and should be! And furthermore, given the irritations and embarrassments involved, they are likely to be considered the lowest of slaves, and treated with great severity and harshness. What a mistake it was that they had been permitted to be free, ever! Usually they are only too eager to be sold from their former city, and serve gratefully in a less hostile, less bitter, less rancorous environment, where they will be simply accepted as the slaves they now are. Similarly, if a fellow captures a woman and carries her out of the city, and enslaves her, he may return with her to the city, she now his unquestioned slave.

Let us now return to our captured free woman, before the "committee of peers." Let us suppose, as will usually be the case, that she is adjudged satisfactory, if only minimally so, as will be made clear to her, to wear a collar in her captor's city. The tarnsman then, and his companions, those who failed to draw the winning lot in the hunting game, are feasted, with their officers, at the table of the very ubar or administrator himself. This is a great honor. The feast is served, of course, by slave girls. One of them, a rather new slave girl, is, as you may suppose, permitted no clothing. She wears only her collar. At the height of the feast she is put through her paces, between the tables. She is then returned to her serving, but you may imagine the difference now in her serving, as she now comprehends what she had to do, and how she is now seen. She will also, later, be expected to dance. She hesitates? The whip cracks. She dances. And after this she is again returned to her serving, simply as might be another dancer, no more and no less. And again, as you may well imagine, there is again a difference, one anew, in her serving, for she has now been forced to dance, a nude slave, subject to the whip, before masters. She touches her collar. She cannot remove it. She now has some sense as to what it means.

After the feast the tarnsman takes her home in his bracelets. She takes her place at his slave ring. The chain is locked on her. She looks up at him. She is his. She serves.

Some free women seek the collar, having come to understand that only in it can they find their fulfillment and happiness, and, paradoxically, at last, strangely perhaps, their most profound freedom.

Sometimes, in a foreign city, a free woman will elude her guards and thrust her way into the precincts of a paga tavern, precincts within which free women are seldom, if ever, found. She picks out a man, perhaps one she has noted earlier, and perhaps even followed, and finds irresistible, and kneels before his low table, unwinding her veils and parting her robes. He considers her. Is she acceptable, is she of interest? Would he have any objection to owning her? Tears form in her eyes. Her eyes plead. She offers him her most precious gift, herself. Will he accept it? "Collar!" he calls to the proprietor. One is brought. He locks it on the neck of the supplicant and conducts her to one of the alcoves, often dragging her, bent over, by the hair, that she may have some understanding as to how her life has now changed. In the alcove then, within moments of the closing of the collar, her training, to her joy, has begun.

* * * *

The free woman knelt very straight. She craned her neck. "I can see very little from my knees," she said.

"You are as a slave," I said. "No one cares whether you can see very much or not."

This was the first time the free woman had been this modestly garbed, such as it was, on one of our jaunts above. I had usually managed to gratify myself by having her slave-garbed in a way far more revealing than I was. I had enjoyed doing this to her, as she was a free woman, and I only a slave. But, instead of being distressed by this, she had always seemed to welcome it. The scantier and more revealing the garb in which I placed her the more she seemed to love it. I did not understand her. But then the notion of being "modestly garbed" is surely a relative one. On Earth, the garb in which we found ourselves, its brevity, its neckline, its lack of a nether closure, and such, would presumably have been regarded as scandalous, particularly in busy, public places. Indeed, even in certain Gorean cities, it might have counted as such. But it was not so here. Men in this city, whatever city it was, whereas they might have regarded our tunics as "appealing," would certainly not have regarded them as scandalous; if anything, for this city, they might have seemed a bit decorous; indeed, many men in this city, I had noted, seemed to enjoy displaying their slaves with a particularly exotic brazenness, often to the mere belly string and slave strip. The girl dare not object, for she is a slave. She knows that it will be done with her as the Master pleases. Too, I had seen more than one nude slave on her leash; that, however, is rare, and is usually done as a punishment. Sometimes, however, after an enemy city has fallen, her women, now enslaved, are denied clothing for some six months; at the end of that time they are inordinately grateful, should the least of tunics be cast to them; supposedly we are not permitted modesty, but we are, of course, sensitive to such things. Indeed, one of the most effective controls our masters have over us is with respect to our clothing, its nature, and, of course, even if we are to be permitted any. In some cities, as I understand it, the state involves itself in such matters; for example, in some cities it is a matter of public ordinance that slave tunics may not be longer than a certain amount; this ordinance is presumably motivated not only by a desire to draw a clear distinction between the free woman and the slave, but to distract the attention of the roving tarnsman, the slaver, the commercial girl jobber, and such, from the glorious free woman, directing it to the meaningless slave, whose charms are more easily discerned.

Whatever be the case here, it is a matter of fact that "slave strikes" more frequently target slaves than free women.

I know this now, but did not realize it at the time. Indeed, I was shortly to be apprised of an exception to this rule, though, at the time, I did not understand that it was an exception.

And, in its way, I suppose the exception, as it is said, "proved the rule." In any event, in contrast to the rule, its anomalous character drew a great deal of attention to the very rule it violated.

Or would, for those who understood such things.

I knew so little of this world!

When I did understand it I became aware, more seriously than hitherto, of the nature of the men in this city—of their skill, ferocity and pride, and their sense of honor.

The men of Gor, our masters, tend to take honor very seriously.

I would learn more of this later.

The slave, incidentally, wants to be owned by a man of honor. We want to be proud of our masters. Too, we are safer with such a man. The man of honor, of course, and perhaps in part because of his sense of honor, holds us in uncompromising, perfect bondage. But that is what we want, for we are slaves.

This, the generally preferred targeting of slaves in raids, and such, I would suppose, has less to do with ordinances, and such, as other things, such as the relative inaccessibility of free women. But I would like to think, too, that it is *primarily* because we are far more attractive than free women.

If free women were really beautiful, why would they not be already in collars?

To be sure, most slaves were once free women. I would have to grant that. On Earth, I myself, though a natural and rightful slave, had been *legally* free. That changed, of course, once I had arrived on this world. I did have to admit, however, that my charge, the free woman, the Lady Constanzia of Besnit, was an extraordinarily beautiful female. She would be a prize for any chain. And she was free, of course. But the nets and ropes of the hunters, I note, most frequently close on the muchly exposed, startled bodies of kajirae, and I would like to think that the reason for this is simple, that we are just, statistically, much more desirable, much better catches. Oh, I suppose there is some pleasure for a brute in unwrapping a free woman, so to speak, like a present, the suspense, the anticipation, and such, hoping to be pleasantly surprised, and so on, but what if he isn't? Then what? Perhaps he can get a few coins on her, as a laundress, or perhaps he might sell her to a woman as a serving slave. But they usually like pretty women as serving slaves.

A word might be devoted to that.

Taste is doubtless involved, as the pretty woman dresses up the compartments of the free woman, much as does exquisite furniture, attractive appointments, and such. But I think, too, free women enjoy ruling women who are superior to themselves in beauty. In the wars between free women and slave girls woe to the slave girl who is the serving slave of the free woman! On such a woman the free woman may to her heart's content indulge her vanity, her arrogance, and her pettiness, and may inflict on her her animosity, and, indeed, her hatred, and her frustration, ventilating these things abundantly and richly, and with impunity, upon the unfortunate, innocent one who is taken as standing proxy for her kind, that kind of which the free woman is so resentful and jealous, a kind of much greater interest and attractiveness to men, the female slave. The serving slave of a free woman is often lashed mercilessly if she so much as looks at a man. Some claim that the keeping of pretty serving slaves by free women is to guard against their own abduction. Should a tarnsman, say, with slave noose in hand, invade their quarters he may choose the slave over the mistress. To be sure, if he prefers the slave he is certain to do so, and she is such that she will rush eagerly to his bracelets, joyful in her femininity and collar to now have the opportunity to serve her natural master, a male. But obviously, if the fellow is interested, he will take both. If he takes one, he will bind her belly up over his saddle, usually that she may be casually and conveniently caressed in flight, that she may be writhing in helpless, raging heat by the time he reaches his camp. If he takes two he will simply chain them one on each side of the saddle, to the booty rings, and thus have a balanced load. If this is done they may be bound in the camp and aroused at his leisure. In the case of taking both the mistress and the slave, the slave, of course, having been longer in the collar, will be "first girl" over her erstwhile mistress. Naturally this is a situation to which she, switch in hand, does not object.

But let us suppose, say, that the tarnsman, the beast, is not satisfied with the "present" he has purloined, it now, unwrapped and examined, having been found wanting.

So let her be a laundress, a field slave, a factory slave, chained to her loom.

But perhaps she could become beautiful in bondage. What then? And there are many modalities of female beauty. And women are very pretty in collars. And as they lose their inhibitions, and such. But there is no comparison, in my view, at least, between the slave girl and the *current* free woman. We are better, infinitely better! At the very least the free woman, once she is in a collar, and finds out what it is all about, will be much improved; she will soon be a thousand times, and more, better than she was when she was only another smug, vain, haughty, nuisance.

The collar is good for us, you see.

So the slave girl is infinitely better than the free woman.

On the other hand, I must grant that the "free woman," once she is no longer free, once she becomes a slave, and learns her collar—once she is no longer free—and has now become a slave girl—will have her value—on the block, and in the kitchen, and in the furs.

That is undeniable.

But then of course she is a slave girl.

* * * *

In any event, the Lady Constanzia and I were similarly attired.

Yes, I thought, she was beautiful.

And how right that collar looked on her neck!

How she had looked at it in the mirror, and adjusted it, this morning—so carefully, so admiringly—with such approving vanity!

She loved it, the pretty little bitch!

To be sure, we were very much the same height. She was perhaps a quarter of an inch or so taller than I. I had little doubt that many men, seeing us, took us for a matched set.

We were similar in hair and eye color, and were similarly figured.

I also doubted now that anyone, even a slaver, would have suspected that the Lady Constanzia was not a slave, without ascertaining, of course, that she lacked the brand. She had something now, you see, of the eagerness, the vitality, the interest, the curiosity, the awakened nature, the readiness to live and experience, of a slave.

Certainly most of the men looking upon us—and there were many—would have taken us both for slaves and—I am confident—attractive slaves.

Certainly there could be little doubt about our charms.

I was a little apprehensive about matters, of course, for it seemed that the pit master had realized what I was doing with the free woman, using her, at least from my own point of view, to take out my little vengeances on my superiors, free women. It was for that reason, I suspect, that he had decided, today, what we would both wear.

I pulled the edges of the slits at the side of the brief skirt a little more closely together, but, of course, as soon as I released them, they parted again.

My flanks were well displayed.

It was not that I minded this so much in itself, for I am not altogether unaware of my own possible charms, and, as a slave, doubtless a vain one, was not above displaying them, and even flaunting them upon occasion, shamelessly and joyously, as that I was somewhat irritated that the distinction between us, she and I, was no longer clearly marked. To be sure, it was she who was in the bracelets, and not I, and it was I who held the leash, and not she. That, I supposed, should be more than enough.

"Do you see him?" she asked, anxiously.

"No," I said, not even looking about. I wanted to get to the docking area. Already the tarns, one by one, were alighting.

"Am I overdressed?" she asked, anxiously.

"No," I said.

"Do you think the tunic is pretty?" she asked.

"Yes," I said.

"Do you think he will like me like this?" she asked.

"Yes," I said. She was exquisitely fetching. The tunics are designed to set off the charms of a slave. And this tunic, to be sure, left little to the imagination.

"I hope so," she worried.

"In a slave collar," I said, "any woman might as well be naked."

"Oh," she said.

The collar, of course, speaks of the vulnerability of the slave. It makes clear her helplessness, her availability. In this sense, in seeing a woman in a slave collar, it is much like seeing her naked, or, if you prefer, potentially naked.

"I can see little from my knees!" she protested, looking up at me.

"It is not yours to look," I said, "but yours to be found, if any should regard you of interest."

"Oh!" she said.

I was hitching her head back, by the leash and collar, close to the slave ring.

"Please, Janice!" she said. "Not so close!"

"Why not?" I asked.

"I want to be able to put my head down," she said. "I want my lips to be able to touch the very tiles of the terrace!"

I looked at her. I did not think it was the tiles of the terrace that she wanted to kiss.

"Please, Janice," she begged.

"So you have already reached that phase, have you?" I said.

"Yes!" she said, defiantly, earnestly.

I gave her the slack she required.

"Thank you, Janice!" she said. "Thank you!"

"I will be back shortly," I said.

"Do you see him?" she asked.

"No," I said, looking about. "Do not get up!" It is customary for slaves not to stand at slave rings. Usually they kneel there, or sit there, or lie there.

"Yes, Mistress!" she said. How naturally, how quickly, how easily, I thought, had that expression escaped her! To be sure, it was part of her disguise, so to speak.

There were still people hurrying over the bridge. There was already a crowd at the docking area, mostly near the warehouses.

I checked the bracelets, and the leash lock, of the Lady Constanzia.

"You have been so kind to me, Janice!" she exclaimed. "I am sorry that I had you whipped!"

That had occurred in my first day in the depths, when she was still the occupant of a dangling slave cage, suspended over a pool to which large aquatic rodents, one variety of urt, had access.

"Do not concern yourself with the matter," I said. "I may have your clothing removed and have you whipped."

"Janice!" she said.

"Then you can see for yourself what it is like," I said.

"Please do not whip me, Janice," she said.

I could do this, incidentally, as she was in my keeping. On the other hand, I had no intention of doing so. I was really rather fond of the Lady Constanzia. She did not seem to me to be a bad sort, considering that she was a free woman.

"Perhaps I shall," I said, lightly.

"No!" she begged.

"Why not?" I asked.

"I want my first beating to come from the hands of a man," she said. "After that, you may do with me what you want."

"I will be back shortly!" I assured her.

I did turn back, at the bridge, to see her kneeling there, in the accustomed place, by the slave ring.

I could also see, now, the scarlet-clad figure for whom she had been waiting making his way across the terrace, toward her. At almost the same time she may have seen him because, when I glanced back, she was kneeling beautifully, modestly, head down, at the ring. Perhaps she would lift her head, seeming surprised, and pleased, when his shadow fell across her body. Some days ago, upon my suggestion, following her urgent request for it, the pit master had permitted her slave wine. Who knew, after all, what might occur in the streets or markets? There were many byways in such a city, narrow alleylike streets, dark doorways, and such, into which a slave, ordered to silence, might be drawn.

"That is what we must drink," I had informed her, noting with satisfaction the expression on her face as she had lifted up the bowl, filled with the foul brew, and had smelled it. "It is not like the delicious beverages quaffed by free women for such purposes, is it?" I had asked.

"No," she had whispered.

"I am told, however," I said, "that the releaser is delicious. When we are given that we know that we are to be bred." This form of mating, as one might suppose, is carefully controlled and takes place under supervision. The slaves selected for breeding are generally unknown to one another, normally hooded and commonly forbidden to speak. In this way it is felt that certain complications may be avoided.

She looked down at the foul brew.

"You need not drink it," I said to her.

"No," she whispered. Then she lifted the bowl to her lips. She put back her head. Then, scarcely pausing to take a breath, she drained the bowl.

"Oh!" she cried, her entire body shuddering.

"That is slave wine," I said, "free woman."

I regarded her with some satisfaction. I thought that she might now understand, a little bit better than before, what it might be to be a slave.

"How can you drink it?" she asked.
"Do you think we are given a choice?" I asked.
She put the bowl down, unsteadily.
"Will it work with a free woman?" she asked.
"If she is a female," I said. "Where do you think slave girls come from?"
"Bracelet me now, Janice," she asked. "Leash me. Take me above now."

* * * *

The scarlet-clad figure had now reached the Lady Constanzia. I saw her lift her head, timidly, to him. How very much she looks like a slave at his feet, I thought. But then, of late, I reminded myself, how much the Lady Constanzia seemed to be like a slave at the feet of any man.

She had had her slave wine. I did not fear now, to leave her at the ring. On the other hand, I thought she would, indeed, be safe in such a place. It was not merely that she was chained there, for safekeeping, but that it was a very public place. Also, the scarlet-clad figure had visited her there several times before and had never, in spite of what I suspected were certain provocations, forced her. It would not have been wise to have done so, of course, for he was not of this city. The forcing of a slave, indeed, even the use of an unoffered slave, by a stranger, an outlander, so to speak, might be taken as some form of presumption or insult. Furthermore, even within a city, such things are often regarded as incivilities, unless taken, perhaps, as legitimate portions of a free man's punishment of an errant slave, say, perhaps, one who might have been regarded as being insufficiently deferential. These men have many ways of reminding us that we are slaves, and one of them is our use. But I thought there might be an even more grievous reason for the scarlet-clad figure's restraint in the matter of lovely, fetching "Tuta." I conjectured that he was the sort of man who would want to own a slave, one who would want to have her fully his, before putting her to his pleasure. I did not know on what business, incidentally, the scarlet-clad figure was in the city. Doubtless it must be soon concluded. I would not have advised him to dally beyond his welcome. Suspicion of strangers, of outlanders, seems to come very easily to the men of this world. Too, neither the Lady Constanzia nor

I knew the name of the stranger, nor even his city. She, as a putative slave, and I, as an actual slave, would not dare to inquire into such matters. One does not wish to be kicked or cuffed. Curiosity, it is said, is not becoming in kajirae.

I quickly turned about and hurried over the bridge, toward the docking area.

Nineteen

There were some folk still crossing the bridge, though fewer now that the tarns had alighted. Some slave girls, too, scurried across the bridge, doubtless eager to see the returned raiders, the mighty mounts, the harvested riches of the venture's predations. I joined them. Slave girls often have the run of the city. On the other hand, male slaves seldom do, for obvious reasons. An exception is the male silk slave, usually the male pleasure slave of a rich woman, but sometimes one belonging to a female entrepreneur, in whose brothel, one specializing in the tastes of women, he serves. Some men are brought from Earth here for such purposes I have heard, but I do not know if it is true. There were certainly no males in my group. We were all women. Had there been males in our group I think they would have soon been spoiled for such an application. Seeing women like us, in the power of men, they would doubtless have soon assumed the whip and become masters.

More than a hundred and fifty tarns had landed in the docking area. Guards held the crowds back. Loot was being unloaded. There was music in the docking area, adding to the celebration. In the city, to my right, the bars, which normally signify times and alarms, were sounding in jubilation.

"See! See!" cried men in the crowd.

Vessels of gold were lifted by raiders, displaying them to the crowd.

Children squirmed in and out among the people.

Many were the colorful robes.

Boxes were being lifted down to waiting hands.

Some of the mighty saddle birds, like gigantic, crested hawks, they are called "tarns," moved about uneasily. Sometimes wings would snap and air would rush about. Once or twice one or another of these mighty creatures put back its head and screamed to the clouds. The music continued. The bars continued to sound, rejoicing.

I saw some of the captives, stripped women, hooded, being led forth, in their chains, from cage baskets, slung to the harnesses of the mighty birds. The women moved uncertainly, unsteadily. Doubtless they were bewildered, confused. Incidentally, even free men, brought to this city on diplomatic missions, on commercial ventures, and such, are brought here hooded. The location of the city is supposedly a secret, known only to its citizens. Only they can come and go unhooded. Naturally, too, there are numerous outposts of the city in the mountains, at which tarnsmen are always on the alert. It is the mission of these men to keep the secret of the city. Such outposts constitute the nodes of an extensive system of reconnaissance and surveillance. From them frequent, randomized patrols are mounted. From them companies of tarn cavalry may be launched to intercept and destroy intruders. Unauthorized strangers risk their lives by even approaching such places. Cleared entrants, usually cleared in their own cities, flying under appropriate passage banners, report to them, for hooding and transport. Few, incidentally, except in armed parties, traverse the mountains on foot. It is difficult and dangerous to do so. They are not only rugged and precipitous, but are apparently alive with animals, such as rock panthers and sleen. It is said that none may pass unauthorized the lines of interdiction, and that, of those who do, none are to return.

I was jostled in the crowd, but none, it seemed, took note of me. Free and slave were there in zest commingled.

"Stay back! Stay back!" called a guard.

One raider, still mounted on the tarn, reached into a saddle sack and hurled a handful of jewels high over the crowd. They rained down. People reached and scrambled for them, laughing. It would not do, of course, for slaves to seek such stones. They are not for us. We would not wish our hands cut off. In many cities we are not permitted to touch money. In many it is a capital offense for us to touch a weapon.

It was hard for me to see in the crowd, for the robes and hoods.

"Oh!" I said, pinched by someone.

I heard a coarse male laugh.

One does not complain, of course, as one is slave. Such small attentions, a pinch, a touch, a stolen kiss, pressed perhaps to the side of one's neck, as one is briefly held, helplessly, must be expected. Indeed, in their way, they are flatteries. The slave who does not elicit such attentions, who is not deemed of sufficient interest to warrant them, may suspect that she will soon be placed by her master upon the block.

I squirmed to a new place in the crowd.

The crowd surged about me.

I could see very little, for the men and, indeed, most of the boys, were much taller than I. The women were muchly of my own size, but even there, the ornateness of the robes, the height of the hoods, sometimes made it difficult to see. I was irritated with them, the free women. They were so ornately, so complexly robed, whereas I had only my slave frock, that scandalously brief, muchly revealing, single piece of cloth, and my collar. But I did not think they were so different from me, really, they, such proud things, so gorgeously bedecked, so smug under those layers of cloth. Beneath the protective, shielding casings of those stiff brocades were there not terrains and latitudes which, shorn of their armor, would prove as vulnerable and soft as mine?

I was momentarily blinded by a flash of light, the sun reflected from a huge silver plate, perhaps a yard in width, held over his head by a mounted raider. The flash was not unlike that from mirrors used as signal devices in the mountains. I had seen such flashes occasionally from the balustrade, presumably the routine signals of guards. Smoke signals, too, are apparently sometimes used, but I had not seen them from the balustrade. At night, beacon fires, which may be shielded and then unshielded, in codes, may be used. The flash of the mirrors, the sight of the smoke signal, the glimpse of a fire, such things, it might be recollected, convey their message at the speed of light, far faster than a tarn can fly, incomparably more swift, even, than the flighted sound of a distant bar.

There were exclamations of astonishment from the crowd. Such a plate might have come from a palace.

Raiders such as these are often gone several days, sometimes even for a season. They have concealed loot camps, many times actually within enemy territory. Then, sooner or later, after they have conducted their raids, they gather together their booty and return home. To be sure, much of the booty may have been disposed of earlier, in other places, but one suspects, the vanity of the men of this world being such, that enough will be retained for a goodly showing on the docks. And, of course, in any event, the saddlebags bulge with gold obtained from the earlier dispositions of loot. One form of booty, on the other hand, does tend to be brought to the city, and that is female booty. This city serves as a clearinghouse for a great deal of such merchandise. In it there are many markets in which such goods are disposed of, on both a wholesale and retail basis.

Some men, somewhere, began singing.

Men from the city were near the front of the line of tarns, conferring there with one who may have been the expedition's leader, and certain others. Such expeditions are seldom purely acquisitive in nature. They may also gather information of political or strategic interest. Even tiny bits of information can be significant, and a number of bits of information, each seemingly insignificant and unrelated to others, sometimes, properly organized and understood, like a suddenly assembled jigsaw puzzle, may yield a picture which is not only clear but meaningful. But now, I supposed, they were engaged in only general inquiries. Indeed, they might be doing little more now than congratulating the leader, and his officers, on their successful return. Full reports could be later rendered.

I saw a fellow standing in the stirrups and swinging a huge double strand of pearls about his head, again and again, and then he flung it out, far over the crowd. It was seized by a dozen hands. It burst. It showered about.

I supposed some of this casting of loot to the crowd was no more than the overflow of good spirits, a manner of celebration, of contributing to the general jubilation. But, too, I suspect, that for some, at least, it represented a release of tension, and constituted a form of relief. It might have been, too, something of an offering of thanks, so to speak, to the fates, or the gods, or the Priest-Kings, whoever they may be, for a safe return. More than one of these fellows had knelt down and kissed the tiles of the docking area, stones of his native city. It is not always the case, you see, that everyone returns from such expeditions. Indeed, sometimes the expedition, itself, does not return.

Captives were now being knelt in lines, perpendicular to the long docking area, facing the warehouses.

They were still hooded.

They were being chained together, by the neck, beginning, of course, at the back of the lines. That is customary. It was in such a way that I, in the corridor of the pens, had first been added to a neck chain. This produces apprehension in a girl, and she is not permitted to turn her head. Then the collar is on her. But, too, she is less likely to bolt. And when the collar is on her it is too late to bolt. She is then part of the coffle. To be sure, these slaves were hooded, and hooded slaves, like other sorts of animals, are less likely to bolt. Some other chains, too, were being rearranged. The hands of those who had been front-shackled were now being back-shackled, shackled behind their backs. No longer, as they now were, would they be able to use their hands to feed themselves. Too, back-shackling better impresses her helplessness on a captive. There were several such lines of captives. In each line there were fifteen to twenty captives. As each line was completed, the captives, now beads on the "slaver's necklace," would be unhooded.

"Beautiful!" called a man. Perhaps he saw one on which he intended to bid.

Captives trembled in their chains.

Interestingly they were all *free* women. At that time I did not realize how unusual that was, not knowing at that time that "slave strikes" are almost always directed against slaves. This was the result, as it turned out, I would later learn, of a special situation. It was a response to a presumed insult on the part of an administrator of a distant city, something to the effect that those of this city, whose name I did not yet know, were at best cowards and petty thieves, capable of no more than making off with an occasional slave. Accordingly that city, smug in its supposed security, had been saved for last, for the final strike of the expedition. The result of the administrator's indiscreet remark was that now more than four hundred of that city's free women, almost all of high caste as it turned out, were now on their knees, shackled, on the docking area. A considerable amount of plunder, presumably for good measure, had been acquired, as well. If slaves had been taken, they had been disposed of elsewhere. That is not hard to do, as there is always a market for them. Too, what room would there have been for slaves? The numerous baskets, the arrayed booty rings, the varieties of saddle straps, and such, were already "taken," so to speak—by free women. I doubted that the administrator of the offending town would again be so bold, so unguarded, in his remarks on those of this city. Too, the nature of the strike had been intended as an insult, saying, so to speak, "You must understand that your women are ours, whether slave or free, if we deign to take them. We usually take your slaves for they are far better than your free women, but, this time, we will make an exception. We will take, you see, what women of yours we please. You cannot stop us."

Involved, it seems was a matter of umbrage, one of offended pride, indeed, a matter construed somehow, correctly or incorrectly, as one of *honor*.

When I became clear on these things later I understood, to my uneasiness, how ruthless and powerful, and bold and skilled, how proud and dangerous, how particular, how touchy, how sensitive, how easily angered, how difficult to satisfy, the men of this city were.

Surely in this city a girl would have to be very careful in her collar.

These men were dangerous, and mighty.

They would not be easy masters.

They would know how to get the most from a trembling, fearful slave.

But to what other sort of man would a girl wish to belong?

Most of the women, I supposed, were soon destined for the block. Perhaps some would be held out for special purposes, gifts, and such. Perhaps some would be retained by the raiders themselves, who might enjoy training them, teaching them their duties, acquainting them with the nature of their new life.

"Excellent!" called out various men.

The catch was good, I gathered.

Even I had to admit that several of the women were quite beautiful. They would doubtless make superb slaves.

The slave, of course, already knows how to please. The free woman must learn.

Some men enjoy teaching them.

To be sure, not every woman was on a chain. Some knelt, even front-shackled, in sirik, head down, near the very talons of the great birds. These were mainly those who had been tied to booty rings or bound across the leather itself. Most were now unhooded.

Some slaves of the raiders had been permitted across the lines and now swam with rapture in the arms of their masters.

I saw one fellow displaying a catch to a slave. "What do you think of her!" he asked. It was a slim captive. She was a brunette. She was in sirik. Her wrists, front-shackled, as is common in sirik, were pulled high over her head. "Pretty," admitted the raider's slave. He then put his left hand on the side of the captive's waist and, with her wrists enfolded in his grasp, bent her backwards, to exhibit the bow of her delights. She was exquisite. Her hair hung back and down. "Yes, very pretty," granted his slave, I thought apprehensively, reluctantly. And, indeed, who could blame her? "Shall we keep her?" asked the raider. "No, no," cried the slave. "Sell her. Sell her!"

I went to my hands and knees to crawl forward in the crowd, that I might the better see. If I knelt in the front, as were many other girls, I should be able to see quite well. It was only a matter of getting there. If one crawls, one is scarcely noticed. On the other hand, it is certainly not advisable to push past free persons. I was in a state collar with my name on it. I was quite vulnerable.

"Oh!" I said, in pain, suffering the petulant blow of a free woman's slipper.

But then I had come to the guards' line. A free man even moved a little to the side, that I might pass him.

"Thank you, Master!" I said, gratefully.

Some chests were being brought forward through the crowd, from the warehouses. Loot was being recorded, and entered into them. They were then locked, and the lids sealed with wax. Signet rings, cylinder seals, and such, impressed their marks into the warm wax.

I was on all fours, at the front edge of the crowd.

"Stand," suggested the free man. "You will be able to see better."

"Thank you, Master," I said, rising to my feet. He placed me before him. He could see easily over my head.

Still, bars in the city sounded.

Reunions, I saw, took place.

Here and there I heard vendors hawking goods. One had pastries, another sweets. Another fellow, somewhere, was selling apricots.

One of the captives in one of the nearby lines suddenly screamed, and struggled, in her chains, to her feet. As she was on a common chain, neck-coffled on it, her action dragged on the neck chains of the girl behind her and before her, half pulling the one behind her to her feet, jerking back, twisting, causing to cry out with pain, the one before her. Swiftly the lash fell, once, twice, sharply on her, and she was again on her knees, her head down, sobbing, cowering, making herself as small as possible, fearing only that she might be again subjected to the lash's kiss.

"They learn quickly," said the man behind me.

"Yes, Master," I averred. It was true. We learn quickly. It does not take us long to understand that we are slaves, fully, and helplessly, and that is all there is to it.

One of the tarns suddenly snapped its wings and a great rush of air blasted toward us. My hair blew back and the tunic was whipped back on my body. The garments and robes of the free persons, too, were swept back. Women cried out and held their veils. Some put down their heads, clinging to the collar of their robes and their hoods. Dust and tiny particles pelted us. There was laughter in the crowd, so unexpected was the rush of air. "Watch out," called a fellow. This time I closed my eyes, and turned away. The blast thrust me against the man behind me. He enfolded me in his arms, sheltering me, and I put my head against his shoulder. Again came the rush of air. My tunic was whipped about my body. Then it was done, the blast. I then, lifting my head a little, my right cheek near his shoulder, pressed back a bit, self-consciously, against his arms. He released me. I could not, of course, have procured my own liberty. The men of this world are much stronger than we. "Forgive me, Master," I said, head down, and quickly turned about again. I had not, of course, met his eyes. One is slave.

"Listen," said a fellow.

"Yes," said another.

At almost the same time I heard small bells. In a moment, too, I detected the odor of incense.

"They are here for their coins," said a fellow.

"I think you had best kneel," the fellow behind me said, kindly.

I knelt.

"I hate such parasites," whispered a man.

"Hush," said another, frightened. "They are the intermediaries between ourselves and the Priest-Kings."

"So they say," said another, under his breath.

Looking down the line I noted that a quiet had come over the crowd, and even over the victorious raiders. Not only had the slave girls knelt, but I noted, too, that the kneeling captives had now lowered their heads.

The ringing of the small bells could be heard quite clearly now. Once again I smelled the incense.

The crowd parted to my left and I saw, making its way through the crowd, some sort of standard, a golden staff surmounted by a golden circle. The circle I would later learn was the sign of the Priest-Kings, the symbol of eternity, that without beginning or end. Emerging through the crowd first were two boys, one ringing the bells and the other shaking a censer, wafting fumes of the incense about. Behind these two came another boy, he bearing the standard of the golden circle. Behind him came a gaunt, hideous man. His features frightened me. I did not doubt but what he was insane. Behind him, in double file, side by side, came some twenty other men. Each carried, before him, a golden bowl. They made me uneasy. Something in their appearance seemed to me unhealthy. They seemed pathological. Some looked simple. Others appeared to be of unsound mind. Some mumbled to themselves, prayers perhaps. They certainly did not look much like the normal men of this world. They were too pale. Were they strangers to the sun and fresh air? They moved poorly. Did they never leap and run, and wrestle? Were they ashamed of having bodies, or of being alive? Had they somehow sought refuge in pathetic lies? Did they think that absurdities conferred dignity upon them? Such, I thought, might not function well in this demanding, hardy world. But then they had perhaps found a way of surviving. Perhaps they, who might otherwise have been dismissed as pathetic misfits, as simple failures in nature, had managed to construct a social niche for themselves, perhaps by inventing and providing a service. They seemed so smug, so furtive, so sly, so sanctimonious, so hypocritical! How serious they were. Did they fear that the world might suddenly find them out and burst into laughter? All these men had shaved heads. All wore robes of glistening white. These were, I gathered, "Initiates," supposedly the highest of the high castes.

How odd, I thought, that it should supposedly be they who had the ear of the mighty and mysterious Priest-Kings. If there were Priest-Kings, I wondered if they knew about the caste of Initiates. Perhaps they would regard them as a joke. Why would the Priest-Kings, I wondered, if they really required intermediaries, and were unable to deal directly with men, and, indeed, if there was any point in them dealing with men at all, have chosen to achieve this end with so eccentric and improbable a caste? Why would they not have chosen some other caste, say, the metal workers or the leather workers, as intermediaries? Those castes, at least, seemed to be populated with men. The leather workers were excellent at piercing our ears, for example, the metal workers at fitting shackles to fair limbs.

Kneeling, partly bent over, I watched this procession wend its slow, solemn way, bells ringing, incense smoking, in front of the crowd. It went to the end of the docking area and then turned about, and made its way back, before the crowd, but between the tarns and raiders on one side and the captives, on the other. The captives, in their chains and shackles, kept their heads down. I noted, spying on their progress, that the members of the procession were fastidiously careful, even scrupulously careful, to avoid any contact with the captives, even so much as the casual brushing of a bared foot, a shackled ankle, a small shoulder, a lovely thigh, with the hem of a robe. Those in the crowd, too, with but few exceptions, exhibited extreme deference to these robed individuals, whom I took to be "Initiates," both free men and women assuming attitudes of deference, most standing with heads respectfully inclined. The slave girls, those near the front of the crowd, whom I could see, as the procession passed, had thrust their heads down to the stones of the docking area. Some trembled. I gathered that a slave's failure to yield suitable deference to such individuals might be regarded as a peculiarly heinous omission, one perhaps jeopardizing not only the girl, who, after all, was but a mere slave, but perhaps the city itself.

The procession had now stopped, in such a way that the twenty or so men with their golden bowls, on the other side of the captives, were now in a single line, all facing the crowd. Before them, toward the center, were the three boys, novices, I supposed. He with the golden standard, that surmounted with the golden circle, was in the center. To his right was the boy with the bells. To his left was he with the censer. Before them, now, was the gaunt man, the standard of the Priest-Kings behind him.

He lifted one thin arm to the sky. A clawlike hand was revealed, the sleeve of the robe falling back to the elbow.

"Praise be to the Priest-Kings!" he called. His voice was sonorous, and wild. In it I thought there was more than a bit of madness.

"Praise be to the Priest-Kings," murmured the crowd.

"Behold," cried the gaunt man. "We are favored by the Priest-Kings!" He half turned to his left, and then to his right, gesturing expansively behind him, first in one of these directions, and then in the other, indicating accumulations of treasure, among and before the tarns and raiders, piles of it, boxes of it, chests of it, bulging sacks of it. He then faced the crowd and lifted his hands to the left and right, indicating the captives, now having been separated from the other loot and brought forward, closer to the crowd, both those in lines, they accounting for the largest number, and those kneeling separately, all bound, many in sirik, in the general vicinity of their captors.

"We thank the Priest-Kings for the favors they have bestowed upon us!" he cried.

"Thanks be to the Priest-Kings," said the crowd.

"We thank them for the gifts they have given us!"

"Thanks be to the Priest-Kings!" said the crowd.

"We thank them for the riches they have given us!"

"Thanks be to the Priest-Kings!" said the crowd.

"And we thank them, too, for these slaves!"

A tremor and moan went through the captives. They were, at this point, of course, free women.

"Thanks be to the Priest-Kings!" said the crowd.

We were to be given to understand, I took it, that these various matters were to be viewed as having all proceeded in accordance with the will of the mysterious Priest-Kings. But who knew? Perhaps they were not even interested in things of this sort. Too, assuming them to be interested, I wondered if there were any independent way of finding out what might be the will of the Priest-Kings, short, that is, of waiting and finding out how things, in fact, came out. It was difficult to know, you see, how such a claim, that things proceeded in accordance with the will of the Priest-Kings, might be evaluated. To be sure, perhaps a Priest-King might show up and say, "No, that is not what I wanted, at all." But how would you know it was a Priest-King? How would it establish its identity? Perhaps it could uproot trees, or kill people, or something. But, could Priest-Kings do such things? And, if so, was it only Priest-Kings who could do them? I expected that, here and there on this world, and doubtless on others, similar ceremonies might take place. The women of city A, for example, might be led to believe that it was the will of the Priest-Kings that they become the slaves of the men of city B, and the women of city B might be led to believe that it was the will of the Priest-Kings that they become the slaves of the men of city A.

To be sure, there is nothing inconsistent in this possibility. I supposed that a woman might, in theory, believe that she, say, because she deserved it, or because it was appropriate for her, was destined to slavery by the Priest-Kings. Perhaps she would accept this in virtue of the supposed wisdom of Priest-Kings. Or, even if she thought this a mere whim, or even an arbitrary decision on their part, merely to demonstrate their power, she might reconcile herself to it, indeed, soon joyously submitting to, and accepting, what she takes to be her decreed fate. Some such belief, I supposed, might assist her in her adjustment to bondage. On the other hand, I think that any reference to the will of the Priest-Kings in these matters is both unnecessary and misleading. Incidentally, I have never personally known a slave on this world who brought the Priest-Kings into these matters. We do not want our bondage, our joy in servitude, our submission, our love, demeaned by attributing it to something alien, something other than ourselves, something outside of ourselves, such as the will of the Priest-Kings, if such should exist. It is too close to us, too intimate to us, too meaningful to us, to be cheapened in that way. It depends not on Priest-Kings, you see, but on what we are, women.

"Our offerings have been accepted, our prayers have been heard," he said.

Now it seemed that these Initiates or at least he who appeared to be chief amongst them was implicitly suggesting that the success of the expedition might well be attributed to their offerings, doubtless ultimately supplied by the faithful, and their prayers, uttered in the safety of their temple precincts. I looked up to see the faces of some of the raiders. Those faces, some of them so young, seemed solemn. Did they not think their own efforts had been efficacious in these matters? Who, after all, rode the mighty tarns, who did battle, who risked their lives, who, sword in hand, bestrode the corridors of burning palaces? And how must such words sound to the lovely captives? Surely they, if none others, must know who it was who gagged and bound them in their beds, and carried them off, surely they must know who caught them, and flung them down and put chains on them, who fought over them with curses, with sweat and steel, who carried them helpless through the smoke of burning houses to waiting tarns. Surely they were under no delusions as to who it was who fastened them on their backs over saddles, who thrust them naked into the cage baskets.

"Let us again give thanks to the Priest-Kings!" cried the gaunt figure.

"Thanks be to the Priest-Kings," said the crowd.

I noticed that one of the robed, shaved-headed boys, the one with the bells, was eyeing one of the captives. She was one of those in the lines. She was a small brunette. Her hands twisted a little behind her, in the shackles. She might have been a little younger than he. I did not think she was aware of his gaze.

I did not scorn the lad for noticing her. If anything, I was pleased he had. It made him seem a little more human. To be sure, I supposed that he had best watch his step. Too, she had best watch hers. Though she was now a free woman, she was a stripped captive, and would doubtless soon be a slave. If he became involved with her I had little doubt that it would not be he, but it would be she, particularly if she were a slave, who would be found at fault. In such a case I do not think any of her sisters in bondage would envy her. The seduction of such a fellow, I supposed, would count as a terrible offense, one perhaps endangering even the city itself. But perhaps he would leave the caste before it was too late, if it were not already too late, before, say, he took his final vows, or performed whatever act or acts it might be by means of which his entry into the caste might be effected. Perhaps, before he became much older, he would come to understand that there were two sexes, really, and that they are formed by nature, each in its own way, for the other. The caste of Initiates, incidentally, provides a socially acceptable refuge for men who may not wish, for one reason or another, to relate to women. It is probably a kindness for a society to provide mercies of this sort. This observation is not intended to reflect on the caste as a whole. It is my surmise, incidentally, that the great majority of Initiates, for better or for worse, abide by, and respect, the regulations of their caste.

The gaunt figure now lifted his grasping, crooked hands to the clouds. "Praise be to the Priest-Kings!" he again called.

"Praise be to the Priest-Kings," repeated the crowd, a low murmur.

"May the blessings of the Priest-Kings be upon you," said the gaunt figure.

"Praise be to the Priest-Kings," said again the crowd.

The gaunt figure then turned a little to his left, to the crowd on his left, and made a wide circling gesture with his right hand. This was done in such a manner that I gathered that something of profound importance was to be understood as taking place. He then faced the crowd before him, directly, and solemnly repeated this gesture. This circular gesture, it seems, reminiscent of the circle surmounting the staff, the symbol of eternity, was the "sign of the Priest-Kings." He was, in effect, blessing the crowd. I wondered if the Priest-Kings would be pleased to have such a fellow, and in such a manner, blessing crowds in their name. To be sure, why should they object? After all, what would it be to them?

The gaunt figure now turned to his right, toward my portion of the crowd.

"Head down, slave girl," whispered the man behind me.

Quickly I thrust my head down to the stones. It behooves a slave girl to be careful of whose eyes she meets, and how she meets them. We must be careful of looking too boldly into the eyes of our superiors, in particular, unknown free men or women. Brazenness can be cause for discipline. We do not wish to be punished. This is not to deny, of course, the expected and appropriate meetings of eyes in thousands of contexts and times, as in attempting to read one's fate in the eyes of the master, in examining them to learn if one is in favor or disfavor, in meeting them when commanded to do so, as when he examines us to see if we are lying, or when he wishes us to see the sternness in his eyes, that he is displeased, as in trying to read his will, that we may serve him better, as in looking up at him in rapture, squirming in his power, as in gazing into his eyes, on lonely beaches and in sheltered glades, with love. But if it can be dangerous for a slave to look too boldly into the eyes of a mere stranger, if such can invite a kick or a cuff, or even a whipping, imagine how wary one would be of meeting, and how one would fear to meet, the eyes of one such as the gaunt figure, the eyes of one seemingly unbalanced, eyes in which, it seemed, only too clearly blazed vanity, cruelty, and madness. I sensed, from the time involved, and from tiny movements, and adjustments, of those about, that the gaunt figure was now no longer facing us. He was through now, it seemed, with our part of the crowd. I lifted my head a little. He was again facing the center of the crowd.

"It is now time to demonstrate your gratitude to the Priest-Kings," said the gaunt figure.

"Perhaps that might be done by filling up the golden bowls," speculated a fellow, under his breath.

"Hush!" said a frightened free woman.

"The Priest-Kings love a generous giver," said the gaunt figure.

"Certainly the High Initiate does," said the fellow.

"Be quiet," said the woman, terrified.

Half of the twenty or so Initiates went then to the raiders, moving amongst them, holding up the golden bowls. I saw coins, and jewels, and jewelry dropped into the bowls. The other half of the Initiates then began to move amongst the crowd. The crowd, too, or, at least, many of its members, put coins, usually single coins, or coins of smaller denomination, in the bowls. These were fetched from purses, from wallets and pouches. Most Gorean garments, other than those of artisans, do not contain pockets.

One of the Initiates was then in our vicinity. I heard coins dropped among others.

The Initiate was careful to avoid me, and, indeed, even free women. They might, however, drop a coin into the proffered bowl from a gloved hand, touching neither the bowl nor the Initiate. There was no injunction, it seemed, against accepting such donations.

The man behind me put a coin in the golden bowl.

"You will see, I trust," said one of the fellows in the crowd, "that this coin is turned over to the Priest-Kings, and does not end up in the temple coffers."

"I did not know the Priest-Kings needed money," said another fellow.

"I wonder what they will buy with this," said another.

"Be quiet!" said the free woman.

The Initiate himself made no response to these remarks. He may not even have understood them. I did note that the fellows who were engaged in this raillery did, all of them, however, place their coins in the bowl. They were, I suspected, taking no chances. What if, for example, as an outside possibility, but one they were not willing to discount, there might be some mysterious connection between the Initiates and the Priest-Kings? Why not, then, put a coin in the bowl, particularly if it were not too valuable a coin? As far as I can determine, most people on this world do, in fact, believe in the existence of Priest-Kings. On the other hand, it seems, also, that they generally regard them as being very far away and not being very interested, if interested at all, in the affairs of human beings. In short, they do not dispute the existence of the Priest-Kings but do not, on the whole at least, depend upon them in any practical way.

The Initiates then reformed their double line and, bells ringing and smoke wafting about, fragrant, from the censer, took their way from the docking area. To be sure, there was at least one significant difference between the procession as it had arrived and the procession as it left. The twenty or so golden bowls which had come empty to the docking area were now leaving it heavy with coin, with jewels and jewelry. Certainly, of the raiders and the Initiates, it seemed the Initiates had had the safer, easier part of things. Indeed, to obtain their share of the riches, they had not even had to leave the safety of the city. Also, it had not even taken them a great deal of time, only a few minutes, really. To be sure, parties of this size, with the bars sounding and such, were presumably rare on the loading docks. For the most part the Initiates would have to make do with what they could obtain from other sources, such as the wages of workers. While not engaged in obtaining their livelihood from more productive elements in society, Initiates, as I understand it, spend a great deal of time in self-purification. In this, interestingly, the study of mathematics seems to be essentially involved. It is not only women, incidentally, which are forsworn by Initiates but also, interestingly, beans. I am unfamiliar with the historical origins of these matters.

"They are gone!" said a man, relievedly.

The presence of Initiates, I have noted, tends to have a somewhat depressing effect on most people. It is generally a relief when they have taken their way elsewhere. Most men of this world, it seems, would prefer that they confine themselves to the precincts of their temples. The uneasiness which many feel in the presence of the Initiates is that which, or is very similar to that which, I think, many feel in the presence of forces, explicit or implicit, which they sense are inimical to life.

The musicians in the crowd were now again striking up a tune. The hawkers were again at work, calling out the nature and virtues of their goods. I again rose to my feet.

I had come here for a specific reason, of course, not merely for the pleasure of participating in the celebration. With my purpose in mind I considered the lines of captives. I was sure that any one of several would do.

"Congratulations, lads!" a man called to the raiders.

Some, seeing him in the crowd, lifted their hand, waving to him.

"Apricots! Apricots!" called a vendor.

"Pastries!" called another. "Pastries!"

"Tastas!" called another. "Tastas!"

"Here is a tasta right here," said the fellow behind me, putting his hand in my hair, pulling my head back a little, holding me by it.

"Yes, Master," I laughed. "I am a tasta!"

He laughed, and released my hair. I remained standing, before him.

I heard a jangle of slave bells. A girl broke through the guards and ran to kneel before one of the raiders. "I am owned by Fabius!" she said. "Consider his tavern!" Her breasts were haltered in scarlet silk. She wore a long slave strip, some six inches in width, also of scarlet silk, secured by a cord, the strip put over the cord in front, taken between her legs, drawn up snugly behind and passed over the cord in back. The free ends of the strip, lovely, before and behind, were something like two feet in length. Her brand was the common kajira mark, the same as mine. Her wrists were braceleted behind her. On both her ankles there were slave bells, and slave bells, too, on her collar. She was, I took it, a tavern slave, a paga slave.

"Perhaps!" laughed the raider.

One of the guards then good-naturedly drew the slave away by the hair and threw her stumbling, with a jangle of slave bells, back into the crowd.

"No!" called another girl, from the side, kneeling, in brief purple silk, lifting small pinioned wrists. "The Golden Shackles! The Golden Shackles!"

I could smell her perfume from where I stood.

I touched my collar. It was a state collar. My work lay in the depths. These others were slaves, it seemed, of a quite different sort from me. Yet we were all slaves, and all owned, in effect, by men.

"Perhaps," called the raider.

Doubtless there were many establishments in the city, I thought, that would be only too willing to assist men such as these in the disbursement of their riches.

The treasure was now muchly assorted, muchly tallied. Already some of it was being carried to the warehouses.

I saw a tarn, now disburdened of its loot, surrendered by its rider into the care of a tarnkeeper, who would conduct it to its cot.

Water bags were visible near one of the warehouse doors.

Captives stirred in their chains.

Some of the crowd, now that bulk of the treasure had been exhibited, began to leave.

I wondered if some of the raiders might go this night alone to the temples, to place there a private offering, no Initiates about. They might stand there alone and give thanks to the world, or the fates, or the Priest-Kings, that they had returned. One controls so little, if anything, of one's own fate. The mystery exists. The Initiates, I suspect, understand it as little as anyone else. It is only, I think, that they pretend to do so. That is how they make their living, by the most demeaning and grievous of all lies.

But others, many others, I suspected, perhaps simpler men, or perhaps more intellectually insouciant or robust fellows, would conduct themselves otherwise, joyously frequenting the taverns, prowling the streets with torches, making loud the night, indulging in riotous thankfulness. They had returned, to laugh, to sing, to drink, to hold yet another slave in their arms. These would be neither the soldiers of Priest-Kings nor the foes of Priest-Kings. They would be rather fellows who had chosen to go their own way. They would respect the mystery, but would not much concern themselves with it. Enough to spill a few drops from the first cup, a libation, honoring Priest-Kings, or perhaps, in the name of Priest-Kings, for what is involved here may have many names, what might hold sway over both men and Priest-Kings, the fates, the mystery. Ask no more then of men such as these than that of which they might be held responsible, ask of them only the sternness of their will, the loyalty of their heart, the skill and readiness of their steel. These things they might pledge and give. As for the rest, let the fates, or the mystery, or whatever it might be, be as it would.

But still others, I supposed, might return quietly to their compartments, to be greeted there by their kneeling slave, to be feasted by her and then, later, in the light of the lamp of love, to recollect, and cherish her, in the furs.

Several of the other tarns, disburdened of loot, had also, now, been conducted from the docking area.

More people had now left.

The guards had relaxed their lines. Some individuals went now to greet personally the raiders. Then, some of the raiders, together with friends, left the area.

I saw the belled slave, she in the scarlet silk, leashed by one of the raiders. It was thusly she would lead him to the tavern of Fabius. He was taking no chances on her slipping away from him when he arrived there. The girl in purple silk was between two other raiders. Her small wrists were pinioned before her. They had her on a double leash. Sometimes superb slaves are sent forth to solicit for the taverns but then, when one arrives there, they hurry away, to find more customers. These two, however, on their leashes, would not be likely to do so. These two who solicited would, it seemed, also serve and, I suspected, profoundly. The taverners might not like this, the time, indeed, perhaps the entire night, of a skilled soliciting slave being spent in service, but I did not think they would object. Men such as these, once they have a girl on their leash, are seldom crossed with impunity. I saw some of the captives watching the two girls being led away, leashed. I wondered if they realized that such a fate might, in time, be in store for them.

I saw two officers beginning to examine the lines of captives. One had a grease pencil. They were followed by a scribe with a tablet, who made jottings as they proceeded down the line. Information pertaining to captives and slaves, their dispositions, and such, is sometimes marked on their bodies. The upper surface of the left breast is often used for this. The pertinent information, displayed in this manner, so conveniently and prominently, is easily read. The left breast is used, I assume, because most men are right-handed. A similar consideration may illuminate the general custom of branding on the left thigh. The brand, in such a location, is more ready to the hand of a right-handed master.

Some dock workers, three of them, were picking up water bags, those which had been placed near one of the warehouse doors. It seemed they would water the captives before they were marched to the pens. I did not doubt but what their flight had been a long and dry one. Too, it is interesting how watering a captive will improve her appearance. Probably they wanted them watered before marching them down the barred corridors. Wholesalers sometimes congregate outside such corridors, leading down into the pens, looking in through the bars, forming conjectures as to the value of the catch.

I stepped a little forward. The guards did not seem to care now.

I walked a bit down the line which would have marked the front of the crowd.

Two of the guards walked away, conversing among themselves.

"Here, slaves!" I heard a fellow call.

It was the vendor of apricots. Quickly I and some four or five others sped to him, to kneel at his feet. He was in an excellent humor. I gather his business had prospered this afternoon.

"Please, Master," we begged. "Please!"

He pointed to his feet, and we crowded, one against the other, to lick and kiss them.

"Up!" he said.

We straightened up.

"Here is one for you," he said, "and one for you, and one for you!"

"Thank you, Master!" we cried. Such things are precious to us.

"Shameless sluts!" cried a free woman, one of the captives, in one of the coffles. She had beautiful blond hair. She was probably vain of it. The officers and the scribe had already passed her point in the line.

I had received an apricot.

"Disgusting sluts!" cried the free captive.

"Please, Master," I cried, "another. Another!"

He looked at us.

"Please!" we wheedled. We almost rose from our knees, so eager we were.

"Very well," he said.

"Thank you, Master!" we cried.

And each of us received another! How generous he was! He took the last apricot for himself, gripped it between his teeth, and held the basket upside down, shaking it twice.

"Thank you, Master!" we called after him, as he left.

"He should have thrown the last one amongst you," said the free woman. "It would have been amusing to see you fight for it, you meaningless she-sleen."

"I wish he had," snapped one of our number, the largest, a broad-bodied girl in a coarse rep-cloth tunic. "I would have obtained it!" I supposed she might, indeed, have won the apricot in any such contest. Indeed, even if she had not won it, she might have taken it away from whoever had won it, unless, of course, the master had prevented it. To us she was quite fearsome, but to a man, of course, she would have been as only another female, to throw to his feet.

"Do not speak back to me!" snapped the free woman.

The broad-bodied girl went to stand near the free woman, looking down upon her. The free woman was kneeling in coffle. She was neck-chained. Her wrists were shackled behind her. Her ankles, too, were shackled.

"Down on your knees!" cried the free woman.

"It is you who are on your knees," said the broad-bodied girl. I sensed she had little affection for free women.

But why should she?

Why should any of us?

Free women were our enemies. They seldom neglected an opportunity to be cruel to us. We were so helpless. They were so imperiously grand in their freedom. We muchly feared them.

"Do not rise up, Lady!" said one of our number, kneeling to the side. "You will be lashed!"

"I, lashed?" she said, incredulously. But she did not rise up, despite the broad-bodied girl's provocation. Perhaps she recalled what had happened to the girl in the other line, the other captive, who had done that.

"Yes, you, lashed," said the broad-bodied girl.

"You have two pieces of fruit," said the free woman. "Give me one!"

"No," said the broad-bodied girl.

"'No'?" said the free woman, stunned.

"No," said the broad-bodied girl, taking a goodly bite from one of the apricots.

"I command you to do so!" said the free woman.

"You are shackled, and you have a chain on your neck," said the broad-bodied girl.

"I shall call one of the guards!" said the free woman. The power of free women, of course, rests ultimately on the might of men. In the end, though this is sometimes obscured by social arrangements, it is the men who are the masters. Were it not for men, free women would be as powerless as slave girls.

"Call them," said the broad-bodied girl, biting again into the apricot.

"Do not call them, I beg of you, Lady," said one of the girls, quickly. "They will beat you."

"I am not a slave," said the free woman.

"They will not mind accustoming you early to the whip," said another.

"Your time of ordering people about is over," said the broad-bodied girl.

"But you may, in some years, become a first girl in some household," suggested one of the slaves in the vicinity.

"Do you beg water?" inquired one of the dock workers of a woman some places earlier on the coffle. "I am to be addressed as 'Sir'."

"Yes!" she exclaimed.
"'Yes', what?" he asked.
"Yes—*Sir*," she said.
He looked down at her.
"Please," she said, "please, Sir. I am very thirsty. Please, Sir—Sir—Sir—Sir!"
"Put your head back and open your mouth," he said.

She then put her head back, and he inserted the spike of the water bag between her teeth. He watered her, briefly. She wanted more. It was not given to her. I saw her tongue try to obtain each last drop, each residual moistness, from about her lips. He then went to the next woman.

"Do you beg water?" he asked. "I am to be addressed as 'Sir'."

"Yes, Sir," she said. She was then watered.

She was watered more liberally than the other woman. She had doubtless learned from the other's experience. Her belly would be nicely rounded. A similar effect is obtained when a woman is wrist shackled and must pull the chain of the shackles back tightly against her waist. I had had to do this in the corridor of the pens, while kneeling, shortly after being ordered from the pitch-dark cell. It is "having one's belly beneath the chain." That is, of course, also a way in Gorean for referring to a girl's bondage. For example, "I am pleased to note that Lady So-and-So's belly is now beneath the chain." "Excellent! How long has her belly been beneath the chain?" and so on. A slaver's practice is often to put binding fiber, or binding leather, about a girl's waist, snugly, and tie her hands behind her back. This, of course, narrows her waist, rounds her belly, and contributes to the accentuation of the bosom. This is not really a slaver's "trick" because it is obvious what is being done. It is, however, attractive. Needless to say, a slave is never bound so tightly or cruelly that she might be injured. It would be stupid to damage her in such a way; as it would reduce her value. This does not mean, however, that she may not be bound tightly. It is useful for a slave to occasionally know herself absolutely helpless.

It would be not only the second woman who had profited from the experience of the first woman, but the first woman, as well. Given the next opportunity to beg water, I had no doubt she would do so as a needful, suitably deferent suppliant. Nor would she forget the word 'Sir'. To be sure, that expression of respect would doubtless soon be changed for another, one even more appropriate, and, indeed, required, for what she was soon to be.

"I must leave now," said the broad-bodied girl to the free woman.

The free woman, on her chain, in her shackles, looked up at her.

Suddenly the broad-bodied girl kicked her in the side and then, biting on the apricot, holding it in her mouth, took the free woman by the hair with both hands and jerked her head back and forth. The free woman cried out in misery, in pain.

The broad-bodied girl then took the apricot from her mouth and bit into it again.

The free woman looked wildly to the dock worker, a few women from her, for protection, for redress. But he, it seemed, had noticed nothing. Masters do not much interfere in the squabbles of slaves, you see, and, for most practical purposes, it seems that this was at least the sort of category in which the free woman now found herself included. She seemed aghast, stunned. She began to shake. She seemed then small, and helpless. We often live in fear, of course, of the strongest girls amongst us. None of us would have dared to interfere, even if we had been so inclined. And the free woman had been insolent. Let her begin to learn her manners.

"Do you beg water?" asked the dock worker of a nearer woman. "I am to be addressed as 'Sir'."

"Yes, Sir," said the woman.

She, too, had learned how to beg water.

"You," said the free woman, to one of the girls who had spoken kindly to her.

"Mistress?" asked the girl.

"Can such things be done to me?" she asked.

"Unless the masters prevent them," said the girl.

"I do not understand," said the free woman.

"Try to be pleasing to the masters," said the girl.

"Numbers," said the free woman, "have been inscribed on my body. What do they mean?"

"They are to be read by the pen masters," said the girl.

"What do they mean?" she asked.

"I suppose, Mistress," said the girl, "that they suggest an initial category for you, your possible disposition, and such."

"'Category', 'disposition'?" she asked.

"Yes, Mistress."

"What are they?" she asked.

"I do not know the meaning of the numbers, Mistress," said the girl.

"You are stupid!" said the free woman.

"Yes, Mistress," said the girl.

"Do you beg water?" asked the dock worker of a woman some four places before the free woman.

"Never, never!" she cried out.

He then went to the next woman in the line. "Do you beg water?" he asked. "I am to be addressed as 'Sir'."

"Yes, Sir," she said.

He then watered her, and proceeded on to the next woman in line.

In a moment, however, she who had refused to beg for water looked wildly over her shoulder.

"But I am thirsty!" she cried.

Some people, it seemed, learn more slowly than others. I wondered if she were less intelligent than several of the others. On the other hand, perhaps she had been testing a limit, and had now discovered where it was.

He paid her no attention.

In a moment, she cried out, "Yes, I beg water! Please, Sir! I beg water, Sir! I beg water, Sir!"

But he continued on his way.

"Please," she wept. "Please, Sir!"

But he paid her no attention. Perhaps she might later obtain water from a trough in the pens. In any event, she would not now be watered. In this incident I suspected she had learned a valuable lesson. Also, she was now doubtless better informed than before as to the nature of her new life.

If nothing else, she had learned that she was not different from the others.

"What are you waiting here for?" asked the free woman, angrily.

"Do you wish to hear me beg for water?"

"Yes, Mistress," said one of our number, she who had just been denounced as stupid, who was kneeling to the side. "We would like to hear you beg for water."

"Slut!" hissed the free woman.
"Yes, Mistress," said the girl.
"Go, all of you!" commanded the free woman.
"No, Mistress," smiled the girl.

It was a small enough vengeance, I supposed, for the insults which the free woman had recently addressed to us, for example, in the matter of the apricots. It was not wholly for such a purpose, however, that I was waiting there.

The free woman pulled in frustration at the shackles which confined her hands behind her back.

The fellow with the water bag had now arrived at the free woman's position, and we slaves, those still there, backed away a little. Those of us who were not already kneeling, and I was one, now knelt. We were in the presence of a free male. The free woman, though her primary attention was on the man with the water bag, from the corner of her eye, took note of our action, it seemed apprehensively.

"Sir!" she said.

"Have you requested permission to speak?" he asked. "No, Sir," she said.

"Then it seems you might consider doing so," he said. She looked up at him.

"May I speak?" she begged.

I supposed that this might be the first time in her life the free woman had ever begged permission to speak.

"You may, if you wish," he said, "speak two words." She looked up at him, puzzled.

"Do you beg water?" he said. "I am to be addressed as 'Sir'."

"Yes," she said, hesitantly, adding, "—*Sir*!"

These were, I gathered, the two words which she was to be permitted.

Two of our number laughed. It seemed she had begged well.

He had the water bag slung over his shoulder. With his left hand, it gripped in her hair, he bent her head back. He regarded her for a moment, for she was very beautiful, and she uttered a tiny whimper of protest, well aware of the display of her beauty and his casual regard thereof. Her long, lovely, blond hair fell behind her, even to her calves. He then with his right hand guided the spike of the water bag between her teeth. Gratefully, head back, she drank and sucked at the spike. It had been long, I conjectured, since she had had water. Water gushed from her mouth, some running over her chin and down the outside of her throat, even under the steel collar with the front and back chain on her neck, to course down her body. He pulled the spike away from her, still holding her head back, though I think she, tears in her eyes, would fain have been permitted more.

She whimpered again, as he had not released her hair. She closed her eyes, perhaps that her eyes not meet his. "There are numbers written on my body," she said. "Please tell me what they mean."

"Have you requested permission to speak?" he asked.

"No, Sir," she said.

"Perhaps you should consider doing so," he said.

"May I speak!" she begged. "May I speak!"

"No," he said.

He released her hair and she bent far over, sobbing, the better I assume to hide her body. But his hand in her hair straightened her up again. She was to remain kneeling upright, it seemed. He released her hair. She kept her back straight, regarded. Again her hands jerked futilely at the shackles. He then crouched down, beside her. She did not meet his eyes. There are many reasons for back-shackling, of course. The primary effects are custodial, psychological, utilitarian and aesthetic. The custodial effectiveness of the arrangement requires no comment. The psychological aspect of impressing the captive's helplessness upon her has already been mentioned. She is, for example, in this arrangement, unable to feed herself in any normal manner or to fend away those who might wish to touch or examine her. The utilitarian aspects of this arrangement are largely accounted for by the conveniences it affords the captor, for example, in facilitating examinations, inquiries, displays, leashings, chainings, and such. The aesthetic aspects, too, are obvious, for such ties, as is the case, for example, with the hands-over-the-head ties, have a tendency to call attention to, accentuate, and enhance certain aspects of a woman's beauty. Needless to say, these various aspects, and others, symbolic and otherwise, do not function independently of one another but tend, naturally enough, to function in such a manner that each deepens and strengthens the effects of the other. The dock worker, his examination completed, now rose to his feet, and went to the next woman in the coffle. "Do you beg water?" he said. "I am to be addressed as 'Sir'."

"Yes, Sir," she said.

As the free man continued down the line we rose to our feet.

"Girl," said the free woman to one of our number.

"Yes?" answered the one addressed.

"I am sorry I called you 'stupid,'" said the free woman.

"That is all right, *girl*," said the slave.

"*Girl*!" said the free woman.

"Certainly," said the slave. "Did you not see how you were looked at? You now, too, are only a 'girl.'"

"I am a free woman!" said the free woman.

The slave laughed. "Girl," she said, "*girl*!"

"I said that I was sorry," said the free woman. "I am hungry. Let me have part of one of your apricots!"

"Do you acknowledge that you are a girl?" asked the slave.

"—Yes," said the free woman.

"Do so," said the slave.

"I am a—a girl," said the free woman.

"A chained girl!" laughed another of the slaves.

"Yes," said the free woman. "I am a chained girl!"

"Only a chained girl!" said another of the slaves.

"Yes, yes," wept the free woman. "I am only a chained girl! I am only a chained *girl*! Now, please, please give me even a part of one of your apricots!"

"Why should we give anything so precious to one who is only a chained *girl*?" inquired one of the slaves.

The free woman cast her a glance of consternation.

"Command me," said the girl who had been first addressed by the free woman.

"Give me one of your apricots," said the free woman.

"No," said the girl.

"Please!" said the free woman.

"Beg your own," said the girl. She then turned away. I, and two others, then remained in the vicinity of the free woman.

"Please give me something to eat," said the free woman to the rest of us.

"You will be fed in the pens," said one of the girls.

"Probably some slave gruel," said another.

The free woman looked at them wildly.

"She has very pretty hair," said the first of the two other girls.

"I wonder if they will have it sheared," said the other.

"Would they do that?" asked the free woman, anxiously.

"They might," said the first girl.

"But, why?" asked the free woman, aghast. I gathered she was, indeed, fond of her hair.

"To make a wig for a free woman," speculated one.

"But I am a free woman!" said the free woman.

"They could even certify it honestly as the hair of a free woman, and then brand you a moment later."

"Brand me?" asked the free woman, weakly.

"Surely you do not expect not to be branded and collared?" said the second girl.

Most of the hairpieces, and wigs, and such, affected by free women are certified as being from the hair of free women. Most on the other hand, I am reasonably confident, are from the hair of slaves.

"They might also use it for catapult cordage," said one of the girls.

The free woman shuddered.

Anything, of course, could be done with her. She was now, for all practical purposes, though her body had not yet been marked, the property of masters.

I touched my own hair, nervously. I, too, of course, could be shorn. Some masters harvest the hair of their slaves every two or three years, understanding this, I suppose, as a part of the productivity of the slave. To be sure, most Gorean masters like long hair on their slaves, and pleasure slaves are seldom shorn, except as a punishment or discipline. Some girls do have their hair cropped, for example, such as might work in the factories, the laundries, and such. Too, girls transported in slave ships are commonly shaved completely, to protect them from vermin below decks. It is not unknown for shorter-haired slaves to ascend the blocks, slaves whose hair, for one reason or another, has been cut short, but they are the exception. Also, they are usually low girls, stable slaves, field slaves, kettle-and-mat girls and such.

"Farewell, *girl*," said one of the two slaves.

"Farewell, *girl*," said the other.

They then left.

I alone, of the original group, was now with the free woman.

That I had lingered would, I supposed, suggest to the free woman that I might have done so for a purpose. To be sure, this was true. But it was not for any purpose which she was likely to suppose.

The information I wished I could not well obtain from either a free person, without great risk, or, indeed, from a slave either, for they would presume that anything so obvious must either be known to me or for some reason forbidden to me. They would not wish to risk telling me what I wished to know. What if the masters should find out? Curiosity, I recalled, was supposedly not becoming in a kajira. Yet we are, I suspect, among the most inquisitive of creatures.

"You dally, slave," said the free woman.

I shrugged.

"Perhaps you enjoy seeing free women in coffle, stripped and shackled," she said.

"It is where they belong," I said.

"Had I my whip," she said, "I would make you rue that remark!"

"That would not make it less true," I said.

She cried out with rage.

"It is no longer yours to hold the whip," I said. "It is now in the hands of others."

She jerked at the shackles, angrily.

"Did you used to whip slaves?" I asked.

"Yes!" she said.

"It is now you who must fear the whip," I said.

She looked up at me.

"It is such that it may now be used upon you," I said. "It will be interesting to see how you like it."

She looked down. She shuddered. "I do not want to be whipped," she said.

"Please the masters," I said.

"They would not give me water, unless I said 'Sir' to them," she said, wonderingly.

"Yes," I said. That seemed like a small enough thing to me.

"I have never before in my life addressed men in such a way," she said.

"With respect?" I asked.

"Yes," she said. "I have strange feelings," she said, "when I address men in that fashion."

"Such feelings are natural," I said.

"But you do not address them as 'Sir'?"

"No," I said. "We address them as 'Master.'"

"I would be terrified to do that," she said, "how it might make me feel."

"You will learn to do it," I said. "And you will also learn that it is a quite meaningful mode of address. They are the masters."

"You are a barbarian!" she said.

"Yes," I said. "I am a barbarian."

"It is thusly fitting that you should be a slave!" she said.

"But not such as you?" I asked.

"No, no!" she said.

"Why?" I asked. "Are you less female than I?"

She looked at me, wildly.

"You have fought your femaleness for a long time," I said. "But the masters will not permit your continuing to do so."

She shook with terror.

"For the first time in your life," I said, "you are going to become a full woman, a true woman, the woman you were born to be."

"No!" she protested.

"What is important here," I said, "has nothing whatsoever to do with one's origins. They may condition and flavor our slavery, and make us of more or less interest to one man or another, but they are, in themselves, of no great importance. What is crucial here is not whether one is a barbarian or not, or comes from this city or that, but what we have in common, whether one is a female or not. That is what is of ultimate importance in these matters, our sex, our femaleness."

She jerked in the chains, helplessly.

She put her head down. She sobbed.

Then she looked up at me. There were tears in her eyes. "But then it would be fitting," she whispered, "that we both be slaves."

"Yes," I said.

"Do you understand the numbers written on my body?" she asked, looking up at me.

"You want to know your category, your future brand, your likely disposition, your period of training, a possible place and time of sale, such things?" I asked.

"Yes!" she said. "Yes!"

"I did not even know they were numbers," I said, lightly.

"You are illiterate?" she said, suddenly, angrily.

"Yes," I said.

"Why have you dallied here!" she said.

"Perhaps to give you an apricot," I said.

"Give it to me!" she said.

"No," I said. I wanted one for myself. The other I thought I would give to the Lady Constanzia.

"So that is why you have remained here!" she said. "Not to feed me, not to help me, unknown to the others, in fear of me, or seeking my favor, but, like them, to torment me!"

"I think you are little to be feared now, free woman," I said. "And, if I were you, I do not think I would overrate the favors you have to dispense. Even men will take from you precisely what they please, and in any amounts or modalities they wish, and at any time of the day or night. And you will strive desperately with all your beauty and intelligence to please them."

"You want only to torment me, like the others," she said.

"You were not really very nice to them," I said.

"But they are nothing, only slaves, and I am a free woman!" she said.

"You, too, will soon be nothing," I said, "only a slave."

She looked up at me, angrily.

"And you, too, will learn to fear free women," I said. "You will learn to fear them terribly."

"Is this your petty vengeance on a free woman," she asked, angrily, "you illiterate, stupid, sleek, embonded, collared little she-urt?"

"I do not think I am smaller than you," I said.

"It is you who are stupid," I said.

"I, you illiterate, collared she-urt?"

"You were brought here hooded," I said. "You do not even know in what city you are."

"I am not stupid," she said. "It is you who are stupid, if you think I do not know where I am!"

"Oh?" I said.

"It is you who are stupid, not me," she said. "Anyone would know where he was, here in this place. Do you think I do not know in what mountains I am? Do you think I cannot tell the coloration of the Voltai, the Scarlet Mountains? Do you think I am totally unaware of the distances and times I have traveled? Do you think I cannot recognize the accents of the men who brought me here? Do you think I cannot understand the emblems and accouterments of the men of this place? Do you think the markings on the tarn saddles are in some foreign tongue? Do you think the songs of the crowd are unintelligible to me? Do you not think I can recognize the seven towers of war, the wall of Valens, the standards on the bridge behind us, the banners about, those that fly even from the warehouses themselves?"

"I do not know," I said.

"I am in Treve!" she cried. "I am in Treve!"

I smiled.

"You tricked me!" she cried.

"Yes," I said.

But my triumph was short-lived, for at that very moment two strong masculine hands closed on my upper arms, from behind. "Do you think it is nice to trick a free woman, tasta?" he asked. It was the voice of he who had been behind me in the crowd.

"No, Master," I said. "Forgive me, Master!"

"Her manner changes quickly," observed the free woman.

"I wondered why you were dallying here," he said.

"Forgive me, Master," I said.

"What a slave she is," said the free woman.

"What was it you wanted to know?" he asked.

"In what city I wear my collar, Master," I said.

"So small and simple a thing?" he asked.

"Yes, Master," I said.

"It seems you might have found that out in a thousand ways," he said.

"I am illiterate, Master," I said. "It is not so easy."

"Why didn't you ask me?" he asked.

"Would Master have told me?" I asked.

"No," he said. "And then I would have beaten you, and then bound you and wired a note to your collar, testifying to your indiscretion."

"Yes, Master," I said, in misery.

"But it is now too late for such things," he said, "for you have tricked a free woman and have now learned in what city you are."

"Forgive me, Master," I begged.

"Close your eyes," he said.

"Yes, Master," I said.

"You have discomfited this free woman," he said.

"Forgive me, Master," I said, frightened, my eyelids pressed shut.

"You are now going to kick and squeak before this free woman," he said.

"Master!" I moaned.

He spun me about. "Oh!" I cried, as I was lifted from my feet.

I heard the free woman gasp.

"Oh!" I cried, again.

"Excellent little tasta," he said.

"Master?" I said. "Master?"

I heard some men laugh, doubtless passers-by.

But then, in moments, my feet off the ground, my arms and legs clutched about him, I began to gasp. Then, a little later, he lowered me to the ground and, mercifully, bundled my head in his cloak, only then permitting me to open my eyes. I could see the darkness inside the cloak, and sometimes, as I was turned toward the sun, the coloring of it, red, and light through the tiny openings in the weaving. And then, shortly thereafter, as he took me again from myself, as men can, and mastered me, I began to kick and squeak.

After a time he was through with me.

"Close your eyes," he said.

"Yes, Master," I said.

He then removed his cloak from about my head.

"The free woman," he said, "will tell you when I am gone. Only then may you open your eyes."

"Yes, Master," I said, lying on the stones of the docking area, my body a medley of sensations, physical and psychological, of confusion, humiliation, fear, and rapture.

"When you return to your kennel tonight," he said, "you are to tell your keeper what you have done today."

"Please, no, Master!" I begged, my eyes pressed shut. "Yes, Master," I said, in misery.

I lay on the stones.

"He is gone," whispered the free woman, after a time.

I opened my eyes, and rose to all fours, and looked at the free woman.

"Are you going to tell your master, or keeper?" she asked.

"Yes, Mistress," I said.

There would be inordinate risks in not doing so.

"Surely you will be whipped, at least," she said.

"Yes, Mistress," I said.

"But you will tell, anyway?"

"Yes, Mistress." Surely she must understand the ease with which the matter could be brought to the attention of the authorities. The simplest, most casual, check could determine whether or not I had complied. I did not know, of course, whether or not that check would be made. But it could be made, tonight, or tomorrow, or months from now. I would not care for it to be made and have its result not in my interest. It might be the difference between a lashing and being thrown to sleen.

"How helpless you are, as a slave," she marveled.

"Yes, Mistress," I said. I knelt.

"What is it like to be so helpless, so vulnerable, so subjugated, so dominated?" she asked.

"Doubtless Mistress will learn," I said, softly.

"Men are such powerful brutes," she said. "Why will they not compromise with us, and do what we tell them?"

"It is we who are slaves who must do as we are told," I said.

"I may be made a slave," she said.

"Mistress may be assured of it," I said.

"Then what was done to you could be done to me," she said. "I would have to obey!"

"Yes, Mistress," I said.

"Men could use me, *me*, a free woman—"

"Once a free woman," I said.

"—to satisfy their terrible, ferocious lusts!"

"Be pleased," I said, "that on this world men are so free, so healthy, so strong. Here their lusts have not been reduced to tepidities."

"I would have to serve!" she said.

"Wholly," I said.

"I would be branded, and collared!" she said.
"Yes," I said.
"It is so different from being a free woman!"
"Yes," I said.
"Then I would have to vulnerably answer to their lusts," she said.
"And how else," I asked, "could your own needs be satisfied?"
She looked at me.
"I do not refer to the tamenesses, the banalities, the lukewarmnesses," I said. "I do not refer to the tepidities. I refer to perilous heights and formidable depths. I refer to matters of force and power, of storms and fire, of songs and blood, of shouting and crying, of laughter and tears, of realities, of victories, of dominance and submission, of owner and owned, of master and slave, of the joy of absolute and uncompromising conquest and the rapture of utter, unconditional surrender."
"I have dreamed of such things," she said.
"So, too," said I, "has every woman."
"I would have no choice," she said.
"No," I said. "You would be only a slave."
"I could learn," she said, "to lick and kiss for a candy."
"Or an apricot?" I smiled.
"Yes," she said.
"You will learn just how precious such small things may become," I said.
"I am sorry that I called out so cruelly to the slaves," she said.
"You yourself will doubtless discover, in time," I said, "what it is to be insulted by, and abused by, and even whipped by, free women."
"I did not understand," she said.
"It is hard to understand, if one is not in the collar," I said.
"Don't go!" she said.
"I must be getting back," I said.
"I awakened in my bed," she said, "as I was being gagged. I could not cry out. It was a young, blond raider of Treve who captured me. I was stripped and bound, and put to his pleasure, in my own bed! Then he hooded me and carried me to the roof where his tarn was waiting. Later I served him nude in his camp, as though I might be a slave. I knelt, serving him his food. I poured his wine."

"And how did you feel about this?" I asked.

I saw she was struggling to speak. Then she whispered, "I loved it!"

I nodded.

"But this distressed me," she said, "that I should have such feelings!"

"Yes?" I said.

"So I was insolent—"

"What occurred then?" I asked.

"He seized me and swathed my entire upper body with coarse rope," she said. "He then put me to his pleasure, briefly and brutally. He then swathed my whole lower body with similar rope. He then left me that way for the night! I wept and begged his forgiveness toward morning, but it earned me only a kick and a warning to be silent. Then, the next day, he put me on the common chain. Afterwards I would cry out to him that I hated him, and then, a little later, I would beg him to keep me!"

"I understand," I said.

"You cannot read the numbers on my body, truly, can you?" she asked.

"No," I said. "I am sorry."

"What kind of slave do you think I will be?" she asked.

"That is easy to see," I said.

"What?" she asked.

"You have beautiful hair," I said. "And your body and face, too, are very beautiful."

"Do you think they will see me as a pleasure slave?" she asked.

"Certainly," I said.

"That is the sort of slave I wish to be," she said.

"Have no fear," I said. "It is in that category that you will ascend the block."

"But I want to belong to he who captured me," she said.

"It is not yours to say to whom you will belong," I said.

She regarded me, in misery.

"Anything could be done to you," I said. "You could be taken anywhere. You could be sold to anyone."

"No!" she said.

"Yes," I said.

"I thought he liked me!" she said.

"That is quite likely," I said, "as he had you serve him in the camp."

"What did I do wrong?" she said.

"It seems," I said, "from what you have said, that you were unpleasant, or insolent. Perhaps you showed him a side of your personality which he did not care for."

She looked at me.

"To be sure," I said, "such things can be whipped out of a slave."

She moaned.

"He may not have wanted to spend the time and effort on you, to reform you," I speculated. "There are, after all, many slaves."

"I can change," she said. "I want to change!"

I regarded her.

"It was not truly I who spoke," she said. "It was not the slave."

"I understand," I said.

"But why would he not want me?" she asked. "Do I not have lovely hair, am I not beautiful?"

"Such things are mere externals," I said. "They are easily come by, in any market."

"I do not understand," she said.

"You have a very superficial notion of what it is that men are buying in a slave."

"I do not understand," she said.

"And what of your personality, your character, your disposition?" I asked.

"I do not understand," she said.

"Do you think men are idiots?" I asked. "Do you think they are satisfied with mere externals?"

"I do not know," she said.

"No," I said. "They own whole slaves."

"Do they not regard us as mere things, as mere objects?" she asked.

"Do you think they would be satisfied for a moment with something that looked like a woman, and moved and talked like a woman, but had no insides, had no feelings, no consciousness?"

"No," she said.

"If they did regard women as mere objects," I said, "it would make no difference to them whether they were dealing with such a simulacrum or a woman. But that is absurd."

"Yes," she said.

"I must go," I said.

"Will I ever see him again?" she begged.

"I do not know," I said.

"What can I do?" she asked.

"There is little you can do," I said. "The shackles and chain are upon you."

I rose. I could see the dock workers preparing to move out the lines of captives.

"What is it like to be a slave?" she cried.

"Much depends on the master," I said.

"I know who I want to belong to!" she wept.

"But who will buy you?" I asked.

She put back her head in misery, the chains moving on the collar.

"Present yourself well on the block," I said. "In that way you should bring a higher price, and thus obtain a more affluent master."

She moaned.

I looked about on the stones, for the two apricots. I seized them up. I split one and pitted it. I slipped the pit into the hem of my tunic. I would dispose of it later in an appropriate receptacle. One does not just cast such things about in such a place, particularly if one is a slave. The men of this world tend to be particular about their cities. In them, it seems, there are Home Stones. "Here!" I said. I placed the pitted fruit on the stones before her. She looked down at it. "Take it," I said. "It has been pitted. You need not fear the disposal of the seed. In time, you will learn to beg your own."

She looked up at me.

"It is nothing," I said.

"Thank you," she said.

"I wish you well, slave girl," I said.

"I wish you well, Mistress," she said.

"Hurry," I said.

I backed away. I saw her put down her head and bite at the fruit.

"Hurry," I whispered.

I heard a whip crack, several yards away. I jerked back, wincing, frightened. It is a very frightening sound. It is particularly frightening when one understands something of what the whip can do to one.

The first line of captives was now on its feet.

I saw the free woman with whom I had entertained converse lift her head.

Again the whip cracked.

The second line of captives was now on its feet.

"Your first step will be taken with the left foot," they were informed by a worker. "You will keep your eyes fixed forward. You will not look to the right or to the left."

At the whip's suggestion the third, and then the fourth, and then the fifth, and then the sixth, rose to its feet.

I hurried away.

The whip cracked again, and the seventh line rose. The free woman was in that line.

"Your first step is taken with the left foot," I heard. "You will keep your eyes fixed forward. You will not look to the right or to the left."

I thought it would be more merciful if they hooded the women.

Again and again the whip cracked, as line after line of the captives, with a rattle of chains and shackles, rose to its feet.

I moved back by the doors of the warehouses.

Now all the lines were on their feet.

Workers with whips coursed the lines, snarling, adjusting posture, lifting chins with whips. Whips cracked, and more than one lash was laid upon a startled beauty who then strove zealously, instantaneously, to be found acceptable. In more than one case the very lash which had struck a captive was pressed to her lips that she must fervently kiss it in gratitude.

"Straighten your bodies!" "Suck in your guts!" "Put your shoulders back!" "More!" "Lift your chins!" "Higher!"

The lines were inspected.

They now stood well.

The captives must be beautiful. They must not dishonor the city in which they had the honor to be chained.

There was the barking of orders.

Again the whip cracked.

The lines then began to leave the docking area, in order, beginning with the line farthest to my right.

I picked out the free woman from the lines. She did not look back. She, like the others, kept her eyes fixed forward—absolutely. Woe betide the captive who might glance as little as an iota to the left or right.

How much more merciful, I thought, if they would just hood the women. It is hard to be blindfolded by, gagged by, or bound by, the "Master's will." In being "blindfolded by the Master's will" one must keep one's eyes closed. I had, just shortly before, been so "blindfolded." In being "gagged by the Master's will," one may not speak, even to request permission to speak. In being "bound by the Master's will," one must keep one's limbs in the prescribed position, as though they were actually so bound, or so metal-clasped, or chained. There are several familiar versions of this. In one the slave crosses her wrists before her body and must retain the position until freed by "the Master's will." In another she kneels, her head down, and clasps her hands behind her back. If she is right-handed, she clasps her right wrist with her left hand. If she is left-handed, she clasps her left wrist with her right hand. Another common version of this sort of "binding" is to put the slave on her belly and have her cross her wrists and her ankles. It is thus as though she were bound hand and foot. She remains this way, as in all these cases, perhaps for hours, until she is freed "by the Master's will." A very unpleasant application of this technique is to put a slave in the sun and spread-eagle her "by the Master's will." One then smears her face, and body, and hair, with honey and leaves her there, her presence being soon noted by a large variety of unpleasant insects. This is, of course, a punishment. After such a bout with thousands of tiny, swarming, crawling visitors, sometimes almost obscuring her, the slave is much improved. The more merciful master, of course, literally stakes the slave out, binding her wrists and ankles widely apart, to the four stakes, before applying the honey. In either case, the girl will be much improved. Even the threat of this sort of punishment, it might be noted, is likely to be effective. And this saves a good deal of unpleasantness all around, and some honey, as well. To be sure, for the threat to be effective, the girl must understand quite clearly, and will understand quite clearly, that the threat is not an idle one. If she entertains any doubts on that score, the master will see to it that they are soon satisfied.

It was workers, not guards, I noted, who prowled the lines, whip in hand. It seemed those of this city, in these remote, isolated precincts, did not fear the theft of these curvaceous prizes. How secure they think themselves, I thought.

The lines would be marched through the city to the pens. I doubted that they would be far. I supposed the captives in their march must endure scrutiny from men, and abuse from free women. Too, children can be very cruel, running out with switches, pelting them with pebbles, and such. This is not prevented for these captives are, in a sense, women of the enemy, and, in any event, will soon become mere slaves.

I looked about the docking area, now empty.

I had never seen the face of the fellow who had stood behind me in the crowd, and who had grasped me by the arms, from behind, after I had tricked the free woman. In the crowd he had been behind me; I had feared to look upon him directly, for he was a free man; later, near the line, again behind me, he had ordered me to keep my eyes closed; then later he had bundled his cloak about my head; then I had later again been ordered to keep my eyes closed, until he had withdrawn. I reddened, looking back to where he had hoisted me upon him, and then, later, put me down to the stones, the cloak wrapped about my head. Yes, I had been well punished. I had been put to his purposes under the very eyes of the free woman. Worse, he had not chosen to be merciful with me. He had made me display myself before her as the helpless slave I could be made to be. Yes, he had made me kick and squeak before her! To what a sweet spectacle she had been treated! But did she also, I wondered, look on in awe and fear, watching me not only kick and squeak, but moan, and wriggle, and writhe, and clutch at him, a spasmodic thrall, a mastered slave, considering that, in some other time and place, it might be she herself who would find herself so responding, so gasping, so eager, so pleading, so helpless, so mastered, in the arms of a man? I had been well used. And tonight I must confess what I had done in the matter of the free woman to the pit master, how I had tricked her, how I had obtained information which my superiors, for whatever reason, had not seen fit to vouchsafe to me. I shuddered. But I had no rational alternative. The failure to confess might mean far worse punishment, perhaps even my death. I would throw myself on my belly before him, kissing his feet, a terrified, contrite slave, begging for mercy. I looked about. The fellow who had put me to his purposes, in whose arms I had been little more than a spasmodic doll, leaping to his touch, could recognize me. I could not, of course, recognize him. This gave him much the advantage over me. I might look into the eyes of many a man, I thought, and not know if he were the one or not. I might look into the eyes of many a man, I thought, wondering if he were the one in whose arms I had leaped so obediently, in whose arms I had been so had. I then quickly hurried back over the bridge to the terrace, to fetch the Lady Constanzia.

I clutched the second apricot. I would give it to the Lady Constanzia. I did not doubt but what she would be deeply appreciative. Such tidbits, such things as a fresh apricot, are rare in the depths, even in the diet of a free woman. I would feed it to her by hand, little by little, as she knelt there, back-braceleted, by the wall, chained to a slave ring. This would contribute to her disguise. Also, of course, as she was a free woman, it would please me to have her take it in this fashion.

Twenty

Tonight the pit master had come with me to the cell of the peasant. Sometimes I thought the prisoner might be dead. He was so still. But then he would open his eyes.

"Greetings, Master," I would say to him, for he was a free man. Then I would attend to my duties in the cell. Later I would return to the quarters of the pit master. I had never again attempted to taunt him, as I had once.

The pit master, tonight, sat for a time, cross-legged, before the peasant. It was almost as though they were both warriors. Neither spoke.

"I am finished, Master," I whispered to the pit master, as I had concluded my duties in the cell.

He rose to his feet.

The peasant looked up at the pit master. "Is it time," he asked, "to do the planting?"

"No," said the pit master. "No."

We then left the cell.

Twenty One

"I am a free woman," said the Lady Constanzia.
"Of course," I said.
We were in the Lady Constanzia's cell. She had eaten, and I was preparing to leave the cell.
She was wearing the brief, white, sliplike garment, of which she was fond. It was not unlike a slave tunic.
"But I want to be a true woman!"
"Dismiss the matter from your mind," I said.
"But what if the free woman is not the same as the true woman?" she asked.
"Obviously it is not," I said.
"I am in anguish," she said.
"Do not concern yourself with such matters," I advised her.
"I must!" she wept.
"The free woman is a political concept," I said, "with a particular political history, relevant to a particular time and place. The true woman is a biological concept, relative to a species, its nature, and the conditions germane to its fulfillment."
"I have been free," she said. "Now I want love."
"Put such thoughts from your mind," I said.
"But I am afraid of love," she wept.
"Of course," I said.
"It makes slaves of us!" she wept.
"Yes," I said.
"Janice," she said.
"Yes," I said.

"I want to be a slave!" she whispered.

"Dismiss the thought from your mind," I said.

"Today," she said, "when we were above, when he came to the ring, I spread my knees before him!"

"You must not do so!" I said. "You are a free woman!"

"Do you think not being branded, not being collared, makes me a free woman?" she asked.

I did not respond.

"Do you think not being legally embonded, in some technical sense, makes me a free woman?"

"Yes," I said.

"I love him!" she said. "I love him!"

"You do not even know him," I said.

"We have talked for days at the ring!" she said. "He cannot even look at me without my wanting to cry out for his touch!"

"It is the slave garb," I said, "the collar."

"In them I am myself!" she said.

"You are a free woman," I said.

"No!" she said.

"Yes," I said. "Hasten now, and don the robes of concealment. The guard will soon be about!"

"No!" she said.

"Very well," I said. "Then I shall not take you again to the surface."

"No, no!" she said. "Please, forgive me, Janice. I am sorry. Forgive me! I will obey! I will obey!" Hurriedly then she put on the robes of concealment.

I then left the cell.

I locked it with special care. I was pleased the guard did not have the key, for I feared that the cell door now was no longer closed on a free woman, but on something considerably more desirable, something considerably more tempting.

Twenty Two

"Master?" I asked.

The pit master, of late, had seemed much lost in thought. Seldom now he read at the table.

Fina, too, his preferred slave, was much concerned.

She was not now present.

I did not know what produced this change in the pit master. Some days ago I had, as I had intended, confessed my trickery with the free woman. I had bellied, cowering, at his feet. But he had only crouched down beside me, and put his great hand on my head, and shaken it a little, almost affectionately. "So, now," he said, "you know you are in Treve?"

"Yes, Master," I whispered.

"Kajirae are such curious creatures," he said.

"Am I not to be beaten?" I asked.

"No," he said.

"Thank you, Master," I said. My good fortune in this matter, I suspected, might have less to do with my deserts than with the preoccupations of the pit master.

Let me speak for a moment of the pit master.

As I had come to know him better, I had come to realize he had a large, deep, unusual mind. I am sure Fina was well aware of this, as well, and it was probably one of the reasons she was so much his slave, so to speak, though hers was a state collar, like mine. I think that we, women, although not immune to male beauty, are less seriously influenced by it than men, the brutes, by female beauty. Indeed, a pretty male face can be aversive to us. The masculinity that attracts us, and can overwhelm us, is one of intelligence, power and virility, one of ruggedness and might. We are looking, so to speak, for our harem master, although we would hope to be the only slave in his harem. We want a man at whose feet we feel it is appropriate that we should kneel, as women, and slaves. We do not want an equal; that is not enough for us; we want more than that; we want a master. We want him to be strong, ambitious, aggressive, possessive, jealous, lustful, dangerous, dominant. We want him to guard us, and protect us, and own us, with masculine ferocity, to see us as his rightful properties. We want to feel ourselves as though we were nothing before his wrath and power. We want to feel that it is the most important thing in the world for us that we please him. We want him to be jealous of us, and fiercely possessive of us; we want to be important to him; we do not want to be ignored or neglected; we do not want to be taken for granted, or just be "there," perhaps almost unnoticed, as are so many "wives" of Earth; the slave, I assure you, receives a great deal of attention, perhaps more than she sometimes cares for; she, in her service, and subject to his command and domination, is muchly noticed; one of the cruelest of punishments he can inflict upon us is to subject us to the same neglect and indifference commonly accorded to an Earth "wife"; how we strive to be pleasing to him, that that will not occur; but it seldom occurs; better the mercy of the slave lash; he must want to keep track of us, for we are his possessions; he must want to know our thoughts, our whereabouts, and our every action. He desires us; he lusts for us; and we are his; and so he is jealous of us and inordinately possessive of us, his relished goods, his coveted prizes, his properties, his slaves; and so he keeps us on a short leash. The pit master, despite the monstrosity of his appearance, was mighty in his manhood. We slaves were helpless in his arms. When I clutched him I must despair of the least shred of dignity. In the arms of such a man a girl is muchly aware that she is in her collar and will shortly find herself subdued, and forced to yield herself wholly, spasmodically, helplessly, whether she wishes to or not, in the most degrading and wondrously joyful of all ecstasies, those of a slave to a master. Beyond, however, the gloriously humiliating, reductive, exultant, grateful, exalting, writhing submissions of a begging slave, Fina, I was sure, was actually enamored of him. She was not simply his obedient ecstasy slut. She was enamored of him, and he of her. But I do not think he knew her feelings toward him. And I do not think he would have believed her, if she had found the courage to declare them. Given his misshapen bulk, its gross disproportions, and his monstrous visage he did not believe any woman could love him. One other feature of the pit master I should mention. His mind was not only large, deep, and unusual, but it was also an independent mind. He thought for himself. How few men and women of Earth, I thought, did that. Is not acquiescence superior to inquiry? Is not cowardice, rather than simple discretion, the better part of valor? Is not conformity to prescribed falsehood less perilous than the seeking of truth? In any event, with respect to the enforcement of commands, customs, and such, the pit master was selective. He was neither legalistic nor rule-bound, but, too, he was neither antinomian nor iconoclastic. He would neither agree to be the same, as most, nor disagree merely to be different, as some.

He would think for himself; he was such a man.

And so, for whatever reason—whether he had understood and been forgiving of a slave's desperate concern to discover in what city she served, whether he had been tolerant of an Earth-girl slave's naive foolishness, whether he was fond in his rough way of her, and thought he would this time excuse her indiscretion, whether he had simply seen no point in punishing me, whether he thought the whole business beneath his attention, or perhaps simply, as I suspected, because he had other things to attend to, which more concerned him—he had not beaten me. I was grateful to him. I did not think him weak. If in his view I had truly merited a lashing, then, even if he were fond of me, as I suspected, I would have received it, and so, too, would have Fina, or any of the others.

The pit master, as we have noted, had not been zealous in enforcing the edicts of the officer, he to whose compartments I had earlier been conducted, he whom I had served, he before whom I had danced, he who had several times made slave use of me, he at the side of whose couch, on the floor, on the tiles, with only a sheet to cover me, my head to its foot, I had been slept in a chain.

Certainly he had been lax in enforcing the officer's instructions in the matter of the mysterious peasant, that huge, vacant creature in the lower cells. He had not regarded such treatment as honorable. In not complying, however, I did not doubt but what he had betrayed oaths, or even codes. "What is one to do?" he had once said in the corridor.

"Master?" I had asked. "It is nothing," he had said. He had then continued on.

"Have you spoken of this to the Lady Constanzia?" he asked.

"No, Master," I said.

"Do not do so," he said.

"Yes, Master," I said, gratefully.

"How is she?" he asked.

"Well," I had said, "Master."

"Good," he had said.

"Master," I said.

"Yes?" he said.

"Is anything wrong?"

"No," he said.

"I am sure Fina would be happy to please you," I said.

"And you?" he asked.

"I, too," I said.

"You need not look upon my face," he said.

"No, Master," I said. "Thank you, Master."

"Go to your kennel, and close the gate," he said, kindly.

I kissed the massive, swollen cheek of the pit master. I did this very gently. Then I stripped and went to the kennel, for we are to be nude within them.

I wrapped the blanket about me, and, from the inside, drew shut the gate.

It locked automatically.

I watched him sit there on the bench by the table, his head in his hands.

Then, after a time, I fell asleep.

Twenty Three

"It is precisely here that you will stay!" laughed the Lady Constanzia.

"Yes, Mistress," I said, irritably.

I knelt by the same slave ring to which I had often fastened her.

My head, by the neck, was pulled back close to the ring. The leash was wound about the ring in such a way as to hold me tightly back against it.

"That will do for the moment!" said the Lady Constanzia.

I could not pull away from the ring.

"She is pretty, isn't she?" said the Lady Constanzia, turning to the fellow with her, the stranger in the city, he who had come again and again to visit her, at this very ring.

"Quite," said he, approvingly.

I was dressed precisely as she had been in our first outings, in the rags I had selected for her, those which I had specially selected, in my slave girl's vengeance on a free woman, to display her as a low slave. I had wished her to burn with shame and humiliation in them but she had loved them. Now it was I who wore them! I, though I was an actual slave, doubtless because I recollected my own intent, felt the very shame and humiliation which I had intended for her, but which she, infuriatingly, had simply refused to feel. I do not think I would have thought much about the garmenture if it had not been for the significance involved, from my point of view, at least. But, you see, there was a principle of sorts involved here. That was what was maddening about the whole thing. It was not so much the fact that I was muchly exposed, for I have worn slave strips, and less, and slaves grow used to such things, and may even revel in them brazenly, as the fact that I was now revealingly clad in the very way I had once intended for her to be revealingly clad. "Is that too tight?" she had asked, as I had knelt, back-braceleted, in the depths. "Yes!" I had said. She had then made it tighter. Then she said, "Suck in your belly." She knotted the rag about my waist. "How is that?" she asked. "Too tight," I said. "Oh!" I said. She had jerked the knot yet more tight. She had then leaped up and clapped her hands, admiring her handiwork. "You are pretty, Janice!" she said. She bent down, and kissed me. Then she leashed me. "Come along," she said, eagerly. "We must go above."

I now looked up at her, irritably, I kneeling at the ring, my head back against the metal.

It is not comfortable, having one's head back in that fashion.

A great change had come over the Lady Constanzia, as you may have gathered, in the last few days. The current reversal of our typical situation had come about in two ways. First, the pit master had been well aware, it seems, and far more so than I had realized, of my little games with the Lady Constanzia, the frequent imposition of my slave girl's vengeances upon her, a free woman. Indeed, he seemed far more aware of such things than the Lady Constanzia herself, or, at least, rather more inclined to object to them, for in her case it seemed that the more she was treated as a slave, the better she liked it. But was she not a free woman? Was she not, thus, entitled to more respect than I had accorded her? And had I not been, in my way, an insolent slave girl? In any event, this morning, he had decided that it was I who would be leashed, and garbed precisely as I had, earlier, chosen to garb her. Second, it had to do with the change which had been taking place in the Lady Constanzia over the past few days. I had, on the whole, refused to recognize that change, but it had been clear enough to the pit master. We had become, it seemed, less a free woman and a slave, as I viewed us, than two slaves. And, if that was so, why should it be I who would be always permitted to act as her arrogant superior, when there was, in effect, little, if anything, to choose between us. Did my insolence not need a corrective? Might I not profit from a lesson? Very well. Today, it would be I who would wear the leash. As you can see, the matter was quite paradoxical. On the one hand, as the Lady Constanzia was at least technically a free woman, might I not be reprimanded for having subjected her to certain indignities, my little slave girl's vengeances on a free woman? And, on the other hand, paradoxically, as she was now little other than a slave, might not I, a mere slave, be reprimanded for having treated her in such a way as to suggest that she might be less than I? In any event, today, it would be I who would be leashed.

"But she may escape, Master!" I had said.

"Do you think there is an escape for you?" he had asked.

"For me, Master?" I asked.

"Yes," he said.

"No, Master," I said.

"Why is there no escape for you?" he asked.

"Because I am a slave girl, Master," I said.

"Lady Constanzia," he said.

"Yes?" she said.

"You wear a single garment, a slave tunic, and are collared," he said. "Do you think there is an escape for you?"

"No," she said.

"Why not?" he asked.

"Because," she said, "I am as a slave girl."

"Today," he had said, "it is you who will hold the leash."

"As you wish," she had said, puzzled, startled, "—Master."

Oh, yes, I think there was a lesson involved, but I think, too, that the pit master had thought the whole thing rather amusing. It was not that he did not like me. Indeed, I think he was quite fond of me. It was, rather, I think, that he had been somewhat irritated with, or, at least, had entertained certain reservations with respect to, my treatment of the Lady Constanzia and, indeed, of the "slave," Tuta. His punishment of me then, it seems, would be this little joke. Had I been a bit arrogant, a bit vain? Then let me be reminded that anything could be done to me, and that I was only a slave. Does a slave require to be humbled? Men such as those on this world are skilled in doing so. Quickly they bring us to our knees. Quickly they remind us of our collars.

"Now," said the Lady Constanzia, regarding me, "let us do what we discussed."

The fellow with her drew forth from his pouch a lock gag. I had worn one only once, in training.

I pressed my head back, against the stone of the wall. I could not pull away from the slave ring, as I was leashed closely to it.

I made a tiny noise of protest as the leather pad, a part of the device, was thrust in my mouth. In a moment, with small adjustments, the entire device, of leather and metal, was fitted to me. It was then locked shut. I looked up at them, reproachfully.

The curved metal bars, well back between the teeth, where they cannot be slipped, holding the wadding in place, close behind the back of the neck. To these same bars, in front, is attached the binding. This binding is of thick, supple leather; it fits snugly, closely, to the contours of a girl's face and mouth; it had been drawn back, tight, on me; that is the way such things are worn; on the outside it is covered with hinged metal plates. It also, like the curving bars, goes behind the back of the neck. The whole then, the wadding bar, anchored deeply behind the teeth, holding the wadding in place, and the binding, with its protective plates, is secured with a single-thrust lock. That had now been done.

I looked up at them.

How pleased was the Lady Constanzia!

The heavy wadding, or packing, was in my mouth, attached to the bar between my teeth. The binding was fastened tightly about my face; I could hardly move my lips within it; I tried to speak but could not, of course, even begin to do so.

They seemed amused.

I knelt there; I was well silenced; I was quite helpless.

I was in lock gag.

One of the advantages of the lock gag is that the girl cannot remove it, any more than a collar. She may thus serve in it with her hands free. To be sure, if the girl is disciplined, such a device is not necessary. An ordinary gag, which she is forbidden to touch, will suffice. Indeed, she may be simply "gagged by the master's will," and thus be forbidden to speak, even to beg permission to speak. There are various utilities of lock gags, which we need not note. One might observe, however, that they are occasionally useful with free female captives or even hysterical slaves. One utility which should be noted, particularly as I suspect that it may have been of interest to the Lady Constanzia and the fellow with her, is that, as the gag, with its plates and such, cannot be removed without a key or tool, it cannot be, say, conveniently undone, or cut away, by anyone who might wish to make inquiries of the captive or slave. A free man, thus, could not easily inquire of me, until the gag had been undone, the whereabouts of, say, a pretty slave and a fellow not of the city, a stranger, one clad in scarlet.

The Lady Constanzia, now that I was gagged, loosened the leash at the ring, so that my head was no longer bound back tightly to the ring. I might now sit at the ring, or kneel near it, or even lie beneath it.

"Do not go away, Janice," she said. "I love you!" She then kissed me and arose, and beamed down on me, she with her hand on the arm of the scarlet-clad fellow. "We are going to have a wonderful day in the city!" she said. "We are going to go everywhere! We are going to see everything! We are going to eat! I will bring you back something, if he permits me."

I looked up at them.

"It would be nice if you could come along," she said, "only that that would not really be nice. I want to be alone with him. We would rather be together, *alone*. You understand."

She then kissed her finger tips and touched the side of my face.

"You will stay here now, and wait for us, won't you, Janice?" she said.

I looked up at her.

Then I shrank back, for I saw a sudden sternness in the eyes of the male.

Swiftly I whimpered once, in affirmation. I knew the signals. Had my response been quick enough? I saw him draw back his hand.

"No, do not strike her!" cried the Lady Constanzia. "She is my friend!"

He then, angrily, took the Lady Constanzia by the hair and bent her backwards, exhibiting the bow of her beauty. She winced, crying out with pain. "Master will do, of course, as he pleases!" she cried. "Forgive me, Master! But I beg you not to hurt her, for she is my friend." He released her hair and she knelt before him and seized his leg, looking up at him. "Please do not hurt her," she begged.

He looked at me. "Do you beg forgiveness?" he asked.

Quickly I whimpered once, and put my head down to the stones.

"And you," he asked, addressing himself to the Lady Constanzia, "do you beg forgiveness?"

"Yes, Master," she said.

When I looked up, I saw her kissing his feet. This startled me, as it was the first time I had seen the Lady Constanzia at a man's feet thusly. How fervently, how humbly, how submissively, she kissed his feet! Did she think he was her master? Did she not recollect that she was a free woman? How like a slave she looked at his feet, how like a beautiful, submissive slave!

"You are both forgiven," he said.

"Thank you, Master!" breathed the Lady Constanzia. He then turned about.

She leaped to her feet, to run beside him.

"Do you not know how to heel a man?" he asked.

Instantly she knelt.

"You need whip-training," he said.

"I would," she said, softly, "that you were my master, and would whip-train me!"

"What?" he asked.

"Nothing, Master," she whispered.

"Is there no word as to when you will be put up for sale?" he asked.

"No, Master," she whispered.

His eyes clouded. I doubted that he could long remain in the city.

Then he said, "Let us enjoy the day."

She leaped up, and kept her distance, waiting for him to turn about, that she might heel him.

He put out his hand to her, gently. "You may heel me another day," he said. "Today, come, walk with me."

Eagerly then, happily then, she took his arm. He seemed tall and stalwart, she, beside him, so small, so soft, so lovely.

They then began to cross the terrace, together, she looking up at him, her hand on his arm.

Few paid them any attention. They might have been merely a master and his slave.

I knelt at the ring and watched them go.

The lock gag was not really uncomfortable. It had, of course, been put on me tightly, effectively. The fellow apparently knew how to do such things. It had not been put on me cruelly, then, nor in such a way as to hurt me. It had been put on me in the usual way such a device is put on a slave—not cruelly, nor in such a way as to hurt her, but simply with a snug, tight, perfect efficiency.

I had worn one once before, in the pens.

It was the same.

To be sure there are few things that so convince a woman of her helplessness than to be gagged. The blindfold is another such device, of course. Imagine the helplessness, dear reader, should there ever be such, of this account, of being gagged and blindfolded, *and bound*. You might then have some sense as to what it might be to be in the power of others, to be as a slave.

Such terrors are not that unusual in a slave. They are useful in her control and domination.

I was muchly bared. I wore two rags. By means of one of these my breasts were haltered high. The other, skirtlike, open on the left, was tied about my waist. My wrists were braceleted behind me. I was chained by the neck to the slave ring.

I watched the scarlet-clad figure and the Lady Constanzia growing smaller, across the terrace. She was exquisite, and, in the past days, had become extremely feminine. It was as though she was discovering herself, and blossoming. She had been learning that men and women were not the same, but extremely different. They are not identicals, but complements. Each sex can be fulfilled only in so far as it becomes true, and honestly and fully true, to its own self. I wondered if the pit master knew what he was doing, letting the Lady Constanzia go free in the city. I watched her figure, tiny now, across the terrace. She wore a brief, modest slave tunic. It was her only garment. It had no nether closure. I did not think that the scarlet-clad figure, who seemed a man of honor, as seem most Gorean males, would take advantage of the lovely, slavelike creature. Indeed, I suspected that it might be he and not she who would be forced to impose fierce constraints upon himself. I suspected that it might be he who would be forced to resist the pleas, and offerings, of a woman who, it seemed, at his feet, could be only a slave. I trusted the Lady Constanzia, you see, less than I did him. He was, I thought, the sort of man who would not, without permission, make use of another's slave. Could he resist the love in her eyes, I wondered, the trembling of her body, so ready for the collar? He might have to cry out with rage, and cuff her from him, or spurn her away, she sobbing, with his foot. In any event, I was pleased that she had had slave wine. But what did I know of these things? Perhaps it was his plan to abduct her, as a slave bauble. Perhaps she would find herself gagged and bound, and held tightly in a closed slave sack. But could he get her out of the city? I doubted it. This was no ordinary city. But would they try to run away together? Was that their plan? What would be the case when we did not return to the depths at the proper time, the fifteenth bar? Was this the meaning of the lock gag, that I might be found here after curfew, and even then would be unable, until the gag was removed, to furnish information? But I did not think they would try to escape. He would surely realize the control of the tarns, the surveillance, the dangers of the mountains. It did not seem likely that any, alone, could survive in them. And if he cared for her, would he risk her, even in an abduction? The quarrels of pursuers might slay her as easily as him. But did she wish, herself, to elude him, and attempt to escape? I did not think so. She was no longer as naive as she had been. Surely she now understood the meaning of her skimpy garment, the significance of the collar on her neck. She had acknowledged to the pit master this morning that she was "as a slave girl." She would know then that there could be no escape for such as she. But an even stronger chain held her, I thought, the growth of her softness, of her femininity, of her desire to serve, of her need for love, the dawning of her very self-consciousness, the coming to understand what she truly was, should be, and wanted. Wherever she was, she would now understand what she was. She had come to understand that she was the sort of woman whose it was to ascend the slave block, humbly, barefoot, and stand there, and be bid upon.

At the very edge of the terrace, the Lady Constanzia turned about and waved to me.

I nodded my head to them. I did not know if they were able to detect the movement, at the distance.

Then they had disappeared.

It was still morning. I looked up at the sun. It would not yet be the ninth bar. The tenth bar signifies the tenth Ahn, or noon. There are twenty Ahn in the day.

I sat back against the wall.

I pretended not to notice as men, passing by, regarded me. Men think nothing on this world of scrutinizing slaves.

Toward noon another slave was chained to a nearby ring, but, an Ahn or so later, her master returned for her and I watched her leave, heeling him. She had excellent legs.

It was now rather warm and so I decided to lie down, at the wall, under the ring, and sleep. The sunlight was red through my closed eyelids. Then I turned to my side, my back to the wall.

I thought of the Lady Constanzia and the scarlet-clad stranger.

In a little while I fell asleep.

Twenty Four

It can not be so late, I thought, the bar ringing so many times, I have not slept that long. Look, the sun is still high. It can be no more than late afternoon!

I saw two men running across the terrace, robes fluttering behind them.

Far off I saw a woman in the robes of concealment rushing away.

I saw a fellow by the balustrade pointing outward, toward the mountains. "Look!" he was crying. "Look!"

I suddenly became aware that the bars were those of alarm, ringing incessantly.

The pad of the lock gag was in my mouth. The curved metal bars were like a bit between my teeth.

I rose to my knees. Then I rose to my feet. I could stand at the ring, as the leash permitted it.

I could hear other bars, too, now, about in the city.

"There!" cried the fellow by the balustrade.

I went to the end of the chain. I stood up on my tiptoes. I even pulled the ring up.

I could see, now, over the balustrade, a line of tarns, perhaps some twenty or so, knifing their way toward some part of the city, to my right, beyond the bridge, beyond the docking area.

They are not of this city, I thought. They are strangers! It is a raid! They have come through the defenses!

I, standing, watched them.

They seemed placid enough, so far away, moving swiftly, in single file, toward the right, toward some other part of the city.

Perhaps they had moved in stages, by night, coming closer and closer to the city, concealing themselves by day in ravines, now, at this time of day, making their dash toward the city. They might have three Ahn until darkness. That was quite possibly the time they had allotted for their work. Then they would doubtless attempt to withdraw, their work done, whatever it might be, under the cover of darkness.

Then I turned and backed toward the wall, in a rattle of chain, for a gigantic shadow, frightening me, fleeting and wild, had been cast upon the wall. It was a tarnsman of the city, hurrying forth, overhead, to intercept the raiders. Behind him there came two more. One of the tarns screamed. It is an incredibly loud, frightening, piercing sound. It rang from the wall.

What could twenty men, or so, do against a city?

The line of tarns in the distance had now disappeared.

Surely it could be only a token raid, a response, a reprisal, at best.

A line of guardsmen hurried across the terrace.

Some men now emerged from buildings. Some made their way over to the balustrade. Others crossed the bridge, toward the docking area. Whatever was going on did not, it seemed, concern this part of the city. I saw even the robes of a free woman coming out onto the terrace.

Some more tarns, from the city, hastened by, overhead.

The bars continued to sound.

"What is it?" cried a man.

"Strangers! Tarnsmen!" he heard.

"A raid," said another.

"Whence?" asked a man.

"Who knows?" said another.

"How many?" asked one.

"Not many," said a man.

"Twenty, thirty," said another.

"So few?" said a fellow. "They must be mad!"

"They cannot be interested in the city," said another.

"There must be a tarn caravan approaching the city!"

"It would have its escort," said a man.

"There are none scheduled," said another, one with the sleeves of a blue robe rolled up.

"What could they want?" asked a man.

"Women?" suggested a man.

I backed away a bit toward the wall. We, I knew, to men such as those on this world, did count as booty, obedient, trainable, well-curved booty. We learned to serve our masters well. And, indeed, women such as I, slaves, as we were domestic animals, constituted booty in a most uncontroversial, immediate and obvious sense, a form of booty as taken for granted here, as, on another world, cattle to Huns, horses to Indians. To be sure, we were not the only sort of animal which counted as booty. Many other sorts would have, as well, even the mighty tarns. And, as I have indicated, we are not specially privileged. Here, on this world, even the free woman counts as booty.

"What was their direction?" asked another.

"There!" said a man, pointing.

"That is it," said a man, convinced.

"The pens!" said a fellow.

"Yes," said another.

"But it is madness," said another. "The pens are guarded."

"They must be mad," said another.

"Look!" said a fellow. "There come our lads!"

"Are they ours?" asked a man.

"See the banners!" said another.

I stood up, again, on my tiptoes, to look, between the men. There must have been nearly a hundred tarnsmen now in flight.

Only too obviously were they on the trail of the earlier party.

"Those poor sleen," said a fellow. "They will be cut to pieces."

Though none seemed to notice me, I thought it best to kneel. There were, after all, free men present.

"They can stop the bars," said a fellow.

"No," said another. "Let the city stay alert."

"It may even be over by now," said a man.

This seemed to me possible, particularly if the strangers had reached the pens. They would be, I assumed, well secured, well defended. Too, tarnsmen and guardsmen from about the city had doubtless rendezvoused at that point by now. But moments ago I had seen tarnsmen even from this part of the city hurrying in that direction.

"We may as well go home now," said a man.

"But why would so few men try to reach the city?" asked a fellow. "And why, so few in number, would they strike at the pens?"

"They are mad," said a fellow.

"Drunk," suggested another.

A man looked down at me, and I quickly lowered my head, that I not meet his eyes.

"It is over now," said a fellow.

"We do not know," said a fellow. "There may still be fighting."

"There were less than fifty, surely," said a man.

"I think it would be over," said another.

At about that time the bars began to diminish, first one stopping sounding, and then another.

"Yes," said a fellow. "It is over now."

They began then, wishing one another well, separating the one from the other, to take their diverse ways from the terrace.

I lifted my head.

It was still bright, still late afternoon.

I wondered if, elsewhere, some skirmish was done, some steel reddened.

It was a strange feeling, being where I was, where it seemed so quiet, the sky so blue and calm, the clouds moving overhead, unhurried, knowing that not far away some terrible action might be ensuant, perhaps at the pens. But the bars had stopped sounding. It was done then. It was over.

I sat back against the wall.

I wondered where the Lady Constanzia and the scarlet-clad fellow might be. One supposed they might have taken cover with the sounding of the bars. Or perhaps she had been braceleted while he went to investigate, perhaps one bracelet put about her left wrist, the other about the linkage of a stout fence, or perhaps she had been knelt before a stanchion, her wrists braceleted about it.

Some folks were strolling now on the terrace. I closed my eyes, against the heat, the sun.

"Look!" I heard. It was a man's voice. It came from somewhere in the vicinity of the balustrade.

I opened my eyes and stood up, by the ring. I looked in the direction in which he was pointing, out, over the balustrade. Several others, too, were looking. Some of these were near the balustrade. Others had turned about, from where they were on the terrace.

"Look!" he cried again.

I could now see, in the distance, that to which he must have reference. It was another flight of tarns. They seemed tiny, so far away. It was difficult to judge their number.

"Tarns!" said another fellow, now, too, pointing. Two more men ran to the balustrade.

The tarns seemed larger now. They must be coming very rapidly, I thought. It seemed clear that there were more tarns in this group than in the first group, perhaps considerably more, but by how much the numbers of this group might exceed those of the first group it would be very difficult to say, that for two reasons, their formation and orientation. They were in single-file, like the first group, but they were not moving to the right, as had the first group, an orientation that had made possible a fairly exact estimate of their numbers. Rather, this time, in file, they seemed to be moving directly toward us. If one had not been looking at an exact point in the sky one might not even have noticed them. Too, they seemed at a fairly low altitude, approaching parallel to the ground. They might not be more than a few yards height above the walls. At times they were difficult to detect for the mountains behind them.

"They're coming this way!" said a fellow.

"Go," said a man to a free woman. "Leave! Get indoors! Get off the terrace!"

I saw a child, with a ball, running toward the balustrade.

"Run!" said a man.

"There is no danger!" said a fellow. "The bars are not sounding!"

"They have to be our lads!" said another. "It is a second pursuit!"

"Disperse! Disperse!" said a guardsman, near the balustrade. "Move! Move!"

The flight did indeed seem to be approaching with great rapidity.

"Go!" said the guardsman. He actually pushed a fellow. That is seldom done with free persons.

If the approaching riders had banners they had not yet unfurled them. To be sure, this is normally done only when recognition is practical, or important. It might be mentioned, too, that the unfurled banner, at high speeds, is difficult to manage. It requires a strong man under such conditions to keep it from being whipped from its boot. It also, because of drag, reduces airspeed. Too, obviously, it handicaps its bearer in combat. His compensation is the banner guard, usually four of his fellows whose duty it is to protect him and the ensign. Actual instructions in flight are usually auditory rather than visual. They tend to be transmitted not by banners, or standards, or even pennons, but by tarn drums, trumpets, and such. Even riderless birds, as I understand it, will often respond to these signals, the charge, the wheel to one attitude or another, the ascent, the dive, the retreat, and such. In measured flight, tarn drums may also supply the cadence for the wing beat.

"Go!" said the guardsman.

"The bars aren't sounding!" protested a man.

"Go!" cried the guardsman.

I saw a woman turn about and began to hurry from the terrace.

"There!" said a man. "See! The banners! The banners of Treve!"

There was a cheer from those on the terrace.

Still the flight proceeded toward us.

"Run!" screamed the guardsman. "Run!"

"No!" cried a man.

"Look!" cried another.

"See the banners!" cried another.

"Run!" screamed the guardsman. "Run!"

Suddenly, overhead, only yards above us, there was a terrible sound of screaming tarns, and a blasting storm of wings. I heard a terrible scream of a tarn and saw one of its wings cut from its body by the almost invisible, swaying tarnwire. I saw another great bird tangled in it, tearing at it, bloodily. Another had thrust its talons about the wire and was wrenching it about. Two birds thrust through the wire, darting within its interstices. The terrace was filled with screaming, running people. There was a mass of color and robes. On the terrace the tarn which had lost its wing was screaming and flopping about. Another tarn broke through the wire. I then saw some five men, suspended from a rope, lowered from a hovering tarn, descend to the terrace. The guardsman who had been at the balustrade rushed toward them. I backed against the wall, to which I was chained. Even so, I was buffeted by people fleeing, seeking the edge of the wall. Some fled over the bridge. Some fled toward the steps at the end of the terrace. I saw more tarns darting through the wire, guided by a fellow, still mounted on his tarn, on the terrace. Some other men were running toward the posts supporting the wire. Another fellow, suspended from the saddle, the tarn hovering, was cutting at the wire with a two-handled tool. Other riders soared overhead casting down wired weights to drag at the wire, perhaps to pull it down, perhaps to increase its tautness, rendering it more vulnerable to stress. I saw one of the tarns on the terrace seize a fellow in its beak, and then half of him was cast to the side. Another tarn had four men grasped in its talons. Its head seemed alert, lifted, its eyes wickedly bright, scanning to the left and right. There must have been some fifty intruders now on the terrace, some in the saddle, others dismounted. I could see more tarns coming over the mountains. Doubtless they would be directed in, through the gaps in the wire. Then I saw, too, shimmering, the descent of a network of wire, it cut from the posts by the men who had scaled them. I saw a woman showered with blood from the mutilated tarn. Its rider, now dismounted, drew his sword, and, with one stroke, cut its throat. The woman fled. I heard orders being issued. I did not know the accents. Save for the intruders the terrace was now mostly empty. Those who had been here, who had managed the matter, had fled. But there were, in many places on the terrace, crumpled forms. I saw the ball which had been the child's rolling in the wind across the terrace. The guardsman who had cried out at the balustrade lay in blood only a few yards from me. Beside him lay two of the intruders. I became vaguely aware, now, that the bars were again sounding. The defenses of this part of the city, I gathered, had been drawn away, to defend the pens. But surely the alarm was now once again out. Surely it could be only a matter of minutes before a defense could be mustered. I smelled smoke. But what if the tarnsmen of Treve, those in the vicinity, were in pursuit of the first flight? What if it had drawn them away? Could they hear the alarm bars behind them, in the city? Could they be recalled? Could a messenger catch up with them? How much time would it take to do so, and then return? And would the officers of the pursuit return to the city? Their priorities might be otherwise. The pursuit of intruders, I knew, was tenacious, relentless. It would be important to the pursuit that the secret of the city be kept. Any who knew it might later be a guide to thousands. However many had slipped into the city might, in accord with some sober military calculus, be left for later. In a sense, were they not now isolated, trapped? There must be tarnsmen left in the city, though. Surely there must be! I was sure, too, there would be numerous guardsmen, spearmen, bowmen. Did they know where the intruders were? It was perhaps two Ahn until darkness. There were now several of the intruders, some mounted, others not, on the terrace. I would have guessed their number at some one hundred and fifty men. One fellow seemed to be in command. He seemed to be issuing orders, fiercely, impatiently, but I could not hear them. I saw several men, in squads, rush away. Some of these squads went into buildings, adjoining the terrace. One went toward the stairway, across the terrace. Another turned about, toward me. I lay down at the foot of the wall, my knees drawn up, terrified, looking down at the stones. They sped past me. When I looked up, I realized the one party had gone to seal off the stairway, and the other, that which had run past me, perhaps without even really seeing me, had gone to the bridge. These were the two principal access points to the terrace. To be sure, it could doubtless be reached in some other fashions, through narrow passageways, over the balustrade from below, descending from adjacent roofs, perhaps through certain buildings.

On the terrace, now discarded, lying among bodies, I saw some of the banners of this city, which had been displayed during the approach to the city. Too, here and there, on the stones, occasionally glinting in the oblique rays of the lowering sun, strands of it, like lengths and tangles of metallic webbing, was tarnwire.

To me this incursion seemed madness.

Surely there were less than two hundred men here.

Obviously they could not take the city.

I saw one of the intruders light a torch. He hurried into an adjacent building. Two others followed him. What could be the purpose of these men here? I had just seen the fellow with a torch enter a building. Indeed, I had smelled smoke, earlier. Certainly fires must have been started. But I did not think they could burn the city, not unless they were prepared, in effect, except perhaps for certain districts, to enter and torch it, building by building. And many Gorean dwellings are not easy of access. In many the only access is in virtue of bridges which are often high above the ground level, bridges which may be easily defended, even destroyed. Whereas the buildings, and towers, might be burned out, it would be practical, on the whole, to do it only from the inside. This was not a place which might be destroyed by a single lamp, brushed by a sleeve from a table, or by the focused rays of a lens, poised over straw, waiting for the sun.

But if they could not take the city, nor destroy it, what was their purpose in coming here?

It must be gold, I thought, or women.

To my left I saw one of the raiders dragging a free woman toward the center of the terrace. Her hood and veils had been disarrayed. His hand was in her hair. He threw her to her knees in the vicinity of the officer. I then saw another raider conducting another free woman forth. Her hood and veils were also disarrayed. She was bent over. She hurried beside him, as she could, his left hand in her hair, her head held down, at his hip. It is a common leading position for female slaves. In the pens I had often been conducted from one place to another in that fashion. It is painful. His right hand held a drawn sword. It was bloodied. This woman, too, was put to her knees near the officer.

Yes, I thought, they are after women, and gold!

But the two women were not stripped. They were not bound, or chained. I did not see them being tied over saddles, or to saddle rings. There seemed no cage baskets with the raiders. I saw no plate, or candelabra, no vessels of silver or gold, being brought forth. Had it not yet been fetched?

And how would these goods, these loots, of precious metal, of soft flesh, of unusual fabrics, of rare spices, be transported whence these intruders derived?

Did they think this would be easy?

At any time the men of Treve might fall upon them!

What an irrational and improbable wager they lay with the fates of the mountains and steel! What an abuse of economic realities was here enacted! Were the odds of defeat so difficult to calculate? Was it so hard to judge of the speed of birds, the distance to safety, the numbers of the pursuit, the determination of the pursuers? What could they hope to obtain here that might render them willing to accept risks so irrational? One man had conjectured that they might be drunk but the bravado of a drunken spree might suffice for the scaling of a wall or the storming of a gate but it would not carry men for days across mountains, hiding by day, moving by night. Then it must be, I thought, as another had conjectured, they must be mad, the whole of them, the several of them, together, they must all be mad. Was a woman or two, a sack of plate, a handful of gems, worth their lives? Did they value their lives so lightly? It must be that, I thought, they must all be mad.

Across the terrace, now, to my left, as I now knelt, my back to the wall, I saw some people being herded out, onto the terrace, from one of the buildings. There were perhaps thirty or forty of them. They were being brought to the center of the terrace, where the officer held forth. They were put in a circle, on their knees, huddling there, crowded together. The two women who had been brought forth earlier were now among them. Men with swords drawn stood about.

But they could not be mad, I thought, not so many.

The women in the group were still clothed.

Surely they would remove their clothing and assess them, and secure those of most interest, those destined then, could they but reach safety, for the pens, and the block.

But they were still clothed.

I saw a fellow drawn forth from the huddled group and thrown before the officer, or commander, of the intruders. Then, a moment later I, shrinking back against the wall, aghast, saw him put to the sword. Then another was drawn forth, he, too, suffering, after a moment, the same fate. There were cries of misery from the huddled group. It surged, uneasily. Intruders at its periphery tensed, swords raised, to strike down the first who might leap up, who might try to run.

I then, to my horror, saw a woman pulled forth from the group. It was a woman! She, too, in a moment, was put to the sword.

I pulled at the bracelets on my wrists. I only hurt myself. Such devices, close-fitting, obdurate, restrain us, with perfection. I pulled against the leash collar with the side of my neck, but it was close about my neck, then above the kajira collar. The linkage of the chain clinked, the ring creaked, pulled up, straightened, from the wall. Then, held as securely as before, as helplessly, I sank back to my knees, in misery. The chain was then slack, dropping down from the back of the leash collar, looping up to the ring.

I saw a slave girl fleeing from one of the buildings. She ran, erratically, like a frightened, confused animal, here and there, on the terrace. She avoided the intruders. She fled toward the bridge. She must have seen men there. She turned back. She started toward the stairway across the terrace, but, in a moment, stopped. There were men there, too. She fled then to the balustrade and crouched down by it, trembling, making herself small. But she was not pursued. I did not understand it. None came after her, with a rope or chain, or even a loop of fine wire. Her legs, I had thought, had been excellent. She had certainly seemed worthy, I would have thought, of interest. It seemed likely that she would, in a neck chain, on a block, obedient to the instructions of an auctioneer's whip, have stimulated spirited bidding. But she crouched by the balustrade now, trembling, neglected.

I saw another man drawn out of the group. He, too, in a moment, was put to the sword.

A shadow moved swiftly across the terrace. I looked up, wildly. It was a tarnsman, aflight, undoubtedly a warrior of the city! The intruders, too, looked upward. Had there been doubt as to their location in the city, which seemed doubtful, it had now been dispelled. Surely guardsmen of the city must have formed by now. And so, too, would have warriors quartered within the walls, though the accustomed precincts of their duty lay not within the city itself. The guardsmen, the warriors, either, would surely far outnumber the intruders. Why did the intruders not fly? Did they not realize the danger in which they stood?

I saw another man put to the sword, then another woman.

I saw two more slave girls flee out of a building. They, too, like she before them, saw nowhere to run. One, a redhead, ran to the wall to throw herself to her belly there, under a slave ring. She covered her head with her hands. She was some twenty yards to my left. The other, a blonde, finally fled to the balustrade to join the other girl there. The drop from the terrace to the next level, below, at the balustrade, was more than a hundred feet. None of the intruders showed interest in the slaves. Yet all, like most in this city, which seemed to have its pick of slaves, were clearly of high quality.

I saw another man drawn out of the group and put to the sword.

This must be some mad form of reprisal, I thought, pulling these people out, butchering them.

Had such a thing been done by the men of Treve in their city?

Perhaps.

But I did not think it likely. The motivations of the men of Treve, as I understood them, were predominantly economic. I did not think they would be above pillaging and burning, but I would not have expected them to behave in this fashion. In particular I would not have expected them to put women to the sword. Women, from the point of view of the men of Treve, and from the point of view of most of the men on this world, as I understand it, are to be seen in terms of other purposes.

Another man was put to the sword.

But if it were mere massacre that was upon the mind of these men, if simple butchery was their intent, why did they not fall upon the huddled, kneeling group as a whole? Why did they not, in some two dozen fierce, merciless strokes, make the terrace run red with blood? Indeed, why had they bothered to bring them forth, here, to the terrace? Why had they not slaughtered them before, in the very vestibules, in the corridors, on the stairways of the buildings themselves?

I saw then another group brought forth from a building. It was smaller than the first group. Perhaps it had been cut off in one of the buildings, a rear entrance sealed. With this group, of some twenty or thirty individuals, including some children, I glimpsed the bared legs and arms of some tunicked slaves, at least five or six of them. The tunics of two, at least, were of silk. These women, these slaves, though animals, were being herded along, shoulder to shoulder, frightened, with the free individuals.

I heard swordplay, from my left, and about the corner of the wall. Some defenders of the city, it seemed, doubtless come across the docking area, were now engaged in contest for the bridge leading to the terrace. It was some fifteen feet in width. I could not see what was occurring. I could hear the clash of metal.

In a moment the sounds were ended. I waited, expectantly, to see fleeing intruders, or triumphant guardsmen, stream onto the terrace. But there was nothing. The challenge then, it seemed, had been repelled. There had not been enough men to force the bridge.

The new group of prisoners had now been flung among the others.

The sun was lower now, over the mountains.

There were cries of misery as another fellow was dragged out of the group and, before the commander of the intruders, put to the sword.

Men among the intruders looked up, tensely, at the skies.

The commander, impatiently, angrily, swept his arm toward the wall. The slave girls in the group, those who could do so, rose to their feet, unsteadily. Others were jerked to their feet by intruders, storming among the kneeling figures. An order was barked. In two cases a blow was delivered. The slaves hurried from the group, to come to the wall, where they knelt, or lay, or crouched down, terrified. They had been separated out from the free individuals. I noted, startled, the brunette, long-haired, her legs muchly bared in brief scarlet silk, in a golden collar, who had been among the first to flee to the wall. She now lay near me, under the first slave ring to my left. She seemed half in shock. She was looking down at the stones, frightened, her legs drawn up. I do not think she knew me. The scarlet silk informed me, and all who might look upon her, that she was to be understood as a pleasure slave. In her ears were large golden rings. They said much about her, what she was, and how men were to view her, and what they were entitled to expect of her, everything, and such. She, like myself, was a pierced-ear girl. Her golden collar, if not the rings, suggested that her master was rich, and, indeed, he was. I knew him. The slave who lay beside me, not even realizing it, was she who belonged to the officer, he whom I had served recently in his compartments. She was the slave I had met long ago on the surface of one of the towers, she whose name was "Dorna." Like myself, she was now only a pierced-ear girl. To be sure, she had silk, and a golden collar.

Smoke was now emanating from three of the buildings bordering the terrace.

A free woman was seized by the hand, and drawn forward, out of the group, to be flung on her knees before the officer. I saw her look wildly to her right, to the wall, where the slaves were, as she was dragged forward. Then she was on her knees. It was she whom I had first seen being dragged by the hair toward the center of the terrace.

A moment later I saw a sword raised over her head. "No!" she screamed. I could hear her even at the wall. She tore down the robes from her shoulders, thrusting them down over her hips, even onto her calves. "I am a slave!" she screamed. "I am a slave!" The sword wavered, then lowered. The officer pointed to the wall. The female rose up, sobbing, and began to run toward the wall. A command arrested her and she stopped. She had not removed her slippers. She kicked them off and then ran to the wall, to kneel there, trembling. The slave girls drew away from her. They feared her, as she must surely be a free woman.

"I, too, am a slave!" cried out another woman in the crowd. It was she whom I had seen being led at the intruder's hip, the second woman who had been brought to the center of the terrace. She, too, tore down her robes. Those near her in the group pulled back, isolating her. So she knelt naked in her heap of robes, in a small open space in the group. An impatient gesture from the commander of the intruders ordered her, too, to the wall. Frenziedly she pulled off her slippers and ran to the wall, to huddle there with the other woman. Four more women, too, then, proclaiming themselves slaves, purchased thusly their release from the group and, in turn, commanded, fled to the wall.

I heard then, suddenly, war horns, trumpets.

Men of Treve, now, in force, I thought, had come to the bridge. I did not know how long a handful of intruders could hold it. Toward the center of the terrace some intruders held the reins of several tarns.

We could hear shouting now, from the vicinity of the bridge.

I also saw intruders pointing out, over the balustrade. There were several tarns in flight, moving rapidly in this direction.

Two of the intruders, from the group at the center of the terrace, hurried toward the wall, swords drawn. The slaves were muchly pinned against it. I, of course, was held well in place by the impediment on my neck.

The slave, Dorna, may not even have seen them coming. She was looking down. It seemed she feared even to move.

One of the fellows with a sword was well to my left, much farther down the wall. The other was less far away. The farther fellow went to his right, the nearer one to his left, approaching us. Roughly did he interrogate those at the wall, including the stripped women, those who had proclaimed themselves slaves. "Where is the entrance to your pits, to your depths?" he cried, sword at the ready. I conjectured suddenly, sick, that this may well have been the object of the intruders' interest. Perhaps some in the group had known one of the entrances but had refused to divulge the information, and had, thusly, honorably, at a stroke of the sword, perished. But most of those who had been slain, I was sure, would not have known any of the entrances. Such things are not public information. But they had been slain, too. I was sick. I had seen even free women put to the sword. How terrible were these men, how desperate, how determined! One, or, at least, one who was free, who might know an entrance, it seemed, would have been well advised to reveal it. The truth or the sword was the choice offered to those hapless prisoners drawn forth from the group and put before the commander. Again and again he had given the sign that had brought the sword down on a bared neck.

"Oh!" cried the slave next to me, in pain, Dorna, kicked like a common slave, though she wore scarlet silk and a golden collar. "Where is the entrance to the pits, to the depths!" cried the intruder.

"I do not know, Master!" she wept. "I do not know!"

This, I was sure, was true. She had been taken from the top of the tower before I had been entered into the concealed shoot which had sped me far below the city, to the net suspended over the pool, that to which the giant urts had access.

"Oh!" she cried, again kicked.

He then turned to me and pulled my head up by the hair. He saw the hinged metal plates across my mouth, those attached to the gag's leather binding, the curved bars, inserted deeply between my teeth, emerging then at the sides of my mouth, curving about my neck, the whole locked behind the back of my neck, secured there with a thrust-lock.

He raised his sword in fury, in frustration, and I closed my eyes. I expected to die. Then I was flung angrily to my left side, and I fell there, on my chain, almost beside Dorna. The intruder was hurrying now about the wall, toward the bridge.

I heard another trumpet.

A tarn now flashed by, a few yards overhead.

It was less than an Ahn now till darkness.

I saw some of the intruders mount their tarns. Some of the great birds smote their way upward through the dislodged wire, to meet the newcomers.

I saw one of the intruders from the group across the terrace, at the stairway, hurrying back to the main group.

Two more buildings adjacent to the terrace were now aflame.

The intruder who had come from those stationed at the stairway rushed before the commander, pointing back toward the stairway. I saw then the commander, with several men, hurrying in that direction. In that direction, I knew, lay one of the entrances. It was the only one I knew, other than that unenviable one which lay at the top of the tower. The men at the stairs, as far as I knew, had not had to defend them, unlike the men at the bridge. Perhaps, disburdened of the necessities of defense, they had apprehended someone who knew, or pretended to know, a ground-level entrance, perhaps the one I knew, to the depths. In any event, the commander had hurried toward the stairway. Almost at the same time a line of guardsmen appeared far to my left, emerging from one of the buildings. They had perhaps forced the rear entrance, and used this as an avenue onto the terrace. An instant later I saw intruders, fleeing past on my left, having come doubtless from the bridge. One, only yards away, pitched rolling to the terrace, the quarrel of a crossbow in his back. In what seemed a breath later I saw guardsmen of Treve, swords drawn, burst onto the terrace, come, too, doubtless from the bridge. One intruder turned to fight, but was cut down by five men. Others hurried across the terrace, toward the far stairway. The men who had guarded the group near the center of the terrace now rushed from the group, some to seize the reins of tarns, others running toward the stairway. There came a cheer from the group, as it rose now to its feet. Guardsmen of Treve raced across the terrace, from the left, trying to cut off the retreat of the intruders. Some men fought at the tarns. Some seven or eight tarns rose into flight. I saw one fellow cut away from the reins of his tarn, and the great bird rose, riderless, following those which had taken flight. Another fellow was thrust from the saddle by a spear, wielded by a warrior of the city. Tarns of Treve flew overhead. The free women who had stripped themselves rose, dazedly, to their feet, by the wall. Dorna lay where she was. She seemed still in shock. I think she may have had only a dim sense of what was occurring. I could not speak to her, for the gag. One of the free women went from the wall, to recover her clothing. It was in the hands of one of the men from the group. But he did not give it to her. She looked at him, startled. His eyes were terrible. He pointed to the wall. Frightened, she shrank back, before him. He pointed to the ground, by the wall. She knelt. He pointed again to the ground, angrily. Then she lay there by the wall, frightened, on her belly. Another woman who had risen up from where she had been by the wall and had gone back to retrieve her clothing was being dragged back, naked, by the hair. She was then brutally thrown against the wall. She was then beside it, down on her right knee, next to it, the palms of her hands on it. And then she sank down beside it, on her knees, her hands on her thighs. Her right side was to the wall. She looked back over her left shoulder, frightened, at the man who had returned her to the wall. Another woman leaped up, but a fellow blocked her way. She stood before him. She regarded him, angrily. But then her lips began to tremble. Then she backed away from him, a foot. Then, suddenly, her head was snapped to the side, lashed to the side by the back of his hand. She spun about and fell against the wall. She was then on her knees by the wall. She looked up at him. There was blood at the side of her mouth. She remained on her knees. He looked down upon her. She crept closer to the wall. The six women who had proclaimed themselves slaves then huddled there, together, against the wall. Men stood about. They would remain, for the time, where they were. The slave girls edged farther away. To be sure, they remained, too, substantially where they were, at the wall, where the intruders had placed them.

I lay then at the foot of the wall.

I could scarcely move. I was alive!

The sun had now sunk behind the mountains. Some lamps were brought, and set in mounts on the wall, and elsewhere about the terrace. Bodies were being removed. Those of the city, and those of the intruders, I supposed, would receive quite different dispositions. Artisans, in the light of lamps and torches, began to repair the tarn-wire. In the morning, I supposed, slaves would clean the terrace.

It seemed very quiet now.

I realized that the bars had stopped sounding.

Dorna still lay quite near me.

It was well after darkness when I heard the sound of accouterments, and the light of a torch fell upon the wall. I struggled to my knees and put my head down. There must be free men present.

I saw a heavy, bootlike sandal, the sort worn by warriors, which can sustain long marches over stony soils, which provides protection from the slash of coarse grasses and the strike of leech plants, nudge Dorna.

She whimpered.

Again the bootlike sandal moved against Dorna's body, prodding it.

"Slave girl," said a voice.

"Master?" whimpered Dorna, questioningly. As she had said the word 'Master' it had not been simply as a customary form of deferential address, suitable for use in addressing any free man by a female slave, but in it, rather, it seemed that she had, to her relief, recognized, or thought she had recognized, the voice of her own master. And I, too, was sure I recognized the voice. He was not looking at me, but at Dorna, at his feet. I lifted my head a little, and then put it down, again, quickly. Yes, it was he, the officer! I did not think he recognized me. But how well I recalled him! In what detail and perfection he had had me! I had served his supper. I had danced before him, as a slave. I had been well put to his uses. He had slept me, later, nude, on the floor beside his couch. Toward morning he had once again drawn me to him and used me once more to slake his lusts. How I had leaped to his touch, how I had clung to him, how I had held him and kissed him, and licked him, and begged him, gratefully, sobbing, not to stop.

"Yes," he said.

He, being a total man, had made me a total woman. He, being a total master, had made me a total slave.

"Have they gone?" whispered Dorna, frightened.

"It is over now," he said.

I thought she sobbed, in relief.

He then kicked her, gently, with the toe of the bootlike sandal.

"Oh!" she said, wincing.

"Should you not be kneeling?" he asked. Quickly she knelt before him.

He regarded her.

She spread her knees.

"Master," she begged, frightened.

"Yes?" he said.

"Were they of Tharna?" she asked.

"They wore no insignia," he said. "There was nothing to identify them officially."

"Were they of Tharna?" she begged.

"No," he said. "They were not of Tharna."

She looked up at him.

"They had not come for you," he said.

"And they were not *his* men?"

"No," he said.

I was not certain that I understood her allusion. I did recall she had had a former master, one she much feared.

She regarded him, anxiously.

"They had not come for you," he said.

"But what was their purpose here?" she asked.

"It lay elsewhere," he said. "It lay in the tunnels, in the pits, in the depths. That is where the last of them died, some forty of them. They fought like crazed men. Few could stand against them. Every trap, every secret device, was sprung upon them. They sought alternate routes. In the corridors they met the war sleen and the hunting sleen of the pits. Tharlarion, even, and worse, were permitted into the tunnels. Perhaps a hundred guards died."

"Master is bloodied," said Dorna.

"The blood is not my own," he said.

Indeed, he seemed there at night, by the wall, in the torchlight, and the light of the small lamps, a very terrible figure. He was tall and broad-shouldered. Behind him there was a shield bearer. Over his left shoulder hung the scabbard of a sword, the hilt of the weapon visible within it. In his left hand he cradled a helmet. It would muchly enclose the head. On it, mounted over the crown, from front to back, was a crest of sleen hair. The opening in the helmet was something like a "Y" in shape. There was blood on the helmet. Blood, too, was on his thighs. I had seen him before not as a warrior. I had seen him in robes on the height of a tower, on a great chair, as might have been some ruler, some dispenser of justice, and I had seen him in the softness of lounging robes, in his own compartments. In his size, his strength, his intelligence, his power, he had been fearsome enough, even then. But I had not seen him until now in the garb of war, in the leather of the warrior, the sword at his shoulder, his helmet in hand. I did not want to look at him now. I was afraid. And I now understood, better than before, how a man might come to power on this world, and the sort of men that might rise to sit upon the chairs of state.

"The intruders wore no insignia," he said, "but they were of Ar."
"Master?" asked Dorna.
"There is no mistaking the accents," he said. "I know them well."
Dorna shuddered, it seemed, in relief.
"And many," he said, "in receiving their death strokes, cried out 'Glory to Ar!'"
Dorna was silent.
"It is strange that they were here," he said, musingly. "They could not have been authorized. They must have betrayed oaths."
"I do not understand," said Dorna.
"It does not matter," he said.
"There is the matter of the slaves, and of the free women, Captain," said one of the men with the officer.
"Let the slaves return to their masters," he said.
A sign was given and one of the soldiers went down the wall, permitting what slaves were there to leap up and speed from the terrace, some through buildings, some over the bridge, others, crossing the terrace, to descend by the far steps.
"This one is chained," said one of the soldiers. I kept my head down. I did not wish to be recognized.
"Let me see her," said the officer.
I winced, my head pulled up, by the hair. Tears sprang to my eyes. I blinked against the torchlight, which fell fully upon my countenance.
"I thought so," said the officer. "It is the Earth-woman slave."
I could not lower my head because of the soldier's grip in my hair.
"Did you know that Earth women make good slaves?" the officer asked one of his men, a subaltern.
"Yes, Captain," said the fellow.
"A stroke or two of the whip and they immediately understand the nature of their new life," said the officer.
"Yes, Captain," grinned the fellow.
"Why did you hide?" the officer asked me. "Were you afraid?"
I whimpered once.
"Is someone to come for you?" he asked.
I whimpered once, again. I did not know if the Lady Constanzia and the scarlet-clad figure would come back for me or not, but this seemed the most likely, and honest, answer I could give.

"Civilians will be soon be permitted to return to the terrace," said the officer.

I whimpered once, acknowledging that I understood him.

At a sign from the officer, the soldier released my hair. I sobbed with relief. His grip had been tight and painful. It is customary on this world, of course, for slaves to be handled in such a fashion, with uncompromising firmness and authority. The men here keep us precisely in line. They do not choose to be weak with us.

"She is a pit slut," said the officer. "If she is still here in the morning, see that she is remanded to custody, pending claiming."

"Yes, Captain," said the man.

After all he had made me do, after all he had had from me, was this, then, all he now had to do with me, hardly even recognizing me? But then I recalled he was a free man, and I was only a slave.

He then turned to regard the girl beside me.

"Slave," said the officer.

"Yes, Master," said Dorna.

"You will return home," he said, "and prepare my bath. You will then wash me. You will then prepare a light collation and serve me. These things are to be done naked."

"Yes, Master," she said.

Slaves are sometimes kept naked in a man's compartments, of course. But, too, after men have risked death, it often pleases them to be served by naked women. Perhaps such a thing, so simple in itself, speaks to them of joy and life. To be sure, the flavor of nudity, as so many other things, depends much upon context. There is the foolishly outraged and defiant nudity of the stripped free woman, in her capture noose, who does not yet know how she appears to men and what will be done with her; there is her trembling nudity when she lies upon her belly in a hunting camp, awaiting her shackling; there is the nudity of the exposition cages, in which one must move and pose for potential bidders; there is the exposure on the slave block itself, as one is auctioned; there is the sweaty nudity of work, as when she scrubs tiles on her hands and knees in her master's compartments; there is the nudity of the slave bathing her master; there is the nudity of the slave in the morning, kneeling before the master, waiting to learn if she may clothe herself; there is the beautiful warmth of a loving slave, nude and collared, serving wine in the light of a lamp of love; there is the nudity of the enflamed slave, aroused in her dance, who will beg for her master's touch; there is the nudity of the women of the enemy serving at the feast of the victors, a nudity that celebrates the prowess of the conquerors and proclaims the fate of fair spoils of war.

There are many nudities, with nuances and flavors.

The common denominator here is the beauty of the woman, the capture or slave. It excites and delights men. Accordingly, they will have the joy of it. They will, as masters, have it subordinate to their will—and as it pleases them—*fully, completely, utterly.*

"Then, tonight," he said, "you will be slept naked at the foot of my couch, chained by the neck to the slave ring."

"Yes, Master," she said.

I did not doubt but what she would be used before being spurned from the couch to the floor at its foot. I envied her a private master.

"Go!" he said.

I wondered if he would grant her a sheet, as he had me. But, I hoped, no more, no more! She, too, was a slave!

Doubtless she would be in the same collar and chain that I had worn. I wondered how many women had been slept thusly, the master done with them, on the tiles beside his couch, their head to its foot. I supposed a great many. He was a powerful Gorean male, and highly placed.

I wondered if I were the first Earth-girl slave who had had that experience.

It did not seem likely.

"Yes, Master!" she cried, and leaped up, and fled from the terrace, leaving through one of the buildings, that from which, earlier, she and others had been herded forth.

I wondered if she would please him as well as I. But, to be sure, much depends on the mysterious chemistries which can obtain between masters and slaves. How else explain the fascination that even a plain slave may sometimes exercise over the most powerful, rich, and handsome of men, to the puzzlement and dismay of beauties languishing in his pleasure garden? How else explain how a slave worthy of a ubar's palace may in a market, unbidden, throw herself in her chains to her belly before an ugly, low-born, monstrous brute, pleading desperately to be purchased? Has she seen in him her master? Similarly, consider the power which such a brute may sometimes exercise over even free, beautiful, high-born damsels, such that, at the very sight of him, they will kneel and beg his collar. In him, perhaps, they, too, have seen their master.

But sometimes, too, a woman's past may enhance how a man sees her in bondage. For example, it is doubtless pleasant for a ubar to have a conquered ubara at his feet, in his collar. She is then, of course, only a slave, but it is understandable that her past, like her hair and figure, may influence how she is viewed. Let her hope that, sooner or later, she will come to be viewed as only another slave. She does not wish to be tormented by her past, nor treated cruelly on account of it. Let the masters be merciful to her. Let them forget her past! Let them now treat her as only another slave! That is now all she is.

Dorna had lost no time in obeying.

I had gathered, from various things I had heard, here and there, that she may once have been an important and powerful personage in some city, perhaps in the city of Tharna, the men of which city it seemed she much feared. But such things, it seemed, must be long behind her. Her life had changed. She now wore a collar. She was now only a slave girl, quick to obey her master. To be sure, her past might continue, in the senses which we have suggested, at least for a time, to exercise some fascination over her master. How amusing to have such a woman as a slave, to have her serve his meals, to order her, at so little as a snapping of fingers, to pose or dance, or to strip and hasten to the furs! But, sooner or later, one supposed, or might hope that, for her sake, her past would tend to be forgotten, and she might, for all intents and purposes, mercifully, if not for this master then for another, become only another slave. The officer was, as I recalled, not the first master she had had. She had had apparently at least one other, he who had first captured her, he who had first put the collar on her neck, one from whom she had been stolen, one whom she feared terribly, with all the terror of her embonded heart. When she had queried the officer as to whether or not the intruders had been *his* men, I supposed this former master might have been the one she had had in mind. On the height of the tower she had been reeling, sick with fear, at the very suggestion that she might be returned to him. And, of course, her fear was quite meaningful. She was only a slave. She could be simply bound and hooded, and returned to him, his then to do with as he pleased. I wondered if, sometimes in her kennel at night, hearing a sound, she might awaken, frightened, pulling the blanket about her, fearing that it might be he, her first master, who had come for her. But he would not, presumably, know where she was. Might she not be anywhere? On this world were there not hundreds of cities and thousands of slaves? No, from him she would in all likelihood be safe, unless her present master, if she might prove somewhat displeasing, might decide, perhaps as a joke, to return her to him. But then, as an option, might he not, under the same circumstances, and perhaps preferably, and perhaps more amusingly, see fit to return her to Tharna? Dorna, I was sure, would do her best to please her master.

"Did the intruders reach the lower corridors?" a man asked the officer.

"No," said the officer.

One of the men with the officer, the captain, was clad not in the gear of war, but wore a blue tunic, and carried, on two straps, slung now beside him, a scribe's box. It was flat and rectangular. Pens are contained, in built-in racks, within it. Depending on the box, it may also contain ink, or powdered ink, to be mixed with water, the vessel included, or flat, disklike cakes of pigment, to be dampened, and used as ink, rather as water colors. In it, too, in narrow compartments, are sheets of paper, commonly linen paper or rence paper. A small knife may also be contained in such boxes for scraping out errors, or a flat eraser stone. Other paraphernalia may also be included, depending on the scribe, string, ostraka, wire, coins, even a lunch. The top of the box, the lid, the box placed on a solid surface, serves as a writing surface, or desk.

"There is the matter of the free women," said another man to the officer.

"Yes," said the officer.

They went then a little to their right, some few feet to my left, as I knelt.

"There are six of them," said a man. He was one of the civilians who had stood guard over the women, keeping them at the wall.

The women looked up, frightened, the torchlight revealing them. Some tried to cover themselves.

"Kneel in a line, here, facing the captain," said a soldier.

"We are unveiled!" protested a woman.

"Hands on thighs," said the soldier. "Backs straight. Do not speak."

Hurriedly they formed themselves, as they had been told. The officer considered them.

"These are the ones?" he asked.

"Yes, Captain," said a man.

"Captain!" cried one of the women.

"Silence," said the soldier.

"Bring a whip," said a man.

"I have one here," said a voice. It was handed to him. The woman shrank back, kneeling back on her heels, pressing the palms of her hands firmly down on her thighs.

"Backs straight," cautioned the soldier.

The women complied.

Again they were regarded.

They trembled.

"What is to be done with them?" asked a man.

"They have proclaimed themselves slaves," said the officer. "Let them be slaves."

"No!" cried the women. "No!"

The lash fell amongst them.

Those who had leaped to their feet were seized and flung back, down, against the others. Some tried two, even three, times, to leap up, to flee to freedom, but they could not penetrate the ring of men. Each time they were thrown back to their knees, with the others. They were then crowded together, one over the other. Down came the lash! They cried out with pain, huddling together. One tried to stand, just a little, her knees flexed, her hands and arms raised to fend blows, but she was then, blow by blow, stroke by stroke, returned to her knees, and then when another blow fell she cried out for mercy, and threw herself to her belly, her hands over her head, sobbing. She had now learned what the whip could feel like. Some of the women knelt, holding out their hands for mercy, but the lash fell upon them, too, and they put down their heads, sobbing, bending over, almost double. Some, kneeling, crying out, sobbing, clasped their hands together, lifting them to the men. But the lash fell. And then they were a small, writhing knot of terrified women, each trying to hide behind the other. The whip, hitting at the edges of the group, the left, the right, forced it in upon itself, and then, sobbing, cowering, they huddled together, tiny, within the ring of angry men.

The lash ceased its whistling speech. To its harsh discourse they had learned now to attend.

"Chain them together by the neck," said the officer. "And take them to the pens. See that they are branded by morning."

Chains were brought and the six women were fastened together by the neck. They were then knelt again before the officer, facing him. How strange it must have been for them, free women, to find themselves in steel collars, linked to other such collars, by chains.

"Please, no more the whip!" wept one, seeing it poised in a fellow's hand.

"Do not whip us more!" begged another, cringing.

"Please, do not whip us!" begged another.

"As slave girls," said the officer, "you will doubtless become quite familiar with the whip."

One of the women moaned. She seemed to me one who might have been cruel to slaves. Now she herself had felt the whip. Had she owned female slaves? If so, she had undoubtedly found the whip effective in controlling them. She would now find that it would be similarly effective in controlling her.

"Are you prepared to obey?" inquired the captain.

"Yes, yes!" said the women.

"Turn to the right," he said.

They then, kneeling, were in a line, one behind the other, their right sides to the wall.

"Keep your eyes straight ahead," said the officer.

The women complied.

"You will learn to be females and please men," he said.

One of the women gasped. Two of the others trembled.

"Sell them out of the city," said the officer. Women wept.

"Do you wish a record made of this, Captain?" asked the fellow in the blue tunic, he with the scribe's box, on its straps, slung at his left side.

"No," said the captain. "Keep no record of this. They have shamed the city, and the Home Stone. Let them go their way. Let them not be remembered. Let it be, in the records of the city, as though they had never been."

One of the women sobbed.

"Put your hands behind your back," said the soldier in charge of the small coffle. "Now hold your left elbow with your right hand, and your right elbow with your left hand." This pins the arms back, the forearms parallel to the ground. Sometimes arms are tied in this position.

The women complied.

"On your feet," said the soldier in charge of the small coffle. "Left foot first, step! Step!"

The coffle was then marched past me. It rounded the corner of the wall and would, I take it, cross the bridge, and the docking area, on the way to the pens.

I felt sorry for the free women, in a way, but I think I sensed, and they sensed, as the men about perhaps did not, for I sometimes think men are very stupid, that the fate inflicted upon them was not as grievous as might be supposed. To be a woman, a true woman, in its total dimensionality, is not only a not unenviable fate, it is a fulfilling, exciting, thrilling, profound, deep, beautiful, and glorious thing. Sometimes I feel sorry for men, just a little, but then I grow afraid, for I remember that they are, after all, the masters.

The fellow with the whip had followed the coffle.

Around the corner, perhaps on the bridge, I heard the crack of the whip, and a cry of fear.

I doubted that the leather had touched anyone, but it could have, of course.

But then, a moment later, I heard the whip again and, this time, a cry of pain.

Yes, I thought, shuddering, men were the masters.

The officer and his companions, that small retinue, then left the terrace.

Shortly after the departure of the officer and his retinue I think the terrace, previously muchly cleared, must have been reopened, for I had scarcely closed my eyes, sitting at the wall, when I felt hands fumbling at the lock gag, opening it. "Are you all right?" begged the Lady Constanzia. Her eyes were wide with fear. "Yes," I said. Her companion, the scarlet-clad fellow, had removed his cloak. It was muchly wound about his arm, constituting in its way, it seemed, an improvised shield. Strangers in this city are not permitted to carry weapons. He wiped the lock gag on his cloak and returned it to his pouch. I was pleased to see it disappear therein. I then began, for no reason I understood, to tremble. The Lady Constanzia kissed me. "They would not let us come to the terrace," she said. "You are sure you are all right?" "Yes," I said. The Lady Constanzia freed the leash from the ring. It then hung loose within the ring. The scarlet-clad fellow turned her about and took her in his arms. She lifted her lips to his. How soft she was in his arms! How she melted to him! She was then, surely, as a slave girl in the arms of her master. I was startled. How could this be? Was she not a free woman? Did she not know better? Had she not been taught? Had she no pride? But I saw her now, before me, as a slave girl in the arms of her master. "I love you, my master!" she whispered. He then crushed her to him. He sobbed. "Master?" she asked. He then, forcibly, put her from him. "It is nothing," he said. She then knelt, as delicately, and naturally, as any slave. He seemed overcome by emotion. "Master?" she asked, again.

"Curse honor!" he wept, suddenly.

I am sure that neither of us understood his outburst.

"When will I see you again, Master?" she asked.

He looked down upon her, tears in his eyes. His fists were clenched.

"Master?" she asked.

"I do not own you!" he cried. "You belong to another!"

She looked up at him, puzzled.

"You are merchandise!" he wept. "You are a mere property!"

"Yes, Master?" she said, puzzled.

"I must remember that!" he cried.

"Yes, Master," she said.

"Your sort, and better, may be purchased in any market," he said.

"Yes, Master," she said.

"Why then," he demanded, "do I feel as I do?"

"How is it that Master feels?" she begged.

"I fear I have grown fond of a slave," he said.

"Cannot one grow fond of a slave, even of so small and unimportant a thing?" she asked.

"Curse the codes!" he cried.

"When shall we see one another again, Master?" she asked.

"Never!" he wept.

She looked at him, aghast. She almost rose to her feet, but she stayed kneeling. I gathered that he had seen to it, in the time they had had together, that she had received training. He had her under discipline, which is suitable, as he thought her a slave.

"Never," he whispered, looking down at the stones.

"If I have displeased Master," she said, in agony, "I will endeavor to improve my behavior!"

"I have dallied overlong in the city," he said. "The extension granted to me, the last for which I might apply, expires tomorrow at sundown. I must, by then, conclude my business, and take transport for the foothills."

"No!" she wept.

He then put his cloak about him, and turned about, and strode rapidly away.

"Master!" she called after him, in agony. "Master!"

After he had disappeared, taking his way through one of the buildings to the left, the Lady Constanzia collapsed to the stones of the terrace, weeping.

Her fate, though she was a free woman, was not that different, I conjectured, from that of many slaves. They could not go their own ways. They were bought and sold, and handed about, and taken here and there. I recalled a slave who had wanted desperately to serve and please a fellow, he whose whip she had first kissed. But her feelings, only those of a slave, had been unimportant. She had been sold from that house. She had been carried far away. She now served here. The case, I thought, was not really so different with the Lady Constanzia, as she was a prisoner. She could not go where she wished. Her disposition, too, as in the case of a slave, was in the hands of others. In the case of a slave, of course, the disposition is in the hands of the master. It is he with whom one must deal, if one wishes to acquire the woman. She is his to keep or sell, as he pleases. The average man of this world would no more think of stealing a slave within his own city, or a host city, one which has extended the courtesy of its walls, than he would of any other act of illicit and dishonorable brigandage. There is sometimes a double frustration involved in these things, that of the slave whose master will not sell her to one to whom she wishes to belong, and that of the fellow who wishes to own her, to whom she will not be sold, for one reason or another, perhaps for spite, perhaps because the owner wishes to keep her for himself, perhaps because the would-be purchaser cannot meet the owner's price. The key to understanding these matters, of course, is to understand, simply, and clearly, that the female is an article of property, that she is owned. In the case of the Lady Constanzia, as she was a free woman, her disposition was, I supposed, in the hands of certain officials of Treve. I almost wished that the Lady Constanzia was a slave, and had a private master, that the scarlet-clad figure might have approached her master with the intent of negotiating her purchase. But perhaps his funds, even in such a case, would not have sufficed for her purchase? Perhaps his funds, those still at his disposal, were required for the discharge of his business here? And he would not steal her, it seemed. No, that would not be honorable. She did not belong to him. He could no more bring himself to steal her than he could have brought himself to steal a silver vessel, a golden plate, from a house in which he had been accepted as a guest. It was little wonder, then, that he, torn by desire and love, in bitter rage, cursed the strictures of honor. By the men of this world we are highly prized. They hunt us down and capture us, and make us serve them, and keep us for themselves. We are treasures to them. They will kill for us. But few of them, it seems, no matter how exquisite we are, no matter how beautiful we are, will compromise their honor for us. And I do not object to this for, without honor, how could they be men, and, if they were not men, true men, how could they be fit and perfect masters for us?

In time, red-eyed, the Lady Constanzia rose to her feet, unsteadily. She took the leash, pulling it from the ring.

"I am sorry," I said to her.

"We had a wonderful day," she said. "We did everything, we saw everything."

"I am sorry," I said.

"I'm sorry we put the lock gag on you," she said, "but we thought it best. We would not have wanted you to furnish information to others, about who I was with, where we might have gone, and such. I did not want to risk being summoned in early. You understand. We did not want to risk you spoiling our holiday."

I nodded.

I recalled the frustration of the intruder who had been unable to question me because of the lock gag. I recalled the look in his eyes, and the readying of the sword, but he had not struck me. He had flung me, rather, angrily to the side. I had lain there, terrified. But I had survived. None of the slaves had been put to the sword. Our collars, it seemed, had saved us. This is not that unusual, incidentally. In the sacking of a city, slaves, like other domestic animals, other valuables, and such, are often saved, while free folk may be put to the sword. Indeed, sometimes free women, I have heard, take the collars from their own girls, putting them about their own necks, that they may increase their chances of survival. They often then, self-collared, knot a rag about their hips, to conceal that they have no brand, and hurry into the streets, to surrender, as a slave, to one of the conquerors. Sometimes their girls pursue them, to point them out to the conquerors. Sometimes they subdue their former mistresses, remove the cloth at their hips, and bind them, and lead them on ropes to the conquerors.

"Can you stand?" asked the Lady Constanzia.

"Yes," I said, rising unsteadily.

In a few moments then we were making our way across the terrace to the broad steps far from the wall.

At the height of the steps I asked the Lady Constanzia to wait for a moment, while I looked back, across the expanse of the terrace. It seemed very broad. Here and there, on the wall, at the bridge, and to the right, and at certain places on the balustrade, were lamps. The sky was dark with clouds. One of the buildings, bordering the terrace, one now rather before me, and to my right, was still afire. Smoke rose from it to the dark sky. Artisans were still working with the tarnwire.

"Strangers held the terrace," said the Lady Constanzia.

"Yes," I said.

Toward its center was the place where the butchery had occurred.

How desperate had been those men. They had sought an entrance to the pits. They had apparently found one. In the corridors, I gathered, the last of them had died.

I looked back to the wall where I had been chained, that to which the slaves had been commanded, that against which the free women, those who had proclaimed themselves slaves, had also been confined. I could see the bridge across the way, that across which the free women, in coffle, had been marched, their arms held up, closely behind them, the elbow of the left arm grasped by the hand of the right, the elbow of the right grasped by the hand of the left. They would be, presumably, in the pens by now. They might already be branded. My thigh tingled as I remembered my own branding in the pens, long ago. It had been quite painful. I had cried out in misery. A branding rack had been used, to hold us steady for the mark. Our hands had been braceleted behind our backs, to a belly chain, that we not be able to tear at the brand. My entire group, it was said, had been excellently marked. Certainly I was. But this was not surprising for the iron masters in such a place, of the caste of metal workers, are skilled. We had all been given the common kajira mark. Perhaps theirs would be the same. They were to be sold out of the city, I recalled. They would find themselves then at the mercy of strangers. Gone would be their privileged status, that of the free woman. Gone would be the protection of the law, of guardsmen, of the shared Home Stone. Let them then salvage what they could of their lives. Let them strive to learn how to please.

I thought of the slave girl, Dorna. The earrings had been quite attractive on her. I suspected that she might now be quite fond of them. That seems to be the way it is with the women of this world. They fear them. Then they love them. To be sure, they also made her only a pierced-ear girl. I supposed that she might now be bathing her master.

I then, on my leash, following the Lady Constanzia, descended the long stairway to the lower levels. I stepped carefully, as my hands were braceleted behind me.

In two places on the steps I saw dark stains, which I supposed to be blood.

"We saved a piece of fruit for you," said the Lady Constanzia. "I put it in my tunic. I will give it to you below."

"Thank you," I said.

We continued on our way.

The Lady Constanzia was crying.

Twenty Five

"Somewhere," said the peasant, dully, "I heard steel, I heard shouting."

"It was far away," said the pit master, sitting, cross-legged, as he sometimes did, before the chained peasant.

The pit master's legs were small for his upper body, almost bandy. He looked like a boulder of sorts, sitting there in the cell.

It was late, the same night as the raid of the intruders. I had been unable to attend upon the peasant until now, as I had been late returning to the pens. The pit master had waited for me.

"Master is all right," I had said, relievedly, returned by the Lady Constanzia, kneeling before him.

"And I am pleased you live, little Janice," said he, "and you, too, Lady Constanzia."

We were both kneeling before him.

The pit master had been covered with grime and blood. He had been cut about the left shoulder. A bloody rag had been knotted about his upper body. His lower body was filthy as it seemed that one or more of the tunnels had been flooded to the height of a man's waist, to facilitate the entry of water urts and tharlarion. These had been, I gathered, by noise and fire, herded toward intruders. But now he was clean and clad in a fresh tunic. That he had been wounded would not now be discernible, the blood stanched, the wound dressed, the dressing hidden beneath the tunic. It was not unusual, incidentally, for the pit master to be careful of his appearance when he came to the cell of the peasant. He would often bathe and attire himself in fresh, clean raiment before presenting himself before him.

It seemed strange that he would accord such courtesy and regard, such esteem, almost reverence, to one who was a mere peasant.

"I am finished, Master," I said.

"What is honor?" asked the pit master of the peasant.

The peasant lifted his head, and looked at him, uncomprehendingly.

"Honor," said the pit master.

"I do not know," said the peasant.

"I do not know, either," said the pit master.

"I have heard of it, once, somewhere," said the peasant. "But it was long ago."

"I, too, have heard of it," said the pit master, bitterly, "but, too, it was long ago."

"Is it not something for the upper castes?" asked the peasant.

"Perhaps," granted the pit master.

"Then it is not our concern," said the peasant.

"No," said the pit master, bitterly. "It is not our concern."

"Is it time for the planting?" asked the peasant.

"No," said the pit master.

We then left the cell.

Twenty Six

"You have eaten nothing!" I chided the Lady Constanzia. She lay in the white sliplike garment, that undergarment resembling a slave tunic, on the mat in her cell, her knees drawn up. Her eyes were red with weeping. She stared outward, though I think she was looking at nothing. I did not even know if she had heard me.

I had returned from my duties in the cell of the peasant, following the pit master back to his quarters. It was late, the same night as the raid of the intruders.

A messenger had been awaiting the return of the pit master. His missive had been delayed, given the disruptions in the city, and those in the pits.

"I will never see him again!" said the Lady Constanzia.

"Eat," I said.

"No," she said.

"Do you wish me whipped, that you have not fed?" I asked.

"Take it to the other girls," she said. "None will know."

I put the plate to one side. My fellow pit slaves would be glad to get it. It was better than their common fare in the pits. They would fall on their knees about the pan, seizing what they could from it.

"I bring you word," I said, "which has but recently been received."

"Is it word from him?" she asked, looking up.

"Alas, no," I said. "But it should make you happy. It is good news for you, indeed."

"What?" she asked, in misery.

"Your ransom has been paid," I said. "The agreed-upon amounts have been lodged with the business council, the entire matter attested to by the commercial praetor. I saw the orders, and the seals."

"You cannot read," she said.

"I could not read the orders," I said, "but I saw them, and the seals."

The orders, bearing the seals, had been delivered to the pit master.

"Rejoice!" I said. "Your sojourn here, in this damp, dismal place, in this cell, behind these bars, will soon be done. You will soon be returned to your native city and your accustomed mode of life."

She put her head down on the mat, and sobbed.

"Do not cry," I said. "This is what you have longed for, this is what you have waited for, this is what you have lived for, what you have hungered for, your freedom, your liberty!"

She wept.

"What is wrong?" I asked.

"Better a chain in a poor man's kitchen," she said.

"What?" I said.

She looked up at me. "You know I am not a free woman," she said.

"You are a free woman!" I assured her. "You must be!"

"Why?" she asked.

I did not know what to respond to her.

"I want to be helpless," she said. "I want to be owned!"

"Lady Constanzia!" I protested.

"Do you not understand?" she asked. "I want, with all that I am, with everything that I am, to love and serve, holding back nothing, ever! I want to give all!"

I was silent.

"Surely you understand these things, Janice," she said.

"I am only a collared slave," I said. "I have no choice in such matters!"

"Fortunate Janice!" she wept.

"Hist!" I said. "I think I hear the approach of the guard. Hasten! Don the robes of concealment!"

"No," she wept.

"You must!" I said.

"No," she said. "Whip me, if you wish, as a slave."

The guard's footsteps came closer.

I seized up her robes of concealment and flung them over her as though they might have been bedclothes.

I then knelt before her, putting my hands out. "Please, Master!" I said. "Here is a free woman! She is not clothed. All is well. I will soon leave the cell! Please do not look. Please do not compromise her modesty!"

But he did look, a little, particularly where one ankle emerged from beneath the robes.

But then he took his way away, continuing with his rounds.

"Thank you, Master," I said.

"Those were the happiest days of my life," said the Lady Constanzia, "with him, in his power, in a collar and the rags of a slave."

I kissed her, trying to comfort her.

"I will never see him again. I will never see him again," she wept.

I picked up the plate, with the untouched food, and left the cell, locking it behind me.

Twenty Seven

"May I speak, Master?" I asked.

"Yes," said the pit master.

I was following him in the corridors, on his morning rounds, the day following the events recently recounted.

"The strangers sought an entrance to the tunnels," I said.

"It would seem so," he said.

"Why?" I asked.

"Who knows?" he said.

"Master knows," I speculated.

"Are you insolent?" he asked, not looking back, continuing to move before me, with those short, irregular steps.

"No, Master," I said. "Forgive me, Master! I beg not to be beaten!"

Twenty Eight

"Is this the Lady Constanzia?" asked the fellow behind the high desk, looking down upon us.

"Yes, your honor," said the pit master.

"Bring her forward," he said. He was, as I understood it, an officer in the business court, that under the jurisdiction of the commercial praetor, subject, ultimately, to the high council.

The Lady Constanzia, clad in new, rich, ornate robes of concealment, fully hooded and veiled, was conducted forward, between two guards, from the pits. There were also, in the lofty, circular, sunlit room, the light coming through high, narrow windows, dust motes visible within it, two guards of the court. A broad, scarlet marble circle was before the high desk of the praetor's officer, and the Lady Constanzia was conducted to its center, the guards then withdrawing, moving back, several feet, leaving her there, alone, on the circle. She seemed small there, even tiny, before the high desk. The pit master, as indicated, was also in the room. I, too, was there. Indeed, it was I who, in my office as keeper for the state of the free woman, had led her here, she leashed and back-braceleted on the way. Though it might be thought demeaning to a free woman to be in the keeping of a slave, it was also thought to be less compromising to her modesty than to be led by a male. Having such in the keeping of a female, too, of course, is likely to be safer than entrusting them to a male who, after all, particularly if irritated or provoked, might be tempted to do far more to her than compromise her modesty. The slave, too, of course, is much more subject to supervision and control than a free man. She may, for example, for any lapse, or putative lapse, be easily put to punishment.

Within the entrance to the court the Lady Constanzia had been freed of the leash and bracelets. One of the guards had inserted these within his pouch. I knelt back, and to the side, on the left side of the room, as one would face the desk. I wore a clean, modest tunic. My hair had been washed and brushed. It had also been tied back, behind my head. In this fashion it was perhaps less distractive, less luxurious and slave-like. But it also, of course, accented my collar.

To the left of the praetor's officer, to our right, as we faced him, below him, on the floor level, on a bench, behind a table, was a court's clerk.

"You are the Lady Constanzia, of the city of Besnit?" inquired the praetor's officer.

"I am," she said.

"You have been the object of a ransom capture," said the praetor's officer.

"Yes, your honor," she said.

He then addressed himself to the court's clerk. "There is no difficulty as to the matter of her identity?" he asked.

"No, your honor," said the clerk. "Her fingerprints tally with those taken shortly after her delivery to Treve by the abductors."

"Have the agents of the redemptor accepted her as the Lady Constanzia?" inquired the praetor's officer.

"They have, your honor," said the clerk.

"In virtue of interrogations and such?"

"Yes, your honor."

"There is the matter of the slipper."

"It is here," said the clerk. He produced a tiny, jeweled, muchly embroidered slipper. It might have cost more than many slaves.

The praetor's officer nodded to the clerk and he carried the slipper to the Lady Constanzia, who took it in her hands, and looked upon it.

"Do you recognize it?" asked the praetor's officer.

"Yes, your honor," she said. "It is mine."

"It matches with that brought by the agent of the redemptor?" asked the praetor's officer.

"Yes, your honor," said the clerk. He then took it back from the Lady Constanzia and returned to his desk.

"The court of the commercial praetor of the high city of Treve," said the praetor's officer, "accepts the prisoner as the Lady Constanzia of Besnit."

The clerk made a notation on his records.

"You are now within the custody of the court of the commercial praetor of Treve," said the officer.

"I understand, your honor," she said.

"There is also the matter of a necklace," said the praetor's officer.

The clerk then produced, holding it out, a large, impressive necklace, with many strands, containing many stones. It was breathtakingly beautiful.

"Do you recognize the necklace?" asked the praetor's officer.

"It seems to be that which I selected in the shop of a jeweler in Besnit, before my abduction," she said.

"It is," he said.

"Yes, your honor," she said.

"And was it not to obtain such a thing that you went to the jeweler's shop?"

"It was, your honor," she said.

"Were you not careless of your safety?" he asked.

"Yes, your honor," she said.

"It was not wise, was it?" he asked.

"No, your honor."

"And then you were captured?"

"Yes, your honor."

"Why did you enter the shop?" he asked.

"To obtain such a thing, or things," she said. "I wanted such things."

"But you were rich."

"I wanted more," she said.

"Such greed," he said, "is unbecoming in a free woman."

"Yes, your honor."

"It would be more appropriate," he said, "in a slave girl."

"Yes, your honor," she said.

"Destroy the necklace," said the praetor's officer to the clerk.

"Your honor!" cried the Lady Constanzia.

"It is paste," said the praetor's officer.

We watched as the clerk struck a fire-maker, one used to melt wax for seals, and set the flame to the necklace. The flames sped from paste stone to paste stone, and the whole was then dropped to the side, flickering and smoldering.

"Such things are seldom used in ransom captures," said the praetor's officer. "They are usually used in the luring of free women by slavers."

We watched smoke curl upward from the necklace.

"It was kept on me until I came to this city, which I now learn, by your words, is Treve," she said. "I thought it a joke, that I should be made to wear it, that all might see me in it, and realize how it had been used in my abduction, and that I wore it, such a rich thing, but, captive, could not profit from it."

"The joke," said the praetor's officer, "was richer than you understood."

"Yes, your honor," she whispered.

"Do you know the identity of your redemptor?" asked the praetor's officer.

"Yes, your honor," she said. "They are my brothers."

"Do you recall," he asked, "when you were first in your house, and mistress of your enterprises, a certain matter of business, from more than three years ago, conducted with the house of William, in Harfax?"

"Your honor?" she asked.

"There was the cashing of letters of credit in Besnit, from the house of William, in Harfax, letters the House of William had drawn on the street of coins in Brundisium, to be used in the purchase of ingots in Esalinus, these to be melted down in Besnit and there, in Besnit, to be formed into the wares for which she is famous, thence to be sent to the house of William, for resale through the house of William to the shops of Harfax and elsewhere, even as far away as Market of Semris, Corcyrus, Argentum, Torcadino, and Ar."

The Lady Constanzia put down her head.

"The gold was fairly purchased at competitive prices," said the praetor's officer. "And the wares were made under the supervision of your house, and according to your specifications. But the wares were mismarked. Their gold content was not that agreed upon. The wares were muchly debased from the original agreements. Your house made an excellent profit on the matter, retaining the extra gold for your own coffers. Testimony from a metal worker, one traveling from Besnit to Brundisium, one who had been engaged in the manufacture of the wares in Besnit, seeing such articles in Harfax, and noting them marked as they were, in a way he knew false, alerted the house of William. They had not hitherto conducted tests, as the reputation of your house, prior to your accession as mistress of its enterprises, had been faultless. The wares were recalled and remarked. Much did the reputation of the house of William suffer. In time the street of coins in Brundisium demanded repayment of its loans. The house of William was in jeopardy. Only two years later did it manage to recoup its losses, and to rebuild its fortunes. You may suspect that much bad blood then existed between your house and that of William, in Harfax."

"Yes, your honor," she said.

"Do you know now," asked the praetor's officer, "who your redemptor is?"

"Surely," she said. "My brothers."

"No," he said.

"I do not understand," she said, puzzled.

"It was naturally intended that your brothers, your own house, should be your redemptor," said the praetor's officer. "Naturally it was with such a redemption in mind that you were abducted for ransom."

"They are not the redemptor?" she asked.

"Surely you were aware of delays in the matter of your ransom," said the praetor's officer.

"Yes, your honor," she said.

"Your brothers refused to pay," said the praetor's officer. "Indeed, from their point of view, why should they? They were now first in their house, and master of its fortunes. If you were to return they would be reduced, again, to second."

Lady Constanzia looked up at him.

"Their sense of honor seems to be equivalent to your own," he said. "They would seem to be the fit brothers of such a sister, and you the fit sister of such brothers."

"Who, then," she asked, "is my redemptor?"

"Kneel," said he, "prisoner."

The Lady Constanzia knelt in the center of the scarlet circle.

"Your redemptor," said he, "is the house of William, in Harfax."

She looked up at him, startled.

"An oath, it seems, was sworn," said the praetor's officer. "This oath was sworn upon the honor of the house of William, in Harfax. It was in this oath sworn that you were to be brought to the house of William as a slave, and put naked and in chains at the feet of the master of the house. Your disposition will be in accord with the provisions of this oath."

She trembled, kneeling on the scarlet circle.

"Do you not wish to leap up, and try to escape?" asked the praetor's officer. "Do you not wish to protest, to cry out, to beg for mercy? Do you not wish to bemoan your fate, to tear your clothing?"

"No, your honor," she said.

"What have you to say?" he asked, puzzled.

"I will attempt to serve my master to the best of my abilities," she said.

"I can guarantee it," said the praetor's officer. Then he lifted up certain papers on his desk. "It is to be done in this fashion," he said to the clerk. "She is to be stripped and branded, and put in a holding collar. She is also to be gagged, for her words, her pleas, her remonstrations or such, will be of no avail, nor will they be of interest to those of the house of William, in Harfax. Let them not then be disturbed by them. She is then to be placed in an outer robe of concealment, the outer robe only, but also hooded and veiled. Then, hands bound behind her, on a rope, at the tenth Ahn, she is to be brought to this place. Here she will be delivered into the hands not of an agent of the house of William but into the hands of one of that house itself, the youngest and least of that house, who has come to Treve for this purpose, to acquire her, to whom she is to be given as a slave."

The clerk nodded, and, lifting his hand, summoned the guards of the court. They lifted up the Lady Constanzia who, it seemed, could scarcely rise unaided. Each guard then took one of her arms. The Lady Constanzia threw a wild glance toward me, over her shoulder, but she could do little more, as the guards held her arms. I lifted my hand to her. She was then conducted from the chamber. There were tears in my eyes. I did not rise, of course, for I had not received permission to do so.

Twenty Nine

I knelt to one side, and back, in shadows, inconspicuously by the wall, in the circular chamber of the court of the commercial praetor. Shafts of sunlight, like golden spears, fell through the high, narrow windows, illuminating the scarlet circle before the high desk.

I heard two of the time bars, far off, across the city, beginning to sound.

The pit master, two guards, and I, I heeling the second guard, had returned to the court but a few moments ago. The guards waited within the chamber, near the entrance.

The high desk stood untenanted before the scarlet circle. There was no need, now, for the presence of the praetor's officer. What business was now to be done could be handled by the clerk, and diverse minions, of the court.

I counted the sounding of the bars, stroke by stroke.

Shortly before the last stroke the outer door to the chamber, that leading to the hall outside, opened. A man entered. He had sturdy legs. He walked angrily. He stopped in the vicinity of the scarlet circle. One learns quickly in the collar to be quite sensitive to the moods of men. In the first glance, a frightened glimpse, I had detected his agitation, his anger. One learns to fear such moods in men. When they are in such moods one knows that one may be kicked, or beaten, though one has done nothing. I was pleased I was back in the shadows. To be sure, I did not think that I was in danger. The entrant did not own me. It was, accordingly, highly unlikely that he would consider abusing me. Too, the pit master, who would, I was sure, protect me, was at hand. Nonetheless, I kept my head muchly down, suitably for a slave.

I heard the tenth bar sound.

It was the tenth Ahn.

The tenth sounding of the bar still lingered over the city when a side door in the chamber opened and the court's clerk, with a folder and papers, entered. He spread these upon the table, that which was, as we were situated, to the right of the currently unoccupied desk of the praetor's officer. He and the fellow who had entered but shortly before conferred briefly over these papers. There were, it seemed, two sets of such papers. They were, it seemed, in order. I did not doubt but what one set was papers of the court, stamped with the sign of the court, and certified with the signature of a praetor's officer, if not the praetor himself. On copies of these papers the fellow who had but recently entered scribbled his signature. He put one copy within his robes. The other set of papers, which had been examined, and in places compared with the first set, was different. It was left open now on the table. In its original form it had been folded and narrow, and tied with a ribbon. The ribbon was blue and yellow.

The court's clerk then went to the side portal. "Bring forth the slave," he called.

A guard of the court entered, leading a small female figure on a rope. She was in at least the outer robe of a free woman, apparently the same ornate, colorful, expensive robe that had been worn that morning. From the fall of the robe on her body I suspected that she was naked beneath it. The rope by which she was led was tied about her neck. I could see beneath the hem of the robe that her feet were bare, slave bare. The robe did have its attached hood, and her features were modestly veiled. Her head was down. About the robes and hood, and veil, holding them in quite tightly against her neck, was a collar. It was a simple collar and I supposed it was a temporary collar, a holding collar. Its engraving was probably no more than some simple legend, such as "If found, return me to the pens of Treve." Beneath the veil, as I recalled, she was to be gagged. I did not doubt but what she was, and, in the manner of the men of this world, quite effectively. Her words, her pleas, her cries, her remonstrations, or such, as I recalled, would not only be of no avail, but were not even of interest to those of the house of William, in Harfax. Let them not then be disturbed by them. Behind the small female figure, rather in the background, was a second guard of the court. The fellow who had but recently entered, in such agitation, so angrily, who had considered, and signed, papers at the desk of the clerk, had, at the call of the clerk to the guard, turned his back and walked through, and outside, the scarlet circle, that before the high desk. He was now some feet on our side of the circle. The small female figure was led to the center of the circle. This time, however, she did not face the desk, but faced the fellow on the other side of the circle. Her head was down. His back was turned. The guard who had led her forward now untied the rope from her neck and withdrew. He went to stand, with the other guard, to the far side of the clerk's table. Their presence was thus unobtrusive. The hands of the small female figure were behind her. I assumed they were tied there. She was now standing alone, in the center of the circle, her head down. She looked very small there. Sunlight fell upon her through the high narrow windows.

"The slave," said the court's clerk.

Angrily, with a swirl of robes, the man turned about and came to the edge of the circle. "I own you!" he cried, his voice thick with rage. It seemed she suddenly trembled, and might look up, but he cried out, "Do not dare to look upon me, you worthless slut, you now-nameless slave!"

The fellow made an angry gesture to the clerk. The clerk summoned forward one of the guards, he who had led the slave into the chamber. The fellow came forward and produced, from his belt, a small key. It was the key, I assumed, to the holding collar. The clerk then looked to the fellow at the edge of the circle. That fellow indicated that the slave was to be turned about, and she was, rudely, so that now, standing, she faced the portal through which she had been introduced into the room. I saw that her hands were now, indeed, tied behind her back, fastened there with binding fiber. The fellow then came forward. He then removed from his pouch a collar and handed it to the clerk. The clerk looked at it. He thrust it before the slave, that she might see it. But then, perhaps because he thought that she, in her distress, her fear, was in no condition to peruse it, he said, "The legend on the collar reads, 'I am the slave of Henry, of the house of William, in Harfax.'" He then handed the collar back to the fellow who, from his previous, angry announcement of ownership of the slave, I gathered must be this very Henry, he referred to on the collar, he of the house of William, in Harfax. He would also be, as I recalled, from the words of the praetor's officer this morning, the youngest and least of that house.

Henry, from behind, above the holding collar, put the collar about the neck of the slave. He did not do this gently. Such collars, too, as it was a common collar, of the sort most frequently found in the north, fit closely. I, Fina, and the others, wore such collars. So, too, I recalled, did Dorna. I assumed most in this city did. He jerked the collar back, firmly. It must have been tight as it had, pinned beneath it, the cloth of the outer robe of concealment, the hood of that garment, and the veil. He pulled it back, again, firmly, and I heard the click of the collar's closure. It is a clear—decisive—*meaningful*—sound. There is no mistaking it. The girl will not forget it. She has been collared. She may hear that sound even in her dreams, and awaken, and touch her throat, and, half-asleep, stirring, ascertain its sure presence. Yes, it is there, and *on her*. And she cannot remove it. She is in a slave collar, in the collar of her master.

Inadvertently, without really thinking of it, my hand strayed to my own collar.

I kissed my finger tips and pressed them to my collar.

I envied girls their private masters.

I belonged to the state of Treve.

The pit master briefly glanced down at me.

Frightened, I returned my hands, palms down, to my thighs. I straightened my body. I looked straight ahead. My knees were slightly spread, enough to show that I was a pleasure slave, but were closely enough placed to accord with the decorum of the praetor's court. I was pleased to understand that the pit master would choose to ignore my slight indiscretion. No one but a frustrated free woman would denounce, or punish, a girl for loving her collar.

I was relieved.

I would not be punished for breaking position.

We then, he and I, the pit master and one of his pit slaves, returned our attention to the floor.

The slave was now in two collars, the holding collar and, just above it, the identification collar, that by means of which she can be identified, as belonging to a particular individual. As soon as the identification collar was in place, the guard of the court removed the holding collar. There had been no moment, then, when the slave had not been in at least one collar. Henry, as we shall speak of him, now adjusted the identification collar on the slave, moving it about, and pressing it down, until it was in place, the lock at the back of the neck.

He then regarded her, in his collar. He then stepped back, away from her.

"You may turn about," he said. "Keep your head down." She obeyed and he, for his part, went back to the edge of the scarlet circle, rather on our side of it. She was then standing in the center of the circle, rather as she had before, save, of course, that she now wore not a temporary collar, a holding collar, but the collar of her master.

"You nameless slut," he said.

She kept her head down.

"Worthless slave!" he cried.

I could not understand his fury. He was facing her, his back to us.

"Kneel," he said, "keep your head down."

She fell to her knees before him.

"Perhaps the slave recalls," he said, "one who was once the Lady Constanzia of Besnit, one who once, when the mistress of a rich house, defrauded the house of William, in Harfax. Much did the house of William suffer, in its resources, and more, in its reputation, in its very name, honored for generations in a dozen cities. Nearly did she bring the house of William to its ruin, but the house, a strong one, survived, and, rebuilt itself, in its resources and its name. Indeed, it is now the most prosperous of the merchant houses in Harfax. In the time of our peril, of our shame, of our sacrifices, we did not, of course, forget the name of Constanzia of Besnit. But, know that even now, now, in a time in which our fortunes have been recovered and more, in a time in which our name shines again, and more brightly than ever, in a dozen cities, in a time in which we have become first among the houses of our caste in Harfax, we still remember that name. No, we have never forgotten the name of Constanzia of Besnit. We remember that name well. And then, wonder of wonders, it came to our attention, as such things may, that the Lady Constanzia, lured like a vulo, and trapped by her greed, was now a capture prize, being held in Treve for ransom. But, lo, would her own brothers not ransom her? But it seemed not. What then was to be her fate? If she were not simply fed to sleen, it would be, presumably, oh, miserable fate, the collar! Well, you can well imagine our reluctance to see such a fine lady, and one so special to us, being simply put upon a block, somewhere, and who would know where, and being sold to just anyone. No, it seemed fitting to us that we should rescue her from such a fate. Was she not, after all, an honored member of our caste? And so we decided to ransom her, if her brothers would not, as an act, if nothing else, of caste solidarity and benevolence. And so she was ransomed. And her ransom was not cheap, I tell you that. Should we not have waited until she was enslaved, and then bid upon her? No, certainly not. She might not have been enslaved. What if she had been simply fed to sleen? But, we had heard rumors that her body might not be without interest, and so we speculated that her captors might see fit to save her for the collar. But would we know where she would be sold? Perhaps not. And auctions are such tricky things. Could we be sure of overcoming all bids? Might there not be others who, for similar reasons, for similar grievances, might be as anxious as we to obtain her? And what if she misbehaved in the house of the slaver and was, say, cut to pieces, and never even came to the block? But more than these fears, I think, was the pleasure, the gratification, which would be felt in our house by our having been your actual ransomer. I think you can understand what an excellent and fitting thing this was. And so she came into our hands, deliciously, *as a free woman*. And what, then, was to be done with her? We had feared, you might recall, that she might find herself enslaved, but our fear, most particularly, most exactly, was that she would find herself enslaved by the will and act of another—and not by our will and act, not by the will and act of the house of William, in Harfax. But our fears proved groundless. She has now been enslaved by our own will and act, by the will and act of the house of William, in Harfax, and is now, specifically, my slave, I who am the fifth son, and least in that house. You understand the meaning of this, too, I am sure, that you are the slave of the least in the house. But do not fear. You will be presented before the first in the house. An oath has been sworn to that effect. Indeed, it is in accord with the provisions of that oath I am come to Treve, to fetch you to Harfax. It is to be mine, you see, in accord with the provisions of the oath, to throw you as my branded slave, naked and in chains, to the feet of he who is first in my house, William, my father."

The slave's head was down.

"You will serve well in the house, I assure you," he said. "You will work long and hard, you will perform the lowliest and most servile tasks."

She did not lift her head.

"You will be kept under the strictest of disciplines," he said.

She kept her head down.

"It will be amusing," he said, "to point you out to our guests, and delineate your history, as, too, you are serving at our meals. Indeed, afterwards, perhaps we will have you accompany our guests to their rooms, seeing to their needs and wants, attending upon them, bringing them fresh linen, bathing them, preparing their couch and, later, naturally, taking your place at its slave ring, a token of the hospitality of the house of William."

She kept her head down.

"Yes," he cried, angrily, "you will serve well in that house! And, that it may be well recalled who you were, and what you did, you will be suitably named. Put your head to the tiles!"

She, kneeling, in the outer robe of concealment, in the hood, in the veil, thrust her head down to the tiles. Her small hands were then up, behind her, high, resting on her back, where the wrists were crossed, tied together.

"I name you 'Constanzia'!" he said, angrily.

The slave was now named 'Constanzia'.

At this point the clerk inscribed something on the set of papers which lay still on the table.

"You may straighten your back, but keep your head down, slave," said the angry Henry, of the house of William, in Harfax.

Instantly the slave, who was now "Constanzia," obeyed.

The clerk now folded the papers together, forming the long, narrow packet as before. He then tied the packet shut with the blue-and-yellow ribbon. He then walked across the scarlet circle, past the kneeling slave, and handed the papers to Henry, who took them, and put them within his robes, as he had his copy of the earlier papers, the court papers. These later papers were undoubtedly the slave's slave papers. Somewhere, I had no doubt, there were similar papers on me. The notation on the papers which had been made by the clerk had undoubtedly been the slave's name, presumably with the effective date of the name, as such names may be changed, as the master wishes. Subsequent names may, of course, be added to the papers, with their effective dates. Different masters, for example, will often give different names to slaves. Blue and yellow are the colors of the caste, or subcaste, as the case may be, of the Slavers. Some, as noted earlier, regard the Slavers as a caste independent of the Merchants, some regard it as a subcaste of the Merchants. The colors of the merchant caste itself are white and yellow, or white and gold. Needless to say, caste members do not always wear the caste colors. For example, a scribe would normally wear his blue when working but not always when at leisure. Goreans are fond of color and style in their raiment. They tend to be careful of their appearance and often delight in looking well. Not all slave papers are bound in blue and yellow, of course. I had seen copies in the pens which were in plain folders, in envelopes, and such. Indeed, some had been merely clipped together.

"I would now be left alone with the slave," said Henry.

"Our concern in this business is now done," said the clerk. "We have another matter to attend to, one which must shortly be discharged."

"I will not be long," said Henry.

"I wish you well," said the clerk.

"I wish you well," said Henry.

The clerk then, followed by the two guards of the court, withdrew.

The pit master and I were well back in the shadows. I am sure the fellow realized our presence in the chamber, but it was not conspicuous. The two guards from the pits, who had come with us, were back by the main portal.

"I hate you!" Henry said to the slave.

She trembled, her head down, her hands bound behind her.

"Oh," he said, angrily, "it is not merely that you were once the hated Constanzia of Besnit! What matter such mild hatreds? We have you now in our collar. You are now under our whip. Let the house be satisfied with what you now are, and what will be done with you. I hold a grudge against you far more profound than that attendant upon the fraud you wrought upon us, even that attendant upon the near ruin into which you brought our house. No, do not dare to lift your head, hated slave!"

The slave kept her head down.

"You do not understand, do you, hated, branded slut!" he cried.

She whimpered twice, in misery.

"Ah," said he, "you have already been taught gag signals! Excellent!"

I did not understand his fury.

"Twice you have caused great injury to the house of William," he said, "once to the house as house, and once to the house through me, one of that house."

He then, in fury, spurned the slave with his foot to the tiles. "Dare not to look upon me!" he cried.

She kept her eyes averted.

Even I was terrified by his wrath.

"Curse honor!" he suddenly cried, his fists clenched.

I was startled by this outburst, and looked up, more closely than before, less unobtrusively, less furtively. His back was to me. I had not heard this voice much before, if I had heard it before, only a few times, and then it had been in calmness, even in humor, sometimes in peremptory command, not as it was now, shaken with rage, almost hoarse with fury. But I thought that I recognized it. Before it had been only a whisper about my mind. Now I was certain. Also, it then became clear to me that the slave, far more familiar with the voice than I, if it was indeed the voice which I thought, must have surely wondered or speculated, or suspected, or entertained hopes, about the identity of its owner long before I. But she could not have been certain of the matter, for the voice was now unnatural with rage, and there might be many similar voices. She had not been permitted to look upon his features. That had been denied to her. She could not then be absolutely certain as to the matter. Indeed, even I had not looked directly upon him.

"What injury you have done to me!" he cried. "It is because of you that I have lost the most exquisite, beautiful, and desirable slave in all the world, the woman I love! Yes, here in this retreat of tarns, I found my love slave. But I must conduct my business! I must ransom the slut, Constanzia of Besnit! I must sign the letters of credit to the state of Treve to redeem her, rather than use them to negotiate for she who is to me beyond compare, who is to me above all others. Curse honor! Were it not for honor I would forget you. I would let you be dragged to any kennel, on any man's chain. Were it not for honor I would remain secretly, at the risk of my very life, in this city, to seek her, to somehow come into possession of her! Were it not for honor I would find my love, and fly with her! Kneel, head down!"

The slave struggled again to her knees.

"We must leave," he said. "The clerk has further business this afternoon."

He then walked a little about the slave, considering her. He crouched down behind her, and put his hand on her ankle. She tried, in fear, to draw it a little away, but he held it. "Do you fear a man's touch on you?" he asked. "You will grow used to it, my dear. Your ankle is not bad. It is trim, like hers. It will doubtless take a shackle well." He then moved his hand a bit inside her outer robe, perhaps to the interior of her thigh. She jerked, putting her head back, and then, swiftly, lowered it again. "You will grow used to it," he said. Then he stood up. "Your body may prove to be, as rumored, not without interest," he said. "But you will never compare to her. You are too unlike her. At best you would be as a moon to her sun. To her you will always be, in my mind, as nothing."

He then walked further about her.

"Would you like to speak?" he asked.

She whimpered once, desperately. Then, after a time, she again whimpered once, even more desperately. Then, in a moment, she began to try to speak, making tiny little futile noises, muffled in the gag.

"But you see," he said, "you may not speak. Were you not informed? Do you not understand that your words, no matter how piteous, will be of no avail? The matter is now concluded. You are branded, branded, you perfidious, dishonest, corrupt, fraudulent slut—yes, at last, after all this time, branded, at last branded!—superb!—it is now done!—the slave mark is now on you, *in* you!—it has been burned deeply into your very body with the fiery iron—understand that, slut!—and you are now, too, in your rightful neckwear, no necklace, my dear, but the collar of a slave—and it is locked on you—and you cannot remove it—and it is my collar!—it is my collar that you wear, slut! You are now owned! I own you! You are now kajira! Kajira! And my dear, my sweet little thing, you are *my* kajira!

"Ah, you would speak? But were you not informed? Your words are not of interest to those of the house of William. Why should we listen to the begging, pleading prattle of a slave? We choose not to do so. Perhaps later you will be permitted to speak, and you will be lashed if we are not pleased with your words." He then walked about her, until, again, he was rather before her, she a little to his left. "Keep your head down," he warned her.

The slave, kneeling before him, head down, pulled at the binding fiber.

"Do you truly think you can free yourself?" he asked.

She ceased her efforts, putting her head down even further. She whimpered twice.

"You might be interested in knowing," said he, "my former lofty, rich lady, that your rival, the one I prefer a thousand times to you, is one amongst the lowliest of slaves, and one, it seems, amongst the most despised of slaves, one clad when most often I saw her only in a collar and rags, and never in more than a simple tunic. Her name, not that it matters, is 'Tuta'."

The slave began to tremble, uncontrollably.

"What is wrong?" he asked, puzzled.

The slave seemed in much agitation. How she pulled at the binding fiber, so desperately, yet so futilely. She made tiny noises, they muffled in the gag.

I myself had drawn back on my knees. What I had feared, what I had hoped, had come true!

He regarded the slave, puzzled, she kneeling, head down, before him.

"I do not understand," he said.

She whimpered piteously, desperately.

"What is wrong with you?" he asked. "Doubtless she wishes to plead," he mused. "It will do her no good." He looked down upon her. "Do not expect the least of kindnesses or considerations in our house, new slave."

She squirmed.

"Perhaps she wishes to raise her head," he speculated.

She whimpered once, desperately.

"So soon she desires to exert the wiles of a slave!" he said, angrily.

She whimpered, in misery.

"Ah, yes," he said, "I have heard rumors to the effect that the Lady Constanzia of Besnit might have slave curves concealed beneath her robes. Would one not have guessed? And how appropriate! And how fortunate for her! Perhaps if she grovels well she may be lashed less frequently! Perhaps she desires to now exhibit them, that they might win for her some lenience? Do you think I am so easily put off, so easily swayed, dear little thing, that I might be seduced from my resolution by the luscious contours of a begging slave? But do not fear, for I have every intention of putting them frequently and well to my pleasure. But they will never compare with those of my love! To her gold, no matter how luscious and exciting might prove to be the curves of your perfidious, despicable body, you can never be more than a meaningless tarsk-bit of shaved copper!"

The body of the slave shook, trembling with emotion.

"See," he said, scornfully. "How quickly she learns! She is clever, no doubt! Oh, yes, she is highly intelligent, but now her intelligence will have a different object, not that of seeking wealth and power, but that of pleasing a master! Scarcely has she been branded and the collar put on her than she hopes to sway me with the pathetic artifices, the piteous beggings, of a trembling slave, but her cunning will avail her naught!"

Clearly the slave wished to raise her head, but dared not do so. I was pleased that I had given the Lady Constanzia some slave training in the pens, in answer to her desperate request that I do so.

She had desperately desired to learn how to be more pleasing to a certain visitor to Treve.

I had found her an apt pupil.

I showed her a few things, but not too many. She was, after all, a free woman.

In particular I tried to apprise her of the psychology of these matters from which, in a sense, all else flows.

"Your internal states," I told her, "are important, your mind, your emotions, and desires."

"In bondage it is your heart, your love, that blossoms," I said.

I spoke to her of nature, and her laws, and of health, and dominance and submission.

On the behavioral level, I called her attention to a variety of attitudes and modalities of deference, some as simple as kneeling and bowing the head.

"Be submissive, and feminine," I had told her.

"Be a slave," she said.

"Yes," I said, "be a slave."

Another thing I told her was to *listen*.

That was because she was a free woman.

One need not tell a slave that. The slave is in a collar. If she is inattentive, she may be lashed. Too, it is extremely important for her to listen to the master, for he *is* her master.

"It is not only we who wish to be listened to," I told her, "but men, as well."

And I did not tell her this but, commonly, aside from considerations of prudence, the slave *wants* to listen. Most slaves soon become loving slaves and it is one of the happinesses of the loving slave to have the master speak to her. And who is more important to her than her master?

We want the master to be kind and loving, but also to keep us under a strict, perfect discipline, even to the whip. We wish there to be no mistake about the matter that we are slaves, fully, nor any doubt about to whom we belong.

That is how we will to have it.

And so it is with care and attention, and pleasure, that we listen to the master.

Too, of course, as we are only slaves, and animals, we are grateful to be spoken to.

In addition, of course, it may be easier for the slave to listen, for she is seldom allowed to speak, unless she has been given permission to do so. Subjected to this condition we are muchly aware of the authenticity and rigors of our bondage. Few things more impress upon us that we are slaves. We are animals and goods. What better to remind us of this than that we may not speak without permission?

"Perhaps you think I can be moved by a piteous glance?" he said.

She made tiny whimpering noises, begging.

"Do you wish to look upon me?" he asked.

She whimpered once, plaintively, desperately.

"We must leave the city by sundown," he said.

She whimpered again, begging.

"You are doubtless curious to see to whom you belong," he said.

She whimpered, once.

"I suppose that sometime, sooner or later, you must be permitted to look upon my features," he said.
She uttered a tiny noise, a single whimper.
"Do you wish permission to lift your head?"
She whimpered once.
"It is not granted," he said.
She moaned.
"It will be rather in compliance to my command that you will lift your head," he said.
She tensed.
"Lift your head," he said.
She lifted her head, commanded, wildly, gazing upon him.
"What misery!" he cried. "Your eyes! They are like hers. They remind me of hers!"
But she now, unbidden, sobbing had flung herself to her belly before him, pressing her veiled, gagged mouth to his sandals, again and again.
"It seems the slut understands in what danger she stands," he said.
She ministered as she could to his sandals.
"She who was the proud Lady Constanzia now has some understanding of her new condition, it seems."
Sobs wracked the figure at his feet, but they were, I think, unbeknownst to him, sobs of joy.
He prodded her from him, angrily, with his foot. "Misery!" he said. "Her very eyes are like those of my beloved slave!"
She lay on her side, her hands bound behind her, looking up at him. The outer robe she wore had become somewhat disarranged, and it was now, as she lay, above her knees. I speculated that she was indeed naked beneath it.
"I see that you can stimulate a man's desire, Constanzia," he said, menacingly, in fury.
Frightened, she tried to make herself smaller, pulling her legs up.
He reached down and seized her, and pulled her up, to her knees, looking closely at her.
"I suppose, too," he said, "your hair will be dark, as hers." Then his voice became soft. It almost broke. "Perhaps," he said, "your eyes, your hair, if it be dark, truly dark, as hers, that you remind me of her,

will gain you, you hated slut, a lenience which you might not obtain by other means. Perhaps, at times, I will give you a tidbit at the table, or perhaps, at times, even hold the whip, for that you remind me of her."

Then he stood up, angrily.

"No!" he suddenly cried, in fury. "You will not weaken me! I shall not be weak! I will not be weak! You have been the enemy of our house, and are now my slave! No lenience for you, hated slut! No indulgence for the new slave, Constanzia!" He looked down at her, in fury. "I should put you to my pleasure now," he cried, "and in the manner you deserve, with ruthless authority, on the very tiles of the court!" But he did not seize her. Rather, angrily, he jerked her to her feet. He then drew a leash from his pouch and put it on her. "We must to the dock," he said, angrily. "Do you step forward, eagerly? So close to me? Do you look up to me so? Your eyes are filled with tears. Well should they be, with tears of fear and misery!" He turned about. She hastened to follow. He turned back. "You do not drag on the leash?" he asked. "You do not require a cuffing, to remind you that you are a leashed slave?"

She shook her head, it seemed, happily.

He drew back his hand, but then he lowered it, angrily. "I would not stand so close to me," he said. "Do you not realize that but a moment ago, but for a wisp of will, blowing one way or another, you would have been put to my pleasure? Do you not think I can sense your nearness?"

But, as she had not been commanded, she stood her ground, near to him. She lowered her head, submissively, as his slave.

"Yes," he said, "I do not doubt that you will prove of interest in the furs, and to our friends, our guests, our business associates, as well."

She shrank back.

"Surely you understand, my dear Constanzia," he said, "that you are now a slave."

She regarded him.

"Indeed," he said, angrily, "what is the meaning of these trappings you wear, this robe, this hood, this veil? Are they not presumptuous on one such as you have become? Do they not do you unwonted honor? Surely you understand that you are no longer entitled to such dignities."

He dropped the leash, and it dangled down from her neck, before her.

He put his hands on the hood.

"It was thought," said he, "that you might first be stripped in Harfax, but surely we need not so long postpone that small detail, so salutary in its effects upon a female."

His hands tightened on the hood.

"Do you not pull back, do you not plead?" he asked.

But she kept her head down.

"What a strange effect you have upon me," he mused. "It is doubtless because of she of whom you remind me. But I ignore this. I steel myself. I remind myself that you were once the Lady Constanzia of Besnit. So may you learn, new slave, what it is to be owned! So let it be told at the fairs, let it be remembered in the annals of the Merchants, that she who was once the proud Lady Constanzia of Besnit, who defrauded and nearly brought to ruin the house of William, in Harfax, was led through the streets of Treve on a leash, naked and bound, then the slave of Henry, least in that house!"

He thrust back the hood. The shape of her head, her throat and such, could now be much better discerned. The color of her hair, on the other hand, as the veil was arranged, it swathing her head, enclosing it save for her eyes and the very top of the bridge of her nose, could not be determined. The veil was not pinned back, nor merely bound about her lower face, the hood concealing the hair, but enclosed it, as noted, save for the eyes and a bit of the bridge of the nose. She was, of course, more revealed than before, the shape of her head, the loveliness of its positioning, its setting, and such.

He thrust the dangling leash back, over her left shoulder.

She shuddered a little.

His hands then grasped her robes, at the collar.

She regarded him.

Then, angrily, he tore them down from her shoulders, and then stood for a moment, as though in awe, she before him, erect, slim, and lovely, the robes hung down now behind her, from her bound wrists, held by the sleeves. She had, indeed, been naked beneath them.

"Ai!" he said. "It would indeed have been the collar for you!"

She straightened herself, even a little more.

Her slave curves were exquisite.

"You are beautiful," he said. "Indeed," he cried, "you are *slave beautiful*! You should never have been a free woman! How absurd that freedom should have been permitted to you! What a woeful mistake! Such a body is born for the collar! It is incomplete without it!"

She stood silent before him, scrutinized, inspected.

"You would bring a high price on the block," he said. But then he said, menacingly, "But you are not for sale."

She lifted her head a little, almost as though proffering her veiled countenance to him, as though she was eager to place the veil which she could not remove within his power.

"Oh, you can whine, and beg, and kneel, and grovel and weep, and plead to be sold," he said, "to anyone other than the House of William, in Harfax, for as little as a tarsk-bit to anyone, for any service, but you are not for sale! We have waited long to obtain you. We have plans for you, slave!"

She whimpered, futilely, fighting the gag.

But she could not speak.

It had been put on her by a Gorean.

"Beg if you wish," he said, "to be the girl of a keeper of tarsks, to be the property of a sewer master, to be sold for the cleaning of tharlarion stables, but you are destined rather for the house you so defrauded, for the house of those you so wronged, for the house of your most dire enemies! You are ours, and you will remain ours, to do with as we please, *and fully*, you may be sure, even though a ubar should bid upon you!"

She regarded him, her hands tied behind her, well and closely held by the binding fiber.

"Let us see if the former Lady Constanzia has been well marked," he said.

There was a tremor in her body, one almost of shyness. She had not long been a slave.

She must submit her brand, fresh in her body, for the inspection of her master.

He had not yet seen it.

Would it be found acceptable? Would it meet with his approval?

She trembled.

She must hope he would find it pleasing.

It seemed she could scarcely move.

"Turn your left flank to me, *slave*," he said.

She complied.

"Ah!" he said, suddenly, appreciatively. "Yes, yes!"

She whimpered, gratefully.

The slave was much relieved.

"Yes," he said, "you are well branded, an incisive, clean mark. There is no mistaking it. And *common* kajira mark! Of course! Excellent, and superbly fitting! The former Lady Constanzia of Besnit—marked as a *common* slave!—Excellent!"

The common kajira mark, of course, which I myself wore, is a lovely brand. It may be the most familiar brand on Gor for a female slave, but that does not make it any the less beautiful. Indeed, I suspect it is the most common brand because it is the most beautiful, or surely one of the most beautiful. Just as the male beasts wish us to be attractive, and dress us for their pleasure, when permitting us clothing, and such, so, too, they brand us for beauty, as well. The brand, small and tasteful, but momentous in its meaning, much enhances the beauty of a woman, both aesthetically and cognitively—in the latter dimension marking her as slave, and thus latently, implicitly, indicatively hinting at, or, better, stating, the pleasures, the joys, one may have of her. The most common brand site is the left thigh, under the hip. This site is analogous to that used on a multitude of other forms of domestic animal, verr, tarsks, bosk, and such. Sometimes boys enjoy surprising slaves in the streets or markets and flip their tunics, to ascertain the brand, and, doubtless, to treat themselves to a flash of thigh. It is a game for them. As they are free persons they could simply put the girl to her knees and issue the command, "Brand," to which the girl must respond by revealing her slave mark. But this would take time. And the pack of them are afoot, racing about and frolicking. It is irritating to be sometimes struck by a free woman or women after this has occurred, as though we could help it! Though we are doubtless quite sensitive to matters of modesty we, as slave, are not permitted modesty. It is one thing to be bared for our masters, and another for strangers.

"Now," said he, "face me, again."

She complied.

He then approached her and reached to the veil.

"It is your face now," said he, "the utmost delicacy, and least expression, of your features, which are to be exposed."

She did not pull back.

"Perhaps you do not understand," he said. "Your features are to be publicly exposed, such that anyone, the least of the workers at the docks, even a male slave, may look freely, and as he pleases, upon them."

She stood a little closer to him.

"You will be able to hide nothing," he said.

She even lifted her chin.

"Are you truly prepared," he asked, "so easily, to be face-stripped?"

She lifted her chin a little more, looking up at him.

"Strange," he said, "that you do not cringe, that you do not try to flee, that I need not use the leash, to hold you here. Have you learned so soon the futility, the meaninglessness, of recalcitrance, of disobedience? Perhaps you have felt the whip. Or perhaps you understand, already, the brand, the collar." He pulled away part of the veil from about her throat, freeing it from under the collar. "It is with pleasure, as you may well conjecture," he said, "that I now bare the face of she who was once the Lady Constanzia of Besnit. I have dreamed of unveiling her, of stripping her face, of exposing it, of making it naked." He continued to unwrap the veil. "In a moment now, my dear," he said, "your face will be naked, as is fitting for what you are now, a slave.

"Aiii!" he cried, in astonishment, dropping the veil to one side.

Instantly she fell to her knees before him.

He tore the gag from her, pulling out the wadding, discarding the binding.

Her head then was down to his feet, she weeping, covering them with kisses. The leash, fixed on her, fell to the floor. "I love you, my master!" she wept. "I love you!"

He drew her up to her knees and he crouched before her, holding her by the upper arms.

"What madness is this!" he cried, in consternation. "I do not understand! Are you not my Tuta!"

"I am whoever you will have me be!" she wept.
"But what of the Lady Constanzia of Besnit!"
"I was she," she cried.
"You are Tuta!" he said.
"She was the Lady Constanzia of Besnit," she wept.
"Tuta was a slave!"
"No! She was free! By the kindness of the pit master she was permitted to go abroad in the city, though only if collared, and clothed as a slave! I assure you there was no danger of her escaping!"
"Tuta," said he, "was right-thigh branded!"
"No," said she. "You assumed that because in certain rags permitted to me you could see only my left thigh, and, it not being marked, you inferred, I thought to be a slave, that I was right-thigh marked."
He stared at her, in disbelief.
"I trust that master does not object to a left-thigh-marked girl," she said.
"No, no," he said. "I am right-handed. I prefer it."
"Good," she said.
"You were the Lady Constanzia?"
"Until this morning, and scarcely an Ahn ago, when I was, by order of the house of William, in Harfax, branded and collared."
"Why did you not tell me you were free?" he asked.
"I must appear as a slave," she said. "And you did not tell me who you were either!"
"Of course not," he said. "What business would it have been of yours? I thought you were a mere slave."
"Yes, Master," she said, happily.
"My Tuta!" he said, beside himself with elation.
"No, my name is Constanzia," she said. "That is the name which has been given to me by my master!"
"Should you not have told me you were free?" he asked.
"But would you have then related to me, would you have felt free to do so, would you have even approached me, would you have considered me? I wanted you to relate to me. I wanted you to approach me. I wanted you to like me. Thus I wanted you to see me not as what I was, in some legal sense, a free woman, but as what I was in my heart, what I had come to long to be, as a full woman, as one who, in

the order of nature, belongs to men, as one who, in the order of nature, is a man's slave."

"And so I saw you," he said.

"And appropriately, my master," she whispered.

"Surely you should have told me you were free," he said.

"No, Master," she said.

"Why?" he asked.

"When I was near you," she said, "I was not free. When I was near you, I was a slave."

They kissed.

"The first moment I laid eyes on you," she said, "I wanted to be your slave."

"And I," he said, "from the first moment I saw you, I wanted you in my collar."

"It is in your collar I am now," she whispered.

"How can you have been Constanzia of Besnit?" he demanded.

"Forget that cold, greedy, proud woman," she begged, "think now only of the slave in your arms, who would die for you."

"The Lady Constanzia of Besnit," he said, "muchly wronged my house."

"She is now your slave," she said. "Do with her as you will."

"I must take you back to Harfax," he said.

"I heel my master with love," she said.

"I must, by oath, throw you naked and in chains to the feet of my father."

"Do so," she said. "I beg it."

"Your life will not be easy in the house," he said.

"I am a slave," she said. "We do not expect our life to be easy."

"What am I to do with you?"

"It is my hope that my master will do with me as he pleases."

"I love you," he said.

"And I love you, too, my master," she said.

"Tuta!" said he.

"Constanzia," she said.

"You will answer quickly enough to either," he said.

"Yes, Master," she said, happily.

There was a sound behind the portal to one side, that through which the clerk and the guards had earlier entered, bringing with them the slave.

Henry looked quickly toward the portal.

She looked over her shoulder, too. Frustration crossed her lovely features.

"I would serve you!" she said.

"Serve me?" he said.

"Surely master knows what to do with a slave," she said.

He threw her then to her back on the tiles. "Spread your legs, slave," he said.

"Yes, my master!" she said, delightedly.

I heard another sound behind the portal. The clerk, I gathered, had returned. The pit master, with the two pit guards, and I, of course, were waiting for him.

"Shameless," said the pit master to me, regarding the pair, she in his arms, on the scarlet circle.

"Yes, Master," I said, happily.

"Yet doubtless he should try the slut out," he said.

"Yes, Master," I said.

"I wonder how she will do as a slave," he said.

I considered the pair. She was gasping in his arms, head back, eyes closed.

"Excellently, I conjecture, Master," I said.

"She looks well, naked, in her collar," he said.

"Yes, Master," I said.

"She belongs in it," he said.

"Yes, Master," I said.

"Ai! Aiiii!" cried Henry.

"Oh, my master! My master!" cried the slave.

Then she wept, pulling at the binding fiber, "I cannot hold you! I cannot hold you!"

He then knelt beside her, and lifted her to a half-sitting position in his arms.

Her head and hair were back, hanging down. Her body was gorgeous with color, a mottled scarlet tapestry. Her nipples were tightly pointed.

"It seems you will do as a slave," he said.

"I desire only to serve and please my master," she said.

He gasped, trying to regain his breath. He put her to her back on the scarlet circle. He, kneeling, looked down upon her.

"I love you," he said.

"And I love you, my master," she said.

Then suddenly, without warning, he seized her ankles and thrust them cruelly apart.

"You are a slave," he reminded her.

"Yes, Master," she said. "Do with me as you will."

"Ah!" she cried.

It took him longer with her this time, and, then, in a few minutes, he stood up, unsteadily.

She looked up at him. "The slave would be grateful if her master were pleased with her," she said.

"The master is pleased with her," he said.

"The slave is grateful," she said.

The portal leading from the chamber opened and the clerk stepped through, taking in, in a glance, the slave, naked on the tiles, and her master standing over her. He did not seem surprised.

"Sir," said he. "The court must conduct further business."

"We are leaving," said Henry, he of the house of William, in Harfax.

The clerk withdrew, presumably to return shortly.

She stretched a little, and lifted one knee, rather saucily, rather provocatively, I thought. "Do you think that I may do as a slave, truly?" she asked.

"It is possible," he said.

"And how do I compare to your Tuta?" she asked.

"There seems little to choose between you," he said.

"But how could I compare with her?" she asked. "I am too unlike her!"

"Not as unlike as you think," he said.

"I am only as a moon to her sun," she pouted, "only as a tarsk-bit, and a shaved one, to her gold."

"Perhaps it was a mistake to remove your gag," he said.

"In your mind, compared to her, I could be only as nothing," she said.

"Be silent," he said.

"Yes, Master," she said.

"Master?" she asked. For he had drawn a knife from his robes.

"Kneel," he said.

She did so.

He then went behind her and cut the remains of the outer robe of concealment away from her bound wrists.

"What are you doing?" he asked, for she had lifted her bound wrists out, away from her body, lifting them up, toward him.

"Are you not going to sever the binding fiber?" she asked.

"What is wrong with it?" he asked. "Does it not bind you perfectly?"

"It does bind me perfectly," she assured him. "I am quite helpless in it."

"Then," said he, "it will remain as it is, until I might be pleased to remove it."

"Oh," she said.

"Do you understand, Constanzia, Tuta—Constanzia?" he asked.

"Yes, Master," she said. "We understand."

The leash still dangled from her neck.

"On your feet," he said.

She struggled to her feet.

He took the leash and drew her to him, quite closely. He then regarded her, about a foot from him, he holding her there, by the leash.

"You have served well in quick usages," he said. "We will see later how you do when put to service for Ahn at a time."

"I know nothing!" she said, in alarm. "I have not been love-trained!"

"I will train you to my tastes," he said.

"Whip-train me," she whispered.

"The training of such as you is always subject to the whip," he said.

"Good," she said.

I recalled, as undoubtedly she had, as well, his often-remarked observation, early in their acquaintance, that she was in need of whip-training. Now, it seemed that that deficiency would be remedied. It would be attended to.

She inched closer to him. She was now almost touching him, looking up at him.

"And as what shall I be trained?" she asked.

"As a pleasure slave, of course," he said.

"You dare?" she asked. "You dare do that to she who was once the Lady Constanzia of Besnit?"

"Certainly," he said.

"Why?" she asked.

"Because that is the way I want you," he said.

"You are a beast," she said.

"I am a man," he said.

"But what of my will in these matters?" she asked.

"You have no will in these matters," he said. "You are a slave. Your will is meaningless; it is nothing."

This was true. The will of the slave did not count. The will of the master was all.

"But would I be a good pleasure slave?" she asked.

"I will see to it," he said. "And you will be not only a good pleasure slave, but, I assure you, you will be a perfect pleasure slave."

"I see," she said.

"Then you are serious," she said. "I, the former Lady Constanzia of Besnit, am to be a pleasure slave, and you will train me as such."

"Yes," he said.

"I see," she said.

"Did you ever doubt it?" he asked.

"No," she smiled.

"Is it not the sort of training you want?" he asked.

"It is the sort of training I beg!" she said, suddenly, delightedly, earnestly. He then crushed her to him.

I had realized, of course, for some time, that there was not only a slave in the Lady Constanzia of Besnit, but a pleasure slave. It had been obvious, for some time, that she wanted desperately to submit herself to the mysterious visitor to Treve, to submit herself in the most perfect and complete way a woman can submit herself to a man, to be his ardent, devoted, helpless pleasure slave.

Then he thrust her from him, reluctantly, an effort which must have cost him much will. "Later, later," he said. "We must from here," he said. "There are matters to attend to. There are others to join, agents of our house."

"Master!" she protested.

"In the first camp," he said, "you and other slaves will be put in cages. I will have you drawn forth from your cage. I will have you brought to me and chained to a stake in my tent."

"And how shall I live till then?" she asked.

"On water," he said, "and a handful of slave gruel."

"Yes, my master," she breathed.

He then stepped from her, releasing a coil or two of the leash, permitting it to slacken.

"Are you prepared to be led forth?" he asked.

She looked down, wildly, in consternation, at the shreds of her robe on the floor, and at the hood, and the veil.

"I am unclothed," she said.

Surely something might be arranged from the remnants of the robe, or from pieces cut from the hood! Indeed, even the veil, a large one, might be wrapped about her body!

"You have your collar," he said.

"Master!" she protested.

"Certainly you do not think I would deny my house this triumph," he said.

She straightened herself, as the leash went taut, between the ring on the leash collar and his fist.

"Yes, Master," she said, answering his earlier question, "I am prepared to be led forth!"

He then turned about and strode toward the door. She hurried to follow him.

"Master!" she said.

He stopped, and turned about.

"Should I try to place a downcast expression on my face, Master?" she inquired.

"You may do as you will," he said, irritatedly.

"Doubtless you should treat me in your house, publicly, as a despised slave."

"I suppose so," he said, "at least for a time."

"They need not know I am your love slave," she said. "I am your love slave, am I not?"

"Yes," he said.
"Am I subject to the whip?" she asked.
"Certainly," he said. "You are a slave."
"Am I to be whipped in your house?" she asked.
"It will undoubtedly be expected, upon occasion," he said. "You were, after all, once the Lady Constanzia of Besnit."
"And who will whip me?" she asked.
"Whoever wishes to do so," he said. "Even other slaves. I advise you, thusly, to try to be quite pleasing, to everyone."
"Yes, Master," she said, trembling.
He turned about, and took a step toward the door.
"Master!" she said.
He turned to face her.
"You will whip me sometimes, will you not," she asked, "that I may know that I am a slave, and that you are truly my master?"
He did not respond.
"Can you not understand?" she said. "I love you, truly love you, helplessly! With slave helplessness! As a slave her master! And I am a slave, and you are my master! I want reassurance. I want proof, in my deepest heart, that you can do with me what you want, and that you will, that I am your slave, that you own me!"
"Be in no doubt as to the matter," he said.
"I would be convinced!" she said.
"On the practical level?" he asked.
"Yes," she said.
"I see," he said.
"Perhaps I will displease you!" she said.
"Then you will find yourself punished quickly enough," he said.
"Could you punish me?" she asked.
"Test me," he said.
"You could!" she said. "You could!"
"And would," he said.
"Yes, Master!" she said, happily.
But I did not think she would wish to displease him. And, too, once she had felt the whip, once it had made it clear to her what she was, once it had confirmed her bondage upon her, once it had imprinted upon her an understanding of what could be done to her,

I did not think it likely that she would be eager to feel it soon again, even lightly, even in the hands of a beloved master, one to whom she had surrendered everything, one to whom she belonged, totally. The whip, as a tool, is a quite effective implement. It serves to keep us well in line. Free women may make men miserable, and even attempt to destroy them, but slaves may not do so. It is ours, rather, to strive to be pleasing to our masters.

"In my house," he said, "it will be I who will first tie you to the whipping ring, who will give you your first public lashing."

"Thank you, Master," she said. "It is your whip which I would feel first, before all others."

It is not that unusual, incidentally, to whip a new slave, upon her first being introduced into a house. To be sure, the custom apparently varies from city to city. In any event, given the background and interactions of the Lady Constanzia of Besnit and the House of William, in Harfax, I did not think that they would wish to wait long before seeing the lash laid to her—well laid—to the back of the new slave.

"Master!" she cried. "Look!"

"What?" he said. "The girl in the shadows, the creature with her?"

"It is Janice!" she wept, joyfully.

"Are you sure?" he asked.

"Please let me go to her, just for a moment, please, my beloved master!" But the leash restrained her. "Oh!" she wept, in misery, held, helpless to approach me. But then he advanced toward me, letting her hurry before him. The pit master, near me, threw his cloak over his head, and turned away, that his features not be seen.

Constanzia knelt before me, I kneeling, too. "It is he, Janice!" she said. "I am a slave! I am his slave! I am happy! I am so happy! I love you, Janice!"

She bent toward me, joyfully. I took her in my arms and kissed her. "I am happy for you!" I said. "I love you, too!"

She then lowered her head to kiss the feet of the depth warden, near me. "Thank you, Master," she wept. "Thank you for everything!"

He kept the folds of his hood drawn carefully about his face.

Then in a moment she was drawn to her feet by the leash, and pulled away. She looked over her shoulder, drawn toward the portal. "I love you!" she said. "I love you!" I called. Then the slave girl, naked and bound, on her leash, was taken from the chamber. I heard the noises of a small crowd outside, and much jeering. Some had gathered, it seemed, to witness the procession of the Lady Constanzia to the docks. I supposed that several of these people would accompany her to the docks, and that, indeed, she might have to run something of a gantlet until her arrival there, perhaps being abused, switched, and spit upon. So much, at least, it seemed, would be owed to the house of William, in Harfax. To be sure, her master would doubtless to some extent protect her, seeing to it that the crowd did not exceed the proprieties customary to such occasions, for example, that they not be permitted to mutilate her or break her limbs. And soon, of course, or sooner or later, she should be relatively safe, being chained and hooded, and inserted into a cage basket, perhaps with other slaves, having arrived at the docks.

Shortly after Henry, of the house of William, in Harfax, had exited with a slave, the door to the side opened and the clerk came through. The pit master went forward then, and, near the clerk's table, conferred with the clerk. Some papers were signed, a copy being retained by the clerk, and one by the pit master.

The clerk then turned toward the portal. "Bring forth the free woman," he called. The two court guards then entered, conducting, between them, a woman in the robes of concealment, fully veiled. She was, however, barefoot. Her ankles were trim. I wondered if she were pretty. The pit master turned to the two pit guards, by the portal leading to the outer hall, that leading thence to the outside, and, with a gesture, summoned them forward. He also beckoned that I should approach. I quickly rose to my feet and hurried forward, then kneeling near him. I noted impatience in the manner, and contempt in the eyes, of the woman in the robes of concealment as I approached. I knew myself despised by her. I did not meet her eyes.

"This is the Lady Ilene of Venna," said the clerk.

The pit master lowered his head, his features shielded within the dark hood.

"Where am I?" she asked, angrily. "What am I doing here?"

The pit master went behind her and, one by one, pulled her hands behind her. There were two clicks.

"I am braceleted!" she exclaimed, angrily. "How dare you put me in such things! Remove them, immediately!"

The pit master was then again before her. He looked down at her feet.

"One slipper," said he, not turning from the free woman, but addressing himself to the clerk, "was used to convince her house that she was in our keeping. The other is in a distant city, where negotiations may be conducted, the authenticity of our negotiators attested to by the possession of the second slipper. It was not thought that, under the circumstances, she required hose."

Bonds are seldom placed over clothing. The free woman, the Lady Ilene of Venna, was under detention, rather obviously as a ransom prisoner, as had been the Lady Constanzia of Besnit, now the slave Constanzia, owned by Henry, of the house of William, in Harfax. Accordingly, her hose had been removed, that her ankles might now from the Gorean point of view be the more appropriately crossed and tied, or shackled. Such things are in part cultural, and in part practical.

I considered her, what I could see of her.

She certainly did have trim ankles. They would look well, crossed and corded together, tightly, or shackled.

I wondered, again, if she were pretty.

Doubtless the guards, too, were curious about that.

The woman tried to pull her feet back, a little, more beneath her robes.

"Who is this misshapen lout?" she asked. "What is he doing here? Why does he conceal his features?"

"You are in the presence of a warden of our city, Lady," said the clerk. "It is in his keeping that you will find yourself until your disposition is clear."

"My disposition?" she asked.

"Yes, Lady," said the clerk.

"What are you doing!" she cried.

"He is leashing you," said the clerk.

"Never!" she cried.

There was a click. She was leashed. "Take it off!" she cried.

"What?" asked one of the pit guards, one who had had his eye on her.

"'What'?" she asked.

"Yes, 'what'," he said. "Your veil? Your hood? Your clothing?"

She shrank back. "Monster," she said.

The pit master gestured to me and I rose, and came forward, and then again knelt, this time before the free woman, putting my head to the tiles before her. "Forgive me, Lady," I said. I then rose up and grasped the leash.

"I will not be led by a slut of a slave!" she said.

The pit master then gestured to the guard who had spoken before, and I willingly surrendered the leash to him.

He stood rather close to the free woman and, the leash wrapped about one hand, put his two hands on her hips. He looked down into her eyes, and she turned her head away. With one hand, the chain of the leash dangling from it, he reached up and, within her hood, the chain trailing, touched the left side of her face. Then he turned it, again, to face him. He then put one finger to the height of the veil, where, near her left eye, rather at the bridge of her nose, he pulled it down, ever so little. It seemed he might think of peering down, within it. She tried to back away, but was prevented from doing so by one of the court's guards. The fellow then crouched down a little behind her, on her right. He transferred the leash to his left hand, and, with that hand, brushed up the hem of the robes a bit and, with his right hand, grasped her right ankle. "Steady her," he said to the court guard behind her, and that guard then grasped her by the upper arms. The pit guard then, holding to her ankle, lifted her foot, lifted it up so that the lower portion of the robe of concealment came forward, to lodgment behind the knee, this revealing something of her calf, and also, of course, her foot, the ankle in his grasp. "A pretty calf," said the pit guard. "Yes," said the court guard holding the woman from behind. "I think she would take a two-ring," said the pit guard, lifting the ankle a little more. "Yes," said the other pit guard. "I would think so," said the other court guard. This was a reference to the sizes of ankle rings. "She is about the size of Janice," said the other pit guard, he not holding the woman's ankle. "What size ankle ring do you take, Janice?" "A two-ring, Master," I said. "See?" said the pit guard holding the woman's ankle. "Yes," agreed his fellow. The woman put her head in the air. I suppose she was not pleased at all to learn that she had this in common with me, that we might take the same size ankle ring. But what would be so surprising about this? Were we so different? And are not free women, as the men of this world sometimes suggest, only slaves without collars? The pit guard then released her ankle, and the fellow behind her released her upper arms. She now stood as she had before. Only I think that now she was acutely conscious of the men about her, and, in particular, of he who held her leash. His fist, the right fist, the leash now again transferred to his right hand, the leash wrapped about it, was only about six inches from her collar ring. He looked down at her. She quickly averted her eyes. "I wonder if she is pretty," said one of the court guards. "'Ilene' would be a pretty name for a slave," said the fellow with the leash. "Yes," said his fellow.

"Please," protested the woman.

"Do you think you might make good company for a lonely man on a long, cold night?" asked the guard, he holding her leash.

"I would be led by the slave," said the free woman hastily, frightened.

There was laughter.

I thought her request a judicious one, particularly if she did not wish to be visited in a cell at night, and forced to strip, and perform as a slave.

"Forgive me, Mistress," I said, accepting the leash from the guard.

"Slut," she said to me.

"Yes, Mistress," I said.

"Functionary," said the woman to the clerk.

"Lady?" he said, politely.

"You will expedite the arrangements for my ransom," she said. "I will soon be ransomed by my beloved sisters. There should be no difficulties in the matter, as we are one of the richest houses in Venna."

"It is my hope," said he, "that these matters may be conducted with the utmost dispatch."

"And if things do not work out," said the pit guard, he in whose hands she had been, in effect, assessed, "I am sure we can think of something else for you."

"Beast!" she said.

"What did you think I had in mind?" he asked.

She turned away, angrily.

"I expect," she said to the clerk, "to be treated with honor, and with dignity and respect, such as comports with my condition and station."

"I understand," he said.

"You may begin," she said, "by removing these horrid bracelets and this obscene leash!"

"They are the devices," said he, "of your current keeper, a warden of the city."

She turned to the pit master.

"Lout," she said.

The pit master lifted his head a little, his features hidden in the folds of the hood. He seldom left the depths, and, when he did so, he apparently exercised certain cautions.

"Remove the bracelets and leash!" she said.

"Remove them yourself," he said.

She struggled, briefly, pulling at the bracelets behind her back. The chain danced on its collar ring. I trusted she would neither mark nor injure her wrists. Such bracelets are not designed to be slipped by a female. They hold us well.

"I cannot do so," she said.

"Then they will remain on you, until I see fit to remove them," said the pit master.

"Tarsk!" she berated him.

The pit master stiffened. He was known as "the Tarsk" to certain scions of the city, I knew. The free woman, of course, would not know this. With her, it was merely a convenient term of abuse, an insult at hand.

The guards present smiled. The two pit guards exchanged glances. With her insult the free woman may have inadvertently placed herself closer to their grasp than she realized.

"I am rich, and of high station," she said. "I shall expect the finest accommodations."

"I have in mind a little place for you," responded the pit master, "one near the water."

"Excellent," she said.

"Sir!" protested one of the pit guards, he who had for a time held the free woman's leash.

"No," said the pit master, his decision having been made.

The free woman, it seemed, would not soon be in a cell, or even an ample-sized, low-ceilinged kennel, one which might be on the guard's rounds, one to which he might hold the key.

The free woman laughed merrily, understanding the pit master's decision as constituting for her some sort of victory, particularly given the disgruntlement of the guard.

"Perhaps later," said the pit master to the guard. "We shall see."

"Our business here is done," said the clerk, he having signed over the prisoner to the pit master. "I wish you well."

"I wish you well," said the pit master.

The clerk with the court guards then withdrew, exiting through the same portal by means of which they had entered the chamber.

The pit master then drew forth from his pouch a slave hood, which I would place on the prisoner. He and the two guards then went toward the door. They conferred there, out of earshot. Perhaps they spoke of the prisoner, perhaps of matters of the pits. I do not know. Too, curiosity is not becoming in a kajira.

I began to open and unfold the hood.

"What is that?" asked the free woman.

"A hood, Mistress," I said. I needed not tell her it was a slave hood.

"What is it for?" she asked.

"Forgive me, Mistress," I said. "It is to hood you. You are to know little of your surroundings, even where you are."

"I am not a slave girl!" she said.

I shook out the hood.

"Wait," she said. "See that guard."

"Which?" I asked.

"There, he who so insolently dared to touch me!"

"Yes, Mistress," I said.

"He is a handsome fellow, is he not?"

"Yes, Mistress," I said.

"The leash is pretty, isn't it?" she asked.

"Yes, Mistress," I said. It was of gleaming chain. The metal collar, with its ring, was also attractive.

"The bracelets, too, are pretty, are they not?" she asked.

"Yes, Mistress," I said. Most slave hardware, it seems, or at least that intended for women, is not designed solely for custodial purposes, for perfection of security. That function goes without saying. It is also designed, commonly, to display the slave, to show her off, to enhance her beauty. Bondage, as a whole, incidentally, has a tendency to enhance the beauty of women, not so much from the emphasis which it places on diet, exercise, proper rest, cleanliness, physical attractiveness, cosmetics, costuming, and such, as for the way in which it returns woman, in an institutionalized fashion, to her place in nature, rightly relating her to men, reducing her inhibitions and freeing her emotions. No woman can be fully fulfilled and happy until she finds herself at the feet of her master. Many women do not know how beautiful they are until they see themselves, bound and collared, in a mirror.

"What is it like to be touched by a man?"

"They make us serve them well," I said.

"Do you think they could make me serve them well?" she asked.

"Do not make me speak," I said.

"Speak," she said.

"Yes, Mistress," I said.

"Slut!" she said.

"Yes, Mistress," I said.

But she had trembled, thrilled.

"I will not be here long," she said. "My beloved sisters will ransom me, almost instantly!"

"Yes, Mistress," I said. I lifted the hood.

"Do you think he likes me?" she asked.

"I do not know, Mistress," I said. "Perhaps he might, if you were concerned to be pleasant—and if you were nude, at his feet."

"Slut! Slut!" she said.

"Yes, Mistress," I said. I then drew the hood over her features, and buckled it shut, beneath her chin.

In the hood, though she was not gagged within it, she remained silent.

I lifted the chain leash. I looked to the pit master, and the guards. They still conferred.

I wondered what the free woman might look like, stripped, on a slave block. She had had a trim ankle, a well-turned calf.

But she was confident that her sisters would ransom her.

I wondered if the guard would make a bid on her.

I then, at a sign from the pit master, brought the free woman forward and, shortly thereafter, she flanked by the guards, I holding her leash, the pit master leading, we left the court of the commercial praetor. We did not return immediately to the pits, as the pit master had certain matters to attend to in the city, mostly having to do with supplies. Indeed, it was, as it happened, only after sunset that we reached the entrance to the tunnels, some branches of which lead to underground routes and defenses, others to the pits. We did stop for a moment on the terrace, to watch a tarn caravan in flight, one of more than fifty birds, one which had left in the vicinity of sunset. Those not of this city with such a caravan, in the carrying baskets, would be hooded. Among these, I was sure, would be Henry, of the house of William, in Harfax, and certain agents of that house. In the cargo of the caravan, too, I was sure, in one of the cage baskets, there would be a slave, also hooded, a girl who had, only this afternoon, been named 'Constanzia'.

Thirty

Fina, the preferred slave of the pit master, burst into the quarters of the pit master. I and two others were present, a guard and another girl.

"Master!" she cried. "They are coming! Members of the black caste!"

The guard thrust the girl from him. He looked wildly at the pit master.

"Seal the passages," said the pit master. "Alert the guard."

The guard swiftly left the room.

The girl whom he had thrust from him looked after him, in consternation, clutching a bit of slave rag to herself.

"Fecha, Janice," said the pit master with a swift gesture, "to your kennels!"

I quickly pulled my tunic off and hurried to the kennel, backing into it, pulling shut the gate after me. I was then locked in. I drew back in the kennel. Fecha discarded the slave rag and locked herself, too, in her kennel. Fina, who had no kennel, but was commonly slept at the slave ring of the pit master, quickly seized up a polishing rag and, kneeling to one side, head down, began to buff a goblet.

But the first figure which entered the quarters was not that of a stranger, but one who had, upon occasion, frequented these precincts before, the officer, he whose name I knew not, but whose rank was captain.

The pit master looked up from some papers which he had but a moment before spread before him. He had also, beneath these papers, I had noted, concealed a stiletto.

"The projected invasion has landed," said the officer. "It has made landfall, as anticipated, at Brundisium."

"It has begun," said the pit master.

"It seems they think it safe now," said the officer.

"And perhaps now, it is," speculated the pit master.

"But an Ahn ago," said the officer, "emissaries from Lurius of Jad have arrived in the city. They have obtained clearances from the administration. They are authorized to enter the depths."

"Members of the black caste, the Assassins," said the pit master. "They are not far behind you."

"You know?"

"I have just received word."

"They wish to take custody of the prisoner," said the officer. "I am sure of it."

"It will be a brief custody, I am sure," said the pit master.

"He is to be removed to Cos," said the officer.

"He will never reach Cos," said the pit master.

"I have heard he is to be removed to Cos," said the officer, firmly.

"Why Assassins?" asked the pit master. "Why those of the black caste?"

"Efficiency, anonymity," said the officer.

"What has Lurius to fear?" asked the pit master. "Is the prisoner not safe here? Has he not enough spies on the continent, even in Ar herself? Has he not a thousand traitors in high places?"

"They approach," said the officer, uneasily.

"Are you armed?" asked the pit master.

"Yes," said the officer, touching his left side, beneath his robes.

"Last night," said the pit master, "I dreamed of honor."

"If he is taken from us," said the officer, "Treve loses a counter of inestimable value."

"And would Cos permit us to retain such a counter?" said the pit master.

"Numbers beyond count have landed in Brundisium," said the officer. "There must be better than a thousand ships, better than a thousand companies."

"What is their destination?" asked the pit master.

"It is rumored Torcadino," said the officer.

"And thence to Ar?"

"Doubtless."

"Such forces might be turned eventually toward the northeast," said the pit master. "The mountains could swarm with them. There could be too many to turn back."

"Ar must fall," said the officer, in a terrible voice. "She is our ancient enemy."

"And what may we expect from Cos, and Tyros, once entrenched upon the mainland?" queried the pit master.

The officer looked down, angrily.

"Ar is divided against itself," said the pit master. "There are traitors in high places."

"Excellent," growled the officer.

"Had there not been he would not have been encouraged into the Voltai, had there not have been we would not have received the information which permitted us to ambush and snare him as we did."

At that point, from outside, somewhere down the corridor, we heard a sounding of metal, perhaps the beating of a sword hilt on a closed gate.

"Open!" we heard. "We have orders! Open!"

"The passage is sealed," said the pit master.

"It must be opened," said the officer. "The administration has cleared them. They have authorization."

"What has Rask said of this?" asked the pit master.

"He has pledged a thousand men to stop them," said the officer.

"And would precipitate war," said the pit master, irritably.

"And what Kaissa would you play?" inquired the officer.

"I have a game in mind," said the pit master.

"Neither of us may betray the honor of our post," said the officer.

"And where is found the house of honor?"

"He is to be surrendered to them," said the officer. "There is no other way."

"You understand what that means?"

"There is no other way."

"There is a possibility."

"None we may with honor pursue."

"Honor has many voices, and many songs."

"Open! Open!" we heard, from down the corridor. There was a repetition of the pounding on the bars of the gate. "Open! Open!"

"We need time!" said the officer.
"They will not have their way this day," said the pit master.
"And how is that?" asked the officer.
"Their papers are not in order," said the pit master.
"I see," said the officer.
"Open," we heard. "Open!"
"Coming, coming, Masters!" called the pit master.

Thirty One

"We have seen a hundred prisoners!" cried the fellow in the black tunic, the leader of the strangers.

"None is he, I am sure of it, Master," said a furtive, twisted fellow, his face a mass of jerking scar tissue.

"If I knew whom you seek, perhaps," said the pit master.

"Gito will know him," said the fellow in black.

"We can kill every male prisoner in the depths," said one of the fellows in black, a lieutenant.

"You have no authorization for that," said the pit master.

"You know whom we seek," said the leader of the men in black tunics. There were twenty-three in their party, the leader, a lieutenant, the fellow called 'Gito', and twenty men. Each of the twenty men carried a sword, a dagger, and a crossbow. Some had their bows set.

"If you have come to take custody of a prisoner, as your orders state," said the pit master, "why have you no chains with you?"

I had noted this, too. One of the men carried a leather sack. It was the only unique, or unusual, object they seemed to have with them.

"Are any of these a preferred slave?" asked the leader of the fellows in black.

The ten female slaves kept in the quarters of the pit master, I among them, had been, at the insistence of the leader of the strangers, brought along in the corridors. Our hands were bound behind our backs. We were stripped. I had not understood why we were taken along. I now began, uneasily, to suspect why.

"They are only slaves," said the pit master.

"Cut their throats," said the leader of the strangers.

We cried out, and shrank back, and might have run, but there was nowhere to run. Men were all about. One fellow took me by the hair, to hold me in place.

"Hold!" said the pit master. "Know that these women are the property of the state of Treve! You are within the walls of Treve. You are sheltered by her Home Stone. You cannot deal with the property of Treve with impunity."

"You have delayed us long enough," snarled the leader of the black-tunicked men. "We came yesterday to the pits, and you put us off with some absurd technicality."

"We have our regulations, Master," said the pit master.

"That technicality was cleared this morning," said the leader of the strangers.

The majority of the men in black tunics, incidentally, save for two who returned to the surface, to repair the fault in their papers, had remained overnight in the quarters of the pit master. It seemed that, as tenacious and terrible as sleen, they would take their repose on the very trail they followed. Too, I am sure they did not trust the pit master. The officer of Treve had left the quarters of the pit master shortly after the arrival of the strangers, putatively to ensure that new papers would be properly prepared, that there would be no further difficulty in the documents, supposedly of transfer or extradition. The men in the black tunics who had remained overnight in the quarters of the pit master, including their leader and his lieutenant, seemed to me strange fellows. They were much unlike many, if not most, of the men of this world. They did not laugh, they did not joke, they did not tell stories. They were silent, frightening, terrible men. I do not think they had Home Stones. If they had some loyalty, and I do not doubt they did, I think it was rather to some bloody oath, or dark covenant, or even to a leader. They attended to their equipment, they sharpened their swords. They drank only water. They ate sparingly. The hospitality of the pit master, offering us to them, was declined. Even the women chained at the wall were not touched. We were, however, denied our blankets, and we must all be chained, even those in the kennels. One of the girls at the wall, Tissia, I do not know what she had done, was savagely kicked by one of the black-tunicked fellows. "Temptress!" he denounced her. She wept and crawled away from him, pressing herself against the wall in her chains. I supposed we were all temptresses, all women. But I could not understand the meaningless savagery of his rejection of her. How different it was from the average response of the average man of this world. The men of this world delight in our femaleness, and in its joyous subjugation, in owning and mastering it. They prize our softness, our beauty, our desirability. And it does not occur to them, in this natural world, to conceal their desires to relate to it in the order of nature, as a dominant sex to one whose biological calling it is to delight, to please, and obey. But these men, these men in dark tunics, were so different! They had us naked in our chains, but then they ignored us. It was no wonder that we drew back in our kennels, and huddled against the wall. Such treatment made us feel small, and ashamed of our beauty. But then perhaps these men had other concerns, concerns which took priority over the curves of chained bond-sluts. Perhaps when their business was done we, or such as we, might be recollected. Perhaps we might then, nude, serve them their food and drink, diffidently. I would fear to serve such men. This morning, before they left the quarters of the pit master each had, in turn, turned away from us, then being anointed, or something, by one of his fellows. Each, following this ritual, had then donned his helmet.

"This one," said the lieutenant, pulling Fina forward by the hair, "was not kenneled."

"Cut her throat," said the leader of the strangers.

"No!" said the pit master, raising his hand.

"Show us the lower corridors," said the leader of the darkly clad men.

"No, Master!" wept Fina.

"They are dangerous," said the pit master.

"Show us," said the leader of the strangers.

"I will show you," said the pit master.

"He is a weakling," said the lieutenant.

"Release the slave," said the leader of the strangers, "but keep her, and the others, with us."

The fellow who had brought Fina forward let her go. She, sobbing, began to back away. But another fellow stopped her, forcibly. He took her by the upper left arm and thrust her forward. She would remain with us.

"You will recognize him, my good Gito?" inquired the leader of the strangers.

"I am sure of it," said the furtive fellow, the side of his face moving under the scar tissue. His face was such that it might once have been thrust into boiling oil.

"Go first," said the leader of the strangers to the pit master.

"Master!" protested Fina, in misery. But she was cuffed to silence.

I had seen nothing of the officer of Treve this morning. He had, I gathered, thought it best to avoid the depths this day. Indeed, the guards of the pits had been dismissed. "We have no need of them," had said the leader of the helmeted, darkly clad brethren.

We followed the pit master, descending toward the lower corridors.

"Cursed Assassins!" cried a fellow from a cell.

In a few minutes we were in the lower corridors. Here and there there was water on the corridor floor. It was cold to my bare feet. Sometimes it splashed, too, on my ankles, from the tread of the men about me. By myself, or with the pit master, I could avoid the water, keeping to the higher parts of the floor, but it was not easy to do so now, I muchly in line, with the other girls, the men about. Here and there the ceiling of the corridor was so low that even I must bend over. Two of the fellows with the leader carried lanterns. The passage was lit, too, here and there, with tiny lamps. Common cord held my wrists behind my back. I was tightly bound.

"Move back the observation panel on that door," said the leader of the helmeted men.

One of the fellows with a lantern undid the panel latch and slid the panel, in its tracks, to one side. He lifted the lantern near the opening and peered within.

"Something is within," he said.

"Open the door," said the leader of the helmeted men.

"There is only a peasant within," said the pit master. "He does not even know who he is."

"And who is he?"

"41."

"'41'?"

"Prisoners in this corridor are referred to only by numbers," said the pit master.

"Let us see him," said the leader of the strangers.

"I do not have the key," said the pit master.

"Why do you insist upon obstructing us in the line of our duty?" inquired the leader of the strangers. "Do you think no report will be made of this to the administration, to the administrator, to the high council?"

"I do not have the keys," said the pit master.

"Keys may be fetched," said a man.

"Tools may be brought," said another. "We may then force the door."

"I weary of these hindrances," said the leader of the helmeted men.

"Shall we go back for the keys, for tools?" asked a man.

"Where are the keys?" asked the leader of the helmeted men.

"I do not know," said the pit master.

"Seize him," said the leader of the helmeted men.

The pit master was seized. Four men held him. He did not struggle. I think they did not know his strength. He did not try to throw them off.

The leader of the helmeted men pulled the pit master's head up, by the hair.

"You are a tarsk, indeed," said the leader of the helmeted men.

The pit master looked up at him, his mouth open, his eyes rolling. He growled, a sound not human.

"Where are the keys?" asked the leader of the helmeted men.

"I do not know," said the pit master.

"Kill him," said the leader of the helmeted men. The lieutenant removed his dagger from its sheath.

"No, Masters!" cried Fina, thrusting herself forward, falling to her knees in the damp corridor. "He has not spoken the truth to you. The keys are here! They are on a cord, about his neck!"

The leader of the helmeted men reached inside the tunic of the pit master and pulled forth keys, on a string. He broke the string, jerking it against the back of the neck of the pit master, freeing it.

"Open the door," he said to one of the men.

The pit master looked down at Fina.

"Forgive me, Master," she said, putting down her head.

The door, after a time, was swung open.

One of the men with a lantern entered first. He was followed by the leader of the helmeted men. Then entered the pit master, who had been released by those who had held him. Some other men, too, entered, including the lieutenant.

The lantern was held up, and the men regarded the sitting figure within.

"He is a big one," said a man.

"So are many of his caste," said another.

The peasant lifted his eyes, blinking, against the lantern.

"Light the lamps in the cell," said the leader of the helmeted men.

The lamps, one by one, were lit. I had usually lit only one, in my attendance here.

Fina and I, and the other girls, as the lamps were being lit, were thrust into the cell and knelt to one side, on the right, as one would look toward the prisoner. In this fashion, our helplessness was increased, we now being subject to a custody stricter than would have been possible in the open corridor. Certainly we would be less tempted to run. Too, this disposition of us freed more men to enter the cell.

"You have misled us again, have you not?" inquired the leader of the strangers.

"I do not understand," said the pit master.

"You are a brave man," said he, "to trifle with those of the black caste."

"Perhaps he whom you seek is not here," said the pit master.

"Who are you?" demanded the leader of the strangers of the peasant.

"I do not know," said the peasant.

The leader of the black-tunicked men straightened up, disgustedly.

"Is it time for the planting?" asked the peasant.

The leader of the black-tunicked men turned in fury to the pit master, who stood to one side, to his left.

"You would palm this off upon us," demanded the leader of the black-tunicked men, "for he whom we seek?"

"I do not understand you," said the pit master.

"You understand me only too well!" cried the leader of the strangers. "You put a madman here, a simpleton, a dolt, one out of his wits, one who does not know his own name, a worthless, meaningless brute, a monster of no consequence, and expect to delude us!"

"We can seek further, if you wish," said the pit master.

"We have it on authority," said the leader of the black-tunicked men, "that he whom we seek is in the depths. Where is he?"

"Who?"

The leader of the black-tunicked men looked about himself, angrily. But he did not respond. Then he turned back to face the pit master. "You trifle not only with me," he said. "You trifle with Cos, with Lurius of Jad."

"I shall be pleased to seek further," said the pit master.

"You are clever, pretending reluctance," said the leader of the black-tunicked men. "The matter of the keys was well done. Not knowing where they were, and all. And this dolt, this garbage, in the lowest corridor, in five chains! So clever!"

"But Captain," said the lieutenant. "Should we not call Gito?"

"For what?" snapped the captain.

"To examine the prisoner."

"Where is our dear friend Gito?"

"He lingers in the corridor. He fears to enter."

"Gito!" called the captain, he who was the leader of the black-tunicked men.

"Master?" inquired Gito.

"Enter, look upon the prisoner."

The small, furtive fellow, with the terribly scarred face, perhaps from scalding, entered the cell.

"Is this he?" asked the leader of the strangers, pointing to the peasant.

"It cannot be," said Gito, squinting.

"Could you recognize him?"

"I could recognize him anywhere," said Gito.

"Look closely upon him," said the leader of the strangers. "Bring the lantern closer," he said to one of his men.

"Do not be afraid," said the lieutenant. "He is chained."

Gito, the side of his face moving, knelt down before the peasant, looking at him closely.

"Well?" demanded the leader of the strangers.

"There is a resemblance," said Gito, slowly.

"Of course there is a resemblance," said the officer, angrily. "These sleen of Treve would have managed that."

Gito continued his consideration of the peasant's countenance.

"No," he said, at last. "I do not think it is he."

He then stood up.

"We must look further," said the leader of the black-tunicked men, turning away.

"Gito?" said the peasant.

The leader of the black-tunicked men turned sharply back, to regard the peasant.

The cell was very quiet.

Gito began to tremble.

"Gito?" said the peasant.

"He knows him!" said the lieutenant.

"Yes?" said Gito, backing away.

"Is it you?" asked the peasant.

"Yes," said Gito.

"He heard the name before. You spoke it yourself," said the pit master.

"Be silent!" said the leader of the black-tunicked men.

The peasant lifted his eyes, seemingly vacant, toward the leader of the strangers.

"You wear black," he said.

"Do you know the meaning of such habiliments?" inquired the leader of the strangers, eagerly.

"No," said the peasant.

"You remember them, such habiliments?" said the leader of the strangers.

"I do not know," said the peasant.

"Think, think!" said the leader of the strangers.

"Perhaps," said the peasant.

"It was long ago," urged the leader of the strangers.

"Perhaps," said the peasant. "Long ago."

"Where is your holding?" asked the leader of the strangers.

"I do not know," said the peasant.

"Near Ar?"

But the peasant was looking on Gito, who shrank back, among several of the men in black.

"Are you not my friend Gito?" asked the peasant.

"He knows him!" said the lieutenant.

"Is your holding not near Ar?" asked the leader of the strangers.

"Perhaps," said the peasant. "I do not know."

"Down with Ar!" said the leader of the strangers.

"No," said the peasant, very slowly.

"Yes," said the leader of the strangers, "down with Ar!"

"'Down with Ar'?" said the peasant.

"Yes, down with her!" said the leader of the strangers.

The peasant seemed puzzled.

"Ar is nothing to you," said the pit master.

"I spit upon the Home Stone of Ar!" said the leader of the strangers.

"Ar is nothing to you," insisted the pit master.

"Be silent!" said the leader of the strangers.

"Is she in danger?" asked the peasant.

"Yes!" said the leader of the strangers.

"Then those who are of Ar must defend her," said the peasant.

"I am sure it is he!" said the lieutenant, delightedly.

"And what of you?" urged the leader of the helmeted men. "Are you not of Ar? Must you, too, not defend her?"

"Is it time for the planting?" asked the peasant.

"Must you not defend Ar?" asked the leader of the black-tunicked men.

"Why?" asked the peasant.

"Are you not of Ar?"

"I do not know."

The leader of the helmeted men stepped back.

"It is he," insisted the lieutenant.

"I agree," said the leader of the helmeted men. He then, with two hands, removed his helmet. A gasp escaped me, and several of the other girls, too, for, on the forehead of the leader, fixed there, presumably this morning, was the image of a black dagger. It was such a thing, it seemed, that these men had placed on their foreheads this morning. The leader of the black-tunicked men now handed his helmet to one of the others. He also drew his dagger. "Bring the sack forward," he said to the fellow with the sack. It was brought forward, and opened.

"He is chained!" said the pit master.

The peasant looked out, as he often did, seeming to see nothing.

He called Gito turned his face away.

"You have played a clever game of double Kaissa," said the leader of the black-tunicked men, "leading us to believe, as though falsely, this was he whom we seek, when it was in truth he, but the game has been penetrated."

"This is not he whom you seek!" said the pit master.

"And whom do we seek?" asked the leader of the black-tunicked men.

The pit master was silent.

"He whom we seek surely could not be confessedly in Treve," laughed the leader of the black-tunicked men.

"That is not he," said the pit master.

"Then it will not matter that he is killed," said the leader of the black-tunicked men.

The lieutenant and several of the others with them laughed. It was the only time I had heard them laugh.

I saw the hand of the pit master steal toward his tunic.

"Someone is coming," said one of the men outside the door.

The pit master drew his hand quickly away from his tunic.

The figure of the officer of Treve appeared in the doorway, he whom I knew well, and he who had, in the manner of these men, known me well, and as a slave.

"We have found he whom we seek," said the leader, "and we will brook no interference."

"I do not come to offer you any," said the officer. "Your papers are in order."

"Where have you been?" asked the pit master.

"I have set guards at all exits to the city," he said.

"For what purpose?" asked the leader of the strangers.

"To prevent the possible escape or improper removal of a prisoner," he said.

"You take great pains to guard the honor of your keeping," said the pit master.

"Yes, and of yours," he said.

"I have not betrayed my trust," said the pit master.

"And I am here to see that you do not," said the officer.

"It seems we have different senses of honor," said the pit master.

"Honor has many voices, and many songs," said the officer.

"It would seem so," said the pit master.

"He does not even know what we will do with him," said the leader of the black-tunicked men.

"Your papers are for transfer, for extradition," said the pit master, "only that."

"They do not specify that the prisoner is to be removed alive, or in his entirety," said the leader.

"I am not fond of those of the black caste," said the officer.

"Nor we of those of the scarlet caste," said the leader.

"At least we have the common sense to go armed," said the lieutenant.

"You do not share our Home Stone," said the pit master. "You should not be armed in our city."

"We have the authorization of the administration," said the leader of the black-tunicked men.

"Who would disarm us?" asked the lieutenant.

"Stand back," said the leader of the black-tunicked men.

"I am reluctant to permit this," said the officer of Treve. "It is one thing, in the honor of a keeping, your papers in order, to surrender a prisoner. It is another to see this done within our walls. I fear lest the Home Stone be stained."

"Is it your intention to interfere?" inquired the leader of the black-tunicked men.

"It does not seem that I could," said the officer. "Such would seem to constitute a betrayal of my post."

"It would, clearly," the leader of the strangers assured him.

The leader of the strangers then returned his attention to the peasant.

"Is it time for the planting?" asked the peasant.

"Perhaps you would have us put more chains on him first?" said the pit master, bitterly.

"That will not be necessary," said the leader of the black-tunicked men.

"You!" cried the pit master, addressing himself to the fellow called Gito. "He is not the one you know. Tell the captain!"

"Where is my friend Gito?" asked the peasant.

"Here," said Gito, from back among those in the black tunics.

"Are you well, Gito?" asked the peasant.

"Yes," said Gito.

"I am pleased to hear this," said the peasant, approvingly, distantly.

"There is no doubt about it," said the lieutenant. "He remembers him. He knows him."

"He should," said the leader of the strangers. "He once, on a hunting expedition, saved Gito from brigands who were torturing him. He took him, half dead, burned, defaced, into his own house, showered him with gifts, improved his fortunes, treated him as a kinsman. He loved few and trusted few, as he loved and trusted Gito."

Gito turned away.

"It is he, is it not?" said the lieutenant.

Gito covered his face with his hands.

"No!" said the pit master.

The lieutenant smiled.

The leader of the black-tunicked men then motioned the fellow with the sack to advance.

"No!" said the pit master, thrusting his own body between the knife and the peasant.

The leader of the black-tunicked men looked to the officer of Treve. "Order this obtuse brute to stand aside," he said.

"Stand aside," said the officer of Treve.

"No!" said the pit master.

"He is armed!" said the lieutenant.

The pit master, from within his tunic, had drawn forth the stiletto which I had seen yesterday in his quarters, that which he had concealed beneath papers.

The leader of the black-tunicked men stepped back, carefully, slowly, not taking his eyes from the pit master. He made no quick moves. When he was a few feet back he stopped. He then transferred the dagger he carried to his left hand and drew his sword with his right. It left the sheath almost soundlessly. It was a typical blade of this world, small and wicked. Such blades are favored by those who prefer to work close to their men. They are also designed in such a way that they may, by a skillful swordsman, in virtue of their lightness, speed and flexibility, be worked within the guard of longer, heavier weapons. Their design is such, in short, as to overreach shorter weapons and yet, in virtue of the weights involved, penetrate the defenses of less wieldy blades. The lieutenant had also drawn his weapon.

"Please stand aside," invited the leader of the strangers.

"Stand aside!" said the officer of Treve.

"No!" said the pit master.

Fina, amongst us, kneeling in the damp straw, bound, moaned.

The pit master did not glance at her. His eyes were on the leader of the strangers.

"Bowmen," said the leader of the black-tunicked men.

Two black-tunicked, helmeted fellows who had their bows set, quarrels ready within the guides, stepped forward.

"No!" screamed Fina.

"Do not lift your bows," said the officer of Treve.

"He is armed!" said the lieutenant.

From within his robes the officer had drawn forth a blade. It had apparently been slung beneath his left arm. It had not been sheathed.

"The first man to lift a bow dies," said the officer of Treve.

"Why do you interfere?" inquired the leader of the strangers.

"It will take only a moment to kill them both," said the lieutenant.

"You are a captain," said the leader of the strangers to the officer of Treve. "You hold rank in this city. Why would you defend this monster?"

"We share a Home Stone," said the officer.

"Is it time for the planting?" inquired the peasant.

"Yes!" suddenly cried the pit master, over his shoulder. "It is time for the planting!"

"You have been kind to me," said the peasant. "But I must now leave. It is time for the planting."

"You may not leave," said the pit master, speaking to the giant behind him, not taking his eyes from the leader of the strangers.

"I must," said the peasant, simply.

"They will not let you!" said the pit master. "These men will not let you!"

"I am sorry," said the peasant. "I must go."

"You cannot!" cried the pit master. "They will not let you!"

"Not let me?" said the peasant, dully, uncomprehendingly.

"No, they will not let you!" said the pit master.

"Look," said the lieutenant, amused. "He is getting up."

There was laughter from the helmeted men.

The peasant now stood. He looked down at the chains, from one side to the other, on his wrists, and ankles.

He pulled at them a little, not seeming to comprehend the impediment they imposed upon him.

"Free yourself!" said the lieutenant.

The peasant pulled against the chain on his left wrist. The links of the chain went straight, lifting the ring from the wall. He similarly tried the chain on his right wrist.

There was laughter from the men present.

"They mock you! They laugh at you! They will not let you do the planting!" said the pit master, not looking back.

"They are not my friends?" asked the peasant.

"No!" said the pit master. "They are not your friends! They would stop you from the planting."

"I must do the planting," he said.

"They will not let you!" cried the pit master.

Suddenly a strange, ugly, total, eerie transformation seemed to come over the gigantic body of the peasant.

"Free yourself!" taunted another man.

"He is growing angry," said another.

Suddenly the veins in the forehead of the giant seemed to swell with blood, like ropes under the skin. His eyes seemed suddenly inhuman, inflamed like those of a mad animal.

The men grew silent, uneasy.

He threw himself again and again against the chains. His wrists bled.

He uttered a low, terrible sound, not like anything even an animal might manage. More like something that might have sprung from the depths of the earth, a rumbling, as of a volcano.

There was an uneasy laugh from one of the helmeted men. The girls, kneeling in the straw, bound, neglected, to the side, I among them, were tense. We shrank back a little. Our knees moved in the straw. It seemed we might be in the presence of a force of nature.

He strained against the chains, uttering terrible sounds, like no human.

"Ai," said a man, watching.

Then it was suddenly, oddly, as though he grew in stature, in power, and strength.

Doubtless it was an optical illusion, given the confinement of the cell, his now being upright, not sitting, his pulsing to his full stature, then bending down, like a bull, straining, muscles bulging, pulling outward. Then straightening up, then again bending down, again pulling forward.

"He will tear his limbs from his body," said a man.

But I did not think the peasant, that violent giant, that simple, outraged behemoth of a man, in his present state of mind, in his agitation, in the singleness of his purpose, in this ferocious, puissant concentration of all of his force, his power, against iron and rock, was troubled by pain, or even capable of feeling it.

Again and again the chains drew against the rings. It seemed that a draft beast of enormous size could have exerted little more stress on that metal.

Some of the men then laughed.

But almost at the same time there was heard the slippage of a bolt, and we saw, on his left, our right, as we looked upon him, the plate to which the ring was attached, jerk outward an inch.

"Ai," said a man, in awe.

The men were then silent.

In the light I saw, on his right, our left, one of the links of chain stretch a little, bending. I do not know if others saw this. The links there could have been slipped apart, but the peasant took no note of this, rather he continued to force himself against the chain, the link bending more.

"I have never seen anything like this," said one of the black-tunicked men, in awe.

"He is amazingly strong," said another.

"The bolts are weak," said another.

"They have been filed from the other side," said another.

The peasant reached down and seized the chain on his right ankle with both his right and left hand. He then crouched down and then began, slowly, to straighten his legs.

"He will break his legs," said a man.

Suddenly the chain snapped from the ring.

"It was rusted in the dampness," said a man.

"We have seen enough of this," said the leader of the black-tunicked men.

"You know he cannot free himself," said the pit master. "You know he cannot do that!"

"Bowmen," said the leader of the strangers.

But the gaze of the bowmen seemed fixed, in awe, on the straining giant. Their bows, the quarrels set, were not elevated to fire, with a vibrating rattle of cable, to the heart. I did not think they even heard their captain.

"Bowmen!" said the leader of the strangers.

His cry shook the bowmen.

"Spare the pit master or die!" cried the officer of Treve.

"Hold your fire," said the leader of the strangers. They had not, however, mindful of the proximity of the officer's blade, raised their weapons, either to the pit master, or to the officer. One could presumably manage to fire. The other, whichever it was to be, would presumably die. The lieutenant moved a little to his left.

"Remain where you are," cautioned the officer of Treve.

He could be outflanked by a thrust from his right.

"You have one stroke, that is all," said the lieutenant.

"Remain where you are," said the officer of Treve.

The lieutenant stayed where he was. He himself had not been authorized to strike by his captain, and the single stroke which the officer might be expected to initiate might well be intended for him.

"You have no objection, I trust," said the leader of the strangers to the officer of Treve, "to the simple removal of your disobedient subordinate from the line of fire?"

"If he is unharmed," said the officer.

"Stand with me!" said the pit master.

"Stand aside," said the officer. "Their papers are in order. You know that as well as I. Be mindful of your post, its honor, and your duty."

"Honor has many voices, many songs," said the pit master.

"Get him out of the way," said the leader of the strangers.

We suddenly heard a second chain snap, that which had been on the left ankle of the giant. The end at the ring with the force of the suddenly parting metal struck down at the stone like a snake, jerking and rattling. It had even struck a spark from the stone.

Several of the helmeted men, cautiously, began to approach the pit master. The officer of Treve stepped back.

"Stand aside," said he to the pit master.

"Stand with me," said the pit master.

"No," said the officer of Treve.

The peasant, his legs free, save for the shackles and a length of chain on each, now turned about and grasped, with both hands, the chain on his neck. He put one foot against the wall. He began to tear back on the chain.

One of the black-tunicked men lunged at the pit master. He cried out in pain, twisting, drawing back, his arm slashed. The pit master drew back his arm, but before he could bring it forward again, three of the black-tunicked men had hurled themselves upon him. Then others followed. The officer from Treve observed this, and did not observe the sign that was given by the leader of the black-tunicked men. Then, suddenly, he himself was seized by two of them. A third wrenched open his hand, his blade fell to the floor. Almost at the same time there was a snap of chain and the neck chain which was on the peasant dangled before him, from the ring on his collar, and he had turned about again, to face us, his eyes wild, saliva running at the side of his mouth. His hands were bloody. Blood, too, was on the chain. The pit master's grip on the stiletto was like iron. They could not pry it from his fingers. But six men held him, helplessly, to the side. The way was now cleared to the peasant.

"Kill him, kill him, kill him!" cried Gito, back by the door. "Do not wait! Kill him!"

In the commotion even those of the black tunics who had been in the corridor had entered the room. Indeed, some had set aside their bows, to assist in the subduing of the pit master. Two, however, remained at the door. I had noted the anguish with which some of my sisters in bondage had observed this. They could not run past the men. They would remain, as we, the rest of us, slave girls kneeling in a cell, bound, our disposition, our lives, in the hands of men. And I am certain that they were as alarmed as I to be where we were. I think it required no great perception to understand that we beheld, unwilling though we might be, sensitive matters, matters which might prove delicate, matters which might deal, even, with states.

One of the girls sprang to her feet and ran toward the door, but she was caught there, and held for a moment, and then flung back, forcibly, cruelly, to the stones and straw.

She lay there, her wrists bound tightly behind her back with simple, common cord, sobbing.

And if she were to run, where would she go, nude and bound, in the depths? Would she not be stopped by the first gate? There would be no escape for her, neither here nor elsewhere, no more than for us. We were collared. We were branded. We were slave girls.

We feared, being where we were, seeing what we had seen. We feared the black-tunicked men. We feared that we might be disposed of. Perhaps it would be decided that we had seen too much. Yet we understood, surely, little, if anything, of what we had seen. How absurd, if for so little, not even comprehended, our throats might be cut! No wonder we were so miserable, so frightened!

The peasant stood there now like a beast at bay. From the shackles on his left and right ankles there hung, their links on the stone, broken chains. Another chain dangled from the ring on the collar on his neck. A link had snapped, but the plate behind him on the wall, too, was half pulled out from the stone. His wrists were still shackled. He did not know that there was an opened link on the chain that held his right wrist. It might have been simply slipped from its joining link. But he did not know this. And the chain on his left wrist still went back to the metal plate, pulled out, though it was, an inch or so from the wall. It seemed the bolt behind the stone had drawn tight against the stone and it could not move further, not without pulling the very stone itself from the wall.

"Bowmen," said the leader of the strangers. The two bowmen advanced. Then they stopped, and set, left feet forward, right feet back, crosswise, braced. The peasant hurled himself again against the chains which held him back. The bowmen were no more than a yard from the peasant. The only light in the cell was from the two lanterns, and the tiny lamps. There were several men about. We knelt back, and to the side. Again the peasant, bellowing, threw himself against the chains. We shrank back, frightened. "He is strong," said a man. Again the peasant hurled himself against the chains. "Kill him," cried Gito. "Kill him, quickly!" "He is chained," the leader of the strangers reminded Gito. "Kill him!" urged Gito. "Prepare to fire," said the leader of the strangers. The bows were lifted. Again the peasant threw himself against the chains. Save for the metal band, the bow, or spring, mounted crosswise, now drawn, and the cable, arched back, the devices, with their triggers and stocks, were not unlike stubby rifles. They were small enough to be concealed beneath a cloak. "Kill him!" cried Gito. Again the peasant threw himself against the chains. I saw the one link bend more. We heard part of the stone scrape outward in the wall. "Kill him," cried Gito. "Kill him, quickly!" "No!" cried the pit master. Again the peasant threw himself against the chains. There was a sound of tortured metal, a scraping of stone. The entire block of stone in which the plate and ring was fixed on the peasant's left, our right, had inched out. "Kill him, kill him!" screamed Gito.

"Take aim," said the leader of the strangers quietly.

"No!" cried the pit master.

The two bowmen trained their weapons on the heart of the peasant.

The officer of Treve stood quietly, angrily, to the side, restrained by two men. His blade, his fingers pried from the hilt, one by one, was at his feet. That mound of a human being which was the pit master struggled. Six men clung to him. Fina was sobbing.

The leader of the strangers, stood to one side. He and the lieutenant, now that the pit master was restrained, had sheathed their blades.

"Do not kill him!" said the pit master, moving like a part of the earth beneath those who clung to him.

"Kill him! Kill him quickly!" screamed Gito, from the back.

Again the peasant threw his weight against the chains. There was another sound of metal and rock.

The leader of the strangers smiled. He lifted his hand.

"No!" cried the pit master.

The two bowmen tensed, their fingers on the triggers, their quarrels aligned to the heart of the peasant.

I saw the chains straighten, the rings straighten; the plate on our right, the peasant's left, out from the stone, and the very stone in which it was fastened, too, drawn an inch or more out from the wall, and the other chain, too, I saw, it still fastened to its ring and plate, these tight on the stone, but there, too, the stone itself, the heavy block of stone in which the bolts of the plate were set, was, like the other, with a scraping and a powder of mortar, a rumbling grating, another granular inch or more emergent from the wall.

Again the peasant lunged against his chains, and there was a squeal of metal and there was, as though reluctant, crying out, protesting, another tiny yielding, a grating of stone, another tiny movement, another tiny fearful slippage, of a ponderous block of stone.

"Do not kill him!" screamed the pit master.

"Shoot!" cried Gito. "Shoot!"

The hand of the leader of the strangers raised just a little, preparatory presumably to its sharp descent, doubtless to be consequent upon the issuance of a word of command.

He smiled.

The chains were tight, straight from the wall. The peasant seemed like a crazed animal, gigantic, leaning forward, straining, bulging with muscle and hate.

"Glory to the black caste," said the leader of the strangers.

"Glory to the black caste!" said the black-tunicked men.

The hand of the leader of the black-tunicked men lifted a bit more. His lips parted, to utter the signal that would unleash the quarrels.

"Aargh!" cried one of the bowmen reeling back, his face a mass of blood within the helmet, the quarrel slashing into the wall to the right of the prisoner, gouging the wall, showering sparks and the other, too, was buffeted to the side by his fellow, his own quarrel spitting, too, to the side, to the peasant's right, striking the wall, bursting stone from it like a hammer, flashing sparks in the cell, then turning end over end, sideways, eccentrically, to our left. The block of stone, broken from the wall, torn out of it, still fixed to the plate and bolts, and chain, had burst forth, showering mortar in the room. As it had left the wall it had, with all the violence of the forces imposed upon it, whipped to the peasant's right, striking the nearest bowman on the side of the head. It had split the helmet and, in the instant before it had split, the metal had been flattened, the skull crushed within. The lights were wild in the cell, the two lanterns being jerked back by those who held them, the light of the tiny lamps obscured by moving bodies. Wild shadows moved about.

"Blades!" I heard. "Lanterns up!"

A dozen blades must have left sheaths.

We screamed. We shrank back. We huddled together, back against the wall.

We then saw, in the light of the swinging lanterns, in the light of the small lamps, the men drawn back, the peasant, standing where he had been, but now bent over, his eyes wild, like something that had tasted blood, a long-forgotten taste, but one which induced a wild intoxication. He was still held to the wall by the right wrist. I doubted that chain could hold him longer now. He jerked back the stone on the chain still clinging to his left wrist. Men leaped back, not to be caught in the trajectory of that jagged, ponderous weight. The one bowman had crawled to the side. "Cut him down!" said the leader of the black-tunicked men. A man advanced, but leaped back as the block of stone on its chain whirled again through the air. It might have been a meteor on a chain. The peasant gave another great cry and with his right arm he lunged against the chain that still held him. The weakened link, that which could have been slipped earlier, it having been opened, but that not known to him, now parted so that the chain was broken.

"He is free," said a man, in awe.

"The chains were tampered with," said another.

Even the pit master seemed in awe. He no longer struggled. Those who were with him seemed scarcely now to restrain him. The officer of Treve, too, seemed staggered by what he had seen. His sword, which had been pried from his hand, lay at his feet.

"He cannot escape," said the leader of the strangers, calmly. "Kill him."

The peasant, now that his hands were free from the wall, took, with both hands, the chain which was on his left wrist, that to which the block of stone was still bolted.

He lifted the stone easily from the floor. It swung on the chain, about six inches from the floor. He was bent over. He was breathing heavily.

None of the men cared to advance.

Gito crept behind the men to our left, and crouched down, by the wall.

The peasant suddenly swung the great stone on its chain about his head in a wicked whirling circle. He stepped out a yard from the wall. The men drew back. Some went to the side. Then the peasant retreated to the wall. His eyes, wolflike, looked to the left and right. He would not permit them behind him. If he should strike a man, of course, that might stop the stone, or even tangle the chain, providing the others with the opportunity they needed, blades ready, to close. But none cared, it seemed, to be the first to tread within the orbit of that fierce satellite, that primitive, improvised weapon.

"You, you," said the leader of the strangers to two of his men. "Sheath your swords, set your bows."

The two men, protected behind their brethren, unslung their bows. Some such weapons are set by a windlass, but those these men carried were more swiftly prepared for fire. They could be drawn with two hands, the bow held down, a foot in the stirrup. It would take a moment, of course, to free the bow, to draw it, to set it, to extract a quarrel from the quiver, to arm it. The long bow, naturally, has a much greater rapidity of fire. This bow, on the other hand, once set, like a firearm, remains ready for fire. It is useful in cramped spaces, in close quarters, in room-to-room fighting. It is an alert weapon, responsive to the trigger; its opportunity need not be more prolonged than the movement of the target across a passageway; it is a patient weapon; it can wait quietly, motionlessly, for a long time, for its target to appear. The two new bowmen set their feet in the bow stirrup, grasping the cable with two hands, one on each side of the guide.

Suddenly, crying out, realizing somehow, in some dark part of that simple brain, in some instinctive fashion, that he had not a moment to spare, risking all, heedless of his back, swinging the stone about his head, the peasant, chains flying about his ankles, charged toward the bowmen. His action, as sudden as it was, took the black-tunicked men by surprise. They fell back before him. The one bowman, his foot locked in the stirrup, looked up only in time to see the great stone whipping toward him; the other was protected by his fellow who received the blow, but, he, too, his foot in the stirrup, fell awkwardly to the side. He cried out in pain. "Blades! Close with him! Close with him!" cried the leader of the strangers. But the stone on its chain, the peasant whirling with it, spun about and about. I saw flesh fly from the thigh of one of the men. He staggered back. Blood splashed on the man to the right of the officer of Treve, he holding his right arm. The sword lay still at the officer's feet. The pit master suddenly, again, began to struggle. The six men about him tightened their grip, clinging to him tenaciously. They clung to him like dogs to a bull. He struggled to throw them from him. The bowman who had been struck lay to one side, his head awry, too far back, still in the helmet, half torn from the body. Swords darted at the peasant but none reached him, he protected in the whirling shield of chain and stone. And then the stone struck against the side of the portal and the stone burst from the portal, a cubic foot of wall there broken from its place, but the stone, too, on the chain, shattered, splitting at the bolts, and fell in two halves away. The chain on his wrists flew about. That to which the ring and plate was attached, bolts still on the plate, struck a fellow across the face, lashing him back. And then the peasant was back again, at bay, against the wall. We cried out, we sobbed with fear. Gito was hiding himself in straw to the left of the portal as one would enter.

"The stone is done now," said the leader of the black-tunicked men, himself now straightening up, lowering the sword he had held before his face, two hands on the hilt. "The chains are nothing."

The peasant was breathing heavily. The door was in front of him, but men with blades blocked his passage.

"Four will advance," said the leader of the strangers. "You, and you, will engage," he said, to two of his men, near him, on the right side of the room, as one would enter it.

"And you, and you," said the lieutenant, to two of the men on his side of the room, the left, as one would enter.

The peasant looked wildly about himself.

He could not defend himself, he substantially defenseless now, against these blades. The chain might be evaded, or it might be stopped or turned, or tangled, by a blade. Too, as he would move to defend himself on one side, the other would close.

"He is dead," said the leader of the strangers, quietly.

Suddenly the officer of Treve kicked the sword at his feet, that which had been earlier pried from his hand, toward the peasant. It slid across the stone. The peasant looked down at it.

"Position to advance," said the leader of the strangers.

The four men formed, one ahead on each side.

"Pick it up!" said the officer of Treve.

The pit master, held by the men at him, looked to the officer of Treve, wildly, gratefully, elatedly.

The peasant bent down and picked up the blade. He looked at it, almost as if he did not understand such a thing. I supposed he may never have had such a thing in his hand before.

The four men prepared to advance looked to one another, and to their captain.

"You do not understand such a thing," said the leader of the strangers to the peasant. "You are of the Peasants. It is not for your caste.

Your weapon is the great staff, perhaps the great bow. You are of the Peasants. You do not know that weapon. You are of the Peasants. Remember you are of the Peasants."

"Yes," said the giant before us. "I do not know this thing. I am of the Peasants."

"Advance," said the leader of the strangers to the four men.

I gasped.

The first darting stroke toward the peasant had been parried smartly.

I had scarcely followed either the thrust or its turning. That single, sharp ringing of steel seemed to linger in the cell.

"Do you call this a weapon?" asked the peasant. "It is only a knife. Yet it is quick. It is very quick."

"Strike!" said the leader of the strangers.

Another man lunged forward and again the blow was turned, almost as though one might blink an eye, by reflex.

"I do not know this thing," said the peasant, looking at the blade, curiously.

Another fellow thrust but this time the thrust was not merely parried. The attacker lay to the peasant's right, his knees drawn up. He coughed blood into the straw.

"But it is quick," said the peasant. "It is quick."

"Attack, attack!" cried the leader of the strangers.

Steel rang out by the wall of the cell. I think I heard blades cross seven or eight times.

Black-tunicked men drew back. Another of their fellows lay in the straw.

"He is a master," said a man, in awe.

Suddenly the pit master, with a great cry, with a great surge of strength, like a moving mountain, like a pain-crazed, maddened bull, threw from him the black-tunicked men who held him, as the mountain might have uprooted trees and tumbled boulders to the valley below, as the bull, rearing up, tossing its head, might have shaken itself free of besetting dogs.

At the same time the officer of Treve threw the two from him who had held him.

The pit master tore a lantern from the hand of a man and dashed it against the wall. Oil flamed for a moment, running on the wall. He then, with one hand, smote lamps from the wall, tearing them away from their holders. The second lantern was seized by the officer of Treve and dashed to the floor. Flame flickered in the damp straw, then disappeared. The last lamp, to the left, as one would enter, was struck from its holder. I heard one of the girls cry out, scalded by the splashing oil. The flame did not take in the damp straw.

"Light! Light!" cried the leader of the strangers.

We heard a man cry out with pain.

In a moment or two one of the lamps was found and lit.

One of the black-tunicked men lay in the portal, his chest bright with blood.

"Where is the prisoner!" demanded the leader of the strangers.

"He is gone," said a man.

Thirty Two

The leader of the strangers, warily, the fellow with one of the lamps, tiny and flickering, preceding him, went to the portal.

"The corridor is dark," said the fellow with the lamp.

"He extinguished the lamps as he passed," said a man.

"He cannot get far, not in the pits," said the leader. "Light more lamps."

The lamps which were still serviceable were lit. One of the lanterns, even, though its glass was broken, was lit.

"There are more lamps, torches, and such, in my quarters," said the pit master, helpfully.

The lieutenant, carefully, crouching beside the fellow, spreading the metal, removed the helmet from the first victim of the peasant, he whose head had been struck by the stone on the chain. The lieutenant laid the bloody helmet to one side. On the broken skull within, on its forehead, distorted by the breakage, was a tiny black dagger, set there this morning.

"Your actions have been noted," said the leader of the strangers to the pit master, "and yours as well," he added, addressing himself to the officer, "and will be duly reported to the authorities."

"Surely Lurius of Jad, the paragon of honor," said the officer, "would not have condoned the murder of a prisoner."

"From whom do you think we obtained our charge?" said the leader of the strangers.

"He cannot escape us," said the lieutenant, standing up. "He is in the vicinity."

"You need only find him," said the pit master.

Neither the officer of Treve nor the pit master were now in the custody of the black-tunicked men. The pit master had, I supposed, slipped his stiletto back within his tunic. He did not have it, at any rate, in his hand.

"I trust we may, from this point further, now that he is free, and dangerous, have the assurance of your support," said the leader of the strangers.

"Do not doubt it," said the pit master.

"He will be trapped against the first gate, that sealing this tunnel," said the lieutenant.

"Arm your bows," said the leader of the strangers. "Fire even at a shadow."

Gito was still half buried in the straw, huddled there, shaking, whimpering, to the left, as one would enter.

The leader of the strangers regarded us. We kept our heads down. We dared not meet his eyes. I think there was not one of us who would not then have rather, a thousand times over, been elsewhere, almost anywhere, in the heaviest of chains in the foulest of dungeons; pitching, sick, bound to our pallets, almost immobile, in the holds of stinking slave ships, covered with vermin; sweating in the mills, chained to our looms; carrying water, shackled, in the fields; even drawing sleds or wagons, padlocked in our harnesses, draft beasts. But we were beautiful, and a different sort of slave. But what would even our beauty, and our hope to please, to be spared to serve, avail ourselves with these men? And we had perhaps, they might judge, seen too much.

The leader of the strangers turned away from us.

The black-tunicked men then, following him, withdrew from the cell.

The officer of Treve followed them.

A moment later Gito, fearing to be alone, scrambled out, to join the black-tunicked men.

The pit master snapped his fingers.

We struggled to our feet, aligning ourselves, standing, the tallest first. Fina was third of the ten, I was seventh.

At a gesture of the pit master, discerned in a lamp from outside the door, held by one of the men, we filed out of the cell. We followed the officer of Treve, Gito, the black-tunicked men. The pit master came behind us.

I tried to free my wrists, but I could not do so. They, like those of the others, had been bound by men, our masters.

The water in the corridor was cold to my feet.

I was sick with fear.

Thirty Three

"The gate has been thrust up," said the leader of the strangers, angrily.

"It seems it was not secured," said the pit master.

"He could be anywhere in the depths," said the lieutenant.

"We will return to the quarters of the depth warden," said the leader of the strangers. "We will make that our headquarters."

"You will be most welcome," said the pit master.

"We will require a map of the depths," said the leader of the strangers.

"None exists in the city, by policy," said the pit master, "just as no map of the city, either, may be prepared."

This, as I understood it, was not uncommon in this world. In some cities it is regarded as a capital offense to make or be found in possession of a city map. The motivations for such policies, one assumes, are military.

"I will be pleased, of course, to furnish guides," said the pit master.

"We shall manage on our own," said the leader of the strangers.

"I know the depths well," said the pit master.

"You two," said the leader of the strangers to the pit master and the officer of Treve, "will remain in our headquarters, as our guests."

"As you wish," said the pit master.

I myself, of course, would not have cared to tread the passages of the depths unguided. I knew some myself, of course, but I knew only areas in which I had been permitted.

"There are many passages," said the lieutenant, uneasily.

"I think we shall find him easily, systematically," said the leader of the strangers. "We shall mark each passage searched. Eventually we shall have searched them all."

"You are thorough," said the pit master.

"Guards are set at the tunnel entrances, of course," said the leader of the strangers.

"Yes," said the pit master.

"He is as good as ours," said the lieutenant.

"Do you have sleen?" asked the leader of the strangers.

"Most were killed in the tunnels, recently," said the pit master. "Two survived."

They were magnificent beasts. It was not surprising that they had been the two which, released in the tunnels, defending the depths, attacking the raiders earlier, had survived. Both of them had taken the peasant's scent, but the leader of the strangers would not know that. One of them was also one of the two which had, earlier, been imprinted with my scent. The other had died in the tunnels, in the fighting.

"There are two who might hunt?"

"Yes," said the pit master.

"Sleen will tear him to pieces," said the lieutenant. "There will be little, if anything, to return to Lurius of Jad, to prove the successful discharge of our office."

"They are to be utilized only as a last resort," the leader assured his lieutenant.

"They will not be necessary," said the lieutenant.

"They are trailers or hunters?" asked the leader.

The distinction, in fact, is sometimes a subtle one, particularly if the beast's bloodlust becomes aroused.

"Hunters," said the pit master.

Sleen are trained variously. The five most common trainings are those of the war sleen, which may also be utilized as a bodyguard; the watch sleen, to guard given precincts; the herding sleen, which will kill only if the quarry refuses to be herded rapidly and efficiently to a given destination, usually a pen or slave cage; the trailing sleen, which is used, in leash, to follow a scent; and the hunter, which is trained to hunt and kill. It is next to impossible to use a hunter as a trailer, because, when the quarry is near, and the killing fever is on it, it will even turn and attack its leash holder, to free itself for the strike on the quarry. A trailer is usually a smaller beast, and one more easily managed, but it is, when all is said and done, a sleen, and trailers not unoften, at the hunt's end, their instincts preponderating, break loose for the kill. When they begin to become unmanageable they must sometimes be killed. The hunters are used generally, of course, in the pursuit of fugitives, free or slave. Unleashed, they are not retarded in their hunt by the lagging of their keepers. I was terrified of sleen. I had seen how they could tear apart great pieces of meat. Most houses in which female slaves may be found, it might be mentioned, as it may be of interest to some, would not have sleen. The sleen is, at least in civilized areas, a rare, expensive and dangerous beast. They do abound in some areas in the wild, as, for example, in the surrounding mountains. The sleen often burrows, and it is predominantly nocturnal. There are also several varieties of the animal apparently, adapted to diverse environments. The most common sleen in domestication, as I understand it, is the forest sleen. It is also the largest, animal for animal. There are also, as I understand it, prairie sleen, mountain sleen and snow sleen. There is a short-haired variety found in some tropical areas, the jungle sleen. And one variety, it seems, is adapted for an aquatic environment, the sea sleen.

"Excellent," said the leader of the strangers.

He then turned to the fellow who carried the sack. "Return to the cell and get the prisoner's blanket," he said. "Put it in the sack, and seal the sack, that there may be no mistake as to the blanket in question."

The man turned about and hurried back to the cell. In a few moments he had returned, with the sack sealed.

"Lead us to your quarters," said the leader of the strangers to the pit master. "We shall organize our searches from that point."

"I should be honored," said the pit master, graciously.

We then continued on. In a moment I had passed beneath the spikes of the lifted gate. I turned my head to the side, just a little. The pit master was now in front. Perhaps one might drift back, to crouch down, and hide somewhere? But they would search all the passages, eventually, and I would be found. Too, I was not eager to be alone in the passages. Indeed, the peasant must be somewhere in them. I heard a cry behind me, from the last girl in the line. I turned more about. Perhaps she, too, had had such thoughts. But there was, I now saw, one of the black-tunicked men at the end of the line. He had apparently taken up his position there when the pit master had moved forward. Perhaps the girl had dallied. She had been thrust forward, I gathered, not gently. I saw him turn and draw down the gate. It was not locked down, but I could not have lifted it, even had I not been bound.

"Move!" he said, irritably.

We hurried on, in front of him, bound, in single file.

Thirty Four

"What time is it now?" demanded the leader of the strangers.

"It is near the tenth Ahn," said a man, inspecting the level of the water in the clepsydra. In the depths one cannot tell day from night, except by the clocks.

We had been returned to the quarters of the pit master better than two Ahn ago.

The officer of Treve and the pit master were sitting at the table, playing Kaissa, which is a board game of this world. They were absorbed in the game. I think they were both skilled.

The leader of the strangers paced the floor angrily. His lieutenant was sitting by, cross-legged. Gito was crouched in one corner, his knees drawn up under his chin. He looked about himself, furtively.

Five of the black-tunicked men had perished in or near the cell, two being struck by the chain and stone, two in swordplay, and one apparently thrust through, in the darkness, the peasant exiting from the cell.

Three more, since that time, as was determined from reports arriving at the quarters of the pit master, now the headquarters of the strangers, had perished. One had been pierced by a concealed spear, spring-released from the side of a corridor, another in crossing one of the narrow bridges over a crevice, it buckling as weight was placed at its center, another when an apparently solid portion of the corridor had fallen away beneath him, plunging him screaming, we heard the screams even where we were, into a nest of tiny, active serpents below, serpents called osts. They are, it seems, highly poisonous. The effects of the poison, too, I am told, are not pretty to watch.

In the case of the first man, the pit master had reminded the leader of the strangers that various security devices in the corridors were armed, especially in view of the incursion of the raiders earlier, and reiterated his offer to furnish expert guidance. "You will remain here," the leader of the strangers had informed him. "As you wish," said the pit master. In the case of the second man, it seemed that he had neglected to lock two small rods in place, toward the center of the bridge, before sliding it out, into place, without which action, it buckles and turns, as on a hinge. In the third case, the man had apparently not noted the small fanglike sign carved into the wall of the corridor, some two inches above the floor. Accordingly it was not surprising he did not locate the lever which would have secured the trap, disarming it. In both of these cases, too, the pit master's expressed willingness to be of assistance was spurned.

"An excellent move," said the officer of Treve, studying the board before him.

"What is the delay!" cried the leader of the strangers. "They should have taken him by now!"

"There are many passages," said the pit master, looking up. The leader of the strangers spun away from him, in fury. The pit master then returned his attention to the game.

A watch of pit guards, as noted earlier, had been dismissed. A second watch, reporting in but a few minutes ago, had also been dismissed.

Where we were, in the headquarters of the strangers, there were, besides the pit master, the officer of Treve, the leader of the strangers, his lieutenant, Gito, and ourselves, the slaves, three men. The others, originally twelve in number, had been divided into four search parties of three men each.

I knelt by the wall. I was chained there, with the others, the ten of us, the pit slaves. I think they wanted all of us together, where we might, collectively, be easily observed. Too we might then easily be removed from the wall, individually, or together. In any event, the kennels were not in use. The slaves at the wall were normally fastened there by two chains, one on the left ankle, the other on the neck. Now, however, each of us wore but one chain. Mine was on the left ankle. In virtue of this arrangement, that of the single chain, we could be quickly, conveniently, removed from the wall. Our hands were still bound. Food had been thrown to us. We fed as we could.

"Capture of Home Stone," said the pit master.

"It is the eleventh Ahn," said a man, looking at the clepsydra.

The leader of the black-tunicked men made a noise of disgust.

His lieutenant was sharpening his sword. Three crossbows, armed, rested on the table.

I lay down by the wall, to rest.

The pit master and the officer of Treve reset the board, for another game. They had played very evenly, as I understood it, first one winning, then the other.

"Your move," said the pit master.

I pulled a little at my bound wrists. The wonder and terror of this suddenly came to me. How was it that I should be here? I did not even know how I had come to this world! But I was here now, helpless, owned, where I must serve, and please and obey, a slave girl on an alien, exotic world. Who had first seen me, who had marked me out, who had first decided this? Who had speculated how I might look in a collar, who had conjectured my lineaments, who had read my body, and my heart?

"The Turian opening?" asked the pit master.

"Perhaps," said the officer of Treve.

I became suddenly angry. How could they play a game, now, at a time like this?

Sometimes I, and others, had served as prizes in such contests, between guards. Sometimes we must lie to one side, or even under the table, chained hand and foot, waiting to see who would be victorious, to whom we would be awarded for the evening.

"You are intent on the Turian," said the pit master.

"Perhaps," said the officer.

I was furious.

I hated the game.

How often I had had to wait for contentments, even such as might be granted to a slave, because of Kaissa! How often I had been uneasy, restless, in my kennel, pressing a tear-stained face against the bars, grasping them, they damp from the sweat of my palms. How I would squirm with need, and must wait! Could they not understand my small cries and moans, and then I would be warned to silence, that I not distract them from their foolish game! Then I would crawl back in the kennel, my fists clenched, trying not to cry.

After a time one of the black-tunicked men said, "It is the twelfth Ahn."

There were more reports during the afternoon.

"Vanarik preceded us," said a man, limping, he whose foot had been twisted in the stirrup of the crossbow, when the peasant had attacked him and the other. His fellow's head had been almost ripped from his body by the stone on the chain. "Two gates fell, one before, one behind. A panel slid upward. Tharlarion entered the area. Before we could kill them Vanarik was pulled from the gate, he clinging to it, not inches from us."

"That would be on level two, in passage eighteen," said the pit master not looking up from the board.

Another of the black-tunicked men died where two passages had intersected. The crossbows had been armed, the men tense. The leader of the strangers, I recalled, had advised them to fire even at a shadow. That shadow had been one of their own men, brought down with three quarrels.

The black-tunicked men had had better fortune in another passage, where five urts had charged them. One of these sleek beasts had been directly killed, by bolts. Two others, wounded, had been turned back. Two others had been, wheeling about amongst them, slashing and biting, destroyed by swords. The men had then pursued the two wounded urts, following a trail of blood, until they had them cornered, quarrels hanging from their flanks, where they slew them, hissing and snarling, against a gate with further quarrels. One of the black-tunicked men had been seriously bitten, and another clawed, but none had perished. The bows had served, in their way, as shields, the urts snapping at them, clinging to them, permitting the defender to draw and hack at their stretched necks with his sword. Sleen would not have made that mistake. They go for warmth and blood.

I found it of interest that so many of the gates in the corridors had not been sealed.

The passages were armed, but they had not been, oddly enough, closed, their gates locked down.

"It is the fifteenth Ahn," said a man.

Clepsydras are of two sorts, the inflow and outflow varieties. The inflow devices add water to a container and the level in the container measures a unit of time; the outflow devices drain water, the time measured then by the level of water remaining in the vessel. The device in the quarters of the pit master was an outflow device. Its accuracy is controlled by two major factors, its shape and the size of the aperture through which the water drains. It tapers toward the bottom to keep the water pressure constant, that being required to regularize the speed of the flow, a larger amount of water over a larger area exerting a pressure equivalent in its effect to that of a lesser amount over a smaller area. The second major factor is the aperture itself. This is a drilled plug which is periodically replaced. If this were not the case the passage of the water, over time, even in stone, would enlarge the aperture, deregularizing the device.

"We found these," said one of the black-tunicked men, reporting back. He held chains.

"Come here!" said the leader of the black-tunicked men to the pit master who, accommodatingly, left his table and game.

"Yes," said the pit master, examining the chains. "These are undoubtedly those which were worn by our prisoner. Surely you can recognize them as well as I." There could be little possibility of mistake, at any rate, I supposed, about the chain with the plate and ring attached. Bolts were still loose in the plate.

"Where did you find these?" demanded the leader of the strangers.

"In a place where there were tools," said the man.

"The workroom," said the pit master. "There is an anvil there, a forge, hammers, chisels. Chaining, unchaining, the fitting with common shackles, and such, you understand, is done there. It is more convenient than going to the surface."

"Are such places not guarded?" demanded the leader of the strangers.

"The guard was dismissed," the pit master reminded him.

"He is now free of his chains," said the leader of the strangers.

"I would assume he still wears the collar, and what is left of the neck chain," said the pit master. "That would be difficult to remove by oneself, with the tools there."

"Are there no metal saws there, or files?"

"No," said the pit master. "It would be dangerous to keep such things in the depths."

Shackles, of course, and links of chain, if one wishes, may be forced apart, or even broken, given proper tools and sufficient strength. There are files and metal saws, too, which can do such work, though it takes more time. I had been in the workroom several times. The tools there were heavy tools. It was not regarded as advisable to have files and metal saws there, things which might be easily concealed.

"We know the prisoner is still in the depths," said the lieutenant.

"There is no doubt about that," said the leader of the strangers.

"It is only a matter of time then," said the lieutenant, "until we have gone through every passage."

"Are there missile weapons in the depths?" asked the leader of the black-tunicked men.

"Only yours," said the pit master.

"Excellent," said the leader of the black-tunicked men.

"Take me to the surface!" suddenly cried Gito, from where he crouched by the wall. "I want to go to the surface!"

"We need not even close with him then," said the leader of the black-tunicked men, paying Gito no attention.

"I want to go to the surface!" cried Gito.

"Call in the search parties," said the leader of the black-tunicked men. "In the morning we will form a single, larger group. Even in the darkness we can blanket an area with quarrels."

One of the men went out, into the corridor. From various points we heard him blowing blasts, on a reed whistle.

"You two will accompany us tomorrow," said the leader to the officer of Treve and the pit master. "We have no intention of leaving you behind. Too, the slaves will be with us. I trust a concern for their safety, or for that of one or more of them, will ensure your diligence as guides. They will precede us, you see. In this fashion we will keep them in view, which will doubtless be pleasant for you, not of the black caste, and there will be no slipping of them away."

Whereas the Gorean slave girl commonly heels her master, her master sometimes orders her to walk before him, for the pleasure of seeing her walk. And if she knows what is good for her she had best walk beautifully. This also gives him an opportunity to assess her interest to other men, for example, to see if men look after her, as she passes. This gives him some sense of her value. How much would she be likely to bring, for example, exhibited on a slave block? This is useful if he should be thinking of selling her, but it is also tends to be of independent interest, and not only to the master, but also to the slave. We are very curious to know, vain beasts that we are, what men might pay for us, if we were to be offered for sale.

But, alas, some men, I fear, purchase girls largely for self-regarding, social reasons, for example, to impress others with their wealth, good fortune, or taste. But then, too, on Earth, do not some men buy a certain car, or a certain house, or a certain painting, and such, largely to impress others? Too, on Earth some men will, in effect, purchase wives, so to speak, though the "exchange of coin" is less obvious. These women, as I understand it, are referred to as "trophy wives." There are differences, of course. On Earth, it is the woman who sells herself and, accordingly, keeps her own purchase price, so to speak. That is not the Gorean way, of course. On Gor the woman is sold by her owner, who keeps her price. I am happy to report that there is no Gorean expression which would be exactly equivalent to "trophy slave," but I am forced to admit, in all honesty, that the concept, in effect, or certainly a similar sort of concept, is not unknown on Gor. In Gorean there is an expression which would rather literally translate as "display slave," and it seems that that is much the same idea, namely, that the woman's value is seen to lie more in the ranges of a decoration, an appointment, an appurtenance, or such things, than in herself, than in the heats, services, devotions, and loves of a whole woman, a living, breathing, loving, passionate, needful female. The palanquins of rich men are sometimes followed by strings of back-braceleted, briefly tunicked, neck-chained display slaves. When the slave is walked before the master, her head and eyes remain forward. She is not to look to the left or right. She is, after all, under the eyes of her master.

I suppose I am beautiful enough to be a display slave, but I do not think I would like it.

When the slave is walked before the master she may or may not be on a leash. It is up to the master.

Most often she is not leashed.

In this way the master may remain rather in the background. Perhaps he is just a fellow going in the same direction? But if the slave is accosted he will probably show up promptly enough, leash in hand.

She will then be leashed and there will be no doubt as to whose slave she is.

One might mention, in passing, that the "concept of the leash" may figure, as do a number of other concepts, in references to bondage. Just as one might refer to a slave as "marked meat," or as a "collar slut," or a "vulo," or a "tasta," or as one might ask someone if a certain girl now wears a collar, or is garbed in the slave tunic, or has bared arms, or a bared face, or in whose bracelets or chains she finds herself, so, too, one might speculate that she is probably on a leash by now, or assert that she is on a given leash, say, so-and-so's leash, or inquire of a slave her master, by inquiring, "Who leashes you," "On whose leash are you," "Who holds your leash," and so on.

"Too," continued the leader of the black-tunicked men, "the slaves may also serve as shields, if we are attacked, either by he whom we hunt, or by other beasts."

"Take me to the surface!" cried Gito, leaping up, hurrying to throw himself on his knees before the leader of the strangers. "Take me to the surface!"

"You are free to leave," said the leader of the strangers.

"Alone?" quavered Gito.

"I have no intention of sparing men to conduct you to the surface," said the leader.

"You are not going to stay here another night?"

"Yes," said the leader.

"In the morning you will leave this place?"

"Yes, to conclude our hunt."

"What of me?"

"You may remain here."

"I will accompany you, of course," said Gito. Then he returned to his place by the wall, crouching down there, watching the portal.

We expected ten men to return, answering the summons of the reed whistle, but only nine came in.

"Where is Emmerich?" demanded the lieutenant.

"Is he not with us?" asked a squad leader, looking back.

"He was following," said a man.

"He may have taken a wrong turn," said the pit master. "The passages can be confusing."

"He will report in soon," said another man, uneasily.

"He may be lost," said another.

"He was only paces behind me," said another. "Is he not here?"

"No," said a man.

"Let us have supper," said the leader of the strangers. "We shall then rest. In the morning we have much to do."

"I shall set a guard," said the lieutenant.

"Two men," said the leader.

"Yes, Captain," said the lieutenant.

"Loose three slaves to serve," said the leader of the strangers.

"Of course," said the pit master.

"That one, which seems to be your favorite," said the leader, indicating Fina. "And this one," he said. Tira, who was blond, whimpered, kicked.

He looked us over. None of us dared to meet his eyes.

"And this one," he said, identifying another. I cried out, kicked.

Thirty Five

I think it may have been some stray sound, not even identified, which awakened me.

I was at the wall, chained there again, by the left ankle. My hands, which had been unbound that I might serve, were now again bound behind my back.

None of those whom I had served, deferentially, I naked, collared, head down, at their very elbows, those morose, black-tunicked men, had so much as touched me. No hand had stolen forth to caress my flank, nor grip my hair, pulling me to them, if only to thrust their face to my throat, my hair about, to take in the scent of one whom they knew must serve them in any fashion they might desire, a female slave. I fear I served clumsily. They frightened me. I almost dropped a dish. But none paid me attention. I was miserable, and alone in my fear. Then, later, happily, we were returned to our chains and bonds.

Sometimes there is a sense of security, being on a chain, even back-braceleted or back-thonged. There is less then to fear. We have been put where men want us, and as men want us. How could we help then but be pleasing? Unless perhaps we were insufficiently quick, if approached, to kneel and put our heads down to the stone? Certainly I felt safer on the wall chain, bound, unnoticed, out of mind, than I had serving, trembling, fearing I might make a mistake, amongst those morose, terrible visitors. Should I be pleased that I was one of the three chosen to serve? Doubtless that spoke well for my attractions, such as they might be. But, too, I had been terrified. The visitors were not, I was sure, normal Gorean men. I feared them, far more than the normal Gorean male. I was not sure how to behave with them. The normal

Gorean male, for example, will accept a slave's obeisance and her humble kissing of his feet, but these men, I feared, might punish her for having approached them too closely. I did not know how to behave with them. They seemed unpredictable. In my collar I felt confused and frightened. I did not know what they might do to a slave.

* * * *

Let me pause for a moment.
I think it is important to do so.
Please forgive me.
In this book, which is an unusual book, I think, and certainly violates many of the little rules and regulations, in their doctrinaire plenitudes, which so constrict the contemporary theory of the novel, beyond which many seem not to see, I have tried to tell the truth, even truths which may seem to some unfamiliar and strange.

Truth is a strange thing.
There is a danger in seeking it, for one might find it.
That one does not like a truth does not make it false.
How few people understand that!
But there are many sorts of truths, as there are flowers and beasts. Some truths are hard and cold, and sharp, and if one touches them one might cut oneself and bleed. Some truths are like dark stones which do little more that exist unnoticed; others are green with the glow of life, like moist grass rustling in the morning sun; some truths are like frowns; and some are like smiles. Some are friendly; others are hostile; and, in both cases, their nature is just what it is, not what they may be said to be. Politics is not the arbiter of truth; it may be the arbiter of comfort, safety, conformity, and success, but it is not the arbiter of truth; the arbiter of truth is the world and nature; they have the last say in these matters.

Many may wish it were not the case; and many will pretend it is not the case; but it is, for better or for worse, the case.

Truth does not care whether it is believed or not; similarly, stone walls and cliffs do not care whether they are noted or not; so then let us leave it to the individual to do as he thinks best. Truth, the stone wall, the cliff, are not enemies; but they are real.

I think then that I should mention, perhaps, particularly given the fact that an earlier paragraph might be misconstrued, and that the frightening condition it references might be understood as being typical of a given form of relationship, that there is a lovelier, warmer, more beautiful, benign sense, of "finding security on a chain." It is one familiar to thousands of loving slaves. In a typical bondage, one is cared for, nourished, sheltered, nurtured, protected, and often loved. Certainly one is, at least, desired and lusted for. How many wives, I wonder, are *lusted* for. One respects wives; one lusts for slaves; wives are free, and are to be treated with dignity and circumspection; slaves are owned, and are suitable objects to be put to one's pleasure. The wife consents, if she feels like it, and is so inclined; the slave obeys. The wife may dole out her favors by carefully measured spoonfuls, like medicine, in a regimen designed to reduce and torment, and thus to control, an angered, frustrated, confused, manipulated, indoctrinated, unquestioning childlike patient; the slave kneels and hopes to be found pleasing. The powerful, healthy man is aggressive and lustful; what is he to do when he realizes at last he has been mistreated, denied, cheated, starved, and shamed; he may rise up with a snarl; let the wife be dismayed to discover she is to her horror then in the vicinity of a man; what does he care; let him kick the pedestal from beneath her, and find her a collar; or let him turn his back upon her inert, righteous petulance and seek something a thousand times more desirable, what he needs, and wants, a slave; the slave does not denounce the lusts of the master; she endeavors to satisfy them, and, in this, finds her own womanhood; she does not want a weaker man; she wants a strong man, and a whole man, one it is fit for her to serve; how absurd, how embarrassing, how psychologically futile, how intellectually preposterous, to reveal one's actual nature, one's health and power, one's lust, to an offended, glorious free woman, or to waste it upon her reluctant, anesthetic body; away with the very thought; what could he be thinking of; let him seek rather a slave; the slave, you see, is the object on which it is appropriate for a man to ventilate his lust. Indeed, it is one of the things she soon learns she is for. She also learns that the human male, when he has what he wants from a woman, and fully, and with perfection, is, within the limits of the mastery, a pleasant, kindly, happy, wonderful thing. She is awed, and fulfilled, by this relationship. And, of course, it is she who, subject to his rule, and responsive to his will, has bought this about, not that she was—you understand—given any choice. She wishes to please him, of course, but she knows also that she is a slave and *must* do so. For even a minor error or laxity she knows she may find herself under the whip. She finds this subjection to male domination thrilling, and reassuring. Her master is not weak. There are clear standards, limits, and requirements. She must be careful of them. Commonly they are made clear to her, and the nature of the penalties which will be imposed for the least infraction thereof. She must be a pleasing slave. She is happy. This is the surely one of the deepest and most profound relationships in which a woman can stand to a man, that of slave to master, and, ideally, that of love slave to love master. It is no wonder then that we sometimes kiss our finger tips and press them to our collars, that we humbly lift and kiss the bracelets that link our wrists so helplessly, so closely, together. Do we not admire the unslippable shackles on our trim ankles, fastening them in such proximity to one another, so inhibiting our movements? They have been put on us at the pleasure of the master. Are we blindfolded? Are we forbidden to speak? Are we gagged? Are our wrists tied behind our backs? Must we kneel naked before him? We are his. Let those who can understand these things understand how it is that a slave can love her bondage, and that she would never exchange it for the jejune inanities and boredoms of freedom—how it is that she can lie contentedly, happily, at the foot of a man's couch, chained to his slave ring. Some, I suppose, will find this incomprehensible. There is nothing for it then, but to allow them to continue in their ignorance. But the woman at last has a place here, a condition, a station. She is now a slave. She now at last "belongs," and in the most profound sense of belonging, that of belonging *to someone*. She now "belongs" in the most profound sense conceivable, that of being *owned*. She realizes, with a radiant warmth that floods her, that illuminates her mind and enflames her belly, that she is now goods, a property, her master's slave. Men have found her of such interest and attractiveness, and they have wanted her so much, and so lusted for her, that they have enslaved her, that they have put her in a collar and made her theirs, that they have seen fit, in their imperious, dominating mastery to own her, and put her to their service and pleasure.

* * * *

I did not know what had awakened me.

Lamps were lit in the quarters of the pit master, serving now as the command center, or headquarters, of the strangers. I could see black-tunicked figures lying about. I could hear the breathing of sleeping men. I think that only I and Gito were awake. He was sitting with his back against the wall, his knees up, he holding them. I could not see the guards at the portal.

I was about to close my eyes and try to return to sleep when I saw the body of Gito, across the way, stiffen. His eyes were wide with terror.

Within the portal, some feet within it, I saw, following his gaze, the immense figure of the peasant, barefoot, in his rags. On his neck was the collar, and a chain dangled from it. The sword which had been kicked to him by the officer was in a rag sling, suspended over his left shoulder. He looked about. I closed my eyes quickly, feigning sleep. When I opened them again I saw that he was before Gito, who was trembling in terror, making himself tiny by the wall.

I am dreaming, I thought.

The peasant sat down, cross-legged, before Gito.

"I must leave soon, my friend," he said softly.

Gito nodded numbly.

"The planting must be done," the peasant reminded him.

Gito nodded.

"I may not see you again," said the peasant. "It was my desire to wish you well."

Gito trembled.

"I wish you well," said the peasant.

"I wish you well," whispered Gito.

The peasant smiled, and put his great hands affectionately on Gito's small shoulders. He then rose, turned about, and, soundlessly, left.

Yes, I must be dreaming, I thought.

But, a moment after the peasant had vanished, I would surely in any event have been awakened, for Gito leaped to his feet screaming. "Awake! Awake! He was here! He was here!"

In the room there was consternation instantly. "What? Where?" cried the leader of the strangers. "There! There!" cried Gito, pointing to the portal. "Where is the guard?" cried the leader of the strangers.

"You were dreaming," said a man to Gito.

"No, no!" cried Gito.

"The guards are not at their post," said the lieutenant.

"To arms!" cried the leader of the strangers. "Out into the hall! Run! Search!"

"The lamps in the hall are out," said a man, drawing back into the room.

"Torches, light lanterns, hurry!" cried the leader of the strangers.

The pit master sat up in his blankets, rubbing his eyes. The officer of Treve, too, bestirred himself.

Gito was jabbering incoherently.

"Bring some slaves!" screamed the leader of the strangers. Five or six of us, including Fina and myself, were quickly freed of our chains and pulled by the hair to our feet, and were thrust toward the portal. We were to be used, I gathered, as shields, or as tests, thrust before the men, of the passages, their possible dangers.

In a moment we were thrust out into the corridor, men, most with drawn swords, some with armed bows, behind us. Lanterns and torches cast light about.

"This way!" cried the leader of the strangers, pushing Fina forward.

Thirty Six

Fina screamed, drawing back.

It was something like half of an Ahn that we had been hurrying through one adjacent passage after another.

I think only the pit master's skill kept us from becoming lost in what seemed sometimes, in our alarm and haste, an eerie, dreadful, unfathomable subterranean labyrinth.

The leader of the strangers had hoped to follow the dark passages, the extinguished lamps indicating the path taken by the prisoner but, at a joining of several passages, it was seen that the lamps of each were still lit, dimly flickering into the distance, thus giving no indication which, if any, might have been trod.

The pit master pressed forward. He had been almost at the elbow of Fina. She was shaking.

"Lift the torch," said the pit master.

The pit master turned over the body in the corridor.

"It is Emmerich," said a man.

There were coarse marks on the throat. The cartilage of the throat had been crushed.

"He was strangled with chain," said the lieutenant.

There was little doubt as to what had left its savage imprint there.

"He has been dead several Ahn," said the officer of Treve. He was of the scarlet caste.

The men looked about themselves, uneasily.

"Where can he have gone?" asked a man.

"He is here somewhere," said another.

"He must be weak," said a man. "He has had nothing to eat."

"When was he fed last?" asked the leader of the strangers.

"He was fed yesterday evening," said the pit master.

"By now his reflexes will be slowed, his actions will be erratic, he must grow weaker soon, if he is not already considerably weakened," mused the leader of the strangers.

"If he has not eaten in the meantime," said the pit master.

"What is there to eat?" asked the leader of the strangers.

The pit master tore back a part of the black tunic.

"Aargh," cried a man, in disgust.

"Peasants are beasts," said a man.

There was no dearth of water in the pits, of course, particularly in the lower corridors.

"We will return to the chamber," said the leader of the strangers.

"Where was the guard?" asked the lieutenant.

"Consider sleen, Captain," urged a man.

Gito pressed closely to the leader of the strangers, looking fearfully about himself. The leader of the strangers angrily brushed him back. Gito retreated, but he remained so close that he might have reached out and seized his sleeve.

In a few minutes we had returned to their headquarters. Within we found two of the black-tunicked men, lying to one side. "Knaves!" cried the lieutenant. "They have slept through the alarm!"

"Kill them," said the leader of the black-tunicked men.

"That will not be necessary," said the officer of Treve. "Their throats have been cut."

"They are the guard," said the lieutenant.

They had not been noticed at the beginning of the alarm, being taken for men asleep. They had not been noticed in our haste to rush into the corridor, in our pursuit of the prisoner. He must have drawn them earlier within the chamber, and put them like that, to one side, as though they slept. If one were to awaken, and see them thusly, lying there, with others about them, men clearly asleep, breathing deeply, one might not suspect anything was amiss.

"He was truly here," said a man.

More than one of them, I am sure, suspected that the alarm had been a false one, occasioned by the trepidation of Gito, awakening from some terrible dream.

"How is it that he can come and go as he pleases?" asked a man.

"He is like the savages of the Barrens," said a man.

"He is a beast," said the leader of the strangers. "He has the cunning of a beast. He has the stealth of a beast. He has the savagery of the beast."

One of the men murmured assent.

"He is not human," said the leader of the strangers. "We are hunting something which is not human."

"Captain," said the lieutenant.

"Yes," said the leader of the strangers.

"Emmerich had a bow, and quarrels. They were not with the body."

"I know," said the leader of the strangers, irritably.

"I think we may then assume," said the lieutenant, "that the prisoner is in possession of, or has access to, a missile weapon."

"I think that is a fair assumption," said the leader of the strangers.

The black-tunicked men exchanged glances.

Gito whimpered.

As the two guards had been slain, and the other man, he who had been missing, had been found strangled in the corridor, there were left of the strangers, other than their leader, his lieutenant and Gito, just seven men.

"He is not human," said the leader of the strangers. "He is a beast, a mad and dangerous beast."

"Let him then be hunted as a beast," said the lieutenant.

"You have changed your position on the matter then?" said the leader.

"Yes, Captain."

"You have two sleen available?" asked the captain of the pit master.

"Yes."

"Hunters?"

"Yes."

"They are similar beasts, similarly agile and aggressive?"

"Yes," said the pit master. "It is unlikely that one could far outdistance the other."

There would be then time only for one shot with the bow.

"Have them here in the morning, ready to hunt," said the leader of the strangers.

"As you wish," said the pit master.

"Set a double guard, four men, in two pairs," said the leader of the strangers.

"Yes, Captain," said the lieutenant.

"It seems he was indeed here," said a man to Gito.

"Yes," said Gito, looking about himself, "yes."

"Why did he come here?"

"He came to bid me farewell," said Gito.

"Why?" asked the man.

"I am his friend," said Gito.

"I see," said the man.

"Secure the slaves," said the leader of the strangers.

"Slaves, prepare to be secured," said a man.

We, those of us who had been freed earlier in the alarm to accompany the men, there were six of us, quickly hurried to the wall and knelt there, close to it, facing it. We were aligned now, spatially, with the others, as we had been before the alarm. I felt my bound wrists pulled up and inspected. They were still well tied. I then, in a moment, felt the ankle ring snapped shut about my ankle. I was then again fastened to the wall. When we were all secured, the men left us, and we lay down, or reclined, frightened, as we might.

"The sleen will finish him, in the morning," said a man.

"Yes," said another.

I saw Gito across the way. I did not think he would sleep. I did not think I would sleep either. But, in a few moments, despite my fear, my aching arms, the hardness of the stone, I had lost consciousness.

Thirty Seven

I did not want to be touched by the animals. I feared them terribly. One must have been fifteen feet in length, and the other close to twenty. I could not have begun to put my arms about one. The leg just above the paw in the larger animal must have been some six inches in thickness. They were leashed, the leashes going to rings on huge leather collars, four to five inches in width, an inch or two in thickness. I dreaded even that they might rub against me, those huge bodies, with their glossy, oily fur. It was easy to see how men might not be able to control such beasts. Their tongues lolled out now. They seemed passive enough, at the moment. Their breathing was heavy, a sort of panting, as they padded along with us, but it was regular, and showed no signs of particular excitement. Perhaps they were merely being exercised. Their heads, broad at the back, tended to taper toward the snout, rather like those of vipers. The length of their body, too, with its six legs, tended to suggest a furred serpent, or reptile. Such things are mammalian or mammalianlike, however, in the sense of giving live birth and suckling the young.

Two of the black-tunicked men clung to each leash. Again the black-tunicked men did not wish pit guards present. Once again they had been dismissed. Even with two men on a leash I did not think they would be able to hold the animals if they should be determined to go their own way. But, to be sure, these were hunting sleen, and not intended to hunt on the leash, but rather only when unleashed.

I cried out a little as one of the beasts brushed past me. I had felt its ribs, like iron bands beneath the smooth, rippling muscles, sheathed in the oily pelt. Even in that brief, smooth touch I had sensed a considerable force, like a wave in the sea. But such beasts are not only powerful. They are extremely agile as well, and can easily top a thirty-foot wall. Over a short distance they can outrun fleet game. Their front claws, used in burrowing, can tear through heavy doors. Sometimes it takes ten spears to kill one.

"We will loose them here," said the leader of the strangers.

We stopped.

We were at the intersection of several passages, at a point we had reached last night, and a point we were sure the prisoner had occupied at least once, for it was here that the extinguished lamps had ended.

The beasts looked about, puzzled.

This was surely not their pen.

In our group were the leader of the strangers, his lieutenant, Gito, his seven men, the pit master, the officer of Treve, and ten slaves, in two groups of five each. The members of each group were tied together by the neck, presumably not merely to control us, as a coffle chain might, but to keep us together, making our disposition as a shield, or wall, more effective. The two groups might precede the men, forming a double wall in the passage, or, if the men wished, one group might precede and the other follow, in this fashion providing protection for both the front and rear. I was in the second group as I had been seventh in the slave line, my position there determined by my height. Both groups, however, at this point, were muchly together. As before, we were unclothed. Our hands, too, as before, were tied behind our backs.

"Bring the sack forward," said the leader of the strangers.

This was done.

This was the sack which contained the blanket which had been taken from the prisoner's cell yesterday morning. It was sealed, and the seal, with its dangling string, had not been broken.

"Loose the sleen," said the leader of the strangers.

The heavy collars were removed from the throats of the two sleen. There is a difference in custom here with various sorts of sleen, which might be remarked. War sleen, watch sleen, fighting sleen, and such, when freed, would normally retain the collars, which are often plated and spiked, for the protection of the throat. With hunting sleen, on the other hand, the collars are usually removed. There are two views on this matter. One view is that the collar might jeopardize the hunt, for example, that it might be caught in a branch, or be somehow utilized to restrain the animal before it has located its quarry. The other is that the removal of the collar returns the beast to its state of natural savagery, that it removes from it any inhibitions which might have resulted from its familiarity with human beings. Certainly it is difficult to recollar a hunting sleen until it has made its kill, until it has been pacified, sated with the predesignated blood and meat. The two views, of course, are not mutually exclusive.

When the collars were removed the behavior of the two animals was significantly altered. They seemed to become a great deal more restless.

Usually, of course, such things hunt in the open.

One urinated in the passageway. Its urine has an unusually strong odor. In the wild, urine and feces are used to mark territories.

The head of the larger animal moved from side to side. The smaller animal began to make tiny, excited, anticipatory noises. I had heard such noises before meat had been thrown to them. Saliva fell from the jaws of the larger animal. It moved between the men to put its head against the thigh of the pit master. It was only he, one supposes, of those in the corridor, it recognized.

I began to cry.

"What is wrong with her?" asked the lieutenant.

"Nothing," said the pit master.

I could not help myself.

"She attended to the prisoner, for months," said the pit master.

"Any might weep," said the officer of Treve, "given the enormity of what you intend."

I recalled the prisoner, as he had been, before he had risen in his chains, in madness, intent upon the planting. He had been little more than a remote, inert form, as simple as rock, as distant as a far-off mountain, sitting cross-legged, chained, on the stone floor of a cell in the lower corridors. He had seldom even seemed to be aware of my presence in the cell. Now he was somewhere out there in the passages. He would not know for a time that the swift beasts pursued him, padding swiftly through the dark halls. Then I did not think he would be aware of it for long. It was not as though he might see them coming, across a plain, from hundreds of yards away. It was unlikely he could run before them, once he realized them behind him, for more than a few minutes. I shuddered, and wept. Might it not have been better, I thought, if he had died in his chains yesterday morning, in the cell, by the knife? How terrible to die beneath the fangs of beasts!

"Be silent!" said the pit master.

"Yes, Master," I said.

"Break the seal, open the sack," said the leader of the strangers.

The seal was broken away by he who had been the custodian of the bag, and the bag was opened.

The leader of the strangers drew out the dark, thick blanket. He thrust it to the pit master.

"Give the command," said the leader of the strangers.

"I beg you not to do this," said the pit master.

"Give the command," said the leader of the strangers.

"I do not advise you to pursue this course of action," said the pit master.

"Give the command!" said the leader of the strangers.

"I will not give it," said the pit master. "It is a simple 'Scent-Hunt' command."

The larger beast suddenly squealed, hearing these words. It looked eagerly about itself. Men drew back. I and others screamed, shrinking back against the wall of the passage. Swords were loosened in sheaths.

"You will be dealt with later," said the leader of the strangers. "You," he said to the officer of Treve.

"I do not set sleen on free men," he said.

"Do not think your place in this city is so secure," said the leader of the strangers.

"Give me the blanket," said the leader of the strangers.

It was surrendered by the pit master.

"It is a simple 'Scent-Hunt' command?"

"Yes."

"Back away, to the sides of the passage," said the leader of the strangers. "We do not know in which direction the trail will lie."

My group was thrust to one side of the passage, and the other group to the other side. We were aligned in our groups, close to the wall, side by side, facing outward. I could feel the rock behind me with my bound hands. The others, too, the lieutenant, Gito, the pit master, the officer of Treve, the black-tunicked men, drew to the side, to one side or the other, leaving only the leader of the strangers, clutching the blanket, and the two animals in the center of the passage.

"Beware," said the pit master. "Where sleen are concerned, there is always danger."

"Do you think I do not know that the pits of Treve are renowned for the reliability of their hunters?" said the leader of the strangers.

"You cannot always depend upon sleen," said the pit master.

"Hi, hi," said the leader of the strangers, slapping his thigh, calling the animals to him.

"Be careful," said his lieutenant.

"Here," said the leader of the strangers, crouching down, thrusting the blanket to the snouts of the beasts. "Here, take scent, take scent."

The two animals, eagerly, tails lashing, thrust their snouts into the wadded blanket.

The larger animal then, as had the smaller, earlier, in its excitement, loosed its urine. This is apparently a behavior selected for in the evolution of the sleen. I do not think that it is simply a device to clear the bladder prior to strenuous activity, for example, to avoid discomfort in the chase. I think, rather, it has to do, at least in part, with the common prey of the sleen in the wild, which is usually the tabuk, a single-horned antelopelike creature. A filled bladder, gored, releases wastes into the ventral cavity, with considerable danger of infection. If the bladder is cleared prior to the wound the chance of infection is considerably reduced. Over thousands of generations of sleen this behavior has, I suspect, been selected for, as it contributes to the survival of the animal, and its consequent capacity, obviously, thereafter, to replicate itself.

"Scent! Hunt!" said the leader of the strangers. "Scent! Hunt!"

The blanket was literally torn from the grasp of the leader of the strangers, who then stood up, watching the sleen. They began to scratch at it, and seized parts of it in their jaws, ripping it. At one point it fluttered, shaken, in the passage, like a flag.

"Scent! Hunt! Scent! Hunt!" urged the leader of the strangers.

The two beasts looked up from the blanket, it torn in shreds beneath their paws.

"They are beauties," said the leader of the strangers, "beauties."

"It is done," said the officer of Treve angrily. "They have taken the scent."

"Watch them!" said a man.

I had never seen sleen hunt in a situation such as this. I had seen them, in a little demonstration which had been staged for my benefit, one I was never likely to forget, seek out and rip apart particular pieces of meat, pieces of meat which had been given particular names. The smaller of the two sleen was one which had been imprinted with my own scent and name. I knew a given command could set it upon me. Both of these sleen had also been imprinted, I knew, with the scent, and some name, or signal, associated with the peasant, and could be set upon him. On the other hand, the pit master had not volunteered the appropriate signals to the leader of the strangers. This was not surprising, of course, given the pit master's obvious reservations concerning the intentions of the black-tunicked men. One does not need such signals, of course, when one has at one's disposal an article of such utility as the quarry's robes, or tunic, or blanket.

"Scent! Hunt!" said the leader of the strangers.

"I do not understand," said a man.

"Surely they have the scent now," said another.

The sleen had not left the area. The larger one snarled, menacingly.

"Scent! Hunt!" cried the leader of the strangers.

The larger sleen turned in a circle, as though confused. Then it ran down the corridor for a few yards.

"It is hunting!" cried a man.

But then the animal stopped, and turned about.

"It is coming back," said a man.

The large sleen thrust past the leader of the strangers and ran a few paces down the corridor behind us. In this it was accompanied by the smaller animal. Then they turned about, together, and returned. They went again to the shreds of the blanket. Then they lifted their snouts into the air, and then they put them to the floor of the corridor.

"What is wrong with them?" asked the lieutenant.

"They seem confused," said the pit master.

"They are stupid animals," said a man.

"Scent! Hunt!" said the leader of the strangers.

The two sleen now turned about, then they crouched down, their bellies no more than an inch or so from the floor. I heard a very low growl from one of them. Their tails moved back and forth. I saw their ears lie back, against their heads.

"What is wrong with them?" said another.

The eyes of the first sleen, the larger, the more aggressive, fixed on the leader of the strangers. He stepped back.

The larger sleen snarled. There was no mistaking the menace in that sound.

I could now detect a rumble in the throat of the smaller animal. It, too, seemed to regard the leader of the strangers.

"Something is wrong," said a man.

The leader of the strangers took another step back and drew his blade. He held the hilt with two hands.

Then the larger sleen, scarcely lifting its belly from the floor, crawled quickly forward a foot or two, snarling, and stopped. His companion, to his right, did the same.

I knew little or nothing of sleen, but the intent, the agitation, the excitement of the animals, was evident.

Again the two sleen, first the larger, then the smaller, approached, and stopped.

"Draw," said the leader of the strangers.

But before blades could leave their sheaths the first animal scrambled forward, snarling, charging, its hind feet scratching and slipping, spattering urine back, just for an instant, on the floor of the passage. The second animal was at its shoulder, scarcely a fang's breadth behind. The leader of the strangers struck wildly down at the first animal, slashing its jaw and the side of its face, turned to orient its jaws to its prey, cutting into it, with his blade, and the force of its charge struck him back and the beast, shoulders hunched, was on him, he on his back, screaming, the other beast now, too, at his body, seizing it in its jaws, tearing it toward itself in its frenzy. The lieutenant and some five of the black-tunicked men, shouting, kicking, crying out with horror, crowded about the intent animals, cutting down at them with blades, trying to stab into those active, twisting bodies. The larger beast lifted its head from the leader of the strangers, its jaws flooded with blood, part of the body in its grip, it bleeding itself from the stroke of the leader's blade. The smaller animal continued to feed, being struck with stroke after stroke. Neither animal, in its excitement, seemed to be aware of, or even to feel, the attack of the other men. Again and again the blades cut and stabbed at them. One man cried out in pain, wounded, by the thrust of another. Then, suddenly, the larger animal, snarling, turning about with blurring speed, caught another man in its jaws, shaking him. A blade then found its heart, and in its death throes, not releasing its new prey, it rolled and shook, and half of it fell free to the side. The smaller animal continued to feed until its vertebrae, at the base of the skull, had been severed.

When it became clear that the animals were dead the men stopped hacking and thrusting at their bodies. Then they drew back, almost as though in shock, their reddened blades lowered. They were breathing heavily, with their exertion. Blood was about, and the parts of two men. I drew back even more, trying not to let it, in its flow, touch me. I understood for the first time now, clearly, that there was a certain pitch in this part of the passage. This could be determined from the path taken by the blood. Some of it now, trickling, running here and there, was better than twenty yards down the passage. One could see the reflection of the lamps in it. I did not look at the pieces of the leader of the strangers, or of his fellow, caught by the larger beast. The two sleen were masses of blood and hacked fur. Two paws, even, had been cut away, one supposed after the animals had died, the hacking, frenziedly, irrationally, prolonged.

The lieutenant looked at the pit master.

"Sleen are unpredictable," he said. "They are erratic beasts."

The lieutenant did not lower his gaze.

"We must sometime find our way out of this place," said one of the black-tunicked men.

"The pit guard will be reporting in soon," said another.

The lieutenant then wiped his blade on the coat of the nearest sleen, and sheathed it.

"Where is Gito?" asked a man.

"He fled," said another. He pointed down the passage. There were no bloody footprints, so his flight had preceded the flood of blood in the corridor.

My neck hurt. When the sleen had attacked there had been amongst us terror and confusion. Some of us had tried to flee to the left, others to the right, whichever was closer to us. As a result we had been tangled, hurt, wrenched, confused, held in place. And the squealing and hissing, the snarling, the crying out, the cutting with the blades, had been so close to us that we might, had we not been bound, have reached out and touched the men, almost the bleeding, twisting bodies of the sleen. We had screamed, and begged to be freed, but none had attended to us, of course. More important business was at hand and we were only meaningless slaves. We were now again against the wall, put there by the men, backed against it, side by side, hands bound behind us, the cord on our neck holding us together, frightened.

"Be silent," said the pit master.

We tried to obey. I bit my lower lip, attempting to control its movement. My shoulders shook. The side of my neck hurt, where the cord had burned it. The floor was sticky with blood.

Two of the black-tunicked men had not joined in the attack on the sleen. They had, in those sudden, unexpected, precipitate, grisly moments, stood back, perhaps fearing to act, perhaps unable to do so. The lieutenant slowly turned to regard them.

"There is no blood on your blades," he said. The men stepped back a little, looking at one another.

"Surrender your blades," said the lieutenant. The men looked at one another, uneasily. "I am now in command," said the lieutenant.

"I suggest," said the officer of Treve, "that you need every man you have."

The two blades were surrendered to the lieutenant.

The lieutenant gestured to the two men who had surrendered their weapons.

"Hold them," said the lieutenant.

The two men were seized, each by two of their fellows.

"I do not advise this course of action," said the officer of Treve.

"There will be blood on your blades," said the lieutenant.

"No!" cried one of the two held men, struggling.

"Let us redeem ourselves!" cried the other.

"You would then be left with only four men," said the officer of Treve.

The lieutenant's eyes were cold. The blade was leveled for its thrust.

I closed my eyes that I might not see the blade, his own, pass between the ribs of the first of the two held men.

Then the lieutenant said, "Release them."

Their fellows stepped away from them.

I expected the two men to turn about then, and run.

But they did not.

Rather they stood where they were. I then gathered something of the discipline of the black caste.

The blade was motionless, steadied on the left forearm of the lieutenant, leveled with the first man's heart.

"Masters!" we heard. "Masters!" It was Gito's voice. He was running toward us, coming from down the corridor. He was distraught, gasping. He ran through the blood, spattering it about. "He is ahead!" he cried. "I saw him! He is ahead!"

"In this passage?" asked a man.

"Yes, yes!" cried Gito, pointing backward.

"Why did he not kill you?" asked a man.

"He is my friend," said Gito. "He is ahead! Hurry! You can kill him!"

The lieutenant did not lower his poised blade. He had not even looked back at Gito.

"Where does this passage lead?" asked the lieutenant.

"To the urt pool," said the pit master, reluctantly.

"And there is an interposed gate?"

"Yes," said the pit master.

"Then we have him!" cried a man.

The lieutenant did not take his eyes from the fellow before him.

The fellow, he at whose heart the steel was poised, trembled, but he did not break and run.

"If you would take him, I suggest dispatch," said the officer of Treve.

The lieutenant then turned to one side and thrust the blade deeply into the body of one of the dead sleen, that closest to him, the larger of the two animals. He then returned the blade to the black-tunicked man. The lieutenant then took the other man's blade, which he had held in his left hand, and did with it the same, returning it also to its owner.

"Your blades are bloodied," said the lieutenant.

"Hurry! Hurry!" urged Gito.

Again the lieutenant regarded the pit master.

"Sleen are erratic beasts," said the pit master.

"Form the sluts in front," said the lieutenant. "Set your bows."

We were thrust a little down the passageway, the first group, that "cord" of five in front, the second group, the second "cord" of five, in which I was one, behind, and in the interstices of the first group. In a moment the bows were set, six of them.

"May I have the first shot?" inquired one of the black-tunicked men.

"Granted," said the lieutenant.

"When the command 'Down!' is heard," said a man to us, "you will fling yourselves to your belly instantly. When the command 'Up!' is heard, you will stand, instantly, arranging yourselves as you are now."

"Yes, Master," we said.

There is a common command, familiar to all female slaves, "Belly," which brings us instantly to our bellies before he who commands us. This particular command expression, however, was not used in this context. I speculate that this was because the context of the two commands, and certainly their connotations, was so different. It is one thing, for example, to aesthetically and beautifully signify submission by bellying, perhaps on the furs at the foot of the couch, we being permitted upon them, and quite another to fling oneself down so that quarrels may be suddenly fired from behind one. Too, normally in a "belly command" one orients oneself toward he who commands, not away from him.

Gito hung back.

The lieutenant took him by the scruff of the neck and threw him some feet down the passageway, before us.

"Proceed," he said.

Gito hurried a few feet down the passageway. The blood was now viscous in places, half dried. In some places, where he had stepped, it was pulled up, like syrup, clinging to his sandals, exposing the floor of the passageway.

Gito turned about, and looked back.

He went a few feet further down the passageway.

He turned back, again.

"This way," he said. Then he said, "Let me behind the wall!"

"You are in no danger," said the lieutenant. "You are his friend."

Gito moaned, and, looking over his shoulder frequently, reassuring himself of our continued presence, made his way down the passageway, staying close to the wall.

"We will pin him against the gate," said the man who had requested the first opportunity for fire.

Suddenly, from down the passageway, we saw, blazing in the reflected light of a lamp, two eyes.

"Sleen!" cried a man, alarmed.

We screamed, and tried to draw back, but were held in place.

"No," said the pit master. "It is an urt."

It was crouched down, before us.

It was large, but not large for those I had seen in the pits. It probably weighed no more than twenty or thirty pounds. Most species of urts are small, weighing less than a pound. Some are tinier than mice.

Gito had fled back. He now hid behind us.

"What is it doing in the passage?" asked the lieutenant.

"Someone must have left the panels open," said the pit master.

"Look," said a man. "There is another behind it."

"There seems much carelessness in the management of the pits," said the lieutenant.

"You have had us dismiss the guards," said the pit master.

"The prisoner must have opened the panels," said a man.

"But the beasts are here, beyond the gate," said a man.

"The gate, it seems, was not locked," said the pit master.

"That would seem an unfortunate oversight," said the lieutenant.

"Yes," said the pit master, "it would seem so."

"Doubtless it was lifted by the prisoner," said a man.

"Doubtless," said another.

"Will the urt charge?" asked the lieutenant.

"I do not know," said the pit master. "I would not approach it too closely."

"It is dangerous?"

"Quite."

"Kill it," said the lieutenant.

"Perhaps your colleague, Gito, can turn it," suggested the pit master.

"No, no!" said Gito.

But the urt did turn then, of its own accord, and scampered back down the passageway. The other, which had been behind it, hesitated for a moment, and then followed it.

"Advance," said the lieutenant.

I felt the butt of a crossbow prod me.

We continued down the passageway. We came, in a moment, to a turning.

"The lamps are out," said a man.

"He must be ahead," said a man.

"He must be trapped," said another.

"Take lamps from the passage," said the lieutenant.

Two of the men went back and fetched the nearest lamps.

"Will you truly walk down this passage, carrying light?" asked the officer of Treve.

"Free slaves, that they may do so," said one of the black-tunicked men.

"They are the shield," said a man.

"You," said the lieutenant to the officer of Treve, "will do so."

"I think not," he said.

"Prepare then to die," said the lieutenant, angrily.

"The pit guard will be reporting in soon," said the pit master.

"You will dismiss them, as before," said the lieutenant.

"They may be looking for us now. I doubt that they would be pleased to learn that you had slain a captain of Treve. Too, perhaps your men would like to leave the depths alive."

The black-tunicked men exchanged glances.

"You will dismiss them," said the lieutenant.

"That is difficult to do until they have reported," said the pit master.

But at that moment we heard, from down the passage, in the darkness, a hideous, but unmistakable human cry, which was followed, almost instantly, by a violent squealing of urts.

"Urts!" cried a man.

"They have him!" cried another.

"Our work is done for us!" cried another, elatedly.

The lieutenant, followed by his six men, thrust about us, and between us, pushing us to the side, lifting the rope on our necks. Gito remained behind us. The officer of Treve and the pit master followed the black-tunicked men in their rush forward. "Hurry!" said Fina, dragging her group forward. Ours, perhaps fearing to be separated in this place, we helpless, urts about, hurried behind. I could see the two lamps flickering down the passage. Also, in a moment, I could see a mound of twisting, squealing urts, clambering over and about something, biting at it. Some scampered about the edge of the group, as though seeking some avenue of approach, some entrance into that heap of squirming, frenzied animals, some ingress into that broiling tumult of glistening fur and slashing fangs, that they, too, might feast. The peasant, I assumed, from the horrifying cry I had heard, must be beneath that terrible living hill of beasts. Behind them I could see the bars of the gate. The gate was down. The darkness of the walk ringing the urt pool was behind. I also became aware, vaguely now, of a woman's screaming. That must be the Lady Ilene, whom I had met in the chamber of the commercial praetor, kept now, I knew, pending the arrival of her ransom, in the tiny cage suspended over the urt pool, that cage which had been for some time the residence of the Lady Constanzia, that cage which could be opened at the tug of a cord.

The lieutenant, the six men, two with lamps, stood back from the pile of frenzied urts. The fur of some of them was bloodied, they apparently having been, crowding in and about, in the haste and excitement of the feeding, bitten by their fellows. "Pull them off," said the lieutenant, to one of the men who had not attacked the sleen.

The woman was screaming, from within, over the urt pool.

The man put aside his bow and reached into the pile of animals, seizing one after another and throwing it to the side. I thought this took great courage. To be sure the animals seemed on the whole hardly aware of him. Some did twist about to tear at him, as might have fighting dogs. As soon as he would fling one to the side it would turn about and try to thrust its snout back into the pack.

The two men with the lamps lifted them higher.

The smell of blood was strong in the passageway. The passageway, too, was loud with the squealing of the beasts. From within, over the urt pool, we could still hear the screaming of the woman.

"It is a dead urt!" said a man, suddenly.

"We heard a cry," said another. "It was human."

The fellow who had been pulling the urts aside now stood back. His hands and forearms were covered with blood, but much of it, I am sure, was from the fur and jaws of the urts. He had been bitten at least twice. His left sleeve was in shreds. The urts now dragged the body of the dead urt, now half eaten, its bones about, to the wall, where they continued their feeding.

"He must have been attacked on the other side of the gate," said a man.

One of the black-tunicked fellows went to the bars of the gate, peering through, into the darkness. "Bring a lamp," he said.

"How did the urt die?" asked a man.

Urts seldom attack their own kind unless their fellow behaves in an erratic fashion, as it might if injured or ill.

"What difference does it make?" asked a man.

"What do you see?" asked the lieutenant of the fellow by the bars. He now seemed to be gripping them with great tightness. Indeed, he seemed to have pulled himself closely to them, even pressing himself against them. Too, oddly, he seemed taller now, as though he might have stood on his toes.

"What do you see?" asked the lieutenant, again.

"There is a quarrel in the urt!" said a man, suddenly, the beasts, in their feeding, moving about.

"Extinguish the lamps!" cried the lieutenant.

I heard the heavy, vibratory snap of the cable, but did not see the quarrel. It must have been fired from only a foot or so behind the bars of the gate. I did see the lamp move strangely in the hand of the fellow who held it, he who had been summoned to the bars. The other lamp, in the hand of the other fellow, had been dashed from his hand by the lieutenant. "Fire through the gate!" cried the lieutenant, wildly. I heard three bows fire, one after the other. Then I heard a fourth. Urts still squealed and stirred to the side.

"Draw back, reload!" said the lieutenant.

Men thrust past us. Indeed, we fell, or my "cord" did. I was bruised by a weapon as someone went past us.

"Get the slaves across the passage," said the lieutenant. "Block it!"

The girl next to me cried out with pain. I think she had been grasped by the hair and pulled to her feet. Certainly the cord on my neck, rasping, jerked upward. I cried out in misery. I crouched. The cord was still taut. Then it grew fiercely insistent. The side of my neck burned. I must rise. I was subject to the cord. I must be compliant. I scrambled to my feet, in misery, in the crowded darkness, obedient to the imperative of my constraint. The rest of the "cord" rose, too. I then heard another girl cry out with pain, perhaps Fina, kicked, and then that "cord," too, to the side of us, to our right, was on its feet.

We were frightened. We gasped for breath.

I think they feared that the gate might be lifted in the darkness. That their foe, blade in hand, in the darkness, might come through, either to do them greater injury or slip past them. But I was sure the gate had remained down. Had it risen, I was sure I could have heard it, in its tracks. Too, the urts were quieter now. We could, however, still hear them feeding.

"An interesting stratagem," said the officer of Treve, in the darkness.

"Excellent Kaissa," said the pit master.

It was only later that I understood their probable meanings. I was, at the time, confused, sick, afraid, almost unable to stand, waiting there in the darkness, with the others, not knowing if something, an urt, or the prisoner, armed, intent, might suddenly be upon us, perhaps slashing to one side or the other, in some eagerness to get at the men.

But he did not come through the gate in the darkness.

The lifting of the gate, of course, would have marked his position, if only for a moment.

The prisoner had apparently lifted the panels to the urt nest, permitting them access to the walkway, the gate having been raised to permit them, or some at least, into the passageway, the gate then being lowered. It is terribly dangerous, of course, to trap an urt against a barrier, as it will then fight with terrible ferocity. To approach the gate would have trapped them in this fashion, thus making them his allies. But his plan, it seemed, had been even subtler than this. Urts on the other side of the barrier, the men approaching, the corridor dark, necessitating the bringing of light into it, he had apparently, probably with his own body, if not blood, lured urts back, close to the gate. He had then cried out, as though under attack, and, doubtless at the same time, during that seemingly agonized, hideous cry, fired into the urts at point-blank range, thereby killing or wounding one of them, and initiating the feeding frenzy. By the time it had been determined that the victim was another urt the men would have been within range. I was sure now that the one man who had clung, so closely, so stiffly, to the bars, had been struck, through them, with a thrust of the sword, to the heart. I was sure he had not come back with us. The prisoner would then have lifted the crossbow, the quarrel set, and fired again, through the bars, at the man with the lamp, the light illuminating the target. He had killed two men in this fashion and, had the urts behaved differently, might have accomplished the destruction of one or two others. The lieutenant had four men left.

Gratefully, something like a quarter of an Ahn later, kneeling on the floor of the passage, I rubbed my wrists.

"I do not think he will fire on you," said the pit master. "There are ten slaves, and he will know that there are several, at least. He is limited in his quiver, and he is not likely to use quarrels on slaves."

"Yes, Master," I said. But I was not greatly reassured by these words. I was more reassured by the fact that I was in a rear group. Yet I had little doubt that he was sincere in his remarks, as he was obviously willing to let Fina be in one of the forward groups. We had now fetched torches and lamps from the passages, whatever was available. Indeed, even the pit master had fetched himself a torch.

"Let us get more men," said Gito.

"We have taken fee," said the lieutenant, "as have you."

"Where is the pit guard?" asked the officer of Treve.

"They have reported in by now, and have not been dismissed," said the pit master. "I would suppose they are searching for us."

"Up," said a man to the slaves, and we rose to our feet.

We were now differently arranged. We were now in five groups of two each, a pair for each of the black-tunicked men, including the lieutenant. Each girl in a pair was tied by the neck to the other with cord. I was with Fecha, on her left, about two feet from her, that much latitude and no more permitted to me by the cord. She had been given a small torch, and I carried a lamp. As we were fastened together we could not well bolt, as coordination in such a matter would be difficult. Too, tied as we were, we constituted, as before, something of a shield, in this case for the one man behind us. We were the fourth group. The pair including Fina, the second group, was appropriated by the lieutenant, who seemed aware of her specialness to the pit master. The pit master, with his torch, stayed close to them. The officer of Treve, too, remained in the vicinity of this group. Gito followed the fifth group, several paces behind. This new arrangement, that of five groups, made possible a more diversified deployment of the men, presumably an advantage on the walkway about the urt pool. On the other hand, it would presumably be less effective in blocking passages or in providing a barrier which could be, at a word, a command, raised and lowered, from behind which volley firing might take place.

"Look," said the man in the lead. He was the second of the two men who had not joined in the attack on the sleen earlier. The first was he who had been given the unenviable task of separating the feeding urts. He had, it seemed, lost a great deal of blood. His bow had been set for him by his fellow.

"The gate is open," said another man.

I did not look at the remains of the man who lay in the passage. The urts had been much at him. It was he who had requested the first shot earlier.

He had been left where he was, that the urts would be less dangerous, from a heavy feeding.

The other fellow who had died at the gate, who had brought the lamp forward, had been hauled back in the corridor. In this fashion, if the urts pressed on us again, there would be meat to interpose between us and their reawakened appetites.

Had it been deemed useful I had little doubt that one or more slaves might have been sacrificed, to accomplish the same purpose.

It would have been easy enough to do, as we were bound, and conveniently at hand, in our neck-cords.

I feared these sober, strange men in their sable habiliments. A normal Gorean male, I was sure, would have defended a jeopardized kajira to the death. But, too, he would not have relaxed the perfection of his mastery over her in the least. Is she not, it might be asked, a desirable, beautiful animal, worth saving for his pleasure?

An Earth woman, incidentally, if rescued on Gor by a Gorean, might be surprised at the aftermath of her rescue. Half hysterical with relief, overwhelmed with gratitude, say, she is prepared to throw herself into his arms and grant him, even though he is a stranger, the inestimable favor of a kiss. Many Earth women seem to think their kisses are of great value, whereas most of them do not know how to kiss. The kisses of a slave on the other hand, so subtle, and humble, and well-placed, coupled with her entire demeanor, the meaning of her collar, and such, can drive a man mad with pleasure. But then that is understandable; she is a slave. To be sure, as the slave is further and further aroused by the master, in his turn, her kisses may become more and more piteously and helplessly orgasmic. But then to her surprise, and, one supposes, consternation, the Earth woman finds herself enfolded helplessly in mighty arms and kissed in turn and kissed as she had never dreamed she might be kissed, with such ferocity, and mastery and power, and ownership, and then as she reels, giddy and dazed, she is taken in hand and turned about, and thrown to the ground, on her stomach; her clothing, she almost failing to comprehend what is occurring, is ripped from her, all of it; she feels the air on her body and the grass on her belly and breasts; she protests; she struggles; she tries to rise; his hand holds her in place; she cannot rise; her wrists are jerked behind her and enclosed in slave bracelets; she is then leashed, and led from the field; if she resists or dallies she will be whipped; if he has a collar with him it will undoubtedly be put on her; he has saved her life and it now belongs to him, and he will do with it what he wants. He will keep her, have pleasure with her, sell her, or give her away, as he pleases.

This will become more intelligible to her as she becomes more aware of the ways of Gor.

Not all cultures are the same.

She is now a slave, with all that that means on Gor.

She will soon learn.

* * * *

"Where are the urts?" asked the lieutenant.

"As they did not pass us," said the pit master, "and they are not here, one gathers they have returned to the nest, or the pool. Some might be on the walkway."

It seemed very dark beyond the gate. I could see the railing about the pool.

It was silent within, very silent.

"Perhaps he is gone," said a man.

"Was he within," said a man, "he would have left the gate down, as a barrier. It would have been dangerous for us to lift it. He would have fired from behind it."

"Are there other gates, accessible from the walkway?" asked the lieutenant.

"Yes," said the pit master.

"Aagh!" cried the lieutenant, in fury.

"Then he is gone?" said a man.

"Are the gates open?" asked the lieutenant.

"No," said the pit master.

"I do not believe you," said the lieutenant.

"He is gone then?" said the man.

"If he was not within he would have left the gate down," said a man, "to make us believe he was within, to slow our pursuit."

"Leaving it up, is to invite us into a trap," said a man.

"Or have us believe it so," said another.

"He is not within," said the lieutenant. "But he has already won his point, buying time, we, like fools, standing about in idle converse."

"I would, nonetheless, recommend caution," said the officer of Treve.

"Step from behind the slaves," the lieutenant ordered the lead man.

Reluctantly he did so.

It was he, I recalled, who had been the second of the two men who had not joined in the attack on the sleen.

"Go to the threshold, stand there," said the lieutenant.

The peasant, I recalled, was not likely to waste quarrels on slaves, at least according to the speculations of the pit master, which speculations I fervently hoped were sound.

The black-tunicked man, on the other hand, would presumably constitute a prime target.

"I do not think he is within," said the lieutenant.

The man slowly, reluctantly, went to the center of the threshold.

He stood there.

It takes time, of course, to reload the crossbow. That interval of time, I gathered, figured in the lieutenant's calculations.

After several seconds, the man standing there in the portal, silhouetted by the light behind him, the lieutenant, unwilling to lose more time, indicated that one man, preceded by his fair shield of two, should enter and go to the left, and another, he, too, preceded by his shield of two, to the right. After an interval of about four paces, the lieutenant, with two slaves, followed the man who had gone to the right, and the other man, with his two slaves, followed he who had gone to the left. The man who had served as point for our advance, with two slaves, remained at the portal, just within it.

I was with the second man who had gone to the left, preceding him, with Fecha.

We moved cautiously, the light lifted.

There were four gates giving access to the walkway, that through which we had entered, and, across the pool, on the other side, three, each leading to a different tunnel.

I heard a girl scream. An urt, on the walkway, at their approach, had scrambled over the railing, and dived into the pool.

Fecha held her torch over the pool. We could see ripples in the water there. And I saw the wet, glistening head of an urt, just at the surface. The head was very smooth. They swim with their ears back, flat against the head. This was not the urt which had just entered the pool. That one had dived in far back and to our right.

"Hurry!" urged the lieutenant to the man before him. He feared the loss of time.

"Move," said the man to the slaves before him. They whimpered, and, lamps lifted, moved forward. The pair ahead of us stopped.

"Urt!" cried Tira, pointing.

"No," said the man. "It is only a shadow."

The lamps and torches threw strange shadows, which moved, as the source of light moved, sometimes giving the impression of a dark body stirring, even moving furtively, or quickly.

I looked above us. The vault of the chamber was lost in darkness. I could see the cage, high, to my left, over the pool, with its various chains and ropes, for controlling its location. There was also the cord which went to the gate latch at its bottom.

"Lift the gate," said the lieutenant to the pit master. The first man and the lieutenant had come to the first gate, reached by going to the right about the pool. The lieutenant did not wish to risk either himself or his man by standing at the gate, lifting it. A bolt from the other side would not be likely to miss. The fellow who had served as a lure for quarrels was still back at the gate we had entered, guarding it with his bow. The man with the lieutenant was the one who limped, having injured his ankle yesterday morning in the cell, apparently having twisted it in the stirrup of the crossbow, while trying to reset the weapon.

"It is locked," said the pit master.

"Determine that it is so," said the lieutenant.

With one hand the pit master bent down and pulled against a crossbar of the gate.

"Try it," said the lieutenant to his fellow.

Reluctantly the man put down his bow and, with two hands, tried to lift the gate.

"It is locked," he said.

I heard urts in the pool below. Some, it seemed, had just entered it, from the tunnel leading to the nest. The noises about the walkway may have aroused their curiosity. Too, once they had come to the tunnel opening, which was beneath the surface of the pool, reached from the nest, on a higher level, on the other side, they may have seen the light from the lamps and torches on the water. Such things were probably associated in their minds with the possibility of food. There were several urts in the pool area, I knew, and, save for their fellow, and what they had had of the man by the gate, they had not eaten for two days. They would doubtless, most of them, be hungry. The guard had been dismissed. When one urt leaves the nest, others tend to follow.

"Hold," said the man behind us.

We stopped.

He looked about himself.

The first man, with the two slaves, who had gone to the left, was now well ahead of us, and had reached the first of the three opposite gates which was accessible from our side of the pool.

He stood to one side, against the wall, back from the gate. He did not care to try it. Given its weight, it was unlikely that the slaves could have raised it, even if it had been unlatched.

"Stand before the gate," he said to the slaves.

The slaves did as they were told.

"What do you see?" asked the man.

"Nothing, Master," said Tira, peering into the corridor beyond.

The man carefully confirmed this, looking about the edge of the wall.

He then, the light behind him, put aside his bow and, crouching down, struggled to lift the gate.

He stood up, wiping his hands on his tunic, recovering his bow.

"It is locked?" called the lieutenant to him.

"Yes," said the man.

"Then it is the center gate which is unlocked!" said the lieutenant. "Hurry!" he urged the fellow before him.

"Move, move!" said that fellow to the slaves before him.

The two parties, the first group from the left, the black-tunicked man with two slaves, and the two groups from the right, the one man and the lieutenant, with the slaves at their disposal, now converged at the opposite gate, the center gate of the three gates across from that through which we had entered, one party to its left, the other, the larger party, to its right. Neither party wished to simply present itself before the opening.

Gito had remained behind. He had not even entered the pool area.

The other fellow, who had been first in our advance, guarded the portal through which we had entered.

I looked up, again, at the cage, hanging there in the shadows, near the ceiling. We had, earlier, heard the free woman screaming. We had heard nothing from her, however, since our entry into the pool area. I was sure she was still in the cage. I thought I could see her small form within it. To be sure, this was difficult to determine in the shadows. I thought that perhaps she was frightened. I thought that perhaps she might by now have developed some sensitivity to the possible indiscretion of unsolicited speech. In the cage women, as in chains and kennels, tend to become sensitive to many things, in particular, that they are females.

"Titus!" called the lieutenant.

"Move," said the man behind us. We hurried then about the pool, he following.

"Lift the gate," said the lieutenant to the pit master.

"It is locked," the pit master said.

"That is absurd," said the lieutenant.

"It is locked," said the pit master, again.

"Illuminate the passage," said the lieutenant, thrusting Fina and her cord-mate before the gate.

The pit master, already before the gate, did not object.

"Look," said the lieutenant, angrily, to the man nearest him.

The fellow looked, carefully.

"The passage seems to be empty," he said, "as far as the light carries."

"Lift the gate," said the lieutenant.

The man put down his bow and, with great caution, crouching down, strove to raise the gate.

"It is locked," he averred, confirming the word of the pit master, who stood by, his torch lifted.

"I do not understand," said the fellow to the left of the gate, Titus, he whom Fecha and I had preceded.

"He could not have passed us," said the fellow at the gate, who recovered his bow, and stood.

The other fellow, he with the lieutenant, looked across the pool, to the portal across the way. The fellow who had led our approach was still there, his bow cradled in his arms. "Herminius is on guard," he said.

"He could not have passed him," said he who had been at the gate.

The lieutenant looked at the pit master.

"It would seem to me that the inference is clear," said the pit master.

There was a sudden, half-strangled cry from across the pool as Herminius, clutching at his throat, legs kicking, seemed, somehow, to fly upward, into the darkness. He was trying to get his fingers, it seemed, at something on his throat.

"He is here!" screamed the lieutenant, gesturing wildly toward the portal across the way. "Hurry! Run!"

The men, two to the left, and two to the right, the man with the lieutenant and the lieutenant, fled about the walkway.

"He is above, somewhere in the shadows!" cried the lieutenant. "Get those torches up!"

I could see the dark, jerking shadow of Herminius over the portal. The two slaves who had been with him had fled to the right, as one would enter the pool area. One had dropped her lamp. We could see the men hurrying about the pool area, toward the portal. "Torches, light!" cried the lieutenant, near the portal.

"Go," said the pit master, "go," pushing Fina down the walkway. Fecha started, too, to follow, and I, corded to her by the neck, hurried with her. A splash of hot oil from the lamp fell on my leg. I cried out. The lamps and torches were wild in the darkness. The pit master and the officer of Treve followed, going about, however, to the left, as one would face the portal from the inside.

I was sure the prisoner had not gone through the portal. He was still in the chamber. Too, Gito was somewhere down the passage and presumably would have cried out had the prisoner passed him.

"Sluts!" cried the lieutenant. "Lift the torches! Lift the lamps! Lift them up!"

Fina screamed and stepped back, turning about. I, too, shrank back, sickened.

Near the portal, at its threshold, there lay two severed hands.

Herminius, it seemed, had not been permitted to interfere with the effectiveness of the noose which had drawn him up, into the shadows.

His body was quiet now, some thirty feet above us. It moved only as the rope, and its weight, would have it.

"He is somewhere up there, in the shadows," said the lieutenant. He took care, I noted, not to stand where he was illuminated.

The bows were lifted. It was almost as though they were alive, seeking prey.

Suddenly in back of us, and above us, over the pool, we heard a bolt, that of the cage latch, jerked loose.

The cord which went to the latch on the bottom of the cage over the pool went, with the other apparatus, chains and ropes, connected with the control of the cage, from the cage to the wall, over pulleys, and then down to the level of the walkway, where it, like the other devices, was secured. The trigger cord, which would release the latch at the bottom of the cage, was intended to be drawn, if drawn, at all, from the level of the walkway, but the cord, itself, naturally, stretched across the darkness, as I have indicated, and came to the wall.

It had apparently been drawn, then, from above, by the wall, in the darkness.

The gate bolt on the cage drawn, the bottom of the cage dropped downward on its hinges, opening the cage. There had been a rattle of metal and a creaking of chain, the cage swinging, emptied of its occupant, and the sound of a body suddenly caught short in its fall. We spun about and saw the Lady Ilene, her small ankles tied together,

her hands tied behind her back, a rope under her arms, swinging over the dark waters of the urt pool. She twisted wildly. She bent her legs at the knees, trying to pull her feet up. We saw her eyes, now that she was lower, over what seemed to be her veil. They were hysterically wild. She spun about on the rope, squirming helplessly. We could now hear tiny, helpless, terrified sounds from her. Her veil, it seemed, had been used to gag her. One did not know if she would have remained prudentially silent, daring not to mix in the business of men, daring not to call attention to herself, a female, or not, but the option had not been granted to her. Urts began to knife instantly toward the vicinity of the pool over which the Lady Ilene was suspended.

"Look to the wall! Look to the wall!" screamed the lieutenant. "It is only a diversion!"

"Ai!" cried a man.

The body of Herminius seemed to rise on the rope, and stand for a moment erect, in the air, and then it seemed to fly outward from the wall. It struck into the water, over the railing, opposite the portal. It would be bloody.

"There, there he is!" cried the lieutenant. "There! Fire!"

I, too, saw for a moment, in the shadows, a huge shape. It had hurled Herminius from the wall as easily as the pit master might have thrown a joint of meat into the pool.

Titus, the black-tunicked fellow whom Fecha and I had shielded, was, I think, a man of suspicious and subtle instincts, of wary caution. He had dallied in moving with us about the walkway. He had let others move first. He had remained back, like a coiled spring, ready to fire. I thought him perhaps the most dangerous of the black-tunicked men. He must have seen the black shadow, too. He had turned back, after the cage had opened, before any of us, before even the lieutenant had called out. His bow was the first realigned with the wall. That must have marked him out as the next to die. He pitched back, over the railing, the fins of a quarrel half hidden in his tunic.

"He has fired!" cried the lieutenant, elatedly. "Find him! Find him! Fire! Fire!"

But suddenly, from a place high on the wall, now feet from where the body of Herminius had been thrown, on one of the ropes which were intended to control the movements of the cage, a dark figure swung over the urt pool. There was a quiver and bow slung at its back, a sword dangling behind it.

"Tensius to the left, Abnik to the right!" screamed the lieutenant. "You have him now. He has no time to reload."

The figure had alighted on the opposite side of the walkway, before the middle gate of the three gates on that side of the pool.

I thought the prisoner might have time to reload, but he, surely would not have time to fire twice.

"Run! Run!" screamed the lieutenant.

One man, Tensius, sped to the left. It was he who had been the first of the two men who had refrained from attacking the sleen, and had later been bloodied, separating the urts. The other man, Abnik, limping, hurried to the right. He it was whose foot had been injured yesterday in the cell, in the stirrup of the crossbow. He had been the man with the lieutenant, in the investigation of the gates.

The prisoner would not have time to fire twice.

"You have him!" cried the lieutenant.

Only a few feet below me urts were tearing at the bodies of Herminius and Titus. The water of the pool was scarlet. The Lady Ilene, out of the cage, tied to it by a rope fastened under her arms, bound hand and foot, gagged, dangled over the urt pool. But she seemed of no interest now to the urts. None circled beneath her. None tried to leap up to seize a foot or leg. Readier meat lay within their province now. I did not know, but I thought that the urts would not be able to reach her. It was a risk, of course, which the peasant had been willing to take. I wondered what thoughts went through her head. She had figured, but a bit ago, as a diversion. Now she had another role to play, I suspected, one which had doubtless been projected for her earlier, one independent of the entry of the determined, tenacious black-tunicked men onto the walkway, the role of a dangling lure, one which might serve, for some purpose, as a distraction to urts. Certainly she had figured at least once in the plans of a man. Perhaps she understood herself better now as a female, and what might be done with her. Surely to the collar would now be but a short step for her. To be sure, she now seemed, as things had turned out, of little current interest to the urts. They, feeding eagerly, had been drawn away from her, to the blood and bodies below the railing. The peasant, presumably, would not have been able to count on that development. It was, presumably, a fortunate one for the Lady Ilene, particularly if the peasant had underestimated the capacity of the urts to leap from the water.

Tensius, from the left, Abnik, from the right, hurried toward the peasant.

But he did not load the bow, for a last shot. Rather, to my horror, he took a quarrel between his teeth and, bow in hand, leapt over the railing, into the urt pool itself.

"He is insane!" cried the officer of Treve.

Almost at the same moment Tensius had come to the place on the walkway from which the peasant had dived into the pool. He looked into the water, in consternation. Abnik, a moment later, came to the same place.

"Fire! Fire!" cried the lieutenant.

Uncertain, Tensius and Abnik, judging as they could the likely path beneath the water of the peasant, loosed their quarrels. They hissed down into the water. "Reload!" cried the lieutenant. He himself bent down and picked up the bow which had been that of Herminius. Its quarrel had become dislodged but, in a moment, it was again fitted in the guide. I did not doubt but what, at one time or another, the lieutenant had been quite practiced with such a weapon. It, like the dagger, would doubtless be familiar to the wearers of the dark habiliments.

"Illuminate the pool!" cried the lieutenant.

We all, then, save the pit master, with his torch, brought our lamps or torches to the railing.

The light reflected up from the surface of the pool. Below me the urts were still feeding.

The lieutenant scanned the water tensely.

No body surfaced, penetrated with quarrels.

There seemed no sign of the peasant.

Then Tensius and Abnik had reset their bows.

"Where is he!" cried the lieutenant, his bow in hand.

But he received no answer.

We waited, about the railing. The urts continued to feed. The remains of the bodies rolled about in the water, under the stress of the feeding. Sometimes they were tugged under, and then, again, in a moment, surfaced. They were pulled back and forth.

The light of the torches and the lamps shone, reflected, from the water.

"He must have drowned," called Tensius, from across the pool.

Certainly one would have expected the peasant to surface by now, if he were still alive. It was, of course, dark in the pool, and the light was uncertain.

"Urts have taken him, under the water," called Abnik.

"Is there an exit from the pool!" demanded the lieutenant of the pit master, standing behind him, his torch lifted. "Of course," said the pit master, "that through which the urts enter it, through their nest."

"Where is the exit?" demanded the lieutenant.

"There, under the water, at the side," said the pit master, indicating an area of the pool to our right, as we faced the pool, we near the portal through which we had entered the pool area, the point indicated rather opposite where the cage dangled.

"Close the panels which permit access to the walkway!" said the lieutenant.

This took but a moment to do, as the pertinent levers were just outside the portal.

The peasant now could not return through the nest, even if he survived there, to the walkway.

I did think it possible, as doubtless so, too, did the lieutenant, that the peasant might now, at this time, the urts otherwise occupied, successfully reach the nest, which would be above water, on the other side of the wall. Indeed that might explain why he had not surfaced. To be sure, he might have surfaced, unnoticed. As I have indicated, the light was uncertain.

"Tensius, Abnik, into the water!" cried the lieutenant, gesticulating to the pool.

They looked across the pool as though their officer might be mad.

"I am bloodied," said Tensius. He had lost blood from the bites of urts, when he had separated them, near the closed gate, earlier.

"It is safe now," said the lieutenant.

The urts did seem to be feeding now. To be sure, I doubted that all of them, and there must have been seventeen or eighteen of them, had had their fill.

"The nest opening is there!" pointed the lieutenant. "Enter it! Find him! Kill him!"

"Would you send them to their deaths?" asked the officer of Treve.

"We have taken fee," said the lieutenant.

I supposed that the nest might be empty now. But it would not be likely to long remain empty.

I shivered.

In dealing with urts there are certain things to be kept in mind. One does not intrude into their nest. One tries to avoid placing oneself between them. And one never denies them an avenue of escape.

"Into the water!" screamed the lieutenant.

The men looked at him.

"It is safe now," said the lieutenant. "The urts feed. Go! Go!"

"He is drowned!" cried Tensius.

"Urts took him!" said Abnik.

"Bring me the body!" said the lieutenant.

The lieutenant, this officer of the men in the black habiliments, seemed as tenacious as might be a sleen itself, this world's finest and most relentless tracker, a sleen on its scent, single-minded, implacable, driven. He wanted confirmation of the kill. Too, I supposed, in a short while, the urts about, it might be difficult to obtain remains sufficient to constitute convincing evidence to a fee giver that the task which had been agreed upon had been successfully accomplished.

Tensius first, who had refrained from attacking the sleen in the passage, but who had later separated the urts, removed his helmet and set aside his bow. The black dagger was still on his forehead, from yesterday morning. He then put his knife between his teeth and, with great care, lowered himself over the railing, and dropped down into the pool. He did this as gently as was possible. Abnik followed him, similarly. The lieutenant remained on guard, with the bow, surveying the water.

"They are brave men," said the officer of Treve.

Tensius and Abnik swam to the edge of the pool, to our right.

They looked back.

The lieutenant pointed to the place where the pit master had indicated lay the underwater entrance to the nest.

I saw Tensius first submerge. He was followed, in a moment, by Abnik.

"Look!" said the pit master.

One of the urts, an arm in its jaws, was swimming back toward the nest.

"Kill it!" urged the pit master.

"It takes time to reload," said the lieutenant.

"It may just brush past them," said the officer of Treve. "It has its meat."

"Yes," said the lieutenant, surveying the surface of the water, "that is what it will do."

"Not if there are young in the nest," said the pit master.

"Are there young in the nest?" asked the officer of Treve.

"Yes," said the pit master.

"It takes time to reload," said the lieutenant.

"It is too late now," said the officer of Treve.

The urt, too, had submerged.

"Space the light about the pool," said the lieutenant, with a gesture of his arm.

The slaves spaced themselves then more about the pool. I remained with Fecha a little to the left of the entrance, as one would enter the area of the pool. The lieutenant was a few feet to our right. The pit master was behind him, holding aloft his torch. The officer of Treve was nearby. Gito was not in the pool area, but back in the passage. I had glimpsed him. He was crouched down, his back to the wall of the passage, looking toward the portal.

We waited, it seemed for a long time.

"Should your men not have returned by now?" asked the officer of Treve.

The lieutenant did not respond. He continued to survey the flickering surface of the pool.

There was a sound of chain as the cage swung a little. It was a few yards away, above us. It had been moved by the weight of the bound, gagged free woman, dangling on the rope over the pool.

She looked at me.

I was suddenly, intensely, ashamed, aware of my nudity. How such as she must scorn such as I! In what contempt must she hold me! How she must despise me! But I was not such as she! I was a slave! I was collared! I must be as men would have me! If they saw fit to deny me clothing then I would not have clothing! If they ordered me to dance, I must dance. If they wished me to serve, I must serve! I was not such as she! But then I, for anything, would not have wished to be such as she! I had learned my womanhood! I would never, never surrender it, not now that I had tasted it, not for all the garbage and politics in the world. I had learned it at the hands of strong men, their precious gift to me, an inestimable treasure, men to whom I would be forever grateful. I had now found myself, and accepted myself, and loved myself! I was not a man, or a kind of man. I was a woman, something radically different and wonderful. I pitied men not being women! But then, suddenly, even though I knew her to be free, I did not sense contempt or scorn in her. It was strange. I quickly looked away. It is seldom wise for a female slave to look directly into the eyes of a free woman. But then I recalled that she had been in the cage. There, suspended in the darkness, helpless, alone, perhaps she had had time to think, to ask herself what she was, and wanted to be, and might be, and where she herself might be found.

"Surely your men should have returned by now," said the officer of Treve.

"It is not clear what has occurred," said the lieutenant.

The urts continued to feed, turning the two bodies about in the water.

I saw another swimming toward the nest, a shred of muscle trailing behind it.

"By now," speculated the officer of Treve, "it seems he should have been taken, or the body found."

"The two of you," said the lieutenant, not taking his eyes from the water, "have been insufficiently cooperative. Your actions, you may be assured, will be reported to the administration."

The pit master continued to hold his torch aloft, as he had, rather behind the lieutenant.

"They must have found him, they must have killed him, by now," said the lieutenant.

"Undoubtedly," said the officer of Treve.

"Perhaps they have all died in the nest," said the pit master.

"He may have drowned," said the lieutenant.

"Possibly," said the pit master.

"Where is he?" cried the lieutenant.

"Somewhere, one supposes," said the officer of Treve.

"Masters," cried Gito, from back in the passage, "let us go to the surface!"

"Go!" said the lieutenant, not taking his eyes from the pool.

"I do not know the way!" cried Gito.

"Where is he?" asked the lieutenant. He received no response.

"He must have drowned," said the lieutenant. He received no response.

"Where are my men?" asked the lieutenant.

"I would not know," said the pit master.

"They are in the nest," said the lieutenant, "waiting for the way to clear of urts."

"Perhaps," said the officer of Treve.

"They are clever fellows," said the lieutenant.

"Doubtless," said the pit master.

"Picked men."

"I do not doubt it," said the pit master.

It was an elite squad, I gathered, which had come to Treve. To someone, it seemed, their mission must have been of great moment.

"They have with them the body, or the head, of the prisoner," said the lieutenant.

"Possibly," said the officer of Treve.

"They will return any moment," said the lieutenant, determinedly.

"Possibly," said the officer of Treve.

"There is something across the way," said the pit master. He gestured toward the opposite wall, several yards from the nest entrance. There, something humped, like a cloth filled with air, had come to the surface.

"Where?"

"There."

"What is it? A dead urt?"

"It is a body," said the pit master.

"Excellent!" said the lieutenant. "It has come to the surface!"

An urt swam to the object and began to bite at it. Once it pulled it beneath the surface. It then emerged, again, closer to us. Another urt then swam toward it.

The object rolled to its back.

"It is Tensius," said the lieutenant.

The eyes were still open, staring upward. One could see the dagger on the forehead. When the body was pulled back, again, one could see that the left leg was gone, and the left hand.

"Urts," said the lieutenant.

I did not know if Tensius had reached the nest or not. I supposed that he might have, as we had not detected a disturbance in the water near the entrance to the nest. But if he had been killed in the nest, why had the urts not fed on him there?

When I looked away from the water I saw that the lieutenant's attention was returned, intently, to the pool. Indeed, he held his bow more at the ready than before.

It was indeed an elite that had come to Treve.

Had the prisoner died in the pool it seemed his body would have surfaced before that of Tensius.

But the body of Tensius, it seemed, had not served as a diversion.

It was merely meat, floating in the water, being eaten.

The moments taken for its identification, the lapse of attention to the tunnel entrance occasioned by its appearance, had been without cost.

The lieutenant lowered his bow.

One could not climb from the pool to the walkway without a rope, or some such device, the tunnels to the walkway having been earlier sealed.

"The prisoner," said the officer of Treve, "may have died in the nest. Too, he may have been trapped beneath the water, wedged under an outcropping, or between rocks."

The latter hypothesis was an interesting one, as water urts sometimes secure prey under the water, saving it for later, rather as certain predatory beasts will bury a kill, or place it in a tree, to be finished later. Some birds impale insects on thorns, for a similar purpose.

"He is alive, somewhere," said the lieutenant. "I am sure of it."

"That seems improbable," said the officer of Treve.

"The body of Tensius shows that he is alive," said the lieutenant. "If he had been killed by urts his body would have made that clear. It would have been a mass of bites, or the throat would have been gone. The condition of the body, on the other hand, shows that it was not attacked by urts until either it was dead or unable to defend itself. And he would not have drowned unless he had been held under the water, in which case the prisoner is alive. I am sure Tensius was stabbed, and the wound washed free of blood."

"Interesting," said the officer of Treve.

"He is clever," said the lieutenant. "He is cunning. He is magnificent prey. It is a pleasure to hunt him."

"Those of the black caste are famed for their prowess in hunting," said the officer of Treve.

"But he has miscalculated," said the lieutenant. "He thought to use the body of Tensius as a diversion, to cover his exit from the pool, but he could not leave the pool. Instead, he has only managed, unbeknownst to himself, to inform me that he is still alive."

"Let us get more men," said Gito, who had crept closer to the portal.

"I need only one clear shot," said the lieutenant.

"He is surely dead," said Gito. "Let us hasten to the surface."

"I have not seen the body," said the lieutenant.

"You truly think he is alive?" asked the officer of Treve.

"Yes," said the lieutenant. "He has now inadvertently informed me of that fact. That loses him his advantage. I am now ready for him, quite ready."

"Come away!" begged Gito.

"I need only one clean shot," said the lieutenant.

The quarrel lay ready in the guide, as quiet as a bullet.

Suddenly from the part of the pool near the entrance to the nest we saw a hand reach up, breaking the surface, and then an arm. A head momentarily broke the surface, and then the body seemed dragged under again. Then it came again to the surface, arms thrashing. It cried out with pain. "It is your man!" said the officer of Treve.

It was the black-tunicked fellow, Abnik, who had had his foot injured in the crossbow's stirrup yesterday morning.

He went under again, seemingly pulled down, and then, choking, spitting water, came again to the surface, closer. "Help! Help!" he cried.

"He is fleeing the nest!" said the officer of Treve.

Abnik tried to swim toward us. It seemed something held him back, under the surface.

"Urts have him!" said the officer of Treve.

"Help! Please!" cried Abnik. Then, choking, he was drawn under again.

One of the girls on the other side of the pool, tied by her neck to her cord-mate, screamed, horrified.

"Keep the torch up!" cried the lieutenant.

I suddenly realized his attention was not on the pathetic figure in the pool but on the waters behind it and about it.

"Help!" cried Abnik.

The water was bloody about him.

An urt beneath the railing turned smoothly in the water, orienting itself toward the figure in the water. It did not, however, approach it. Rather it twisted about, suddenly, and returned to its work at hand. We saw the figure of Tensius pulled under, beneath the railing. Then it surfaced, again. The side of its face was gone.

"Help!" cried Abnik.

We could now see, surfaced behind him, the head and neck of an urt, one that was very large.

Then it dove down again and Abnik cried out in misery.

"Please!" he wept.

His face was contorted. It was hideous. His hands clutched at the air as though he might gain purchase there to drag himself to safety.

"Help! Help!" he cried.

The attention of the lieutenant I noted, to my horror, was not on the struggling figure of Abnik. He was intensely considering, rather, the waters to the side and back.

The head and neck of the urt surfaced again, behind Abnik.

I screamed.

"There it is!" cried out the officer of Treve. "Kill it! Kill it! Save your man!"

"Do not be foolish," said the lieutenant, without taking his attention from the pool. "Do you not understand what is occurring?"

"Please, help me!" cried Abnik.

"Give me the bow," said the officer of Treve. "I will kill it."

But the lieutenant, angrily, pulled the bow away.

The pit master stood rather behind the lieutenant, his torch lifted. I could see the urts below us, at the bodies near the wall, beneath where we stood.

"Kill the thing!" said the officer of Treve. "Kill it!"

"No," said the lieutenant.

"Save him!" begged the officer of Treve.

"I have taken fee, as has he," said the lieutenant.

"Kill it, kill it!" said the officer of Treve.

The man in the water, thrashing about, screamed in misery.

"No," said the lieutenant.

"It is an easy shot," said the officer of Treve, desperately. "At this distance you could not miss!"

"I will not waste the quarrel," said the lieutenant.

"Help!" screamed Abnik.

"He will die," said the officer of Treve.

"I am hunting," said the lieutenant.

"Shoot!" begged the officer of Treve.

"No," said the lieutenant.

It took time, I knew, to reload.

The lieutenant did not even see the hands of the man in the water raised to him, supplicatingly. Nor did he see the fear in those eyes, the terror and pain. His attention was elsewhere, on the waters behind the figure and the thing at his back. But it might have been to his advantage had he paid closer attention to the figure in the water for suddenly the thing behind Abnik rose up in the water and, at the same time, we saw the quarrel of a bow emerge and the cable snapped forward and the quarrel took the lieutenant in the side of the throat just under the chin and tore upward through the skull breaking the helmet away from the head and we saw, below, for one terrible moment, cowled in the head and pelt of an urt, the pelt about his shoulders, the eyes, and the fierce visage, of the peasant, and then that head descended again into the water, and it seemed, once more, eerily, only the head and shoulders of an urt. It moved slowly away, across the pool. It then, near the entrance of the nest, slipped under the water.

The pit master now leaned forward, over the railing. Abnik was now rolling lifeless in the water, lost in the midst of the urts and bodies.

"Is there a way from the urt nest, other than to the pool and walkway?" asked the officer of Treve.

"Ways are barred," said the pit master.

"But there are ways?"

The pit master shrugged.

"Water must be brought to the pool," said the officer of Treve. "A drain? A conduit?"

"They are impassable," said the pit master.

"Do you believe that?" asked the officer of Treve.

"They are impassable by an ordinary man," said the pit master.

"I see," said the officer.

"They are barred, they pass through tharlarion nests."

"Is there any possibility that the prisoner could escape?" asked the officer.

"None whatsoever," said the pit master.

"Could he live in such passages?"

"Perhaps, on urts," said the pit master.

"There is no way out?"

"No," said the pit master.

"Would it be wise to use men, pursuing him in the passages beneath the city?"

"I would not think so," said the pit master.

"What has happened?" called Gito, from down the corridor.

"It is over," said the pit master.

Gito crept to the portal, and then he cried out with horror.

The pit master looked down at the body of the lieutenant.

The officer of Treve, crouching down beside the body, carefully removed the helmet. It was already partly forced off. Its crown was filled with blood and hair.

"He was an excellent officer," said the pit master.

"Of his caste," said the officer of Treve.

"It is strange," said the pit master. "Had he chosen to save his man, by firing on what we took to be the beast, he would have killed the prisoner."

"Yes," mused the officer of Treve.

"What would you have done?" asked the pit master.

"I would have tried to save the man."

"Even at the risk of losing the quarrel, and not having time to reload before a putative attack?"

"Yes," said the officer of Treve.

"But he did not do so."

"No," said the officer of Treve.

"Why?"

"Castes differ," said the officer. He then, with his thumb, wiped away the dagger on the lieutenant's forehead. "He is no longer hunting," he said.

"The prisoner did not flee," observed the pit master. "He returned for him."

"He, too, it seems, was a hunter."

"Do you think it an inadvertence on the prisoner's part that the one man's body, that of he called Tensius, was returned as it was to the pool?"

"Certainly not," said the officer of Treve. "He wanted the officer to know that he was still alive, that was the point of that, in order that the assassin be tensely ready, that he be extremely watchful and alert, and that the preciousness of his quarrel be fully appreciated. He might have but one chance to loose it. He must retain it for the perfect shot. He must in no event waste it."

"But how would he know the officer would not protect his man, that he would not be fired on in the cowl and pelt of the urt?"

"He knew the caste he was dealing with," said the officer of Treve.

"The officer assumed, naturally enough, that the man in the water was only a diversion. Accordingly, he did not even consider him, but directed his attention elsewhere."

"And thus permitted the prisoner to approach unseen, to a point at which a miss was impossible."

"It is hard even to understand such Kaissa," said the pit master.

I understood very little of these things. It did seem to me that the peasant had surely manifested a subtlety, acumen, and terribleness far beyond what one might commonly expect of his caste.

"It is interesting," said the officer of Treve, "that so many of the gates in the passages were unlocked, but the passages remained armed."

"He would use the men of the dark caste to clear the passages before him, of course," said the pit master.

"But the three gates here, across the way, were locked."

"Yes, that is interesting," agreed the pit master.

"You are certain that there is no possibility of escape through the urt nest, through drains, or sewers, or such."

"I think I hear the guard in the corridor," said the pit master. "They have found us."

"I noted you held your torch behind the officer," said the officer of Treve.

"Did I?" asked the pit master.

"That silhouetted his head and shoulders well, even if an approach had been made under water."

"I suppose it might have," said the pit master, "now that I think of it."

"Were the chains of the prisoner tampered with?" inquired the officer of Treve.

"That seems unlikely," said the pit master.

"There is one thing I do not understand," said the officer of Treve.

"What is that?"

"They were prize sleen, trained to perfection. How could it be that they became confused and attacked the captain of those of the dark caste?"

"As you know," said the pit master, "such beasts are unreliable."

"I do not think so," said the officer.

"Oh?"

"How could they make such a terrible mistake?"

"Perhaps they did not make a mistake," said the pit master.

"I do not think they did," said the officer of Treve.

"Perhaps you are right," said the pit master.

"But the blanket was taken from the cell of the prisoner. It was kept, all the while, in a sealed sack. I saw the seal myself."

"It was taken from the cell of the prisoner," said the pit master. "But that does not mean that it was the blanket of the prisoner."

"The hunters insisted on spending the first night in the depths," said the officer of Treve, "presumably to guard against the prisoner being secretly removed."

"I suspect that was their motivation," said the pit master.

"Accordingly," said the officer of Treve, "the blankets of the captain of those of the black caste and the prisoner might have been switched early the next morning, before those of the black caste arrived at the cell."

"An interesting possibility," said the pit master.

"And the captain of those of the dark caste then, by using his own blanket, unbeknownst to himself, set the sleen upon himself."

"That is a possibility," admitted the pit master.

"You are guilty of collusion in the escape of a prisoner," said the officer of Treve.

"We need not regard him as having escaped," pointed out the pit master. "Too, it was not I who kicked a sword to him, putting it within his grasp."

"I am not fond of murder," said the officer.

"I only dreamed of honor," said the pit master. "But I think you may have looked upon her, in a cell, face to face."

"Sir," said one of eleven men, the current posting of the pit guard. They were now in the passage. Gito was far down the passage, crouching down. "We searched long for you."

The pit master put his torch in a rack, beside the portal.

"The guard reports for duty," said the man.

"Feed the prisoners," said the pit master. "Secure the passages, return to your normal duties."

"Are you safe?" asked the man.

"Yes," said the pit master.

"There is not one amongst us who will not take up arms on your behalf," he said. He looked about himself, and toward the darkness of the pool area. He touched his blade, slung over his left shoulder.

"That will not be necessary," said the pit master. "Our guests have gone."

The officer of the guard turned about arid went down the corridor, past Gito. His men followed him.

"I wonder if we have done well here," said the pit master.

"I do not know," said the officer of Treve.

"I wonder if what we have done here truly comports with honor," said the pit master.

"I do not know," said the officer of Treve.

"Nor I," said the pit master.

"She has many voices, and many songs," said the officer of Treve.

Before we left the pool area the pit master, by means of the ropes and chains controlling the cage, brought the helpless Lady Ilene, she dangling on the rope, to the wall, where he lifted her up and put her on her knees, on the walkway. He freed her hands and feet, cutting the cords of twisted cloth, taken from her garments, which the peasant had used to bind them. When he freed her of the gag, being careful, in observance of her modesty, not to look upon her features, she pleaded desperately to speak, but this permission was denied to her.

She then, kneeling before the pit master, put her head down to the bloody walkway.

"She may soon be ready for a cell," said the officer of Treve.

"Or even shackles," said the pit master.

"Perhaps," said the officer.

The Lady Ilene was then reinserted into the cage, and the cage restored to its place over the pool.

I saw her kneeling in the cage, her small hands on the bars. The light cord ran from the walkway, up, through its rings, over its pulleys, to the latch at the bottom of the cage, that securing its gate.

The urts were still feeding.

The pit master lifted up the body of the lieutenant, and thrust it over the railing.

There was a splash in the dark waters below.

The pit master then cut the cords, in the center, that held the pairs of slaves together.

We then left the pool area.

The slaves preceded the pit master and the officer of Treve. We did wait for a moment, when the pit master stopped beside Gito, in the passage. "You will come with us," he said. "When we come to the sack in the passage, where it was dropped, you will pick it up, and bring it along."

"Yes, yes, Masters," said Gito anxiously. He then hurried along with us.

Thirty Eight

"It is there," said the pit master to the messenger, indicating the sack.

The pit master had been engaged in a game of Kaissa with the officer of Treve.

"The messenger is here," Fina had announced.

The pit master had then risen, to attend to the business at hand.

"This is to be transmitted to Lurius of Jad, Ubar of Cos," said the messenger.

"As indicated on the orders," said the pit master, signing them and stamping them.

I did not want to look at the sack. In it was the head of Gito.

"He is your friend?" the pit master had asked Gito, in one of the passages, shortly after we had returned from the pool area. Gito had retrieved the sack, and was holding it, opened, as he had been requested.

"Yes," had said Gito.

The pit master had taken him by the throat, and pressed him back against the wall of the passage. The sack had slipped from his hand.

"And you are his friend?" asked the pit master.

"Yes, yes!" said Gito.

"And I am your friend," had said the pit master. He had then lifted Gito up by the throat, holding him against the side of the passage. Gito squirmed, held so. I do not know if Gito, unable then to speak, held by the throat, saw the stiletto leave the tunic of the pit master or not. Surely he must have felt its point enter his body, on the left side, below the ribs. The point then, with terrible slowness, as Gito squirmed like an impaled urt, moved upward, behind the ribs, until it entered the heart. His head was shortly thereafter twisted and cut from the body. It was kicked into the opened sack by the foot of the pit master. The sack was then closed, and was later sealed, with a wax disk and string. The pit master cleaned his blade on Gito's tunic. The body itself was later given to tharlarion.

I watched the messenger leave.

The pit master then returned to the game.

"A water urt was found in the valley three days ago," said the officer of Treve, studying the board.

"That is interesting," said the pit master.

"Naturally I had the outlets from the sewers checked," said the officer.

"Of course," said the pit master.

"A bar was found broken from the stone, and another, beside it, bent to the side," said the officer, his fingers poised over a piece on the board.

"Creating an opening large enough for the passage of a man?" asked the pit master.

"Yes," said the officer, moving the piece.

"Large enough for a large man?"

"Quite," said the officer.

"Interesting."

"I thought you said there was no way out from the passages."

"There was no way, when I spoke," said the pit master.

"A way was apparently made," said the officer. "A ruined bow was found at the spot, the metal, and quarrels, used as tools, also the blade of a sword, and of a knife, blunted, broken from their hilts, these things used in furrowing stone, in scratching out the mortar."

"Imperfect tools for such work," said the pit master.

"Yes," agreed the officer.

"You have repaired the damage?"

"Of course."

"I think we may assume that our friend has left us."

"Yes," said the officer.

"But he is now, it seems, unarmed?"

"It would seem so," said the officer. "To be sure, in the hands of such a man a branch, a stone, could be dangerous."

"What do you conjecture are his chances of survival?" asked the pit master, studying the board.

"You are joking?"

"No."

"He has no chance," said the officer.

"Oh?" said the pit master.

"He will be detected by patrols," said the officer.

"I would not count on it," said the pit master.

"No man can live alone in the mountains," said the officer. "He will starve. He will die of exposure. He is, for most practical purposes, unarmed. Sleen will kill him."

"I see," said the pit master.

"He cannot escape the mountains," said the officer.

"Nor could he escape the depths," said the pit master.

"He is no more than a wild beast himself," said the officer, "a madman, roaming in the mountains."

"That is true," said the pit master.

"He will die," said the officer.

"But his blood will not be on our hands," said the pit master.

"No," said the officer.

"He is a remarkable man," said the pit master. "He is cunning, and brilliant, and ruthless, and powerful. He is a relentless, implacable foe. He is generous and loyal to those he thinks are his friends and would be merciless with those he deems his enemies. It would not be well to betray such a man. I fear his vengeance would be terrible."

"He will die in the mountains," said the officer.

"It would be well for some if he did," said the pit master.

"He is harmless now," said the officer. "He does not even know who he is."

"And some had best hope he never remembers," said the pit master.

I did not understand these things. It was the talk of masters. I was to one side, kneeling by a lamp, sewing a rent tunic for one of the guards. I had been taught to sew in the pens. Such skills are expected of us, as I have indicated. I had been ordered to kneel, and then the garment had been thrown to me, with instructions to repair it. "Yes, Master," I had said. But I enjoyed performing such tasks for the masters. I had learned to sew well, and must, in any event, comply, and the guard, too, was handsome. That he had selected me out to sew his garment, I was sure, was not without significance. Too, my needs, those of a slave, those which put me so much at the mercy of men, had begun, powerfully, irresistibly, to arise in me again.

"I have never known such a man," said the pit master. "Have you, Terence?" I was startled. This was the first time I had ever heard the name of the officer.

The pit master moved a piece.

"That is an interesting move," said the officer.

"Have you?" asked the pit master. "Have you ever known such a man?"

"No," said the officer of Treve, Terence.

"Do you know any who could stand against such a man?" asked the pit master.

"One, perhaps," said Terence.

"Who?" asked the pit master.

"One I met long ago, when I was a mercenary tarnsman," said Terence. "I was in Port Kar."

"A den of thieves, a lair of pirates," said the pit master.

"It was at the time of the naval engagement between Cos and Tyros and Port Kar," said Terence.

"As I understand it, you had some role in that."

"Yes," said Terence.

"One which did not endear you to those of either Cos or Tyros," said the pit master.

"It was the first time tarns were used at sea," said Terence.

"What was his name?" asked the pit master.

"Bosk," said Terence, "Bosk, of Port Kar."

Two guards were at the far end of the long table, also involved with Kaissa.

"What is the war news, from the surface?" asked the pit master.

"Dietrich of Tarnburg has seized Torcadino," said Terence. "In the north, Ar's Station is under siege."

"Dietrich's action stops the drive to Ar," said the pit master. "That will give Ar the time she needs."

"Ar deserves no such good fortune," said Terence.

"The siege of Ar's Station, on the large scale of things," said the pit master, "seems surprising. I would think it would be unimportant."

"One would think so," said Terence. "One trusts that it will remain so."

Besides myself, of the pit slaves, there were now in the chamber only Fina, Kika, and Tira. Most of the slaves were about their duties in the corridors. Two had been permitted to the surface for holiday. One, Tassy, had been thought in the view of the pit master to have shown too little deference to a particular prisoner. She had, accordingly, last night, been put in with him. I had seen her pulled back by the hair, screaming, from the bars, her hands trying to reach through them. This morning I had seen her lying at his thigh, in the straw, docile and timid. I feared she had become his slave. Fina was kneeling near the pit master, cleaning leather. Kika and Tira were washing suls. These would be later baked, and used in the evening feeding.

Terence thrust a piece to a new position on the board.

"A strong counter to my move," said the pit master. "I fear I must think again."

"Guard your Tarnsman," said Terence.

I bent to my work. I made my stitches small, and fine, and closely and evenly spaced. I hoped the master, the guard, for whom I labored would be pleased. I did not wish to be beaten.

"Ai!" said one of the two guards to the side, at the far end of the table, responding to some move in his own game.

This utterance was followed by a sound of chain as the woman near them lifted herself a little, looking up. She was now half lying, half kneeling. Her legs were together. Her weight was muchly on her right thigh and hip. The palms of her hands were on the floor. The sound had been the consequence mainly of the movement of the chain on her neck, the links moving against one another, and the terminal link pulling at the holding ring of the metal collar, but there had been, too, the movement of the links on the floor of the chamber, those of the chain which joined her ankle rings, and that of the chain which joined her wrist rings. She was the only free woman in the chamber. Too, perhaps paradoxically, she was the only woman in the chamber who had not been given clothing. The rest of us had our tunics. She was chained where she was, to a ring, near the guards, because she, or, perhaps more accurately, her use for the evening, was to figure as prize in the guards' game. She must also, though free, address the pit slaves as 'Mistress', and wait upon us, as we might please. She was the girl,

Ilene. She had learned much in the cage. The pit master had decided that it would not harm her, to spoil her for freedom. What could her sisters do, after all, if what was returned to them was, at that time, little better than a needful female slave? She would still be legally free, and that would suffice for the justification of the ransom's collection, a ransom measured, interestingly enough, to a rate appropriate to a free female. What did it matter if, returned to her house, she might writhe and squirm in tears in her bed, striking her pillows in need? I think she now feared only that the ransom might be paid. I myself was not certain that her fears were justified. I had gathered that her sisters might be loath to pay and, also, now having tasted the wealth and power of the house, might be unwilling to do so. I expected that it would eventually be her fate to ascend the slave block, to be auctioned. Such a fate is quite common with those in her predicament. And once the collar was on her neck her sisters need fear her not at all. Indeed, they might even keep her in their own house, as a slave. I was a little bit angry that she had been selected as the prize in the guards' game. I think that was not so much because she was beautiful, which she was, as because she was free. Her being a free woman gave something of a fillip, it seemed, to her use as a prize. Once she was collared, of course, if that should occur, she would have to compete with such as I on a more even basis. Her treatment, her caresses, her rewards, and such, would then be more clearly a function of what she was in herself alone, more clearly a function of whatever intrinsic merit, quality, or worth she might possess in herself alone, as a female, as a slave.

"Surrender your Home Stone," said the other guard. "You are done, finished!"

"Hold, hold," said the first fellow, irritably, he who had uttered the exclamation only a moment ago.

"Your Ubar and Ubar's Builder are forked," said the other guard. "Any honorable fellow in these circumstances would hasten to resign."

"I will defend the Home Stone while yet a Spearman remains," said the other, irritably.

"Very well," said the other.

"I retain two Physicians to your one," said the first.

"So it will be a lengthy endgame," said the other.

"I may even tease out a draw," said the first.

"—Masters," said the Lady Ilene, suddenly, falteringly.

"Did you request permission to speak?" asked one of the guards.

"Forgive me, Masters," she whispered, frightened. "May I speak?"

"Yes," said the fellow.

"Thank you, Masters," she said. The Lady Ilene, you see, was not always granted permission to speak. She was, accordingly, appreciative. That permission could have been denied to her, of course, even as it might be denied to a slave.

But perhaps we should all be grateful when granted permission to speak.

Women love to speak.

It is one of our great pleasures.

Therefore, that we must request this privilege well reminds of who is Master.

I really thought they were more harsh with her than with us. A slave is almost always allowed to speak. It is merely that she is expected to ask permission to do so. The Lady Ilene, on the other hand, had seldom been granted that permission. I wondered if she realized, though she was a free woman, that that was part of collar training, or slave training.

I was pleased that they had given her permission to speak. It was clearly, this time, more than usually, quite important to her.

Indeed, so concerned she had been that she, doubtless in a momentary lapse, occasioned by her agitation, her sense of vulnerability, had failed to enunciate a standard permission request. I had seen that she had been frightened, but a moment after the utterance of the word 'Masters'. She had not, clearly, or at least clearly enough, though there had been supplication in her voice and tears in her eyes, requested permission to speak. Had she forgotten that she was naked and chained to a ring at their feet?

But they were kind to her.

"So speak," said the other guard.

"I have a question," she said.

"What is it?" asked the first guard.

"What, Masters," she asked, "—what, Masters—what if there is a tie, a draw, Masters?"

"Then we share you," said one of the fellows. "Now be silent."

"Yes, Masters," she said, and lay back down, quietly, on the stones, naked, in her chains, to await their pleasure.

She had hoped, I was sure, that the first guard would win. It was he who had so initially terrified her in the chamber of the commercial praetor, who had placed his hands upon her hips and looked down upon her, who had reached within her hood to turn her face to his, who had dared to threaten the integrity of her veil, who had brushed up the hem of her robes and had calmly examined an ankle and calf.

I had realized even then that she had found him despicably handsome. Even then it had been clear to me that she had wondered what it would be to be in his arms. She had inquired if I thought he liked her, and my response, I fear an unpleasant one, had been to the effect that he might if she were inclined to be pleasant and was nude at his feet. This response, of course, had incensed her. "Slut! Slut!" she had cried. "Yes, Mistress," I had said, and then hooded her.

She was looking up at him now. Her eyes were moist. Her lips were slightly parted.

I saw she was apprehensive, but curious, and eager, as well.

Her hair had been nicely brushed and combed. She had been washed.

I did not think she had any reason to be afraid. She had nothing to fear, saving perhaps failing to please.

It seemed likely that he would win, or, at least, not lose, and in that case he would be one of the two who would share her.

She was a prize for men. But then are not all women, in their way, prizes for men?

I looked at her.

Her head was now down, her eyes closed. I think she was trying to understand her feelings.

She addressed them as "Master," you see, as she addressed us as "Mistress." She served in the chamber, though free, as, in effect, a slave of slaves, that her character might be improved, and that such experiences might to some extent mitigate the abruptness of any possible transition to bondage, when such behaviors would not only be suitable for her, but required. And she would address free men as "Master," similarly, that she might become accustomed to that form of address, it perhaps becoming incumbent upon her one day. Too, the pit master thought it fitting, as she was a female.

"Capture of Home Stone," said Terence.
"Ah," said the pit master, leaning back.
Terence began to reset the board.
"No," said the pit master, lifting his hand.
"Do you not wish to play again?"
The pit master shook his head.
"Is your heart not in the game?"
"Did we do well?"
"I think so."
"It is my hope that we did well," said the pit master.
"Let us play again."
"No."
"It will take days for the object to reach Lurius of Jad," said Terence, "and days for his response."
"That is not important," said the pit master.
"I have seen that the papers have been arranged," said Terence, "those attesting even to the departure of those of the black caste from the city."
"I have never lost a prisoner before," said the pit master.
"He will die in the mountains," said Terence. "He will never reach Ar."
I recalled that there had been some speculation that the holding of the peasant might be in the vicinity of Ar. To be sure, he himself had not seemed sure of it.
"I think you do not understand," said the pit master. "I betrayed my trust, my post, my oath to the city."
Fina looked up from her work.
"What we did may well be in the best interests of the city," said Terence.
"That does not alter the fact that I betrayed my oath."
"Would you have had murder done?" asked Terence.
"No," said the pit master.
"You did what you had to."
"Of course."
"Dismiss the matter then from your mind," said Terence.
"I must now do again what I must," said the pit master.
"I do not understand," said Terence.

"What I must do is quite clear," said the pit master. "The moves were determined from my first action. I have known that from the beginning. It is a forced continuation."

"I do not understand," said Terence.

"There are no alternative moves."

"Let us play again."

"No."

Fina seemed frightened. She had stopped her work.

"I will take my leave," said Terence. "I wish you well."

"I wish you well," said the pit master.

Terence then gathered together his things, and left the chamber.

The game between the two guards, unexpectedly, I gathered, did turn out to be a draw. He with the advantage had apparently been overconfident, or careless, in the endgame. The draw turned, apparently, on a single Spearman. Some games are such, that the outcome depends not on the pieces of power, which may balance one another, but on the smallest move of the most insignificant piece on the board. I suppose that this may upon occasion be true in greater games, as well, that even a child, or slave, properly placed, at a critical juncture, might serve to topple empires. The free woman knelt before the two men and kissed their feet. She was then freed of the neck chain, pulled to her feet, turned about, and thrust toward the portal. This was not done ceremoniously. She might have been no more than a slave. She then hurried, in her manacles and shackles, as she could, toward the guards' quarters, to prepare wine for them. They followed, their arms about one another's shoulders. She knew the way. She had served on the mats before.

Fina seemed frightened.

I did not understand her apprehension.

I returned to my sewing. I hoped the guard for whom I labored would be pleased. I did not wish to be beaten. It was my hope, as well, that he would ask for me, and that the pit master would see fit to assign me to him. Oh, how I would run to his mat! How I longed to lie in his arms, and be reminded, once again, of what I was, a slave.

Thirty Nine

I became aware of it only dimly at first.

The sound seemed far off, a pounding, perhaps even a shouting.

Terence, the officer of Treve, had not visited in the depths for several days, not since the last game of Kaissa he had played with the pit master.

The pit master had been unusually sedulous in his duties the past days. Too, he had seemed involved in various mysterious arrangements of which we pit slaves could make nothing, comings and goings, and conversations with various functionaries.

I knew, of course, that by now the grisly gift transmitted to Cos must have arrived.

Again I thought I heard the pounding, far off.

I changed my position, on the tiles, beside the divan of Terence. He had summoned me to him yesterday evening. He had made me serve him exquisitely well. He had accepted only perfections of service from me.

I had seldom been more aware that I was a slave than in his presence.

He was attracted to me, I am sure, as a female fit for the purposes of men, but I think, too, he took a rather special pleasure in using me, as one may, with one woman or another, for one reason or another. The special little pleasure he had in me, a particular pleasure with me, as he might and doubtless did have other particular pleasures from other women, aside from the usual marvels, excitements, and gratifications of our slave usages, his to command and ours to provide, again and again at the cost of our own delicious, complete conquest, had to do with the fact that I was from Earth. He seemed to have some sense of what, politically, educationally, and culturally, was being done to the men of Earth, to destroy them, and cripple them, and deprive them of their masculinity. Accordingly it was with a particular pleasure that he made me, a woman of Earth, now taken from Earth, now collared, now in Gorean bondage, throb, and kick, and spasm in his arms, squirming, and crying out, leaping and writhing, gasping, and moaning, licking and kissing, a ravished, subdued, begging slave. "You are pretty in your collar, little slut," he would whisper. "Thank you, Master!" I would moan. "You have nice slave curves," he would say. "Thank you, Master!" "Are there others like you, on Earth?" he would inquire. "I do not know, Master!" I would cry. "I do not know!" "How fortunate are the men of Earth," he would say, "to have women such as you in their collars." "Have mercy, Master!" I would beg. "Have mercy, Master!" And then he would ruthlessly force again and again upon me the ecstasies of the surrendered woman, those of the subjugated female, those of the utterly vanquished slave. Afterward, sometimes when I lay at his thigh, clasping his leg, daring to press my lips to him, again and again, softly, humbly, so gratefully, so very gratefully, he would say bitterly, "I should whip you." "No, Master," I would whisper. "Please, no, Master."

I opened my eyes. There was no light now in the room. The tiny lamp had flickered out long ago.

After his uses of me he had, as he had before, put me to the tiles, beside the divan. I lay on its left side, as one would look toward its foot. I was chained there, as before, by the neck. My head, too, as before, was toward its foot. It is not uncommon to sleep the slave with her head at the feet of the master. Most usually there is a slave ring fixed in the couch itself, or on the floor, at the foot of the couch, to which the slave is chained. She is thus commonly slept on the floor, at the foot of the couch. She is also, commonly, when the heat of the master is upon him, used there, by the slave ring to which she is chained. It is a great honor, of course, to be allowed upon the surface of the couch. When one is granted this privilege, one commonly kneels at the foot of the couch, at the left side, as one looks toward its foot, and kisses the coverlets or furs, and then enters upon its surface. One enters at that point, first, because it is the foot, and, second, because most masters are right-handed, and it is thus, as they turn to their side, more convenient for them to stroke and caress the slave. To be sure, it is not at all unknown for a master who is fond of his slave to permit her to share his couch. She is well aware of the privileges entailed, and realizes that they are subject to revocation.

I had been given a sheet.

I now sat up, holding the sheet about me.

It was clearly a pounding. Someone was at the door. Too, someone was calling out, insistently, urgently.

I was afraid, for it was quite early in the morning.

His brace of yellow-clad slaves, and Dorna, as well, had been sent, braceleted and coffled, as an evening's gift to one of the off-duty shifts of the wall guard. I did not think Dorna was much pleased with being coffled with the lesser slaves, or with being charged with the recreation of common soldiers. I was sure, however, that the second or third could make her squirm, as she was handed from one to the other. She was now, of course, a slave, and her slave needs, now ignited, would sooner or later, if not now, give her no choice in such matters. We learn to beg in the arms of any man.

I was afraid to awaken the captain.

I clutched the sheet more closely about me. I thought there were strange things going on in Treve, of late, things I did not understand, but which made me afraid.

Late last night, when he had finished with me, he had knelt me beside the divan. He had then put the chain on my neck. He had then looked down at me, I kneeling before him, he seated on the divan. He had leaned forward and taken my head in his hands, brushing back my hair a little. It was a gesture which seemed tender for so strong a man, one so imperious and brutal.

"Janice," had said he.

"Yes, Master?" I had said.

"Do you ever expect to see he who was your charge, the prisoner, 41, the peasant, he of interest to the black caste, again?"

"No, Master," I said.

"If, perchance, you saw him again, do you think you would be able to recognize him?"

"Yes, Master," I said.

"How long did you attend upon him?"

"Months," I said.

"You could then undoubtedly recognize him," he said.

"I would think so, Master," I said.

"You are doubtless one of the very few people who could do so," he said.

I supposed this were true. The pit master, and he himself, of course could recognize him. Too, I would suppose certain guards could do so, and, of course, the other pit slaves had seen him, at least twice, once in the cell, once in the vicinity of the urt pool. But I did not doubt that I might be thought to be more familiar with the prisoner than any, save, of course, the pit master himself. Certainly I had little doubt that I was more familiar with him than he who now interrogated me.

"That makes you very special," he said.

"Master?" I asked.

"You were even purchased to attend upon him," he said.

"Yes, Master," I said.

"And many know that," he said, "not only here, in Treve, but also elsewhere, for example, even those in the pens where you were first collared, and trained."

"Are these things important?" I asked.

"Probably not," he said.

"The prisoner died in the mountains, did he not?" I asked.

"Undoubtedly," he said.

"Am I to be afraid?" I asked.

"Curiosity is not becoming in a kajira," he said.

"Please, Master!" I begged.

But he took me then by the shoulders and threw me, with a rattle of chain, to the tiles beside the divan. He rose, angrily, from the divan. I lay there then at his feet, trembling, reminded that I was a woman, and a slave. "Forgive me, Master!" I begged. He drew back his foot to kick me, and I tensed, but he did not kick me. Rather he turned to one side, and, in a moment, cast me a sheet. "Thank you, Master," I had said.

I could hear the pounding at the door, the cries. I was sitting up, on the tiles, the sheet clutched about me. I was afraid, afraid to awaken the captain, afraid not to awaken him, afraid of what was occurrent in Treve, unknown to me, afraid of what might be the purport of that insistent pounding, those urgent cries.

I quickly knelt beside the divan and put my hand on his leg. "Master! Master!" I said. "Master! Awaken! Please, awaken!" I shook him then by the shoulders. "Master!" I said. "The door! Someone is without!"

He awakened suddenly, sitting upright.

"The door, Master," I said. I had been frightened by the quickness of his response, once awake. It was the way one might awaken in a camp, perhaps, if an alarm had been sounded.

In a moment he had left the bed and thrown a robe about his broad shoulders.

I could not hear the rushed conversation at the door. I knelt beside the divan, holding the sheet about me.

In a moment he had returned to the room and hastily donned a tunic. He slung a sheathed sword about his left shoulder. When the blade is in use the sheath and belt are discarded.

He looked down at me.

"Master?" I asked.

"You had best come," he said. He unlocked the chain from my neck. I had only time to seize up a bit of silk and follow him. I ran after him, catching up with him only in the corridor. Two pit guards, I knew them both, I had served them both, were with him.

"We came as soon as he left," said one of the men.

"You did well," said the officer. Then he addressed himself, striding down the hall, to the other guard. "What of the girl?" he said.

"He left her chained in the chamber, as you anticipated," said the guard.

"Fetch her," said the officer. "The keys are in the chamber. Hurry. You know where he will be."

"Yes, Sir," said the man, turning about, hurrying away.

"Master!" I cried, gasping, trying to keep up.

"Be silent," he said.

In a few moments we were outside the tower and hurrying through the streets. It was gray, and cold, and there was a fog about. We began to ascend winding stairs, and were soon traversing high bridges. I did not look down, save at the narrow passages I trod. I am frightened on the higher bridges. We heard the first bar sound.

Forty

I knew the place. I had been here once before, on the height of this windy, lofty tower.

It was here that I had received the state collar of Treve. It was here that the great chair had been set on the dais. It was here I had first stood before the officer of Treve. It was here I had been suitably humbled, and whipped. It was here I had learned that it was not the practice of this city to compromise with its slaves.

Too, it was here that I had trod, hooded, a plank, one extending out, unbeknownst to me, over a terrible drop, hundreds of feet down, to jagged rocks below. I had removed the hood, and seen, to my horror, my situation. The jailer, the warden of the cliff cells, Tenrik, in whose care I had first been in this city, had come out upon the plank and brought me back to safety, before I might fall. Later, bound hand and foot, I had been carried to the wall again, that I might realize what could be done with me, that I might be cast down from that terrible height. I had been informed, too, that sleen came to the rocks below, at night, to look for bodies.

"Hold," said Terence, softly. He put out his hand, arresting the advance of the guard, who was to his right. I, behind them, stopped, too.

It was dark at so early an hour, but not absolutely so. We could see a figure, a large figure, a grotesque, monstrous figure, seemingly part human, seemingly part animal, bent over, near the wall, before us and to our left. It was at the place where the plank had been run out, near the place where I, bound hand and foot, had been once held in the arms of the jailer, Tenrik, he standing on the wall itself, the winds blowing against us. Something dark lay at its feet. I supposed it to be a cloak and hood, discarded.

The figure, as it could, was standing, just within the retaining wall. I did not know if it were praying, perhaps to the Priest-Kings, perhaps to other, stranger gods, or not. Goreans pray standing.

Fog swirled about it, like smoke, or clouds, wind-twisted, about a dark rock.

Perhaps it was not praying.

Perhaps it was only offering its homage to the world, to the environing mystery, that immensity from which we derive, one which spawns us and then abandons us, the unfathomable, uncaring immensity, leaving us conscious in the loneliness, in the knowledge that our laughter and our tears are of no importance, that our sorrow and pain is, in the end, when all is said and done, meaningless, that we are a joke told by accident, a cruel but touching, infinitely precious joke, told by no one to no one.

The officer of Treve, Terence, quietly removed the sword belt, the sheath and sword, from about his left shoulder, handing it to the guard, to his right.

He would, I gathered, attempt to approach the figure.

I saw nothing near the figure, but I did not think it was totally alone. I supposed that many thoughts, or memories, were with it. At such times perhaps one stands in crowds, the crowds of oneself, together with one's infancy, one's childhood, one's youth, one's past, one's present, one's weakness, one's strength, in the lonely, crowded, empty silence. At such times who knows what whispers to one. Too, perhaps honor, or duty, stood at its side, invisible to others.

Suddenly the figure spun about. "Do not approach," it warned us.

The officer of Treve stepped back.

"Tal," said the officer of Treve.

"Tal," said the figure. "Do not approach." It seemed a strange time and place for such greetings.

"Reports are to be made, on the depths," said the officer of Treve.

"They have been prepared," said the figure. "Other dispositions, too, have been made. You will find all is in order."

"Come back with us," said the officer.

"You have had me watched," said the figure, angrily, accusingly.

"Come back with us," said the officer.

"Sir?" asked the guard, to the officer's right.

"No," said the officer to him.

"Do not approach," warned the figure. From its tunic it drew forth its stiletto.

"Back," said the officer to the guard, who stepped back.

"You, too!" said the figure.

The officer, reluctantly, for I suspect he had planned to rush forward, stood back.

"Leave," said the figure.

"No," said the officer.

"I would be alone," said the figure.

"You are not alone," said the officer.

"Go!" said the figure.

"I have authorization to this surface," said the officer.

"Stay back!"

The officer stopped.

"Who is with you?" asked the figure.

"Demetrion," said the officer.

"It is Janice, too, is it not?" asked the figure.

"Yes," said the officer.

"Was your service satisfactory, Janice?" asked the figure.

"It is my hope it was, Master," I said, frightened.

"If it was not, you must expect to be severely punished, or slain," he said.

"Yes, Master," I said.

"You are standing," he observed.

"Forgive me, Master!" I said, falling to my knees. Had I been trained for nothing?

"You will stand back," said the figure to the men.

"We are back," the officer assured him.

The figure then returned the stiletto to his tunic. He then stepped up, to the wall about the surface of the tower. It was there that Tenrik had once held me. I had been ordered to look down. I had seen the rocks hundreds of feet below.

This was a place not only for the discomfiture of slaves.

It was also a place of execution.

From this place criminals and traitors were sometimes cast down, to the rocks below.

It was for that reason, doubtless, that he had come here.

"Hold!" cried the officer, Terence.

The figure paused on the height of the wall, and turned to face us. There was no way, now, in which we could reach him before he would have time to act.

I wondered if the officer should have come to the surface of the tower.

Perhaps he should not have come.

Our presence here, I feared, was cruel, and intrusive.

"We have not yet concluded our Kaissa match," said the officer.

Most Gorean matches, as I understand it, consist of an odd number of games, for example, eleven or twenty-one. Needless to say, the matches sometimes take days to finish. Their current match had been set at eleven games. Each had, if I had not lost count, won five games.

"I wish you well," said the figure.

"Hold!" cried Terence. For the figure had turned to the outside, standing on the wall, that unlikely brick-and-mortar margin, that brink of forever.

"I have lost a prisoner," said the figure.

"It is nothing," said the officer. "So, too, have others, thousands of others!"

"I have betrayed my trust, my post. I have betrayed my oath. That is not nothing."

"Come down," said the officer.

"I am a traitor to my word, and to the city. I have shamed the Home Stone."

"No," said the officer.

"It has been defiled."

"No!" protested the officer.

"Such a stain can be cleansed only with blood."

The figure turned again toward the mountains.

"Hold!" cried the officer.

"Master!" cried a voice, that of Fina, running across the surface of the tower. Yards behind her came the guard who had been sent to fetch her.

The pit master came down from the wall, in fury. He grasped Fina in his arms, who was weeping, who clung to him.

The pit master turned a baleful glance upon the officer. "I left her chained!" he said, in anger.

"That she could not follow you, of course," said the officer of Treve. "But she has been freed."

"I will die with you, Master!" she wept. "We shall die together, in one another's arms!"

"No," cried the pit master, in fury, thrusting her from him. She fell to the stones, and grasped him about the leg.

He shook himself free and glared down at her. "Return to the depths, now!" he said.

"No," said the officer. "Do not do so!"

"You have no right to do this!" cried the pit master.

"I have every right," said the officer. "You do not own her. She is the property of the state of Treve. We are not in the depths now. And my rank, I remind you, considerably exceeds yours. Who do you obey, Fina?"

"You, Master!" she cried, defiantly.

"Very well," said the pit master, regarding the officer. "For the moment, you win."

He could, of course, come again to this place sometime, unbeknownst to us, or to another. Indeed, he might thrust himself upon that slim blade concealed within his tunic.

"Come, Master!" cried Fina, leaping up, and springing to the wall itself, where he had stood.

"Come down!" cried the pit master, in horror. He put out his hand, but he was afraid to approach her, for fear she might leap down, or he might, inadvertently, cause her to lose her balance. "Come down, I beg you!" he wept.

"You beg a slave?" she laughed.

"She should certainly be beaten," said the officer.

"Come down!" cried the pit master!

"Let her jump," said the officer. "She is only a slave."

"She is Fina!" he wept.

"Come up, Master," she laughed. "Let us die together. Let us leap to the rocks below, caught one last time in one another's arms!"

"No!" he cried.

"I love you!" she cried. "I will not live without you."

"You cannot love me," he wept. "I am a beast, a monster, hated and shunned, so born, and so condemned to live."

"You will never know the beauty, the shining beauty, the truth, I see within you!" she cried.

"I give you my word," said the officer, "within the rights of my code, and sworn in the name of the Home Stone itself, that if you shall accomplish upon yourself this injustice, I shall see that she will be free to follow you, whether it be from this ledge, or by the cord or knife."

"No!" cried the pit master.

"It is so sworn."

"Come, let us die together, Master," said Fina.

"I, not you!" he said.

"We," she said.

"No!" he said.

"Then I alone!" she said. "Do you think that I can live, having caused you to compromise your honor?"

The pit master turned about, crying out with misery, his fists clenched.

"Keep her in chains," the pit master begged the officer. "Guarantee to me her life."

"That of a mere slave, do not be foolish."

"So you would set me this dilemma," said the pit master, "that either she must die or I must lose my honor?"

"And if she is to be the reason you cannot retain your honor, it seems that she, herself, is resolved to die."

"Come down," said the pit master to Fina.

"Master?" she asked the officer.

"Remain where you are," said the officer.

"Sleen!" cried the pit master.

"It seems we have reached an impasse," said the officer, lightly.

"And how is it to be resolved?" asked the pit master, in fury. I feared he might extract that stiletto from his tunic and drive it into the heart of Terence.

"Easily," said Terence, "by Kaissa."

"Kaissa?"

"Of course."

"I see."

"Slave," said Terence to Fina. He snapped his fingers. "Come down!"

Fina came down from the wall.

The pit master hurried forward, to clasp her to him, but the officer interposed himself. "No," he said, sternly. "You do not own her. She is the property of Treve. Do not touch her." The pit master, bewildered, stepped back. Fina, too, was startled. The officer took her firmly by an arm and thrust her, as a slave, to Demetrion. He was the guard who had come first with us to the surface of the tower. He who had fetched Fina was Andar. "Bind her, hand and foot, and kneel her to the side," said Terence to Demetrion. Then to Andar he said, "Fetch a lantern, and a board, and pieces."

Fina, in a moment, was kneeling to one side, her wrists tied behind her back, and fastened to her crossed, bound, ankles. She could not rise to her feet. It is a quite common tie. It is often used in training, to accustom women to kneeling before men. She had first been put on her stomach. The hands are tied behind the back first, and then the ankles tied, and brought up, behind, and fastened to the bound wrists. The woman is then put to her knees.

Andar, a little later, brought a lantern, and the board and pieces.

"The match is apparently of importance to you," said the pit master, bitterly, sitting down, cross-legged, before the board.

We heard the second bar sound. Tarn wire swayed overhead.

"You understand what is involved here," said the officer.

"Yes," said the pit master.

"And you," asked the officer of Fina.

"I think so," she said.

"If you win," said the officer to the pit master, "you may gleefully splash yourself upon the rocks at the foot of the wall, thereby bringing joy to the hearts of local wild sleen, and the slave, bound by her fear of compromising your honor, which compromise would then be in violation of our arrangements, will not seek to follow you in the path you have chosen. If I win, you will accept my concept of what is honorable in this matter, and so, too, will the slave."

"Agreed, for myself and for the slave," said the pit master.

"And no action pertinent to these matters is to be taken until the game is done?"

"Agreed, for myself and the slave," said the pit master.

"And this is sworn?"
"It is sworn."
"By the Home Stone?"
"By the Home Stone itself!" said the pit master, angrily.
"Excellent," said the officer.
He then picked up the board, with the pieces on it, went to the wall, and threw the entire board and pieces out into space, over the wall.
"What have you done!" cried the pit master, in horror, rising up.
Fina was laughing and crying.
"I do not feel like playing now," said the officer. "Perhaps some other time."
"No, no!" cried the pit master.
"As you may recall," said the officer, "no action pertinent to these matters is to be taken until the game is done."
"Play!" demanded the pit master.
"I think not," said the officer.
"You have tricked me!" cried the pit master, in fury.
I began to cry, too. The game, I realized, would never be played.
"Sometimes," said the officer, "the best Kaissa is no Kaissa."
"It seems you have won," said the pit master.
"It is all of us who have won," said the officer. "Untie her," he said to Andar.
Andar undid the knots which restrained Fina, and she, unbidden, leapt up and threw herself into the arms of the pit master, sobbing and laughing.
He held her to him, in confusion, in fury, in consternation.
"Up, Janice," said the officer, and I sprang to my feet, joyfully.
"It is chilly here," he said. "You must be half frozen. It is well you are with us. Else you might be picked up as a stray by the watch."
"Yes, Master," I said.
"Perhaps you can warm some wine in my compartments," he said.
"Gladly, Master," I said.
"You do not mind if I return her to the pits later in the morning, do you?" inquired Terence of the pit master.
"She is to be returned by the tenth Ahn, as you know," said the pit master.

I did not understand that. It sounded as though something had been arranged.

"Granted," said Terence.

"You tricked me," said the pit master.

"Do not despair," said the officer. "One cannot leap to one's death every day."

"How am I to live with myself?" asked the pit master. "My honor is by my honor betrayed."

"How could that be?" inquired the officer.

"As you have arranged it," said the pit master, bitterly.

"You did not lose a prisoner," said the officer. "You saved a prisoner. He would have been murdered had you not acted as you did. In this, in protecting the prisoner, in preserving him, you kept the oath, in a manner far more profound than you realized."

"I did not keep the oath," said the pit master.

"Then the oath, my friend," said Terence, "kept you."

"I do not understand," said the pit master.

"We are sometimes moved by forces and understandings deeper than we can understand. You acted in such a way as to fulfill your office more grandly than could have been possible in any other course of conduct."

The pit master held Fina to him. He looked at the officer, puzzled.

"In thinking you betrayed your oath, you were mistaken. Rather you were bringing about the very ends which it envisaged. Do you think that the meaning of an oath is the words it wears? It is rather what it celebrates and intends, the meaning behind the meanings of the words. Repudiated in words, it was revered in deeds. Denied, it was fulfilled. Forsworn, it was kept. Honor rejected was honor transformed, honor restored. How often do we seek to do one thing and discover we have done another? How often we achieve ends which we do not intend. You have not betrayed the Home Stone of Treve. Rather you have kept her from the stains upon her which a venal administration would authorize."

"I would return to the depths," said the pit master.

"Hold!" said a voice.

Instantly Fina and I knelt.

It was the watch, four men and a subaltern. Two held lanterns.

"Ah, Captain, it is you," said the subaltern. He looked through the darkness, studying the visage of the pit master, in the light of a lantern. "And you, Sir," he added. Fina and I were then illuminated in the light of the lantern. Demetrion and Andar stood to one side.

"These slaves are with you?" asked the subaltern.

"Yes," said the officer.

"It is early."

"It will be light soon," said the officer.

"Is all well?" asked the subaltern.

"Yes," said the officer. "All is well."

The watch then continued on its way.

The pit master reached down to pick up his cloak and hood which he had discarded on the stones, near the wall.

"Master," said Fina. "I am cold."

The pit master held the cloak and hood. "But I may be seen in the city," he said.

"I am freezing," smiled Fina.

He then had her stand and put the cloak and hood about her.

He would not cover his features now. He would return to the depths, through the streets of the early morning, as he was. He would not hide his face.

"Come, walk beside me," he said to Fina.

"I will heel Master," she said.

The pit master and the officer of Treve then embraced. The pit master was weeping. Then, shaken, he left the surface of the tower. He was followed by Fina, on his left, three paces behind.

"Are we to keep him under surveillance any longer?" Demetrion inquired of the officer.

"No," said the officer. "It will not be necessary."

Demetrion and Andar then, Andar bearing the lantern, left the surface of the tower, as had the pit master and Fina.

"Master," I said.

"Yes," he said.

"What is special about the tenth Ahn?"

He looked at me.

"Oh, I know, Master," I said, "that curiosity is not becoming in a kajira, but I would know. I would know."

"Your life is going to change, Janice," he said. "You will have to leave Treve."

"Master?" I said.

"You, and the other pit slaves who were in the depths recently. The pit master has made arrangements for you all, and I have made them, unbeknownst to himself, for him. I will see to it that he will be able to take Fina with him."

"What of you?"

"I, too, and certain other men, will be leaving."

I suddenly began to understand what might be the nature of the arrangements, the dispositions, which the pit master had been concerned with recently.

"You cannot leave the city of your Home Stone!" I said.

"We have received word," he said, "that a delegation from Cos will arrive in Treve shortly."

"What will be done with me, and with Fecha, Tira, and the others?" I asked.

"Other than Fina?"

"Yes," I said.

"You are going to be sold," he said.

"Sold?"

"Of course, my pretty little property," he said.

"I do not understand," I said.

"Surely it is not so difficult to grasp," he said. "You were sold before, you know."

"Of course, Master," I said, falteringly.

"It is not just you, Janice," he said. "All the pit slaves who were recently in the depths will be sold, as well. Even Fina, in a sense, will be sold, purchased from the state, but I will see that she comes within the keeping of the depth warden. She will make a lovely gift for him, I would think."

"And the rest of us?" I said.

"To be sold in different cities," he said. "You will be scattered, papers will be changed. You will disappear to the eight winds. It will not be possible to trace you."

"I understand," I said. We had seen too much, or knew too much, and I, doubtless, most of all. Had the black-tunicked men been successful in the depths I suspected we might all have had our throats cut, even the other girls, whose understanding of these things must be even less than mine, which was negligible. The black-tunicked men are trained to kill for a purpose, and to think as little of it as others might of the cutting of wood.

"None of you will be sold publicly, of course," said the officer of Treve. "We will not risk that. The sales will be discreet, and private. They will be purple-booth sales."

"That is a great honor, Master," I said.

"You are all excellent-quality merchandise," he said.

"Thank you, Master," I said.

"See that you, in your performance in the booth, do not disappoint the buyer's agent."

"Yes, Master," I whispered.

"You may rise," he said.

I rose to my feet. I held my arms folded about myself, for the air was chilly here, on the surface of the tower, in the early morning. He had gone to stand near the wall, looking out toward the mountains.

"This all has to do with the prisoner, the peasant, does it not, Master?" I asked.

"He died out there, in the mountains," said the officer.

"But you do not know that," I said.

"No man could survive alone out there," he said.

"Perhaps some men, Master," I said.

"Yes," said he, "perhaps some men. And yes, my lovely Earth-woman slave, my lovely Gorean slave girl, it does have to do with the peasant, all of it has to do with the peasant."

"Are we to return to your compartments?" I asked. "Am I to warm wine for you?"

"Yes," he said.

"It will be light soon," I said.

"I shall miss you," he said.

"And I shall miss you, Master," I said.

"There is nothing more to be done here," he said. He then turned about, and I followed him.

We heard the call of the watch, that all was well in Treve. I did not know, however, if it were true or not. I did know that the surface of this tower, in the coldness of the morning, had, as the tops of certain peaks in the distance by light, been touched by honor.

Forty One

I lay on my stomach, on my mat, in the house of my master. My eyes were filled with tears. Aynur had laid the switch to me well. This evening she had had Tima and Tana tie me to the whipping post in the garden. The other women, the flowers of the garden, had been summoned forth to watch. My crime, as it had been announced to the flowers, was that of having approached the wall. The roughness on the bottoms of my feet, no longer bleeding then, had been shown to the other girls.

"The barbarian is stupid," had said one of the girls.

"They all are," said another.

"Why would she go to the wall?" asked another. "She cannot climb it."

That was true.

But I had wanted to press my hands against its solidity, knowing there was a world on the other side of the garden, and that I was then a little closer to it. One could hear the noises, the cries, from outside. One knew there was a world there, teeming, busy, with its sights, and sounds, and smells, a turbulent, active world, one different from that of the garden. I wanted to be on the other side of the wall. I wanted to be there, where I might run through the streets in a tunic and collar, where I might drink water from the lower basins, where I might press through crowds, carrying a package or vessel upon my head, unable to defend myself against the touches of men, who might touch me as easily as one might pet a dog. I did not object to such things, for I was less than a dog. I was a slave. Too, such things are flattering. They bespeak one's appeal. They say, you are attractive, you excite them. You are not without interest to masters. They would not mind using you, perhaps even owning you. I wanted to be seen by men, and found desirable. I wanted to see the desire in their eyes, and sense their heat. I wanted them to turn their heads to look after me, as I made my way down the street. I wanted them to wonder what I would look like, naked, in their own collar, on their own furs, at their feet, their property, one who must serve them to the best of her abilities in whatever manner they might please. I wanted to be on the other side of the wall, even if it meant being forced to labor long hours for a harsh master. I did not fear rising before dawn, and taking up a basket, and hurrying through the gray streets to the market. I did not fear the public washing places, the shallow cement tanks where one might launder. I did not fear the needle, the broom, the kettles, the yards, the sheds, the kitchen. I would be grateful at night even for a rush mat. Better to be chained in a hovel, subject to the whip of the least in the city, than a flower in the garden!

Doubtless the girls had been puzzled as to why I was switched as hard and lengthily as I had been by Aynur, only for going near the wall. They did not know, as did Tima and Tana, and Aynur, about the tall, long-haired man who had come to the garden, who had commanded me, he to whom I had fearfully, but eagerly and gratefully, surrendered, serving him with all the desperate, pleading needs of my body. Had the flowers known that would they not have cried out that I should have been even more grievously punished? How starved we were in the garden. I wondered if there were not many amongst us who would have welcomed being thrown to galley slaves.

I lay on the mat, chained in its vicinity by the left ankle, to a ring on the floor. If I had been so chained during the rest period this afternoon, I would not have been able to enter the garden, to approach the wall, to encounter the stranger. It would have been better, doubtless, if I had been chained where I was now. I was not clear on how he had gained admittance to the garden. It must be, of course, that he was known in the house, to the master, or the guards. Aynur, for example, had obviously recognized him. Indeed, she had seemed to be very familiar with him. That frightened me. I wondered if he were known to the master, my current rights holder. I had never seen the master, but I supposed that he had seen me. It might have been he behind the screen when I was first stripped and exhibited in the house. On the other hand it could have been an agent, or house master. I did not know. I knew very little about the master. I did know his name, and it was clear that he was very rich, which seemed unusual, I gathered, for the current state in the city, which was occupied, I gathered, by foreign troops. He had dealings in slaves it seemed, and had extensive agricultural holdings. He also had something to do with at least certain theaters and theatrical companies in the city. It was said he was welcome, even, in the central cylinder of the city. The name of this city, if I have not mentioned it before, is Ar. It is nominally governed, as I understand it, by a ubara, whose name is Talena. The actual governance is presumably in the hands of a military governor, one named Myron, who bears the title of Polemarkos of Cos, or, more strictly, Polemarkos of Temos, which is the third largest city on the island of Cos. He is said to be cousin to Lurius of Jad, the Ubar of Cos. I had heard of Lurius of Jad in Treve. It was he who had sent the black-tunicked men to that city. My master, interestingly, had shown no interest in me, nor, indeed, as far as I know, in any of the other slaves. We, or most us, did not understand this. Aynur may have understood, but she never spoke to us about it. His name is Appanius, Appanius of Ar.

"My dear Gail," said Aynur.

Immediately I tensed with terror, on my belly, on the mat. I feared to be struck again.

She had approached, barefoot, as are most slaves, softly on the tiles. I had not heard her.

"I am sorry I displeased you, Mistress," I said. "Please do not strike me again!"

"You are only a pretty little barbarian slave," she said. "How could you know what you were doing? Here, I have brought some soothing lotion for your back. Lie still."

"Mistress?" I said.

"Ah," she said, "is that not better."

"Yes, Mistress," I said, tensely. The lotion was cool on my striped back.

"Mistress?" I asked, frightened.

"You should not have gone on the stones," she said. "You might have injured your feet."

"Yes, Mistress," I said.

"Your feet are to be soft and pretty," she said.

"Yes, Mistress," I said.

"You are a pleasure-garden girl, you know," she said.

"Yes, Mistress," I said.

She continued to apply the lotion.

"After this," she said, "if you want to go into the garden during the rest period, you should ask me, first."

"Of course, Mistress," I said. "Forgive me, Mistress."

"And if, in the future, you should see someone in the garden, someone you suspect may have no right to be there, you should hurry in and inform me."

"Yes, Mistress," I said. "I am sorry, Mistress, that I pleased him."

"You are only a little barbarian," she said, gently. "You could not please such a man."

"Yes, Mistress," I said. I was not truly sorry, of course, that I had pleased the visitor. I had been hungry to do so. Too, I was sure that I could please him at least as well as she. Indeed, some men like barbarians. They put us through our paces quite well. And I had little doubt that I could tell when a man was pleased and when he was not. One does not wear a collar long before one becomes quite adept at such determinations. Indeed, if they are not pleased, we are likely to soon find out about it, at the receiving end of the leather, of a switch, or strap, or whip.

"That is better, isn't it?" she asked, leaning back, putting the lotion to one side, wiping her hands on a towel.

"Yes, Mistress," I said, gratefully.

"I will return in a moment," she said, "with your supper."

When she returned I sat up, and ate. She had brought some choice viands, perhaps begged from the meals of men. Too, she had a small, shallow bowl of wine.

"Thank you, Mistress," I said, finishing this repast. "I am terribly sorry I did wrong earlier. I did not wish to annoy you, or displease you. You are very kind."

"Now," she said, "let us remove this heavy, ugly shackle from your ankle."

She opened the shackle and put it, on its chain, the chain running to the ring, to one side. She held the keys to such things.

"Now," she said, "you may come and go as you please, within the quarters, of course."

"Thank you, Mistress," I said.

No other girls were now with us in the rest area, not even Tima and Tana, who were her assistants.

"You are very kind," I said.

"It is nothing," she said, kissing me lightly on the cheek. She then gathered up the dish and bowl and left.

I lay back down on the mat.

I did not understand this change in Aynur's behavior. I was sure she had been outraged at finding me in the arms of the tall, long-haired man. I had little doubt that he came sometimes to see Aynur. Earlier, in the garden, she had seemed almost insanely jealous of his attentions to me. Indeed, she had even been humiliated before me, and her assistants, by being put to her knees by him, and by having to fetch his sandals, sandals which he then, pointedly, had me tie. I would not have thought that such insults would have been easily passed over by a woman such as Aynur. Too, she would have her needs, doubtless as keen and stressful as those of others. In this house, in the garden, there was much pain. Sometimes, to be sure, we entertained, in the house or garden, some singing and playing, others, such as I, fetching food and drink, attending on the guests, then all of us, later, as we might be selected, or allotted, or assigned, serving, as slaves. But it was not enough for us. Could that not be told simply by looking at our necks, and seeing that there were collars there? Did this detail not serve as token, if none other, that slave fires had been lit in our bellies? Had men not seen to it?

After a time the other girls began to enter the room, one or two at a time. I took little notice of them. Under Aynur's supervision they surrendered their silks and jewelry. Soon, when the house master made his check, with his lamp, we would all be on our mats, even Aynur. I heard a guard close the gate to the garden. I heard the bolts thrown in the locks. In this house we were not to speak after the nineteenth Ahn. I recalled the tall, long-haired man. I wondered what he had been doing in the garden. He was apparently known in the house, but I had not seen him before. How I had leaped to his touch, how I had obeyed him! How I must have amused him, in his arms, I so unable to conceal myself from him. How well he knew me now, as the slave I was! He had frightened me, with his questions. He had wanted to know the location of the pens in which I had been trained, even the accents of my original captors. He had wanted to know if I could read a certain word, which I could not, and if I could recognize a certain sign. The sign, of course, had been the sign, or name, of the city, Ar. I knew that. It is on many seals, and such. And most frighteningly he had wanted to know if I had ever heard of a slave named "Janice," if I had ever been in Treve. I think I was entitled to be afraid. It was not as though I could run, or hide. I had never even been allowed out of this house, save in the garden. Doors were bolted, gates were locked. There were walls, and guards. And even more devastatingly I was a slave. There was no escape for me. I did not control my own destiny. It was in the hands of others, the masters. I was afraid. I was miserable.

"Extinguish the lamps, my lovely sisters in bondage," said Aynur, pleasantly.

One by one the lamps were extinguished.

Aynur seemed in a good mood this evening. I am sure that that anomaly was muchly appreciated by all of us. On the whole, Aynur was quite strict with us. We must, for example, for the inspection of the house master, kneel with our knees in a line, and spread to the appropriate angle. Our backs must be straight. Our chins must be elevated to the proper height, our hands must be placed exactly so on our thighs, and so on. She was quick with her switch. She kept us under excellent discipline.

I lay there on the mat for a little while in the darkness.

The room was very quiet.

I was exhausted, and my back still hurt, despite the soothing lotion.

I decided that there was no reason to be afraid, really.

After all, the man had gone away, and I was safe in the house.

Too, more importantly, I had denied knowing a "Janice." I had denied ever having been in Treve.

That should finish the matter.

I fell asleep. I am sure it was well before the mat check.

Forty Two

"Shhh," I heard. "Do not make any noise."

I awakened on the mat. It must have been well after the mat check.

It was Aynur's voice.

It was dark in the room. I could hear the breathing of several of the other flowers, asleep nearby on their mats.

"Mistress?" I asked.

I was still on my belly, from the switching I had received the preceding evening.

"Place your wrists, crossed, behind your back," said Aynur. I complied and, in an instant, with a double loop, they were corded together.

"Do not make any noise," said Aynur.

"What is it?" I whispered, frightened.

"You are to be taken to see the master," she whispered. I was startled to hear this. Was this how he had his girls brought to him, in the darkness of the night, secretly? Or, did this have to do with other business, clandestine business perhaps, nocturnal interrogations? Perhaps he was curious to know what had transpired in the garden. Indeed, perhaps the stranger was with him and I must now be brought before them both.

"Should I not be silked?" I asked.

"You will go as you are," she said.

Aynur then reached before me and thrust a wad of cloth into my mouth. This she bound in place with a folded scarf, knotted behind the back of my neck. The original wad of cloth, now held in, as I struggled with it, moving it about in my mouth, expanded to fill my oral cavity. "Be very quiet," said Aynur. "Do not make any noise." It was an effective gag. Even had I dared, I could have done little to make myself heard. "Get up," said Aynur. I rose to my feet. I felt her hand on my back. "Move," she said, "barbarian." I was pressed toward the door. The door was now unlocked. I preceded her, directed by her, down the main corridor, and then into a side passage, past several doors, and then into a small room. It was dark. Aynur closed the door behind us. Surely this was not the compartments of the master!

"Sit," said Aynur.

I sat down.

"Cross your ankles," said Aynur.

I did so and Aynur, in the darkness, bound them together.

A moment or so later a fire-maker was struck in the room and a man, masked, lit a tiny lamp on a table. There was another man in the room, as well, also masked.

Near the table, on the floor, there was a slave box.

"This is the slave," said Aynur. "I deliver her to you, Masters."

I struggled suddenly with the bonds, but could not free myself.

The men regarded me, bemused.

I tried to speak but was prevented by the gag. I could utter only small sounds, pleading sounds, questioning sounds, sounds of misery and fear.

"You have done well, slave," said one of the men.

"Thank you, Master," she said.

Then Aynur turned to me. "Do not fear, barbarian slut," said she, "but after today, sooner or later, I would have found a way to get you out of the garden! Do not think to lie again, filthy little slave, in the arms of my Camillus!"

I supposed that guards might be sometimes suborned, with the promise of the gift of dangerous, delicious, clandestine favors, and such, to cooperate in such matters. Intrigues in the gardens, in the slave quarters, can be quite fearful.

"See her struggle," said Aynur to the guards. Then she again addressed herself to me. "One of the guards, one who leaves the city tonight," she said, "will be thought to have stolen you from the slave quarters, doubtless for your golden collar."

I looked at her, angrily, over the gag. Did she truly think I might be stolen only for my golden collar?

"I myself will return to the quarters, locking the door behind me. How surprised, how horrified, will we all be in the morning!"

Again I struggled, but Aynur had tied me quite well.

"But I have been saved the trouble of arranging these matters," she said, "for others, it seems, are interested in you. Tonight's events have been planned, it seems, for some time, but only this evening was I contacted by a guard, he who leaves the city this night. You can imagine with what joy I attended his proposals."

I looked to the men. It was hard to read their eyes. I did not think they were guards in the house.

One thing unnerved me, terribly. Though I was stripped and bound before these men, I did not seem to find myself regarded with the interest, curiosity, or relish I might have anticipated, that which one might expect to be accorded to such as I, a naked, bound slave. I hoped, of course, that this might prove to be an ordinary, if unusually daring, case of slave theft. Stealing slaves, as you might expect, is a not unusual practice on this world. Among many young men the theft of slaves, and even of free women, from enemy cities is regarded as a sport. Among slavers it is regarded as a business. The prevention of slave theft is one reason for the presence of slave rings in public places, for the fastening of slaves to the foot of couches at night, and so on. I did not much fear slave theft as it would extract me from the boredom, if security, of the garden. Indeed, I welcomed the prospect for I hoped that it would, sooner or later, bring me within the grasp of a master who would know how to handle me, and would do so, with audacity and command. But I did not think these men were simply interested in picking up a pleasure-garden girl, even one who might be of unusual interest, either for their own house or to put on the block in some foreign city, hopefully turning a tidy profit on her. I might be beautiful or not, but I did not think these men were interested in that sort of thing. They did not seem to regard me with an interest which suggested they wanted me for themselves, nor, as far as I could tell, did I find in their gaze any speculations as to how I might appear to possible buyers, or to an unknown principal.

"Put her in the box," said Aynur.

I was lifted up and put in the box. For a moment I was sitting up, wildly, within it, but then, by one hand in my hair, pulling back and down, and the other, lifting my ankles, and forcing them back, I was brought down in the box, on my back. I tried to rear up, but I was pressed down, rudely, uncompromisingly, just under my throat, by the hand which had governed my ankles. My bound ankles were then pulled forward and down, in such a way that the soles of my feet were on the floor of the box. I whimpered, frenziedly, pleadingly. I lay in the box then, on my back, my knees drawn up. It was small. I was cramped within it. The lid was shut. I heard bolts snap. It was a sturdy metal box, and is, in itself, its own security device. Its occupant need not be bound. It had four sets of perforations, for the admission of air. One was to my left and one to my right, where my head was. The others were to the left and right, near my ankles, as I lay. In this fashion, whether a girl's head is to the left or right, as she is inserted into the box, there will be breathing holes in the vicinity of her face. I could see out through the perforations, by turning my head one way or the other. These perforations, in each set, were so arranged as to form a cursive *kef*, which is the first letter in the word 'kajira'. The cursive *kef*, in variations, is also used as the common slave mark for kajirae. On my left thigh, just below the hip, I bore the same mark, put there by a slave iron.

"Bury it deep!" laughed Aynur. "Cast it into the foulest carnarium!"

I struggled inside the box. I whimpered madly. It would be only too easy, in the dead of the night, to bury the box somewhere outside the walls, in some remote place, or to cast it into one of the carnaria, the refuse pits outside the wall, into which garbage, and excrement, and all filth, as from the emptying of the giant vats of the *insulae*, might be thrown. But could they not, if this were their intent, strangle me first, utilizing some convenient string or cord, or smother me with a blanket or cushion, one easily found, perhaps one almost at hand, or even enter a blade swiftly, mercifully, into my heart? Surely that would not be difficult. They were armed!

"Before such things are considered," said one of the men, "we must make certain that she is the correct slave."

I turned my head to the right, in misery, looking wildly through the tiny perforations at Aynur.

"She answers the description," said Aynur. "She had a private sale. She came to the house at the time in question."

"One not of the house was within the house today," said one of the men to the other. "He may have spoken with her."

"He was alone with her in the garden," said Aynur, angrily. "He undoubtedly spoke with her!"

"Not necessarily," said one of the men.

Aynur looked down, angrily.

Sometimes the masters use us in silence, neither permitting us to speak, nor, for their part, deigning to speak to us. This is a very humiliating way in which to be handled, but in it we are left in no doubt as to the fact that we are mastered. Human speech does not pass between us. We are put in one position or attitude, or another. We must obey the slightest signs and indications. It helps to remind us that we are animals.

"I think we should assume words passed between them," said the other man.

"Not necessarily," said the first. "It is sometimes amusing to treat a pleasure-garden girl, or a high slave, as though she might be a low slave, or even the most worthless of common slaves."

I supposed this was true. The difference between a high slave and a low slave, of course, is only the whim of the master. It is they who decide on which step of the dais, so to speak, we may kneel, or even if we may approach the dais at all.

"Surely we are not prepared to take the risk," said the other.

"No," said the first. "It has been resolved that we shall not wait."

"I have delivered her into your hands," said Aynur. "Pay me."

"Are you standing?" asked one of the men.

Aynur fell to her knees, angrily. Then she put out her hand, palm up.

"Pay me!" she said.

I sensed that one of the men removed some coins from his wallet. I heard the clink of metal.

Aynur seemed quite pleased. Her hand was out.

I saw a hand poised over hers, as though to drop coins into her opened palm.

"You are certain," asked the man, "that you wish these coins to touch your hand?"

"Master?" asked Aynur, pulling back her hand suddenly, as though it might have been burned.

"It is nothing to me," said the man. "But I thought it might be something to you."

Aynur, suddenly, angrily, fearfully, held her hands behind her back. They might have been braceleted there.

Aynur, though she was first amongst us, was nonetheless a pleasure-garden girl. Pleasure-garden girls are commonly forbidden to touch coins. Reasons for this are obvious, for example, that they might receive gratuities from guests and hide them; that they might take money from guards, or others, to further intrigues or to attempt to influence masters; that they be denied the power which coins might bring, in bribing guards or tradesmen, and so on. Indeed, slaves are commonly forbidden to touch money except under certain conditions, as when being sent to the market, and so on. In this house, as in many others, slaves, at least those of the pleasure garden, were not permitted to touch money. It can be a capital offense to do so, hands may be cut off, and such. Legally, of course, the slave can own nothing, not even as little as a tarsk-bit. It is, rather, she who is owned.

"No!" said Aynur, suddenly. "I do not want the money!"

"As you wish," said the fellow. I saw the hand, presumably holding coins, withdrawn. I heard them clinking again, presumably being returned to a wallet, falling in with others. Aynur was furious.

But she was a slave. She was slave helpless. Even so little as a word, or a veiled hint, to the house master, by someone, might call attention to her. Would it be worth her life, say, to retain the coins? Could she successfully hide them, if they were sought for? Could she dispose of them, without being found out? Would her denials be credited, if it were stated by some authority that she had taken them? Who were these men? Did they, perhaps, have the confidence of the master? Might they not even be his agents?

"I shall, with Masters' permission," she said, angrily, "return to the rest area."

"You may find that difficult," said one of the men.

"Masters?" she asked, frightened.

"I think you will find that the guard has closed the door, after you," said the man.

"No!" cried Aynur, in horror.

The door, of course, locked automatically.

Certainly a guard had left the door open, and certainly he might have closed it later, following our exit. It would presumably be the same guard who had contacted her earlier, and who had left the door open for our exit, he who had apparently been suborned, he who might even, by now, have left the house, to depart the city.

"Masters!" protested Aynur.

Her terror was fully justified. She could not return to the rest area. She was locked out, and within the house. In the morning she would be found in the hall. She would then be punished, perhaps by being thrown to leech plants, perhaps by being fed to sleen.

"Yes?" said one of the men.

"What am I to do?" she begged.

"You may do whatever you wish," he said, "but if I were you, I would accompany us."

"You have arranged things thusly!" she said.

"Yes," he said. "If you remain here you will surely die, and thus you would be wise to come with us. In this fashion, of course, you place yourself in our power. And if this is not the slave we seek, if you have delivered the wrong girl to us, if it turns out that you have been mistaken, or have sought to trick or betray us, you will be in our power, answerable, and fully, to our displeasure."

She moaned.

"Stand," said the other man. "Bracelets!"

Instantly Aynur stood and turned toward the door, placing her hands behind her back. I saw her wrists locked in slave bracelets.

"We have brought a cloak for you," said the first man.

Aynur moaned.

He put a cloak about her shoulders, gently, as though she might have been a free woman. Then he turned her about, rudely, and, considering her, hooked it shut. He then pulled the cloak's hood up and over her head, and down about her features. I saw her eyes within the shadows of the hood. She was looking down at the slave box. I did not know if she could detect my features within the perforations, or knew that I was looking out, or not. Her eyes were filled with fear. One of the men opened the door and looked out in the hall. He then returned to the room. He and his fellow then lifted up the slave box. I whimpered, helplessly. I felt myself carried through the door. Aynur, I was sure, hurried closely behind. An outer door had been left unlocked. In a few moments I was being carried through dark streets.

Forty Three

I lay in the iron box, my knees drawn up. I was no longer bound or gagged. I was in some basement beneath a basement, I thought. We were still within the city, I was sure. I had no idea where in the city, in what district or quarter, we might be. Indeed, had I known, the names would have meant nothing to me. There had been very little light in the streets after we had left the vicinity of my master's house. The streets had soon become very narrow and crooked. The footing, too, must have been uneven, judging from the movements of the box. We had evaded the watch once, but only soon after leaving my master's house, by withdrawing into a deserted courtyard. As we had not later encountered the watch, or guardsmen, I conjectured that our present district or quarter must be a poor one, one far from affluent areas, perhaps even a dangerous one, one on which the city might not care to waste its forces. We had entered a building. I had been carried down a long, winding flight of stairs. Then, in some subterranean area, a trapdoor had been lifted, and I had been carried down, further. I had been told, and it was doubtless true, that cries from such a place could not be heard outside, that they would be unavailing, even the most piercing screams. Indeed, the place had doubtless been chosen, at least in part, because of this property.

I moved a little in the box, to ease my body. Its iron sides were so strong. I was so cramped within!

Such boxes are sometimes used for slave discipline.

I had been taken out of the box at various times, to be fed and watered, and permitted to relieve myself, on a leash, only to be returned to it later. Too, once, while I was out of the box, the golden collar had been cut from my neck. Even the filings from the saw had been gathered in a silken napkin, laid under my head and neck, my hair tied up, over my head. The collar, even the filings, were of value. The two men continued to wear masks. Their accents were like those of most of the guards in the house, but I did not recognize them as from among those guards. They were, I think, local hirelings, indeed, ruffians of some sort, brigands. It was only too clear that they were interested in the collar, for its gold. But then, too, of course, it would make sense that it be removed, as it bore on itself, engraved upon it, the name and house of my master. After the golden collar had been cut away, and the napkin, with its filings, carefully gathered up and folded, I had been led, held by the hair, my head held at the hip of one of the men, to an anvil. My head and neck were laid upon it. Out of the corner of my eye I saw a sturdy, rounded bar of iron. This bar was bent into a curve, but the curve was not closed on one side. It was shaped rather like the letter C. This was put about my neck. I saw a heavy hammer rise. Then, as I closed my eyes, this bar, with powerful, expert strokes, was shaped about my neck. The C had now become a closed circle. The curve was regular; the two ends were flush. It had been well put upon me. I suspected that my captor, he who had wielded the hammer, might be, or might once have been, of the metal workers. I could no more remove the collar, of course, than I could have opened a link in a heavy chain, one which might have held a ship, with my fingers. No longer, then, did I wear a collar of gold. I now wore a simpler collar, indeed, a collar that was no more, in fact, physically, than a ring of iron. To be sure, legally, socially, and psychologically, a collar is a collar, and it marked me as a slave. Indeed, it marked me as a very lowly slave, or, more likely, one who had now been put, for one reason or another, in a temporary collar, perhaps for purposes of transit, or prior to her sale, or such. There are also strap collars which are similar, in which a flattened strap of metal is beaten around the neck, usually also for similar purposes. "Do not fear," had said one of the men to me. "Even this will be removed, if your ankles are to be tied together and weighted, and you are to be cast into a carnarium."

It was three days ago, I think, that I had been brought to this place.

From where the box had been put on the floor I could look out through the perforations and, in the light of the lamp in the room, it set on a small table, see Aynur.

Shortly after we had first come to this place the box had been put on the floor and one of the men had ascended the stairs again, to pull down the trapdoor, and lock it shut, from the inside.

When he came downstairs, putting the key away in his wallet, he went to Aynur, who was standing, and brushed back her hood. He then unhooked the cloak and opened it, holding it open for a time, regarding her. She was in her silks, again, the sleeveless, silken scarlet vest, tied shut with a mere string, and the belly silk, scarlet, too, in the Harfaxian drape, fastened at the left hip with a golden clasp. Her earrings, her bangles and bracelets, her armlet, her talmit, had been removed before the mat check. My ornaments, including even the tiny golden earrings, had been removed earlier, before I had been switched in the garden. It is common to account for, and lock up, such valuables at night. One would not want, for example, a girl trying to barter such things, bracelets and such, for, say, the caress of a guard. Before coming to arouse me, on the pretext of taking me to the master, I supposed that she must have donned her silk. That would have been safer than wearing it under her silken sheets. For mat check, Aynur, under the lamp of the house master, under her sheets, was to be as bared as any other girl. She was, when all was said and done, only another flower. Let her beware then lest the house master should in his check lift back the sheets and not find her naked.

The fellow then slipped the cloak from Aynur's shoulders. It fell back, behind her, on the floor.

"Turn about," he said.

She obeyed, and, in a moment, he had unlocked her slave bracelets, those which he had put on her in the small room, those lovely, linked, twin confinements by means of which her wrists had been pinioned behind her. He returned the bracelets to his wallet.

"Go to the straw by the wall," he said. "Stand there, in the light of the lamp."

She did so.

I realized that Aynur was a quite beautiful woman, and, without her talmit, and her switch, and, now, in the presence of the men, did not seem, really, different from the rest of us.

"May I speak?" asked Aynur.

"No," said the man.

Yes, she seemed rather like the rest of us now.

"She is a high slave," said one of the men to the other.

"That was before," said the first man.

"She was first girl in the house of Appanius," said the other.

"Do you think you are a first girl, and that you are now in the house of Appanius?" inquired the first man of Aynur.

"No, Master," she said.

"Do you think you still wear the talmit?" he asked.

"No, Master," she said.

"Are you a high slave?" asked the first man.

"Yes, Master," she said, hesitantly.

"No, you are not," he said.

"Yes, Master," she said.

"Are you a proud woman?" asked the first man.

"I do not know, Master," she said, uncertainly.

"If you are," he said, "you will soon be cured of that."

"Yes, Master," she said, frightened.

"We do not coddle slaves here," he said.

"No, Master," she said.

"You have ten Ihn," he said, "to strip, and kneel where you are, on the straw."

Frenziedly Aynur fumbled with the string at her vest, at last jerking the vest open and slipping it back. With her right hand she seized the golden clasp at her left hip and opened it, flinging the silk to the side and dropping to her knees.

"On your back," said one of the men.

Swiftly Aynur obeyed.

She then served them.

After a time, I heard one of the men ask her, "Are you proud?"

"No, Master," she cried. "No, Master!"

And then I realized that Aynur, indeed, was now no different from the rest of us. She was now only another slave, at the mercy of masters.

That had occurred, I think, three days ago, at any rate within a few minutes of our having come to this place. I could now see Aynur through the perforations of the slave box. She was sitting at the wall, naked, on the straw, her knees drawn up, her head down, hair before her face, her wrists up, tied together, over her head, fastened to a ring in the wall. I thought the men were very cruel to her. Surely they showed her little mercy. I sometimes felt sorry for her, even though she had brought me into their power. These men, masked ruffians, brigands, I thought, were not gentle with slaves to begin with. They were the sort of men who would master a woman with great strictness, the sort of men whom we know we must please and obey, with no nonsense about it. But, too, I think they were cruel to her because she had not kept properly the office of the first girl, because she had dishonored her trust, because she had entered into an intrigue, because she had coveted gold, because she had betrayed her master. Such things tend not to be overlooked by the men of this world. They tend to disapprove of such slaves. She was now theirs, and helpless. I did not know what they would do with her.

I looked at her, through the perforations in the slave box. She now had her head turned toward me, looking at me, or the box. I did not know if she could see me within or not. Much would depend, I supposed, on the light. She shook her head a little, to move the hair from before her face. She would certainly realize that I would understand, if only from the voices, and the sounds, what had been done to her, and the sort of treatment which she had been accorded. Many times she had been made to thrash, and squirm, and howl with pleasure, within feet of me. She had been forced, many times, to show herself, to prove herself, helplessly, irreservedly, a female and a slave before me. Perhaps that cost her much, I such a lowly slave, and only a barbarian. Was she not made to squirm and thrash before me like the commonest pleasure slave in a tavern or brothel? Did she not kick and howl like the lowliest kettle girl? But why was I not used? These men had not so much as touched me. Her feelings must be complex, and mixed. She was a passionate woman, and all her passion had been liberated by her slavery. She, then, like the others, must have been starved in the gardens. How often could she have lain in the arms of her Camillus? Surely, seldom! And now she found herself, suddenly, at the mercy of masters who were callous, lustful brutes, being put frequently, mercilessly, to their pleasure. Her needs now, it seemed, were richly satisfied, and, as the men would have it, ruthlessly so. But her pride had been stripped from her, and before one she despised. With what joy and anguish must she have suffered, never knowing, too, what her fate was to be. And I, my feelings, too, were mixed. I envied her her uses, and had even, upon occasion, begged that I, too, might serve, but, for some reason, this had been denied to me. My slave needs were aroused, but I must not satisfy them. Once I was cuffed when I begged too hard. Too, I did not know for what I had been brought here, or who had arranged that it be so. And I did not know, either, what my fate was to be. The tiny things said to me upon occasion, or overheard, served in no way to allay my fears. I looked out at Aynur, through the perforations. She turned her head away. Her golden collar, too, had been removed, cut from her neck, the filings, even, gathered in the napkin. She, too, now, as she sat at the wall, her hands bound together, over her head, fastened to a ring, wore on her neck only a simple collar, like myself, a rounded, shaped bar of metal. And these were fitted closely to our necks.

We heard, suddenly, a tapping from above, on the other side of the trapdoor. It was not an ordinary tapping, but manifested, rather, a certain pattern, a complex pattern, which was thrice repeated. I did not doubt but what it was a prearranged signal.

The men looked at one another.

Then one came toward me, carrying the cloak which had originally been put about Aynur in the house of Appanius. As he neared the box, I could see only his feet. He tossed the cloak over the box. I could then no longer see out through the perforations.

I heard the other man climbing up the stairs, toward the trapdoor.

Forty Four

I lay tensely in the box, on my side, my head lifted, trying to listen.

The men conversed with the newcomer in hushed tones. I could not determine what they said.

At one point the box was struck and I jerked back. One of the men had apparently kicked it, the cloak spread over it, indicating it.

"Masters?" I heard Aynur ask, fearfully.

Then I thought that she was being removed from the wall. I also heard, a moment or two later, two small clicks, from which sounds I gathered that she had been braceleted. I also heard a stirring of straw, and supposed that she was pulled forward, presumably to kneel, as free men were present, closer to the box.

A moment later the box, with the cloak, was turned, so that my head was oriented away from the men, toward the opposite wall. The cloak was then lifted away from the box. But I could see nothing but the room through the perforations before me. "Close your eyes," said a voice, that of one of the men whose captive I was, he whom I took to be first of the two. I closed my eyes. I heard the locks undone, the lid put back, on its hinges. I was on my side in the box. I felt a hand in my hair. I winced, as it urged me up. Too, it turned my head toward the wall, away from the men. "Kneel upright, back straight, head down," said the voice. I was then kneeling in the box, my head down, my eyes closed, facing the wall, away from the men. I felt my wrists pulled together, behind my back, and corded together. The cord was then run down to my ankles, which were crossed, bound together, and tied to my wrists. "Put a knife to her throat," said the man who was near me.

I was afraid, but it was Aynur whom I heard whimper. Certainly I felt no blade at my throat. "We will now see if you have given us the right girl," said one of the two men, he whom I took to be second of the two. He was some feet away, in the room. "Let us hope, for your sake, you have delivered the right slave to us."

"I have tried to do so, Master!" wept Aynur.

"Have you sought to trick us, or betray us?"

"No, Master!"

"Have you made a mistake?"

"I hope not, Master!"

"Is she the right girl?"

"I hope so, Master!" cried Aynur.

"If she is not, you will die," said the man.

I heard Aynur cry out with misery, as though her head had been jerked back by the hair.

I was startled as a cloak, doubtless that which had been put on Aynur in the house of the master, and which had just been over the box, was put about my shoulders. Too, it was loosely draped about me. I felt it on my calves, as I knelt. I was then lifted from the box, in the cloak, and turned, and knelt, facing the men. I kept my eyes closed, as I had been commanded. A slave does not disobey such commands. Too, now that I was again kneeling, I kept my head down. Disobedience is not permitted to us. We are kajirae.

"Lift your head," said the man near me.

I obeyed, but kept my eyes closed.

"It is she, is it not?" said the other man, eagerly, addressing himself, doubtless, to the newcomer in the room.

"Open your eyes," said the man near me, just a little behind me, to my left. I gather he may have received some sign from the newcomer.

I opened my eyes, and found myself kneeling some feet before a seated man. He was in a dark cloak. Its hood was thrown back, but I could not ascertain his features, as he was masked, as were the other two. Aynur was before me but to the left. She was kneeling, naked, her hands behind her, presumably braceleted. Her head was cruelly held back by the hair, by one of the two men whose captive I was, he whom I took to be second amongst them. He was crouching a little behind her and to her right. His left hand was in her hair, holding her head back, and his right hand grasped the hilt of a knife, its blade at her throat. I looked again, wildly, frightened, at the seated man.

I saw him nod.

"It is she!" said the man holding Aynur. He released Aynur and sheathed his knife. Aynur's head came forward, and she sagged, shuddering.

"Do you dare to look boldly on your master, slave?" inquired the man behind me, to my left.

Quickly, frightened, I lowered my eyes. Why had he spoken of this man as my master? I did not think that he was Appanius of Ar. Had I now a new master? But perhaps this was in the sense that Aynur now had a new master, or masters, that she now belonged, in effect, to those who had captured us. But I, what of me? Would I not, too, in that sense, belong to them? But it seemed not. It seemed, rather, that it was to he who had come most recently down the stairs that I belonged. My submission, my obedience, all that I was, it now seemed, was his. I had been stolen, it seemed, and he was my new master.

And so it was that I knelt before him, in that secret place, far below the streets of the city, bound hand and foot, the cloak about my shoulders, concealing my body.

I knelt very still.

I did not move as I feared to dislodge the cloak. I was afraid it would slip from my shoulders. I did not know what the sight of my body might do to him, a man of this world, what activities, what agencies, what behaviors, it might precipitate. These are not tamed men, these Goreans. They are brutes, beasts, men of power, men of passion and violence, of inordinate desire, men who relish and celebrate women in every fiber of their being, who take them in hand, and deliciously, completely, uncompromisingly, own them, and master them.

He regarded me, not speaking.

Aynur had lifted her head. Perhaps she, naked and braceleted, envied me the cloak. One of the men, he who was first amongst the two, as I understood it, was still behind me, a little to my left. The other was before me, still a bit behind and to the right of Aynur. But both were now standing.

Both Aynur and I were helpless. We might as well have been chained in a market, or have been in heavily barred, triple-locked capture cages.

"Would you care to see her?" asked the man near me. He bent down, and his large hands, reaching about me, were on either side of my neck, on the edges of the cloak, near my throat. With a simple movement he might have drawn the cloak down and away, slipping it back and to the sides. I tensed. But the seated man made a tiny gesture, a negative gesture. The man behind me removed his hands from the cloak and straightened up.

"She is pretty," said the other man, encouragingly.

I did not understand why the cloak had been put about me. I did not understand why, now, it had not been removed. Nor, I think, was this clear to those who had been my captors.

I bit my lip, a little. I knew what it was to be looked upon, to be assessed, to be examined, as a female and a slave. But now I was frightened, for I feared my value to this newcomer, he who had been announced to me as my master, had little to do with whatever features or properties I might possess as a woman in bondage, with such things as beauty, intelligence, character, personality or talent. There was, I feared, a different interest in me, one which might be far more sinister or insidious, one far less immediately intelligible than those associated with the typical, obvious values of a slave.

"Very pretty!" urged the second man.

I had been taught to present myself well in chains, or ropes. I had been taught to turn well on a slave block.

But it seemed such things were of little interest to the newcomer.

Desperately I looked at him, trying to read his eyes. You must understand that we literally belong to the masters, and that they may do with us as they please. I hoped that he would be kind.

"She begged for use," said the man behind me. "She had to be cuffed."

I feared I detected contempt in the eyes of the newcomer.

I put down my head.

"She is a hot little slut," said the second man.

I looked up, angrily. Could I help myself? And had I not been enslaved? And had my needs not been ignited and enflamed by men? Had they not detected and revealed my most profound erotic secrets? Had they not released me from myself? Had they not, indeed, forced me, with whip and chain, to become my true self, the needful, hungering, passionate self of my dreams? They had not permitted me to hide! Why then was I to be criticized? It was they who had put me in the collar!

"We have kept her starved of sex," said the man behind me, "as you ordered."

Why would he have ordered that?

Our eyes met and I quickly lowered my eyes and head, before that fierce gaze. I looked down, fearfully, docilely, humbly. I was a slave.

The seated man then, suddenly, rose to his feet.

I looked up, frightened.

But he paid me no attention.

He reached within his cloak and drew forth a leather pouch. It seemed heavy. It was apparently filled with coin. He tossed this to the man behind me whom I then understood as being surely he who was first of the two who had captured Aynur and myself. The captor did not even count the coins. That the sack had been given to him by the man in the mask was apparently a sufficient guarantee of the integrity of the transaction. They, I gathered, unlike Aynur and myself, had some sense of he with whom they dealt. They might not know his identity, but they were apparently adequately assured of the validity of his credentials, at least as being those of some contact in question, of his reliability, of his right to conduct certain businesses.

"There were two collars of gold," said the man behind me.

The newcomer made a tiny gesture, granting them such trivial objects. The collars would doubtless be melted down. Either was doubtless worth more than many slaves, doubtless more than I and perhaps more even than Aynur.

No longer did we wear collars of gold.

No longer were we pleasure-garden girls.

Now, about our necks, as though we might be the least of common girls, were hammered simple rings of iron.

"What of this slave?" asked the second man, indicating Aynur.

Aynur turned wildly toward the newcomer.

He would make no claim upon her.

Aynur, wildly, desperately, in terror, threw herself to his feet.

"Please, Master," she begged, "keep me!"

But he stepped away from her, and, when she looked up, it was the two captors who stood over her.

"Have mercy, Masters!" she wept.

"You have served your purpose," said the second man.
"A girl may serve many purposes!" she wept.
"What should we do with her?" asked the second man of the first.
"We could always put her in the slave box, and return her to the porch of the house of Appanius," said the first man, musingly.
"Please, no, Masters!" said Aynur. "My perfidy would be clear to all! I would be nailed to the gate!"
"It might be dangerous to return her to the house," said the second man.
"That is true," said the first.
"It would be better," said the second, "to bind and gag her, and put her in the slave box, and then cast the slave box into one of the more remote carnaria."
"We could save the slave box," said the first, "and, at night, simply weight her and cast her into the carnarium. She would disappear without a trace."
"Yes," said the second, thoughtfully. "That is much better."
"No, no, Masters!" wept Aynur.
"We could then sell the slave box," said the first.
"Yes," agreed the second.
"Have mercy, Masters!" cried Aynur.
"You are a treacherous slave," said the first man.
"No, Master, no!" she cried.
"You are disloyal," said the second man.
"No, Masters, no, no!" she cried.
"Do you deny the words of free men?" inquired the second man.
"I beg humbly only to correct the misapprehensions of Masters," she wept. "I was treacherous. I was disloyal. But I am no longer treacherous! I am no longer disloyal! I have learned my lesson. Forgive me, Masters! Give a foolish, disobedient slave the opportunity to redeem herself! I will never again betray a master!"
"What are you?" asked the first man.
"A slave, Master!" said Aynur.
"And what else?" he asked.
"Nothing else, Master," she said. "Only that, Master!"
"Are you determined now to be a good slave?" inquired the first man.
"Yes, Master! Yes, Master!" wept Aynur.

"Perhaps we should then cut her throat before we cast her into the carnarium," said the first man.

"No, Master! Have mercy, Master!"

"What are you good for?" asked the second man.

"All the things that a slave is good for!" she wept.

"You are cold," said the second man.

"No," she said, "I have a thousand heats and a thousand flames!"

"Do you think you could please a man?" asked the first man.

"Desperately and fervently," she said, "in all the ways that a woman can please a man! I beg only the opportunity to show you!"

"Let us leave her fate in the hands of the other slave," suggested the second man.

"No, no, no!" cried Aynur, turning white. "No, Master! Please, no, Master!"

"But she was first girl over the other slave," said the first man.

"So much the better," said the second man.

"You were, as I understand it," said the first man to Aynur, who seemed now unable to rise even to her knees, "a poor first girl, one not only unpopular in the garden, but even one richly hated therein, one who ruled it strictly and cruelly, personally, arbitrarily, using your modicum of power as an opportunity to satisfy your vanity, bestowing favors on your sycophants, indulging in petty vendettas, stealing from, and abusing, those whom you disliked. Too, you tried to seek power from guards, and even, through them, to contact, and influence, others, others, even, outside the house. Your pettinesses, and administered punishments, often founded on nothing more than your whims and tastes, were notorious in the house."

Aynur moaned.

"And, in an abuse of your power, you tricked this other slave, and illicitly, treacherously delivered her, for putative gain, into our hands, in this act betraying both your office and your master."

Aynur's wrists seemed small, behind her back, pinioned there by the bracelets.

How helpless we are, bound!

"So it seems fitting then," said the first man, "that your fate be now put in the hands of she whom you tricked, she whom you betrayed into our grasp."

"Do not entrust my fate to her, Masters!" wept Aynur. "She hates me. Please, no, Masters! I am, when all is said and done, only a slave, and I am naked, and braceleted, at your feet. Have mercy on a slave, Masters!"

"What is to be done with her?" asked the first man of me.

I was startled by what had occurred. I knew that Aynur despised me. I knew that she hated me. I knew that she had willingly delivered me into the hands of these men, neither knowing nor caring what they sought of me. I knew she wanted me out of the house. I was sure she welcomed this opportunity to rid herself of me. She would not have cared, I was sure, if they had simply, once outside the house, cut my throat, or, for some reason, cast me into some pit, one of the great carnaria outside the city. She did not wish me well. She was my enemy.

"Shall we weight her ankles and hurl her into a carnarium?" asked the second man. "Shall we throw her to leech plants? Shall we stake her out to be eaten alive by insects?"

I was silent, disconcerted.

Suddenly Aynur, on her belly, oriented herself toward me. She looked up at me, tears in her eyes, lying before me on the stones, a prostrate, naked, braceleted slave. I might have been a queen, kneeling over her, concealed even in the heavy, dark cloak.

But there were rings of metal on both our necks.

"We can expose her in the mountains," said the second man. "We can leave her bound, at the mouth of a larl's cave."

"My life is in your hands," wept Aynur. "Please, sweet, beloved Gail, my favorite, beloved sister in bondage, be kind, be merciful!"

Aynur did not now have her talmit, that symbol of authority. She did not now have her switch.

"I am sorry I was cruel to you!" said Aynur. "I am sorry! I am sorry!"

No longer was she first girl. She was now naught but another slave. And a rather pretty one. There was no special reason, I now saw, why she should have been first girl, any more than several of the others.

"Please, beloved Gail," she wept.

"She is beautiful, Masters," I said, suddenly. "You do not wish to hurt her."

He who was first among the captors looked at me, startled. The newcomer, too, who had paid little attention to these matters, turned, now, to regard me.

"She is your enemy," said the second man. "How shall we kill her?"

"She is only a slave," I whispered. "She wants to love and serve."

"Yes, yes," whimpered Aynur, her head turned to her left, her cheek on the stones.

"Do you not understand?" asked the second man. "We are granting you a rare privilege. We are permitting you to dictate the manner of an enemy's death. You may never again receive such an opportunity. Relish your revenge! Let it be sweet!"

I put my head down. I wanted none of this.

"Beg!" said the second man to Aynur. She cried out, kicked. "My life is in your hands," wept Aynur to me. "Permit me to be spared! I beg my life!"

"How do you address her?" inquired the second man of Aynur. She wept, again, again kicked.

"Mistress! Mistress!" she said. "I beg my life, Mistress!" I was in consternation.

I was now as Mistress to the proud Aynur!

"If I am to die, please let it be done quickly, mercifully, Mistress," said Aynur.

"Speak!" the second man ordered me.

"I am a slave, Master," I said. "It is neither mine to prescribe, nor dictate, the manner of another's death. It is rather mine to obey, to serve."

Aynur lay helplessly before me. All that had seemed cruel and hard about her before was now gone. She was now no more than the slave she was. The cruelties, the artificialities, had been broken away from her. She was now utterly vulnerable, and soft, and tender, and beautiful. Now she was no more than a helpless slave girl.

"What is to be done with her?" inquired the second man.

I looked down at Aynur, and she looked up at me, piteously. No longer was she the Aynur of old.

"We are both slaves, Masters," I said. "That is all we are. That is our destiny and nature. We beg to love and serve. That is what we wish, to be pleasing, and to be loved. Please be kind to us. Please show us mercy. We beg it."

"What of her?" said the second man. He indicated Aynur, roughly, brutally, prodding her with his bootlike sandal.

"If you do not want her," I said, "do not hurt her. If you do not wish to keep her for yourselves, do not kill her. Sell her. Surely she will bring you a good price in a market."

I sensed the men looking at me.

"I am sure that she will do her best to be a good slave," I said.

"Is it true?" asked the second man, of Aynur.

"Yes, my masters," whispered Aynur.

"For the time, then, at least, we will spare her," said the first man.

Aynur shuddered. I feared that she might faint.

I was acutely aware of my own helplessness, and bondage, how my ankles were crossed, one lying over the other, the two looped with cord and bound together, how my wrists were crossed, and bound. I pulled a little and, in an instant, had come to the last of the slack, an inch or so, in the cord which fastened my wrists to my ankles. I was conscious of the cloak, so precariously about my shoulders, and my nudity beneath it. It was total power the men held over Aynur and myself. This was not merely a matter of their much greater size and strength, enabling them to handle us as though we might be children, enabling them to do with us as they wished, nor was it a matter merely of the implacability of our bonds, denying us even the most meaningless opportunity to try to defend ourselves or to flee; it had rather to do with the marks on our thighs, the collars on our necks, that we were slaves. It was that which, more than anything else, more than their incomparably greater physical strength, more than the sternness of bonds, made us wholly, helplessly, theirs.

The second man bent to Aynur's ankles and bound them together.

"Thank you, Mistress," breathed Aynur.

I winced, seeing how tightly her ankles were bound together.

The man then knelt across her body and thrust the slave bracelets higher on her wrists. He then, with cord, tied her wrists together. He jerked the cords tight. He then removed the bracelets from her, putting them in his pouch. He then drew her to her knees and gagged her.

I dared not cast a glance at my master. He was standing to one side.

I feared to be overly bold. I did not wish to be lashed.

The slave box, by the first man, with his foot, was thrust before me and to my right, rather toward the foot of the stairs. It scraped on the stone flooring. It was not far, then, from where my master was. It was to his left. He paid it no attention.

The second man then lifted Aynur up in his arms. I saw her eyes, over the gag. He carried her to the slave box. He sat her in the box. He put one hand in her hair and the other on her ankles. I again saw her eyes. In them there was terror. Neither of us knew, truly, what her fate was to be. It was my hope that they would spare her, if only for the whip and collar of another, one who would see, even casually, to her perfect mastering. He put her down in the box, on her back, her knees up. He shut the lid of the box, and locked it. Through the perforations in the box, in the form of the kef, I could see her face.

In what perfect custody we are kept!

The newcomer, my master, and the two captors then exchanged further words, *sotto voce*.

I saw then the slave box lifted by the two men. It had stout, leather handles at each end. It was carried up the stairs, and then, the first man opening the trap, thrusting it up, through the opening. The trap was then closed. I heard the steps of the men, heavy with the weight they were bearing, cross the floor above, and then, in a moment, as they set themselves to a new flight of stairs, diminish.

I was then left alone, in the subbasement, with my new master.

Forty Five

I thought that I would attempt to charm or placate my master. I would dare to lift my eyes, timidly, to his. I would smile, a timid smile, hoping to please him.

I lifted my head.

"Slut!" cried he in rage.

I understood nothing of his fury. It made no sense to me. Why should he be angry with me? Why should he be cruel to me? I thrust my head down, instantly, terrified.

I had only smiled at him.

How had I done wrong? How was it that this should have so offended him, have so enraged him?

"You worthless slave and slut," he whispered. In his voice there, was almost unbelievable hatred.

No longer dared I hope that he might be kind. I hoped rather now only that I would be permitted to live.

"You smile at me," he snarled, "not even knowing who I am!"

I kept my head down. I trembled.

"Lift your head!" he snapped. I obeyed.

"Back, back, further!" he said.

My neck then hurt. I saw, above me, the wretched, peeling ceiling of that dank place.

He approached me and handled the collar.

"Fitting," he said, contemptuously.

It was a ring collar, hammered about my neck, suitable for the lowest, the most miserable, the most worthless of slaves.

"So," said he, contemptuously, angrily, "you begged use?"

Of course I had begged use! Was I to be blamed for what I was, for what I had become, that which I had earlier been only secretly, only in my dreams? And were not the masters, too, to blame? Had they not released the slave? Did he now think I could simply return her to her dungeon, where she had languished, neglected and denied, after I had met her, and, in her, my true self? Once one has found oneself can one forget oneself? It is a bit late for such things then. It is one thing never to acknowledge oneself; it is one thing to pretend and hide; it is one thing to avoid meeting oneself; but it is quite another to forget oneself once one has met oneself; one cannot, so to speak, then unmeet oneself; one may hide from the truth; one may attempt to avoid it; one may even arrange one's life in such a way as to minimize the possibilities of learning it, at least explicitly, face to face, in its full glory; but once one has seen it, one cannot simply unsee it; one cannot unlearn it; it can no longer be repudiated; incantations can restore neither virginity nor ignorance. And, too, I loved my sex, my truth. I would cling to it forever. No one could force it out of me. I was not discontent to be a woman.

With his left hand he grasped the cloak at my throat, holding me by it. With his right hand, he struck me thrice, first with the palm of his hand, then with the back of the hand, then, again, with the palm of his hand, lashing my head back and forth.

I looked up at him, my face stinging. I tasted blood in my mouth.

"Yes," said he, angrily, "you would crawl to any man as a slave."

He then, in fury, tore open the cloak and exposed me, before him. He regarded me.

"Yes, yes," said he. "You are a slave, a slave! That is what you are, a slave! It is no wonder that you worthless little things bring a good price on a market block!"

He then thrust me to the floor.

I lay there, afraid to move.

I heard him rummaging about the room. Then I heard the snap of a slave whip. I moaned. I tensed. He came and stood near me.

"Please be kind to me, my master," I said.

"Barbarian slut," he said, "Earth-girl slave, Earth-girl thrall!"

He knew then that I was not native to this world. He had understood this, perhaps, from my accent.

Yet I was not sure of this.

Could he have known this independently?

As he had spoken to me I had been at first startled. Then I had grown troubled.

Now that I had been several months on this world I was much more aware of the subtleties of diverse accents within the language of the masters, that language which I must learn, that I might the better obey, that I might the better understand what was required of me. This accent was not that of the local guards, those I had encountered in the house, nor that of the captors, nor that of those of Treve. Indeed, it reminded me in ways of my own early accent in this language, not with respect to my native tongue, which still influenced how I spoke the language, of course, but with respect to that which I had originally absorbed in learning the language, now so long ago. My speech had, however, over the months, been heavily influenced by my time in Treve, and, in the past weeks, doubtless, by that of this city itself.

The whip snapped again, a strict, sharp, loud sound, like the report of a firearm, a sound that seemed to ring explosively from wall to wall.

I was terrified.

I did not want to feel it on me.

But the blow did not fall on me.

"You crawl to the feet of any man," he snarled. "Crawl then, slut, to my feet, as well."

"I am bound, hand and foot!" I wept.

"Crawl!" he commanded.

I could move only a bit at a time, laboriously, painfully, over the stones, toward him.

"You are slow!" he said.

The whip snapped again.

"Forgive me, Master!" I said.

At last I lay at his feet, on my side. I turned my head, that my lips might touch his sandals. But he stepped away from me, angrily.

"You are not yet at my feet, are you?" he asked.

"Forgive me, Master!" I said.

Again I tried, inch by inch, to reach him. But this time he seized my ankles and turned me to my stomach. My ankles were then up, behind me, fastened to my wrists. I saw the coils of the whip lying beside my head, to the left. I heard a knife slip from a sheath, a soft sound. I lay very still. The masters may do as they please. I did not wish to move unexpectedly, suddenly, and risk being cut, by accident. My ankles were held still, my left ankle in the grip of his left hand. A blade of apparently incredible sharpness moved through the bonds, quickly, deftly, on my ankles. They seemed to spring away. I then lay on my belly, facing away from him, my legs freed. The blade was returned to its sheath. I saw his hand pick up, again, the whip.

He stood up, he turned about, he moved back.

He was silent.

I was not unmindful, I assure you, of the command which had been imposed upon me, and had not been rescinded. Too, men such as these, who relate to women in the modality of the master, are not patient.

I was then on my knees before him.

"You crawl quickly to the feet of a man," he sneered.

I had crawled to him on my knees. My hands were still bound behind my back. I knelt before him, and put my head down, to his feet.

"Yes, Master," I said.

"You may beg use," he said.

"I beg use," I said.

I was very much aware that my ankles were freed.

"Why do you beg use?" he asked.

"I fear to be whipped," I said.

"And if you were not afraid of being whipped?" he asked.

"I would still beg use," I said.

"Without even knowing who I am?" he asked.

"Yes, Master," I said.

"Slut and slave!" said he, in fury.

"Yes, Master," I said.

"You are worthless," he said. "You are unutterably contemptible!"

"Yes, Master," I said.

"I always knew it," he said.

"Master?" I said.

"From the first!" he said, angrily.

"Master?"

"Earth-slut!" he said.

"Yes, Master!" I said.

I was startled. Had I not heard this voice before? "Look up!" he commanded.

His eyes, within the mask, were fierce.

The whip, coiled, was thrust roughly before me. Instantly I licked and kissed it.

How long it had been since I had knelt before him! How long it had been since I had kissed that whip!

"I love you, I love you, my master!" I cried.

"You know me, do you not?" he said.

"Yes, Master!" I cried. I dared not lie to my master. I knew him now as well as if his features had been bared from the beginning. To be sure, I had never known his name, or his city. I had known little more of him than, in my heart, he was my master. It was he to whose whip my lips had been first pressed on this world!

He tore the mask away from his features, casting it aside, looking down at me.

How fierce were his eyes!

That he had worn the mask suggested to me that perhaps it had not been intended that I recognize him. I hoped I had not placed my life in jeopardy by my admission that I was cognizant of his identity. But he must know that. Too, I dared not lie to him. He was my master.

How terrible seemed his anger!

"I love you!" I said.

"Liar!" said he, in rage.

"No, Master!" I protested.

He glared at me.

"You are my master!" I cried. "You have always been my master!"

"Liar! Liar!"

"No, Master!" I wept.

"But one thing you say is true," he said.

"Master?" I asked.

"That I am now your master."

In his voice there seemed terrible menace.

"The slave rejoices!" I said. "She begs to serve!"

"How clever you are," he said.

"I do not ask that you like me, even a little," I said. "I only beg, unilaterally, with no hope of the least reciprocity, that you will permit me to be your helpless love slave!"

"It is little wonder, with your cleverness," he said, "that you learned the language so quickly, that you so quickly and well learned the lessons of the pens."

"I am well advised," I said, "to learn the language of my masters as quickly as possible. It is not pleasant to be beaten. And surely I am not to be blamed if the slave in me was a little closer to the surface, a little more eager, a little less repressed than that in some others."

"You belong in the collar," he said.

"Yes, Master," I said.

"How well you look on your knees, bound."

"Thank you, Master."

"It is where you belong."

"Yes, Master."

He looked at me. It was difficult to read his eyes, his visage. He loosened the coils of the whip, but then, to my relief, slowly, wound them back together again.

"Am I to be whipped?" I asked.

He did not respond.

"I did not expect to see master again," I said.

"Nor I you," he said, "slave."

"Is it but coincidence," I said, "that she who has come into your power is I?"

"Not at all," he said. "It is only to find you that I have come to this part of the world."

I looked at him, suddenly, in wonder, and joy.

"Master has sought me?" I asked.

"Yes," he said.

He must then, I thought, share something of my feelings for him. Not lightly did one undertake lengthy journeys on this dangerous world.

"You have come far to acquire me," I said, shyly.

He regarded me, not speaking.

"I thought that master did not care for me," I said. I recalled the neglect, the contempt, the cruelty with which he had treated me in the pens. Of all the guards it seemed it was he alone who despised me, who held me in such disdain.

"You are a worthless slut," he said.

"Yes, Master," I said, contentedly.

"Do you know my accent?" he asked. "It is not unlike your own."

"I can recognize it, of course," I said.

"It is an accent of Cos," he said. "Your accent, too, despite the barbarian influences, and others, is substantially a Cosian accent, for it is there you learned your Gorean. You were trained in pens in the capital city of Cos, Telnus."

"Yes, Master," I said. This was the first time I had heard the location of the pens in which I had been trained. They were in a city named Telnus, on Cos, which I did know was an island.

"There has been a great war," said he, "between Cos, and her allies, and Ar, and her allies. The victory has come to Cos, but for various reasons, having to do primarily with the volatility of mercenary forces, it is thought that the permanence of this victory is not assured. You know in what city you are?"

"In Ar," I said. I knew that. I knew, too, something of the occupation, and of the hardships in the city, though we had been much sheltered from the consequences of such in the gardens.

"What you perhaps do not know," he said, "is that Ar was betrayed in this war, by traitors in high places."

"No, Master," I said.

"Without such treachery it is unlikely that Cos could have secured her success."

I was silent.

"In particular, it was needful to deprive Ar of competent leadership."

He was then silent.

"Master?" I asked. But it seemed he felt he had spoken more than he wished.

"It was not easy to find you," he said. "There were attempts made to conceal your whereabouts. Interestingly, the clue to your location came, so to speak, from the other side, from the side of those favoring Ar, or perhaps one might say, better, from the side of some who are suspected of favoring Ar, whose activities, unknown to themselves, are closely monitored."

I understood very little of what he was saying.

"Must we speak of such things, Master?" I asked.

"You do not know your role in these things, do you?"

"No, Master," I said, "nor is it important."

"Sometimes," said he, "the slightest movement of a leaf, stirring in the wind, is important. Sometimes the particular position of a grain of sand may be of the utmost consequence."

"Love me," I said.

"Love you?" he asked.

"Please," I said.

"I do not understand," he said.

"Have you not come from far away, perhaps from halfway across a world, to find me?"

He looked at me.

"You have now found me," I said. "I am yours."

"I know that you are mine," he said.

"To do with as you please."

"I know that," he said.

"I beg to be done with then as master pleases," I said.

"Oh?" he said.

"Yes, Master," I said.

He smiled, bitterly.

"I love you," I said.

"Liar!" he cried.

I looked down. I felt helpless. I did not know how to make him believe me. How could I convince him of the authenticity of my feelings? How could I prove to him that I was his, wholly, and in the most complete and perfect way a woman can give herself to a man, as his love slave?

Unbidden then I lay before him, on my back, my bound wrists under me, nestled in the small of my back, my left knee lifted. It was one of the ways in which I had been taught to lie before a man.

"You are a bold slave," he said.

"Beat me," I said, "if you are not pleased." This, too, this saying, I had learned in the pens.

"I have dreamed," said he, "of you before me, so."

"Oh, Master," I said, "I do love you!"

He regarded me angrily, skeptically.

"If you do not believe me, Master," I said, "do not concern yourself with the matter. I am before you, as a slave. Simply put me to your purposes, that I may serve the imperious will of my master."

I felt overwhelming desire for him. My entire body seemed aflame. I was hot. I lifted my body to him. I was juicing, as a slave.

"I am not a man of your world," he said to me.

I lay before him, eager and ready for my subjugation. I wanted to be overwhelmed, to be carried away, to be loved with need and desire onto ecstatic madness. "Do you think I want the tepid caresses of tamed men?" I asked. "Do you not know, truly, what I want and need, that I want, and need, a master!"

"I have not been sent here for the purpose of acquiring a slave for my personal delectation," he said.

"You have been sent here?" I asked.

"Yes," he said.

"Why?" I asked.

"Oh, I have come of my own will, as well," he said.

I recalled that he hated me.

"Master?" I asked.

"Do not think that I did not want to come," he said. "No. It was others, who could also recognize you, who did not wish to come. It was I who was eager to come."

"Who could *recognize* me?"

"Yes," he said.

"I do not understand," I said.

"Surely you must understand why I have been sent here," he said.

"No," I said.

"Do you not know, truly, why I have been sent here?" he asked.

"No," I said.

"To kill you," he said.

Forty Six

I lay there, suddenly numbed and cold.
He had turned away from me.
"You know why you were sold to Treve, of course," he said.
"No," I said.
"Anyone with similar properties would have done," he said, "but it was you whom they purchased."
I lay on the stones, looking at the ceiling above me.
"They wanted one to attend upon a prisoner, one who would be utterly ignorant of the affairs of our world, one who could be depended upon to innocently and naively discharge the duties of a keeper, relieving free men of that responsibility, thus, too, enabling the contacts with the prisoner to be the better limited, particularly those of free persons, one who would be unlikely to have any relationship, either before the collar or after it, with the parties in question, one who, a slave, would be completely within the power of the authorities, one who could not, rationally, be expected to participate in any way in the affairs in question, for example, in bargaining, in tendering or accepting bribes, and such."
He cast down the whip, into the straw. This frightened me. I would rather he had held to it.
"We have our sources of information," he said. "It has come to our attention that the prisoner has escaped. This was a long time ago. It seems almost certain he would seek to return to Ar. His presence in the city could significantly alter matters. Furthermore, there is some reason to believe that he may now be in the city."
I understood almost nothing of this.

"Strangely enough," he said, "it seems he is unaware of his own identity, the result, I take it, of some trauma or injury. Further, perhaps in part due to the consequences of the aforesaid trauma or injury, he may no longer be easily recognizable. In short, at present, it seems he knows neither himself nor is he known by others."

He turned to face me.

"You, of course," he said, "could recognize him instantly, for you know him as he is now, from Treve."

I lay on the stones, frightened, bound.

"It is he who was Prisoner 41, in the corridor of nameless prisoners, in the pits of Treve. We have all this from the administration in Treve. Indeed, you are apparently one of the very few people who could recognize him, and the only one whose location we know."

He approached me, a step or two.

I rose to my knees, frightened. I pulled at the cords on my wrists.

"You might suggest, of course," he said, "that your life be spared, that you might identify this fellow for us, the party of Cos, that we might then repair the oversight of Treve, by removing him from the picture, but we have considered, and rejected, that possibility. As you are a slave, and he is a free man, you cannot be trusted to identify him. You would surely suspect that you would be marking him out for death. You would then, presumably, pretend not to recognize him, even if you did. Too, you would be clever enough to know that your life might then be worthless, that either we, or those of Ar, learning of what you have done, and, in particular, as you are a slave, might deal with you summarily, and those of Ar rather unpleasantly. As a slave, too, you would know the penalties for bringing harm, either directly or indirectly, to a free person."

I shuddered.

"I see you do," he said.

"The danger then," he said, "is that you might identify him for others, for those favorable to the cause of Ar. The underground in Ar, you see, the resistance to the occupation, in particular, a band of brigands, the Delta Brigade, mostly veterans of the campaign in the delta of the Vosk, must not locate him. He could be used, you see, even in his current state, as a rallying point for resistance."

I recalled the man in the garden, and his questions, which had frightened me so. I doubted that he was in league with the Cosians.

"Accordingly," he said, "given the information at our disposal, and your putative location, I have been sent to Ar to preclude that possibility."

Then I rose, unsteadily, to my feet. I backed away from him.

"There is no escape for you," he said.

I felt the wall behind me.

"It was for this purpose," I asked, "that you had me at your feet, begging use?"

"I have wanted you there, begging use," he said, "for a long time."

"I had thought," I said, "that when you had come here, looking for me, that you might care for me."

"I hate you," he said.

"Or," I said, "that even if you hated me, that you wanted me, that you desired me, that you would have me at your feet, helplessly subject in all things to your imperious will."

"You may scream, if you wish," he said, "but it will not be heard. You may run about, if you wish, but it will do you no good."

I regarded him, in misery.

"Kneel here," he said, pointing to a place at his feet.

Obediently, helplessly, I approached him and, cold and numb, knelt before him.

"Put your head back," he said.

I did so.

"Farther," he said.

I complied.

I felt his hand in my hair, holding my head back, painfully. I saw the movement of his arm. Then I saw the blade, removed from his sheath, held before my face. I recalled how easily it had parted the cords on my ankles.

"Do you wish to say anything?" he asked.

"You are my master," I said. "I love you."

"You lie to the end," he said.

"I do not lie to my master," I said.

I felt his hand tighten in my hair. My head was pulled back, farther. I heard the blade touch the collar, beneath it. Then I felt its edge, like a fine, hard line, at my throat. I closed my eyes.

He suddenly cried out in rage and drew the knife away.

He leaped to his feet and, in fury, fled to the other side of the room. He threw down the knife. He struck the wall with his fists.

I collapsed to the stones, scarcely believing myself alive.

"How absurd," he cried, in anger, "to love a slave!"

"Master?" I said.

He spun about. "Yes!" he cried. "I love you, you worthless slut, you meaningless thing! I have loved you, madly, insanely, uncontrollably, recklessly, violently, from the first moment I saw you!"

"Master," I breathed, unable to believe my ears.

"Yes!" cried he. "Call me 'Master'! It is fitting, for you are a slave, and will never be other than that!"

"Yes, Master!" I said.

"You are no more than a branded slut, no more than meaningless, worthless collar meat!" he cried.

"Yes, Master!" I cried.

"You are unworthy to be a free woman!"

"I hope so, Master," I said.

"What?" he cried.

"—I hope so, Master," I whispered.

"Slave!" he sneered.

"Yes, Master," I said. "It is true. That is what I am."

"Disgusting!" he said.

"No!" I cried. "No!"

"Do you dare speak back to me?" he cried.

"With master's permission!" I cried.

"You will never be a free woman!" he said.

"Nor do I wish to be a free woman!" I said. "I have been free! I know what it is like! I am content to be a slave, and wish to be a slave! I am fulfilled in bondage, in ways that you, a man, or some men, may never understand! Oh, yes, you enslave us for your gratifications and pleasures, you monsters, you beasts! But what you do not know is that we love our bonds, and our belonging, and our being owned, and being helplessly subject to the magnificence, the glories, even to the whip, of your total, uncompromised mastery of us! Do you not know we want men to be strong, and our masters? Let the twisted and hormonally deficient conceal their seekings of power under the pratings of rhetorics. Let others of us who long to love and serve, and obey, and be desired, dream of masters!—yes, masters!—*our* masters!

He looked down upon me, and I realized that these things to him, a man of Gor, were not that strange.

He knew something of our needs.

He was not a stranger to the nature of females.

"I am a slave," I whispered.

"It is well known to me that you are a slave—*legally*," he said. "I can see the collar, the brand."

"It is more than that," I wept. "I am a slave inwardly, in my need, and in my love, and in my nature! It is what I am! Despise me for it, if you wish! I am a natural slave, a rightful slave, and here, on this world, in my collar, I have found myself at last! Hate me! Hold me in contempt! But I am a slave, and I love being a slave! I love it! I love it! Do not try to force me to be what you want me to be! Rather accept me for what *I* want to be, and am!—one who knows she belongs at the feet of men!—and desires to be at the feet of men!—their slave!—*their loving slave!*"

"I do not understand myself," he said.

"Master?"

"How could I care for you?"

"It is my hope that you do, at least a little, my master."

"You are no more than an Earth slut, a barbarian!"

"Yes, Master," I said. "Forgive me, Master!"

"The lowest of the low," said he.

"Yes, Master," I said, "Forgive me, Master!"

"You are not even of Gor!" he cried.

"I have been brought to Gor," I said. "I have been collared here, and made a slave here! Surely now I am of Gor! How could I be more of Gor, than as a Gorean slave girl, hoping like other Gorean slave girls to be found pleasing by her master?"

"You do have a beautiful face," he said, "perhaps the most beautiful I have ever seen, and you have a quick wit, and a luscious feminine mind, and superb slave curves, a body that drives me mad with desire, and your responses would shame those of a she-sleen in heat."

"It seems the slavers knew their business, Master," I smiled.

"We do," he said, "*slave*."

"Do not treat me as might a man of Earth a woman of Earth," I begged. "Treat me rather as a man of Gor a woman whom he owns—one whom he will well master."

He glared down at me.

"Please take me not as you would have me, but as I am."

"You are a slave," he said.

"And I rejoice that I am, Master."

"Slut," he said.

"Forgive me my slavery," I said. "I am a woman!"

"How I have fought my weakness, my loving you!" he exclaimed. "I put you from me. I avoided you. I held you in contempt. I abused you. I kept you at a distance. I treated you with coldness and cruelty! But each instant I was fighting myself, wanting to seize you, to sweep you into my arms, to crush you to me!"

The room seemed to rush about me. It grew dark for a moment. I gasped for breath. I feared I might lose consciousness.

"Yes," he cried. "I love you!"

I fought to remain conscious. Then, again, I was fully conscious. I regarded him, he in such misery, such torment, across the room.

"I must not love you!" he cried. "I must not permit myself to do so!"

I struggled to my knees.

I was in the presence of a free man, indeed, of my master.

He looked at me, wildly.

"But I cannot help myself," he said. "I love you!"

"You gave no sign of this, Master," I said.

"I do not know whether I hate myself or you," he said, "or both, I for my weakness, you for having done this to me, and for being the most exciting and desirable female in all the world!"

"Master finds me of interest?" I asked.

"To see you is to want you!" he said, in fury.

He turned about, again, and again struck the wall. "I must not love you," he cried.

"Surely some men, Master," I said, "love their slaves!"

"You are a mere collared barbarian!" he said.

"Yes, Master," I said.

He spun about, in fury. "And in hating you, and loving you," he said, "I sensed the role you had to play, and the dangers which might attend upon it. I knew that those in the house, of those of Cos, might be among the very few who could recognize you again. I therefore guarded my feelings, confessing to no one the torment in my heart, occasioned by a mere branded slip of a slave. Thus it was that in recruiting one to seek you out and cut your throat it was I who came first, and naturally, to the attention of my superiors, they aware of my hatred for you, my loathing for you, but not of my lust for you, my unquenchable desire for you. Indeed, other guards declined the office, unwilling to hunt you down and cut your throat, which says much for your popularity, you rampant, exquisite, arrant little charmer."

"I am grateful for your deception, Master," I said. "I owe my life to you."

"I did not know how I would behave until the moment I had the knife at your throat," he said, "but then I knew I could not, at least at that moment, end your life, even though you were the most unworthy of slaves."

"'At least at that moment'?" I asked, uncertainly.

"You are a slave," he said.

"Yes, Master," I said.

We are subject to the masters in all things.

"I have dreamed of owning you," he said.

"I am yours," I said.

He retrieved the knife and replaced it in its sheath. I was pleased to see it disappear therein. He reached down and recovered the whip. He coiled it. He then came to where I knelt and put the coils under my chin, lifting it up.

"Yes," he mused. "I think anyone would find you quite pretty."

I did not speak.

"Those from whom I purchased you said that you begged for use, and had to be cuffed."

"I begged for use," I said. "It is not my belief that I had to be cuffed."

"You should be whipped," he said.

"As master wishes," I said.

But he turned about, and put the whip, coiled, on the small table in the room.

Then he returned to stand before me, musingly.

"You would crawl, begging, to the feet of any man," he said.

"Yes, Master," I said.

"You would have begged use from me, even without the threat of the whip, even before you knew who I was," he said.

"Yes, Master," I said.

He then struck me, lashing my head to the side, with the back of his hand. I lost my balance, and fell to my side, to the stones. I lay there, a chastised slave.

"Forgive me, Master," I said. "Recall that I am only a slave."

"On your knees," he said.

I struggled, again, to my knees. How could he blame me for crawling to men, for begging use? Did he not understand that I was a slave, truly! Did he have some unreasonable concept of what I should be, something in his mind, something with little, if any, relation to my realities? Could he not accept me as I was, truly, a helpless female, and slave? Other men had not been critical of this!

"I am appetitious, Master," I said. "I am the prisoner of my needs. I am subject to the forces within me. I cannot help myself. I am what I am, nothing else. Please do not expect me to be other than I am."

He regarded me.

"It is my hope," I said, "that you will permit me to be what I am. Please do not ask me to pretend to be other than I am."

"How strange that I should care for you," he said, "for that is what you are, truly, a mere slave."

"That I am a slave," I said, "I trust does not make me less attractive."

"No," he said. "It makes you a thousand times more attractive."

I smiled, shyly.

"Why do you smile?" he asked.

"Perhaps master's anger with me, with my needs, my appetites, and such, has less to do with his criticality of such things in a slave, for he surely realizes that they are expected, and even required in her, as it has to do with other matters."

"Yes?" he said.

"Perhaps master is jealous, perhaps he is angry that I might be found pleasing by others."

"Beware," he said.

"Perhaps he is possessive," I said, "perhaps he wants me, somehow, all to himself."

"Be silent," he said, angrily.

"Yes, Master," I said, falling silent.

How attractive he was!

I spread my knees before him, scarcely aware of my action.

"There!" he said, suddenly, pointing. "See! There! That is what I mean, you little barbarian slut!"

"Forgive me, Master!" I said. "Shall I close my knees?"

"Close your knees?" he said.

"Yes, Master," I said.

"Do not dare to close your knees," he snarled, "slave! You are before your master!"

"Yes, Master," I said, happily. I saw that he would be strict with me, that he would truly own me, that he would get much from me.

How pleased I was to belong to him!

He was such as knew the handling of a slave.

I would be helpless in his hands.

"I own you," he said.

"Yes, Master," I said. "I am yours, totally yours!"

"Do you wish to be totally mine?" he asked.

"Yes, Master!" I said.

"Liar!" he said.

"No, Master!" I said.

"But whether you wish it or not," he said, angrily, "it is true!"

"I know, Master!" I cried, delightedly.

"Seeing you I become enflamed," he cried. "I cannot help myself! No longer can I resist!"

"Take me!" I wept.

"Slut, slut!" he murmured, lifting me by the arms half from my knees.

"Yes, Master," I begged him. "Own me! Own me!"

In his heat, his frenzy, he pressed me back to the stones, making use of the slave.

"You are my master!" I cried.

"You are my slave!" he cried.

"Yes, my master!" I wept.

He then confirmed upon me, in merciless rapture, his ownership. I was in no doubt of it.

I had felt the first time I had seen him, the first time I had knelt before him, looking up at him, the first time I had kissed his whip, that I was somehow his, that it was to him that I belonged. And I am sure I would have felt this way even had I not been in chains, even had I not been within the institution of bondage, where such as I was subject to explicit legal ownership. But more astonishingly rewarding to me was the now-present suspicion, if not revelation, that the chemistries involved, the fitting together of parts, must have been mutual. As I had looked up and seen my master, so, too, he must have looked down and, at his feet, seen his slave.

Again I squirmed. Again I writhed, in his arms.

Again, to my joy, he showed me no mercy.

I screamed out, in the dark basement, my love for him, and again, and again, my submission.

Later he thrust me to his feet, and I lay there, in my collar, like a dog.

I was enraptured, that he permitted me to remain near him, he finished with me, I, only a slave.

"How is it that I could care for a slave?" he asked, lying on his back, staring at the ceiling.

I did not respond.

"I love you," he said.

"When you tire of me," I said, "you may sell me."

"I will never tire of you," he said.

I kissed at his ankles.

I whimpered.

"You are insatiable," he said.

"I beg that my hands might be freed, that I might caress you," I said.

"Ah," he said, absently, "I did forget to free your hands, did I not?"

"Yes, my master," I smiled.

"Since when does a slave require her hands to be freed, that she may caress her master?" he asked.

"True, Master," I laughed.

I rose to my knees beside him, and put my head down, to his body.

"You learned the lessons of the pens well," he said.

"Thank you, Master," I said.

Slaves must be superb lovers. If they are not, they may be whipped.

There are a thousand ways to please a man, even when one is bound.

In scarcely moments, however, he had again seized me. I looked up into his eyes, those of my master.

I was then put again to his purposes.

I later lay at his side, at his thigh, docile and grateful. "I love you, I love you, my master," I murmured.

"We shall see," he said.

"Master?" I asked.

He rolled over, and reached to one side, drawing to him his belt, with the sheathed knife upon it.

He then extracted the knife from the sheath.

I regarded this action with apprehension. Had he now recalled, in some fearful sense, I wondered, the putative object of his venture to this city?

Had he tired of me so soon?

Surely it was not necessary to kill me. Surely he could simply give me away or sell me!

Had he dealt with me as he had, merely for his amusement, only as one might toy with a meaningless slave?

Did he hate me so?

Had he now determined to comply with the wishes of his superiors, those who had dispatched him to this city, now that he had made me squirm, and cry myself his? Had such compliance been within his intent from the beginning?

"Kneel," he said. I faced him, frightened.

"Turn about," he said. Apprehensively I did so.

Then I cried out with relief, as I felt the knife part the cords on my wrists. My hands came forward, weak, freed, and I was on all fours, beside him, shaken.

"What is wrong," asked he, "slave?"

"Nothing, Master," I sobbed, in relief.

"Ah!" he said.

"Yes, Master," I said.

"Turn about," he said.

I was then, again, kneeling, facing him. I rubbed my wrists.

Suddenly I was startled, for, on the stones, the knife lay before me. He was lying on his back, looking up, at the ceiling. His hands were behind his head, pillowing it, his elbows to the side.

I looked down at the knife.

"You see the knife?" he said.

"Yes, Master," I said.

"Consider it," he said.

"Yes, Master," I said, puzzled.

"Do you think you could seize it, lift it, and, before I could resist, or defend myself, plunge it into my heart?"

"I have no wish to injure my master," I said.

"Do you think you could do what I said?"

"I do not think so, Master," I said. Surely at my first movement he could turn and seize me.

"Pick it up," he said.

"Surely I may not touch it, Master," I said. "It is a weapon." In many cities, it is a capital offense for a slave to touch a weapon.

"Must a command be repeated?" he asked.

"No, Master," I said. I lifted the knife, timidly.

"Approach," said he. "Hold it with both hands."

I knelt over him then, the hilt of the knife gripped in two hands. That was well, otherwise I think my hand would have shaken miserably, helplessly.

"Put it to my heart," he said.

"Please, no, Master!" I begged.

He turned his head to regard me, and I, quickly, frightened, put the knife over his heart.

"Could you now thrust downward before I could resist, or defend myself?" he asked.

I considered the position of his hands, behind his head, the quickness with which the knife might thrust down, the nature of the blade, its sharpness.

"Yes, Master," I said.

"None know you are here," he said. "You could find your way out. You could frequent dangerous areas, where you might well be seized as a strayed slave, not to be returned to a master, but to be sold illicitly, in a black market. You might be out of the city in a week."

"I do not even have clothing, Master," I said.

"Surely you have seen naked slaves in the street," he said.

"Yes, Master," I said. I had seen them, at least, in Treve. I myself, on the other hand, had never been put naked into the streets. It is normally done as a punishment. Normally, too, the slave is locked in the iron belt.

"You would have to be careful not to be picked up by a guardsman," he said.

"I do not understand what master is saying," I said.

"Surely you have lied to me," he said, "suggesting that you might care for me."

"No!" I said.

"The knife is in your grasp," he said. "You need pretend no longer."

"I love you, truly," I said.

"You are a barbarian," he said. "I am a Gorean."

"You are a man," I said. "I am a woman."

"Barbarian," he said.

"Do not hold my origins against me," I said. "I am now only a Gorean slave girl, and am as eager, or more eager, to serve you as any girl of your own world!"

"You could not care for me," he said, "for I would be a stern master."

"Be so," I said.

"I am not the sort of male which I have heard you women of Earth prefer," he said.

"Do not believe all you have heard, Master," I said.

"Oh?" he said.

"Do you think we truly prefer manipulable weaklings who have surrendered their dominance?" I asked. "Do you think such can exact from us the depths of our womanhood? I cannot speak for all women of Earth, but I can speak for one, for myself. I want a man of strength, of power, one who will relish me, and desire me, with might and passion, one who will put me in my place, and keep me there, as a woman, and will see to it, to his joy and fulfillment, and mine, that I am well mastered. I want a man so strong, so intelligent, so energetic, so powerful, so overwhelming, so uncompromising, so mighty, that I can, before him, be no more than his abject slave."

"You are truly a slave," he said.

"Yes, Master," I said.

"Do the women of Earth desire true men?" he asked.

"Master?" I asked.

"In the biological sense," he said, "as opposed to some political sense or another, whatever is current."

"Yes, Master," I whispered. "We cry for them, in the darkness, Master."

"My life," he said, absently, gazing at the ceiling, "is now worth very little."

"Master?" I said.

"I have not complied with the orders set to me," he said. "I have betrayed my superiors. They are not such, I assure you, as to look lightly upon such omissions. I can no longer return to Telnus. There is little, if anything, left for me now. Presumably I will be hunted down, and slain. If you were with me, you, too, would die."

"Then I, too, would die," I said.

"Lie no longer," he said. "You may now kill me."

"I do not lie," I said. "And I would rather plunge the dagger into my own heart."

"You may kill me," he said.

"Never," I said.

He closed his eyes.

"Strike," he said.

The point of the dagger was over his heart. In an instant I might have leaned forward and, with all my weight, slight as it was, moved that thin blade deeply into his body, to the hilt, even through the heart.

"No," I said.

He opened his eyes.

"No," I said. "Forgive me, Master."

"Must a command be repeated?" he asked.

"Repeat it a thousand times," I said. "I will not do it."

"You disobey?" he asked, puzzled.

"Forgive me, Master," I said. "Yes, Master."

"Why?" he asked.

"I love you," I said.

"You are prepared to die, for having been disobedient?" he asked.

"Yes, Master," I said.

He regarded me.

It occurred to me that if he slew me, he would, in this way, fulfill his orders. What would it matter to his superiors how it was that I came to be slain?

"Strike," he said.

"No," I said. "Forgive me, Master."

"There is no other way," he said.

"But there is another way, Master," I said.

"What?" he asked.

"This!" I cried, and lifted the knife, it held in both hands, and turned it toward my own breast. I closed my eyes. I plunged the blade toward me.

But it never reached my heart for his mighty hands, moving like lightning, seized my wrists. I cried out with pain, helpless in that grip. The knife fell to the stones. "Little fool!" he cried. He pulled me to my feet by the wrists, and regarded me, fiercely, and then forced me back down, on my knees, before him.

"Hear me!" he said.

"Yes, Master," I said.

"You may not take your own life," he said. "I forbid it."

"Yes, Master," I said, frightened.

He then threw me to the stones, angrily, before him. He reached down and retrieved the dagger, which he replaced in its sheath. He then threw the sheath and belt to the side. He picked up his cloak, and dropped it down, beside me.

"Keep your head down," he said.

I dared then not lift my head.

"Why did you not kill me?" he asked.

"Because I love you," I said.

"Even though you knew your failure to obey could cost you your own life?"

"Yes," I said.

"Interesting," he said.

"I would rather die than injure you," I said.

"Why?" he asked.

"I am master's slave," I said.

He crouched down beside me and, with his fingers, lifted my chin, and looked deeply, inquiringly, into my eyes. Then I averted my eyes, for it was hard for me to look into the eyes of my master.

"What sort of slave are you?" he asked.

"Master, please!" I begged.

"Speak," he said.

"I confess myself master's love slave," I whispered.

"My love slave?" he said.

"Yes, my master," I said. "I know that you may not care for me. I know that you may despise me, that you may hate me. But it does not matter. I do not care. As worthless as my love may be, that of a meaningless slave, know that it is yours, unstintingly, irreservedly, all of it. It is yours, entirely. I am your love slave."

He lifted up the cloak, and put it about my shoulders.

I looked up at him, through tears.

"I am unworthy to be loved," he said. "I have betrayed my honor. I have not obeyed my orders."

"Is it well that the entire world should fall into the hands of Lurius of Jad?" I asked. "Is he not mad? Is he not a tyrant?"

"He is my ubar," he said.

"Honor," I said, "has many voices, and many songs."

He looked down at me, startled. "That is a saying of warriors," he said. "It is from the codes. It is a long time since I have heard it. I had almost forgotten it. Where did you, a slave, hear it?"

"In Treve," I said.

"A den of thieves!" he said.

I did not respond. Who knows within what houses may be heard the voices of honor? Who knows within what walls may be heard her songs?

"I do not think we can leave the city," he said. "We have no passes."

"We must then remain here," I said.

"For those of the black caste to come, to kill us?"

"It would seem so, Master," I said.

"He who was Prisoner 41, in the Corridor of Nameless Prisoners, in the pits of Treve, may be in the city," he said.

I recalled the peasant. That seemed unlikely. How could any man have survived in the mountains, alone, for most practical purposes unarmed. Too, what difference could it make, really, if he were in the city, a mere peasant?

"You could recognize him, if you saw him?"

"Yes, Master," I said.

"We must try to escape from the city," he said.

"Yes, Master," I said.

"I wonder if I should keep you," he said.

I threw off the cloak and flung myself naked to his feet. I held to his ankles. I pressed my lips to his feet. "Please keep me, Master!" I begged.

"I must guard against weakness," he said.

I kissed his feet.

"You are dangerous," he said. "It is the soft foes who are most dangerous."

"I am not your foe, Master," I said.

"I wonder," said he, musingly.

"Do not fear me, Master," I said.

"You cannot help what you are," he said.

I licked and kissed at his feet.

"Still," said he, "the problem is not at all insoluble."

"Yes, Master," I murmured.

"Women such as you prove to be exquisitely pleasing," he said.

"Yes, Master," I whispered.

"Subject, of course, to the proper controls, and handling."

"Yes, Master," I said.

"Do you think your life with me would be easy?" he asked.

"No, Master," I said.

"You realize that it is likely that I will be sought, and slain, and that you, too, if you are with me, would share that fate?"

"Yes, Master," I said.

"You may now leave," he said.

"Master?" I said.

"I give you one last chance," he said, "to leave this place, to fall into the hands of another."

"Keep me," I begged.

He looked down at me.

"It is what you wish, truly?" he asked.

"Yes, Master!" I said.

"Very well," he said.

"Thank you, Master!" I said.

But his eyes seemed now stern.

Suddenly I was no more than a frightened slave.

"Master?" I said.

"You have had your opportunity to elude my clutches," he said quietly, evenly. "You did not avail yourself of it."

I looked up at him, frightened.

"It is now too late," he said.

"Yes, Master," I said.

"To all fours," said he, "and face away!"

I complied, frightened.

"Strictly," he said, "you have not been entirely pleasing this afternoon."

"How have I displeased my master?" I asked.

I heard the whip removed from the table.

I did not dare look back.

"You were ordered to strike me, to slay me, and you did not do so."

I was silent.

"That was disobedience," he said.

"Yes, Master," I said.

"And you strove to take your own life, which is not acceptable in a slave. She may not do that. She does not own herself. It is, rather, she who is owned."

"Yes, Master," I said.

"To be certain," he said, "I am not unmindful of extenuating circumstances in both these cases, that in each case it was the welfare of your master which motivated you."

"It was, Master!" I said. "I beg forgiveness, if I have been displeasing!"

"And what is to be done when the slave has not been fully pleasing?" he asked.

"It is up to the master," I said. "He may take action or not, as he sees fit."

I heard the coils of the whip shaken out.

I tensed.

"You will receive three blows, only," he said.

That I thought was light, indeed. The beating was then, I realized, more symbolic than anything. It was little more than a way in which he chose to inform me that he did not expect me to be disobedient, or even displeasing, in any way, a way in which I would be apprised of the consequences which might attend such failures on my part.

The whip cracked and I cried out in alarm. But it had not touched me.

"The first blow," he said, "will be for disobedience, the second will be for your attempt to take your own life."

The sound of the whip's report still terrified me.

I realized that, next, it would fall upon me.

The blow fell upon me, and I thought it light, not that it did not hurt, you understand.

My back stung.

Tears came to my eyes.

But I was not displeased that I had refused to strike him. I would have refused again. The blow was little more than a formality. Still I had been whipped.

I cried out in misery, feeling the second blow.

It was not light.

He apparently was quite clear about informing me of his displeasure that I had tried to turn the dagger against myself, even if it had been only my intent to relieve him of his dilemma, to resolve, at a stroke, so to speak, the fearful predicament in which he found himself, to protect him, to save his life, by recourse to the obvious, simple expedient of sacrificing mine.

"Master!" I whimpered, in protest.

"Be silent!" he said.

Tears fell to the stones. I did not wish to feel another blow like that. Now I was truly whipped.

"Prepare for the third blow," he said.

"Master," I cried, "may I speak?"

"Yes," he said.

"For what is the third blow?" I asked.

"What?" he asked.

"Why am I to be given a third blow?" I asked. "What is its purpose?"

"You are to be given a third blow," he said, "because I choose to give you one, and because you are a slave, and that it may serve to remind you of what you are, my little charmer, that you are a slave."

"Yes, Master," I whispered.

I lay then on my stomach, my head to the side, tears bursting from my eyes, my fingers scratching at the stones.

I tried to understand what I felt.

I almost lost consciousness.

My back seemed unbelievably afire.

The leather had struck like lightning on my back. How it had fallen upon me! How it had lashed down!

I lay there then, a slave who had felt the lash. I sensed that the blow, in its way, had been sparing. But it had been sharp, and it was not one I was likely to soon forget.

I heard the whip replaced on the table. "We must leave soon," he said.

I scarcely heard him.

How frightened I was, and how miserable, whipped. I realized now that no matter how much he might love me that I was still his slave, and that he would not be lenient with me. How quickly I would kneel, how quickly I would leap to serve, how desperately, how fervently, I would try to please! I loved him, but, too, I knew him now as my genuine master, one who would not hesitate an instant to correct my behavior, to subject me to discipline, if I should fail to be pleasing.

"Up, my little charmer," he said. "We must be on our way." I rose to my knees swiftly, and turned about, looking up at him.

He smiled, seeing that I would obey with alacrity.

He had donned his tunic.

I had not so much as a slave strip.

"They will be searching for you," he said. "What was your name in the gardens?"

"'Gail'," I said.

"They will then be searching, I wager, either for a slave named 'Janice', once serving in Treve, or a slave named 'Gail', from the gardens of Appanius. What is your name?"

"Whatever master pleases," I said.

"A most judicious response," he said.

My back hurt. I wondered what he would name me, or if he would concern himself to name me. I supposed he would name me. It is convenient for a girl to have a name, by which she can be commanded, and summoned, and such. If he named me, that was then who I would be.

I looked to the two cloaks, the one he had worn, the other which had been put about me after I had been removed from the slave box, and set before him, on my knees. It was his own cloak which he had earlier put about me, almost tenderly, perhaps to shelter me from the dampness of the basement. The other cloak, that which had been put about my shoulders by he who was the first of the two captors, lay to the side.

"Should I don this cloak, Master?" I asked. I did not think he would march me in the streets naked. Without wishing to sound vain, I thought, genuinely, I might attract attention. Constanzia and I had attracted attention in Treve, even in common tunics. I did not doubt but what the Lady Ilene, who was now quite likely to be a slave, would have as well.

I had referred to the cloak which lay to the side, the smaller of the two cloaks, that which was not his, that which had earlier been put about me by the first of the two captors. It was a woman's cloak.

He shook his head.

It would remain here then. Perhaps it might be recognized, if only by the captors.

I touched his own cloak. I felt it lovingly. How warm it would be. I looked up at him. I would love to have it wrapped about me, I naked within it. It would be almost as though I were within his bonds.

I lifted the cloak a little. I did not dare, of course, to put it about me. When a slave is naked before her master, she does not simply cover her body. She must receive permission to cover herself from the master, even if it is by so little as a word or a glance.

I looked up at him.

"You are well trained," he said.

"I had excellent trainers," I said.

"Stand," he said. I stood instantly.

He indicated that I should turn about, and I did so. Slave bracelets were snapped about my wrists. He then turned me about, again, so, that I faced him, my wrists pinioned behind me.

He surveyed me, his slave.

"You are incredibly beautiful," he said.

"I am pleased if master is pleased," I said.

"We shall ascend the stairs," he said. "We shall go forth to the world, together."

He then kissed me, and then put his cloak over me, over my head, blanketlike. The cloak, as he had thrown it over me, would come high on my thighs. It would be as though I might be a new purchase, naked from a sales barn, being fetched back to a domicile, the master's cloak, for want of something better, cast over me.

I stood there.

I then felt the cloak being gathered about my throat, and, in a moment, I felt a collar being put about my neck, over the cloak. The collar was snapped shut. This fixed the cloak in position. It served then as, in effect, a slave hood. I then felt a leash clip snapped about what must be a collar ring.

"You are now hooded, and braceleted and leashed, my beauty," he said.

"Yes, Master," I said, happily.

"As is suitable for you, a slave," he said.

"Yes, Master," I said, happily.

"There is no escape for you."

"Nor do I wish one," I said.

"It is night outside now," he said.

"Yes, Master," I said.

"We shall go forth together," he said.

He then lifted me in his arms and carried me up the stairs. He stopped at the top of the landing and set me down, steadying me with one arm while he raised the trap. He then carried me upward again, through it, and closed it behind him. In a few moments, after ascending another flight of stairs, and moving through a large room, we were outdoors, on the street.

"It begins," he said. "Are you ready, my love?"

"Yes, my love, my master," I said.

I then, hooded within the cloak, braceleted, leashed, followed him through the streets.

Printed in the United States
123139LV00001B/37/A